TEARS UNTIL DAWN

Visit Paul Henke on his website
for current titles and future novels at:

www.henke.co.uk

or email Paul at

henke@sol.co.uk

TEARS
UNTIL
DAWN

Paul Henke

To Allan,

A merry christmas

Paul Henke.

GOOD READ PUBLISHING

First published in 2005 by Good Read Publishing
A Good Read Publishing paperback

10 9 8 7 6 5 4 3 2 1

A CIP catalogue record of this title is available
from the British Library

ISBN 1–902483–07–3

Typeset by Palimpsest Book Production Limited,
Polmont, Stirlingshire
Printed and bound in Great Britain
by Antony Rowe Ltd, Chippenham, Wilts.

Good Read Publishing
PO Box 1638
Glasgow
G63 0WJ

This book is dedicated to the people who lived, fought, loved and died during the Second World War. They gave so much to give us the freedom we take for granted to day.

Acknowledgements

I would like to thank Anne Buhrmann for her excellent work tidying up my prose and editing the manuscript. Also my thanks to the staff at Palimpsest who are as helpful as ever. The others I need to thank are Bruce Macaulay for his jacket design, Jeanne-Marie Jackson and Rosemary Bowe for their feed-back and very apt comments and to Lindsay Falconer for her invaluable last minute input. Finally thanks to my wife, Dorothy, who never fails to praise my fragile ego while criticising my efforts – always constructively, of course.

Prologue

"*WINNING WITH NIXON!*" The silver-haired gentleman grimaced at the newspaper headline. *Here's hoping the man lives up to his slogan.*

He sipped a glass of water to wash away the taste of the antibiotics. Sir David Griffiths wasn't a good invalid at the best of times – but the result of the presidential election in America three days ago had affected his already bad mood.

The bout of bronchitis, his second that winter, had weakened him, and David Griffiths hated the feeling of weakness, especially when there was so much to do. He didn't trust Nixon – the few times they'd met, the man had come across as self-serving and dishonest even. Shaking his head David wandered across to the window and looked out at the landscape.

His house, *Fairweather*, was located in fifty acres of rolling Sussex countryside. In the distance he could see the undulating grey of the English Channel. The days were turning colder. A log shifted in the fire and sent sparks flying up the chimney, causing him to glance inwards. *Fairweather*, he knew, would not survive his death. A family of twenty could be accommodated there quite easily, along with the necessary servants needed to keep such a place ticking over. A mausoleum, he thought – only the foolhardy few could afford to maintain such a house these days.

Already he had received an offer to sell some of the ground for housing development. His reaction had been a vehement no. Fortunately his wife, Madelaine, had agreed.

David tented his fingers, seeing visions behind his closed eyes. This room, his study, had been the scene of so many interesting and exciting events over the forty years he had owned the estate. The house had been lucky to survive the Second World War. If you

1

knew where to look you could still see where the bomb had landed.

Sighing, he turned away from the window and glanced across the book-lined study to his ornate desk, which dominated the room. Many far-reaching decisions had been taken at that desk. He looked at the glass of water on its gleaming surface and then at the discreet but well-stocked bar. He considered pouring himself a whisky but thought better of it. There would be hell to pay if Madelaine caught him drinking, especially on top of the blasted antibiotics he was taking.

A knock on the door brought him out of his reverie. 'Come in.'

The door opened and the reporter Tim Hunter stepped into the room. Sir David was gratified that *Time* magazine had sent one of its rising stars to interview him. Their conversations, recorded by Hunter, would eventually form the basis for a history of the Griffiths family – a story which encompassed the events of the entire twentieth century – warts and all. So far he had enjoyed the reporter's company, found his questioning incisive and intelligent. Hunter was a handsome young fellow, Canadian by birth. In the time they had spent together Sir David had asked some questions of his own; Hunter had lived in Boston with his mother and maternal grandparents, since the death of his father at sea fifteen years earlier following a severe storm off the coast of Newfoundland.

'I hope I'm not disturbing you, sir?'

Sir David waved a deprecating hand. 'Not at all, Tim, come in, do. I could use some company. Help yourself to a drink.'

'Thanks, sir, but it's a bit early for me.'

'Oh?' Glancing at the clock, Sir David saw it was still a few minutes before five o'clock. 'So it is. With the dusk falling, I thought it much later. What can I do for you?'

'I wanted to ask a few more questions about the Duke of Windsor.'

'I thought you might. That was a black affair. If the real facts had emerged about our ex-king there might well have been civil war – we'd have fallen right into Hitler's trap.'

Hunter nodded. 'I surmised as much. You couldn't have been very pleased to act as nanny to a man you despised. How on earth did Churchill convince you to shadow your ex-king?'

'Winston,' Sir David smiled, the memories lighting his eyes, 'had a most persuasive personality.' Although David was eighty-seven years old his memory was as sharp as ever. 'At the time I thought I was

2

too old for the job but Churchill waved that argument away. I suppose, in view of what happened, he was proved right.

I haven't gotten to that part of the archives yet.'

'You'll enjoy it. Now, young man, you've been seeing a lot of my granddaughter, Sian. Don't you think it's time you told me your intentions?'

Much to Hunter's relief there was a knock on the door and the butler appeared. 'Excuse me interrupting, sir, but the Prime Minister is on the telephone. He says he needs to talk to you urgently.'

Sir David strode across the study and into the hallway. He was away for several minutes. When he returned he was looking pleased with himself. Hunter watched as he walked straight to the bar, found a bottle of Islay malt whisky and poured himself a stiff drink.

'Anything wrong, sir?'

Adding a dash of soda, Sir David looked at him and smiled. 'I think you'd better have one as well.'

'Why? What's happened?'

Whatever the reporter was expecting it wasn't Griffiths' next statement. 'The Prime Minister has threatened us with a "D" notice. It would prohibit us from publishing the book. He was very apologetic. Ingratiatingly so. But he argues that the material is too damaging to the Crown. To the House of Windsor.'

'What did you say, sir?' Hunter poured himself a drink too. The same malt, less soda, plenty of ice.

'I told him that our Queen is loved, revered even. That the sins of the uncle would not tarnish her reign, or that of her father. That the electorate was sophisticated and intelligent enough to recognise the actions of one selfish and egotistical man for what they were. But he was adamant. The papers covering the period are still locked away under the fifty-year rule.'

'How did he know about the book?'

'I told a friend in passing a few days ago. I expected the PM to learn about it.'

'What shall we do?'

Sir David took a mouthful of whisky. It slipped down like nectar, not burning his gullet, as it would have done in recent days. He grinned, determination and enjoyment reflected in his smile, 'I love a good fight. And if I can't win fairly, I cheat.'

David's Story

1

AND SO THE darkness of war had fallen yet again. Hours after we declared, in fulfilment of our promise to Poland, the French followed suit. Conciliation was available right to the end, but Hitler would have none of it. To my fellow politicians, the situation was clear. There could be no wavering, no shadow of doubt. But we were very aware of the huge responsibility we bore. The British were still coming to terms with the inhumanities of the last war.

For years Germany had come to be seen by many as a victim of the dictates of the Treaty of Versailles. Appeasement was disguised as mercy and forgiveness. The view that Germany had suffered too came to dominate our policies. Had Hitler been a normal, nationalist leader, committed only to restoring his country's pride, that view would have held. But Hitler and his Nazis were far from normal.

As Member of Parliament for Eastbourne, I was in the House of Commons when the joint Anglo-French declaration was made. Decisions followed swiftly. Our two governments agreed we would avoid bombing civilians and refused to countenance using poison gas or germ warfare. We asked Germany to give similar assurances. No such declaration was received and I left the Commons with a heavy heart.

My heart would have been heavier still, were it not for Churchill's news. I was overjoyed when he was made First Lord of the Admiralty, the post he had held twenty-five years earlier at the outbreak of the last war. We were deep in discussion, debating the creation of the new war cabinet when he received the phone call telling him of his appointment He hung up the receiver with a chortle and said, 'I'm back, Griffiths, I'm back!'

Two days later he collared me in one of the bars in the House. 'David, I need a word.'

I looked at his scowling, wrinkled features. 'You appear to be less than your usual sunny self, Winnie.'

'This is no time for frivolity, damn you. We have a problem of amazing delicacy, which urgently needs attention. If I recollect correctly during the last lot you worked in Military Intelligence.'

I nodded. 'More by accident than design. But I did my bit. Why?'

'We have urgent need of you again.'

'I don't understand. As an MP I'm hardly in a position to contribute to the intelligence services.'

He nodded slowly, then gripped my arm. 'I'll get us a couple of whiskies. What I have to tell you is of the . . . utmost importance,' he paused and then added, 'and not to be repeated.'

We sat in a corner, away from prying eyes and ears. While we waited for our drinks, Churchill lit one of his foul cigars.

'So what's this all about?' I asked once the drinks were placed before us. I took a sip of my malt while Churchill gulped at his.

'I appear to have made a grave error of judgement, David, and I need your help.'

I raised an eyebrow, but he missed the irony as he always did when it was directed at him. Taking another mouthful of whisky he swallowed loudly. His next words came as no surprise. 'As you know, I have always been highly supportive of His Royal Highness, the Duke of Windsor.'

My hackles rose immediately. 'You know my views on our ex-king, Winston – the man is a Nazi sympathiser. Look at the way he was received in Austria and Germany. Good God, man, he's even been known to give the Nazi salute in public. The adulation he's been receiving across Europe was bound to affect an ego the size of Windsor's. And Wallis revels in it too. Loathsome woman.'

'Steady on, man – information has come to light *proving* what you say. I fear the worst, frankly. We can't ignore the situation any longer. Windsor's actions and opinions have been kept very much out of the public domain until now. But unless he returns to Britain soon there will be no escaping where his true loyalties lie and that could spell disaster for the war effort.'

It was well known in certain circles that our ex-king was a fascist at heart. He openly said he believed the *true* enemy of world peace was communism. Since his exile to France he had been courting Hitler and his regime at every opportunity. Indeed he had become friends with many of the ruling party of Germany. His close friend Charles Bedaux had facilitated his entry into German society. A Frenchman who also enjoyed American citizenship, Bedaux was immensely wealthy and a known supporter of Hitler. The relationship between Windsor and Bedaux had been giving the British government sleepless nights for some years. As the bags under Churchill's eyes testified.

'If, God forbid, the Duke declares that a truce should be called for and that he will negotiate with Hitler, then this country will split right down the middle, Griffiths. There are enough right-thinking people who recognise Hitler's regime for the evil that it is, but many others believe fascism is what is needed to counteract communism.' Taking another mouthful of whisky Churchill looked in surprise at his empty glass. 'We cannot allow fascism to flourish otherwise we will lose the liberties we have fought for and cherished all these years. Democracy is the true bastion against totalitarianism, whether the regime comes from the left or the right of the political spectrum. It is the *only* safeguard.'

'So if Windsor comes out in support of Hitler, you fear there could be a civil war?'

'Easily. Mosley's Blackshirts have plenty of support from people who are not currently active members but could be persuaded. Mosley fervently supports Windsor, as you know. If the Duke openly declares for fascism, for *peace*, millions could flock to him. Blast it, where's that waiter?' The man appeared and took Churchill's barked order for another large malt. When he had left, Churchill lowered his voice. 'Civil war could possibly be avoided, but the collapse of the monarchy would be inevitable,' he said with a weary shake of his head. 'That is unthinkable. The monarchy must be protected at all costs. Our King and Queen are too important to this country and the Dominions. So Windsor has to be stopped.' He glared across the table at me.

My own fears were confirmed by what he had said. 'I admit he's a danger, but I don't see where I fit into all this. Nor why you asked about my Military Intelligence connections.'

'As you know Windsor hasn't returned from France since the abdication. We are trying to bring him back. To that end we have offered him one of two positions. Either Deputy Regional Commissioner in Wales under Sir Wyndham Portal or an appointment as a Liaison

9

Officer with the British Military Mission in Paris. With a suitable rank, of course.'

'It's obvious which one he will choose. Paris.'

'We think so too. Wales is a make-believe post, which he should see for himself. But we have a real task for him in France.'

'I still don't see where I fit in.'

'If he goes to Paris, as we expect, we want you to go with him.'

'What!' I sat up straight, jerking my glass, which would have spilled if there had been more than a drop left.

'I thought that would get your attention,' Churchill said dryly.

I beckoned to the waiter for a refill, buying time while I considered his preposterous suggestion.

'If this is your idea of a joke . . .' I finally managed, the words sounding inadequate even to me.

'Of course I am not joking,' he replied indignantly. 'This is not the time or place for humour. We face desperate times, believe me. The conflict won't be over before Christmas, either this year or next. We must prepare for the long haul and we must ensure with all in our power that we win.'

'Damn it all, Winston, I still don't see why you want me with Windsor. I can't abide the man.'

'Which is precisely why we want you with him. You have no loyalty to him. We want you to report back everything he says and does.'

I shook my head. 'I'm a Member of Parliament. I'm with the War Committee. I have work to do here.' I gestured about me.

'Humbug, Griffiths. Parliament will argue and debate while the War Cabinet decides. The only laws we will be passing in the House will be to tighten our security, all of them repressive and restrictive, but necessary in wartime. Most of the MPs' workload will involve giving moral support to their constituents. The only big debate will be about the war effort. Do we fight, surrender or sue for peace? The latter two are unthinkable. Now that Australia, New Zealand and Canada have given their instant support to the Mother Country we cannot hold back. The real democrats in the world recognise the dangers. Our course as a parliament is set.' He paused, puffed on his cigar and added, 'Trust me, you will serve your country better by doing as I ask. Your age is no obstacle. You look years younger than you are. You're well known in the right circles. You've met Windsor before. Toady up to him a bit. That's all we want.'

'All?' I was flabbergasted. Windsor was anathema to me. 'I need to think about it.'

'Pray do. Only make the right decision. This is of huge importance to the country. You could have no more vital a task right now. And it may not be for long.'

'What do you mean?'

'I am working on a plan to spirit the Duke away for the duration.'

'Where to?'

'Bahamas? Kenya? Anywhere. It will have to be a suitably gilded cage but we'll find one.'

'Tell me about the position you have for Windsor in France.'

'Ahh! In two days we are sending one hundred and fifty-eight thousand men to France. They will be known as the British Expeditionary Force. Their role is to bolster the French defences under the command of General Gamelin, the French Supreme Commander. We are also sending twenty-five thousand vehicles and any number of RAF squadrons.' He paused ruefully. 'It means we will be issuing a general call-up. Everyone over twenty. No exceptions, except those in reserved occupations and the clergy. Those who don't wish to fight can have their names placed in a register of conscientious objectors. We'll use them in other ways.'

'Winnie, stick to the point,' I said exasperatedly.

'We know all we need to about the British Expeditionary Force but we have no real intelligence about the state of the French Forces.'

'Why don't you ask them?'

'We have – and been told precisely nothing. We've requested permission to send British officers to inspect the Maginot Line, as well as the French lines. But we were refused point-blank.'

'What has that to do with Windsor?'

'His contacts at the top level in France are legion. We're sure he'll be allowed to visit the places we can't access. Once there he is to note everything he sees and report back to our Imperial General Staff.'

'Will he do it?'

Churchill nodded. 'The Duke is a vain, egotistical and, I am sorry to say, very shallow man. I've come to realise it was a good day for the country when he abdicated. We now have a stalwart King and a wonderful Queen. So matters, to date, have turned out for the best. Windsor will do as we ask because we will appeal to the very traits which make him unsuited to be the Head of State. In spite of his failings, don't underestimate his intelligence. He can be witty, charming, and has an amazing capacity for remembering facts. He's not to be taken lightly. Do so at your peril.'

I stifled a sigh. Everything Churchill said made sense. But did I really want to go gallivanting around France with the Duke of Windsor? Analysing my emotions, I made an astonishing discovery. I was excited by the thought. A last adventure before it was too late? Before I was *really* too old?

I think Churchill sensed the change in me for his eyes twinkled in my direction. I thought of my wife, Madelaine, and my responsibilities – the bank, my constituency – and sighed, shaking my head. 'I don't know, Winston. I really don't.'

'Say nothing for now, David. Come and see me tomorrow with your decision. I'll be at the Admiralty. Eleven sharp suit you?'

I nodded. 'All right. But don't expect me to say yes. I don't want you to be disappointed.'

Lumbering to his feet Churchill waved his cigar in the air. 'You'll make the right decision. I know you will.'

I waved my hand distractedly. Damn Churchill! I knew I should talk to Madelaine but she was visiting friends and wouldn't be home until late. There was nothing for it. With a sigh I heaved myself out of the wing-backed leather armchair and headed for the door. Fresh air and a drive south would help clear my head.

I was soon on the road. I had recently indulged myself with a new car, a Triumph Dolomite roadster made by British Leyland. The balmy autumn night meant I had the roof down with the heating on full. The steady throb of the six-cylinder engine and hum of the wheels gave me a feeling of power. For a short while I forgot about the perilous state of the world and the part I might have to play in it. On an open stretch of road I put my foot down and took the car over 75mph before being forced to slow down for a bend. As my headlights cut a swathe of white across the landscape I remembered the parliamentary debate we'd had. Within days new rules were to be introduced regarding light. Headlights were to be reduced to mere slits, all street lights switched off, windows of houses to be covered with blackout curtains and the edges of the windows painted black to ensure no chink of light showed. Heavy fines would be imposed on those who transgressed a myriad of petty rules, which were, on the whole, fairly useless as far as the war effort was concerned.

I was halfway home when a sudden thought shattered my peace of mind. By mercy of a late birth my son Richard was safe. But my nephew, Alex, was twenty-two years old! He'd be called up! The lad had come down from Oxford that year after studying aeronautical engineering and had joined my brother Sion, in his aircraft manufacturing company. Was his a reserved occupation? Did he serve the war effort better by designing planes or flying them? Goddamn it all to hell! Fear left my mouth dry and my palms wet. Not for myself but for the youngster, and all those other young men who still had so much to live for. The Great War should have been a salutary lesson, so why was this happening now? Should it not have been our duty to save the younger generation this horror? We would have to answer the history books for our failure.

The Windsor situation was forgotten as I thought about the future. Once again I said a silent prayer thanking God that Richard was too young.

The gates of *Fairweather* appeared and I swept into the drive. Arriving home always gave me such pleasure, even under these circumstances. I took the car around the back and into the converted stable block. Madelaine's car wasn't there yet.

It was nearly 11pm and I expected the household to be in bed as I let myself in through the kitchen door. To my surprise I found Susan sitting in the kitchen, a cup of hot chocolate cooling on the table in front of her. I stood for a moment, watching my darling girl. She had been through such a lot in recent years. The death of her beloved Phillipe during the Spanish Civil War had scarred her terribly. Their tiny son, John Phillipe, born after his father's murder at the hands of the fascists, was a constant reminder of her loss, as well as her greatest joy. In recent months she had recovered, both physically and emotionally. Despite my paternal bias I knew her to be beautiful. What lay ahead for my wonderful, brave daughter?

When she smiled at me her whole face lit up.

'Dad! We weren't expecting you! What brings you home?'

'Something's come up that I need to discuss with Madelaine.'

'Sounds intriguing. What is it?'

'I'll tell you when Madelaine gets home. Ah!' At that instant her car came sweeping round the back and she came into the kitchen moments later.

'Darling, what a lovely surprise!' She kissed my cheek. 'I wasn't expecting you for at least another two days.'

'I was just telling Susan that I had something to talk to you about. Shall we go into the study and get a drink?'

'It's cold in there, darling, there's no fire. We're better off staying here,' said Madelaine. 'Susan, would you be a dear, and fix us some drinks?'

'Right away. What would you like?'

'After an abstemious evening, a gin and tonic would go down rather well.'

'Dad?'

'Whisky and soda, please.'

'Coming right up. Only don't start until I get back.'

I smiled at her retreating back. 'She seems more like her old self.'

Madelaine nodded. 'Yes, thank goodness.' Madelaine's relationship with Susan was a source of constant wonder to me. Susan had been born twenty-nine years earlier in America. When her mother died, she came to live with us in England. As she was illegitimate it had been necessary to adopt her, so that she was legally recognised as my daughter, and she had changed her name by deed poll to Griffiths. Thankfully Madelaine had been very fond of her from the beginning.

Madelaine stood at the fireplace, her figure still slim and youthful, and let down her hair. It was long and wavy, reaching just beyond her shoulders and framed her beautiful face. I loved the way she looked – her wide mouth, dark green eyes and fair complexion. After all these years I still found her enchanting. I knew I was one of the luckiest men alive to have such a contented marriage.

Susan returned with the drinks and we sat at the kitchen table while I recounted my conversation with Winnie. Our drinks sat untouched. When I finished I took an appreciative sip of my whisky and looked from one to the other. For a few seconds neither spoke.

Then Madelaine asked, 'What do *you* want to do?'

I shrugged. 'I'm torn, I must admit . . .' I broke off and looked into the distance for a second. Madelaine broke the spell.

'The adventure of it all appeals to you. Is that what you were about to say?'

I looked into her eyes, acknowledging her astuteness.

'A last adventure? To show you aren't too old?'

I squirmed. That was too close for comfort. Susan came to my rescue.

'Dad's not old!' she protested, but stopped when I shook my head.

'Madelaine's right. It's nonsense. They need to send someone younger and fitter. No. I'm needed in Parliament and at the bank.' As I spoke, the words felt like a hollow excuse. I was Chairman of Griffiths, Buchanan & Co, Hill St, Mayfair. The bank was the cornerstone of a business empire I oversaw. But the fact was, apart from major strategic decisions taken every few months, my best friend Angus Frazer ran the operation smoothly, thanks to the senior managers we had in place. Much of the decision-making within our companies was done as low down the totem pole as was reasonable. We were interested in results; how they were achieved was up to the line management. It was a good philosophy and one taught to me by my dear friend and mentor, John Buchanan. We operated on the lines of command found in naval vessels, both Royal and Merchant. To date it had stood us in good stead and allowed me enough time to devote to my parliamentary duties.

Was I really needed or was I merely making excuses? Looking at Madelaine's face my mind was made up. I would decline Churchill's offer.

I arrived at the Admiralty with time to spare and paced the pavement outside for a few minutes. As I went in through its imposing doors, a commissionaire checked my name on a list, glanced at my newly issued identity card and sent me through. A messenger led me up to Churchill's office. The young fellow was prattling on about some VIP or other but I took no notice, busy with my thoughts. Which was a shame really. Listening to his nervous excitement I would have been better prepared for what lay ahead.

2

I WAS USHERED into Churchill's outer office. His secretary immediately walked around her desk and said, 'They're waiting for you, Mr Griffiths. Can I get you anything? Tea? Coffee? Isn't this an honour?'

I couldn't think why it was an honour, so replied, 'Nothing, thank you. I don't think I'll be here that long.'

I walked into the large room overlooking the Strand and paused in the doorway. A second man was standing with his back to the room, looking out of a window. The brightness of the sunlight was in sharp contrast to the gloom of our surroundings. I didn't recognise him, registering only his average height and build. Churchill was by his desk, a paper in his hand.

'Good to see you, Griffiths. Your Majesty, may I introduce Sir David Griffiths?'

I straightened my back and did my best to keep the shock off my face. The messenger's prattling voice and the secretary's feeling of honour now made sense. The King was in the building!

George VI advanced towards me, his hand outstretched. 'Griffiths.'

'Your Majesty.' I shook his hand. His handshake was firm and dry. 'I'm honoured, sir.'

'I wanted to come and speak to you myself. To press upon you the urgency and delicacy of the task Winnie has entrusted to you. I fear the worse. It is of vital importance, not only to the Monarchy, but also to the country itself, that the matter is dealt with in a sensitive but firm manner. You've been fully briefed I take it?'

I looked at Churchill who gave a slight nod. My mouth was as dry as dust and I had an urgent need to run my tongue around my lips. I somehow managed to desist. 'Sir?'

'Yes, Griffiths?' The King raised a quizzical eyebrow.

I mentally cursed Churchill and knew I was trapped. 'We were to finish the briefing this morning, sir.'

'Good. Do this for us, Griffiths, for the country, and you will not find me ungrateful.'

'Thank you, sir. I wasn't looking for gratitude. Doing my duty is enough.'

'Good man. You have a baronetcy, I believe?'

'That's right, sir. For services rendered in 1926.'

His Majesty smiled. 'You rarely use your title, I'm told.'

'It's useful for getting a table in a busy restaurant and impressing my tailor,' I smiled in return.

'My brother is something of a snob, I fear. We wish you to use your title more often. Winston, I have to return to the Palace for a meeting with the Prime Minister. I'll leave you to give him the details. Thank you for your time, Griffiths.'

We shook hands and he departed. I knew enough about royal protocol to realise that I had been set up. There was no way the King would come to see me, or Churchill, for that matter. I had been tricked. But it would never be referred to . . . ever. Except this once. Between us.

'Damn you, Winnie, you knew I was going to refuse. But it would have been impossible to deny the king.'

Churchill had a lit cigar in his mouth, jutting pugnaciously between his lips. When he removed the cigar, he had the effrontery to laugh. 'Of course I knew. But you should know me by now – I'll do whatever it takes. We are heading for desperate times, believe me. Do not denigrate the value of this undertaking. I will say no more. Make your own judgement and don't be clouded by my feelings about Windsor.'

'My own opinion of the man couldn't be much lower – his abdication was the best thing that happened to this country.'

'It is true he's his own worst enemy. Now he has to be protected from himself. He should not be underestimated. He's highly intelligent but also one of the most self-centred men I have ever met. But, Griffiths, he was my . . . our . . . king. As such he deserves special consideration and I will do everything in my power to keep him safe. Which is why I want you with him. The Duke and Duchess of Windsor are at La Cröe, their villa on the French Riviera. We have been in regular contact with the Duke and have asked him to return immediately to

England. He refuses to do so unless his brother the King personally sends a plane and invites him to stay at Windsor Castle. This the King steadfastly refuses. We have sent the Duke cajoling letters and made coaxing phone calls in an attempt to get him to return. He prevaricates constantly. I don't know what game he's playing but he *must* return. It will be your task, along with Walter Monckton, to persuade him to do so. Do you know Monckton?'

'By reputation only.'

'He's a friend of the Duke's and has acted as a go-between for the King and his brother for years. He knows what to do. You depart tomorrow, in an RAF Leopard, for the Riviera. You and Monckton will carry papers giving you diplomatic immunity. So far the Hun hasn't ignored such niceties.'

Churchill continued his instructions. He showed me the letters and wires sent to the Duke; the grovelling nature of their content appalled me. I was definitely the wrong man for the job. I would find it hard to hide my true feelings about him.

The First Lord of the Admiralty seemed to sense my mood. He stopped talking for a few seconds, looked at me steadily and said, 'Don't forget, David, he was our King. He deserves our respect for that, if nothing else.'

I returned Churchill's gaze and said, 'Respect should be earned, not expected as a right. However, I will behave accordingly.'

'Good. Once you join his entourage you must work to stay there. The man is capable of alarming bouts of pettiness. The slightest thing and he is quite likely to ask for your removal. If we persuade him into the position as Liaison Officer in Paris you will be a member of his staff. You'll need a suitable rank, of course. I was thinking colonel. I know you've never been in the services but you did sterling work during the Great War. With the rank of colonel you won't have to do much saluting.'

'What unit?'

'Intelligence.'

'Is this a real appointment or a sham? By that I mean will I be subject to army discipline? Can I come and go as I please? Within reason, naturally.'

'Being in the Intelligence Corps gives you a great deal of latitude. You will have written orders, stating that you report directly to me and only me. There is no chain of command. However, in answer to your question, you will be on the books. Which means you will be subject to the Army Act.'

I grinned. 'I hope I get paid a damn sight more than the king's shilling. I have my tailor's bills to think about.'

Churchill smiled back.

We finished the briefing and I stood to go. A large wall chart in his office showed what I took to be the relative strengths of the fleets and I studied the numbers with some satisfaction. 'We still have the biggest navy in the world.'

'It looks that way but those figures apply to Britain and the Commonwealth. Our fleet is scattered across the world.'

I did a quick tally. 'Nevertheless – four hundred and seventeen ships. Pretty impressive.'

'Of course, we have one less since the aircraft carrier *Courageous* was sunk.'

I nodded. She had been the second casualty of the war. Two weeks previously the liner *Athenia* had been sunk by a U-boat with the loss of one hundred and twelve lives. It meant all-out war on shipping and we had responded accordingly. Unfortunately the *Courageous* was torpedoed with the loss of five hundred and nineteen of her crew. It had been a dark day and was a foretaste, I was sure, of much more to come. Our fleet had sunk the U-boat, U39, only three days earlier. 'What do the numbers conceal?'

'The hulls are old. Many of them are left over from the last lot. America has the same problem. But then it's true of most of the other navies. We'll need to re-build as fast as we can but we've not enough ship-building yards.'

'Germany has fewer than a hundred and fifty hulls.'

'One hundred and forty, to be precise. Whilst France has two hundred and seventeen, mainly in the Mediterranean, to counter the Italian fleet. We are vastly superior to Germany in terms of numbers. But don't forget, we will be fed as a nation by what we bring in by sea. Our merchant ships will be sitting ducks for the U-boats, especially if they hunt in wolf packs like the last time. Right now Germany has only twenty-three ocean-going submarines. The rest are too small and slow with poor endurance.' Pressing a button on his desk he summoned his secretary. 'Bring the papers for Mister . . . I mean, Colonel Griffiths.' Churchill chuckled, 'Colonel Sir David Griffiths, I should say.'

Armed with my orders I left the Admiralty for the outfitters, Gieves and Hawkes. In view of the urgency of my requirements they altered a uniform intended for someone else. By evening I was standing in front of a mirror admiring myself in my colonel's uniform.

I met with Walter Monckton at an airfield in Kent the following morning. The Duke's friend was a few years younger than me, a personable chap with an engaging smile and we hit it off right away. It was his task to persuade the Duke to return to Britain while I hoped to use the trip to ingratiate myself with the Prince so that when it was suggested I join his staff in France he'd have few, if any, objections.

We flew out in a minuscule and very fragile RAF Leopard. It was an uncomfortable flight but we finally arrived at our destination, an airfield a few kilometres along the coast from Nice. A car met us and took us to the gleaming white villa, La Cröe, where Windsor lived in voluntary exile.

We were shown into a large, airy room at the front of the house with breath-taking views over the blue Mediterranean. In the distance we could see yachts of all shapes and sizes, sailing slowly by in the light breeze. It was sunny and warm, the brightness in sharp contrast to the atmosphere we'd left behind in Britain. There the sombre mood of war was already making itself felt. I shook away my gloomy thoughts as the door opened.

The man who entered held out his hand to Monckton. 'Good to see you, Walter. Back for another bash at persuading HRH to return to Blighty? I hope you have more success than I've had.'

'We'll do our best, old chap. Let me introduce you to Colonel Sir David Griffiths. David, this is Major Edward Dudley Metcalfe, known to all as Fruity.'

I'd known immediately who he was. Metcalfe was one of Windsor's few true friends. They had met in India in the early twenties. A cavalry officer, Metcalfe had gone on to manage the Prince's polo stables. He shared a passion for hunting and polo with Windsor and often escorted him when he was night clubbing around London.

Despite his innocent-sounding nickname, Metcalf was also Sir Oswald Mosley's brother-in-law and a member of the January Club, a right-wing association affiliated to Mosley's Blackshirts. Fruity had never, to the certain knowledge of the British Establishment, shown any strong right-wing feelings. He was a follower, not an innovator. He had been best man at the Duke and Duchess's wedding at Château de Candé, Tours, in June of '37. I wondered, if the chips were down, where his true loyalties lay – with his ex-King or his country?

'Please, call me David, ' I insisted.

'We didn't know anyone was coming with you, Walter, old boy.' Metcalfe's smile was friendly enough but there was an edge to his voice.

'We thought that two heads were better than one. We *must* get David to see sense and return with us.'

From my briefing with Winnie, I knew that the Duke, christened Edward Albert Christian George Andrew Patrick David Saxe-Coburg-Gotha, was known as David to his family and friends.

Metcalfe nodded. 'I agree whole-heartedly. I can assure you I've done my best but you know how obstinate he can be sometimes.'

'We all know how stubborn he is, Fruity, but the consequences of him not returning are too awful to imagine. Damn it all man, his country needs him. Ah, there you are, sir.'

At forty-five years of age the Duke was still in his prime. I knew he kept fit playing tennis and golf and, when he had the opportunity, polo and fox hunting. He was a couple of inches shorter than my six feet, slim and narrow shouldered.

'Your highness, allow me to introduce Sir David Griffiths.'

The hand he extended to me was stained yellow with nicotine. 'How do you do, Griffiths? I had no idea, Walter, you were bringing a friend.'

'Sir David is a fellow traveller from London, a friend of Winnie's. He had a few days free and I brought him along. Hope you don't mind, sir.'

The Duke looked at me vaguely, 'Haven't we met before?'

'Yes, sir. Once at my mother's and again at a garden party at the palace.'

'Your mother's?'

'The Baroness of Guildford. After my father died my mother married John Buchanan.'

Snapping his fingers the Duke turned on a warm smile. 'I remember now. You're the banker. I never forget a face.'

If proof was needed of Windsor's remarkable memory this was it. As Winnie had said, the man was not to be underestimated.

'You're most welcome. I hope you'll be comfortable in our wee home. If there is anything you need just tell one of the servants. As you see, we live very simply here. A little golf, swimming from the yacht, excellent cuisine, and best of all, not a stuffy courtier in sight.' He laughed and we joined in. 'Have you met my darling wife yet, Griffiths? Wallis dear, do come and meet our house guests.'

The Duchess joined us, smiling warmly. 'How do you do? I hope you have plenty of gossip to share with us over dinner. We're dependent on our friends for news of home, as long as this ridiculous and unjustified vendetta continues. Not that life here is without its little blessings. I trust you have a pleasant stay, Sir David. But you must excuse us. Come, my dear, it's time for your afternoon nap.'

We watched them depart and then Metcalfe said, 'I'll show you to your room. How do you find the lovely Wallis?'

I thought carefully before replying. 'The photographs I've seen of her don't do her justice. She's an intriguing woman. She has presence, a dignity. I couldn't understand how a man could give up his royal birthright, his sovereignty, for a woman, but having seen them together I think I'll be far less judgmental in future.'

Privately, my opinion of her was unchanged. Wallis was the same height as the Duke, with an angular, heavy-jawed face and a large nose. She was far from pretty and spoke with a harsh American accent, which grated on the ear.

'Mmm. Wallis in Wonderland, we call her. But a word of warning, Griffiths. As far as His Highness is concerned she's the perfect woman; he won't tolerate any slight towards her.'

I nodded my appreciation of his warning.

The villa was spacious, luxurious and well staffed. The few changes of clothes I'd brought I hung in a heavy oak wardrobe and then went out onto the balcony to admire the view once more. Nothing had been said so far about the reason for our visit. I was leaving it to Monckton to set the pace.

The sun was setting to my right and the wind had dropped away to a beautiful, still evening. I became aware of the murmur of voices below and was about to step back inside to avoid being accused of eavesdropping when I realised how ludicrous that was. I ought to be listening.

I heard Monckton's voice first.

'Damn it all, David, I'm speaking as your best friend. You only think of yourselves. Don't you realise there is a war going on and that women and children are being bombed and killed while you talk of your *pride*? What you said to Walter just now was nuts. Did you really think they'd send a plane to take a few of your staff back to England? Of course not! Walter has come in person to persuade you, along with this Griffiths fellow. How much more do you want?'

The Duke's petulant, reedy voice replied, 'Why Griffiths?'

'According to Walter he's reliable and the soul of discretion. He holds the rank of colonel, is trusted by the government but best of all he's a friend of Winnie's. It's at his behest that Griffiths has come to help persuade you to return.'

'Well, if Winnie sent him then he's all right, I suppose. Churchill has proven to be a loyal friend throughout our trials, and has stood by me through thick and thin. Unlike that fool brother of mine!' There was no disguising the bitterness in the Duke's voice. 'We'll talk no more of this matter until after dinner to-night.'

I heard footsteps below and then silence. The cicadas' evening stridulation was starting up, a soporific background noise as the sun sank beneath the horizon.

I dressed for dinner and joined the others on the terrace for cocktails. It was such a far cry from sombre London that I had to stop from pinching myself.

A white-coated waiter served us gin and tonics. I found myself warming to the Duke at first, as he was an engaging and entertaining host. However, the conversation soon turned to world events, specifically the dangers of communism versus the wonders fascism had wrought in Germany.

'Look at the mess the country was in before Hitler took over, stagnant industry, hyper-inflation, massive unemployment. In the past eight years an economical miracle has been achieved. Wouldn't you agree, Griffiths?'

'No right thinking person could deny it.'

'See.' He leapt on my words. 'All right thinking people agree. Which is why this deplorable war with Germany is wrong! Unthinkable! It must be stopped.'

'David,' said Monckton, 'that's all the more reason why you *must* return to England and argue your corner. It's the only way. You can achieve nothing from here.'

The Duke paused and looked first at Monckton and then at me. 'What do you say, Griffiths?'

'I agree with Walter, sir. Either of the two positions you've been offered allow you to influence events.' I had no idea how prophetic my words would be.

Lighting yet another cigarette, Windsor appeared to be thinking about what had been said but then he smiled. 'Come. No more talk of the war and the role I should play until after dinner. I believe it's now ready.'

The meal was superb, the wines the very finest that France could supply. Wallis told me the final course was a speciality of the chef's, white grapes stuffed with soft cheese. Delicious, the finishing touch to a repast fit for a king. I thought that a special effort had been made for their guests but to my surprise I learned that the Windsors dined in similar splendour every night.

'Enjoy your meal, Sir David?' Wallis smiled at me.

'Very much,' I replied with honesty. 'I can't remember the last time I ate so well.'

'Cigarette, Griffiths?'

'No, thank you, sir. I don't smoke as a rule. Only the occasional cigar after dinner.'

'You're in luck. We have some Monte Christos in the humidor. Come through to the terrace. We've drinks set up outside.'

Scraping back my chair I made to follow the rest of them, but Wallis remained seated.

'Stay a moment, Sir David. I haven't had the opportunity to thank you for your efforts on my husband's behalf. On reflection, I think the position in Paris would suit him best. It will be so good for him to have a role to fulfil once more. Left on his own with too much time on his hands he broods terribly over the dreadful slights we've had to bear. He's often close to despair, you know. Visits from friends like Fruity and dear Bedaux have saved his sanity.'

'He won't regret the decision, Ma'am. By touring the Maginot Line, and reporting his findings, he would have the opportunity to make a real difference. Communications are vital. Accurate reports on manpower and artillery could possibly avoid massive and point-less loss of life. An incisive situation report from His Royal Highness would go a long way towards winning back the favour of the powers that be. Has he decided?'

'I'm still working on him.'

'You must be a great comfort to him at a time like this.'

Wallis stared penetratingly at me and I wondered for a moment if I'd overstepped the bounds. She smiled a little sadly and said, 'I have a framed verse from the Duke on my dressing table, Sir David. It reads:

> *"My friend, to live with thee alone*
> *Methinks were better than to own*
> *A crown, a sceptre and a throne." '*

She laughed hollowly. 'It is very tiring living up to the romance of the century. Come, Sir David, let us join the others. I do hope David doesn't drink too much again tonight.'

Whiskies and port, walnuts and olives were served outside. I was astonished to see it was well after 3.30am before noises were made about retiring. Apparently this was quite normal in the Duke's household. Thankfully, by the time we went to bed, Windsor had at last agreed to return to England. In the meantime he would consider which of the two positions he would accept. I hoped Wallis' influence would prevail.

We spent a further frustrating three days doing nothing. Finally the Duke and Duchess departed, with Metcalfe and their cairn terriers in one car, while I followed with the luggage in a second. Monckton had returned to England by plane to prepare for the ex-King's arrival. Nothing was to be left to chance. I travelled as part of the entourage, to ensure the Windsors completed the journey to London.

Prior to leaving La Croë, the Duke had insisted that a destroyer meet him and take him back to England in style, as befitting his rank. At Cherbourg we went aboard the Royal Navy's latest destroyer, HMS *Kelly*. Much to the Prince's delight he found it was commanded by his cousin, the RN's youngest captain, Lord Louis Mountbatten. I had known that Churchill was going to use Mountbatten but had been instructed to keep the information up my sleeve. If the Duke had balked at the last moment I was to have used the information to persuade him to carry on to Cherbourg. Winnie had also sent along his son, Randolph, with a personal message of welcome from the First Lord of the Admiralty. I could see that the Windsors were delighted with the treatment they were receiving.

On board ship I changed into my colonel's uniform, then regarded myself critically in a mirror. The tight jacket helped to keep my stomach in, although it hadn't spread too much, in spite of relatively sedentary years. My eyes were still clear and blue, though my nose was slightly more prominent than I would have liked – it had been broken years earlier in a brawl in New Orleans. An aquiline profile, I assured myself. My hair was still dark, the grey sideburns cut short.

Susan admired my strong jaw and the wide, Griffiths mouth. She said I looked like a pirate. Madelaine said I looked more like a reprobate. Personally I thought I looked like a City banker, albeit descended from a sword-waving cut-throat. I grinned at my reflection. *Rejected by God, hardened in sin and highly unprincipled.* There was life in the old dog yet.

Churchill had really laid it on thick. An honour guard stood in the gloom of the blacked-out city of Portsmouth to welcome His Royal Highness. The Royal Marine band broke into "God Save the King" and Edward inspected the guard. I walked behind him. When we finished and started towards the car Wallis stepped up next to him and took his arm. I realised she was soothing him.

'The short version, by God. Damn cheek, Griffiths, don't you think? The monarch gets the full treatment, other royalty only six bars. I'd become used to the full measure. I should never have returned,' he added petulantly.

I suppressed a grin; it was too late now. He was safely back on British soil.

They climbed into a car accompanied by their three terriers. We watched them depart. A major sticking point had been the King's refusal to allow his brother to stay at Windsor castle and his adamant refusal to receive Wallis. However, rooms at the Ritz Hotel, paid for by the government, had overcome the problem. I would also be staying at the Ritz. Unfortunately, His Majesty's Government was leaving me to pay my own bill. What the hell, I thought, as I strode towards a waiting staff car, I could afford it and the truth was I was enjoying myself.

3

THE FOLLOWING MORNING I telephoned the Duke in his room, offering my services by inviting him to lunch at the United Services Club. I made it clear it would be my treat. I sugared the invitation by telling him that Winston would join us at his earliest convenience. After all, it wasn't really my place to invite ex-Kings to lunch. I wasn't senior enough nor on friendly enough terms to do so. The frosty reception to my invitation quickly thawed at the mention of Churchill's name.

At the club Edward was greeted with a good deal of deference and he lapped up the fawning adoration he received. Many of its members were ex-military officers and it seemed to me that when they joined the services they were brainwashed into revering royalty. A couple of gins further helped to put the Duke into a good mood. Luckily Churchill joined us before we went into lunch and immediately arranged for a private dining room to be set at our disposal. We had finished our soup, an indifferent leek and potato, when another guest arrived – General Sir Edmund Ironside, Chief of the British Imperial General Staff and Inspector-General of the Forces.

Ironside explained the problems we were encountering with the French, insisting it was imperative that we inspected their front-line as well as the Maginot Line to assess the situation. That was where the Duke could help. He would join the Military Mission at the villa in Nogent-sur-Marne to the east of Paris and work with the officers and men there to establish a working relationship with the French High Command at Vincennes.

The Duke picked that moment to drop his bombshell. 'We've decided to take the job in Wales.'

A silence greeted his announcement, quickly broken by Churchill. 'I am sorry, sir, but you're too late, the post has already been filled.'

The Duke, his temper never far away, fairly blazed with fury. 'How dare you give away the position Wallis and I had decided upon?'

His stance surprised me in view of my conversation with Wallis after that first dinner but I kept my face impassive.

Churchill rallied quickly. 'I'm sorry, sir. We couldn't wait any longer. The war has injected a deal of urgency into such matters. Besides, your talents are far better suited to the job in Paris. Trust me.'

'But damn it, Winston, we saw the Welsh job as a way for Wallis and I to settle back into life in Britain. Give me time to re-establish myself with my people. To have Wallis accepted at last.'

A possibility which had been pointed out by his brother, who had blocked the appointment. The King was no fool.

'We understand that, sir,' said Churchill, looking at Ironside and me for confirmation. We both nodded. 'But the fact of the matter is we urgently need your help in France. It's vital. Far more important than Wales.' Churchill used all his considerable powers to cajole Edward into taking the job.

'We will,' said Ironside, 'be sending an intelligence officer with you, of course. Griffiths here will accompany you and help with your work. We need to know the French dispositions, their strengths and weaknesses and have the information immediately despatched back to us. Our Expeditionary Force can then be deployed to best advantage. Provided,' he added with a despondent air, 'the French agree.'

'Before I depart I would expect you to get agreement for me to visit the French zone. Otherwise it would be a complete waste of my time,' said Windsor thoughtfully.

'Steps have already been taken. We suggested it would be good for French morale to have you visit their troops, especially at the front, as you are so popular with the people of France.'

That statement went down well. God, but the man's ego was phenomenal. During our conversation we had been served tough beef with boiled potatoes and tasteless vegetables. We all passed on the pudding. Churchill and the Duke had brandies with their coffees while Ironside and I declined. I paid the bill.

I returned to the Ritz with the Duke and was surprised when he invited me up to his suite for a drink. I wanted to say no but thought better of it. I had come to realise that the Duke of Windsor craved company and Wallis had gone shopping with some friends. In the interests of cementing our relationship I accompanied him.

Their suite consisted of two bedrooms and a large lounge. An adjoining room had been turned into a temporary pantry where the Duke's butler held sway over two other servants.

In the lounge Windsor stood by the window and looked down at Hyde Park. After a few seconds of silence he turned to me and asked, 'Griffiths, what do *you* make of it all?'

'Well, sir, I think it's important work. We need the information. Much depends on the disposition of our forces and without knowing the strength of the French army we don't know where to deploy them.'

He looked over his shoulder, but not at me. He was frowning. 'Where are those damn dogs?' He called out, 'Pookie, Preezie, Detto, come here.' There was no answering yap. The butler appeared.

'Your Royal Highness, I'm sorry to say the cairns have been taken into quarantine. They were reported as having come in from France and taken an hour ago.'

'How dare those uniformed buffoons think they can treat me like this? Find out where they have been taken and get them back. Immediately!'

The butler hesitated, coughed, then finally said, 'I know where they are, sir. The address is next to the telephone. But . . . I have been instructed to tell you that not even . . . for the King himself would the dogs be allowed to break the strict anti-rabies quarantine.' The man licked his lips and said, 'I was told to tell you, sir, that no man is above the law. I'm so sorry, your Royal Highness.'

Edward's shoulders slumped and the anger drained out of him. 'Very well, just bring me a drink, a gin and tonic. You, Griffiths?'

'A whisky and soda, please, sir.'

It was the beginning of a long afternoon. In the following hours, I learned a great deal more about the Duke's support for Germany and fascism. I was beginning to have grave doubts as to the wisdom of trusting Windsor with such an important and sensitive task, but naturally kept my fears to myself. Wallis arrived back in time for tea and I excused myself while the Duke brought her up-to-date about their dogs. I was not unhappy to see how upset she was at the news.

The incident, though of no real consequence, showed the arrogance and unmitigated gall of the man. Our quarantine laws were the strictest in the world and had eradicated rabies from Britain over a decade earlier. Yet he thought he could flout the rules as it suited him.

In my own room I lay on the bed, my hands behind my head, deep in thought. Somehow I had become aide-de-camp to Edward. It was a role I was unsuited for but one I was prepared to endure for the moment. With that thought I fell asleep.

Over the next few days we had a number of varied and lengthy discussions with the incredibly busy Hore-Belisha, the Secretary of State for War. I could see that the Minister was often annoyed with Windsor but the Duke appeared not to notice. If he did, he was so full of his own self-importance that he didn't give a hoot.

One such meeting was particularly sensitive. The issue of the Duke's rank had arisen. 'Hore-Belisha,' began the Duke, in his usual supercilious fashion, 'I am a Field-Marshal in the Army, and that is the rank I wish to retain.'

Hore-Belisha was too wily a politician to show the incredulity he must have been feeling at such unmitigated gall. 'Sir, as heir to the throne you were given the honorary rank of Field Marshal of the Army. You hold many other titles including Air Marshal of the Royal Air Force and Admiral of the Fleet. None of which positions you are trained to hold. The titles mean, sir, with all due respect, that military senior officers would pay you deference on the parade ground or in the mess. Nothing more.' There was a steely glint in Hore-Belisha's eye and I could see he was holding his temper with difficulty.

'I must have a suitable rank.'

'Of course, but you must see you cannot carry out the duties of a lower rank when under the command of a real major-general.' The Minister paused. I realised that this obstacle had been foreseen. 'You can, however, hold the *honorary* rank of major-general, under the command of Major-General Richard Howard-Vyse once you arrive in France.'

Disappointment was visible on the Duke's face. However, he merely nodded and then said, 'It would be a good idea if I visited the Commands in Britain before leaving for France. You know, to give me contact with the troops and help me get into the role. I would, of course,' he added, 'like Wallis to accompany me.'

Hore-Belisha gave a thoughtful nod. 'I shall have to ask permission, sir. Leave it with me.'

The Minister might have fooled Windsor with his anodyne reply but he didn't fool me. The Duke's intention for such a tour was obvious – to raise his and Wallis' profile with the British people. I was prepared to bet he wouldn't be given the go-ahead.

Finally Windsor was satisfied. When he left the room, the minister indicated that I should remain. Once we were alone, Hore-Belisha gave a huge sigh of relief. 'We appreciate your help here, Griffiths. He's the most difficult man to deal with. I wish to underscore the need to keep an eye on him. You know our fears with regard to his fascist views?'

'Winston has made them clear enough.'

'What do you make of his request to visit the Commands?'

I wondered how far I should go. 'I've spent a good deal of time with the Duke and Duchess over the last few days. I find their political views, on the whole, abhorrent. He boasts about his German heritage, with no thought of the offence it causes those who lost loved ones in 'fourteen to 'eighteen. He is anti-Semitic and virulently fearful of communism. Moreover, he remains extremely bitter over the abdication. In truth, the Duke desperately wants peace between Britain and Germany. I think he sees himself as able to deliver that peace. If he tours the Commands . . .' here I was about to put my neck squarely on the line, 'I wouldn't trust him not to pass information to the Germans.'

Much to my surprise Hore-Belisha nodded. 'Those were precisely my thoughts. This is a hell of a situation. The best we can do is contain it. Let us hope we are both wrong and he performs his duty well.'

'What will you tell him about his tour of the Commands?'

'That there's no time. That he must go to France as soon as possible.'

On that note I left. I spent a few hours at the bank in meetings with senior staff before driving to *Fairweather*.

I knew I could rely upon the discretion of Susan and Madelaine and so, over dinner, I told them what had been happening. They were aghast. After dinner we sat in the study and talked about the way the war would go.

'I need to get involved,' Madelaine announced. She smiled at my reaction. 'My languages must be of some use – I'm still fluent in French and German and I used to work for the Foreign Office itself. Naturally it was a long time ago, but there must be something I can do.'

If that's what she wanted I wasn't going to stop her, although I had always thought she enjoyed running the house.

31

'This place runs like clockwork,' she disabused my thoughts, 'and apart from some charity work I have plenty of time on my hands. I thought I would contact the Foreign Office and see if they had anything to offer.'

'Do you want me to make enquiries?'

Madelaine shook her head. 'I know who to talk to. You don't mind, do you?'

Did I? Probably. But I was being ridiculous. I smiled wryly. 'Of course not.'

'Liar,' she leant across and kissed my cheek. 'But thank you for understanding. If things get as bad as Winnie predicts then all of us will be needed sooner or later.'

Susan had been looking into the fire in a sombre mood. 'Madelaine is right. I have skills to offer and it's time I volunteered too.'

'What about the baby?' I asked, startled. Susan had been through enough during the Spanish Civil War and had barely escaped with her life or her sanity. The thought of her putting her life in danger again was unbearable.

'I'm a pilot, Dad, and a damn good one. I can't just sit at home and knit socks for the war effort when I have the skills I do. It said on the wireless today that volunteers with flying experience are being called for.'

'Sweetheart, please. There's no call for you to volunteer. Besides, as a woman the RAF won't accept you.'

'They asked for men *and* women. I don't know what job I'll be offered but the obvious one would be ferrying aircraft around Britain. I know I won't be fighting in France and, to be honest, I don't want to. I've seen enough of war. But I can help.'

'What about John Phillipe?' I repeated.

Susan sighed, and I knew from her answer she had thought long and hard about her son. Separation from him would not be easy for her. 'He's safe here. And he's got Connie to look after him.' His Spanish nurse, who had escaped from Spain with Susan, had become an integral part of the household, as well as Susan's dearest friend. She would have been at dinner with us that evening except she had gone to the cinema in Brighton to see Judy Garland in the new Technicolor film, "The Wizard of Oz". Connie loved John Phillipe almost as much as Susan. She was right. The child wouldn't suffer unduly.

'I'll make enquiries,' I said.

'Thanks, Dad.'

Madelaine had obviously been thinking along similar lines. 'Another thing we can do,' said my wife, 'is to offer the house as a refuge for evacuees, children leaving the cities. Particularly from London. We have plenty of room. If we keep the west wing for our own use we still have eight bedrooms available. Each can hold anything from two to four beds.'

It made sense, although I wasn't too sure how I felt about a horde of brats running around *Fairweather*. 'Have you discussed this with Gibbs?' Our butler was in charge of the other servants – the decision would have far-reaching consequences.

'I mentioned it in passing,' said Madelaine.

'And what did he say?'

'Yes, madam. If madam wishes.'

That sounded just like Gibbs. A butler of the old school. He would, I felt sure, rise to the challenge. 'How would you go about getting children sent here?'

'The evacuation is being organised by schools. I gather children from the same area are being sent to small towns and villages all over the country, so at least they'll have some friendly faces with them. I'll sort it out.'

I was sure she would.

We spent the weekend in discussion, about how best to accommodate child evacuees and how to utilise the land to better effect. I talked to my neighbour who farmed two thousand acres and suggested he use my fifty acres to cultivate some crop or other. We made an agreement, shook on it, and I left him to it. In accordance with Home Office guidelines, he planned to turn our pasture into fields of potatoes.

On Sunday morning we went hunting. I enjoyed a good ride across the Downs, though no fox was caught. In the afternoon we walked as a family through the woods. John Phillipe spent most of the time being carried on my shoulders, making horsy noises and telling me to trot on. He rewarded me with a light kicking if my pace slowed laughing with delight. The sound of his voice brought a large grin to my face. He was such a sunny child, so loving and warm. We would all be lost without him. Despite her own grief, Susan had made sure her son's emotional needs were met, telling him every day how much she loved him. Madelaine and I, for our part, gave the child as much affection and reassurance as possible.

The evening was spent in quiet contemplation and discussion of what the future possibly held. The following morning I left early to return to the Ritz. I wanted to be on hand as soon as the Duke was up and about. Luckily, he wasn't by nature an early riser.

I was sitting in the lobby, in uniform, reading the *Times* when he appeared. 'Morning, Griffiths.'

'Morning, sir,' I replied, rising to my feet.

He briefed me on his agenda and we departed by car to meet with Hore-Belisha again. I wondered what the meeting could be about this time.

Windsor was given the news that a tour of Britain's Commands was not possible. Time constraints didn't permit it. If he was disappointed, he didn't show it.

Waving a nonchalant hand the Duke announced, 'I have decided to waive my right to my salary as a major-general. I would like you to make the announcement to the press. Something along the lines of my generous gesture to the war effort.'

Hore-Belisha looked for a long moment at his well-polished brogues, then summoned his Military Secretary and explained the Duke's proposal to him.

'I'm sorry, your Royal Highness, but no member of the royal family has ever been paid for their services to the army. It has always been seen as a part of your duty to your country in time of need. So the gesture is hardly unique.'

Disappointment showed on Edward's face. 'In that case I wish to be given an honorary colonelcy in the Welsh Guards.'

I could see the Minister working to contain his anger. 'Again, I am sorry, sir, but I cannot appoint honorary colonels. That is in the gift of the King only.' Before Windsor could say anything further, Hore-Belisha rose to his feet. 'Gentlemen, you must excuse me. I have to be at Number Ten in fifteen minutes. The War cabinet is meeting.'

'Before you go, Hore-Belisha,' said the Duke, 'I wish to wear my decorations on my uniform and I wish to have Fruity Metcalfe as my equerry.'

In a hurry to deal with more pressing and important matters the Minister agreed. 'Yes, yes. Now I must go.'

That was our last meeting with Hore-Belisha. Windsor had no further excuse to delay his departure for France.

On the morning of the 29 September, in a force six gale, I arrived at Portsmouth railway station and took a taxi to the harbour. HMS *Express* had been put at our disposal to take us across the Channel. I was standing at the top of the gangway when the Duke and Duchess, their three cairns, obviously rescued from quarantine, and Fruity Metcalfe arrived; a second car, stuffed full of luggage, followed. The Windsors were safely ensconced in the Captain's cabin while I was invited to the open bridge to witness our departure. It was windy with occasional squalls of rain but not cold. I enjoyed watching the organised bustle of the ship getting underway.

After a quick dash to France and a train to Paris, we arrived late that night and booked into the Trianon Palace Hotel in Versailles. On the train I had spent time in the lounge with Metcalfe discussing the war in general and Windsor's mission in particular. I had an inkling that Fruity was not all that he appeared and suspected that he and I worked for the same outfit – Intelligence. As I was reporting to Churchill could he be working through the chain of command? It was just a feeling but there was something about the fellow that I couldn't quite put my finger on.

Later the following morning we reported to the No. 1 Military Mission, La Faisanderie, Nogent-sur-Marne. We were immediately shown into the office of Major-General Richard Howard-Vyse, where the Duke was met politely but left in no uncertainty about who was in charge. Howard-Vyse issued orders, not requests.

'And you are certain, sir, that you will be able to remember all that you see?' Howard-Vyse asked the Duke.

Windsor smiled disarmingly. 'I have endured years of training. Richard, when I was a child I would be introduced to a room full of guests. I would then be taken to an anteroom, where I would be expected to remember everyone's names, where they stood and what they wore. As a result I never forget the names of people I meet. I have, I would suggest, a memory uniquely suited to that of a spy.'

The small gathering guffawed politely.

My presence in the Duke's entourage was now taken for granted and I no longer had to be with him constantly. As a result I spent some time at the Military Mission, discussing the war with some of the other officers. They were all in bullish mood, believing it highly unlikely that Hitler would be able to break through the Maginot Line and take France or anywhere else in Western Europe. I admired their optimism but didn't entirely share it.

That evening I dined late with some of the officers in a local restaurant. Afterwards a group of us adjourned to the Ritz for a nightcap. The Paris hotel had an ambience far superior to the London Ritz. In the foyer I noticed a heavy-set man with combed-back hair shaking hands with the Duke of Windsor. Keeping my back to them, I watched in the mirror that lined the length of the bar. I felt I knew the man but couldn't place him for a few seconds. Then it hit me. Of course! Charles Bedaux.

The Duke's friend was a wealthy industrialist, favoured by large companies all over the world for his innovative method of increasing productivity. His conveyor belts meant he was loved by factory owners and hated by the workers. I knew that he had done a great deal of work in Germany, helping Hitler to rebuild the country, but also to rearm. It was rumoured in the City of London that Bedaux was one of the few men outside of Hitler's immediate circle who had direct access to the Führer.

There was evident warmth and friendship between the Duke and Bedaux. After a few moments Wallis Simpson and Fruity Metcalfe joined them. Bedaux walked them across the foyer and, with a beaming smile on his face, ushered them through the front door.

Back in my room I used a code book to create a simple message for Churchill, on my sighting of Bedaux. In the morning I handed it into the Signals Office and went to the intelligence briefing, which Howard-Vyse had instigated as soon as he had set up shop. There were ten officers and thirty men in the Military Mission. Their task was to act as the channel of communication between the Commander-in-Chief of the British Expeditionary Force in France and General Gamelin, Chief of Staff of the French National Defence Forces. It had been emphasised that their main task was to discover all they could about the French defences and relay the information back to Britain. The prime mover, the linchpin, the real reason for the existence of the Mission was the Duke of Windsor. He never attended the morning briefings; they started too early for him.

4

I MET METCALFE a few days later for dinner and drinks at our hotel, during one of the rare evenings that he wasn't chaperoning the Duke and Duchess. After I plied him with a few strong whiskies, he relaxed enough for me to dare ask, 'Was that Charles Bedaux I saw with the Duke a few nights ago?' I feigned indifference to his answer, but Metcalfe was not slow in replying.

'Yes. They have been great pals for years. Do you know him?'

I shook my head. 'No. But I know *of* him. In certain circles he's quite famous. He works for some of the richest men in the world, I hear. Very wealthy in his own right, isn't he?'

Metcalfe nodded enthusiastically. 'He's proven to be a stalwart friend of David's, supported the Windsors loyally throughout their travails. He gave them his castle, Château de Candé, to use as a retreat following the abdication and for their wedding.'

As a banker I held files on many people and companies, which had proven invaluable. So much so that we now employed two full-time staff to ferret out information on individuals and to collect snippets from newspaper and magazines about them and their businesses. Such information had saved us a fortune in the past. I knew we had a thick file on Bedaux, though I didn't know its contents. But that was about to be rectified. The file was on its way.

I did remember some salient facts however. 'Bedaux was born a Frenchman and took American citizenship, didn't he?'

'That's right,' said Metcalfe cheerfully. 'He's an odd fellow. His knowledge of Europe and our Colonies is staggering. Frightening almost. I don't know whether he was simply trying to impress the Duke and Duchess but he can give chapter and verse on military strengths of the European nations, from our own to Norway and across to Greece. He's dead set against the war and he and David are agreed on practically everything. Bedaux believes Germany should be allowed to expand eastwards and that we should support them against Bolshevism.'

'Did Windsor agree?'

'Oh yes. That has long been his view. David fears the disintegration of the British Empire if we waste our men and resources fighting Hitler. He makes no secret of his views, as you well know.'

Metcalfe looked over my shoulder and said, 'I say, who is that lovely creature walking towards us?'

I turned my head. My daughter Susan was bearing down on us with a wide smile. 'Hullo, Dad. Hope I'm in time for cocktails.'

My heart lifted at the sight of her. When I'd asked for the file to be brought to me I had no idea she would be the courier. I'd expected my brother or one of his pilots to fly across.

'What a pleasant surprise! I expected your Uncle Sion.'

'He's with me – he's registering.'

At that moment my brother strode into view. A couple of years younger than me, he was an inch shorter but with broader shoulders. People often remarked on the resemblance between us – his face, though fuller than mine, had the same blue eyes. At that moment he also had a wide grin plastered on his face as he approached, hand outstretched.

'It's good to see you, Bro'.'

'Sion, my dear fellow, let me introduce you to Fruity Metcalfe.'

They joined us for dinner. Wisely neither Sion nor Susan mentioned the reason for their trip. It was a sociable affair, the food and wine excellent. As soon as it was polite to do so, we excused ourselves from Metcalfe and went up to my room. I always enjoyed seeing Sion. We were both extremely busy, but took time to stay regularly in touch.

My brother was a successful aircraft manufacturer and superb pilot. Flying was his passion. Susan had caught the bug from him and he had taught her to fly. His company, Griffiths Aviation Ltd, was one of the three most important aircraft designers and builders in the UK. The war had started with three fighting aircraft of distinction, the Spitfire, the Hurricane and Sion's plane, the Griffin.

Sion's business was doing well. The Air Ministry had just placed an order for more Griffins and Sion had been asked to produce as many aircraft as possible – and to keep making them.

I knew he and his wife Kirsty were anxiously awaiting news of their son's call-up. 'What's the situation with Alex?'

'No news as yet. His job has been deemed a reserved occupation and so they won't call him up. Mind you, he's champing at the bit to go. And I can't say I blame him. Kirsty wants him to stay at home, but you know how it is.'

'I know. At that age you think you're invincible. The reality is so very different, as we saw last time.'

Sion took a mouthful of whisky and said, 'Each generation has to learn for itself. Usually the hard way.'

Susan gave a wry smile. 'You grow up hellish quickly once you're exposed to war.'

We nodded soberly. Her time fighting as a pilot during the Spanish civil war had been horrific. It had left her physically scarred and emotionally damaged. Thankfully she was over the worst of her mental anguish but the scar on her abdomen would be with her for life.

'One major piece of news,' said Sion. 'We're moving from Biggin Hill. It's too exposed to attack from the air. If the balloon goes up we'll be in the front-line.'

'When did you decide such a big step?'

Sion shrugged. 'It's been on the cards for a while. We're bursting at the seams as it is, so it's a good time to make the move. We're developing a new fighter as well as converting the Griffin V to a bomber. Both are ready to go into production.'

'What'll happen to Biggin Hill?' Ever the banker, I couldn't help adding, 'What about the expense?'

Sion shook his head. 'The government is funding the whole move. They're buying the field and the buildings and expanding the RAF base there.'

'Where are you going?'

'St Athan in South Wales.'

'Where the hell's that?' I asked, frowning.

'Near a village called Llantwit Major.' Sion could see from my face that I still had no idea where he was talking about. 'Ten or twelve miles west of Cardiff.'

'What about a skilled workforce? And housing for them?'

'Housing is a serious difficulty. As to a skilled workforce, that's an ongoing problem. Our men are drifting away on a daily basis as they get called up. We're having to replace them with women, who need training. It'll be the same at St Athan. There's a reasonable catchment area, but it'll still mean bussing workers in. Wherever we go it's a factor. We just have to deal with each problem as it arises.'

I nodded. Sion was good at that.

Susan had an announcement too. 'Dad, I came over with Uncle Sion so I could tell you that I've joined up.'

I was aghast. 'You've done *what*?'

'Joined up.' She spoke nonchalantly but I could sense her excitement.

'As what exactly?'

Her reply didn't surprise me. 'A pilot for a new service ferrying aircraft from the manufacturers to the squadrons. Retired pilots and some women are being taken on.'

'Don't worry, David,' Sion tried to reassure me, 'Susan'll come and work for me. Though she'll be expected to fly for other manufacturers as well.'

I tried to think of an argument I could put forward to dissuade her but knew I'd be wasting my breath. Instead I managed a smile and said, 'Take care, sweetheart.'

Susan smiled. 'You know me, Dad. Always careful.'

I smiled wryly. I *did* know her. That was why I felt such concern. I prayed the war would be over quickly. For all our sakes.

'Did you bring the file on Bedaux?'

Sion nodded. 'It's in my bag. You can read it later. I've also got a letter from Madelaine.'

Sion and Susan intended to stay in Paris for a day and take in the sights. I arranged to meet them for breakfast before bidding them goodnight. Then I settled down with the file. When I'd finished reading, it was nearly two o'clock in the morning. What I'd learnt about Bedaux was disquieting, to say the least. Windsor was swimming in deep and dangerous waters.

With a guilty start I remembered the letter from Madelaine. Tearing open the envelope I read it quickly. She wrote that she had a meeting shortly at the Foreign Office for a possible position in the FO. Arrangements were being made to convert *Fairweather* for evacuees from an East End school. She ended by suggesting we take a flat in town for the duration. I heartily concurred.

Late the following morning we journeyed to General Gamelin's headquarters for lunch. It was a successful social affair and, as far as we were concerned, highly productive. It was agreed that the Duke should undertake a series of morale-boosting tours, to start on Friday. His initial visit would be to the First Group of Armies in the sector, immediately to the right of the British Expeditionary Force. Passes and documents were issued for the Duke, Metcalfe and myself. We returned to the hotel highly satisfied.

'Fruity,' said the Duke, 'I think it would be a good idea if your batman didn't accompany us.'

'Why ever not, sir?' Metcalfe asked, askance.

'It'll leave more room for a few of my things, don't you know. I'd ask Griffiths here, but he outranks you.'

'But we're taking two cars. There's plenty of room,' Metcalfe argued.

'Please don't be tiresome, old boy. It's only for a few days. And I must have room for the odd object or two. You know how I hate tea not made in *kettly*.' The Duke had a childish habit of giving his possessions nicknames. *Kettly*, his favourite teapot, had apparently survived since his days in the nursery.

I could see that Metcalfe was going to argue further, but the Duke had that set expression to his mouth and Fruity knew it would be futile. He yielded with bad grace.

Later that evening I discovered Metcalfe in the bar of the hotel, nursing a large whiskey.

'Long day?' I asked.

Metcalfe looked at me with an expression of resignation. 'Something like that. Some days he's difficult, on others he's bloody impossible.'

I shook my head in sympathy and thought *Thank God for Wallis and the abdication*. It was the first but not the last time that I found myself being grateful to Mrs Simpson.

The day before we set off on our tour Poland surrendered to Germany. The news left a pall hanging over us, as we finally departed. Our party consisted of the Duke, Metcalfe, two batmen, two drivers and myself. Our first stop was at the British Expeditionary Force headquarters in Arras. We spent a pleasant hour in the mess where Windsor lapped up attention from officers senior enough to know better. However, their fawning put the Duke in a good mood for our visit to the French First Army under General Blanchard. We arrived in time for dinner, an informal affair where the Duke was greeted as the guest of honour. Speaking fluent French, he was an immediate hit with his hosts who, though welcoming, weren't as obsequious as their British counterparts. I wondered for a cynical moment if the decapitation of their own royalty had tempered their views somewhat.

We stayed for two days and saw the best of everything that the First Army had to offer. Nothing was kept from us. We looked over the anti-tank defences, visited the large fortifications and went as far as the western edge of the Ardennes. From there we visited the French Ninth Army under General Corap, a wily old bird who tolerated rather than welcomed us. However, the Duke charmed him sufficiently so that we met many of the Ninth's divisional commanders and were able to talk war and invasion with them. We spent the night in a hotel in Charleville, where we treated some of the senior French officers to dinner. The following morning we had the first of many rumpuses that would plague this and similar visits.

We were checking out of the hotel. I had paid my bill when I over-heard Windsor talking to Metcalfe.

'This will *not* do,' said the Duke, the whine in his voice rising as it did when he was unhappy about something or other. 'You must do something.'

'Sir, what can I do?' Metcalfe protested. 'The bill has to be paid. The invitations were made by you. *I* don't have the money. You can reclaim the cost from the government.'

'Little chance of that. Please ensure this does not happen again. Get funds before the event, there's a good fellow.'

I had made the grave error of loitering to listen and was spotted by Windsor. 'Ah, Griffiths, kindly pay the hotel account. You can reclaim the cost.'

It wasn't the money, it was the arrogance of the man that got under my skin. I paid with bad grace and stomped from the hotel to the car, without as much as a thank you from Windsor, who accepted anything done for him as his due.

Back at La Faisanderie Windsor and I began work on the report. As he had claimed, the Duke's memory was remarkable. He recalled details that I had missed although in my defence there were certain things I remembered that he had failed to spot.

It took two days until our six-page account was finished. Entitled "Report on Visit to the First French Army and Detachments D'Armée des Ardennes by His Royal Highness the Duke of Windsor, October,

1939", it detailed precisely the capability of the French in the sector. I considered it an excellent piece of intelligence gathering. It was given, under the classification *Secret*, to Howard-Vyse, who was delighted with our observations.

'I found,' the Duke reported to Howard-Vyse, 'the French to be most helpful and pleasant. They are determined, if possible, to give the Germans battle in Belgium.' Windsor smiled and added, 'Of course they will burrow like rabbits at the sound of the first shell, but then, French logic as ever dictates never die unless you have to.'

That evening I dined alone. I was out of sorts and didn't want any company to distract me from my thoughts. In the long days I had been with Windsor I had learned a great deal more about his thoughts and ambitions. There was no doubt that he still believed himself to be a king beloved by the British, who had romantically forsaken everything for the love of a good woman. He saw himself very much in the role of peacemaker, the saviour of his people. His Nazism and pro-German attitude were never far from the surface.

I was becoming increasingly worried about these intelligence tours we were making. It had taken only a short while touring the French front-line with him for me to think the unthinkable. *What if the information we were passing to Britain also found its way to Germany?*

Draining my glass of excellent red wine I went outside for a walk to clear my head. My steps took me as far as the Ritz. Call it instinct. I knew the Windsors were dining there with Bedaux.

Our report had just been lodged and that evening, almost immediately afterwards, Windsor was meeting with one of Hitler's confidantes. It was infuriating – who knew what secrets the Duke was passing over with the salt? I didn't like it.

I loitered outside the Ritz for some time and just as I was beginning to feel foolish I saw Bedaux come out. He walked to the Gare du Nord, with me on his tail. It was a long way and I was surprised he didn't take a taxi. I watched as he booked a first class seat on the train to The Hague the following morning. As soon as he left I did the same.

The train departed on time. I sat at one end of the dining car while Bedaux was at the other. I ignored him completely, avoiding potential eye contact. Breakfast was silver service and excellent. I had the opportunity to consider how rash I had been in following Bedaux, but I wanted to know where he was going. With the report just completed and his immediate departure after meeting with Windsor, Bedaux's trip to Holland seemed ominous.

In the middle of the afternoon we drew into Amsterdam station. I rushed ahead then waited at a kiosk, watching Bedaux hurry in the direction of the taxi rank. Within moments he was talking to the cabbie.

He asked for the German Embassy.

We left the station in tandem, as I leapt into the taxi behind. I buried myself behind my magazine, keeping an eye on the car ahead.

As Bedaux's vehicle slowed down I said to the driver, 'Keep going, I'm early. Drop me a hundred metres past the embassy and I'll walk back.'

Back at the imposing gates of the embassy, I was in time to see the door close on the broad back of Charles Bedaux.

I looked at my watch – just after 4pm. I was in luck. Most of Europe's Dutch embassies were situated in the same street and soon people began to leave, going home. Trams came more frequently as the daily migration of embassy workers picked up. I stood in a tram queue opposite the German embassy, my felt hat pulled low over my forehead. A tram came and went, leaving me standing in isolation. I walked briskly along the street and crossed the road, whipping off my hat and hiding it under my overcoat.

I moved with the crowd, weaving in and out of other pedestrians, keeping close enough to miss nothing. After about forty minutes I was opposite the embassy gates when the main door opened to reveal Bedaux. He paused in the doorway and turned to shake the hand of the man with him. I recognised him immediately – the German ambassador, Count Julius von Zech-Burkesroda, late of the embassy in London.

I'd seen enough. A tram pulled up and I leapt aboard. I got off at the next stop, hailed a taxi, and was soon back at the train station. My luck continued. The evening train for Paris was due to depart in ten minutes and I was soon settled on board.

Loud alarm bells were ringing in my head. As I sat in splendid isolation in the first class compartment I pondered what I should do. One thing was certain; I had to tell someone of my fears, but whom? At times like this I needed Madelaine's wise counsel. The thought had barely formed when I made up my mind. The Duke was not due to visit the Maginot Line for another fortnight. I could make my excuses for not being in Paris for a few days. According to the conductor my best bet for a quick journey home was to change at Antwerp for Ostend. I should be in time to catch the midnight ferry. At Antwerp I purchased a few necessities before boarding my connection.

The trains kept to their timetable and a few hours later I found myself leaning on the taffrail of the cross-channel ferry, watching the lights of Ostend fade away. The night was distinctly chilly and I went below for a nightcap. In the first class lounge I watched contentedly as a party of revellers drank too much champagne and danced the night away to a four-piece combo of indifferent quality. The Straits of Dover were flat calm, the ferry steaming at a sedate pace, scheduled to arrive in England at the reasonable hour of 06.30.

I retired to my cabin and slept well, waking to the knock of a steward bearing a cup of tea at 05.45. I shaved, put on a fresh shirt and went up top. Dawn was breaking as I stood on the starboard side of the ferry and watched the looming white cliffs of Kent harden in the growing light. There was the usual hustle and bustle in port before we disembarked for the boat train to London Victoria.

According to Madelaine's letter, she would be at the Home Office for her interview that morning. I would meet her there. I just hoped my sudden appearance wouldn't put her off her stride.

We arrived at Victoria just after 09.30, a mere five minutes late. A cab took me to my club, the United Services in the Mall. From there I telephoned the Foreign Office and established that Madelaine was due shortly. I asked that a message be given to her, after her appointment.

I sat at a writing desk and began to put my thoughts down on paper. I was sipping a mid-morning coffee when I was called to the telephone.

'David? Darling, you're back!'

'Hullo, my dear,' I replied. 'Just for a day or two.'

'Wonderful. I'll grab a taxi and be with you shortly.'

Madelaine swept through the revolving doors a few minutes later. She looked as radiant as ever. We embraced warmly then retired to a quiet nook by the fire. We had a lot to catch up on.

'What happened at the interview?'

Madelaine smiled and shrugged. 'I don't know yet. They were more interested in my current situation than the work I used to do for them.

45

Claimed my experience with the FO was too long ago to be relevant. My age came up too, so I'm not hopeful.'

'The damn fools would be lucky to have you. Want me to have a word with Winnie?'

Madelaine looked thoughtful for a moment and then shook her head ruefully. 'I'd rather you didn't. Better to get something on my own merits.'

I laughed.

'What's so funny, may I ask?' Already nettled, her anger was simmering below the surface.

'You're the one who's always extolled the virtue of the old boy network. In your case, old girl. If you think you can contribute to the war effort then let's get you doing something.'

She thought about it for a few seconds and then nodded happily. 'I suppose you're right. Don't bother Winnie, though. I'll use my own contacts.'

'What's happening at *Fairweather*?'

'We've converted the bedrooms into small dormitories. All our furniture has been put into storage and I've had bunk beds installed. Gibbs and Connie are rising to the occasion, as you'd expect. A number of schoolmasters are also coming, to continue with the children's lessons.'

'How many children are we housing?'

'Thirty-eight, plus six teachers. Other children will stay locally and come to us for their school lessons. I've found a small flat in Old Pye Street, which will suit us, although there's no room for servants. Is that all right?'

'Well done, darling, of course it is! You have been busy.'

'There's plenty to do. Now, what's happened your end?'

Madelaine listened attentively, her head cocked slightly to one side as she concentrated on what I had to say.

'It's all very circumstantial,' was her opinion when I'd finished. I was about to protest but she forestalled me. 'But damning, nevertheless. What do you intend to do?'

I shrugged. 'My instinct is to tell Churchill but you know he has a blind spot when it comes to Windsor. What do you think?'

'I think it's your duty to make him see the truth.'

She was right. I telephoned to make an appointment.

There may have been a war and high royal drama seething around us but domestic issues still required our attention. That afternoon we visited the flat, where I signed the lease. It was being let empty and we agreed on items of furniture we'd have delivered from *Fairweather*. We had two bedrooms, a study, living room, dining room and kitchen, more than sufficient for our needs.

I presented myself at Admiralty a few minutes before my 17.00 meeting with Churchill.

5

Winnie was in a foul mood, hunched over his desk, puffing on a cigar, angrily making annotations in a file.

His greeting was curt. 'Why are you here, Griffiths?'

'And a good day to you too, Winnie. Shall I come back later when you're in a better frame of mind?'

He scowled at me and said gruffly, 'Help yourself to a whisky and pour me one while you're at it.'

It was the nearest he ever came to an apology and I accepted it for what it was. While I poured the drinks I considered the responsibilities weighing on his shoulders. 'Is something wrong? What's bothering you?'

He looked penetratingly at me from under beetling brows before replying, 'I know I can trust you, Griffiths. This is privileged information. We have just received the Germans' invasion plans.'

I stopped what I was doing and looked at him in utter astonishment. 'How on earth . . .'

He interrupted me. 'The information is highly reliable. The German generals have been delaying day on day – Hitler is furious. He's insisting they attack on the twelfth of November.'

'Who's our source?' I handed him a glass half-filled with malt whiskey.

'Since early 1936 a German by the name of Paul Thummel has been passing secrets to the Czechs. As a high-ranking officer in the Abwehr, stationed actually in Berlin Headquarters, he's privy to many of Germany's most sensitive and highly classified secrets. Now that Czechoslovakia to all intents and purposes no longer exists *we've* taken him on. He's known as "A54" and his information has proven totally reliable to date.'

'Do we know which way they'll come?'

'Yes. The main offensive will be on Germany's right wing, under Army Group A, who will attack across the Belgian plain towards the coast. Army Group C is to pin down the French at the Maginot Line, while the smaller Army Group B would face the Ardennes in a secondary role, preventing an Allied counter-attack.'

I walked across to the wall map and swept my hand over the western end of Belgium. 'Army Group A would then pour down in a huge sweep into France, cutting off the French army and the Maginot Line?'

'That's about the sum of it. They'll mop up and effectively France will have fallen.'

'What do *our* generals think? Can the Germans do it?'

'Possibly. But we'll give them a very bloody nose if they try it. Once Army Group A is on the move we could counterattack and go back through the Belgian plain and head for the Ruhr. Hit Germany where it hurts most. That's our plan, although I doubt we'll get to implement it.'

'Why ever not?'

'Chamberlain is still trying to find a peaceful solution.'

I shook my head in despair. 'The man's a fool. The Nazis only understand force.'

'Hitler believes that a short, sharp shock will have us suing for peace as soon as France capitulates.'

'And will it?'

Churchill smashed his fist onto his desk. 'Never! Not as long as I have breath in my body.'

I grinned. Good old Winnie, never one to miss an opportunity for passionate rhetoric.

'What brought you here? Why have you left Paris?'

'I have news, Winnie, and I'm afraid you're not going to like it.' As succinctly as possible I related Bedaux's trip to the German embassy. Churchill had the good grace not to interrupt, although I could see from his face that he was furious.

When I finished there was a deadly silence. Then . . . 'Are you suggesting,' he thundered, 'that the man who was our king has deliberately passed information to our enemies?'

I felt uncomfortable under his gaze but I held it. 'It could be that Bedaux alone is guilty – that the Duke's only crime is indiscretion. But I don't believe it.'

Churchill's shoulders slumped and he took a long pull at his drink.

'Tell no one else of your suspicions, Griffiths, until we find a way to curtail the problem.'

I felt anger course through me. No action was to be taken? 'Winnie, I'll tell you this once and for all. Windsor is a scoundrel. He is not to be trusted. He could be doing untold damage, yet you intend sitting back and letting him sell out our people?'

'He was our *king* for God's sake and that means something to me, if not to you. I refuse to believe he is a traitor to this country. Return to your post, Griffiths and do the job you agreed to.'

If I alienated Churchill now, who knew what the result would be? I left a short while later, assuring our First Lord of the Admiralty that I would return to Paris within the next two days.

The following morning I retired to *Fairweather*, where I made arrangements for the furniture that we wanted to be taken up to London. I looked the house over. It was already developing a different atmosphere as valuables were put away and rooms were turned into classrooms.

Much to my surprise, Gibbs appeared to be in his element, taking everything in his stride as he and Connie made their preparations. I spent a little while with John Phillipe, now a year and nine months old. The little tyke was into everything. He certainly had the Griffiths colouring, our black curly hair and blue eyes. His cheeks were red from teething I noticed.

Susan was away for a few days helping Sion to move from Biggin Hill and wouldn't be back until after I'd returned to France. The obligatory weekly letter from Richard could be condensed to a request for ten shillings which I duly despatched, thankful he was safely tucked away at Eton.

Connie confirmed that once the move to St Athan was completed she and John Phillipe would move to South Wales, so that the baby could spend as much time with Susan as possible. As soon as John Phillipe was put to bed I left for London. I wanted to spend the time I had left with my wife. The future was looking bleak and I felt sure we would be apart for much of it.

I arrived back in Paris to the worst possible news. There was deep gloom in the bar of the hotel; the battleship HMS *Royal Oak* had been sunk by a German torpedo, whilst still in her home base of Scapa Flow. More than eight hundred men were reported dead. We had thought it impossible for a U-boat to penetrate the base's defences and believed that the battleship's armour would prevent a torpedo damaging the great ship. Less than four hundred men had survived.

An hour later the Duke and Duchess arrived on their way to a masked ball. Their gaiety and laughter offended me and I left the bar before they could see me. The news of the *Oak*'s sinking seemed already forgotten. Without doubt, they were the most selfish people I had ever met.

The following morning we left for another tour. Our first port of call was to General Gort at the BEF HQ in Arras. On this occasion we visited the British defensive lines around Lille before returning to Paris. Never one to put too much effort into anything, it would be another eight days before the Duke sallied forth once again, this time to inspect the French Fourth and Fifth Armies on the Vosges sector, the western end of the Maginot Line, facing the eastern Belgian border. The Duke had now seen more of the inadequate French lines than any other Briton, with the exception of Fruity Metcalfe and myself. The reports we wrote were detailed and made grim reading. The French lines were badly drawn, poorly armed and based on fixed positions, which were no longer appropriate in modern warfare. If I could see that with my limited knowledge, surely our generals understood the situation?

Throughout this time I was aware that the countdown to all-out war had started, if Hitler's timetable was being adhered to. Within a fortnight the Germans would start the big push, unless some miracle happened.

Whenever we were in Paris, the Windsors met with Bedaux and his wife, either for luncheon or dinner. The Duke clearly had every opportunity to tell Bedaux what we had seen whilst at the front-line and I had no doubt that that was precisely what he was doing. On the 6th November I was waiting in the Ritz when the Windsors arrived to dine with Bedaux. They were using a small, private dining room on the first floor. I immediately enquired about the room next door and hired it for dinner for one.

I ordered my meal and sat toying with the stem of a wine glass, waiting for the waiter to return. The room was some five metres square, ornately furnished and capable of sitting eight. Each dining room was connected to the next by double doors that could be thrown wide open, doubling the space available. I poured myself some wine and stood up, walking soundlessly to the door adjoining Bedaux's room, glass in hand. I placed my ear to the door and could hear a low murmur of male voices but couldn't make out the words. I squinted through the gap between the doors and could see light. After a few moments I realised that I could also see Bedaux's back and someone's hand waving to Bedaux's left. Kneeling down by the keyhole I looked through. I could see the Duke's face in profile.

I heard the door behind me opening and I leapt to my feet, crossing over to the window. The usual routine was for a waiter to stay in the room to serve the guests, the food being kept warm in a special portable oven. I dismissed the man and told him that I would send for him when I was ready. As soon as he was gone I was back at the door. By listening intently, my eyes closed, I could pick out a few words. They were obviously discussing the war but I couldn't hear enough to know what they were saying. It was hopeless. I gave up, returned to the table and ate my rapidly cooling beef Stroganoff.

After a few minutes I stepped over to the door, this time taking my water glass with me. I put the open end against the crack and my ear to the base. After a few moments I began to pick up some words and by concentrating hard could make some sense of what was being said.

I switched to the keyhole and tried there. The acoustic was slightly clearer and I heard Windsor say, 'Take this letter. You know what you must do.'

I put my eye to the keyhole and was in time to see the Duke hand over a sheet of paper to Bedaux. The Frenchman read it quickly, nodded and folded the paper in half and in half again, creating a thin strip some seven inches long and two inches wide. Bedaux fiddled with the inside of his jacket and cursed. I put the glass back over the hole and listened intently.

All I heard the Duke say was, 'It'll be safest.' But that made no sense to me.

'Yes. I'll do it before I leave here. Excellent! A sharp shock and we are looking at a new world order, my dear David.'

'I hope you're right, Charles . . . I hope you're right.'

They shook hands, rose from the table and Windsor, with Wallis, left the room. How could I get my hands on that letter? Short of shooting the man I could see no way.

An expertly palmed fifty-franc note later and the receptionist told me Bedaux had ordered a taxi the following morning for the railway station. I was up early and outside the Ritz when Bedaux appeared, carrying a small portmanteau. I had come prepared, with a small bag of my own, plenty of cash and my passport and papers.

This time Bedaux left the train at Brussels. I followed him across the station and watched as he climbed onto the express for Cologne. I was stymied.

How could I follow him into enemy territory? The last thing I wanted was to be interned for the duration of the war. But it was enough. There was no doubt that the purpose of the journey was to deliver the letter to someone in Germany. I wondered who the recipient would be. The evidence was circumstantial – the letter could have an innocent purpose. But with only days before Germany attacked, if Churchill's information was correct, then there *had* to be some significance to the missive. The thoughts swirled round my head, with no likelihood of my solving the problem. I took the next train back to Paris.

The following day we learnt of the bomb that had devastated the *Burgerbräukeller* in Munich, only minutes after Adolf Hitler had left, killing dozens of his supporters. Churchill sent me a coded message to say that the attack by Germany was off – postponed for the foreseeable future. Was that good news or bad and, more importantly, was it in anyway connected to that damn letter? I wondered if my dislike of the Duke was clouding my judgement but then dismissed the thought. I'd been in his company for too long not to know how Windsor thought and where his loyalties lay. My concerns led me to seek a private meeting with Howard-Vyse.

'I take it,' I began, 'that you know who I really am. My purpose for being here?'

Howard-Vyse smiled and nodded. 'For a banker you're adept at keeping an eye on our esteemed ex-king.'

There was, I thought, a hint of sarcasm in his voice.

'Does that present you with a problem?'

'Good Lord, no, far from it,' he sounded genuinely incredulous. 'He needs watching, is all I meant to imply.'

'As you say. Though I have no proof as yet, I believe that Windsor is relaying information to Bedaux, who is passing it to Germany.'

Howard-Vyse stood up and paced his office for a short while, deep in thought. He paused at his desk and picked up a letter. 'Look here, Griffiths, I want you to read this.'

It was from Field Security Police in London. Intelligence reports from Holland and France had made it clear that Bedaux was a potential threat to the Allies. They requested in the strongest terms that Major-General HRH the Duke of Windsor cease all activity and contact with Charles Bedaux immediately.

I handed the letter back to Howard-Vyse. 'About time too.'

'I take it,' he said, 'that the French reports they mention are yours?'

'Probably. Though you know how it is. Others have possibly submitted similar reports.'

Shrewdly Howard-Vyse said, 'Like Fruity Metcalfe?'

I smiled. 'I was thinking the same thing. I've often wondered what game he's really playing. You heard about his latest trouble?'

The major-general nodded. 'He isn't getting paid. I gather he's somewhat cut up about it.'

'I think it's Windsor's indifference that really hurts.'

'It would make sense if he *is* reporting back to the FSP. They'd pay him some sort of small retainer to keep an eye on things. Why isn't Windsor paying him?'

I laughed at the notion. 'He's the meanest man I know. He only thinks of himself and his personal well-being.'

'I take it you've heard the latest fuss he's creating? The French army has called up his personal chef and he is insisting that he be returned forthwith. The man's become a serious nuisance. It's embarrassing. I shall have to have a word with him. The Germans are bombing the Maginot Line while the French are lobbing shells back at them. Men are dying and all Windsor cares about is his blasted chef.'

'I take it this is why he's being kept away from the front-lines?'

Howard-Vyse nodded. 'Indeed. I need you to have a word with him about Bedaux. Explain that he must stay away from the bounder, for his own good.'

I shook my head. 'Sorry, but I can't do that. Windsor will as soon shoot the messenger as ignore the message. He would simply insist that I no longer be part of his entourage. The only man he's likely to listen to is you.'

The major-general tapped a tattoo on his desk with his fingers and then nodded. 'I suppose you're right.' Looking at me with his hawkish gaze he asked, 'Do you really think our former king is betraying us?'

I had asked myself this question a thousand times. I hated the conclusion I had come to. 'You're asking me whether Windsor is simply indiscreet and Bedaux is taking advantage of their friendship?'

'Is that likely?'

'It's possible, except for one thing.' I described the letter I'd seen Windsor passing to Bedaux and the latter's sudden departure for Germany.

'What do you suggest?'

'Warn the Duke. Let's see which way he jumps.'

'I shall put it in writing immediately. Thank you for being so frank. It's a devilish situation.'

As Christmas approached the Windsors were to be seen everywhere. Visiting the French troops, waving and smiling for newsreel cameras and newspapers, handing out presents to the men in the trenches. They were fêted wherever they went. I sent a telegram home, missing the family dreadfully. As I thought about them I reminded myself of the hundreds of thousands of men stuck in the trenches and what hell they must be going through. When would mankind finally learn to live with one another in peace? It was, I suspected, a question that would still be asked long after I was dead.

Throughout this period I knew that Windsor had continued seeing Bedaux, discretely, but nonetheless regularly. I reported back to Winston but received no instructions.

Then, with total disregard for his orders, Windsor brazenly invited Bedaux to a party just after Christmas. I was among the guests, senior officers of the French and British armies, as well as General Sikorski of the Free Polish Forces.

I found myself standing next to the gruff and burly Sikorski when the Duke joined us, with Bedaux in tow. I had contrived never to actually meet the man, although I had seen the two of them together often enough. After a brief introduction Bedaux's first words to me came as something of a shock. In much the same way as I had researched his background, Bedaux had obviously familiarised himself with mine.

'You know, Colonel Griffiths, that I too served at Fort Vaux during the Great War. I thought it had been too badly damaged to be of any further use.'

How did he know that I'd been to Vaux? Windsor must have told him. If proof was needed that the Duke was supplying information to Bedaux then this was it. I made a non-committal answer, excused myself and walked away.

I sent an encrypted message to Churchill, telling him of my discovery and emphasising Windsor's total disregard of Howard-Vyse's orders not to see Bedaux. On the point of sending it I had second thoughts. Our First Lord of the Admiralty had ignored my last message. It was time to see him in person.

6

I HAD WIRED Madelaine my arrival time and she was at the new flat in Old Pye Street to meet me. Our own furniture helped to make the rooms more welcoming and I gladly accepted a small whisky and soda before phoning Churchill. I was out of luck. He was at the House.

Westminster wasn't far from the flat and I still had my pass. Technically I was still the Member for Eastbourne. I had obviously informed my constituency party that my new duties meant I had to quit parliament and the bye-election had been called for a few weeks hence. I'd had mixed feelings about leaving but now I was sure I was doing something far more important.

It was bitterly cold and I stepped out with my hat pulled down over my ears and the scarf Madelaine had insisted on around my throat. I rehearsed what I was going to say to Churchill all the way to Parliament Square. Once there I paused and looked east towards the barrage balloons swaying at the end of their ropes. Intended to be blown up by falling bombs, protecting lives and property, they seemed puny obstacles against any attack. I felt a black mood descend over me.

I finally tracked Winnie down in one of the bars, where he was deep in discussion with one of the party whips. When I arrived he scowled at me but indicated I should join them.

'It won't be popular,' Churchill continued, 'but rationing is the only way forward.'

The Whip nodded. 'Everyone's in agreement. It'll come into force on the eighth. Here's the list and the allowance.'

Winston glanced at it briefly before handing it to me. I read it with interest. Rationing meant compulsory registration of every household. The weekly allowances per person were disheartening but as Winnie said, absolutely necessary – butter 4oz, sugar 12oz, bacon or ham, uncooked, 4oz. There were plenty of items not rationed although they were on a second list for potential future rationing. These included offal, rabbit, poultry, fish and sundry other items. It was a depressing reminder of what lay ahead. The Whip left a few minutes later, leaving Churchill and I alone.

'I'll tell you now, I don't like it, Griffiths,' he said.

'What don't you like, Winnie? Rationing? The war? Or are you talking about the style of my suit?'

'I'm talking, you facetious oaf, about your latest letter regarding His Royal Highness.'

I leant forward and said, 'Even you can't ignore the facts any longer. I've told you precisely what's going on. I believe Windsor is a traitor. You can believe what the hell you like.'

Wearily he shook his head. 'Acting upon your suspicions would be dangerous constitutionally. All we can do is keep an eye on him.'

Churchill's scowl deepened and he gestured to a waiter. I declined the offer of a drink. 'We have no way of proving if the letter was meant for the Germans. What do you want me to do, Winnie?'

'Do? Why, stick with Windsor, of course. We need you more than ever.'

'In that case I want a personal letter from you instructing him not to see Bedaux again. He totally ignored Howard-Vyse's missive.'

'I'll see what I can do. Now, you must excuse me. I have other work to do.' He drained his glass and lumbered to his feet, making for the door. I watched him go. How could a man as far-sighted as Winston be so blind to one individual?

I returned to the flat with a heavy heart. Before going back to France I intended having a few days with the family. Madelaine had telephoned Richard's house-master and arranged for him to have the evening off, although this was only his first week back after the Christmas holiday. We motored down to Eton to collect him.

As wrapped up as I was in the mission, I had missed the boy. Richard would be fifteen in three days. Already he was almost as tall as me and showed no sign of stopping. He had the Griffiths' dark curly hair and blue eyes and Madelaine's chin and high cheekbones. His personality showed traits inherited from both of us. The combination made him determined and tough. Although still young, he had a streak of potential ruthlessness that I knew would stand him in good stead throughout his life.

Our vehicle, like all the others, had tape over the headlights leaving a thin sliver of light to drive by. Naturally our conversation, from the moment we picked Richard up, centred on the war. We drove into town, picking our way carefully through the dark streets. The pavements thronged with people and driving was hazardous. I was relieved when we arrived at the West End. Bernard Shaw's long-running play, *Pygmalion*, was still showing in the Lyceum and we had made it in plenty of time. We ordered high tea in the theatre's restaurant and eventually steered Richard's talk from the war to what was happening at school. To my great pleasure I learned he had been short-listed for the First Cricket IX, although the final selection wouldn't take place until March. Academically he was doing well, in the top three in every subject except Latin, in which he was consistently amongst the bottom few. I don't think he appreciated my "*Nil desperandum*" crack.

'What about extra coaching?' Madelaine suggested.

'Mother!' Richard looked at her with all the condescension a fifteen-year-old could muster. 'Please! I can't stand the master. And as I have no desire to be either a doctor or a solicitor there's no point.'

'What *do* you want to do, son?' I asked.

Richard licked cream and jam from around his lips, thought for a few seconds and then replied. 'I'm not sure,' he said vaguely. 'Perhaps an engineer or I thought an architect might be a good wheeze.'

'A good wheeze?' Madelaine was aghast. 'It takes commitment to become an architect, my lad, believe me.'

His shoulders slumped. 'Fact is, I don't have any bally inclination for anything in particular. Except to fight in the war, to kill the Hun!'

Young lads were echoing Richard's sentiments all across the country, caught up in patriotic fervour – just like the last time. They all wanted to "do their bit". Two million young men between the ages of nineteen and twenty-seven had received their call up papers. I thought of their parents and sent another prayer of thanks heavenwards that Richard was so young.

The play was superb and we left in plenty of time to get Richard back to Eton before lights-out. We were travelling along Oxford Street when air-raid sirens sounded and huge searchlights lit up the sky, their fingers of light searching for aircraft.

We needed to get into the underground, so, like many other drivers, I pulled over and abandoned the car. We stumbled along in the dark, following the crowds like lemmings. Bond Street Station was on our left and we followed the crowd inside. Police were blowing their whistles and yelling at the multitudes to hurry along. Cautiously we made our way down the stairs to the Central Line platform. There, along with hundreds of other people, we sat on the stone floor and waited patiently for the all clear. Spirits were high, the Bulldog British at their best.

I turned to Richard, 'I think, old son, that you'll be late.'

He grinned at me. 'Gosh, Dad, wait until I tell the others. They'll be green.'

The words were barely out of his mouth when there came a thunderous crash. The station shook and dust floated down from the ceiling. Lights flickered and went out. People screamed. Madelaine's hand found mine and I gripped it tightly, praying harder than I'd ever done in my life. We sat in the darkness for what seemed like hours until a stentorian voice yelled the all clear.

Slowly we made our way back up the stairs. I managed to get a look at my watch and was shocked to see that less than fifty minutes had passed since the siren had started.

The street was bedlam. It was clear a bomb had exploded just along from the underground entrance. A fire was raging in a tall building nearby. Fire appliances were already on the scene and firemen were doing their best to contain and put out the blaze. A police sergeant was waving us away, telling us to hurry before the façade collapsed.

An ambulance arrived with clanging bells but without its usual flashing lights. In the light of the fire we could see bodies being brought out. We made our way to the car in a subdued mood. Much to my relief it started at the turn of the key and we drove away. I concentrated on driving as we picked our way along the dark street.

After a few minutes Richard, who was sitting alongside me, said, 'I've never seen a body before.'

Madelaine leaned forward from the back seat. She placed her hand on his shoulder and drew a finger along his cheek. 'We'll all have to get used to it.'

'The bloody Hun,' he spoke with feeling, clenching his fists. 'I hope that it's not all over before I can do my bit.'

'Don't talk nonsense,' Madelaine said, alarm in her voice. 'You've years of precious education to go yet. And with luck it will all be over soon. Won't it, darling?'

Reluctantly I shook my head. 'No, I don't think so. Not unless we move soon – while we still have the numerical advantage of our fleet and armies.'

'Why don't we attack?' Richard asked.

'The PM won't allow it. There are too many politicians against all-out war. They argue that it's better to settle matters diplomatically than to fight.'

'What do you think, Dad?'

'In principle they're right. In reality they're wrong. Hitler is not the kind of man you can talk to. If we acquiesce to his terms we betray every decent moral principle. There's nothing on the table that wouldn't result in the capitulation of Britain and France to Germany's demands. But Chamberlain can't or won't see it.'

'So what's to happen?'

'I don't know, son. Hitler has very cleverly sliced up Europe, piece by piece. He's got the taste for conquest now, so I don't see him stopping.'

We arrived back at Eton and saw Richard to his house, arranging to pick him up again on his birthday. This time a few of his friends were coming along to enjoy, as he so succinctly put it, "a good nosh".

The journey back to our small flat was uneventful and we had a nightcap before turning in. The following morning we were enjoying a leisurely breakfast when the telephone rang. It was the Foreign Office for Madelaine. I handed her the receiver. She exchanged only a few words before hanging up.

'Well?'

She smiled. 'I've been offered a job as Liaison Officer for the FO as a Wren First Officer.'

'Well done, darling,' I smiled. 'Any idea what it'll entail?'

She laughed. 'None whatsoever. It's a new post. I'm to report to the Admiralty on the morning of the eleventh, Richard's birthday.'

'That's wonderful!'

I accompanied Madelaine that Thursday, intent on speaking to Churchill. The First Lord of the Admiralty was sitting hunched over his desk, an all but forgotten cold cigar clenched in the corner of his mouth, as he read the file in front of him. He waved me to a seat and I waited impatiently for him to pay some attention to me. After a few moments he handed me a file. 'Here, read this while I continue perusing the rest of this blasted bumph.'

Intrigued I took the proffered sheets of paper and began to read.

It was the translation of an incident report, describing a situation which had happened the previous day in Eastern Belgium. Considered so important, obviously, that the report had already been sent to the French and to us. I read it through with mounting excitement tempered by caution. If something appeared too good to be true, by my maxim, then it generally was.

A German light aircraft had crashed after straying over the border into Belgium. The pilots had been arrested. One of them had been discovered trying to burn a bag of documents. The documents were thought to be the *complete German attack plans for Western Europe*.

As Churchill read each sheet of paper he passed it to me. When we were finished I sat back and looked up at the ceiling, deep in thought. Churchill for his part got to his feet and paced the office, hands behind his back.

'Well?' He barked the word at me.

I gave my carefully weighed judgement. 'It's baloney.'

'Others disagree.'

'That's as may be,' I said, frowning, mustering my thoughts. I got to my feet and stood examining the wall map of Europe for a few moments, identifying the places involved. 'A light plane is flying from Münster here,' I pointed, 'to the High Command Headquarters in Bonn, here. They claim bad weather forced them to lose their way and crash all the way over *here* at Mechelen-sur-Meuse, well inside the border. It's ridiculous. Impossible. I've flown with my brother Sion often enough to know a bit about planes. The aircraft was an ME108 Typhoon and just happened to be piloted by a highly experienced major whose co-pilot *also* happens to be a major. The Typhoon is modern, fast. The pilots are arrested for violating Belgium airspace. They have a conversation with the German Military Attaché, *and* . . .' I paused and rifled through the papers, 'the German Assistant Air Attaché *and* a German Lieutenant General. They must have known that listening devices would have picked up everything they said, surely? Yet what do they discuss? The disaster that's befallen Germany because her *war plans have been seized*. Look at this pathetic attempt to destroy the papers by setting light to them behind a convenient hedge! If they were as important as they claim, the courier should have opened the petrol tank, doused the papers and destroyed them in seconds. That's what I would have done.'

'Humph,' Winston snorted. 'The documents disclose plans which tally exactly with what we would expect the Hun to do.'

'I'm telling you it makes no sense. Yesterday the weather here was crisp and sunny and I expect it was much the same in Belgium. Their original flight path covered a total of eighty miles, forty of which meant following the Rhine, a river a mile wide – unmissable – even in the dark. The crash was not at the Belgium-German border but the Belgium-Dutch one. They strayed some sixty miles west, not an error a pilot of that rank would make.'

'I agree,' said Churchill. 'Now, when do you head back to France?'

'It's my son's birthday. I'd like a few more days here before I return. After all, I missed Christmas and the New Year for no good reason.'

'Your job is vital.' Churchill stopped pacing and pointed his cigar at me. 'It's up to you to save HRH from himself, if need be.'

I couldn't believe he was still trying to protect the man. 'It's time you took your blinkers off and saw the man for what he really is. Good day to you, Winston.' I stalked from the room without a backward glance, leaving Winnie standing by the fireplace, his unlit cigar in his hand, at a loss for words, for probably the first time in his life.

Our outing with Richard and his chums was highly illuminating. We spent the whole evening talking about the war, all four boys fervent in their desire to take part. Madelaine and I were equally keen that the sooner it all ended the better. Naturally, our young guests were unable or unwilling to see our point of view and so it made for a lively debate. The evening passed all too quickly.

The next morning Madelaine looked particularly alluring in her wren officer's uniform with its two, thick, wavy, light-blue stripes sandwiching a thin one.

'I feel a fraud,' she said, standing in front of the mirror in the hall and straightening her skirt. 'I don't deserve the rank of first officer.'

'Of course you do. You speak fluent German and French and are one of the most organised people I know. What other rank could you be?'

She smiled and pecked my cheek. 'We are doing the right thing, aren't we? Volunteering like this?'

'It's our duty. Hundreds of thousands of men are needed at the front and so we need an infrastructure to support them. Women will be doing war work as job vacancies arise and our navy, army and air force will need support staff too. The only people able to fit the bill are women and retired military personnel. So I don't see we've much choice.'

'You will take care in France, won't you?'

I laughed with genuine humour. 'My job is to be with Windsor. The man is a coward and will *never* risk his life. He cannot even abide to have his small comforts disrupted. No, he'll be away before the going gets too tough.'

'Then you make sure you do the same.'

'I will, my love, trust me.'

A vicious cold snap had come out of the northeast. The day I left to return to Paris the Thames froze over for the first time since 1888. The Channel was flat calm and the passage to Boulogne passed pleasantly enough. Our train was full of forces personnel, even the first class compartments were jammed with officers of various nationalities, both army and air force. The majority of them were from the colonies, Australia, New Zealand and Canada. Many of our Indian regiments were represented too, by white officers as well as a few turbaned Sikhs. The officers were a congenial bunch and deferential to a colonel in uniform, particularly one who stood more than his share of rounds in the bar. As a result we de-trained in a merry and boisterous mood and went our separate ways.

I didn't see the Duke for a few days. Taking advantage of the cold but sunny weather he was indulging his passion for golf – with Bedaux!

In the last week in January Windsor announced his intention to return to London. He made it clear that he expected Metcalfe and I to travel with him as part of his entourage. So I found myself on the return journey less than a week later. Edward booked into Claridges' and, as I thought it wisest to stay near him, I did the same, telephoning Madelaine once I was there.

On the first night she appeared late at the hotel, looking tired. She took a glass of white wine from me and sipped it appreciatively. 'It's a madhouse over there.'

'What are you doing?'

'Mainly translation work. I've already got six girls working for me, all fluent in either German or French.'

'What needs so much translation?'

Madelaine smiled. 'I suppose I can tell you. We have agents all over France and Germany. Hundreds of them. Mainly low-level, but we do get snippets of useful information amongst the dross. Of course orders or requests have to be translated from English, coded, and dispatched. It's boring work, but useful I suppose.'

The following evening Edward had an invitation to Lord Beaverbrook's home for dinner. The newspaper magnate remained a firm supporter of the Windsors. I knew the Beaver and inveigled an invitation for Madelaine and myself. It wasn't difficult, as my bank, Griffiths, Buchanan & Co, had helped him with many of his financial transactions.

It was an interesting gathering. Along with the Windsors, the Metcalfes, and the Beaverbrooks we met Walter Monckton and his wife. The Beaver was a staunch supporter of Chamberlain and yet I knew that Windsor detested our Prime Minister. As we sat down to dinner I couldn't help wondering where the evening's conversation would lead. I didn't have long to wait.

Rationing meant the meal was simple, even frugal, and as a result we were soon at the port. In the past the women would have left us to our worldly discussions, but times were changing and they stayed with us.

'We must,' said Windsor, 'open a dialogue with Germany. The war should be ended at once.'

'I agree wholeheartedly,' said Beaverbrook. 'And you can help.'

'How?' There was a glint of eagerness in Edward's eyes as he leaned forward.

'Get out of your ludicrous uniform and stump the country. Spread the message. I can help you enlist some powerful allies in the City and of course, it goes without saying that my newspapers will back you one hundred percent.'

Edward and Wallis smiled. This was precisely what they wanted to hear.

'If it's done properly,' the Beaver continued, 'goodness knows where it could lead.'

The thought *back to the throne* hung in the air. Madelaine and I exchanged worried glances.

The conversation continued, the Duke becoming highly excited. 'This is precisely what I've been wanting and working for. We must work with Germany to save the world from the Bolsheviks. A strong Germany at peace with a strong Britain is what's needed.'

'What about,' Madelaine asked, 'the other countries in Europe?'

Windsor frowned at the interruption. 'I don't understand. What about them?'

'What's to become of them?'

Windsor waved a deprecating hand. 'Germany will be freed to fight for her *Lebensraum*, while we will be able to concentrate on our colonies in Africa and the East. We can unify them under one governing Head of State.'

It was clear to me who he saw in that role. The conversation went round the same track several times before we could take our leave. Monckton and his wife left with us. Outside, a London smog was developing and we hurried along the streets in the direction of the hotel, feeling very subdued.

Monckton broke the silence. 'What we just heard was high treason.'

7

RETURNING TO FRANCE Windsor was in a foul mood. At times like that it was better to stay out of his way and so once on the train Fruity Metcalfe and I retreated to the lounge bar.

'What's eating at HRH?' I asked.

'He had a meeting with Chamberlain and talked to him about Beaverbrook's idea.'

'The result wasn't quite what the Duke had hoped?'

'You could say that. Chamberlain vetoed the idea entirely. David has it in his head that Chamberlain doesn't like him and is responsible for him being frozen out.'

'Is that why HRH in turn detests Chamberlain?'

Metcalfe nodded.

'The Duke is treading on dangerous ground. If he isn't careful he could find himself buried under it. We British are slow to rile. But once we are, then God help those who either stand in our way or are against us. I don't believe Chamberlain will last until the summer.'

Metcalfe looked piercingly at me for a few seconds. 'What do you think will happen?'

'The Germans will invade another country. Then Winnie will take over.'

Metcalfe looked penetratingly at me and nodded. 'I've thought so for some time.' He surprised me.

When we reached Paris information had arrived at the Military Mission. The Germans planned to invade through Belgium. I knew the source, of course – the documents captured from the crashed plane. I told Howard-Vyse of my disquiet. He listened intently to my arguments.

'If you're right, Griffiths, and it's a set-up,' he said, 'then what *are* they planning?'

I stood up and wandered over to the huge map that dominated one wall. Lifting a pointer I said, 'According to the pilots' documents they intend to attack here, opening up a front from Lille to Revin at the edge of the Ardennes. Simultaneously a second front will be opened up here by Army Group C.' I pointed at the Maginot Line. 'The Hun comes through and sweeps west all the way to the Channel, meeting up with the German Army Groups A and B heading south-west across the Belgium plain. If those plans are false, as I believe they are, what does that leave?'

The major-general was a professional to his fingertips. 'Hold at the Maginot Line and attack through the Ardennes. Once through, go east and west. It's the route I'd take if I knew how dire the defences were along the Line and through the Ardennes. Thank God, the Hun doesn't know it.'

'Are you sure about that?'

'It's impossible! We've only learned how dire the situation is thanks to the Duke of Windsor's tours. The Germans can't possibly know. It's impossible.'

'And if, as I suspect, Windsor has passed the information to Bedaux who in turn has told the Germans?'

'He was our *king* for God's sake. He would never betray us like that. I refuse to believe it.'

There are none so blind as those who will not see. What was it about Windsor that nobody was prepared to acknowledge the truth?

We continued with our tours around the French Lines and the British Expeditionary Force. Windsor acted as he always did when he didn't like a suggestion or an order. He ignored it. We went around the most sensitive areas with impunity.

A month later I went back to Blighty for a spot of leave, glad to get away. If anything, my attitude to the Windsors had hardened. I was so glad to be able to unburden myself to Madelaine.

'You're not alone in your suspicions, if that's any comfort,' she said, while we lay in bed together. 'Perhaps I shouldn't be telling you this but we have a very able spy in the German embassy in The Hague. He has passed information to a Major Langford, an intelligence officer based in Holland. Langford sent an encrypted message to a man I do work for called Colonel Vivian.'

'I know him. Good man.'

'He thinks highly of you too, darling. Langford has learnt that Bedaux is visiting the Hague embassy almost every two weeks and crossing into Germany almost as regularly. Bedaux's verbal information has been transcribed and the reports read by our man in The Hague. He says it's the very best information, detailing defence strengths and weaknesses as well as manning levels at every location. It goes on to say that the source of the information is *definitely* someone with the BEF.'

'Why doesn't somebody just stop Bedaux?'

Madelaine snuggled closer to me. 'If they get rid of him, then whoever is giving away our secrets could still find somebody *else* to work with. Somebody we know nothing about.'

'It's Windsor,' I said bitterly. 'I'm sure of it. The Duke is the only person who fits the bill.'

'Not true, darling. Don't let your prejudices run away with you. The Prime Minister, Winnie and Howard-Vyse know all the facts. They've simply decided not to act yet.'

Was she right? Was I allowing my unreasonable prejudices to sour my opinion of Windsor? I thought about it and then shook my head. Before I could say a word, Madelaine spoke.

'What's troubling you?'

I sighed. 'Who else could be passing on the information? Howard-Vyse is a patriot to his fingertips. Come to that, so am I. Ergo, it can *only* be Edward.' I kissed her. 'Enough talk. Why don't you lie back and think of England?'

'You really are a terrible cliché. But I love you.'

The following evening we went to the cinema to see "Gone With the Wind". Vivien Leigh, who played Scarlet O'Hara, reminded me so much of my dear, irrepressible Susan. I wished with all my heart that she would find her Rhett, a man who would appreciate her fire and determination and could accept her for who she was. The film was wonderful and it was a treat to forget the worries and cares of the war, if only for a few hours.

The Russo-Finnish war ended after fourteen weeks of bitter fighting. The Finns had done incredibly well to hold out as long as they did. Although the Russians won – and extracted harsh terms – it was at great personal cost. They had lost an estimated one million men. The weaknesses of the Red Army were finally clear for all to see and must have given Hitler hope for any future attack.

I returned to France. The Windsor's hedonistic lifestyle continued unabated. The Duke's open support of Germany grated on my nerves and, unable to stand being near him, I wrote to Churchill asking to be relieved of my task. I received a curt missive back, telling me to stay put.

At the start of April I was surprised by another message from Churchill, instructing me to go to Holland to meet Major Langford. The information the major had was too delicate to trust to the usual methods of despatch; I was to collect it personally.

I had agreed to meet Langford at the main railway station. The journey took far longer than usual. Part of the line had been bombed and we were diverted around it. We arrived almost six hours late but I found him in the buffet, nursing a cold cup of coffee. He was a tall, good-looking man with a pencil-line moustache and a receding hair-line. His handshake was firm and dry and he wasted no time getting down to business.

'I've written it all down. The most sensitive information is in the letter so whatever you do, don't lose it.'

'Care to tell me what it contains?'

'Are you MI?'

'I was in the last show. Now I work directly for Winston.'

That seemed to satisfy him for he asked, 'What do you know about a man named Bedaux?'

My eyes narrowed and I wondered what I should say. 'He's obviously working for the Germans. And he's getting his information from a high-level source in France.'

'I don't understand why he hasn't been stopped,' said Langford. 'Unless to protect the *source*, as you delicately put it. My contact in the German embassy is fearful that Bedaux might one day bring information exposing him. If he does it'll be curtains for him.'

'Is it likely?'

Langford ran his index finger over his moustache before replying. 'The information Bedaux is bringing to the Germans is so good it can only come from somebody very highly placed. It's not beyond the realms of possibility that my contact be made known to this person.'

'Do you have any idea who it might be?'

'He was referred to as "Willi", by a member of the embassy staff. We're almost one hundred percent certain who it is.'

I looked into Langford's penetrating brown eyes. *This man is no fool.* Slowly I nodded.

8

MAY FOUND ME back in England again. I sat alone in the flat, a scotch and soda in hand, the curtains open and lights out, straining to catch a glimpse of the searchlights sweeping the sky. The poor old East End was getting it again. Madelaine had phoned to say she would be late. There was a flap on and her whole team was needed. The clock in the hall was striking eleven when she finally appeared.

'Tough day?'

'A long one, certainly. What about you?'

'I've been at Winston again to put me to work with SIS. I've had about enough of Windsor and his blasted wife. He's carping on constantly about being dethroned for no good reason. If he says one word that suggests for a second that he hasn't been wronged Wallis leaps in with her penn'orth. They're getting on my nerves and I'm going to tell him one day soon just how I feel about him.'

'You can't!' Madelaine was aghast. 'He's your senior officer.'

'He's a spoilt popinjay who needs taking down a peg or two.' I sighed. She was right of course. She usually was. But at least I felt better now I had that off my chest. 'What have you been up to?' I asked as I poured her a gin and tonic.

'I'm not sure I can tell you.'

'As your senior officer, I *order* you to tell me.'

Madelaine snapped me a mock salute and said, 'Aye, Aye, sir. Seriously, darling, we've had some highly reliable information in and the powers-that-be appear to be ignoring it.'

I took a stab in the dark. 'Is it by any chance from Number 54?'

She looked at me in utter astonishment.

'Winnie told me about him some time ago. What's he come up with this time?'

'He's reported that Hitler is going to attack on the tenth of this

75

month. He's detailed precisely how they are coming and the route they are taking. He's even given us the operational name, *Falle Gelbe*.'

'Plan Yellow- an innocuous name for such a major event. How do you know they're ignoring it?'

'The information has been pored over and then dismissed as nonsensical by Chamberlain. He's instructed the Secretary of State for War to do nothing.'

'Is the man mad? Does the invasion of Denmark and Norway mean nothing? Hitler is coming and it's only a question of when.'

'I won't argue, but the PM is having none of it. His dithering is going to cost us dearly if we aren't careful.'

The phone rang. Glancing at my watch I said, 'It can only be Winnie. Time means nothing to that man.' I went through to the hall and lifted the receiver.

I immediately recognised the growl. 'Griffiths?'

'Winston. What can I do for you?'

'I've given your request a considerable amount of thought and have decided you would serve better being seconded to the Secret Intelligence Service, as you asked. However, you will still be reporting to me. Your primary task will be field support of agents. Money, false documents and so on. Your office will be here at the Admiralty.'

'And what about the problem of Windsor?'

'He's my problem now, not yours.'

I thanked Winnie and replaced the receiver. Madelaine was standing in the doorway looking quizzically at me. I passed on Winnie's message, still struggling to take it in myself.

She smiled wanly. 'We'll be working in the same place which, after all these years of seeing you off to work, somehow seems ironic, don't you think?'

I nodded. Ironic indeed.

When we arrived at Admiralty, Madelaine hurried away to her office deep in the building. The hall porter looked my name up on a list and directed me to the second floor at the rear. I found myself in a long corridor with doors on either side. Each door was identical apart from the notation, a letter C followed by a number. Some were unnumbered. I knocked on C3 and entered. A young lady in Wren's uniform was seated at a desk, buffing her fingernails. She looked up enquiringly.

'My name is Colonel Griffiths . . .'

The words were hardly out of my mouth when she leapt to her

feet with a look of dismay. 'I am so sorry, sir. I wasn't expecting you for at least another hour. Oh, bother! I'd planned to have the kettle boiled and everything. I even got some biscuits. Bother!' she repeated.

I smiled. 'It's all right. Wren . . . ?'

'Leading Wren Flower, sir. Gladys Flower.'

'Well, Leading Wren, the tea can wait. I see this is your office. I take it that's mine?' I nodded at a door to the side of her desk.

'Yes, sir. Let me show you.' She opened the door and I followed her in. The room was about twelve foot square, bare walls painted lime green. A window overlooked a small yard. There was a desk, a chair and a filing cabinet. It was a near replica of the Leading Wren's, except for the typewriter sitting on her desk.

'How long have you been here, Gladys?'

'At Admiralty, sir? About three months.'

'I meant in this office.'

'Since yesterday teatime, sir.'

'Do you know what your job is?'

'No, sir.' She smiled and added, 'Apart from making tea that is.'

I smiled back involuntarily. I guessed she was in her mid-twenties. Pretty with fair, short, wavy hair, a pert nose and a cheeky smile. Her brown eyes twinkled with mischief and a real *joie de vivre*.

'In that case why don't you put the kettle on while I think about what we need to do? We could start with acquiring a telephone directory for this building.'

'I thought of that, sir. I've ordered directories for all government departments in London as well as Ministry of War establishments across the country.'

'Good girl. Where are you from, Gladys?'

'Barking, sir. In the East End.'

I nodded. I guessed from somewhere around there from her accent. I noticed she wasn't wearing any rings. 'Not married or engaged, Leading Wren?'

'Not me, sir. I enjoy myself too much to get tied down to one bloke.'

On that note she left the room while I sat in a hard-backed chair that was distinctly uncomfortable. One thing I would see to immediately was better furniture. I knew that in the basement of the bank we had finer desks and chairs waiting to be thrown out. I made the necessary phone call.

Gladys came in with a pot of tea, a cup and saucer and a plate of biscuits on a tray.

'Bring your chair and tea and we'll have a confab. I'll tell you what very little I know about what we're doing here. Incidentally,' I added, as she came back with her chair in one hand and cup and saucer in the other, 'I've ordered new furniture. Bigger desks, matching filing cabinets, a couple of book cases and some leather seats for guests.'

She looked startled. 'How did you manage that, sir? All requests for office furniture are on hold. We keep getting told, "There's a war going on, in case you haven't noticed".'

'I'm having them brought over from my bank.'

'I've never been in a bank. I use the Post Office myself. I had no idea they sold furniture.'

'They don't. When I said "my bank" I mean it literally. I own most of it.'

She goggled at me. 'You *own* a bank?'

'Yes. Well, a good part of one.' I was feeling uncomfortable with the discussion. It sounded as though I was bragging, which I hadn't intended doing. 'Anyway, forget about the bank. Our job here, basically, is to support field agents for SIS.'

'Spies?'

'Well, yes, in a sense I suppose they are.'

'What will that entail, sir?'

'It'll mean getting money, supplies and papers to our men and women working behind enemy lines. I need a lot more information. I'll phone Winnie and ask him.'

'Winnie? You mean the First Sea Lord?'

'Yes.'

She shook her head and daintily nibbled at a Rich Tea biscuit. I knew Churchill's extension and dialled the number.

'Winston? David Griffiths.' I looked up startled as the Leading Wren sat forward with a jerk, spilt her tea and coughed, almost choking on her biscuit. I frowned at her and she pulled herself together long enough for me to continue. 'When can I see you? Half an hour? I'll be right down.' I replaced the receiver and asked, 'Are you all right?'

She nodded. 'Sir, I mean, sir . . . That's the First Sea Lord . . .'

I was puzzled by her reaction so merely nodded.

She took a deep breath and said, 'Sir, with all due respect. You're only a colonel and he's well . . . well . . .'

'The First Sea Lord. Yes, I know. He and I go back a long way.' I left it at that. 'As soon as you've finished your tea, talk to the hall porter and tell him about the furniture arriving. Perhaps he can arrange for somebody to give a hand with it. And ask him what we do with this old stuff.' I paused, and then sat back with a frown. 'See if you can get me meetings with senior staff at SIS. Freddy Winterbotham is head of the Air Intelligence Section. He'll do for a start.'

She nodded brightly and made a notation in a shorthand notebook. 'I'll find as many names as I can, sir, leave it to me.'

I nodded. She was a highly intelligent and capable woman. We would get on well together.

A short while later I went down to Churchill's office.

'David. Settling in all right?'

'Yes. I wanted more detail as to what you expect of me. I thought I would meet with heads of sections and discuss their requirements with them, but first I need to find out who does what. I'll also need some sort of authorisation. Otherwise they aren't going to tell me anything.'

Churchill surprised me by smiling and nodding. 'You've cut straight to the chase. Here's a list of those people you need to speak to, along with their phone numbers. Some of them you'll see are in other buildings around London. This is a letter of authority. Phone them or get your little wren to do it for you. Use my name to get the meeting and take this letter with you.' He handed a second sheet of paper to me.

I read it through quickly. It was, effectively, my *carte blanche*.

'We have,' he said, 'too diverse an intelligence organisation. Air, naval and army intelligence all work separately. My fear is that information is slipping between the cracks with potentially devastating effects. I want you to co-ordinate information between the three services.'

I frowned at him, 'I thought my task was to supply our agents in the field.'

Winston leaned back heavily in his chair and rubbed his chin. 'That's the official line. Unofficially, your task is more important. There is too much inter-service rivalry and jealousy. Too many fiefdoms being protected by small-minded officers who are only interested in their careers.'

'That's a bit harsh, isn't it?'

'Maybe. But there's more than a grain of truth in it. Unless we all pull together we'll be in dire straits. You know that I want a rapid attack through Belgium and into the Ruhr. Cutting off Hitler's main source of armaments would force him to sue for peace. Belgium won't hear of it, insisting that strict neutrality is the only way for them to survive.'

'Like Norway and Denmark?'

'Precisely. Belgium and Holland can't or won't see that they're next. Neither can Chamberlain. In spite of the fact that a month ago he claimed in Parliament that Hitler had "missed the bus".

'The idea that our strategy is strangling Germany's economy is pure bunkum. When Hitler is ready he will attack through Belgium and across the Maginot Line. We need to be ready for when he comes. We mustn't allow any piece of intelligence to slip through our fingers. Such information could be *vital* to our very survival.'

'I can't intercept every bit of intelligence that arrives. It's impossible!'

'I don't expect you to. Recruit suitable personnel. You know what I want. I leave it to you to get it done.'

I nodded. Fair enough. 'Office space?'

'On your floor there are seven empty offices. The hall porter has the list. You'll have them allocated to you.'

'Supposing,' I said slowly and thoughtfully, 'I find something that needs actioning, what do you want me to do?'

Churchill reached into an inside pocket and extracted his leather cigar holder. While he went through the ritual of lighting up, I waited patiently, recognising his usual ploy of giving himself time to think. 'Pass the information to whomsoever you think is appropriate and,' he pointed the cigar at me, 'tell me.'

We ironed out a few more points and I rose to go.

'Any ideas where you'll recruit from?'

I stopped with my hand on the doorknob and looked back at him. 'Of course. From the existing SIS staff.'

Churchill threw back his head and laughed. 'I knew you were the right man for the job.'

My office was in a state of minor chaos when I got back. The furniture had already arrived and Gladys was supervising its installation. I left her to it and went out into the street. It was a beautiful spring day. I looked up at the blue sky and white clouds scudding before the wind and a feeling of sadness engulfed me. With my new position came responsibility for the lives of so many brave young men and women. How many of them would die before the conflict was over? Hitler's destruction of our fragile peace sickened me.

As usual, when I needed to think, I went for a walk. I strolled down The Mall and into St James's Park. It was all very well for Churchill to say get on with it but I was aware that I would be ruffling feathers and treading on some big feet which matched equally large egos. Canny old bird that he was, Winnie knew that. Which was why he'd picked me. A career officer would never be able to do the job – his loyalty to his service would always come first. Despite my rank, I had no such shackles binding me.

Once round the park and I'd cleared my head. I strode purposefully back to my office. Gladys was waiting for me.

'Sir, here's a note. It came with the furniture. There are also paintings sent by the bank. They're in your room.'

The note was from Angus, reminding me of the board meeting in a week's time, should I be free to attend. He also suggested meeting for drinks at the club.

'Gladys, phone the bank, please, and tell Sir Angus Frazer's secretary that I'll be at the club at eighteen hundred hours. Now, let's see these paintings.' There were three. One was a scene from Nelson's battle at Trafalgar, a second of Wellington at Waterloo and a third showed the trenches at the Somme during the Great War. 'Gladys, get the hall porter to send up one of the janitors to hang these on the walls. You can have the one of the Somme.'

'Thank you, sir.'

She was looking at me strangely. 'Are you all right, Gladys? You seem a little quiet.'

'Oh, sorry, sir. I looked you up in Who's Who while you were out. I've never met a millionaire before.'

I laughed. 'We're the same as anybody else. Here, take this list. Make appointments with each of the people on it and get me in to see them ASAP. Starting this afternoon, if you can. One hour apart. I'm just going to check out the other offices we've been allocated.'

Each office was a mirror image of C3, and ran both sides of the corridor. The numbered ones opened into outer offices while unnumbered doors gave direct access to inner sanctums.

During the course of the next twenty-four hours I met senior personnel in Naval Intelligence, Army Intelligence, Air Intelligence and SIS.

Army Intelligence was represented by Major Blakely, who gave me some interesting information: General Oster, Second-in-Command of the whole of the German Abwehr and a staunch but secret anti-Nazi, had confirmed that we could expect to be attacked on the 10 May, just as Agent 54, Paul Thummel, had predicted.

'Has anyone else seen this?' I asked.

'It's been passed to the War Office.'

'And?'

'No action to be taken,' said Blakely and shrugged. 'We can only report what we learn, sir, it's up to the High Command after that.'

He was right, of course.

'It can be very frustrating. We knew about the German attack on Norway and Denmark but chose to ignore it. I'm worried that the same will happen again.'

I shared his fear. I'd inform Churchill. Perhaps there was something he could do about it. I made our intentions clear to each of the officers I saw. If there were any objections, none came my way. Although I suspected they'd start squealing when I started appropriating some of their staff. At each meeting, I surreptitiously asked about their personnel – expertise and ability. I built up a useful picture and took names. I would only need a few. They in turn could recommend others to me.

Freddy Winterbotham was the most forthcoming. 'Sir, you may like to see this report.'

An RAF reconnaissance Spitfire had reported spotting a vast column of four hundred panzer tanks moving around the Ardennes near Luxembourg. The clouds of dust and noise made by the vehicles could be seen for miles.

'The pilot flew over the column a number of times. That was very brave of him.'

'He returned with holes in his wings and rudder.'

'What have you done with the information?'

'Passed it to the War Office.'

'Right. Thanks. Can I keep this copy? I want to show Winnie.'

'Good. If anyone can take any action it's him.'

And so the days continued. It very quickly became obvious that collating evidence from all the forces in a central office was extremely worthwhile. On the 8th of May the War Office issued an intelligence assessment, headed "No Sign Of An Imminent Invasion". I'd appropriated a map that stretched from the Russian border, south to Turkey and Greece, west as far as the Western Approaches and north to Iceland and Greenland. Using it, I read again the different intelligence reports we'd received since No 54's. To me they all pointed to one thing. Germany was mobilising yet again. Only this time the targets were France, Belgium and Holland. I was sure of it. But what was the significance of the movements of the panzers?

I spent hours poring over the map and the reports. I wasn't a strategist by any stretch of the imagination. We had highly educated and trained senior officers whose sole raison d'être was to plan battles and foretell attacks. These men had spent their adult lives in war games and studying historic wars. Many had seen action in the Great War, the Middle East and Africa. So how could I presume to know better then they? The fact was, I couldn't. But something was niggling at me.

It was past the cocktail hour and I gave up. I decided to walk back to the flat having first ascertained that Madelaine had already left the Admiralty for the day. Passing the House of Commons I decided on impulse to go to the visitors' gallery. Ingress was simple as I was immediately recognised.

The veteran Tory, Leo Amery, was on his feet, directly behind the Prime Minister, who sat hunched in his seat. Support for Chamberlain's laissez-faire stance was waning daily. Voice filled with fury, Amery addressed him directly. 'In the words of Cromwell, depart, I say, and let us have done with you. In the name of God, go!'

Uproar followed until the Speaker called, 'Order! Order!'

Another Tory, Sir Roger Keyes, dressed in his uniform of an Admiral of the Fleet, took the floor and joined in the general condemnation over the bungling of Norway, now occupied by the Nazis. Chamberlain looked as though he was about to burst into tears and for a few seconds I felt sorry for him.

I asked the man sitting next to me what had brought on the debate.

'The PM called for a vote of confidence on his handling of the invasion of Norway.'

I listened avidly. As many Tories as Labour and Liberals were condemning the government. When it came to the vote, 281 voted for the government and 200 against. But 41 Tories voted against and 60 abstained. It was a sorry day for Britain – the vote showed again how divided our leaders were at this time of great peril.

I went home in a bad mood, had a late and frugal supper then went to bed. I awoke in the middle of the night. One second I had been fast asleep, the next I was wide-awake. I lay there for a few moments listening to the quiet of the flat. Madelaine was breathing gently beside me and I strained my ears, wondering if I'd been disturbed by something as mundane as a burglar. But all remained quiet. Suddenly I knew what had jerked me so unceremoniously from my slumber. I eased out of bed, found my dressing gown and went into the living room. I checked the time and saw it was only a few minutes after 2am. I'd been asleep less than two hours.

I sat by the window and opened the curtain, looking out on a dark London. Not even the searchlights brightened up the sky. I had woken with one word in my mind. One thought. Windsor! I'd been dreaming about our forays along the Allied lines. I tried to remember exactly what he had presented in his detailed accounts but it was no use. Yet there was something niggling at me, and it was definitely connected to the German troop movements we'd had so many reports about.

After half an hour I gave up and went back to bed. I spent a fitful night, eager to get back to Admiralty. After a hurried breakfast I rushed out of the door, leaving Madelaine to follow later. In my office I checked the intelligence reports and compared them to my wall map.

Phoning Churchill's office I discovered that he wouldn't be in until later as he'd had a late night sitting in the House. I told his secretary what I needed and she promised to messenger them up to me. Ten minutes later I signed for a folder of reports and sat down to read them.

Windsor's memory had been superb. The detail and accuracy of the information contained was first class. I began to put it all together, making notes on sheets of foolscap paper, pinning them to the map. Anti-tank emplacements, troop and gun strengths, machine-gun enfilade areas, barbed wire, ditch and wall obstacles. Deconstructing the reports took most of the morning. I told Gladys I didn't want to be disturbed. Though the phone rang in her office I took no calls. There was a lot of detail but finally I was satisfied. On the German side of the lines I pinned up the intelligence reports we'd received on troop movements. Once I'd finished I sat and looked at the wall for what seemed an eternity. I *knew* it was telling me something. But what?

Then it clicked. I leapt to my feet with an oath. Hurriedly I checked the papers we had rescued from the downed German aircraft, now headed "The Mechelen Incident". Germany's attack plan was a mirror image of ours. Our plan to go through Belgium and Holland and into the Ruhr was the exact reverse of Germany's plan to invade France and the Benelux countries. *But if Hitler had the same information we did, what would he do then?*

Simple! Feint along the lines and come through the Ardennes. Which was why the panzers were moving in the forested area around Luxembourg. The Maginot Line, with its fixed positions pointing forward, was an anachronism. If I knew that I'd direct my armies to sweep around the eastern edge. Attack from behind. Bring my armour and main armies through the Ardennes and send them east and west. Our forces would be caught in a pincer movement.

I stood up and paced my office. If I was right, Windsor had betrayed us for sure. But absolute proof would *only* come with war!

I called Churchill's office. 'Winston? Can you come up to my office, I have something to show you. You know I wouldn't ask if it wasn't important.'

I heard Churchill snort and slam down the receiver. Something else was rattling the old boy but I was sure he'd be up any minute. I opened the door to Gladys' office. 'Leading Wren, the First Sea Lord is on his way up. Show him straight in, will you?'

Gladys goggled at me and then composed herself. 'Yes, sir. Oh, sir, I have these messages for you and the files you asked for.'

'Thanks.' I took them and perused the messages. Nothing important. The files were of greater interest. I thought I'd identified three people, a man and two women, who would fit in with what we were doing and had asked for their personnel files from Registry. I had been expecting an argument about my entitlement to read them and so was pleasantly surprised to have them. Placing them on my desk I stood looking at the wall map, composing my arguments and conclusions for Churchill. A few minutes later I heard his growl in the outer office.

He came barging through the door before Gladys could announce him. 'Well?'

'Take a seat, Winnie. This will take some time.'

'I don't have time. I'm needed in the House. With the vote of confidence gone so badly for Chamberlain we're riding deep waters.'

'This is important. I want to explain what I've got here.'

He sat down, looked around him and said, 'Nice furniture. Where did this lot come from?'

'My place. Now let me explain this map and my findings.'

He sat hunched forward as though about to leap from the leather easy chair he was sitting in. I began with the information we'd learned from the Mechelen papers. Then I went through, step by step, what we knew about the French positions and their front-line. As each piece of information unfolded Winston became more alert. It was not the first time I had seen him thus – he had a first-class tactical brain.

When I had finished he was leaning back in the chair, his hands on his knees, staring at the map. After a few seconds of silence he said, 'It makes such frightening good sense. With our forces massed ready to move across the Belgian Plain we'll be taken by surprise. And our forces are there precisely *because* that's our preferred route to the Ruhr. And so we think the Germans will come the same way. But there's no reason to think that the Germans have the same information as we have.'

I didn't answer but just looked at Churchill. He glared back and finally snapped, 'All right, all right, damn you. He *may* have betrayed us.'

'The question is – what are you going to do about it?'

'I'll take it to the War Office.' Pausing, he said, 'No, better still, I'll call a Chiefs of Staff meeting for early tomorrow morning. Seven ack emma sharp. You can present the information. Bring your map with you.'

I nodded. Fair enough. If I was wrong I could always go back to banking.

'What's happening in the House?'

Churchill looked a little sheepish, if that was at all possible for such a bulldog countenance.

I laughed. 'You're lobbying for support.' I held out my hand. 'Good luck. I hope you oust Chamberlain. We need a leader, not a vacillating coward.'

'Thank you, David.' He shook my hand warmly. 'Thank you very much. I won't forget this.'

I spent the next twenty minutes reading the personnel files of the three people I'd liked the look of when I'd visited the different SIS sections. I wrote brief identical memos to each of their section heads, explaining that I was acting under the orders of the First Sea Lord. If there were any objections they were to be taken up with him.

By the end of the day I had three new people added to my section.

The following morning I was out of the flat before 6am. I arrived at the Admiralty to find Leading Wren Flower already there.

'I didn't expect you in so early,' I said, pleased all the same.

'Someone needs to make the tea,' she smiled.

'I'm sure you'd be wasted doing anything so mundane. Do you know where the meeting is to take place?'

'Yes, sir. There's a conference room next door to the First Sea Lord's office. I've taken the map off the wall and rolled it up.'

'Good, let's get on with it.'

I never had an opportunity to give my views.

Just before 07.00 the Chiefs of Staff began to arrive. As we sat around a large conference table, reports and rumours began to come in. It seemed the Germans had invaded Holland and Belgium at 04.00. It was the devil's own job trying to part fact from fiction. On the face of it, it looked as though the Germans had kept to their original plan and were indeed heading across the Plains and into the Maginot Line. *Why didn't I believe it?*

For half an hour we tried to telephone the French for an update on what was happening. Finally it was agreed that the Chiefs of Staff should leave and return to their own offices. High drama became high farce, as it emerged that the night watchmen had left and the day men hadn't yet come in. All the doors were double and treble locked and nobody could leave. In the end I opened a window and watched as our highest-ranking Admirals, Generals and Air Marshals clambered out. So much, I thought, for national security.

When they left, I'm afraid to say my composure broke. I was so sure I was right. Angrily I tore the map off the wall and dumped it into a wastepaper bin. Stalking from the room I was dimly aware of the Leading Wren pulling the map back out again.

9

WINSTON WAS PRIME Minister! Hallelujah! His first act was to put together a coalition government with Labour's leader, Clement Attlee, as Deputy Prime Minister and Lord Halifax remaining as Foreign Secretary. Chamberlain, much to my disgust, was to stay in the War Cabinet.

I'll never forget watching Churchill give his speech in the House, John Bull come to life. Churchill embodied the fighting spirit of the British – listening, you felt his faith in the people alone could carry us through. His words were rousing and passionate, yet one phrase has always stuck in my memory – "I have nothing to offer but blood, toil, tears and sweat." I could feel an excitement in Parliament that had been missing up until then. At long last we had the political leadership we deserved and needed.

We were so busy in the office, I decided to change one of the leather chairs for a sofa so that I could stay overnight if need be.

The reports coming in made no sense to me. I appeared to have misjudged the situation. The German military attack was proceeding exactly in accordance with the Mechelen papers. The main thrust of the German advance seemed to be through the Low Countries, intent on engaging the BEF and French on the plains of central Belgium. From there we now expected them to push into Northern France. Our forces were already mobilised and heading to meet the threat with the French alongside us.

A new form of warfare was being faced for the first time: Paratroopers. Thousands of them dropped onto selected targets in Holland and Belgium. They landed with devastating effect on Rotterdam while panzer forces attacked the German-Dutch border. The *blitzkrieg* was so effective that the German ground forces linked up with the paratroopers in only three days.

In spite of the evidence coming in I still couldn't believe what was happening. Had I been wrong about Windsor all along?

The French Seventh Army arrived at Rotterdam to help the Dutch city survive the attack. Later that same day the Dutch surrendered. The fall of Rotterdam had taken a mere five days.

Reports were coming in from Allied Forces sources as well as civilians caught up in the fighting. The news was all bad. The Germans were breaking through on every part of the front using the combined tactic of paratroopers and lightning attacks by panzer tanks. I received sporadic reports that convinced me the main attack was still to come – and that it would be through the Ardennes.

I used my office to try and keep tabs on the Windsors. One report particularly sickened me. Its ultimate source was Mrs Clare Luce, the wife of Henry Luce, the owner of the American magazine *Time*. She recounted an incident to Diana Cooper, the wife of the British Minister of Information. After a dinner she'd attended at the Windsor's residence, they had been listening to the news about the bombardment of English towns and villages along the south coast. Mrs Luce said she hated to see the British so wantonly attacked and killed. Wallis had replied that she could not feel sorry for them after what the English had done to her. The report had come from the Minister himself, he was so incensed by her attitude.

Three days after Winston took office he sent for me at No. 10 Downing Street. Without preamble he said, 'It seems I owe you an apology, Griffiths. I've come to the conclusion that you're right about the Windsors. They do represent a grave threat to this country. They and their friends can no longer be permitted to endanger us all. And so I have taken steps.'

I did my best to keep the surprise from my voice. 'What have you done?'

'I've had the Duke of Buccleugh fired from his position as the Lord Steward of the Royal Household and Sir Oswald and Lady Mosley arrested and imprisoned under new defence laws we pushed through the House yesterday. Did you hear about Vernon Kell?'

'The head of MI5?'

'The same. He's been dismissed. I think he's been leaking secrets to the Germans. I've also got rid of Sir Samuel Hoare. He's been sent to Spain as Ambassador.'

I knew Hoare had been the Air Minister as well as a friend and confidant of Edward. 'Why Spain – such a prestigious position?'

Churchill looked uncomfortable for a moment and then replied, 'It was the best I could do under the circumstances. Though I'd have preferred to send the Hoares to a penal settlement.' Churchill sighed and said, 'I have a very delicate task I need performed. I've wracked my brains wondering whom to send – it's a lot to ask of any man.'

As he began to speak, I knew exactly what was intended – part of me had always known it was a possibility.

'You understand that nobody on earth can ever know. Not even your wife.'

I nodded numbly. 'Why not send him into exile somewhere?'

'That's still a possibility. Consider this a contingency plan. It must be done while they're still abroad. *How* you do it, I leave to you. And you know that officially you're on your own, David. What do you say?'

I sat pondering the question for a few seconds. 'I'll agree on one condition.'

Churchill nodded but then growled, 'I don't like conditions, you know that.'

'I'll make my plans but we wait. Despite everything, I still think the Germans will come through the Ardennes. Our forces are speeding at a rate of knots to the West and into Holland and Belgium. Once we're trapped there I believe the Hun will smash through and come in behind us, behind the Maginot Line. If they do, it would constitute enough proof that Windsor has betrayed us. Then I'll carry out your request.'

It was the PM's turn to think for a few moments but then he said, 'I agree. Discuss this with no one. If you need to speak to me urgently phone or leave a message, using the word whisky and I'll know what it's about.'

'Winston,' I said heavily, 'you've been reading too much John Buchan.'

Once I'd left him I was no longer sure I *could* carry out his instructions. Was it regicide to kill an ex-king?

General Heinz Guderian's 19th Panzers battered their way through the lightly defended Ardennes and were in Sedan by the 13th of May. Thirty-six hours of frenetic forest fighting followed, but the under-strength Allied troops were overwhelmed. Lack of concealment, poor anti-tank ditches and badly trained French crews meant their defence was as weak as Windsor had stated in his first report. I was now convinced he had sold us out to the Hun.

We had only one weapon to throw into the fight. The RAF. For our pilots it was little short of a massacre. The reports of losses came in daily and they were horrifying. In only a few short days 45 of the 109 Allied aircraft attacking the panzers were shot down. At that rate the backbone of the RAF would soon be broken. I was summoned to Churchill's office. His troubled face showed exactly how grave the situation had become. 'Just had a call from Paul Reynaud, the French Prime Minister. Reynaud says they are defeated. The Hun has broken through near Sedan and is pouring through in great numbers with tanks and armoured cars. Guderian's panzers have flooded across the Meuse and are charging into the hinterland of northern France.' He looked at me steadily, 'You were right. Windsor did betray us. How quickly can you get to Paris?'

It seemed the whole of Europe was on the move. Refugees were clogging the roads, bombing had made the railroads unusable and cross-channel ferries were subject to attack by German planes. My brother Sion was my only hope. I took the train to South Wales.

Arriving in Cardiff I changed to a branch line to Barry. From there I managed to get a taxi to St. Athan, where I was dumped at the main gate. My uniform and identity card got me inside the wire fence and I was directed to a distant corner of the huge airfield, where a large complex of corrugated iron huts had been erected. Outside one door was the company sign – *Griffiths Aviation & Co Ltd*. The door led to a small office where a pleasant-looking woman was typing furiously.

'May I help you?'

'I've come to see Mr Griffiths.'

'And who may I say is calling?'

'I'm his brother David . . .'

The words were barely out of my mouth when the door opened and Sion appeared.

'Bro'! What a pleasant surprise! Come in! Mavis, get my brother . . . what? Tea or coffee?'

I settled on tea. His office was lined with drawing boards, each with a scale plan of an aircraft. Sion pointed at one of them enthusiastically. 'The latest modification for the Griffin X. We're using the Rolls-Royce Merlin engine as standard to speed up production. With a hydraulically retracting undercarriage, and the slightly swept back profile of the wings we're about the fastest plane in the sky.'

'Do you have a trainer?'

'A two-seater? Oh, I get it. I might have guessed this wasn't a social call. You want taking somewhere.'

'Paris. It's important. I wouldn't ask but the chances of getting there any other way are pretty slim.'

Sion's mouth widened into his usual infectious smile. 'Okay. No problem. It's nearly tea time so will tomorrow suit you?'

'First thing before breakfast?'

We agreed and Sion showed me around his new airfield. They were in the process of erecting large hangers. A metal skeleton was being bolted together and then covered with corrugated iron sheets. Once it was in place a concrete floor would be poured and allowed to set for two days before any machinery was fitted.

'We have one production line up and running. Come on and I'll show you.'

It was an interesting tour. The third and final hangar was where each plane's electrics were fitted, after which it was ready for its inaugural flight. There were upwards of eight hundred people working there. Whereas months earlier the workforce had been mainly male, women now made up the bulk of the employees.

'I refuse to release any of the men until I've trained a woman to replace him, but that only creates problems. Some of the men volunteer and are away before we know it, in spite of the fact that they have a reserve occupation.' Sion shrugged. 'I can't say I blame them. I wish I were younger. I'd be with them.'

'Don't be daft, man. Your work here is far too important. Anyway, you've said it yourself often enough, flying is a young man's game.'

Sion sighed. 'I guess you're right. Come on,' he smacked me on the shoulder, 'let's go to the house. It's over by that copse of trees.'

As we wandered across the grass towards the lighted window in the distance, we talked. 'Any problems with air raids?'

'Not so far, thank God. Not like at Biggin Hill. I don't know if the Hun has yet to learn we're here or whether it's too far for him to come.'

'The latter, I should think.'

'That's what I thought.' He opened the kitchen door and called. 'Kirsty, look who's here.'

My sister-in-law appeared through the door opposite. She took one look at me, broke into a beaming smile and rushed over to give me a kiss and welcome hug. 'If we'd known we'd have killed a fatted calf or two,' she said in her soft Scottish brogue. 'Instead I can offer you some mutton broth.'

'Where's Peter?' Peter Cazorla was Sion's right-hand man. A Mexican by birth, he and his wife, two sons and two daughters were an integral part of Sion's life.

'He has a house on the other side of the airfield,' Sion replied. 'It's safer that way.'

'Safer?'

'In the event of a bombing raid, it's unlikely they'd hit both homes – one of us would survive, we hope. It means the work could continue.'

It made sense but was a terrible reminder of what we were facing. To lighten the mood I reached into my bag and extracted a bottle of port and another of malt whisky. 'Let's have a drink and you can bring me up to date on the family.'

Sion told me their news, pride and anxiety mingled in his voice. Alex, their eldest son, had celebrated his twenty-third birthday a few weeks earlier. He was already a skilled pilot but had been prevented from joining up because he was also a trained aeronautical engineer. A week earlier he had presented himself at the Air Ministry in Holborn and enlisted. Alex had played down his engineering skills, played up his flying prowess and was now in the RAF, being fast-tracked to a fighter squadron.

Their daughter Louise, not yet nineteen, had volunteered to become a nurse. She was training at East Glamorgan hospital in Church Village, about ten miles from St. Athan.

Paul, the youngest at seventeen, was ready to go up to university and had gained entrance to Oxford. He was reading mathematics.

Sunrise was at 05.33 and we took off straight into it. I was sitting in the front of the plane with Sion directly behind. The aircraft's controls were replicated in both positions to enable the trainee pilot to follow through as they learned to fly the Griffin. The cloud base was thick at about 8,000ft and the sun's rays striking the billowing mass created an awesome study in white and grey. I sat uncomfortably with my overnight bag on my knees, thinking about its contents, a very special bottle of the Duke's favourite one-hundred-year-old port.

*   *   *

Staying below the cloud we were treated to the panoramic view of the Bristol Channel stretching left and right. We hit England at Weston-Super-Mare and crossed Salisbury Plain twenty minutes after take-off. Sion had taken the precaution of informing Air-Traffic Control that we would be in the air, destined for France. The last thing we wanted was to be shot down by our own ack-ack or be bounced by an early morning patrol. Salisbury Cathedral spire was a beautiful landmark and we passed directly overhead. We turned a few degrees to hit the Needles on the eastern side of the Isle of Wight before darting across the Channel for the French coast. My eyes continually monitored the dials in front of me, and the sky around me. The altimeter stayed rock steady at 7,200ft, the speed at 320 knots and the revs at 2,100. Though I checked constantly, the oil pressure needle flickered minutely, the trim stayed steady and the compass pointed at 120 degrees. The only dial moving was the fuel consumption. Sion hadn't lost his touch.

We saw no other aircraft but flew over a squadron of destroyers making their way up-Channel. A light flashed at us and we answered. By now the cloud was breaking up so we went up another 2,000ft.

'There's France, Bro',' said Sion on the intercom. 'Dieppe to port and Le Havre to starboard.'

'Beautiful, isn't it?'

'That it is.'

The cloud cleared completely as we approached Paris. The Eiffel Tower was a finger in the sky, marking the city for many miles around. Landing at a military airfield to the west we taxied off the runway. We bounced across the grass and stopped where indicated. Sion slid back the canopy and climbed down stiffly. He took my bag and I clambered out.

We exchanged wry grins. 'Not as nimble as we used to be,' he said.

After breakfast, the Griffin was refuelled, Sion and I shook hands and I watched him take off. As the plane gained height the wings waggled and I waved, though I doubted he could see me.

A decrepit taxi took me into the city and straight to the Military Mission.

Howard-Vyse greeted me with a handshake and the words, 'I wondered where you'd got to.'

'Blighty. Winston had a job for me. I've a letter from him.' I handed over an envelope with the seal of the Prime Minister on the flap.

Ripping it open he quickly scanned its contents. 'Do you know what's in here?'

I shrugged. 'I haven't read it but I assume it's along the lines of giving me every help required apart from manpower.'

Howard-Vyse nodded. 'So what can I do for you?'

'I've been giving it some thought on the flight here. I'd like a car, a pass, a map of France and the whereabouts of the Duke of Windsor. I understand he's left Paris for an unknown destination.'

'Your intelligence is certainly up-to-date. He left yesterday for Biarritz.' The General's voice held more than a hint of scorn. 'As soon as the Germans broke through at Sedan he was off. You know, Griffiths, I hope I never see that man again.'

'How big an entourage did he take with him?'

'His entire party consists of Wallis, his chauffeur and three maids. What are you up to, Griffiths?'

'Better you don't know. Can you let me have a weapon of some sort? Something more substantial than my Webley? A Lee-Enfield, if you have one? I shouldn't need it, but I'd rather be safe than sorry.'

'Actually, I have something better. It's just arrived.' He pulled open the lid of a wooden box. Inside lay three guns I'd never seen before. 'This is the new Lanchester, made by Sterling. It's a machine gun with a mag of fifty rounds. We've been issued with them for close defence.' The General fumbled slightly with the magazine, then showed me how to cock it and pointed out the selector switch for single shot or automatic fire. 'More use than a rifle, I should think, and only three-quarters of an Enfield's length. Easier to carry in the car. Take three full magazines as well.'

'Thank you, Richard. I shouldn't need it but you never know.'

'As for transport, the best I can give you is a Citröen Tourer. It's a two-seater so we don't use it much. That do?'

'As long as it goes. Do you have a current map of France?'

'I'll get you a Michelin Guide. I don't know what you're up to David, but good luck.'

We shook hands and I left, shown to the car by Howard-Vyse's batman. There was no key, only a starter button on the floor. The engine needed cranking but when I pressed the button the motor burst into throaty life. I eased the clutch in, engaged the gears and moved smoothly away. The car was a joy to drive.

It took me an hour to get out of the city. You would never know there was a war going on, everything seeming so normal. At the southern outskirts of Paris I stopped at a garage, squeezed in the last drop of petrol, filled up two jerry cans and purchased a quantity of food. Cheese and bread would make up my staple diet, supplemented with a bag of fruit.

Once in the countryside, I found a thick wood and I pulled over to study the Michelin Guide more closely. I would be travelling through Orléans, Poitiers and Bordeaux. I made a rough estimate of the distance – the best part of four hundred and eighty miles. I checked the odometer. So far I'd managed forty odd in nearly two hours. I needed to get a move on. However, there was one thing I had to do. I took the machine-gun, checked it, cocked it, and fired a short burst at a tree. It pulled right and upwards but handled easily enough. Satisfied, I placed it on the seat alongside me and covered it with my coat.

The day was warming up nicely and I spent a few minutes folding down the roof. Behind the front seats was a small ledge, where I put my bag. I threw my uniform jacket over it, loosened my tie and settled behind the wheel. There was something about a trip like this that appealed to my restless nature. Normally a journey through France would have excited me, but this time I was dreading my arrival and what I had promised to do.

The Michelin Guide proved invaluable as I wound my way south and slightly west. I made good time, occasionally chewing on a piece of bread and a mouthful of cheese, or eating an apple or dried apricot. By the middle of the afternoon I was approaching Poitiers. The traffic I had passed so far seemed normal, with none of the panic I knew to be clogging up the roads in the north. The towns and villages appeared peaceful enough, although of course there was a lack of men around the streets.

The day had stayed fine and warm and I felt a drowsiness and lethargy seeping through me. The road meandered alongside the River Clain and as I went over the brow of a hill I saw the small town of Châtellerault straddling the highway. I pulled into a garage, filled up the petrol tank and then parked outside a small bar. Straightening my tie, I put on my jacket before entering. Two old men sat at a table and watched me approach the counter. I ordered a coffee and enquired after the toilet. It was out at the back; a small shed with a hole in the ground and bars either side to hold on to. So much for French sophistication.

I washed using cold water from an outside tap and used my hand-kerchief to dry my hands and face. My coffee was waiting for me when I re-entered. I drank it quickly, gave the bartender a franc and left. Apart from me asking for the coffee not another word had been spoken.

Feeling refreshed I pushed on. But within a short distance my eyelids were drooping once more and I decided I'd better pull over and have a nap. I stopped a few miles from Poitiers, put the roof up, closed the windows, closed my eyes and promptly fell asleep. I awoke with a jerk, feeling disorientated. Climbing out of the car I stretched aching limbs. I was getting too old for gallivanting around Europe like this. As was so often the case, the spirit was willing but the flesh was becoming weak.

After getting the circulation moving in my arms and legs again I climbed back into the car. Back on the road I put my foot down. I wanted to get to Bordeaux before I had another stop. I was making good time an hour later when there was a bang and the car settled down a few degrees at the rear and the back wobbled left and right. Damnation! A blow-out at this time! Pulling off the road and under some trees, I rolled up my sleeves. The spare tyre was fixed to the boot lid. I expected to find the jack and handle inside. But search as hard as I liked, there wasn't one.

I hadn't seen another vehicle for miles. I'd passed a few farm-houses ages back but there was no habitation in sight. I had two choices. Either I waited and flagged down some help or walked to the nearest house or village, which was probably ahead of me. Sighing, I decided on the latter. I hid my bag and machine-gun, strapped on my Sam Browne over my jacket and had gone about a dozen paces when I stopped. A moss-covered boulder was protruding about a foot from the ground. Trees lined both sides of the road and I stood looking at them for a few moments, a wild idea taking hold. Was it possible . . . ?

I retraced my steps, found the machine-gun, chose a target, cocked the weapon, flicked the selector switch in front of the trigger guard to automatic fire and pulled the trigger. From a distance of less than a yard I couldn't miss. I cut across the branch, spraying chips of wood in all directions. Two bursts left the branch sagging. I leapt up, caught a twig and worked my way along, pulling the branch down. It bent and then suddenly snapped off. I just managed to dart aside as it fell to the ground. Heaving and straining I dragged it over to the rock. Jumping in the car I positioned it with the rear a few feet from the rock. Fitting the branch under the back axle and over the rock I pulled down. After much heaving the car lifted a few inches. Good, that part worked. I lowered the car back to the ground and began skirmishing the area. Finding nothing of any use I used the machine-gun once more and dragged a second, bigger branch over to the rock. Placing it across the end of the first I pushed down. The car lifted easily. But when I let go it fell back again. I had already used up one complete magazine and was reluctant to use a second, but what was I saving it for? This was rural southern France. All the fighting was hundreds of miles away to the north. I fired a third time.

I still needed to use my own weight to lift the car in spite of the branches. Eventually, I could stand next to the car and push down one-handed to raise the back axle a few inches. I began casting around for useful stones. It took forever but I eventually found the one I wanted. Putting it under the car next to the axle, I raised the rear. Awkwardly I slid the stone further along until it was under the axle, then lowered the car until it was sitting precariously on the stone, the rear wheels clear of the ground.

Using a spanner, I eventually got the bolts holding the wheel off, skinning two knuckles on my right hand. As quickly as I could I removed the wheel, put on the spare and replaced the nuts. Raising the car, I gratefully removed the stone and lowered the back wheels to the ground. With a good deal of satisfaction I climbed behind the wheel and resumed my journey. I was aware that the sun was setting and a glance at my watch showed me that I'd been delayed for almost three hours.

By now I'd had enough. I was dirty, tired and hungry. In the dying light of the day I checked my Michelin Guide and saw that Saintes was the next town. I decided I'd stop there for the night.

On the outskirts I saw a watering trough and pump. Pulling over I used it to wash the grime off my hands and face. Then, before I went any further, I hid the machine-gun in the boot under the burst wheel, put on my jacket and spruced myself up. At the town centre, next to the post office and town hall, was the Hotel Delafond.

They had a room free but the kitchen was about to close. I ordered a meal in my room, along with a bottle of Bordeaux. The bathroom was at the other end of the corridor, and I soaked in the hot water for a few minutes, easing out the kinks in my body.

A tough steak of uncertain origin doused in an over-rich sauce, and vegetables that saved the meal from being inedible were followed by an excellent local cheese and biscuits. The wine was superb.

I slept like a log.

10

I ARRIVED IN Biarritz, twenty miles from the Spanish border, just after mid-day. It was a beautiful town with wonderful beaches, the rolling Atlantic lapping gently onto the sand. The day was warm, a soft breeze coming up from the south. I headed for the Hotel du Palais, the largest and most expensive in town, where I established that the Duke and Duchess were indeed in residence before signing in myself.

In my room I dumped my bag and went out into the town. Travelling light, I needed new clothes. I found a gentlemen's outfitters and bought a lightweight suit, as well as a tuxedo with all the trimmings. That evening I sat nursing a cocktail in the bar, ready to greet His Royal Highness, the traitor king, as I had dubbed him.

I was able to watch the doorway reflected in the mirror lining the wall behind the bar. It was well after 21.00 when Wallis appeared, chatting animatedly with another woman. I waited, expecting Windsor to appear at any moment. After a while the two women went in to dinner. I frowned. Perhaps Windsor was ill and had taken to his bed? Or maybe he was out meeting some of his many cronies elsewhere in Biarritz? I was about to ask Wallis when I changed my mind. Instead I went to the front desk.

'I say, was that the Duchess of Windsor I just saw?'

'Yes, Sir David. She's gone in to dinner.'

'Where's the Duke? He's a friend of mine.'

'I'm so sorry, Sir David, he's returned to Paris. Urgent war business apparently.'

I nodded my thanks and returned to the bar. Damn, damn, damn. I'd had a wasted journey. Well, there was nothing for it but to enjoy my evening and return to Paris the next day. I ate a superb meal while sitting on the terrace, listening to a string quartet play soothing music. But instead of it being balm to my soul I sat seething at the wasted effort. Only later, as I sat on my balcony, a large whisky and soda in my hand, watching a full moon rise out of the Atlantic, casting its light like a torch across the ocean, did I find my black mood lifting.

In the morning, before I left, I had a new tyre fitted to the wheel and bought a jack. I didn't want to have to go through the same performance again. I filled up with petrol, checked the oil and water, bought provisions and bottles of cold drink and set off to retrace my route.

By the time I reached Bordeaux the wind had veered and was sweeping in from the Atlantic. A cold front was approaching and squalls of rain soon arrived. The Citroën's heater was ineffective, the windscreen wipers barely adequate and there was a leak in the canvas roof that dripped onto my left shoulder. The temperature dropped rapidly and I was soon shivering. Visibility worsened as the afternoon darkened quickly. Lightning flashed overhead, followed a few seconds later by a deep clap of thunder. Late afternoon I was near Niort when a second thunderstorm appeared. This time forked lightning flashed across the sky as the thunder rumbled. The storm was directly overhead and lashing down. The wipers were fighting a losing battle. I had difficulty in seeing out of the window.

A second roll of thunder sounded like artillery fire and lightning struck an elm tree over to my right. Out of nowhere a horse bolted over a fence in front of the car and I swerved to avoid the beast. Smashing through a fence, I came to a sudden halt. The last thing I remember was my head hitting the steering wheel.

When I came to I was aching all over. I sat up straight and wished I hadn't moved. My head was throbbing. Reaching up I could feel a bump like an egg in the middle of my forehead. I looked about me. I was in a corn field. The engine had stalled but the wipers were still clicking irritatingly back and forth.

It was pouring with rain and I was quickly sodden through as I examined the car. One headlight was broken but that seemed to be all the damage. Crossing my fingers I tried the motor. It burst into life. I turned the car and drove towards the gap in the fence. There was no way I could get up there and onto the road. Instead I began to follow the field around. Twice the car stuck and I had to collect branches to stuff under the back wheels to get enough traction and momentum to keep moving. Each time I seemed to get wetter, if that was possible. By the time I got back onto the road I was saturated to the skin, my head was throbbing and my vision was blurring.

There was no point in going any further and I stopped in Niort. I found a small hotel and booked in. The rooms were cold, shabby and the plumbing left much to be desired. Exhausted, I went to bed and shivered all night. I left after a breakfast of hard-boiled eggs, cold meat and lukewarm coffee. By the time I reached Poitiers I knew I was in trouble. At Châtellerault I was shivering as though I had the ague. Sweat beaded my brow and my vision was blurring. I drove into the town and quickly found the largest hotel. Thank goodness it was utterly different from the one I had stayed in the night before, warm, welcoming and helpful.

I went to bed and a doctor was sent for. He confirmed that I had a mild fever, made worse by the bump on my head, and recommended complete rest for a few days. I didn't feel like arguing and succumbed to his ministrations. My fever held and I was laid up for over a week. During that time the doctor visited me regularly. But the owner's wife was a treasure – she nurtured me like a son, with hot soup and plenty of liquids. Grand-mère Simonet had three grandsons away fighting in the north. Her eldest son had been killed in the Great War and was buried in a mass grave somewhere. Her surviving son was working for the government in Paris. Her concern for her family reminded me of my own mother. Grand-mère Simonet's youngest grandson was obviously her favourite. She had raised him herself after her son had died and her daughter-in-law had remarried and moved away, abandoning the boy. She feared greatly for all the boys and talked about them endlessly.

I sent a telegram to Madelaine letting her know what had happened but had no way of knowing if it reached her. Radio reports and gossip from Grand-mère Simonet kept me abreast of events. The French gun emplacements at the Front were being obliterated by the deadly combination of dive-bombers and accurate German artillery fire. Reinforcements were being hampered constantly by having to fight against the tide of refugees streaming away from the front. Innocent civilians, fleeing the war, were being strafed by German fighters as they sowed mayhem across the north of France.

It was announced that the French Seventh Armoured Battalion had rushed into battle and was stalling the German panzers at Sedan. The next day revealed the awful truth. The Seventh had been obliterated.

A few days later came the news that the Allies were on the run, smashed by a combination of superior forces, better weapons and greater "luck".

I knew it wasn't luck. The Germans had known *precisely* where to attack.

By now the Hun were moving across France almost as fast as their panzers could travel, sweeping everything before them. Whole armies were being wiped out or forced to surrender. Astonishingly, after disarming the enemy troops, the Germans left them behind their lines to fend for themselves. Many took off, heading south and away from the conflict.

The Hun had reached Arras. It was time to get out of bed and return to Paris where I could possibly do some good. Still feeling as weak as a kitten I left Châtellerault with the good Madame's wishes echoing in my head. The storms of a week ago had long passed and I drove through warm sunshine along roads that became busier by the mile. I was amazed that the tide of refugees had already reached this far south. Forcing myself to keep going, late in the night I finally arrived at Paris.

I went first to the Military Mission but apart from a skeleton staff no one was there. I was told that the hotels were full and I decided to accept their offer to bunk down there for the night, exhausted and grateful. I slept on a camp bed in an anteroom until woken by a corporal bearing a cup of tea sometime around 07.00.

Madame Simonet had cleaned my clothes and uniform, so when I reported to Howard-Vyse a short while later I was at least presentable. Briefly, I described the fiasco I had endured then asked, 'What's happening here?'

'I've been ordered to destroy all the Mission's records. You may like to read these.' He thrust a signal pad into my hand. 'Tell me what you make of them.'

I couldn't believe what I was reading. The BEF was being herded like cattle into an area around Dunkirk. The entire army was about to be crushed when General Guderian's forces crossed the Canal du Nord, the last line of defence against the panzers. Once they swept across the canal the Germans would capture over three hundred thousand British troops and leave Britain undefended.

In utter astonishment I turned to the next signal. Our range of listening posts, known as Y Service, had picked up the Germans' encoded signals, forwarded them to the code-breaking centre at

Bletchley Park, and sent them out to the High Command. On 23 May a direct order had been sent from Hitler to Field Marshal Kleist to stop the attack *before* crossing the canal. It was utter madness!

The remainder of the signals were depressing in the extreme. Boulogne was isolated by German tanks. Three battalions of British motorised infantry barely reached Calais in time. Worse, the whole BEF was short of food and ammunition. The only defensible area left now was at Bray Dunes, Dunkirk.

At the Mission we worked round-the-clock. Liaison between the French and British forces was paramount, as the Allies now attempted the impossible – to save an army. All thoughts of Windsor were forgotten.

At 11.42 on the 24th of May, in plain language, the Germans broadcast to their forces telling them to halt the attack along the line of Dunkirk-Hazebrouck-Merville. For three days nothing happened, apart from some skirmishing between forward posts on both sides. Then, simultaneously, two events occurred. The Belgians surrendered and Churchill launched Operation Dynamo – the evacuation of the British Expeditionary Force from Belgium.

On the morning of the 28th of May Fruity Metcalfe came in to the Mission in high dudgeon. 'Bloody Windsor has done a bunk.'

'He's done what?' I was aghast. The man was a *serving major-general in the British army*. No one, not even an ex-king, walked away without permission or orders.

'I had dinner with him last night and asked him what my orders were for today. He said to phone at nine-thirty, which I did. The concierge informed me that at six o'clock this morning the Duke and all his servants left for the South of France.'

So Windsor was not only a traitor, he was also a coward.

'That's not all,' Metcalfe said, close to tears. 'He's taken both cars, disabled the two-seater runabout and poured the store of petrol we had down the drain. It's as if he *wanted* me caught by the Germans.'

I looked Fruity in the eye. 'Or perhaps you know too much, old bean, about his meetings with Charles Bedaux and the information Windsor had passed to him. Come and look at this.' Showing Metcalfe the huge map that covered the whole of Northern France, I explained how the Germans had attacked and the routes they had taken. He had far more military knowledge than I and saw immediately the point I was making.

'They *knew*,' he said in a ghastly whisper.

'I was sent to the Gare du Nord early this morning to make evacuation arrangements,' I said. 'I was accosted by an old Red Cross nurse, a Frenchwoman. Know what she asked me?'

Metcalfe shook his head, despair in his face.

'*Qui nous a trahis?*'

'Who has betrayed us?'

'Precisely. The whole populace is asking how it happened. Written in chalk on the sides of the French army vehicles is *Vendu pas vaincu.*'

'Betrayed not beaten. Damn the man!' Metcalfe spoke his anguish. 'I have to go.'

'Go? Go where?'

'Back to Blighty, of course. Where I can serve my country.'

And he was as good as his word. I later discovered Metcalfe left the building, stole a bicycle, then hitchhiked and walked all the way to Cherbourg. He escaped to Britain where he joined Scotland Yard.

Time was running out. I needed to speak to Howard-Vyse. I knocked on his door and he, courteous as ever, pointed at a seat for me to take. 'I need permission to leave, sir.'

'Leave? But we're evacuating. I understand a plane is arriving to take us out first thing in the morning.'

'Metcalfe has just told me Windsor has left Paris. He's gone AWOL. Apparently he's gone south. I suspect it's back to Biarritz. I *must* go after him.'

Howard-Vyse said sadly. 'You may go. I'll give you a written order to that effect. Whatever you're up to, it must be important. I have to say, David, you're a very determined man. Don't you ever give up?'

I smiled. 'Sometimes, when the risks are too great. But not this time. This time it's become personal.' We shook hands, and I collected my gear, including my carefully packed overnighter with the special port. I added another two magazines for the Lanchester and I went out to the Citröen. I hadn't asked permission to take it but didn't doubt for a moment it would be granted.

This time the roads were jammed with refugees. I had the devil's own job fighting my way through onto open roads where I could get up a bit of speed. The further south I went the easier the roads became but even so, I'd travelled less than two hundred miles by nightfall and weariness was overtaking me.

Try as I might I couldn't find a bed in a hotel. Town after town there were no vacancies. South of Poitiers I gave up. I pulled into a copse of trees, near a small stream, and made camp. This time I'd come prepared.

Cockcrow woke me around dawn. Blearily I looked at my watch. Almost 05.00. I had an army stove with me and lit the white block of fuel to boil water, then shaved in cold water while the kettle boiled. With coffee, bread and cheese inside me, I set off again. My next intended stop was Biarritz.

I was too late. Windsor had left that very morning, with his entourage, for La Croë, his house on the French Riviera. The frustration I felt was almost overwhelming, but I forced myself to swallow my anger and think dispassionately. I booked into the hotel and pondered my next move. This game of cat and mouse – did it mean Windsor sensed something afoot? Or was it his usual yellow-bellied habit of watching his skin that made him move so often and unexpectedly?

I spent a day at Biarritz, had the car checked out at a garage and replaced two tyres. At the main post office I sent a message to Madelaine to let her know I was all right. She would be worried to death. My trusty Michelin Guide told me I had to drive 500 miles or more across Southern France to reach La Croë. I set off on a beautiful, hot summer's day. The roof was down and I wore casual civilian clothes. For a few moments it was as if the fighting was a dream.

The roads wound through some of the most beautiful scenery in the world. Now, so far from the fighting, there were no problems in finding a bed and three days later I arrived at Béziers on the Mediterranean coast. I drove along the coastal highway with the deep blue sea on my immediate right, though from time to time it swung inland and the Med became a distant haze.

Eventually I reached Arles, dumping my luggage in a small hotel before wandering out to a local bar. It was packed with gloomy French people, talking, naturally, about the war. Suddenly a hush. Over the radio came the gravelly voice of Winston Churchill.

"Even though large tracts of Europe have fallen under the grip of the Gestapo, and all the odious apparatus of Nazi rule, we shall not flag or fail. We shall go on to the end. We shall fight in France. We shall fight on the seas and the oceans. We shall fight with growing confidence and growing strength in the air.

We shall defend our island whatever the cost may be. We shall fight on the beaches. We shall fight on the landing grounds. We shall fight in the streets and the fields. We shall fight in the hills. We shall never surrender. And even if, which I do not for a moment believe, this island, or a large part of it, were subjugated and starving, then our Empire beyond the oceans, armed and guarded by the British fleet, will carry on the struggle until in God's good time the New World with all its power and might sets forth to the rescue and the liberation of the old."

When Churchill finished you could have heard a pin drop in that bar. Suddenly a few of the patrons erupted into wild cheering while others demanded to know what was said.

One voice was heard above the others. 'Jeanne-Marie, translate for us.'

An attractive young woman replied. '*Certainment.*' She translated almost verbatim Churchill's words. As she did so the gloom that had hung over the place when I'd entered dissipated. Churchill's speech, so powerful, so magical, had turned fear into faith.

I spoke to Jeanne-Marie a little while later and learned that she was married to an English Spitfire pilot by the name of Barry Jackson. She had been visiting her family when the war had started and was stuck in the South of France.

'I hope your husband is all right.'

There were tears in her eyes when she nodded. 'So do I, monsieur.'

She was indeed a beautiful young lady.

When I left Arles the following morning I cut inland to Aix-en-Provence. I was 10 miles away when the car broke down, steam hissing out of the radiator. I didn't need to be a mechanic to know the cylinder-head gasket had gone. It took three days to effect the repairs. I also had them give the car a complete service and fix the light.

Finally I arrived in Antibes and went straight to La Croë. The house appeared abandoned. Exasperated, I drove to Nice to speak with the Consul General, Hugh Dodds.

My letter of authority quickly gained me entry. I was treated with the greatest courtesy; Dodd's small talk about his uncle by marriage, my friend Winnie, was almost more than I could bear. I thanked him profusely before blurting out, 'Look here, Hugh, where will I find the Windsors?'

'They left France yesterday.'

'Goddamn it, where the hell have they gone now?' I asked in disbelief.

'They crossed the border into Spain.'

The consul couldn't have known the impact his words had.

Did I dare follow the Duke to Spain? I was *persona non grata* with Franco. If he caught me there he wouldn't hesitate to throw me in jail, even have me killed. It seemed only yesterday I'd rescued my daughter, Susan, from Franco's clutches. A leading figure in the resistance, she had been condemned to die in front of a firing squad. Diplomacy had failed – If I hadn't acted Susan's life would have been lost and for what? The vengeful satisfaction of another amoral tyrant? Ever since our escape I had been a thorn in his side, denouncing him and his policies in Parliament. If I was caught in Spain a firing squad was the best I could hope for.

Dodds continued. 'We've been trying to persuade him to return to Britain. Winston has instructed it. But I couldn't get him to comply. I wanted him to take a merchant ship to Gibraltar but he was having none of it. I did persuade him that it was too dangerous to stay here –that's why he left.'

'Where in Spain is he headed?'

'Madrid. The Duke has many friends and relatives amongst the aristocracy there.'

I hadn't forgotten. I clenched and unclenched my hands, wishing they were round our odious little ex-king's neck. Sighing, I got to my feet. 'It looks like I've no option but to follow. Let Winston know I was here, will you? Tell him I'm still following the trail. But warn him I might have to stop at the border. He'll know why.' Churchill knew the full story and probably wouldn't blame me if I didn't go to Spain. If I decided not to carry on, I'd go to Marseilles and take a boat to Gibraltar. That way I could always get back to England.

We shook hands and I left. Now I was headed west, with about six hours of daylight remaining. I couldn't cross the Spanish border as a British Officer serving in the army. I also couldn't take a Lanchester sub-machine gun with me in case I was searched.

By now roadblocks were beginning to appear with regular monotony. Each time I was stopped, my ID as a British Colonel got me through. Near the Spanish border I buried my uniform and the Lancaster in a wood. Apart from my passport, I hid my papers and

ID by taping them behind the cylinder block of the engine. My Webley I managed to jam into the spare tyre, along with its extra ammunition.

And so I joined the thousands of others who were fleeing war-torn France and queued up for ten hours to cross the border into Spain. Customs took a cursory look at my passport and waved me through.

I was appalled at what I saw as I passed through the countryside. The civil war had only just ended and every town and village showed some mark of destruction. The people looked half-starved, many wore rags and all had the hollow-eyed look of the ill-used and downtrodden. Pride welled up in me once more for Susan's involvement in the war against Franco.

Armed soldiers were everywhere but they made no attempt to stop me. Two days after crossing the border I arrived in Madrid and made straight for the British Embassy. As Winston had told me, the new ambassador to Spain was Sir Sam Hoare, exiled from Britain for his fascist views. I had known him for years so a meeting with him presented no problems.

After the customary exchange of courtesies I asked casually, 'Is Windsor in the city?'

Looking surprised, he nodded. 'At the Ritz.'

Where else, I thought. 'While I was outside I glanced through the *Times* you have in the waiting room. Is it true that if Windsor returns to England he's to be arrested?'

Hoare looked uncomfortable. 'Apparently. I've been wiring Churchill for clarification but all I've got so far is that the Duke *must* return to Britain soonest. What's your interest in the Duke, Griffiths?'

'I was on his staff for a while at the Military Mission in Paris.' Knowing Hoare's views I added, 'I have a great deal of admiration for the Duke. And,' I added for good measure, 'for his views. The sooner we get him home, the sooner we can negotiate a peace with Germany.'

Hoare smiled delightedly. 'My dear chap, I had no idea you thought as we do.'

I contrived to look embarrassed. 'It's not the sort of thing I like to talk about. One's political viewpoint is strictly personal. At least where I come from.'

'There is a grand reception tonight, here at the Embassy, for their Royal Highnesses. I'd be delighted if you'd come.'

I beamed my acceptance, shook his hand and left. My next stop was the Ritz. Thankfully I got a suite without any trouble, and sent for room service to have my clothes pressed. The Duke's bottle of port I placed in the wall safe, along with my Webley and other papers.

I presented myself at the Embassy in good time and joined the line-up to be introduced to the Duke and Duchess. When I finally got to the front of the queue, a smile plastered on my face, I took Windsor's small hand in mine and shook it heartily.

'I'm delighted to see you again, sir.'

He smiled back. 'Griffiths! What a pleasure. You must come and see us. And soon. We'll talk later.'

I passed on, grabbed a flute of champagne from a proffered tray of glasses, and mingled with some of the other three hundred or so guests.

A short while later I was sent for and I crossed the room and joined the inner-circle of those guests who were fawning over the Windsors. They in turn were lapping up the adoration and subservience. I was welcomed with wide smiles and all-round introductions.

Sickened by the toadying, I sought a moment's solitude in the library. High wing-backed leather armchairs were strategically placed around the room and I sat in one of them, in the window with a panoramic view of the city. I think I must have dozed because the next thing I was aware of was voices, yet I hadn't heard anyone enter.

I was about to make my presence known when I realised one of the voices belonged to Windsor, the other to the Ambassador, Hoare.

'David, you *must* return to England. I implore you. It's too dangerous to stay here.'

'Dangerous? Why?' The Duke's petulant whine was made worse by stress. 'The Spanish have offered me the Palace of the Caliph at Ronda for an indefinite period. I have spoken with Wallis and both of us agree it is a singularly fine offer.'

'That may be so,' said Hoare, 'but your government is against it. Leaving your post was a terrible breach of army protocol, sir. Churchill is threatening to have you court-martialled if you don't return imme-diately. Return home now and you will be given the post of Governor of the Bahamas – a jewel of an appointment, sir.'

'When will you understand, Sam, I have my destiny to fulfil? I have to negotiate a peace settlement between England and the Germans. That way, Germany can attend to the real problems we face from the east. The whole of Europe must see reason. How can we fight the Bolsheviks with our young men destroying themselves in a senseless conflict? If I head the Peace Movement, there's no limit to what I may aspire to.'

'Even the throne?' Hoare asked.

With fury shaking his voice, Windsor replied, 'It was mine by right. It still is.'

I had been sitting there for too long, had heard too much, to give my presence away, and so I sat quietly.

'I've had a message from our German friends,' Hoare whispered urgently. 'From a Swiss informant who has worked with our Secret Service for years. If you do not return to England and accept the position in the Bahamas he says you will pay the price for your pride. A fatal price.'

Hoare's warning was met by silence. I would have given anything to see the Duke's face just at that moment but couldn't move for fear of being discovered.

'They wouldn't dare,' Windsor said in a strangled voice.

'David, you must leave Spain for your own good. Keep negotiating with Churchill. Get an agreement that will allow you to live comfortably in the Bahamas. If you don't, sooner or later they'll get you. Face facts, man.'

'What do you suggest?'

'Leave Madrid and go to Lisbon. Board ship there and travel to London as quickly as possible. Come to some arrangement with Churchill before it's too late.' After a pregnant pause he spoke again, softly. 'Come, sir, we must return to our guests.'

I heard them leave and stayed where I was for a few more minutes. Finally I got up, stretched my cramped limbs and headed for the door. If Windsor did intend going to Portugal then I needed to act fast.

11

I SEARCHED THE city for a cut-glass decanter I deemed acceptable to the Windsors. That evening I phoned the Duke in his room.

'Sir? It's Griffiths. I have a present here for you, from Winston actually, a bottle of port he tells me is over one hundred years old, from his family cellar. He asked me to bring it as a token of his affection, to drink a toast with you to your future. I also took the liberty of purchasing you an antique decanter. After all, we should do this properly.'

I heard no suspicion in his voice. I heard greed. 'That would be most agreeable. Come to our room in forty-five minutes.' He hung up without so much as a thank you.

Dressed for dinner, I picked up the bottle and the decanter and went along to the Windsors' suite, where a flunkey opened the door. I found the Duke in his dinner jacket, smoking a cigarette, standing at the window looking out at the gardens.

'Ah, Griffiths, good to see you. Are these for me?' He smiled, holding out his hands.

'Yes, sir. This decanter has been authenticated – made around 1725. And here's the port.'

'Let me get it decanted.' He pressed a bell next to the fireplace and the flunkey reappeared. 'Ladbroke, be so good as to decant this port.' He held out both items. 'And no sampling.' It was not said in jocular fashion and Ladbroke merely nodded, withdrawing silently.

We discussed Madrid, its poverty, the heat, the dust, the huge German presence in the city, but not once were the war or England mentioned. Ten minutes later Ladbroke reappeared with the decanter filled with port and three glasses on a tray.

'The Ambassador is here to see you, sir. I brought a third glass.'

'Put the port on the table and take away the glass. He won't be staying long.'

'Yes, sir.' Ladbroke bowed slightly before leaving.

'We can't waste good port, can we?' Windsor smiled at me.

I smiled back at him, with some relief.

Sam Hoare was shown in. 'Good. Two birds with one stone. I thought I might find you here, Griffiths.' He handed me a sealed envelope. 'This came today in the diplomatic pouch.'

I took the proffered missive and was about to put it in my pocket when I noticed the word *whisky* written in the bottom right-hand corner. The envelope looked official but gave no clue as to whom it was from. The word whisky did.

Hoare had taken the Duke off to a corner of the room and was talking quietly to him. I ripped open the envelope.

Dear David,

So sorry not to have seen you the last time you were in London. Please make an effort to come by the next time. I have decided that it would be better not to have the older dog put down as his brother might miss him. I know they don't get on well now, but you never know what the future might hold. However, there is one caveat; if he doesn't travel well, we'll have no choice. He'll have to go!

There was more drivel in the same vein and it was signed *Uncle Wilfred*

The message was clear. The Duke was to live as long as he returned to England. I looked at the decanter and sighed. The best laid plans . . .

The other two broke off their conversation and came across the room towards me.

'I have decided,' announced the Duke, 'to return to England after all. We travel via Lisbon tomorrow. Now that's decided, Griffiths, perhaps you'd be so good as to pour the port. I shall send for a third glass.' Typical of the bloody man to change his mind, I thought.

As Windsor pressed the bell, I lifted the decanter and held it over the fireplace. As I tilted the lip towards the glass it fell onto the stone and shattered, spraying port everywhere.

'Hell and damnation,' I said loudly.

Windsor was white with fury and had the greatest difficulty holding his temper.

'I'm frightfully sorry, sir,' I said, 'I'll replace the decanter tomorrow. As to the contents, when you get to Lisbon, the home of port, I shall arrange to have a two-hundred year bottle given to you.'

If Windsor was mollified he didn't show it. His curt nod left me in no doubt as to his fury. I made my farewells and left. Sion would have enjoyed the irony – I'd nursed that bloody poisoned port all the way across Europe only to smash it myself! In a foul mood I went down to the bar and threw back two whiskies before I got myself under control. Then I laughed. As I replayed the scene in my head, Windsor's rage at the smashed decanter seemed unbearably funny. My "clumsiness" had saved his life, the fool. I felt quite light-headed.

Dining in the restaurant proved a grave mistake. I was sitting in a corner when a Spanish uniformed officer approached me.

In stilted English he asked, 'Is your name David Griffiths?'

Immediately I sensed danger. 'No. It's Metcalfe. I am with the Duke of Windsor's party. Why?'

'It is just that you remind me so much of someone I met during the war a few years ago. I could have sworn . . .'

I summoned up a smile and said, 'Easily done, old boy. Easily done.'

The officer returned to his own table, but kept glancing my way while I ignored him.

I finished my dinner aware that at any moment the officer could go to the desk and check my name. Leaving the restaurant, I took the lift to the second floor and quickly walked the corridor to my room. Time I made for the border. Throwing some of my gear into my case I looked out over the balcony. It was quiet below, the balconies to my right and left empty. A little way off was a lawn with cultivated patches of flowering bushes and trees. I threw the case at one and had the satisfaction of seeing it land amongst some greenery.

Emptying the safe of my papers, I slipped the Webley into my waistband at my spine. Opening the door to the corridor I looked out. It was empty. I hurried towards the lift, saw it stopping at my level and instinctively dashed through the swing doors to the stairs. I didn't wait to see who was getting off and took the stairs two at a time. When I reached the ground floor I kept going. In the basement another corridor led right and left. Heading right I found a door leading to the outside and a set of steps up to the gardens. I paused in the shadows, making sure nobody was about. Orientating myself, I identified the bush my suitcase had landed in. Hefting it in my left hand, I took the Webley from behind my back and placed it in my right-hand pocket. I kept a firm grip on the butt.

The Citroën was parked on the street outside the hotel where I had left it. I threw the case in the back, climbed in, started the engine and with a sigh of relief pulled away from the curb. I was getting too old for this malarkey.

Once clear of the city I stopped the car and checked the map I'd bought when I first entered Spain. Portugal was my best bet. Southwest out of Madrid as far as Trujillo and then I'd have a choice. I hoped I'd get far enough to be able to decide.

I had filled the car with petrol after my arrival in Madrid. All being well I had enough fuel to get me to the border and into Portugal. It was a balmy night. A waning moon was casting a bright light across the landscape and I was moving, leaving my fears and worries behind me.

I'd been travelling for about two and a half hours. The time was fast approaching midnight when I felt my eyelids drooping and I jerked awake. I decided to get some sleep for a few hours. I had just passed through the small town of Talavera de la Reina and was in countryside once more. Turning off the road onto a track, I drove out of sight, found a clearing big enough to turn the car and switched off the motor. The peace was wonderful. I lay my head against the seat and within minutes fell asleep.

I awoke with a stiff neck and a dry mouth. Looking at my watch I saw it was coming up to 03.00 and climbed stiffly out of the car to unbend my aching limbs. After relieving myself, I set off again. The road wound through the mountains, an irregular serpentine of dangerous bends and deadly drops.

Dawn broke and with it a glorious sunrise that burst over my left shoulder and reflected off the high mountains to my right. The Sierra de Gredos was awesome in its splendour.

Progress was slow. I was held up by overloaded lorries belching smoke, donkeys with pannier baskets full of olives and twice by herds of goats. There were few places to overtake on the single-track road and each delay made me more nervous.

All day I kept driving. In one small village I purchased some bread, goat's cheese, olives and a bottle of water. The makeshift meal stopped my stomach rumbling but a full belly did nothing for my peace of mind. My imagination was running riot. I was sure the officer had identified me. A fascist state like Spain would have no difficulty in setting up roadblocks and sealing its borders, certainly along the main routes. Perhaps, I'd made the wrong decision. Maybe I should head south, get close to Gibraltar and hire, buy or steal a boat. Jake Kirkpatrick, one of my best friends, still lived in Southern Spain, near Cádiz. Unfortunately, he was in America with his family, mixing pleasure with business, otherwise I wouldn't have hesitated in making a run for his place.

It was evening when I arrived at Trujillo. The town could trace its existence back to Roman days, but its architecture testified to its Moorish history. I stopped in a side street and climbed wearily out of the little car. I was at a crossroads. Should I go directly west to Cáceres and make a run for the border, or go south to Mérida and then west to Badajoz, on the Portuguese border? Crossing at Badajoz meant getting past the Customs post that was bound to be there. If an alert had gone out for me then it made sense that the major crossing points of the border would be warned first. But the up side was that according to my map the roads were far better and quicker.

With my Webley hidden under my jacket I walked into the Plaza Mayor. A statue of Pizarro, the conqueror of Peru and Trujillo's most famous son, showed him astride a horse, cutting a gallant figure in his armour, as he looked sightlessly to the west.

Small bars and restaurants were beginning to do brisk business as people stopped for an aperitif before heading home after a long day. One was busier than the rest, No 13, the Hostal Pizarro. Luckily I wasn't superstitious. I ordered a coffee and a bocadillos, a long roll of bread filled with ham and cheese. After a second coffee it was time to go. Before departing I bought four bottles of water. Hunger I could cope with. Thirst was a different matter. Nobody had taken any notice of me as far as I could tell. But I didn't want to push my luck too far.

Back at the car I topped up the petrol tank using one of the cans, leaving another full. More than enough for what was left of the journey.

It was dusk by the time I drove out of town. There was very little traffic about at that time of the day and I made good time to Cáceres, some forty miles west. The road was straight and narrow. I drove along the flat with my headlights cutting a swathe of light in front of me.

From Cáceres the road began to meander down towards sea level. This was rural Spain, where the people's day was governed by nature and their animals. I passed farmhouses and a number of tiny hamlets but saw nobody. The next habitation of any size was Valencia de Alcántara. It was the last town before the border.

I wound my way along the single-track road, as the lights of Valencia faded behind me. I was now within ten miles of the border and could expect to come upon the Customs post at any time. Most of these smaller crossings were closed at night, with a gate padlocked across the road. Usually they were unmanned or else a single, sleepy Customs officer was left on duty.

A three-quarters moon had risen, casting a white light across the landscape. It was time to move more stealthily. I stopped the car, switched off the lights and waited a few minutes for my eyes to grow accustomed to the dark. It was now approaching midnight and I had all night to cross into Portugal. I wasn't going to rush it.

It was true what they said. Paranoia helps to keep you alive. It took nearly an hour but finally I reached the border. The Customs post was lit, with armed soldiers manning the gate. Far from being sleepy, they appeared wide-awake.

Either side of the road were rocky hills. I could try and hide the car and make my way over the hilltops. I was fairly certain I wouldn't get lost, but on the other hand there was the danger of tripping or falling and doing myself a serious injury. I didn't relish the idea of dying of thirst or starvation. I also had no idea how far it was to the nearest town or village once I did cross the border. It could be miles.

The border was about half a mile away with a last bend in the road about three hundred yards short of the Customs post. It was down-hill all the way. I sat behind the wheel, released the brake, and let the car roll forward then stopped by the bend, hidden by a low hillock.

There was one wooden building, on the right hand side of the road. From my vantage point I could see there were at least two rooms, the main one glass-fronted. Just beyond the middle of the building a five-bar gate straddled the road. To the right the border appeared sealed off by the terrain while to the left I could see a wire fence stretching up the undulating hill as far as a steep, rising cliff.

I counted three soldiers and an official in Customs' uniform. He had a sidearm, while the soldiers carried rifles. They all looked young, but age meant nothing in a country that had survived such a horrendous civil war. For all I knew they could be hardened veterans.

I wasn't without advantages. First of all they weren't expecting me, secondly the light at the post was ruining their night vision and thirdly, until they'd identified me, they were hardly likely to shoot. I could be an innocent traveller after all. But I would need more than luck to pass those guards. I emptied the water bottles I'd bought in the cafe and filled them with petrol from the can, stuffing the necks with pieces of cloth torn from one of my shirts.

I fed a shirtsleeve into the jerry can and left it by the roadside. With two bottles in each hand I headed across the rough ground towards the right of the Customs building. It was treacherous underfoot. Small rocks turned my heels and more than once I slipped and almost fell. I moved cautiously, watching the post at all times.

If they'd had the lights out they would easily have seen me crossing the open ground, but not one of them even glanced in my direction. I moved obliquely, staying at least a hundred yards away. Halfway across I began burying the bottles of petrol under rocks, at strategic positions. Soon I had all four in a line, placing the last one on the left side of the Customs post. There were no windows in this side of the building so I was safe for now.

A cloud floated across the face of the moon and cast a deeper shadow. Cigar lighter in hand I made my move. I lit the rag in the last bottle and hurried across the broken ground to the next. Cupping the flame behind my hand I lit it then hurried on to the third. Again I lit the rag fuse, keeping a wary eye on the soldiers who were now in clear view. When I'd reached the fourth bottle the first bottle of petrol went up. There was a small explosion and rocks flew into the air.

The soldiers rushed around the front of the building. My blasted lighter malfunctioned as I tried to light the last rag. I shook it and on the fifth flick it came to life. I lit the cloth just as the second bottle went up. Bent double I hurried back towards the car. The third bottle erupted into flame as I reached the can and lit the sleeve. Clambering into the car, I started the motor and went slowly forward. My lights were switched off and I was careful not to gun the engine. The three soldiers were now behind the building, looking at the third fire when the fourth bottle exploded. I watched them nervously moving away from the post towards the flames.

I was about three hundred yards from the building when the can went up with a mighty boom. The three soldiers were behind me now, about four hundred yards away. The Customs official still stood at the front of the building, looking towards the last explosion.

I was within ten yards of the man before he became aware of me. He looked at the car in sheer amazement. I stopped alongside him, Webley in hand.

'Open the gate.'

He looked at the soldiers walking in the opposite direction towards the glow of the fire from the can and then back at me. I cocked the Webley, the sound magnified in the peace of the night. Nodding, he moved towards the gate where he fumbled with the lock. I looked back over my shoulder. The soldiers had spotted me and were rushing back towards the post. The Customs official looked towards them, then back at me and dived through the door. I could have shot him, but what was the point?

I was close enough to the gate to see that it was made of wood. I didn't hesitate; putting the car into gear I slammed my foot to the floorboards. She lurched forward, picked up momentum for a few yards and then smashed into the gate. I took the impact on my arms, my elbows bending as I was thrown forward before pushing myself back in my seat. The car faltered for a second and my heart was in my mouth but the engine picked up, the tyres gained traction and I accelerated away. I heard shots fired behind me but none of the bullets came my way.

As the car careered around a bend at speed I almost lost control. I eased my foot on the accelerator and kept going. Two hundred yards further on I came to the Portuguese Customs post, but it was unmanned and there was no gate to hinder my passage.

Next stop Lisbon and a ship back to Blighty.

Alex's Story

12

THIS WAS IT. This was what training school had taught him. His first dogfight and Alex had the German pilot firmly in his sights. The satisfaction he felt was deep but tightly controlled. He pressed the firing button. Nothing happened. He pressed again, sweat beading his forehead. The Messerschmitt saw him and dived away while he peeled in the opposite direction. He mashed the fire button again and still nothing. A split-second glance inside the cockpit told him his gun control button was still switched off. Shame coursed through him. For a few seconds he flew in a straight and steady line.

'White Three, White Three, break left, break left.' The instruction came over his radio but it wasn't until it was repeated did he remember *he* was Three.

He pushed over hard and the plane's port wing dropped as he headed towards earth. Not a second too soon – a stitch of bullets appeared along his tail as he frantically jigged right and left, trying to shake his attacker.

'Hang on, White Three, I'll get the bastard.'

Alex's mouth was dry as he recognised his squadron leader's voice. His heart pounding, he threw the little plane across the sky. He couldn't see the 109, but his training told him to keep changing course. Dive, swoop, turn. Do anything but *don't* give the other pilot the seconds he needed to take aim.

There he was! Behind and high, coming at him like a falcon diving onto its prey. Alex pulled Gs, as he looped the loop and then barrel-rolled at the top.

'All right, White Three, he's gone. I think I scared him off.'

'Thanks, White Leader.' Alex hoped his voice didn't sound as shaky as he felt.

Arriving back at Northolt, Alex landed and taxied over to dispersal, where he was met by the aircraft's ground crew.

'Everything all right, sir?' Flight Sergeant Andrews asked him.

'Yes, Flight, thanks. I'm needed at de-briefing.' He could feel eyes on him as he walked away. Did they realise he'd forgotten his gun switch? Of course they didn't. He shook himself out of it.

Squadron Leader Hugo Wakefield greeted him. 'You all right, Alex?'

'Yes, sir. Thank you. And thanks for today.' Alex smiled even though he found it hard to do.

'Think nothing of it, old chap.'

Alex had nothing but admiration for Wakefield. His squadron leader had won a DFC while flying Gladiators in Norway and was one of the few who'd survived the experience. As they settled in his office Wakefield smoothed his receding hairline and luxurious walrus moustache. His generous height meant the cockpit of his Spitfire fitted him like a second skin, but it certainly didn't affect his flying ability. After today Alex admired the gentle giant more than ever.

The debriefing didn't take long. As Alex was about to leave Wakefield spoke kindly. 'Don't worry, son, you won't forget again.'

'Sorry, sir?'

'Your gun switch. That was the problem wasn't it? Had the snapper in your sights but didn't fire? Like I say, it won't happen again. Now off with you, we're going down the pub in half an hour. We've been stood down.'

Alex looked straight into his leader's eyes. There was no use in trying to pretend otherwise. Besides which, Alex had always been a bad liar, a trait he'd inherited from his mother.

He walked back to his primitive quarters cursing himself. At twenty-three years of age Alex Griffiths was a veteran of three weeks. He had been fast tracked through training because of his flying experience with his father's planes, particularly the Griffin X. He had known how to navigate, night fly and deal with emergencies. What he hadn't known was how to fight or how to fly aerobatics.

One week at basic training and he had been sent to advanced training school. Only a month later and he had been assigned to a squadron. It was practically unheard of, but good pilots were in short and desperate supply. Typical of the RAF, the squadron flew Spitfires and not Griffins. Luckily Alex had had the good sense not to boast about his flying prowess, which was just as well. It seemed younger pilots could fly rings around him where it mattered – in a dogfight. He couldn't wait for his next chance to prove himself.

The hut he was living in had a long corridor with eight bedrooms along one side. At one end were toilets and a urinal, at the other, three baths. His room was big enough to hold a bed, chair, small table, wash-hand basin, wardrobe and a chest of drawers. Opposite the door was a window, which he flung open to let in some fresh air.

Looking in the mirror he castigated himself again for a fool. He'd had the Hun dead to rights and he should have notched up his first kill. Damn! Damn! Damn! He was twenty-three – an Oxford graduate for God's sake. To have made such a basic mistake . . .

After a quick bath, dressed in civvies, he went out to meet the others standing outside the Officers' Mess, smoking and chatting. The squadron had the use of two cars, one belonging to the Squadron Leader, the other to Alex. Within days of his bowling up at the base his car had been commandeered for communal use. It hadn't occurred to Alex to protest at the arrangement.

The 1933 Hillman Minx was designed to seat four, three passengers and the driver. In fact the most it had carried back from the pub at any one time was fifteen. The squadron was still valiantly attempting to beat the record.

The keys, as always, were in the ignition. Flight Lt Ken Bertram pulled rank and climbed behind the steering wheel. Alex, a mere Flying Officer, sighed and climbed into the back. Seven more squadron members climbed aboard and the car took off with a jerk.

Yells of "Steady on", "Go easy", and "Watch where you're putting your bloody knee", were amongst the more polite phrases wafting out of the open windows as they arrived at the gatehouse. The sergeant on guard duty heaved a sigh, raised the barrier and waved the car through. Ten minutes later they pulled up outside the *Duck & Hound*.

Within minutes, pints of beer were lined up on the bar. Alex fiddled with his pipe and finally got it drawing to his satisfaction. As he listened to the banter and the talk going on around him he smiled. He loved the life and he loved flying. Although he had only been with the squadron three weeks, he felt a great sense of belonging.

He stood at the corner of the bar, watching the others joshing around, his pipe in his right hand, his glass in his left. The barmaid, Mary, stood next to him on the other side of the bar, wiping off beer stains. Blonde, with a busty figure, and a silly giggle, she was almost pretty. She had a wide mouth, a pert nose and the worst bitten fingernails Alex had ever seen. As they talked his eyes kept being dragged to her low cut blouse. *They said that for a pair of nylons . . .*

'You been at it then?' she asked Alex, her voice bubbling with suppressed laughter.

'What do you mean?' Alex blushed. "At it" had only one connotation for him.

'My, you do talk posh,' she replied. 'You know, flying. Killing the Hun.'

Alex reluctantly raised his eyes to her face once more and shrugged. 'I guess you could call it that.'

'I think you're awfully brave. You wouldn't catch me up in one of them planes.'

'No, I don't suppose I would. Look here, Mary, I was wondering . . .' he paused, unable to go on, his lips suddenly dry.

'Yes?' She moved her upper body towards him, pushing out her chest.

'Service! Come on, Mary, leave the poor boy alone and get us a pint.'

With a pout she said to Alex, 'I'll be right back. And you can ask me what you like.' She poured another round of beers and returned to Alex with a pint in her hand. Placing it on the bar in front of him she said, 'You were saying?'

Alex's eyes never wavered. 'Em . . . The pictures. The flicks. Wondered if you'd like to go, on your day off. That is, if you'd care to.'

Mary batted her eyelashes in what she hoped was a coquettish manner. 'Why, are you asking me out, Mr Griffiths?'

Now that he'd broken the ice and dared suggest they go out Alex was no longer so tongue-tied. 'As a matter of fact, I am. What do you say?'

'Sunday's my day off.'

'I'll meet you at six. Here? Or at your home?'

Thinking of the shabby council house her parents lived in she shook her head. 'Here'll be fine. Don't be late.' With another wiggle of her chest she moved away. All the flyboys were the same. They were so easy. But this one looked and talked nice. She needed to get a move on – her period was late and she wasn't entirely sure *who* the father was. She was pretty certain it was that nice young boy Hugh who'd got himself killed in France. She sighed. War was hell.

Alex drank too many beers, as did the rest of the squadron. The journey back to camp took nearly half an hour. The Hillman struggled under the weight of eleven pilots, with a further two either side on the running board. The record stood for another day.

Alex was woken up by a determined prod in his shoulder. 'Your tea, sir. Are you awake, sir? Mr Wakefield sends his compliments. It's just coming up to four ack emma. Another nice day and you're due at dispersal at four-thirty.'

Alex groaned. 'Please stop wittering, Garfield, for God's sake.'

'Yes, sir.' There was no disguising the lack of sympathy in the batman's voice.

Alex forced open his eyes and looked at the batman. 'All right, I'm getting up.' He forced his way out of bed and stood blearily in front of the wash-hand basin, reaching for his toothbrush. God, another dawn!

The tea was hot, sweet and wet and brought him round to a semblance of alertness. Washing and dressing quickly, he hurried over to the mess. The day was utterly still, without even a breeze to stir the leaves. The mess hall and anteroom had not yet been cleared from the night before and the stale smell of booze and tobacco smoke hung in the air. The ashtrays were still overflowing; magazines, newspapers and empty beer tankards littered the place. Alex crossed quickly to the dining room.

A steward was serving tea and toast to the dozen or so pilots seated at the long table. Hardly anyone spoke. It was too early. Alex found the magazine he'd been reading the day before and read the same article again. He sipped his tea, ate his toast and couldn't remember what the article was about when he rose to leave.

The steward appeared in the doorway and said, 'Hercules Squadron transport outside, gentlemen.'

With groans and scraping chairs the pilots got to their feet. Outside the grey light of day was taking on colour. They scrambled into a five-ton lorry and thumped the back of the cab to indicate they were ready to go. At the dispersal hut Alex removed his collar and tie and put it in his locker before tying a white silk scarf around his neck.

Twisting his neck back and forth constantly looking for the enemy meant the scarf was no mere affectation. Slinging his parachute over his shoulder and taking his helmet in his hand, he walked outside. His Spitfire was waiting for him a hundred yards away.

The perfect peace of the morning was about to be shattered. He heard a voice yell, 'Clear? Contact.' Then came the distinct sound of a starter pinion and reduction gear engaging. An airscrew turned, the engine fired twice but failed to pick up. The primer pump and starter trolley were used again. This time the Merlin engine exploded into life with a spurt of flame and a cloud of exhaust fumes.

Alex as usual was awed by it all. The sound of twelve engines being warmed up by the fitters, all at one thousand two hundred revs, was enervating. An occasional backfire ripped through the air and flashes of blue flame from the exhausts were clearly visible in the half-light. At Alex's aircraft the rigger was standing holding a wingtip, while the fitter, his face reflecting the red cockpit lights, continued with his checks. Finally satisfied, he gave Alex a thumbs-up and closed the throttle. The engine spluttered to a halt. All the engines died away and peace reigned once more.

Hanging his parachute on the port wing, Alex climbed onto the wing and into the cockpit. He hung his helmet on the stick and plugged in the R/T lead and oxygen tube. Checking to see the bottle was full, he fitted the mask to his face and checked it was working. Pure oxygen filled his lungs. Pressing the fuel gauge button he checked it also read full. His pre-flight checklist continued. Brake pressure, fine. Trim, just right. Elevators were one-degree nose heavy and full rudder bias would help with the take-off. Finally he checked the airscrew was at full, fine pitch.

He was ready to scramble.

Climbing out of the cockpit, Alex waved his thanks to the two men and walked over to the dispersal hut. There he put on his Mae West while Ken Bertram telephoned Operations. 'Sir? Forty-five Squadron, now at readiness. Twelve aircraft. Goodbye, sir.'

The pilots sat in their scruffy, dilapidated easy chairs. Some slept, or pretended to. Alex closed his eyes and rested his head back, thinking of the barmaid. He must have dozed, for the next moment the shrill ring of the telephone had every pilot wide-awake and sitting up. Alex checked his watch – 06.15. The call had come unusually late for the day's first scramble.

The orderly looked at the pilots and shouted, 'Squadron scramble, base angels fifteen.'

As one, the pilots rushed for the door. Alex was the first out and sprinted across the grass. Already his ground crew was starting the engine. He shucked on his parachute, pulled the straps tight and climbed up onto the walkway. The rigger had already removed the starting plug and pulled the trolley clear before climbing onto the starboard wing. The fitter was on the port wing, helping him into the cockpit. They held his Sutton harness straps over his shoulders while he fixed the leg to the shoulder straps and inserted the pin.

'Okay!' Alex yelled, excitement and anticipation coursing through his veins.

The fitter and rigger leapt down, grabbed the chock ropes and waited.

Alex waved. 'Chocks away.'

The two men tugged the ropes and the chocks flew clear. Alex took the brake off and eased open the throttle. As the plane moved forward the fitter and rigger held each wing and walked with the plane. Alex was flying as number two to Ken Bertram and quickly identified his taxiing plane.

'Okay, Hercules, here we go,' said Wakefield.

This was a squadron formation take-off and Alex concentrated on following Bertram. As the plane picked up speed the heavy feel of the controls lightened. The Spitfire strained to leap into the air. A bump and Alex's plane was flying just as Bertram's left the ground. The wheels went up and the planes tightened their formation as the squadron clawed for height. It wasn't long until they had their first sighting.

Control radioed in. 'Hercules leader, this is Sapper. Two hundred plus, approaching Beachy Head at angels fifteen. Vector one four five. Over.'

'Sapper, this is Hercules, message received and understood.'

'Hercules, this is Sapper. Bandits include many snappers. I say again, many snappers. Keep a sharp watch. Over.'

'Sapper, this is Hercules, understood. Am steering one four five and climbing hard through angels eight. Over.'

Alex checked his altimeter. It showed 10,250ft. Switching on the oxygen supply, he turned the tap to emergency and felt the flow inside his mask and over his cheeks. The flow was okay and he turned it back to sixteen. Concentrating on Bertram's plane, Alex cast a glance around the sky. Other squadrons were racing to join with them. Below and to the left he saw six Hurricanes levelling off.

'Hercules, this is Sapper. You're very close.'

'Sapper, this is Hercules, I see them. Okay. Tally-ho! Tally-ho! Christ, there are hundreds of the bloody swine.'

Alex looked ahead. The sky was alive with planes, like swarms of locusts. For the most part they looked like Heinkel He 111s and Junkers 88s. Above them were the snappers, Messerschmitt 109s. Alex knew they were as fast and deadly as the Spitfire, though the British plane was more manoeuvrable with a tighter turn.

Alex moved out from Bertram, wiped a sweaty palm on his knees, changed hands on the column and wiped the other palm. In the back of his mind he was analysing his emotions, as he'd done on previous encounters. Whatever he was feeling, it wasn't fear. Well, not much. Just enough, he thought, to give him an edge and heighten his senses.

'Hercules from leader. In we go. A first burst and away. Watch for snappers.'

The R/T burst into life. Urgent voices broadcast their warnings.

'Snappers coming round at five o'clock. Another ten or more are three o'clock high. Here they come. Break Green Section. Break, for God's sake.'

Alex was forty feet from Bertram and holding station. He checked the gun button was set to fire and the reflector sight was on. He and Bertram were closing rapidly on the bombers below. Picking his target, Alex lined up on a Heinkel, the distance closing rapidly. A quick glance around the sky and behind assured him there was nobody on his tail. Steady, steady. Now!

He pressed the gun button and all hell broke loose. The light plane shuddered as De Wilde ammunition streaked across the sky and hit the bomber. Bertram's Spit peeled away but Alex kept going. He saw pieces of plane drop off the Heinkel, changed his aim and saw the engine on the port wing burst into flame. He kept firing, walking the bullets along the wing. With a start he realised he was too close and pulled back hard on the column, flipping the Spit to starboard as he did so.

He missed the bomber by inches. Cold sweat burst out on his forehead. Christ, but that had been close.

He flung the plane to port, jinked right and searched the sky. As he went round in a tight turn he glanced down and saw the plane he had attacked drop towards the ground, its angle of descent increasing. He didn't wait to see it crash for now the sky was filled with individual dogfights. It was every man for himself and he made no attempt to find Bertram.

Alex's plane was down to 4,500ft. He pulled up in a tight climb, needing height before he attacked again. Ahead he saw a Spitfire turning desperately away with a snapper on his tail. The German passed in front of Alex's gun sight and Alex fired. His bullets smashed into the cockpit, disintegrating the glass. The plane turned to port and fell from the sky, a dead man's hand on the column.

Suddenly Alex was aware of a pounding in his tail and he flung the Spit into a tight roll as he desperately tried to escape from the attacking German plane. Just as he thought he'd made it another stitch of bullet holes appeared in his port wing. He rolled to starboard and dived for the deck. By now the fight had gone well in-land and Alex knew instantly where he was. Biggin Hill, where his father's factory and airfield had been, was only a few minutes flying time away. He knew this area like the back of his hand.

The Spit juddered again as the Hun shot up its tail. He had one hope. *Come on, you bastard, come on,* he thought. *Follow me.*

The Spit's altimeter was unwinding as though the plane was in free-fall. Still the Me109 stayed on his tail. Yes! Just another few seconds. There was the Hill. Alex turned to port, slewed tightly to starboard, and passed two hillocks, their tops now higher than his cockpit. Staying at that height he flew under the electricity wire stretched between two poles. It was virtually impossible to see. The German wasn't so lucky. At the last second he saw the pole on his starboard side, knew what it was and tried to pull up. His propeller hit the wire and flew apart. Alex watched as the Me109 eased into a glide and headed for a flat field. It landed on its belly and skidded across the open ground.

Alex began to climb but his controls were feeling sluggish and he decided he had better land soon. Looking down he saw the German pilot climb from his cockpit just as a group of men rushed the plane. They appeared to be armed with pitchforks. Alex over-flew the downed plane and waggled his wings, acknowledging the waves from the farm workers.

By now his Spit was growing heavier by the minute. He'd lost hydraulic power and the rudder was feeling sloppy. He did the arithmetic. He was too low and losing too much height. He opened the throttle and pulled back on the stick. He'd gained what? A hundred feet? Not enough. Well, maybe. Just maybe.

"Biggin on the Bump", as it was known by the RAF, lay ahead. He passed over a main road and knew it was exactly two miles to the perimeter. Sweat poured down his cheeks and irritably he loosened his oxygen mask. *Come on, old girl, come on.* Not far now. There was the oak, fine to starboard. He grinned. It was looking good. The engine coughed and he frowned. What the . . .

A quick glance showed the fuel gauge registering empty. He tapped it. Nothing. Come on. Just a few seconds more.

'Biggin Hill, this is Hercules Blue Two,' he said, suddenly remembering his call-sign for the day, 'am approaching the field from the south.' As he spoke he was busy lowering the undercarriage.

'This is Control, we've been watching you. We're ready. Good luck.'

The Spit sailed over the southern fence and floated onto the centre of the runway. The engine coughed, spluttered and failed. Ice-cold, his senses more alert than they'd ever been in his life, Alex went in.

The front wheels touched down, the rear wheel kissed, and he was racing along the middle of the runway. As the starboard wheel collapsed the plane tilted hard over to the right. His wingtip touched the ground and sparks flew as it scraped along the concrete. The Spit slewed hard to the right, and began to turn. It slid off the runway and onto the grass, where the starboard wheel struts caught in the soft earth. The plane twisted right, its starboard wing breaking off, and then landed on the canopy and tail before somersaulting upright. The force caused the port undercarriage to collapse and the plane landed on its belly, still spinning round, still travelling in excess of 30mph when it hit the side of a building.

Alex didn't see or feel the heat of the flames erupting around the engine. Nor did he hear the bell of the fire engine as it raced towards him. He was out cold.

13

ALEX AWOKE TO pain that seemed to stretch from his head to his feet. Blearily he focused on the face looking down at him. It was, he thought, ugly enough to pose as a gargoyle.

'How're you feeling?' The words were softly spoken and kindly asked.

'I don't know, yet. I hurt like hell, if that's what you're asking.'

The face parted in a smile, showing crooked teeth. 'I'm not surprised. Your injuries are painful but not life-threatening, you'll be glad to hear.'

'Where am I?'

'In the hospital at Sevenoaks. Do you remember pranging?'

'Sure. The plane flipped.'

'Good. Do you remember the whole thing?'

Alex thought for a second before trying to nod. 'Hell! That hurts! Yes, I remember. I'd been attacked by a Messerschmitt. I went low, under some power cables. He crashed. Then I lost power. Just made the Hill.'

'Good. At least your head hasn't been damaged, although you've a nasty swelling on the side.'

Alex moved a hand tentatively to the side of his head. He felt the bump above his right ear. He was surprised to see that his right wrist was bandaged, as were his left hand and arm. 'Who are you?'

'I'm Dr Ben Llewelyn. That bump on your head is just one of many superficial injuries. You've torn ligaments in your right leg, your left knee is badly twisted, you've cracked a rib, dislocated your right shoulder, sprained your right wrist and worst of all,' the doctor didn't attempt to pull any punches, 'you've sustained third-degree burns to your left hand, arm and neck. Your scarf saved you from the worst of it, but even so, it's a bit of a mess.'

'Will it heal?'

Llewelyn grimaced. 'Hard to say. We know a lot about burns these days. There'll be some scarring but hopefully it won't be debilitating. We keep the wound dry and let it heal naturally. As long as you wear a cravat the scars won't show. You were lucky. If you hadn't been so low on fuel you'd be dead now. Burnt to a cinder. As it was, the fire had only just taken hold of the fuselage when they rescued you.'

'As you say, I was lucky,' said Alex dryly. He gestured his impatience. 'And my ability to fly?'

The doctor smiled. 'I'll have you back in a cockpit within a month. That do you?'

'Thanks, doc, I appreciate it. By the way, what day is it?'

This time Llewelyn threw back his head and laughed delightedly. 'You crashed this morning. The time is ten past three.'

'Good.'

'Why? Do you have an appointment?'

Alex looked sheepish. 'Sunday actually.'

'Well you can forget it. You're going nowhere for the next week, unless it's to a convalescence home. So you can forget your date, Pilot Officer. Goodbye for now, I've other patients who need my attention.' With that he left Alex alone.

Lying there, Alex was suddenly aware that the last thing he wanted was a date, even with Mary and all her charms. He hurt all over.

The next time he awoke, he hurt more than ever. This time he was able to identify the location of each pain, the worst being in his ribs.

After a while a nurse appeared, gave him some painkillers and bade him goodnight. After a fitful night he fell into a deep sleep around dawn. At 6.30 am he was rudely awoken, to be told that breakfast was due in fifteen minutes. When it came he wished he'd been left to sleep through it.

He was given more painkillers, his bandages were changed and he passed most of the day half-asleep. That evening Sqd. Ldr. Hugo Wakefield visited him.

'So, Alex, the rumour is you're going to live.'

Alex mustered a smile. 'Looks like it, sir. What about the others?'

Wakefield grimaced. 'Johnno and Frank bought it. Steve is missing, presumed dead. Geoff won't ever fly again.'

Alex closed his eyes, the pain more acute than ever. 'Christ. The price we paid was a heavy one.'

'The Hun fared worse. The squadron is claiming sixteen kills and four probables. You've got three confirmed. Another two and you'll be an ace.'

'I was lucky. Incredibly so.'

'That's as maybe. But I'd rather have a lucky pilot than a skilled one. You're off for at least a month. You'll have to stay here, I should think, as you'll need medical attention. Is there anything I can get you?'

With regret Alex thought of his assignation with the barmaid. 'Just one thing, sir. Let Mary at the pub know. I was supposed to meet her on Sunday evening. To go to the flicks. Tell her I'll see her when I get out.'

Wakefield nodded, grinning. 'Being led by your more intelligent organ like all the pilots, Alex. Why am I not surprised? I'll see she gets the message.' As he was about to leave he paused in the door, 'By the way, old chap, I've put you in for a gong.'

Alex's next visitor didn't appear for another three days. He became aware of a presence next to him and opened his eyes.

'Hullo, son.'

'Dad! Dad, what on earth are you doing here?' Alex blinked away the drug-created fog that surrounded his brain and tried to sit up.

'Take it easy, son,' Sion placed a hand on Alex's arm. 'Stay still. I flew to Biggin Hill to deliver a Griffin X. It was an excuse to visit you. Your mother wanted to come with me but our new staff have just arrived and she's up to her eyes with it all. Once we heard you were okay we thought it best that she stay in Wales. She sends her love. How are you?'

'I'll be okay. A few bruises, that's all.'

Sion could see the pain etched in his son's face but hid his worry behind a grin. 'Good. I spoke to the hospital about shifting you somewhere else but they said you couldn't be moved because of the nursing you needed.'

'That's that then.'

This time, Sion's smile was for real. 'Hardly. What it boils down to is that any qualified nurse can look after you. So long as they can change your bandages.'

'What use is that? You can't hire a private nurse. There are none to be had.'

'Of course not but Connie's at *Fairweather*. You can go there.'

Alex's smile equalled his father's. 'That's a brilliant idea, Dad. Let's go.' Alex threw back the bedclothes and made to get out of bed.

'Take it easy,' Sion said. 'We've still got arrangements to make.'

It took an hour but Alex was finally discharged. He was taken outside in a wheelchair, his right leg heavily bandaged and sticking out ahead of him. He was in a good deal of discomfort but did his best to hide it. Sion handled him as gently as possible, trying not to show his worry.

When they arrived at *Fairweather*, Connie and Mike O'Donnell were there to greet them.

'I wasn't expecting you, Mike,' said Alex, holding out his hand. The handshake held a lot of affection. Mike was like a second father to him.

'I flew a second plane to the Hill with your dad.'

Mike O'Donnell was Sion's closest friend and had worked with him for years. Alex admired him tremendously. He was a good man to know in a crisis. A brave man too; Mike was the holder of the Victoria Cross from the Great War. He and Sion had been in many scrapes together over the years. The ties of affection were tightened by love – Mike had recently married a cousin of Sion's by marriage. He had settled in South Wales some months earlier, where he helped his bride Betty to run a wireless factory owned by David. Recently they had diversified to manufacturing R/T sets for the Royal Air Force and the Royal Navy. The radio transmitters were valve operated but recent experiments on things called transistors were showing encouraging signs – Mike insisted they were the future.

'I didn't think Betty allowed you such a long leash,' said Alex with a grin.

'You cheeky young pup, if you weren't in that chair I'd show you what's what. You should show some respect for your elders.' Though his wavy brown hair was turning grey at the temples, Mike's deep-set brown eyes still twinkled with a well-developed sense of the ridiculous, a legacy of his Irish heritage. 'Don't you forget I used to dangle you on my knee when you were just a wee thing, you tinkerous spalpeen.'

Alex faked a groan. 'Not that old hogwash. Connie, don't listen to a word he says. He makes it up whenever it suits him.'

It had been several months since Alex had seen Connie – she was as beautiful as he remembered. She had intrigued him ever since she had escaped from Spain with his cousin Susan towards the end of the Spanish Civil War. He knew she had been through a great deal in her life, but she seemed happy to have settled at *Fairweather* to be with Susan and John Phillipe. Susan was often away working, ferrying aircraft around Britain, and particularly taking Griffins to operational squadrons. She had spoken several times to Alex about how glad she was of Connie's support and the affection she had for her son.

Alex took in Connie's trim figure, her black wavy hair, tied with a bow behind her neck. Somehow he sensed her primness hid something deeper, much deeper. During her time at *Fairweather* she had blossomed. The horrors she had lived through were fading into the past. Right now her blue eyes showed only the concern she was feeling for Alex.

'Let's go in,' she said. 'Help me lift the wheelchair up the steps. You'll see a lot of changes since the last time you were here, Alex . . .' She trailed off as the front door burst open and a gang of children ran headlong outside. 'Not so fast, boys. Be careful!'

The boys wavered on the steps, looking agog at the wounded RAF officer and the two older men wearing flying jackets.

'Go, be off with you,' said Sion.

They turned as one and ran for the woods on the other side of the paddock.

'They're good boys,' said Connie. 'One or two amongst them aren't to be trusted but on the whole they're a pleasant lot.'

'How many have you got altogether?' Alex asked.

'Thirty-six.'

'Ah, and I came to recuperate in peace and quiet.'

'Don't worry, we've organised things quite well. The west wing is out of bounds to the children. They all share the rooms in the east wing and the centre bedrooms. Downstairs we have two classrooms. There are two teachers here from their old school. There had been six but four have joined up. They are housed in the servants' quarters as most of the staff has also gone. Can you put Alex in the drawing room while I see about some tea and toast? That's all we can run to for now.' Connie hurried away.

'Is it,' asked Alex, watching her retreating back, 'natural for a woman to be bossy or is it the nurse in her?'

His father laughed. 'It starts with the former but in Connie's case she's had extra training.'

137

Gibbs, the butler, entered the drawing room with a tray laden with tea things.

'Good to see you, Gibbs,' said Sion. 'I hope you don't mind Alex staying with you for a while.'

'Not at all, sir. It is always a pleasure to see the young gentleman. I hope you get well soon, Mr Alex.'

'Thank you, Gibbs, very civil of you. I'll try not to be a nuisance.'

Connie came in holding John Phillipe's hand. 'Look who I've got here, John Phillipe. Say hullo to Uncle Alex.'

The following morning Sion and Mike left, with a promise to return the following week as they had more planes to deliver.

Alex had youth on his side and he healed quickly. His cracked rib was bound and gave him the most discomfort. Within a week the pain in his dislocated right shoulder had faded to an ache. His torn ligaments and twisted knee were bearable, while his sprained wrist was usable, bandaged tightly. The hardest injury to bear was the burn.

He knew he had been lucky. The fire-tender had been on the scene quickly and extinguished the conflagration before it had taken hold. The plane had caught fire but the sparks had lit nothing more than fumes and a minute amount of petrol, which had spilt onto the port side of the fuselage and had caused the injuries to Alex's left side. Even so, he had been protected for the most part by his flying jacket and silk scarf.

Connie diligently changed the bandages each morning, satisfied with the progress he was making. But she wanted to warn him. 'I've seen injuries like this before, Alex, and there will be some scarring.'

Alex forced a grin. 'I'll have to be careful not to appear in public without my shirt,' he quipped. 'Let me take a look.' Struggling to his feet he hobbled over to the mirror and looked critically at his left arm and neck. The skin on his neck was beginning to heal, regenerating itself. There were a number of ugly lesions that would be a reminder of the accident for as long as he lived, but a cravat or rollneck sweater would hide the worst. His arm was tender to the touch but the red, cooked look was already beginning to fade. What worried him more was his hand – it was stiff and he kept flexing it, feeling needle-like tingles shooting through it.

'Not a pretty sight, but at least the pain is fading,' he smiled at Connie's reflection.

She nodded. 'I have also seen a lot worse.' She came and stood next to him and gently touched his right shoulder.

They exchanged reflected smiles in the mirror and Alex suddenly felt awkward. He looked away quickly, before she saw the attraction he felt for her. He was more aware than ever of her figure, hidden though it was in a high-necked and practical dress. Connie seemed to sense something too for she suddenly turned away.

'Lie on the bed and let me massage your knee.'

Alex lay back and stretched out his legs. Connie sat on the side of the bed and began to tenderly manipulate his left knee, as she had done every day since he arrived. But now there was a difference in the air. The tension between them crackled like electricity. Alex watched her through half-closed lids. He felt himself responding in a way he hadn't done before.

In a husky voice he said, 'I think you'd better stop.'

With relief Connie removed her hands and looked into Alex's eyes. His fingers touched her arm and she seemed to accept the caress, but suddenly she pulled away and stood up. 'No, Alex. Now be a good boy. I've other duties to see to.'

Fury shot through him mingling with his desire. 'I'm no boy, Connie,' he said, frustration making his voice sound harsh. He searched her face. Her features were so emotionless; it was obvious she was forcing herself to hide her feelings.

'You're still a boy to me, Alex. Now, I have to go.'

He lay back feeling aggrieved, turning his head from her as she hurried from the room.

In a foul mood he got off the bed and went downstairs. In the drawing room he switched on the wireless and listened to music being broadcast from the Savoy in London. His thoughts were full of Connie. It took a few seconds to realise that the music had stopped and an announcer had come on.

'. . . *has been named Operation Dynamo. Hundreds of thousands of our men are trapped between the Channel and the French port of Dunkirk. The Prime Minister has ordered every available ship to the area to help evacuate the army. Along with our brave lads are the men of the French and Belgian armies, all trying to get to Britain so that we can continue the fight against Nazism.*'

Alex stood transfixed. If the troops weren't rescued then Britain would be over-run. It was unthinkable! He dimly heard the telephone ringing and a few seconds later Gibbs came in looking for him.

'Mr Alex, Lady Madelaine is on the line. She is enquiring after your health.'

'Thank you, Gibbs.' Alex went into the hall and lifted the receiver. 'Hullo, Aunt Maddie, how are you?'

'I'm fine. More importantly how are you doing?'

'Getting better. My ribs only hurt when I laugh. The burns are the worst of it, but Connie is looking after me.' They exchanged a few more pleasantries. 'Where's Uncle David?'

'Oh, you know your uncle. From what I can gather, he's following the Duke of Windsor halfway across France. He appears to be heading for the Riviera from Biarritz. Winnie sent him, though God knows why.'

After a few more minutes Alex hung up, deep in thought. His aunt had known more of the seriousness of the situation in France. Every kind of boat was crossing the Channel it seemed. Well, he might not be able to fly a plane yet but he could damn well steer a boat.

Alex limped quickly up the stairs and into his room. Sitting on the bed he removed the bandages from his knee and right leg. He flexed both. They were tender but not too painful. He took the bandage off his right wrist and manipulated his hand. Not bad. Not good, but bearable, he thought. Craning his neck he looked at himself in the mirror. He'd leave the bandage on. He rubbed his hands along his ribs and pressed. A slight twinge, that was all. He undid the bandage and took a deep breath. That was better. Hardly a thing. Hell, it had been a week since he'd been shot down and he always healed fast.

Hurrying down the stairs he favoured his right leg, allowing for the torn ligaments by holding onto the banister. He went through to the kitchen. 'Gibbs! Gibbs!'

'Mr Alex?' The butler came out of his pantry, slipping on his jacket as he did so.

'Is the boat in Brighton?' Seeing the puzzled look on the butler's face he added, 'The *My Joy*. Is she still berthed at Brighton?'

'Why, yes, Mr Alex. But she hasn't been used since last year.'

'But my uncle has her checked regularly?'

'Oh, yes. Once a week a member of the household goes down, runs up the engine, pumps the bilges. Otherwise the batteries would go flat.'

'Is she topped up with diesel?'

'I think so. I can easily check the household accounts and see when diesel was last bought.'

'Please do that. Then see Connie. Ask her please to put together a basket of useful medical items. Bandages, plasters, painkillers, ointments. Christ, I don't know. Whatever she's got. And blankets. Lots of blankets.'

'Certainly, Mr Alex but might I enquire why?'

'*Operation Dynamo*, Gibbs, *Operation Dynamo*. Our boys in Dunkirk need us. So jump to it. I'm going on ahead. Send the stuff down as soon as you can. I'll check over the boat and see she's ready to sail.'

'Are you intending to go alone, sir?'

'Don't worry, I'll manage, I won't need the sails. I'll motor across. Where are the keys to the boat?' Gibbs handed him the keys and he limped quickly to the garage where he selected the runabout. As usual the keys to the car were in the glove compartment. Quickly he left the estate and drove through the village of Ovingdean. He hit the main road and turned right for Brighton and within minutes he was at the marina. The *My Joy II* was unmistakable. 60ft long and 12ft broad, she had been built locally of oak ribs with Canadian rock pine planking. She was technically a motor sailer, needing the screw to compensate for her shallow draught. She carried three sails, a foresail, mainsail and mizzen. The mizzen was a steadying sail, which Alex knew he could hoist once clear of the harbour.

He climbed on board and unlocked the door to the wheelhouse. The *Joy* had the musty smell of disuse. Her wheelhouse was set back a third of the way from the bow and was big enough to sit four or five people. The wheel itself was on the port side. Right of it was the handle that moved the engine from ahead to astern. A compass sat next to the wheel, and had been swung to point to magnetic north.

Alex had been on the boat often enough to know how things worked and where they were stowed. Below the wheelhouse on the port side was the navigating office. Inside he found a chart of the English Channel and checked courses and distances to Dunkirk. One hundred and ten miles approximately. He remembered being told once the *Joy* could cruise at eight knots. Assume seven, it made the maths easier. Sixteen hours. He looked at his watch: 17.05. Away by 18.00. ETA 10.00.

He needed provisions. In the galley he opened doors and drawers but all food items had been removed. Damn! What did he need? Tea, bread, butter, jam, cheese, milk, eggs. Not much, just enough for a few days. He'd send whoever brought the medical supplies to get the provisions.

Alex went forward into the engine room. He checked the oil, primed the electric start, waited a few seconds for the diesel to warm up and then pressed the start button. The engine burst into life immediately with a deep-throated roar. Good old Uncle David. The Perkins S6 was the latest and best that money could buy.

Back in the wheelhouse Alex switched on the electric pumps and heard the water gushing over the sides. Up forward was a hatch leading below, to the sail locker. He opened it and clambered down the ladder. Identifying the mizzen, he awkwardly shoved it through the hatch onto the deck, cursing his weakened wrist. He stopped for a few seconds for a breather. His wrist was hurting and both legs ached, but at least his ribs were behaving.

Back on deck he threaded the sail onto the mizzen mast and shackled it to the up-haul. Next he dipped the diesel tanks and the fresh water tanks. Both were full. Even as he worked he saw other boats being manned, started up and departing the marina. Cries of good luck wafted across the still evening air as boat followed boat.

Alex removed the springs so all that was holding the boat along-side were the head and stern ropes. Suddenly he was aware of figures walking along the wooden pontoon and he stopped what he was doing. Much to his surprise he saw Connie, his father and Mike coming his way.

'Hullo, son, thought you'd go it alone, did you?'

Alex beamed at Sion. 'Hi, Dad, you coming for the ride?'

'Try and stop us. Give us a hand with this lot, will you?' said Mike.

Over his shoulder he had slung a General Purpose Machine Gun and belts of cartridges.

'Where on earth did you get that from?' Alex asked.

'Connie was in a bit of a flap when you left. She knew we were arriving at the Hill and telephoned. She just caught us. When she told me what you were up to I spoke to the CO. He lent it to us. We've more boxes of ammo, but it needs fitting to the belts. We've brought spare belts as well. Connie has a medical chest and every spare blanket she could lay her hands on. There's some food, tea and tinned milk, as well. So how about it, Connie?'

Connie smiled at Mike, avoiding eye contact with Alex. 'Are you saying you'd like a cup of tea?'

'I'm saying just that, *acushla*,' said Mike. He turned to Alex. 'How are you feeling?'

Alex moved his arms and legs. 'Not too bad. I'll live. We're ready to go. So Connie might as well go ashore and we can make the tea once we're clear of the harbour.'

His father grimaced. 'She says she's coming with us.'

14

THE DEBATE LASTED several moments. Alex argued bravely but it was no use, Connie had made up her mind. Her nursing skills could mean the difference between life and death for some poor squaddy she said. Alex gave in with bad grace. Thankfully he didn't catch the looks that passed between his father and O'Donnell, nor see their wry grins.

Once clear of the harbour, they hoisted the mizzen and the slow roll the boat had been experiencing ceased. It was still a few minutes shy of 18.00, the sun was high in a cloudless sky and, according to the almanac, sunset wasn't until 21.06.

'What's the plan?' his father asked.

If he was surprised at being deferred to, Alex didn't show it. 'We stay close inshore, under the cliffs to Beachy Head, then pass Dungeness before we go straight across to Calais. From there we follow the French coast to Dunkirk.'

'That's what I figured. Ah, tea! Thank you, Connie.'

'My pleasure, Sion. Alex, yours is down in the galley.' She spoke coldly. The argument they'd had still rankled. She disappeared below again, without a backward glance.

'I still think it would be better if she stayed behind,' Alex said plaintively. 'Can't you tell her, Dad?'

'Don't drag me into this, son. Personally, I think Connie has a lot to contribute on this trip. God alone knows what we'll find when we get to the other side. Whatever it is, it isn't going to be pretty. Connie's already seen war close up, so she knows what she's letting herself in for. And with all due respect, Alex, you haven't.'

Alex gave the wheel to his father and went below. In the galley Connie was busy unloading supplies. She didn't look up when he entered.

Suddenly he could bear it no longer. 'I'm sorry, Connie, honestly

I am. It's just . . . well, I care about you. I don't want anything to happen to you.' He stood beside her, looking miserable.

Connie's face softened and she turned to look at him. Her long-lashed, wide-set eyes, which dominated her face, changed from anger to sympathy. 'I don't want to seem presumptuous, Alex, but I need to be very straight with you now. I know you have feelings for me but I'm not for you. You must find another girl.'

Alex stepped up to her and put his hand on her arm. 'Don't say that, Connie. I've learned that life can be dreadfully short. We have to grab our happiness where we can. You know we may not survive this.'

Connie tore her gaze from him. 'I know. But I'm . . . how do you say . . . damaged goods, Alex. Go and find yourself a nice English girl to marry and have babies with.'

'Damaged goods? What do you mean?'

Connie shook her head vehemently. 'Leave it, Alex, please.'

Up on deck Alex found O'Donnell threading rounds of ammunition into canvas belts. The GPMG had been fixed to the roof at the back of the wheelhouse. From there it could cover three-quarters of the sky. The missing segment of its arc was from dead astern round to the port beam.

Her engine throbbed steadily as the *Joy* cleaved her way through a calm sea. The Channel was filled with small boats, coasters and ships, all heading in the same direction. Every Royal Naval destroyer had been tasked to the job of evacuating the British Expeditionary Force from France.

With binoculars to his eyes, Alex scanned the sea. 'There are ferries, fishing boats, river cruisers, canal boats . . . just about anything that'll float is heading for Dunkirk.'

Five blasts on a foghorn sounded across the water and six destroyers in line astern steamed past, about a mile away. They were going at over 30 knots, black smoke belching from their funnels, in a formidable display of power. Only those who had seen great warships sunk knew how ethereal that power truly was.

Hastings was to port as the sun set. They debated whether or not to put on the navigation lights and decided that a collision with another boat or ship was more likely and more dangerous than the possibility of being attacked by night flying aircraft. So the white masthead lights were switched on, together with the port and starboard navigation lights. Other boats did the same.

The long night wore on; each person was busy with their own thoughts. Connie made soup and sandwiches while the men spelled each other on the wheel. They kept a sharp lookout for other surface vessels coming their way and an equally sharp lookout for enemy aircraft.

Abreast of Dungeness they turned to 085 degrees magnetic and cut across the Channel. All the other ships and boats were following the same well-worn path. Navigation meant simply following the crowd.

Dawn began to break that chill summer's morning around 04.00. Mike and Connie stayed below, trying to get some rest while Sion and Alex shared the wheelhouse together.

'I've never told you how proud I am of you, son. I want you to know that.'

'Thanks, Dad.' Alex pulled a wry face. 'But I'm pretty proud of my old man as well.'

Sion grinned. 'I guess we've done all right so far. All we have to do now is survive the next twenty-four hours.'

'From your mouth to God's ear, Dad.' Alex paused. 'I know this won't be a picnic. I've fought over the skies of France and seen some of the death and destruction that's going on. If I don't make it, I want you to tell Mum how much I love her.'

'Sure I will, son. The same goes for me.'

Alex nodded awkwardly, a lump in his throat. He held out his hand to his father. Sion grasped it and pulled his son close, giving him a hug. He let go abruptly when Alex winced from the pain in his arm and neck.

They switched off the navigation lights and checked their position. Calais was dead ahead.

A sound like thunder wafted across the gently undulating sea. Heavy gunfire! Alex pointed at the sky over France. A dogfight was in progress. Aircraft were criss-crossing, diving, swooping. A bright flash was the exploding and disintegration of a plane, in all probability a Hurricane, thought Alex. An Me109, belching smoke, was heading into the Channel. They watched as the pilot struggled to climb out of the cockpit. He was taking his time, as though he was having difficulty. Alex had his binoculars trained on the plane and found himself urging the man to get free. Finally he saw the pilot fling himself over the side and tumble through the air. His parachute opened, but failed to flare fully. Alex realised he was watching every

146

pilot's nightmare – a roman candle. Hitting the water from that height would be like hitting concrete.

'He's dead. There's no point in looking for him.'

The *My Joy II* sailed serenely on while overhead the battle of the skies continued.

The sea was filled with ships and boats of all shapes and sizes. Horns sounded and cries wafted across the water. Miraculously there were few collisions, only the odd bump and scraping of paintwork.

Connie entered the wheelhouse with bacon sandwiches and cups of tea. The men ate ravenously, restocking their depleted energy after the long night. O'Donnell stood at the door, the GPMG cocked and ready to fire, eyes scanning the skies continuously.

Out of the east came a flight of aircraft. Alex focused his binoculars on them. 'Focke-Wulf Fw190s,' he said calmly. 'And the bombers, Messerschmitt Me410s. Here they come. They're going for the destroyers.'

A wall of anti-aircraft fire poured into the sky from the sleek grey hulls. To an onlooker it seemed impossible that any plane could survive but Alex knew that appearances were deceptive. The planes were weaving through the mass of unaffected sky and pressing home their attacks with chilling success. Two French destroyers took hits, black, oily smoke pouring from gaping holes in their sides.

One Me410 was hit in the starboard engine and was flying low to avoid further damage. It was jinking left and right as if to avoid gunfire but the naval vessels were ignoring him, as he no longer posed a threat. The plane was down at about 200ft and escaping out to sea before it would turn and head back to safety, away from Dunkirk.

It was heading straight for the *My Joy*.

'Come on, you beauty. Come to me,' said O'Donnell, coaxingly, sighting along the GPMG at the Me410.

'Mike,' yelled Alex, 'try for the port wing. The pilot has armour plating underneath his feet and seat.'

'Thanks, Alex.' The gun barrel moved a fraction. The plane was coming in fast, turning gently to port to head south, when O'Donnell opened fire. He kept the trigger pressed as the stream of bullets smashed into the Me410's port engine. The pilot saw where the danger was coming from and tried to deepen the plane's turn, dropping the port wing, obstructing it from the bullets using the fuselage. He was too late. The engine burst into fire, the Messerschmitt dropped further and the port wingtip touched the water. The plane cart-wheeled, breaking up as it bounced on the sea. Miraculously it missed the boats in its path. There was wild cheering. Horns sounded joyfully and many of the occupants of the boats waved to the *My Joy*.

'Good shooting, Mike,' yelled Sion. 'It's good to see you haven't lost your touch.'

'Dad, you take the wheel, will you? I'll get the port and starboard ladders out. Once we get in close enough I'll put the tender over the stern. The men can climb into it and onto the deck.'

'Good idea, only I'll do it. You take the wheel. With all due respect, son, I've got two good hands.'

Alex nodded. His father was right. He threaded the boat towards the beach to the south of Dunkirk. The *My Joy II* drew only four feet six inches and could go in close. Lines of men were waiting patiently, wading out into the water until it was as high as their chests. Some carried their rifles above their heads, others were holding up wounded comrades. The lines snaked out to boats and ships, which floated as close in-shore as they dared go. Alex steered parallel to the beach and then deftly swung the wheel to port, stopping the engine only a few feet from one line of exhausted soldiers.

Sion was already yelling at them to come round to the port side as well. Men were passing up their rifles and then climbing up the ladders on both sides. O'Donnell stayed, manning the GPMG, while Sion and Connie put the tender over the stern and tied it lengthways to the hull. Soldiers began to climb into the little boat and up onto the aft deck.

'Connie,' O'Donnell yelled, 'we need you.'

The wounded were helped below. It took nearly fifteen minutes to fill the boat, with men crammed in every conceivable space. *My Joy* was dangerously overloaded as Alex took her back out to sea. She had gone down almost a foot and moved sluggishly in response to the wheel. The tender was now being towed behind, three grateful soldiers sitting in it.

From below came the cries of injured men. Occasionally Connie's voice could be heard, ordering hapless helpers around.

Six men were squashed in the wheelhouse while out on deck the soldiers sat in serried ranks. Exhausted, hollow-eyed, they looked the epitome of a defeated army. The boat headed straight across the Channel towards Dover. On the way she came across three small rowing boats, which they took in tow. Sion collected the rifles from the men inside the hull and distributed them to those sitting on the upper deck, loaded, cocked and ready to fire.

'Remember,' Sion called loudly, 'don't fire until I give the word. A single shot from a .303 isn't much use. But twenty rounds all fired at once *could* be effective.'

The men nodded wearily. O'Donnell stood at the GPMG, scanning the sky. The destroyers and larger ships were taking the brunt of the attacks by the Germans. Planes were diving, bombing and shooting. Ack-Ack fired back with mixed success. An RN destroyer received a direct hit in the magazine and the ship erupted in a huge ball of fire. She had been steaming away from the shore, full of rescued men. Many hundreds were killed, as the ship didn't stay afloat long enough to launch the lifeboats.

Alex had the throttle wide open but even so the *My Joy* was only managing six knots. They had forty-four miles to go to Dover, the best part of eight hours. It was going to be a long day!

Two hours after they left France Connie came up to the wheelhouse. She pushed a bloodstained hand through her hair. Alex looked at her questioningly.

'Four wounded. Three should be all right, but I'm worried about one of them. He's nineteen, hardly more than a boy. He needs hospital treatment. How long to Dover?'

'About six hours, give or take. Should we hand out some water to the men on the deck? They must be as thirsty as hell.'

Connie got two buckets of fresh water and some mugs. She and Alex went round the deck, offering a drink to those who were awake. Those asleep were lolling against the shoulders of the man sitting next to them. One man reached for the mug offered by Connie. The soldier sleeping next to him slumped forward and didn't stir. Connie quickly knelt by his side and checked for a pulse. There wasn't one. When she sat him up she saw that his clothes were saturated in blood.

'He's dead.'

'Poor bastard,' someone said.

There was nothing to be done but to leave the body where it was – a grim reminder of the horrors of the past days and weeks.

Connie continued handing out water, refilling the buckets as they emptied. As far as the eye could see, small boats and ships were trailing towards Dover. In some of the larger vessels hundreds of soldiers were being rescued while in others there were as few as two men.

A squadron of Spitfires screamed overhead, speeding towards France. Some of the men on the deck looked up and waved. In the distance the chalky white cliffs of Kent formed a white line on the horizon that was hardening by the minute. Alex aimed straight at the cliffs. Dover was five miles to the left of where the boat was headed but he intended to take the boat in close and get some protection from the towering rock.

Others had the same idea. An armada of small boats reached the shore and followed the coastline towards Dover. Alex took the boat alongside the outer mole and tied up. In an orderly fashion the soldiers climbed off the boat and trundled away, disillusion in the set of their shoulders and the dragging of their feet. They all murmured or nodded their thanks. Four men from the West Sussex Regiment took the body of their dead comrade away with them.

An air raid siren sounded and the soldiers swarming across the harbour walls were suddenly galvanised into action. Anti-aircraft guns in emplacements around the area opened up, pouring their deadly hail at incoming bombers. Suddenly the guns stopped as a squadron of Griffins tore into the orderly ranks of the bombers, forcing them to scatter or drop their bombs off-target.

One German aircraft, its wing on fire, flew into the cliff and erupted in a fireball. As the fighting continued, the German bombers scattered, heading back to France. British fighters hurried them on their way, with short, sharp bursts of fire.

Nobody questioned what they would do next. Already they'd removed the head and stern ropes and the boat was making sternway from the side, heading out to sea once more. Connie went below. When she returned to the wheelhouse she had steaming mugs of sweetened tea and a plateful of fried egg sandwiches. The men fell on them like ravenous wolves.

The sun was low in the western sky as they turned from the white cliffs and headed back to France. When they reached Dunkirk it was dusk. The whole town was ablaze. Intermittent firing could be heard, along with the regular sound of an exploding shell. The BEF was fighting a desperate rearguard action.

Nightfall meant a respite from the bombers and fighters. But street fighting kept up apace. Dead bodies littered the beach as the *My Joy* slowly approached, Alex at the wheel. Mike manned the gun once more and Sion pointed a torch ahead of the bow. The navigation lights were off. They made too much of a tempting target for a sniper.

'Stop!' Sion called. 'We're there!' He looked down at the upturned face of a young man, standing up to his neck in water. 'Ready to come aboard, soldier?'

'Yes . . . yes . . . please, sir.' His teeth were chattering. 'I'm . . . I'm free . . . freezing.'

Sion reached down. 'Give me your hand.' He lifted the soldier onto the deck and helped him over the guard-rail where Alex waited with a blanket.

Already the patient soldiers were climbing on board, helping each other, lifting up the wounded. The boat quickly filled and Alex backed the *My Joy* away from the beach. Spinning the wheel, he aimed the bow for England once more.

With no likelihood of air attack, Mike went below and put the biggest pot he could find on to boil. Into the water he poured tins of condensed milk and half a jar of drinking chocolate, then added as much sugar as he felt they could spare. Once it was boiling, he took it and the six mugs they had to the upper deck. He worked his way around the soldiers who sat uncomplaining, thankful merely to be alive. Some of the men said they hadn't eaten for two days and had had nothing hot to drink for three or more. Mike made another two pots and cut up the last of the bread.

Connie was working on her patients in the forward cabin, helped by Sion. She had already removed bullets from two men and was bandaging a third, who'd broken his left arm.

'Are there any more wounded?' she asked, wiping her hair from her eyes with the back of her hand.

'No. I've checked. We don't want the same mistake as last time.'

Shaking her head, Connie said, 'There was nothing I could have done for him anyway.'

'You should try and get some sleep,' said Sion. 'Close the door and stay in here. You won't be disturbed.'

Connie smiled. 'I'm okay. But I will just sit down for a few minutes rest.' She did so and closed her eyes, leaning back on the pillows on the bunk. Within seconds she was fast asleep.

This time they headed straight for Dover, cutting off the angle and saving some precious time. They went alongside the mole more or less where they'd landed earlier and watched as the troops went ashore in the strengthening dawn.

Sion spelled Alex on the wheel and his son went below into an empty cabin. He threw himself on a bunk and instantly fell asleep. O'Donnell was already getting some rest. With the coming of daylight the risk of air attack would become acute again.

My Joy chugged across the Channel a third time. As they approached the French coast they were horrified to see so many damaged ships, many capsized in the shallows having been caught by the German bombers the day before. The fighting was more intensive than ever and the sounds of small arms could be heard clearly in the heavily destroyed town. The Germans were steadily advancing, pushing the British, French and Belgian armies into the sea.

Aeroplanes droned overhead and Alex, a cup of black tea in his hand, strained his neck to see what they were. The unmistakable outlines of Griffins and Hurricanes at about angels 10 greeted him. He saw them peeling off and yelled, 'Here come the Hun! Keep a sharp lookout!'

Dogfights covered the sky. Some German planes got through to drop their bombs on the bigger ships. One bomb hit a small coaster, which began to sink almost immediately. The crew took to the lifeboats and Sion altered course to go to their assistance.

As the *My Joy* drew near the first boat a man waved to them and yelled, 'Don't bother. We'll row from here. Keep going!'

O'Donnell waved an acknowledgement. 'You heard, Sion?'

'Yeah. They're right. Let's keep going.'

They drew in to the coast. In spite of all the men who had already been lifted off there were still long lines waiting. They squeezed in seventy-four bodies this time before starting the trip back. As on the previous journeys, Sion had men sitting on the deck armed with rifles ready to fire, while Alex and Mike handed out mugs of sweet tea along with two Digestive biscuits for those who wanted them.

It was mid-morning and they were halfway across the Channel when they were pounced on. An Me109 came out of the sun straight at them. O'Donnell opened fire with the GPMG while Sion called on the men to hold their fire. 'Steady lads. Steady.'

The enemy aircraft opened fire and a line of bullets stitched across the water towards the boat. Alex turned the wheel hard to port just as Sion gave the order to shoot.

Thirty rounds of .303 ammunition filled the sky like a cloud of locusts. Some of the bullets hit the aircraft though most missed. But it was enough to force the plane away to starboard, the bullets it was firing missing their stern by inches.

'Get ready in case he comes round again,' Sion yelled.

The plane was banking and climbing. Alex put his head out of the window to take a look. 'He's coming back! He's turning for his run in.' As he spoke another aircraft caught his eye and he looked to the right of the German plane. 'There's a Griffin! He's onto him! Oh, my God! He's got him! The Me109's tail's been shot up!'

A ragged cheer went up as the German pilot bailed out and floated down to the sea, only a hundred yards ahead of the *My Joy*.

15

'DON'T STOP!' A voice yelled.

'Run him down,' said another.

'Let the bastard drown,' said a third.

'Dad?'

Sion spoke quietly. 'If it were you in the water I'd want you picked up. He's somebody's son.'

Alex nodded. He manoeuvred the boat alongside the pilot whose life-vest was keeping him afloat.

'Watch out for the parachute and its lines,' Sion said. 'The last thing we need is a fouled screw.'

Sion and Mike used a boathook to snag the pilot's harness. They pulled him to the side and, with the help of a couple of squaddies, hauled the German onto the deck. 'Okay, Alex, let's go. Go astern. Keep the bow pointed at the parachute until we're clear.'

The pilot, far from being grateful, showed his scorn for his rescuers by the expression on his furious face.

'Do you speak English?' Mike asked the man.

The pilot pursed his lips in distaste. '*Ja*. I learn English good. Ready for when we conquer you, English filth.'

'Hear that, lads?' O'Donnell asked the others crowding the deck. 'He says he's going to conquer us.'

'Never,' said a voice. 'We'll be back. And when we are you and bleeding Hitler will be sorry.'

The pilot could barely control his anger – wet, straight from the water, his voice dripped contempt. 'You talk like fools. Our superior equipment and training will guarantee us victory.'

One soldier pointed his Lee Enfield at the prisoner's head. 'Shut up or you won't be here to see it, you stupid kraut.'

'We should have left him to drown,' said a corporal.

'That's enough, corporal,' said Sion. 'Now he's on board we have to treat him as a prisoner of war.'

The pilot looked at Sion through slitted eyes. If he was grateful he didn't show it. Sion ignored him and looked ahead. The white cliffs were beginning to appear. A few moments later there was a commotion behind him and he turned to see what was going on. The pilot had been grabbed by a few of the soldiers – they were about to throw him over the side.

'Stop it!' roared Sion. 'Or I'll have you shot! This is murder.'

'Aye, it is,' said a sergeant. 'Attempted murder at least. He'd taken this pistol from under his vest and was about to shoot you. That's why we jumped him.'

The blood drained from Sion's face. 'Is this true? You were about to shoot me? An unarmed civilian?'

The man looked at Sion with contempt. 'It is my duty to kill the enemy.'

'We saved your life back there. And this is how you repay us? It would have been murder!'

'I do my duty!' the pilot yelled. 'My duty, do you hear?'

'What shall we do with him?' asked the sergeant.

'Shoot him,' said one of the squaddies.

'Throw him over the side,' said another.

'Is that what we should do with you?' Sion asked the German.

'You would not dare,' said the pilot. 'You do not have the courage, and that is why we will win the war.'

'It's funny,' said Sion, 'how you Germans keep underestimating us.'

'Okay lads, it's up to you. You can throw him over the side, with or without a bullet in him. What's it to be?'

The soldiers looked at one another. Now that the heat of the moment had passed they didn't have the stomach to kill in cold blood.

Sion recognised their mood and said, 'Tie him up. We'll hand him over to the authorities when we get to Dover.'

The contempt on the man's face was too much for Sion. Grabbing him by the throat, he said, 'Count yourself lucky, you little bastard. And don't confuse compassion with weakness. We don't kick our enemy when they're down.'

The pilot looked coldly at Sion, not yielding an inch. After they had trussed him up and dumped him in the bow, the men settled down again, staring at the sky, watching for more enemy aircraft. Behind them, over Dunkirk, they could see aircraft still diving and weaving in a desperate dance of life and death.

None of the planes came their way as the cliffs drew closer. Eventually they were in their shadow and paralleling the coast. Other boats had followed the same track and a small armada built up as they approached the harbour entrance. In the last hour they had taken in tow half a dozen small boats that had either broken down or had been rowed all the way from France.

Alongside the outer mole the men disembarked with tired nods and heartfelt gratitude to their rescuers.

'Dad, I'll go and find someone to take our German friend off our hands. Can you check the diesel and water? I'll also see about some food.' Alex leapt up onto the stone breakwater and hurried off. Exhausted soldiers were trundling away, some with rifles slung over their backs. Most were without weapons, having abandoned their guns on the shore around Dunkirk.

Two soldiers were marching towards him, rifles slung over their shoulders, their clean uniforms and polished boots evidence that they hadn't come from France.

'Excuse me,' said Alex. 'I've got a German prisoner . . .'

'That's why we're here, the lads gave us the nod.'

'Follow me, he's on the boat over there.' Alex led the way. The pilot was sitting with his back to the forward flag mast, his hands tied behind him. 'Watch yourselves. He tried to shoot my father after we rescued him.'

'Thank you, sir, we know how to take care of the likes of him.'

'Where can we buy some food? We need to get back across.'

One of the soldiers looked at him in surprise. 'You ain't heard? It's all over. The Prime Minister announced it on the wireless. All the ships and boats are being pulled back. *Operation Dynamo* has been a great success, he says. Over three hundred thousand men have been rescued.'

Wearily Alex nodded. God help the poor men who had been left behind.

It was an anti-climax. The four of them sat forlornly around the table in the salon, mugs of tea laced with rum in their hands.

'Looks like we'd better head back to Brighton,' said Sion.

'Damn!' Alex said with feeling. 'Just one more trip, that's all we needed.'

'You heard the last wireless report,' said O'Donnell. 'Scores of ships have been sunk. The French lost seven destroyers, we lost two and had three badly damaged. But the PM said that we saved an army in five days, which will enable us to keep fighting. We will never surrender, Winnie says, and I for one believe him.'

'Stirring stuff, but I think,' said Alex, 'that I'll get some sleep. The last few days have kept my mind off most of my aches and pains but they're playing me up now.'

Connie put her hand to her mouth. 'Oh! I should have changed your bandages. But I was so busy with the wounded . . .'

'That's all right,' Alex managed a smile. 'I'm healing. They needed your help. I just need to change the bandage on my burns.'

'I'll do it,' Connie stood up. 'I'll just fetch the first aid kit.'

'We'll leave you to it,' said Sion. 'Mike and I can check the boat for fuel, water and oil. What about food?'

'There's nothing. I gave it all to the men,' said Connie.

'I'll nip ashore for milk and a few things,' said O'Donnell. 'It's about thirteen hours to Brighton. There's no point in going hungry.'

'I'll come with you,' said Sion and the two men clambered ashore.

With just the two of them, Alex removed his shirt and Connie carefully undid the bandages. 'We have no fresh bandages so I'll have to re-use these.' She nodded approvingly. 'It's healing nicely. I think you'll be lucky and it won't scar too much.'

'Thanks, Connie, that's due to your ministrations.'

She was leaning over him. Alex moved his head and kissed her softly on the lips. She jerked back as though she had been scalded. 'Alex, don't. Please don't.'

'Connie, what the hell is the matter? You react physically to me as if you were revolted, but I *know* you care for me. Tell me what's wrong, dammit.'

'You wouldn't understand, Alex.'

'That's not an answer,' he spoke hotly.

'It's all I can offer. Please, don't ask me again.'

'Connie, you aren't making any sense. Why won't you talk to me?'

'Leave it, Alex, please.' While she was speaking she continued re-bandaging Alex's hand, arm and neck.

He sat stony faced and silent as she helped him back on with his shirt. When she'd finished he nodded his thanks. It was only when she'd left that he noticed the damp patch on his sleeve. Was that a tearstain?

The return to Brighton was uneventful. They stayed in close to the shore but it seemed that now the BEF had been kicked out of France the Germans were leaving England alone, at least for the time being. They steamed overnight and arrived back in Brighton in the early hours of Wednesday, the 5th of June. Sion and Mike drove back to Biggin Hill to return the GPMG and the car they'd borrowed. They would have to return to South Wales by train.

Alex settled into the routine of the house. The children stayed away from the west wing and he had peace and quiet to heal. He saw Connie daily when she came to change his bandages but they spoke only of his wounds. She was always busy. Keeping out of his way, more like, thought Alex. He didn't try to make another pass at her, though he yearned to get her on her own and find out what the problem was. He was, by nature, a confrontational character.

A month to the day that he was shot down he returned to his squadron. They had been relocated to Biggin Hill and he saw that the airfield was more dilapidated than ever. Burnt buildings, smashed vehicles and destroyed aircraft littered the aerodrome. He reported to the Flight Office, wondering how many of his friends had bought it while he had been away.

'Good to have you back, Alex,' said Hugo Wakefield, shaking his hand. 'Welcome to Biggin.'

'Thanks, sir. Nice to be back.'

'You'll see a few changes since you were gone.'

Alex nodded. It was little more than he had been expecting.

'Since the last time, Taff's bought it. Hippo is in the hospital and Lance is on sick leave. Seb and Dutch are missing, but we think they bailed out over France. There's a rumour that a couple of flyers are on their way back and we're hoping it's them. We've six replacements. All as green as grass and twice as keen. I want your help to lick them into shape.'

' Mine, sir?' Alex was surprised.

'Yes, yours. You've had front-line experience; I want you to explain to them what it's like.'

'But, why me? Surely an older, more experienced pilot would be better?'

Wakefield shook his head. 'I considered it but, coming from me, it seems like more of the same old stuff. Senior officer knows best and all that. You, you're different. You're nearer their age, the same rank, *and* you've been in combat. They might listen to you. Tell them about your mistakes and the things you should have done better. Tell them that it's all right to be scared, but that you have to overcome it somehow. Tell them,' he paused and looked sternly at Alex, 'tell them how it really is. It might save a life or two. God knows, we can't afford the attrition of pilots at this rate for much longer.'

Alex nodded. 'I'll do my best, sir.'

'Good lad.' Wakefield smiled at him. 'I knew you would. Now, cut along to the mess. Drinks and tiffin in ten. By the way, remember I put you in for a gong? They've given you a Mention instead.'

Alex nodded. Somehow, with so many of his friends dead or missing, a Mention in Dispatches seemed irrelevant!

The squadron was stood down for the day. They would be required at dawn the following morning. The four surviving members of his squadron greeted Alex with delight. He met the new pilots, all of whom seemed hellish young to him. After lunch he was told to muster with the newcomers in one of the Nissan huts.

Wakefield introduced him. 'You've met Flying Officer Griffiths. He's going to tell you what it's like in combat. Listen to him. He's been there, done it and survived. He may save some of your lives.' With that he left.

Alex coughed, shuffled his feet and got on with it. He told of the confusion, the frantic searching of the sky for the enemy before he fired at you, of the inevitable fear when in combat. He spoke hesitatingly at first, but then warmed to his subject, holding their attention. After about twenty minutes he asked, 'Any questions?'

At first there were none. But once one of them had broken the ice the questions came thick and fast. Alex answered each one honestly and directly. Wakefield returned an hour later.

'How's it going, Alex?'

'Fine, sir. We're just finished.'

'Good. I hope,' he looked at the keen, young faces in front of him, 'that you've all taken to heart what Alex has told you. We've come a long way since the last lot, but we're still a young service. Survival means learning from our lessons. Don't be a hero. In doubt, run away. Far better to live and fight another day. Training you has cost the country a great deal of money, but more importantly, it has taken time. Time we don't have. There's nothing to stop the Hun coming across the Channel. Winnie says that we need to rebuild our army, navy and air force before we can counterattack. So our task is to live. Remember that. Right, that's enough lecturing. I want you all in the air in fifteen minutes. We're going to practice a bit of aerial combat.'

Alex's new plane was Spitfire M for Mother. As he approached it he couldn't help comparing it to the Griffin, which had a more robust look about it. The Spitfire's narrow undercarriage gave the impression of a thoroughbred, nervous, skittish, and raring to go. Settling into his seat, he soon had the Merlin engine roaring into life at the touch of a button, sending thick clouds of smoke and a stab of flame from the exhausts. The cockpit was enveloped with the smoke, which quickly dispersed as the engine settled down to a steady roar.

The view was bad while on the ground. He had to swing the nose from side to side to see what was ahead while taxiing, moving forward cautiously, knowing that if he hit the brakes too hard the plane would tip onto its nose. He checked the glycol temperature. 107 degrees. Too high. He needed to get airborne to reduce it to its normal range. Alex let off the brakes and slowly opened the throttle, with mixed emotions. This was his first time in the air since his prang. His mouth was dry but when he analysed his feelings he knew that it wasn't fear he was experiencing, more an anticipation, excitement at getting back into the air. The plane accelerated down the runway and lifted gracefully into the sky. He took the wheel in his left hand and used his right to pump the undercarriage up. He looked over his shoulder. Precisely where he expected to see him was T for Tango.

Alex felt the tiny cockpit fit around his shoulders like an overcoat and settled down, getting the feel of his new charge. At 400mph and a height of 15,000ft, he and T for Tango set about a series of manoeuvres and practice dogfights.

After an hour they were recalled to the airfield. The pilot of T for Tango was a new recruit, a young man of nineteen, "Ginger" Robarts. With his slight frame and vivid ginger hair, he was instantly recognisable. He fell in beside Alex as they walked towards the dispersal hut.

After a few seconds of silence, Robarts couldn't contain himself any longer. 'How did I do?'

Alex frowned, jerked out of his usual reverie about Connie. 'Oh, fine. Watch below a bit more. And keep jinking. Don't fly straight for more than a second or two.'

They debriefed and went back to their quarters. After a shower Alex went down to the bar for a drink. The others had already gathered there, ready to bring Alex up to date. Stories, exaggerated and occasionally understated, were told about the month that Alex had been away. He was reticent to talk about his experiences on the *My Joy* but they were wheedled out of him.

'Heard about Mary?' Ken Bertram joined him at the bar, a pint of beer in his hand.

'Mary who?' Alex asked, the name meaning nothing to him.

'The barmaid down at the old *Duck and Hound.*'

'Oh, her. Sorry. What about her?'

'She's up the duff. Was about to marry one of our young sprogs when she let it slip. He escaped just in time. Guess you had a lucky escape too.'

Alex nodded, swallowing with a dry mouth. He took a hefty swig of beer. 'What's become of her?'

'Gone away. Nobody knows where. Pity really. She had a lovely pair of charms to gawk at.'

Alex smiled at Bertram. The Flight Lieutenant was in his late twenties. He had been a lecturer at Newcastle University and a member of the university flying club when war had broken out. He hadn't hesitated to volunteer, claiming the atmosphere of the campus was stifling his adventurous nature. Bertram was growing a moustache with few evident signs of success and often stroked his upper lip as though to convince himself the fungus was still flourishing.

Bertram gestured at the other pilots in the mess. 'What do you make of them?'

'Bloody young.' Alex sighed and added, 'But then we all were once. You either grow up fast or you grow up dead in this business.' He spoke with all the authority of a veteran of only a few of months.

Bertram smiled. 'Ever the philosopher. How's the arm and neck?'

Alex shrugged. 'A bit tight along the left side here,' he pointed at his neck. 'But it's okay I guess. I keep stretching the skin. Turning my head. You know how it is. If you can't see behind you it's curtains.'

Bertram nodded. He knew only too well. 'Well, I think it's an early dinner and an early night. We're up with the dawn chorus as usual.'

The next week brought a lull in the fighting. A few harassing attacks took place over southern England but on the whole the Luftwaffe left Britain alone. The Germans were too busy consolidating their position in France. Marshall Henri Petain, the former hero of Verdun, assumed supreme power. He was made President and Prime Minister with the title of Chief of the French State. The traditional French cry of "Liberty, Equality and Fraternity" was replaced by the Fascist slogan "Work, Family and Fatherland".

In the middle of August, what was to become known as the "Battle of Britain" began in earnest.

Over a thousand enemy planes attacked the south of England every day. The skies were a maelstrom of diving, soaring aircraft, each vying for the advantage of seconds that enabled the enemy to be shot down.

In accordance with standing orders, the Hurricane Squadrons attacked the bombers while the Spitfires and Griffins attacked the escorts. Often, in the mêlée of the fight, these roles were reversed.

Alex was airborne on his eighth day in a row at a few minutes before noon. It was the third time that day his squadron had scrambled. The Radio Direction Finding (RDF) stations for Area 11 were busy. Wave after wave of German bombers, with Me109s as cover, had attacked Britain's aerodromes in the south east. In accordance with *Reichsmarschall* Hermann Göring's promise to Hitler that he would sweep the British from the skies, the Germans were relentless. They were targeting 11 Group's airfields, including Biggin Hill, Kenley, Hornchurch, North Weald, Tangmere, Debden and Northolt. The RAF's Hurricanes pounced like birds of prey out of the sky from 25,000ft straight on to the bombers. They in turn were pounced on by the Me109s, which were attacked by the Spitfires and Griffins.

Despite the Herculean efforts of the fighters, the air stations were bombed repeatedly. In No 11 Group alone, during a period of only thirteen days, forty-five pilots were killed and eighty-three injured. The RAF was fighting for its very survival and losing.

Alex was aware of all this as he levelled off at 26,000ft. Ginger Robarts was flying on his port wing, number two to him.

Below he could see the Junkers and Dornier bombers, coming in wave after wave. The Hurricanes were already diving in front, coming straight into the noses of the enemy aircraft. Alex felt alive, excited and fearful all at once. This was it. Not for a second did he think of his own mortality, only of the Hun.

The Me109s were already pouncing when Alex called, 'Tally ho! Follow me down.'

Lining up a 109 in his sights Alex let loose with a long burst, only to see the plane twist hard left and his bullets rake the starboard wing, the plane diving away. At least the 109's target, a Hurricane, was saved. A slight adjustment to port and another 109 was in his sights. He let loose again, this time the German dived, escaping his attack. In frustration and anger Alex pulled hard on the stick and sent his Spitfire in an almost vertical climb, straight at the belly of a Junkers 88. The twin-engined bomber was opening its bomb doors as Alex opened fire. His bullets bit the underside of the plane, raking the length of the fuselage. The Spitfire turned onto its starboard wing and dived away, only yards from the bomber. At that moment a bomb still inside the bay exploded and the plane disintegrated, scattering burning fuel and pieces of metal across the sky. Robarts was still with Alex and his plane was hit, the engine stopping almost instantly.

The plane turned in a steep dive towards the South Downs, 20,000ft below.

Alex heard Robarts yelling. His Spitfire was trailing smoke, easing up in a swoop at about 9,000ft when Alex turned and dived after him, his intention to cover the pilot down.

'Yellow Eight, Yellow Eight,' Alex said urgently into his radio, 'I'm right behind. Bail out now. I'll cover you down.'

Recently, the Germans had started to machine-gun pilots as they dangled helplessly in the shrouds of their parachutes. Airplanes were plentiful, trained pilots were scarce.

Alex saw the canopy being flung back and Robarts struggling to climb out. Alex sat a thousand feet above and a half-mile behind, warily watching the sky. The battle, as so often happened, had moved away and the two planes appeared alone.

Twisting his neck, Alex saw the 109 come hurtling out of the sky, straight at Robarts' Spitfire. In desperation, opening the throttle wide, Alex turned to intercept. The Hun was oblivious to everything except his target. Still too far away to be effective, Alex opened fire, hoping to draw the enemy away, to distract him. But Alex went unobserved. In horror he watched Robarts look up and see the German bearing down on him, opening fire, the bullets feeding along the tail towards the cockpit. Ginger dived over the side and curled up into a ball, plummeting to the earth.

Horrified, Alex turned in fury after the 109. The German, suddenly aware of the Spitfire on his tail, began diving and weaving in a desperate attempt to escape. Alex stuck to his tail like glue, firing off a few rounds every time he thought he might hit the other plane.

Lower they flew, the land changing from a patchwork quilt to individual trees and houses. Rage burned through Alex. 'You murderous bastard. I'll get you.'

The 109 jinked to port and Alex followed a mere two hundred yards behind. Opening fire, he saw bits of wing fall off the other fighter. The German desperately corkscrewed right but inspiration was with Alex that day and he stayed on the Hun's tail. Firing once more, he saw a trail of smoke trailing out of the 109.

'Got you, you swine,' Alex said. Still he stayed behind the enemy. With satisfaction he saw the canopy being pushed back and the pilot clambering out. 'No you don't.' In a killing rage Alex lined up his sights on the back of the German, now only a hundred yards away and opened fire. His bullets shredded the pilot's body, blood and flesh disintegrating. Alex watched in horror, mesmerised, flying ever closer to his target, his finger still on the trigger. The 109 began to break up as the body fell over the side. With a jerk, Alex saw he was heading at the ground now only about three hundred feet below and desperately hauled back on the column. The Spitfire, as responsive as a thoroughbred horse, clawed for the sky, missing the side of a farmhouse by what seemed like inches.

Alex was sweating. His body ached from the tension, and his eyes smarted. God, that was horrible. But the bastard deserved it after what he'd done to poor Ginger. He turned back to Northolt, low on fuel and almost out of ammunition.

Only eight bombers made it through. The airfield had taken another pounding but it wasn't as bad as it could have been. The runway had been damaged but not irreparably so, and there was still enough room to land. One hangar had received a direct hit; the rest of the bombs had fallen around the edge. When he had lined up to land and his wheels were down, Alex received a green light and he went in. The plane landed with a bump and he taxied over to the dispersal stand. He sat in the cockpit for a few moments as his fitter and rigger arrived to help him. Wearily he climbed out, hanging his parachute on the wing, ready for the next time.

'All right, sir?' Leading Aircraftman Andrews, the plane's fitter, was a cheery soul from Falkirk in Scotland.

Alex shook his head. 'We lost Pilot Officer Robarts.'

Andrews and the rigger pulled faces. They'd liked Robarts, he was always smiling and had a wealth of daft stories to share with the men.

Alex trudged over to the operations hut to report to the squadron intelligence officer.

'Robarts bought it,' Alex greeted Flying Officer Gavin Edge.

Edge was a fighter pilot who'd been shot down over France. He'd been picked up by the BEF and brought out with them. Now he was champing at the bit to return to flying duties but the powers-that-be thought he needed longer to recuperate.

He'd been with the squadron long enough to know how close Alex and Ginger had become. 'Sorry, old man. How did it happen?'

Alex told the story.

'Right. Now let's go through the kills. Here's your form.'

Taking the buff form Alex duly filled in the details, covering the date, time, weather and his aircraft number. Once he'd done that he was prompted by the other man's questions. 'What did you see? What did you do? Were the hits definite or did the plane escape?'

Bit by tiny bit a story built up of the engagement. Alex had two confirmed kills. These, added to his other three, two unconfirmed and one damaged made him officially an "Ace".

'Congratulations, Alex,' said Edge, holding out his hand.

Alex took it wearily, his heart not in it. 'Thank you.'

'You'll get your gong now. Not just a Mention.'

Alex nodded and turned away from the table to leave the hut. The phone rang and Edge picked it up. Alex was almost out the door when Edge called after him cheerily. 'Wait, Alex. That was the Home Guard. They've picked up Ginger. He's all right!'

16

THE FIGHTING INTENSIFIED if that was possible. Squadrons were being called up five, six times a day. It was relentless. The losses amongst British pilots were horrendous. Hurricane, Spitfire and Griffin pilots became "Aces" in a matter of days, shooting down the necessary five planes to qualify. As bad as the British and Commonwealth pilots were finding it, the German losses were even greater. But still they came, pounding the south-eastern corner of England, wiping out the airfields and squadrons at every opportunity.

On the 20th of August, the pilots of Hercules Squadron were finally stood down and forty-eight hour passes were issued.

'What are you planning to do, Ginger?' Alex asked.

The two men, always close, had become practically inseparable.

'Nothing. I'm staying here with a good book. Leicester's too much of a fag to get to.' He waved Evelyn Waugh's novel "Scoop" in the air.

'Any good?' Alex asked with feigned nonchalance, taking it from his hand.

'It's quite funny. A satire about the conceited idiocy of the newspaper . . . Hey!'

Alex flicked the book into a wastepaper basket, hitting it more by luck than judgement. 'If you mean the fatuity of the press, say so. Let's go. You're coming with me.'

'I am? Where to?'

'To my uncle's place near Brighton.'

'He won't be expecting me.'

'He's probably not there but if he is we'll have a rare old time. He's got some incredible tales to tell. Hurry up, Ginger. The old two-seater is lumbered up and ready, so go and pack a bag.'

Ginger scowled for a second and then got up from his seat with a martyred air. He retrieved his book, tucked it under his arm, gave Alex a mock Nazi salute and walked away. Alex grinned.

They stopped for a beer at a thatched-roof pub near Crawley. The sun was hot, and they sat outside in their shirtsleeves, their uniform jackets slung on the chairs behind them. Alex was fiddling with his pipe.

'Why on earth do you smoke that filthy thing?' Ginger asked.

Alex stuffed the end into his mouth and sucked in, drawing air through it. Taking out a penknife to clean around the bowl, he looked at his friend. 'No idea.' He frowned. 'Adds a certain insouciance to my . . .'

Before Alex could finish Ginger burst out laughing. 'Balderdash. You spend so much of your time playing with the bloody thing all you do is get filthy. Look at your hands.'

Alex looked at the ash stains on his fingers and under his nails and pulled a wry face. 'I actually can't stand the sodding thing.'

'Then throw it away.'

Alex looked at the offending article and sighed. He snapped the stem in half and dumped the pieces in an ashtray. 'Let's drink up and get a move on. Tea at *Fairweather* is served punctually.'

As they traversed the drive Ginger said, 'Wow! Is this your uncle's place?'

'Impressive, isn't it?'

'That's an understatement.' Ginger looked out of the corner of his eye at his friend. 'You kept quiet about this, in the mess.'

'And that's how I want it to stay,' Alex said grimly.

He went round the house to the back door. A gang of children were outside, kicking a tin can in a desultory fashion.

'Who are they?'

'Kids from a school in the East End. They've been evacuated here for the duration.'

'Grubby looking lot,' was Ginger's dismissive opinion.

Alex was more compassionate. 'It must be tough, leaving their families, not knowing if their homes have been bombed, their parents killed.'

Ginger squirmed and said, 'I suppose so.'

The boys had stopped kicking the can and watched as Alex's car pulled up away from the area they were using. Alex got out of the car and nonchalantly opened the boot. Reaching inside he lifted out a football and began bouncing it on the ground. The boys looked at him agog. Alex said nothing, just kept bouncing the ball. The tension grew and the boys began to fidget. They were itching to get their hands on the football, their feet moving slowly but inexorably towards Alex.

There were thirteen of them, of all shapes and sizes, in short trousers, open-necked shirts and sleeveless woollen pullovers. Alex looked at them in feigned surprise. The ball bounced with a resounding and satisfying smack of stitched leather against cobbled stones.

'Want something?' Alex asked them.

One of the boys, about eleven or twelve, smaller than the rest, answered, 'Yes, sir. Please, sir. We'd like to play with your ball.'

'What? This one?' Alex laughed, unwilling to tease them any further. 'Seeing as it's yours, I don't see why not.'

'Ours?' one of the lads asked.

'Sure. Only don't play around here. Use the field by the side of the paddock. You know which one?' He tossed the ball to the boy who'd first spoken. 'Catch.'

The boy caught it adeptly and they all ran off, yelling at the top of their voices. The noise brought Connie out to see what was going on.

She stopped dead in the kitchen doorway when she saw Alex, a mixture of anxiety and relief on her face. Then she walked towards them, drying her hands on her apron. He almost put his hand out to touch her, but checked himself at the last moment.

'Hullo, Alex.'

'Hullo, Connie. This is my friend, Ginger. Ginger meet Connie.'

'Pleased to meet you,' said Ginger.

The two men lifted out their bags from the car and walked towards the door. 'Anybody else staying?' Alex asked.

'Susan will be here later on.'

'Good.' Seeing Ginger's quizzical look he explained, 'My cousin. She's a pilot too.'

Ginger nodded sceptically. His look clearly said, '*A woman pilot! This should be interesting.*'

'You're looking well,' Alex said to Connie, who smiled in acceptance of the compliment.

Her eyes showed relief that Alex was making an effort to act normally around her. 'I wish I could say the same for you. You look exhausted. We've been following events on the wireless. It must have been hellish.'

Alex nodded. 'A few days off will soon put us right. Isn't that so, Ginger?'

His friend said in a quiet voice. 'Who's that?' He was nodding towards the imposing figure of Gibbs who had materialised in the kitchen.

'Hullo, Mr Alex,' Gibbs said.

'Hullo, Gibbs. This is my friend Ginger. Ginger, this is *Fairweather's* major-domo, Gibbs.'

The butler cut an imposing figure in his morning coat. 'How do you do, Mr Gibbs?' Ginger said nervously.

'How do you do, sir?' said the ever-courteous Gibbs. 'I have just received a telephone call from Sir David, Mr Alex; he will be arriving later this evening.'

'Good show,' said Alex. 'Knowing Uncle David we'll soon have a party going.'

In the distance they could hear the sound of an engine and soon the windowpanes rattled as the house was buzzed by an aeroplane. Connie smiled. 'Looks as though Susan's arrived.'

'Come on, Ginger,' said Alex. 'Dump your bag. We can take care of it later. I'll introduce you to my cousin. You'll love Susan. I don't think I've ever met anyone more straightforward, male or female.'

Outside, Alex and Ginger climbed into a beat-up, old Land Rover. The engine burst into life with a noxious cloud of fumes from the exhaust and Alex drove out of the yard. In the distance they could see a small bi-plane landing and beginning to taxi towards the hangar, situated at one end of the grass runway. By the time they reached the hangar Susan was striding towards them, a bag hanging from her hand.

Her black hair was cut short in the latest fashion, and her tailored trousers and jacket were immaculate despite her time in the cockpit. She was looking radiant. Introductions were made, Susan slung her bag into the back of the Land Rover and climbed in after it, chatting easily with Alex. Ginger was remarkably quiet, frantically thinking of things to say and wishing like hell that Alex would come to his rescue.

Back at the house, Susan said, 'Your friend doesn't say much, does he?'

Alex grinned. 'The strong silent type, that's Ginger.'

'No, I'm not,' Ginger protested.

'Not strong?' Susan teased. At which Ginger blushed furiously.

'It's tea time,' said Alex. 'Let's go in.'

Walking through the hall Ginger stopped to admire the paintings of airplanes festooned artistically around the dark-panelled walls.

Frowning he moved from one to the other. 'Griffins! Going back thirty years. How amazing!' Then the penny dropped. 'Griffiths! You're related to Sion Griffiths?' Ginger looked at Susan and Alex in surprise. He was even more surprised by her reply.

'He's my uncle,' said Susan.

'Your uncle?'

Alex shrugged sheepishly. 'Which makes him my father. Only don't tell the lads.'

Ginger looked at his friend in something akin to awe. The great Sion Griffiths was Alex's father and he'd had no idea!

'It's not something I boast about,' Alex went on. 'I don't even think the CO has any idea. And I want to keep it that way.'

'Why?' Ginger was genuinely perplexed.

'How would you like to live in the shadow of a legend?' Susan asked mildly. 'Now let's hurry. I'm desperate to see my little boy.'

They went in to tea. Connie was already there with John Phillipe, who had recently celebrated his third birthday. Susan scooped him up for a heartfelt cuddle, and then let him lead her from the room to show her his toys. Ginger, sensing the tension between Connie and Alex, took his cup and excused himself – he said he wanted to take another look at the paintings of the planes.

Alone, Connie and Alex felt horribly awkward in each other's company. A few seconds of attempting to make small talk left Alex wishing he hadn't come. He took his cup and went to stand at the open French windows, looking across the fields to the Channel in the distance. Connie sat in disconsolate silence and watched him.

When the silence had become unbearable, Alex spoke, 'I'll leave first thing in the morning, Connie. I'm sorry . . . really sorry . . .' He searched his mind for careful phrases, words which would convey how he felt. Connie's head remained bowed, her body saying more clearly than words that she didn't want him. His temper flared and he began again, knowing he was making a mistake.

'I can't help it, Connie. I haven't been able to think of anything but you these last few weeks. Now I've seen you I'm more sure than ever that I love you.'

Connie's head jerked up, her eyes searching out his. 'Love!' Connie spoke with scorn. 'What do you know of love? What do you know of anything, of hardship, of fear? Of *life*? '

'How can you ask me that question?' Alex was angry. 'Every day I live is a bonus. Each time we take to the air we wonder if we'll be coming back. Every time we scramble it's *you* I think of.' Finally she raised her chin and looked at him. ' I know you've suffered, Connie – Susan hinted as much. Was there another man? Is that why you can't love me back?' He looked at her so ardently, so baffled with longing and love, that she looked away.

How could she tell him about her past? About the heart-sickness that festered in her when she thought about the rapes? How in her lonely bed she dreamed terrible dreams, powerless to stop the Africanistas coming for her again and again . . . How quickly his feelings for her would change if he knew what had happened, how they had used her. How could she make him understand? Better for him to believe her heart broken. She couldn't allow herself to be hurt again.

Connie moved towards the door. Her voice was heavy and tired, her eyes blank and empty. 'This crush of yours grows tiresome, Alex – it's pure fantasy.'

Susan found Alex an hour later, sitting in the garden with his head in his hands. 'What's wrong? You look the picture of unhappiness.'

He said nothing, just stared at the ground.

'Come on, Alex, you can tell me. You know I'll help in any way I can.' She ran her hand gently across his back. She was very fond of her younger cousin.

'Tell me about Spain, Susan.' Abruptly he stood up, wiping his eyes, and faced her. 'What happened to Connie back there? Why is she so fearful? I can't get close to her yet I'm sure she likes me.'

Susan closed her eyes for a second. 'I can't tell you, Alex. That's for Connie to share. But I will say it was bad, very bad. Please, don't give up on her. She deserves happiness.'

Alex looked closely at his cousin, wondering what the hell had happened to Connie that was so dreadful. Slowly and resignedly he nodded. 'Okay, if you say so. But Susan, you know as well as I do, that I may not have much time. We fighter pilots aren't exactly known for our longevity.'

Susan shuddered. 'I know. But please, be patient.'

The dinner gong sounded. It was really the call to cocktails and so he took time to wash and shave before going downstairs. His Uncle David had arrived with Aunt Maddie and the evening was set to be a pleasant occasion.

Ginger was standing next to Susan, looking at her with more than friendly interest. He, like Alex, was dressed in a blazer and tan slacks. Susan looked very fetching in a black skirt and pink blouse, the simple style effortlessly elegant.

Madelaine was as radiant as ever in a high-necked, calf-length dress of turquoise silk.

'Aunt Maddie,' Alex greeted her warmly, kissing her cheek.

'Alex, my dear, it's lovely to see you.' She kept the worry out of her voice but not her eyes. Her nephew was looking tired.

'Let me get you a drink,' said his uncle.

'It's okay,' Alex smiled. 'I'll get it.'

In a corner of the room was a small but extensive bar and Alex helped himself to a large scotch. 'Anybody need a refill?' There were no takers.

Alex froze with his glass to his mouth when Connie came in. She had piled her hair up. Her black, full skirt flared slightly as she walked, showing her shapely legs. Her trim waist accentuated her full figure and Alex found he was staring at her. She smiled at him and Alex found his heart flipping.

'Drink?' he asked.

'A sherry, please.'

As she took the glass she was careful not to touch his fingers.

When they sat down to dinner, the conversation turned to family matters for a few minutes before returning to recent news of the war.

'We're losing the air war,' said David. 'It will come down to who can keep flying the longest and the most.'

'We've pilots coming in from all the Dominions,' said Madelaine. 'Surely that'll be enough?'

David shook his head. 'I fear not. What do you boys say?'

Alex shrugged. 'It's touch and go. As long as they attack the squadrons we'll be fighting a desperate battle.'

'That's true,' said Ginger. 'We need them to go after other targets.' Aware the others were looking at him, he blushed, afraid he'd spoken out of turn.

'What do you mean?'

Ginger leant forward and quietly said, 'The docks. The towns and cities.'

'But the loss of life,' said Susan, 'would be terrible.'

Ginger nodded grimly. 'It would be worse if we were wiped out. Then there would be nothing to stop the Germans walking into Britain.'

'The lesser of two evils? That's an interesting idea,' said David thoughtfully. 'The question is how do we make them change their target?'

'Easy,' came the startling reply. With everyone at the table looking at him Ginger grinned sheepishly. 'Well, it would be relatively easy anyway. I think.'

'What do you propose?' Madelaine asked.

'The Germans are big on revenge. If we want them to attack our cities . . .'

'. . . we attack theirs,' David finished for him.

'Exactly, sir. If the bombers were diverted away from us then we'd have the chance to re-group and train up our pilots. Mr Churchill has called the air battle the Battle of Britain, and he's right. If we lose this fight we're finished.'

'That reminds me,' said David. 'Winnie's broadcasting in,' he looked at his watch, 'fifty minutes time. Let's get the meal out of the way and listen to him in the study.'

In good time they were seated in David's comfortable study, glasses of port and Madeira at hand. At nine o'clock precisely the BBC broadcast from Parliament.

In a confident and exuberant manner, the Prime Minister broadcast to the nation. '*Never,*' he said ponderously, '*in the field of human conflict was so much owed by so many to so few.*'

His words were greeted by loud cheering from all the MPs in the House of Commons. '*Today I have signed ninety-nine year leases with the United States, giving them naval and air bases in Newfoundland and the West Indies. This transaction means that these two great English-speaking democracies will be entwined to mutual advantage for a hundred years. No one can stop it. Like the Mississippi it keeps rolling along.*' There was more of the same, each sentence interrupted by cheers.

For the family in the study at *Fairweather* their emotions ran just as high, the ladies were wet-eyed, the men forcing themselves to keep stiff-upper lips.

The following morning dawned warm and sunny. The consensus

of opinion was that the perfect Saturday meant doing nothing. Alex borrowed Ginger's Evelyn Waugh and sat in a deck chair on the patio, while Ginger went horse riding with David and Susan. Alex found he couldn't concentrate, thoughts of Connie persistently intruding. It had been his firm intention to leave that morning but Ginger wouldn't hear of it. And the fact was, Alex didn't really wish to leave. The adage "faint heart never won fair lady" haunted him. If only he could get Connie on her own. Perhaps he could talk some sense into her. But she was deliberately avoiding him.

He gave up all pretence of reading. Hearing bickering he got to his feet, following the childish voices. An argument was in progress about a game of football. The teams were uneven, five against six, so he solved the problem and joined in. Soon he was lost in the game. The goal posts were discarded jumpers, there was no offside rule, and touch was when the ball hit the side of the field. The kids gave Alex a run for his money and he was soon working up a sweat.

Mid-morning Connie appeared carrying a tray of freshly made lemonade and biscuits. Alex took the last glass, wiped his forehead with the back of his hand and said, 'Thanks, I needed this. Nice kids,' Alex waved airily behind him.

Connie seemed happy to talk. 'They are. Though none of them are angels. We had an episode or two of pilfering in the beginning until Gibbs sorted it out.'

'What did he do?'

'Caught two of them in the act and gave them each six with a belt across their behinds. They couldn't sit down for days. But at least it solved the problem.'

'Good for Gibbs. I'm surprised he's taken this invasion by the children with such equanimity.'

'He likes them really. And they are in absolute awe of him, which I think he enjoys to a certain extent.'

'*I'm* in awe of Gibbs, so I don't blame the kids.'

'He's very sweet once you get to know him. I'd better get back. I'm teaching some of the local girls first aid.' With that she left, feeling Alex's eyes burning into her back.

Lunch interrupted the game. Alex's side lost, nine goals to twelve.

During the afternoon Alex dozed in a deck chair, barely stirring until Susan came along. She was looking a little frazzled.

'What's eating you?'

'Your friend. Whenever I turn around he pops up.'

'He's in love,' said Alex with a grin.

'In love? Don't talk nonsense. He hardly knows me.'

'What's that got to do with it? It's the effect you have on all hot-blooded men, and you know it!'

Susan had the good grace to smile sheepishly. 'Well, a girl has to keep her hand in.'

'Susan, you know you can wrap men around your little finger if you put your mind to it.'

'At one time, perhaps, but not now. I've a child. I'm practically a matron.' What had begun as a joke suddenly became earnest. 'Truth be told, I'm feeling lonely. I need a good man. There's nothing like a war for focusing the mind on what's important in life. If *you* want Connie,' she abruptly changed the subject, 'you'll need to fight for her.' Susan gave a radiant smile and departed, leaving a thoughtful Alex staring after her.

After dinner they had again adjourned for drinks into the study when they heard a distant explosion, followed rapidly by another. They went out onto the patio to see what was happening. Searchlights were traversing the sky, bouncing off the underside of the clouds, looking for their elusive prey.

'There's one!' Susan yelled, pointing to the south east.

A searchlight had picked up a bomber and was holding it like a butterfly pierced by a pin. The ack-ack opened up, exploding around the plane. In desperation the bomber weaved and dived across the sky but the light held it in its grip. Shells were exploding all around it and suddenly an engine burst into flame.

'A Dornier,' said Ginger. 'Good shooting. Look! It's diving straight down. There's another and another.'

It was now obvious that a large force of German aircraft was crossing into Southern England, heading for the aerodromes that housed the RAF. David stepped off from the patio to look back at the house, checking to see that the blackout curtains were effective. A chink of light showed at the bottom of an upper window but was barely discernible. Even so, he'd mention it to Gibbs in the morning. The sound of a thousand engines droned overhead. Bombs were dropped by stricken aircraft, the pilots jettisoning their payloads. None came near Ovingdean.

The first wave passed but a second followed a few minutes later.

This time they were much closer, almost overhead. The searchlights were picking up aircraft as the ack-ack fired incessantly. One plane had its starboard engine on fire and was diving away from the formation, still trapped by the light as more flack hit home. 'It's coming this way!' David yelled. 'My God, it's going to crash!

17

THE PLANE SEEMED to be only feet above the roof when Alex and Ginger heard the telltale whistling. Alex yelled, 'Down everybody, it's a bomb!'

Grabbing Connie by the arm he pulled her to the ground. Ginger pulled Susan down with him. David and Madelaine were slower. The bomb hit the eastern corner of the house, smashing through the roof and knocking down some of the end wall. But the feared explosion didn't come.

Shakily they got back to their feet.

'A dud,' said David.

'Not necessarily,' said Alex. 'Some of them have delays on them, so that they go off hours later.'

'Killing the men trying to dismantle it,' said Ginger.

'Stay here,' said Alex, 'while I go and see what's what.'

'Oh no you don't,' said his uncle, grabbing his arm. 'I'll go. You go and see to the children. Make sure nobody's hurt.'

Susan and Connie were already hurrying inside, thoughts of John Phillipe uppermost in their minds.

'But . . .' Alex began.

'David's right, Alex. To put it bluntly, he's more expendable than you are.'

'Thank you, my dear,' said David dryly, 'for putting it so succinctly.'

Madelaine tucked her arm through his and said, 'But to me you're irreplaceable. We'll call the bomb squad.'

The two pilots watched as the older couple walked away, David arguing that Madelaine should stay behind. Suddenly he stopped and looked back, 'Get shotguns and go and see if any Germans survived the crash. And be careful,' he warned.

'We'd better do as he said,' said Ginger. 'Where do they keep the guns?'

'In a locked cupboard next to the tack room. The matching Purdeys are in a special safe in the house. Only Uncle David has the key.'

Armed with guns and torches, the two men climbed into the Land Rover. Alex drove away from the house in the direction of the downed plane. In the middle of a ploughed field the vehicle's lights were reflected off some white markings. As they drew nearer they saw the aircraft had landed with the wheels up and somehow, miraculously, not burst into flame.

They approached slowly, Alex twisting the wheel back and forth, plying the headlights along the fuselage.

'A Junkers eighty-eight,' said Ginger.

'Means a pilot and a bombardier. See anything?'

'No.' Ginger switched on his torch and shone it at the Perspex-covered cockpit. 'Somebody's still inside.'

Alex stopped the Land Rover and switched off the engine. The silence was deafening. 'Anybody there?'

Nobody answered and they cautiously approached the door on the starboard side. Shining the torch inside they could see the pilot, with the bombardier sitting alongside. Both were motionless. Alex fiddled with the door and found out how to open it. He reached inside and touched the nearest man. Both bodies were already going cold.

'We can phone the police from the house,' Alex said. 'What a bloody waste. All this death and for what? More heartbreak and destruction.'

The house was in chaos. The children had been taken from their beds, dressed and were lining up to walk into the village. They set off with their teachers, to be billeted among the locals.

'I've telephoned the army base at Brighton,' said David. 'They're sending a couple of engineers to take a look. Presumably they're bomb disposal specialists. They told us to stay well away. It could go off at any time.'

Alex nodded. He'd been to a few lectures, but his knowledge of bombs was restricted almost entirely to how to drop them.

'They reckon it's a thousand-pounder. If it goes off, it'll take the house away,' said David. 'I've told Gibbs not to go back inside. Possessions aren't worth anyone's life.'

While they were talking they had been moving away from the

property. Now they stopped and looked back at the damaged house. In the clear night they could see the broken corner of the roof and the demolished end-wall.

A few hundred yards further on they joined Madelaine, Susan and Connie. John Phillipe lay in Susan's arms, his head snuggled against his mother's neck.

'We'd better go down the front drive and wait for the Army. See what they have to say,' said David.

Alex found himself walking alongside Connie, trying to make out her face in the darkness. For a second, just before the bomb had hit, he had thought he was about to be separated from her forever. Did she care for him at all?

'Uncle David, what about getting the cars?'

'I asked the army. They said that the vibration of the engines starting-up could be dangerous. That it was better to leave things like they are.'

Alex didn't agree but knew too little about it to argue. They stopped halfway to the gate.

'You know, this is ridiculous,' said Alex. 'Ginger, let's go back and get the deck chairs and a few blankets. We can't stand here all night.'

'You'll find deckchairs in the summer house,' said Madelaine.

'Do be careful.' Connie looked at Alex who smiled in return.

At the house, Alex pointed the way to Ginger. 'The summer house is over there. I'll go in and get blankets, cushions and things.'

The two men made numerous trips, bringing back food, a primus stove and a bottle of brandy. They had just settled down, with drinks in their hands and blankets over their knees when headlights appeared in the driveway. A small khaki-painted van came up the drive. It pulled up alongside and a head appeared through the window. A cheery voice asked, 'Where is the blighter then?'

'I'll show you,' said Alex.

'Thanks, cock. Just tell us. It'll be bleeding safer.'

'It'll be easier to show you,' said Alex. 'Incidentally, let me introduce you to my uncle. This is Colonel Sir David Griffiths.'

The man's jaw dropped and the smile left his face. 'Sorry, sir. I had no idea.'

'That's all right,' said David. 'Just do your job. Follow Flying Officer Griffiths and he'll show you the way. What's your name?'

'Sergeant Bacon, sir. And this is Lance Corporal O'Toole.'

A vague outline on the other side of the van nodded.

'Follow me.' Alex led the way and the van went after him, across the lawn to the side of the house.

When they were about fifty yards away Alex stopped and pointed. The two engineers climbed out of the van and gently closed the doors.

'We'll take it from here, sir,' Bacon said in a quiet voice.

'Tell me, sergeant, how likely is the thing to go off?'

'We can't say. The swine are getting cleverer. It could be a dud or it could have a delay clock in it. Or it could be the mechanism is jammed and the slightest thing could set it off.'

'Such as?' Alex asked in a whisper, following the example of the sergeant.

'Noise, or a jar. Stay here, please, sir, while we take a look.'

The two engineers walked quietly away. Alex stood waiting, his imagination working overtime. The slightest thing could set the damn bomb off! He took a few paces back. After what seemed an eternity the two engineers returned.

'It's a thousand-pounder, all right, and it's sitting over a hole. Could that be the basement?' asked Bacon.

'Probably. What now?' Alex asked.

The answer was a complete surprise. 'We wait.'

'What on earth for?'

'The delay clocks are only good for a maximum of twelve hours. We wait for twelve hours after the bomb was dropped. Which was when, precisely?'

'I'd say give it until ten ack emma.'

'Right. It'll also be daylight and we can see what we're doing. In the meantime, keep everyone away. If it does go off, the whole house will be flattened. We'll be back in the morning.'

With that the two soldiers departed and Alex trudged back to the others to tell them what was happening. The group spent an uncomfortable night, dozing in their deckchairs and blankets. Dawn found them a dishevelled lot, wanting their breakfast. Alex elected to return to the house to find a kettle, tea, bacon and eggs. Ginger helped by bringing out the utensils needed for a makeshift meal.

At 09.30 the army returned. This time there were five of them. Three belonged to the newly named Pioneer Corps as evidenced by their cap badges showing a rifle, shovel and pick, with their motto *Labor Omnia Vincit* – Work conquers all. Their task was to ensure the bomb would not move when the engineers began taking it apart.

Ten o'clock came and went. The soldiers stubbed out their cigarettes and went to work. The group waited in anxious anticipation. Around lunchtime one of the Pioneer Corps soldiers returned.

He saluted David and said, 'Won't be long now, sir and the engineers can start. We're almost finished shoring the bastard up. Beg pardon, ma'am.'

'That's all right,' said Madelaine, 'I have heard the word before.' The nervous young man returned her broad smile. 'Would you like some tea?'

'Oh yes, please, ma'am, that's why I came over, like. We're getting right thirsty up there.'

Connie busied herself with a billycan and infused the tea. She handed cups, sugar and a can of condensed milk to the soldier.

'How long will it take to dismantle?' asked David.

'Depends, sir, on what we find. When the sergeant goes in we'll all come down here and leave him to it. He'll be talking to us on a line, telling the corp every move he makes.'

Madelaine asked, 'Why does he do that?'

The soldier looked uncomfortable for a second before replying. 'In case anything goes wrong, ma'am. He tells the corp *exactly* what he's doing. That way if he makes a wrong move and the thing goes off, well, next time we'll know what not to do.'

Later, four of the soldiers returned, one reeling off a field-telephone cable. The corporal sat in the back of the van, his feet on the ground, a notebook in his hand. Connected to the sergeant by ungainly earphones and speaking tube, he listened intently to what Bacon was telling him, giving the others a highlighted commentary.

'That's the cover off.'

'He's cut the wire to the primary detonator.'

'He's found the delay clock. It's jammed! That's why the wee bugger didn't explode.'

Suddenly he tensed over the telephone. 'Say that again.'

'Right. Got it! Go careful, Fred. There's another mechanism in the bomb, which Fred don't recognise. He's unscrewing it now.'

The explosion was hardly louder than a grenade going off. *Fairweather* was still standing, even the birds were singing in a distance copse. Alex and the other soldiers began running after the corporal, who had ripped off his headphones and was charging towards the house.

The sergeant's arms had been blown off and a piece of shrapnel had pierced his chest, killing him. Corporal O'Toole hung his head, fighting back the tears. 'Bloody bastards,' he screamed.

'What happened?' Alex asked. 'Why didn't the rest of the bomb go off?'

'It couldn't,' the corporal said, bitterness in his voice, 'Fred saw to that. The bit what went up was designed to kill the likes of him and me. The Germans are always trying something new. To get us.'

'What do we do now?' David asked, coming upon the group.

The corporal took a deep breath and said, 'We move the bloody thing. It's safe now.'

'How can you tell?' Alex asked inanely.

'Because, sir, if the bugger didn't go off then it ain't ever going to go.'

The sergeant's mutilated body was wrapped in a blanket and placed in the van. The Pioneers began to remove the innards of the bomb, including the explosives. The task accomplished, they departed, Alex and David waving them goodbye.

'They,' said Susan, 'are amongst the bravest men I know.'

From the house David telephoned Gibbs and told the butler it was safe to return.

Susan and Connie busied themselves in the kitchen, making dinner, while the men went outside to examine the damage and to assess what was needed to put things right. It was a sad end to Alex's and Ginger's weekend pass. They returned to Biggin Hill and settled down to flying – each scramble a desperate attempt to stay alive.

With September came a change of tactics by the *Luftwaffe*. Instead of continuing with their policy of bombing the RAF fighter stations, the Germans switched targets to Greater London.

It had all come about by a fluke, but one that gave the RAF a breather to regroup and rebuild. German bombers had carried out a poorly executed night raid on industrial targets in Rochester and the oil tank farm at Thameshaven. Two of the bombers over-flew their targets and jettisoned their bombs over London, killing nine civilians and injuring others. In retaliation, the infuriated Prime Minister ordered Bomber Command to attack Berlin over the following nights.

Although the attacks were largely ineffective, they caused

Reichsmarshall Herman Göring to take personal control of an assault on London. On the 7th September, three hundred and forty-eight bombers, protected by six hundred and seventeen fighters, attacked London. Every plane that could be scrambled took to the air. There was nothing left in reserve.

Alex was now leading two flights of six planes. Ginger was his wing. As they gained height to get above the incoming formations, other aircraft joined up with them until they made a squadron of twelve. London's East End was taking a pounding when the cry of "Tally-ho" went up and their planes dived into the fray. Within minutes it was every man for himself.

Alex dived down at a Dornier, guns blazing, using short bursts. He saw his bullets strike the wing of the plane, missing an engine by inches. As the enemy turned in a desperate attempt to lose Alex he followed, lining up his sights to fire at the pilot. Before continuing with his attack he followed the golden rule of survival and looked over his left shoulder. All clear. Then his right. He was in time to see an Me109 flash across the sky and turn onto his tail.

Forgetting the bomber, Alex pulled the stick back hard and turned in a tight, vertical circle. He knew the Messerschmitt couldn't follow, although the German did his best, letting off a few bursts of machine gun bullets at Alex's Spit. The Me109 pilot gave up after a few seconds and dived after easier, unsuspecting prey.

Alex let out a long sigh of relief, found another target, and swooped on his prey. He watched as bombs dropped from the belly of a Junkers Ju88. The German was concentrating on the task in hand, not looking behind him.

Alex checked there was no one on his tail, above or below, and pressed on with his attack. A stream of bullets battered the Junkers' port engine and almost immediately it burst into flame, black smoke pouring from the cowling.

The bomber dived away and Alex altered his angle of attack for one more quick burst before he would need to go round again. Even as he did so a second Spit came up from below, firing at the Ju88. Alex didn't see where the bullets struck but the plane deepened its dive and headed down towards the ground. Alex didn't wait to see where it crashed. Realising the fight had taken him to the north east of London, he turned east, back towards the fray.

There were confused yells over the R/T which Alex half ignored. 'Look out! 109s at nine o'clock high.' Alex looked up in time to see dozens of them half roll and commence their attack. Christ, thought Alex, is there no end to the bastards?

He decided on his target. A 109 was fixed on the tail of a Hurricane and giving the British pilot a hard time. The Hurricane desperately dived and jinked, trying to lose the German fighter. Alex came up under the German, aiming at the 109's underbelly. Pilots of fighter planes are not gentlemen, he remembered an instructor telling him. They are aerial assassins.

He could clearly see the rivulets of oil along the enemy's fuselage, cast a quick glance around the sky to ensure *he* wasn't a target, and opened fire. The De Wilde ammunition streaked across the sky. The noise in the cockpit was horrendous, like a jack hammer, thundering away. His Spit was now less than a hundred yards away and closing fast. Alex had the satisfaction of seeing his bullets tearing into the 109, causing the pilot to break off his own attack and dive to escape. Out of the corner of his eye Alex saw the Hurricane burst into flame and hoped the pilot would manage to get out. He concentrated on the task in hand.

Lining his sights up on the German he fired again. The 109 burst into flame and Alex, realising he was now too close, pulled hard on the stick, half-rolling to port to miss the burning Messerschmitt. His wing tip missed the tail of the other plane by inches as Alex jinked left and right, not flying a straight line for more than a few seconds.

It was just as well. A stream of bullets passed ahead of his Spit as, from below, an Me109 suddenly appeared in his sights. He had time for a quick burst but missed. He turned away, his mouth dry, his palms sweaty. That had been a close call! *Wake up Griffiths*, he told himself, *or you'll wake up dead!*

Things were thinning out and the sky appeared empty. He searched in vain as he flew over Tilbury, the dock area a blazing mass of fires and black smoke. Movement caught his eye and he turned to port, looking down. There! Going like a bat out of hell for the coast was a Dornier III. Alex's only thought was to get the murdering swine.

A quick glance around the sky showed he was alone apart from the target. A short roll and into a dive and the Spit went down like an avenging angel. Alex could see thin, dark grey smoke coming from the plane's exhausts as the pilot over-boosted his engines in an attempt to escape.

Sheerness was ahead and flack opened up, aimed at the German. The plane continued turning, left, right, never steady for more than a few seconds. Alex caught up with the bomber fast, with plenty of height.

Lining up for a quarter attack, Alex anticipated the German's next jink to starboard. Return fire from the rear gunner was coming close when Alex, allowing for deflection, began shooting. He kept up a long, steady burst, the bullets stitching along the fuselage and across the starboard wing. Then holes appeared in Alex's port wing and he flung his plane hard to starboard in a half roll, pulling back hard on the stick, sending the plane in a steep climb. He continued round, repositioning the Spit for another attack.

Ignoring the return fire he came in again on the quarter and again began firing short, sharp bursts, hitting the fuselage once more. The aspect of the target changed and Alex found himself directly astern of the Dornier. Abruptly the firing from the other plane ceased and as he flew closer Alex saw that the rear-gunner's window had been shot away. The gunner was either dead or wounded.

The chase had Alex totally focused on the target. By now the smoke from the starboard engine was thick and black and the nose of the Dornier had drooped. He moved his sights and fired again at the fuselage, using short sharp bursts. He could see where the bullets struck. He changed his aim, going for the port engine. The bullets, in one sustained burst, marched across the wing and smashed into the port cowling. A thin wisp of grey smoke appeared between the engine and the fuselage. It looked good. Alex stopped shooting and watched as the bomber banked to starboard. The plane was losing height, the starboard engine still burning. Alex throttled back to look closer and saw a German jump out of the plane and a parachute open. One bloody son-of-a-Hun who wouldn't be returning to the Fatherland, thought Alex.

Alex slowed further and let the bomber ease forward. There were no other parachutes and he saw that the plane's nose was lifting again and it was turning back towards the coast. Alex's eyes turned to slits and anger coursed through him. *No you don't, you swine.* Checking the deflection of the sights, he lined up on the cockpit and opened fire, pressing the button hard, feeling the plane judder, the noise like a cacophony of drums in his ears. He saw his bullets smash the glass of the cockpit and the plane go nose down again. Abruptly the firing ceased and he looked at his hand in bewilderment. He pressed again. Sod it, he was out of ammunition. As the thought took hold he felt his plane juddering and he looked out to port in bewilderment. Holes appeared along his wing. He cursed himself. Of all the damn fools! He'd behaved like a beginner, forgetting the cardinal rule of all fighter pilots – *never stop looking for the enemy.*

Alex saw the red streaks flashing past the cockpit as he instinctively turned away. The smell of phosphorus came to him as explosions occurred behind and the plane rocked.

Was this how he would die?

18

ONCE YOU WERE pounced the odds became stacked against you. If he were to survive the next few minutes he would have to fly like he'd never flown before.

He looked over his shoulder and saw an Me109 right on his tail, less than fifty yards away. Even as he looked he saw the flashes of grey smoke from his cannons and felt the hits somewhere in the fuselage. Out of ammo and pounced out of a blue and clear sky! What a stupid, bloody, *bloody* way to die! He turned the Spitfire as tightly as possible. The Me109 tucked in behind him and followed him round, letting loose with a few short bursts every few seconds. Round and round the two planes went, Alex tightening the turn as much as possible. He thanked God that whatever damage had been done hadn't affected the controls. He pulled the turn even tighter and glanced at the gauges.

Oil pressure was okay at 75lbs. Glycol temperature was high at 108 degrees Fahrenheit and the oil temperature was creeping up too. The Merlin engine was beginning to rebel. It was too bad, he had no choice. He tried tightening the turn yet again, even as his eyesight began to darken around the edges. He guessed he was pulling over six Gs. Maybe closer to seven. Not now, he thought, yelling, fighting back the desire to close his eyes and let events take their course. He held the blackness at bay for a few seconds longer.

The Spitfire juddered, a high-speed stall only seconds away. Alex knew that a good pilot could hold the Spit on the judder, out-flying any other plane in the sky. His head felt too heavy to turn to look over his shoulder and he concentrated on holding the plane just as she was. Sweat poured from him, as he managed to move his head far enough to look for the 109. There it was, still on his tail, still firing . . . but missing!

The two continued circling. Alex knew he couldn't stop. If he did he would be dead. He leant forward to ease the G force as his vision began to tunnel once more. He focused on the two advantages he had. The Spit could turn inside a 109 so, as long as they continued, the German couldn't fire on him. And more importantly, the Hun was on the wrong side of the Channel. He would be getting short of fuel soon.

The other plane was so close that Alex could see peeling paint around the black cross on the port wing. He couldn't be sure but he thought the 109 flickered for a few seconds and he smiled grimly to himself. No chance. The Hun was flying the plane on its limits and had no chance of getting closer. The Spitfire gained slowly as the Me109 flickered again and the German was forced to ease the turn to prevent a high-speed stall. *Damn*, thought Alex, *the bastard is bloody good.*

Sweat was pouring into Alex's eyes and he blinked them to clear his sight. The 109 pilot suddenly pulled up out of his turn and tried to gain height on the Spitfire, flying into an almost vertical turn. Alex watched him intently. It was almost time to make his break. By now Alex was further behind him and as the other plane reached the apex of its circle Alex made his move.

He pushed the stick over and rolled the plane onto its back. He centred the stick, took off the bank and pulled through hard, in a half roll. Throttling open he pushed the Spit into a vertical dive. As the earth sped up at him he put the stick over again and he turned the ailerons down to the deck. Each part of the manoeuvre was executed automatically. He was operating on pure instinct, knowing what was needed to survive.

If the Hun had been quick enough to follow and was on his tail then so be it. The die was cast and there was nothing more Alex could do except pray.

His speed was building up at a tremendous rate and the stick forces were increasing alarmingly. The ailerons were getting as heavy as dammit and it was taking brute strength to hold the Spit as she was. Alex glanced at the altimeter and was appalled to see that the plane was passing through 6,500ft. The air space had gone in an instant. Inside the cockpit the noise was overwhelming and he had to swallow and yell to clear the pressure building up on his ears. He eased off the bank and stopped the turn, using the trimmer carefully. He throttled back, bleeding off the speed, praying the plane could continue to meet the terrible stresses he had imposed for a while longer.

Frantically he looked around the sky. It was empty. Nothing behind, and a quick roll showed nothing underneath. He'd made it! He guessed the German had been low on fuel and had scarpered back to France.

Down at ground level he continued flying fast, never staying on a straight heading for more than a second or two. He was exhausted. A combination of the adrenaline and the terrifying stress had taken its toll. Looking around the outside of the plane he could see a sodding big hole in the middle of his starboard wing and a peppering of smaller ones all over the aircraft. He shuddered. Christ but that had been close!

He was below the level of the treetops, determined not to be pounced again. Any plane screaming down out of the sky to attack him would be committing suicide, flying into the ground even if Alex was shot down. He checked the revs, 2,740. A bit high. He throttled back again to plus 4 boost. The compass was swinging erratically, albeit around 225 degrees. The big question was, now that he looked like living a bit longer, where the hell was he?

The ground ahead rose gently and the Spit flew between two woods, about half a mile apart. A church steeple appeared ahead and he increased height by about fifty feet. It was no longer any use to drop low enough to read town and village names. They'd been removed by order of the War Office to prevent any invading army from knowing where it was.

A village appeared and people stopped, looked at him and waved. He was too tired even to waggle his wings. He scanned the landscape for a clue to his whereabouts.

A main road! He could see the white line down the middle. Working on the premise that all roads led to Rome, only in this case to London, he turned gently right and followed it. He flew over another village, larger than the last one. A quick glance at the gauges showed that the Merlin was behaving itself, operating within its limits. Scanning the sky he could see nothing and he took the plane up to 500ft. He took the boost back to zero and the revs down to 2,000. The Merlin ran as smooth as silk and Alex was able to relax a little and concentrate on his navigation. There was not another plane in the sky except for a few smoke trails well over twenty or twenty-five thousand feet. Checking the fuel, he frowned. He had less than fifteen gallons left.

Finally he saw a hillock to his left and smiled with relief. Alex turned ten degrees to port. Almost immediately he could see planes circling, waiting to land at the Hill. He entered the circuit and called control.

'Sapper, this is White 2, I need to come straight in.'

'Good to have you with us, Homer White 2. Roger. You are cleared to land. All other aircraft continue in the circuit.'

Nobody was going to argue. They all knew that if Alex needed in then there was a very good reason. He took his speed down to 170mph, checked the wheels were down and the green light was on the panel. The pitch was fully fine and he turned crosswind on finals. As he put his flaps down the plane shed speed rapidly to 90mph. He opened the hood as he crossed the hedge at the end of the field and eased the stick back a touch. Closing the throttle, the plane dropped and was at the point of stalling. The aircraft sank lower, the wheels touched and momentum dropped off rapidly. He taxied across the field, out of the way of the other aircraft, which were landing right behind him. Undoing his oxygen mask, Alex let the slight breeze cool his face as he approached his usual dispersal point.

The plane landing right behind him came up on his port side and the pilot waved. Alex waved back, a grin on his face. Ginger had made it, thank God.

With his aircraft shot to pieces, the consensus of opinion amongst the other pilots was that Alex was damned lucky to be alive. Alex agreed. That night in the mess he drank far too much beer in celebration.

Because of the state of his aircraft, Alex was unable to fly for the next few days. Instead he helped out in various duties. He worked with the Intelligence Officer, Gavin Edge, debriefing the pilots when they landed, sorting out the wheat from the chaff when it came to pilots' kill claims. He also manned the R/T, vectoring in planes from information passed from HQ. Although he knew it was useful work, he hated it and champed at the bit to be flying again. In many ways waiting for his fellow pilots to make it home was harder than being up there with them.

Several days after his close escape he and Ginger were standing at the NAAFI van, drinking hot, sweet tea, watching the skies. Ginger had been on two sorties that morning before being finally stood down. Their eyes restlessly searched the horizon.

'Who's missing still?' Ginger asked.

'Mark and Algernon.'

'Bugger. Bugger, bugger, bugger,' said Ginger, then for emphasis, 'Bugger. Algie's due to go north any day now.'

There was no need to elaborate. Going north meant going to a training squadron to prepare pilots for the real business of flying fighters against the enemy. The only risk you ran there was from a bullet fired by an over-excited pupil. Alex thought back to his conversation with the older pilot – he had hardly been able to control his relief. 'He said his wife was absolutely delighted to be getting away from here.' He sighed. 'They just found out she's having a baby.'

'Christ, he's just got to get back. He has to!' Ginger's anguish reflected Alex's feelings. So many of their friends had died. The statistics were unbearable. If you stayed in a front-line squadron long enough you died. It was inevitable. Nobody was born with sufficient luck to escape the statistics. A training squadron or promotion out of the front-line were the only escape routes. Algie had been lucky to get the chance – it seemed unthinkable that fate would be so cruel.

They stayed there watching the sky in vain, each plunged into his own gloomy thoughts. After a while Alex said, 'Let's go to Control. They may have heard something.'

In the control hut they found squadron leader Wakefield pacing the floor. It was a routine he followed after every scramble – three steps, turn around, a glance at the wall clock and then at the R/T operator, who shook his head before the pacing continued.

'Any word, sir?' Alex asked.

'Some. We know they are both down. One parachute. We don't know whose yet.'

Neither Alex nor Ginger said a word, but they both prayed it was Algie's. Mark Braidwood was newly arrived from Canada. A pleasant fellow and competent pilot, but an unknown. He hadn't had time to make friends in the way Algie had. Besides, he was unmarried. All the squadron liked Algie's wife, Muriel.

The phone rang. Wakefield swept up the receiver. 'Hullo. Hercules Squadron.' He listened for a few moments. 'Right. Thanks.' Replacing the receiver he said, 'We're stood down until the dawn patrol.'

They turned to leave and the phone rang again, jangling their fraught nerves. The Squadron Leader put the receiver to his ear, identified himself and thanked the caller. Alex and Ginger had paused in the door, searching their senior officer's bleak face.

'Mark Braidwood jumped clear. He's all right.'

'Algie?' Alex asked.

Wakefield shook his head. 'Braidwood saw him jump. His 'chute candled. His body's been found. They're bringing it back now.'

'Christ,' said Alex, 'who's going to tell Muriel?'

Wakefield tapped his chest. 'Goes with the stripes. I'll see her as soon as I can.'

'She's at home. Probably packing right now. They were planning to go in the next few days.' Alex felt the tears in his eyes.

Wakefield nodded. 'They were to come to the mess tonight for a few drinks and a bite to eat. A farewell after all the treats she's made us.' He sighed heavily. 'I'd better get over there straight away. I'll take the chaplain with me.'

Alex and Ginger walked out in silence. Halfway to the mess, Alex said, 'I wouldn't want his job for anything.'

'I'm not going to get married,' Ginger suddenly announced, 'not until this lot is over. It's not fair on the woman.'

'I reckon you're right there,' said Alex, thoughts of Connie intruding on his grief. 'I don't know about you, but I need a very large drink.'

Pilots flying the next day were normally only allowed beer. The rule was changed that night. The first whisky was raised in salute to their dead comrade. The rest were consumed for their effect. Wakefield made an appearance an hour later, his expression grim. Nobody asked him how it had gone. It was plain to see.

'G and T, a large one,' he told the mess man. He drank it in one long swallow and placed the glass on the bar.

'Another, sir?'

'Please. Keep my glass topped up, there's a good fellow.'

A few drinks later and the mood changed. So many friends and colleagues had died and even in their going there was a sense of pride within the squadron. Each scramble meant a confrontation with mortality. Each time a man climbed into his plane he consented to die, for his country, his values and beliefs. Knowing that helped, or so they told themselves. Helped in some ways, but not in others. Algie had been a regular officer and had served in the RAF for nearly ten years. He had been due his half stripe in six months, followed closely by his own squadron. Some deaths hit harder than others.

Someone started tinkling the piano's keys and soon a singsong began. Smiles and laughter followed, though both were subdued and strained. Alex knew it was the mess's way of trying to cope. Brooding did no good. It destroyed morale and sapped their fighting spirit. They were warriors. If they were defeated then Britain was lost. Without air cover nothing could stop the Germans from invading and they all knew it. The responsibility weighed heavily that night.

Alex staggered to his bed, bleary eyed and bouncing off the corridor's walls. He flopped down onto his bed and passed out. A hand shaking his shoulder brought him round. To Alex it seemed like only ten minutes later. Dawn was breaking. Washing and dressing, he felt like hell. He was in no condition to fly.

Wakefield was in the mess and after one look at Alex said, 'You're stood down for today. I'll make an exception just this once. I know Algie's death hit you hard. But young Griffiths, don't make a habit of it.'

Regular patrols were followed by mad scrambles. Some flights were boring, others were heart-stoppingly terrifying. Day by day he thanked God when he woke to a new morning.

Autumn brought no respite except for the airfields. The switch from attacking the RAF to attacking the cities was almost complete and gave Britain a chance to rebuild her squadrons.

Franklin D. Roosevelt won a third term as President of the USA, having pledged that there was no plan to go to war under any circumstances. Then Neville Chamberlain died of cancer, aged seventy-one. No one in the mess mourned his passing, all of them remembering Munich and his "peace in our time" statement.

'Thank God for Winnie,' someone shouted and glasses were raised to the health of the Prime Minister.

At the end of November there came a hiatus in the air war over Southern England. The squadrons gave sighs of relief as fewer interceptions occurred and on the night of 30th November a miracle happened in London. There were no air raids. People looked at each other in wonderment and asked what was happening. It didn't take long to find out. Goering had changed his tactics. His bombers were tasked with the obliteration of the industrial heart of Britain and began to attack the provincial towns and cities. Coventry was blitzed with 600 tons of high explosives and thousands of incendiaries, devastating a vast area and killing many thousands.

Next Birmingham, Manchester, Sheffield and Glasgow were given the same treatment. Every night four hundred plus bombers attacked the shores of Britain, indiscriminately killing men, women and children. The Luftwaffe returned to London after a short respite but on a reduced scale. Churchill, in the House of Commons, announced that civilian deaths from bombing had fallen from 6,000 per week to 3,000. He went on to say that it was taking "a ton of bombs to kill three-quarters of a person."

'That's lucky,' said Ginger as they listened to the wireless in the mess, 'that leaves a quarter to keep fighting. I wonder which quarter?'

'Idiot,' hissed Alex with a grin, 'shut up and listen to Winnie.'

Buckingham Palace had six bombs dropped on it, one of which destroyed the Chapel. A defiant speech from the King brought a cheer from the proud people of England, Scotland and Wales.

For the squadrons the short respite of reduced duties was very welcome but the action flared up again with a passion. Alex downed an Me110 over the Channel and scored numerous hits without an actual kill, though he did share two. His own plane was shot up on three separate occasions, though he managed to return to Biggin Hill each time. The question of Christmas leave was coming up and straws were being drawn for those who wanted to go home. Priority was given to those men who were married. By some miracle, both Alex and Ginger's names were drawn and they were told they could have a week's leave, covering Christmas, to return by 29th December.

Ginger was returning to Leicester, eager to see his elderly parents, until the morning the CO sent for him. When he returned to the mess he was white-faced. Facing death on a daily basis they should have been prepared for the precariousness of other peoples lives. But Ginger's words shocked Alex to the core.

'My parents. A direct hit. Both dead.' Ginger lost his battle with the tears he had been willing not to fall. 'Damn! Why didn't I go home last time?'

'Dolman,' Alex spoke to the mess man, 'a large brandy for Mr Robarts and put it on my bill, please.' A few seconds later Alex thrust the glass into his friend's hands, 'Here, take this.'

Ginger gulped his drink. 'I told them to go to Mum's sister in Yorkshire, but no! Dad wouldn't leave his blasted allotment. He was an obstinate old sod. Fought in the first lot, at the Somme. He was the one who convinced me to join the RAF rather than the army. Proud as punch they both were when I became a pilot officer.' Taking another swig he choked on the drink. 'Damn! I hate the bloody Germans.

Bastards.' He blinked rapidly, his eyes threatening tears. 'Excuse me, Alex, I'm stood down for today.' Alex watched his friend leave, knowing there was nothing he could say and precious little he could do, apart from being there for him. Time was the healer.

In the second week of December the pilots were sitting around a blazing fire in the dispersal hut. From the turntable of an old gramophone player came the scratchy tune and lyrics of that year's hit song, *Whispering Grass*. Nobody paid any attention, especially Alex who was still resolutely trying to put Connie out of his mind. She was a distraction he could do without. Blue cigarette smoke filled the stuffy room and Alex thought yet again about taking up the habit.

The phone rang and the telephone orderly answered it. The pilots watched in anticipation. 'Sir, ops want us airborne by 14.45. A patrol line at 18,000ft over Ashford and down to Folkestone.'

'Thank you,' said Wakefield, 'tell the flight sergeant.' Looking at his watch the Squadron Leader said, 'Right, lads, it's now one minute to twenty past. Press tits at 14.35. Any questions?'

There were none.

Alex went out to his aircraft and strapped in. He ran through his checks and waited for the signal to start. The weather was fine, high cloud cover above 25,000ft, no precipitation expected.

Twelve Merlin engines roared into life at the same time, making a spectacular din. The planes taxied out and lined up for take-off.

'Okay, Hercules, let's go,' Wakefield said over the R/T.

As one the planes rolled forward, across the turf and into the air. In spite of himself Alex couldn't help feeling a surge of pride. Sunset was at 15.51 and already the sun's rays were bouncing off the underside of the dark clouds high above. The Spits manoeuvred into battle formation and headed south east towards Ashford.

'Sapper, this is Hercules, is there anything happening anywhere?'

'Negative, Hercules. The board is clear right now. There's bad weather over Germany so it may be keeping the Hun at home.'

'Let's hope it stays that way,' said Hugo Wakefield. 'Keep your eyes peeled, lads, I don't trust the Germans an inch.'

As the minutes passed the sun sank lower and it looked like the passing of a peaceful day. Alex's mind was wandering, enjoying the incredible beauty of the setting sun and the changes of colour contrasting between the earth and the clouds. Glancing down again he saw a glint of light but thought nothing of it for a few seconds.

By now the sun was touching the horizon and the land was in deep shadow. There was the glint again. Odd, he thought.

The sun's rays were just showing and they were at 18,000ft. So there was no sun down at ground level. Impossible. It meant only one thing. Aircraft.

Craning his neck he looked again. Nothing. Yes! There it was, another flash but longer, more obvious. Was it the sun reflecting off the Perspex windows of an aircraft? Tensing and leaning forward Alex stared down. He saw it! An aircraft.

Excitedly he used the R/T. 'Hercules Leader this is Blue One. Aircraft below, at eight o'clock. Heading towards the coast.'

After a few seconds Wakefield called back, 'Blue One, are you sure? I can't see anything.'

'Pretty much. I saw a flash and now I'm pretty certain I can see the plane. And another one! Now at nine o'clock. It's an Me110. Twin rudder and fins. No doubt.'

After a few seconds Wakefield said, 'Well done Blue One, I've got them.'

'Sapper, Hercules Leader, tally-ho.'

'Hercules, how many?'

'Fourteen, I think. All 110s.'

'Good luck, Hercules.'

'Right, Hercules, stand by to go in twenty seconds. Hold it! Hold it. Echelon port . . . Now!'

The Spits were perfectly lined up. Alex felt the blood lust rising in him and thought of Ginger and his parents. Cold anger surged through his veins. *This is where I earn my fourteen shillings a day.*

The Huns were at about 11,000ft, stooging across Britain's countryside as though they owned the place. Alex, like the remainder of the squadron, cast anxious looks above and behind. Was this some sort of trap? If not, what in hell were the Germans thinking about?

'Standby, Hercules,' said Leader. 'Let's go.'

The squadron got into position behind the Me110s, incredulous at their good fortune. Alex picked a target, realised he was closing too fast and throttled back, staying in the formation, each pilot watching Leader. The 110 was now in his sights and growing bigger all the time.

'Steady . . . Steady . . . Now!' Wakefield gave the order.

A dozen Spitfires opened up at the same time, each hitting their target. Alex relished the noise, vibration and recoil, seeing his bullets smashing into the 110 near the tail and then working along the fuselage and into the cockpit. Black smoke poured out and the plane dropped into a dive. Alex hauled back on his stick to regain height, half-rolled to port and followed after the Me110. Messerschmitts were dropping from the sky. Others, with smoke pouring from them, were jinking like mad and diving for the ground with a Spit on their tail.

Alex caught up with his target around 6,000ft and sent another long burst into the fuselage. He watched as the fuselage broke off just in front of the tail assembly and the plane plummeted to earth. With his blood up, Alex turned towards a fleeing Me110 he had seen out of the corner of his eye.

Two unattacked planes were fleeing for their lives. Wakefield was chasing one, Alex the other. The Germans were crossing the coast as the Spits, on full boost, got within firing range. Alex let loose a quick burst but missed. Still with a height advantage he poured on the speed. Another short burst and this time he clipped the tail of the 110.

A quick glance at his gauges showed everything was all right, with plenty of fuel for at least another ten minutes of hard flying. Closer now, closer. He was concentrating on the target so much that he missed the mushrooming explosions around the German plane until the second salvo. With a jolt he saw flame erupt from the bottom of his target. Steaming down Channel, in line ahead, was a small flotilla of destroyers. They were firing with everything they had and giving the Me110 a hard time of it. The German tried gaining height, lifting the belly of the plane. A shell exploded inside the cockpit, killing the pilot and the plane plunged down towards the sea. Alex's joy was short-lived, as he suddenly became aware of shells exploding around his own aircraft.

The stupid bastards were firing at him! *Stop it*, he screamed at them, as his Spit rocked from a near miss. In the distance he saw another explosion and wondered who had been hit.

19

He turned into a dive and went down for the sea, hoping the dark would hide him. More by luck than judgement he pulled up at 100ft and streaked back towards the white cliffs of Kent. As he flew he was cursing the Royal Navy and their stupidity for all he was worth. He had very nearly bought it. Killed by his own side! The bloody fools. It wouldn't be the first time, or the last.

He could see the white glow of the chalk cliffs and began to climb. His left leg was shaking and he kneaded it with the knuckles of his left hand. Reaction was setting in. From killer to killed in a matter of seconds, that was all it took.

Faintly he heard the message over his R/T, 'All Hercules aircraft, this is Sapper, pancake, pancake. Well done, all of you.'

As his plane passed through 9,000ft the dark turned to a pearly grey and a red thin line appeared on the horizon to Alex's left.

'Hercules aircraft.' The R/T came across stronger now he'd gained more height. 'Pancake, pancake. Let's be having you lads.'

There was silence and then Sapper said, 'Got you, Green Two. Come on in. Who's left out there?'

'Sapper, this is Blue One.'

'I hear you, Blue One. Faint but clear. Transmit so I can get a bearing and I'll vector you back.'

'The boy stood on the burning deck, the silly ass,' Alex declaimed.

'Got you, Blue One. Vector two nine five.'

'Wilco, Sapper.'

'Well done, Blue One. Beer and party when you get back. The bar is confirmed open.'

Grinning, Alex looked out to starboard and saw a flash of lightning streak across the sky. Its power and beauty were awesome. Feeling very small and humble in his aircraft he flew towards Biggin

Hill. As ever, he wondered what the score had been. He had one definite kill. How many more Huns had been shot down?

In a good mood he landed and taxied to dispersal. His fitter and rigger met him and took over the plane while he went for his debrief. In a jolly voice he strolled in and asked, 'How did we do?'

The gloomy silence that greeted his words said enough.

'What's up?'

'Hugo Wakefield's not answering his R/T,' said Flying Officer Edge, the Intelligence Officer.

The smile and blood drained from Alex's face. 'I saw him. We chased two of the Huns out . . . Oh, my God.'

'What is it?' Edge asked.

'We followed the two Germans and chased them into the arms of some of our destroyers. The 110s were low and the one I was chasing was blown out of the sky. They began firing at me and I only just managed to avoid being hit.' He remembered the explosion he'd seen. 'Another plane exploded about a mile from me. I thought it was the other Hun, but it could have been Hugo.'

'Damn!' Edge reached for the telephone and rang the base Commanding Officer, Group Captain Fox. Quickly explaining the situation he replaced the receiver. 'He's alerting the navy now. They can look for him. Right, let's get on with the debrief.'

In a subdued mood the pilots drifted away to the mess. Alex shook his head in bewilderment. His emotions were careering out of control. From the high excitement of shooting down an enemy plane, to the low of barely escaping with his life, the joy of his return followed by the news of Hugo's uncertain fate – his senses and emotions were left reeling.

They waited for the call. When it came their worst fears were confirmed. Hugo Wakefield had, against all odds, survived his plane exploding and had parachuted into the sea. There, supported by his Mae West, his only injury a bruised shoulder, Squadron Leader Wakefield had died of hypothermia.

Alex's first pint of ale barely touched the sides.

A week later the King visited Biggin Hill, to present personally the medals recommended by Wakefield. Among the pilots honoured was Alex. It was an odd ceremony. The men were lined up in their best uniforms and inspected by King George with all the rich pageantry that Britain was so renowned for. At the same time the base was on high alert in case they were called on to scramble and so there was an added tension to the solemn occasion. In due course, along with seven other pilots, Alex's name was called and he stepped forward, saluted and received his honour – a silver cross with horizontal violet and white stripes. The Distinguished Flying Cross was given for acts of valour, courage or devotion to duty performed while in active operations against the enemy. It was a proud moment he shared with his comrades. He wished his parents and Connie could have been there too.

It was a red-letter week for Alex. He received his second stripe and was promoted to flight lieutenant. This was another excuse for a party and drinking too much beer. In the middle of the festivities, Squadron Leader James Cutler, Wakefield's replacement, arrived. The rumour mill said he had joined the RAF in 1924 and had been earmarked for high command. But something had gone wrong apparently – indeed he would have been out of the service if the war hadn't come along and given him another chance. Speculation was rife. Alex took an instinctive dislike to the man, with his pinched mouth and Brylcreamed hair. Knowing how difficult it would be for anyone to fill Wakefield's shoes, he decided to give him a chance.

The war in the air continued, the strain showing as men and machines continued to be blown out of the sky. Alex had never been so glad to see Christmas. After much badgering, Ginger had agreed to go to Sion's place in Wales for the holiday. Early on Sunday morning, the 22nd of December, the two pilots stood at the window of the mess, watching a few intermittent snow-flurries sweep the airfield.

'Shouldn't we get going?' Ginger asked. 'It's a long drive.'

Alex grinned at him. 'Who said anything about driving? Hark!' Raising a finger he pointed skywards. 'That's our taxi, if I'm not very much mistaken.'

A head appeared around the door and an orderly said, 'Plane coming in. Visitors it looks like.'

They watched a twin-engined Griffin V land on the turf and taxi across the field. There was no mistaking Susan's tumble of raven curls when she climbed down from the plane and took off her helmet.

Before they could save her, Susan was dragged off to the mess for coffee and was surrounded by pilots who wanted to get to know her better. After about fifteen minutes Alex thought it was time to rescue his cousin and stepped in.

'Lads, you've all met Susan and now it's time for her to go.'

'What do you mean, time to go?' Mark Braidwood protested. 'And besides, what's it to do with you, Griffiths?'

Alex grinned. 'Susan is my cousin. And she's taking Ginger and me away from all this for Christmas.'

'What!' Gavin Edge looked from Susan to Alex.

Susan nodded. 'It's true, though I try not to brag about it too much.'

'More likely it's because of the shame of having Alex in your family,' said Braidwood, turning his attention to Alex. 'You have this angel in your family and kept her to yourself? That's an outrage, Griffiths.'

Susan laughed before tucking her arms through Alex's and Ginger's. She led them away, leaving a stunned silence behind them.

A short while later they were airborne. 'We're going to *Fairweather* to pick up Uncle David and the rest of the gang. It's to be a big gathering this year. As Madelaine says, we may not all be together next year.' She didn't voice what they were all thinking. They may not all be *alive* next year.

Though most of the Griffin Vs had been modified as bombers, some were still configured to carry passengers, including the plane they were in. The only concession to the war was that the plane was now armed. In minutes they were landing at *Fairweather*, where the party was waiting to depart. They didn't even wait for more fuel but turned round and left immediately. As Alex made sure that David and Madelaine were settled he turned to see Connie securing a squirming John Phillipe on the seat next to her. This left him a seat next to Richard, now fifteen years old and champing at the bit more than ever to fight for his country.

Ginger had somehow contrived to sit in the co-pilot's seat alongside Susan, while the remainder were in the main cabin. As the plane taxied for take-off, Susan glanced over her shoulder and called, 'Keep a sharp look out. Quarter the sky and if you see anything yell out. I'm going to stay at around 2,000ft and go like a bat out of hell. Flying time will be about half an hour.'

Levelling off the aircraft she turned to Ginger, 'Do you want to fly?'

He nodded. 'Thanks. I'll give it a go.'

'Okay. You have the plane.'

Ginger took the controls and flexed his fingers around the stick.

'Come left five degrees,' said Susan, looking up from an air map and staring out the Perspex canopy. 'Once we pass Southampton we'll head for Salisbury and leave it on our right. You okay back there?' She looked over her shoulder.

In the cabin the others were looking out of the small round windows, religiously combing the skies.

'We're fine,' said Alex. 'I can see a flight of Spits at angels fifteen, almost directly astern. Nothing else in sight.'

'Good. Let's hope it stays that way,' said David.

The afternoon was waning and the sun edging down to the horizon when Cardiff came in sight. A short while later, after a completely uneventful flight, the Griffin landed at St Athan.

There was a festive feel in the air in spite of the horrors facing Britain. Kirsty – ever resourceful – greeted her guests with the statement, 'I've had to replace the dried fruit in the Christmas pudding with carrots but I did manage to save some oranges and lemons.'

'What about the turkey, Mum?' Alex asked.

'We got two. And there's plenty of potatoes and Brussels sprouts.'

'Yuk!' said Alex. 'I hate sprouts.'

'Tough,' said his mother, 'because you're eating them.'

Alex grinned behind Kirsty's back, put his finger to his mouth and simulated vomiting. Ginger grinned at his friend's antics.

'What are those white buildings on the edge of the field we saw as we came in to land?' David wanted to know.

'They're prefabricated houses. An idea I had. I'll show you in the morning.'

'Where's Louise?' asked Alex.

'On duty, I'm afraid,' said his mother. 'She sends her love. She won't escape the hospital until New Year's Eve now.'

'And Paul?'

'On his way. He's been visiting some friends,' Sion answered.

'How's he doing?' Alex turned to Ginger. 'My brother's just gone up to Oxford. His first term. Reading mathematics.'

'Oh, Paul's fine,' said Kirsty. 'He appears to have taken to university life like a duck to water.'

'Good. I hope he knows to make the most of it,' said Alex with all the wisdom of his twenty-three years.

That evening, in front of a roaring log fire, they gathered over pre-dinner drinks. Ginger and Alex were both in uniform. Alex's ribbon, sewn on his left breast, was gleaming against the blue of his tunic.

His father raised a glass in toast. 'Congratulations on the medal, son, and on your second stripe.'

The others joined in the toast, his brother adding, 'Jolly well done, Alex.'

Alex grimaced and replied, 'Thanks, all of you. Just lucky, I guess. Uncle David, you know better than any of us what's going on. What news is there?'

David stood to one side of the fire, a glass of whisky in hand. 'We've recently attacked the Italians near a place called Sidi Barani in the Western Desert and taken over a thousand prisoners. This is the start of the fight back. And the Albanians have smashed the Eyeties – at Koritza in Albania. With the RAF bombing the retreating Italians it should soon turn to a rout.'

'They don't really seem to have the will for a fight,' said Sion.

'They don't,' said David. 'Mussolini made a grave error siding with Germany. Most Italians appear to be against the war.'

The discussion expanded to cover world politics as well as the tactics Britain was employing to defeat the Nazis.

It was Kirsty who asked the important question. 'Will the Americans come and help us?'

David shook his head. 'No. It's highly unlikely. Roosevelt won the election on a promise *not* to go to war. He can't back down now. It'll take a miracle before America joins us. We have to do it ourselves.'

'We have the Empire,' said Madelaine.

'Yes. Thank God,' said David. 'They are pouring aid to us but it's still touch and go. And of course we've got the Free French, the Poles and the others who got out before Germany put a stranglehold on Europe. This will be a war of attrition. Whoever has the most men and raw materials will win.'

'Our problem,' said Sion, 'is the *lack* of raw materials. Everything, from iron ore to coal, is being imported and the amount we're losing due to sunken shipping is horrendous.'

'What's to be done?' Susan asked.

'We need better air cover,' said Alex. 'We're all agreed on that but we don't have the range to be of much use. Besides, how do you locate a submarine and drop bombs on it? It's all so hellish complex.'

'Alex is right,' said David, 'up to a point. It's also a question of attrition. We need more ships that can steam in excess of eighteen knots. That'll mean they can avoid the U-boats and only have to worry about surface raiders. It's then that the RAF will come into its own, bombing the Germans' surface ships. We have far too many tramp steamers ploughing across the ocean at eight or nine knots. If they're detected by the Germans they don't have a chance.'

'What about this deal Churchill has made with Roosevelt?' Madelaine asked.

David grimaced. 'It's a lousy deal. Fifty over-age destroyers, in exchange for British bases in the Atlantic and Caribbean. It's the best the Americans can do as it doesn't need Congressional approval.'

'Anybody for a top up?' Sion asked.

'I'll do it,' said Alex, getting to his feet. 'It's all right, Dad, I know where the booze is kept. Anybody else?'

Glasses were refreshed. Alex's more so than the others. He wondered for a few moments if he was drinking too much and then dismissed the thought. He and other pilots like him were under great strain. A little too much whisky now and again – where was the harm?

Dinner that evening was rabbit stew, shot on the airfield. Kirsty used all her considerable culinary skills to make the meal as enjoyable as possible. Her guests all congratulated her – it was one of the best dinners they'd had since the war began. A lot of wine and port helped the food to go down.

By bedtime Alex was three sheets to the wind and went to his room on unsteady feet.

The following morning, with a cold wind sweeping in from the Bristol Channel, the men went for a walk. Alex to clear a thick head, the others to see Sion's set-up. Two planes were being produced, the Griffin bomber and a fighter. Both were proving very popular with pilots, as they were highly manoeuvrable and comparatively fast. In a far corner they came across a long, low building.

'What's in there?' David asked.

Sion smiled. 'My *pièce de résistance*,' said Sion. 'Remember the problem we had housing staff? This is the solution.'

They went inside. It was a hive of activity.

'What's going on?' Alex yelled above the noise, a pounding in his head beginning to manifest as a headache.

'We call them prefabricated houses,' Sion yelled. 'Let's go outside and I'll explain.'

To Alex's great relief they went out into the comparative quiet of the fresh air.

'Housing here is a huge problem,' Sion began, leading the way back to the house. 'When we first came we managed to beg, steal and borrow enough bricks and stone to build our place and put the offices on the site. However, it was a different story for the work-force. We needed housing and we needed it fast. We had plenty of capacity for drains, water and electricity, but nowhere for people to eat and sleep. So we developed this idea. We tackled the problem just as we would building an aircraft. We designed the complete house, each one identical. Two bedrooms, a kitchen and lounge, bathroom and separate toilet. Come on, I'll show you.'

Sion let the way to a corner of the airfield. Houses had sprouted up like mushrooms. He pointed at an empty concrete base. 'Each house is made of an aluminium frame and asbestos sheets. It has two thousand components, including fitted cupboards and a stainless steel kitchen sink. I admit they're rabbit hutches, but we can put one up in four hours once the base is in. Follow me.'

He led the way inside one of the houses. 'All ready to move into. Those with children have priority, others share. Some of the houses have three men in them, one in each bedroom and the lounge. It's better than a barracks or a dormitory. Of course, a lot of women are here now, replacing the men as they're called up.'

'Pretty neat, Dad,' said Alex. 'I'd have thought other places could use something like this.'

'We've told the Ministries of Works and War but they don't seem interested. Still, you never know, they may come round later. Let's go back to the house.'

Outside the wind had backed and was coming from the north. A biting, bitter cold lay over the airfield, the thin smattering of snow turning to ice. They hurried back to the warmth of the kitchen, to find it full of tantalising smells. A suggestion of a festive drink was quickly taken up and the men retired to Sion's study, which also doubled as his office. Soon they were sipping single malt whisky and the talk turned to the war once again.

After lunch Alex went to bed, pleading tiredness but it was obvious that it had more to do with what he'd had to drink. Sion was becoming concerned about his son's drinking habits. He was imbibing far too often.

Work at the airfield continued right up to Christmas Eve and stopped only for two days. On Christmas day a late breakfast was followed by dinner served at 5pm. It was a boisterous affair, with everyone determined to enjoy the happiness while it lasted. The pudding, flavoured with hoarded currents and carrots, was a great success. To great yells of glee, they each found a silver sixpence in their portions.

After dinner, Alex waylaid Connie as she came out of the kitchen. Pulling a piece of mistletoe from his pocket he put his arm around her waist. 'As it's Christmas?' he asked hopefully and clumsily planted a kiss on her lips.

For a second Connie returned the gesture then pushed him away. He staggered slightly.

'Alex, you're drunk.'

'Just a bit merry,' he slurred. Clumsily he put his arms around her again. 'We don't need bloody mistletoe.' This time he pulled her roughly to him and kissed her hard, forcing his tongue between her lips.

Instead of melting against him, Connie pulled back with a look of horror on her face. 'Don't ever do that again,' she said harshly.

Angry now, Alex grabbed at her again. This time she slapped his face. The shock brought them both to a standstill.

Ruefully, Alex rubbed his cheek. 'I guess I asked for that. You've made your feelings clear. I apologise. I'll never force myself on you again.' With as much dignity as he could muster he walked away, swaying slightly. He didn't look back and see the tears in Connie's eyes.

Boxing day was their last day together as a family. No one spoke of it but everyone knew the future was so uncertain that within days any of them could be dead. Following the pattern of the last few days, Alex went to bed after lunch, very much the worse for wear. Around the middle of the afternoon, Sion roused Alex from his bed and insisted he join him for a walk.

Snow was forecast for later. The wind had dropped and the sky was a pale blue, with a thin covering of high cloud.

'What did you want to talk about, Dad?'

Sion kept his eyes to the ground, and his shoulders hunched against the cold. After a few seconds he stopped walking and looked up at his son. 'You. Son, you're drinking far too much. We all know the strain you're under, but you seem to be out of control. Think about the effect of so much alcohol on your system – it fogs the brain. In your position it couldn't be more dangerous. Carry on the way you are and your reactions will be so slow you'll be dead in a fortnight.'

'Dad, don't talk utter rot. I'm only drinking while I'm away from the squadron. We hardly drink when we're operational. It's beer only and not even that if we have an early morning patrol to do.'

Sion wasn't convinced, but wisely said nothing. What *could* he say? 'Well, take it easy, Alex, please. We have enough to worry about without wondering if you're fit to fly as well.'

Alex clapped his father on the back and said with forced jollity, 'Don't worry, Dad. Trust me.'

Back at the house, Alex filled a hip flask with whisky, making sure no one was about. Before dinner his parents were delighted to see he limited himself to a single drink. They weren't aware he was sneaking off to the toilet to down large mouthfuls of neat malt.

Dinner consisted of Christmas Day's leftovers, a favourite with them all. Afterwards, they joined in a game of charades, much to their amusement and pleasure. Connie and Alex barely exchanged a word.

Farewells were poignant and tear-filled. By evening Alex and Ginger were back at Biggin Hill, with a dawn patrol ahead of them. After a couple of beers in the mess they went to their rooms early. Ginger to get some sleep, Alex to finish the contents of his hip flask. When he was roused at 07.00 he was bleary eyed and hung-over. One advantage of winter, he thought, was that sunrise wasn't until eight o'clock, so the patrol was at a civilised hour.

By the time he was in the air his mind was as clear as the day. Apart from a few clouds in a washed out, pale blue sky, conditions were perfect. The wind was still and from his vantage point the fields and hills, lightly dusted with snow, looked as pretty as a picture post-card. As he flew automatically, his eyes darting across the dials, monitoring the plane's performance, he thought of Connie. He had behaved abominably. He had deserved to be rebuffed but she had shrunk from him, her eyes showing something like fear. Despite his drunkenness all his longing and desire for her had been in that kiss – and she had responded, if only for a few glorious seconds. What the hell was the matter with the woman?

'Violet One, Violet One, do you read, over?'

It took three transmissions for Alex to break out of his reverie and remember his call sign for the day.

'Sapper, Violet One, over.'

'Wake up, Violet One. Bandits at angels fifteen, over Dungeness. Vector one six zero.'

Alex repeated the information, acknowledged the message and turned onto the heading. His wingman, Red Harris, was a New Zealander who had recently joined the squadron.

'Violet Two, keep a sharp look out,' Alex told him.

'Wilco,' came the laconic reply. Harris always spoke as though he hadn't a care in the world.

'This is Sapper, fifty plus snappers reported. All squadrons are scrambled. Do you see them, Violet One?'

Alex had been desperately searching the sky. As the question was transmitted he made out the Me109s, below and ahead.

'Sapper, this is Violet One, I see them. I reckon there are closer to a hundred snappers. No bombers.'

'Understood. Good luck. Out.'

There was nothing for it but to attack. Alex turned up the oxygen flow and transmitted to his wingman. 'Red, stay close until we mix it. After that . . . well . . . good luck.'

'See you in the bar for a pint, mate,' said Harris.

Around them other Spitfires were forming up. They fell into formation and the attack began. Within seconds the aircraft were scattered across the sky, each pilot fighting for his life. The ether was rich with different languages and accents. French, Polish, Dutch and Norwegian intermingled with the accents of Canada, Australia, South Africa and New Zealand. Of course the Welsh, Scots and English were well represented too. The babble was distracting but at the same time comforting. If you could hear the voices you were still alive.

Alex increased speed and the angle of his dive. He checked the deflection on his sights and with the cockpit of the Messerschmitt firmly in the centre he opened fire. Keeping the trigger closed, he watched as massive pieces of the enemy cockpit flew apart.

'Violet One, Violet One, pull up, for Christ's sake. Alex! Pull up!'

With a start, Alex heard his Number Two scream his name and

was shocked into alertness. He was closing on the target at a rate of knots, still firing, in danger of hitting it. He let go of the trigger and pulled hard on the stick, throwing the plane into a tight right turn as he did. Sweat popped from his head as he threw the Spitfire across the sky and away from the Me109 that was now filling his view. As he turned, the tip of his port wing touched the spinning propeller and was shredded.

20

THE SPIT SPIRALLED down, Alex fighting the controls all the way, his altimeter unwinding as the plane picked up speed. Pushing hard on the rudder, he turned into the spiral and took control of it. He had seconds in which to decide – jump or fly. Indecisive, he chose the latter only when he knew it was too late to parachute to safety. The spiral stopped and the little plane swooped over a hedge, inches above the earth. Alex's heart was pounding and his mouth was bone dry.

As he checked the instruments he found his left knee was shaking and a throbbing had begun between his temples. For the first time ever, he was airsick all over his left sleeve.

'Alex, are you all right?'

'Yeah, Red. Thanks.'

'Strewth, I thought you'd had it. You appear to have lost about six inches off the wing.'

'Thanks. I see that.' Alex tried to lick his parched lips.

'What do you want me to do?'

'Get back up there. I'll be okay. I'll head for base.'

Alex heard the relief in Harris' voice. 'Wilco. Good luck.'

Alex didn't bother acknowledging the transmission but set a course to the north, hedge hopping, and staying low. He quickly recognised where he was and adjusted his course. A short while later he was lining up to land at the airfield.

He taxied over the field and to the dispersal point. The throbbing across his forehead had moved and now sat in the back of his skull, pounding like a hammer. Shutting down the engine, he pushed the canopy back and climbed wearily out.

'Sorry about the mess,' he said to his fitter, waving vaguely behind him. 'I puked.'

'We'll have it cleared in a jiffy, sir.'

'Sorry about the wing, too.'

'Leave it to us, sir.'

Alex nodded and walked away. The Intelligence Officer debriefed him carefully before crediting him with the kill of the Me109.

'You look like something the cat's dragged in, Alex,' the IO said as they finished. 'Get some rest until we know the situation with your plane.'

Squadron leader Cutler had arrived back at the airfield only minutes earlier and walked into the hut just in time to hear Edge's comment.

'What's up with your plane, Griffiths?'

'The port wing is damaged, sir.'

'A new Spit arrived last night. You can take it. H for Harry. We've more planes than pilots. Check her out.'

'Yes, sir,' Alex said stiffly, stomping out of the hut. Bugger him, he thought. I'll get something to eat first. He looked at the mess on his sleeve. And wash the puke off.

He sponged off the sleeve before going to the mess. It was now 09.45 and as always he was amazed that so much had happened in such a short space of time. Faced with bacon and powdered eggs he opted for a slice of toast and a cup of tea. He was about to go and check the new plane when Cutler appeared.

'Have you been over H for Harry yet?' he greeted Alex.

'Not yet, sir. I'm just about to.'

'Flight Lieutenant Griffiths, when I tell you to do something I expect my orders to be carried out straight away.'

'But, sir, I needed to get cleaned up. I was damn lucky up there today.'

'Spare me the excuses, Griffiths.' Cutler raised his hand and looked angrily at Alex. 'Just do as I say.'

Seething with indignation, Alex stalked from the room. Damn the bloody man!

It took an hour but the plane checked out after a short flight and a few bumps and grinds – landings and takeoffs. Satisfied, Alex finally made it to his room and threw himself onto his bed. He needed sleep badly but the more he wished it the more evasive it became. After nearly forty minutes he gave up and staggered over to the basin to wash his face. With water dripping from his chin he looked at the hollow face that gazed back at him. The dark smudges under his eyes were testament to more than his lack of sleep. He turned away from his image and reached for a towel. Almost of their own volition his fingers opened his sock drawer and paused. Licking his lips he stood irresolute. What the hell, it would be hours before he was required again. The squadron had been stood down until the evening. With trembling fingers he reached into the drawer and withdrew his hip flask. Unstoppering it, he gave a mock salute to his image and tilted the flask into his mouth. The dribble of whisky that barely wet his lips left him craving more.

Hurriedly he packed a small bag with a civilian jumper and coat and slipped the flask underneath. Grabbing his car keys he hurried from the hut and out to the car park. Minutes later he had left the airfield and was motoring at high speed through the lanes towards Westerham a few miles south. He stopped at the pub at the edge of town. Quickly changing out of his tunic jacket he slipped on his jumper and sports coat. In the pub he asked for a bottle of whisky, accepting an inferior blend instead of the malt he'd wanted.

About to leave he turned back to the bar. 'Give me a large whisky and soda, please, barman.' Paying for the drink, he drank it in three long swallows.

As Alex left the bar he heard the barman say to his wife, 'Another poor flier. Alive today, dead tomorrow. Poor sod!'

Driving back to the airfield he was cutting the corner of the bend at the bottom of the hill leading up to "The Bump" when an oncoming bus caused him to swerve to avoid an accident. The back wheels of his car skidded and he felt the rear slide, turning into the high bank of the hedgerow. He turned into the skid momentarily, regained control and twisted the wheel the other way, taking the car safely round the bend. The alcohol in his blood made him reckless and instead of slowing down after his near miss he accelerated. Twice more he nearly lost control but managed to avoid crashing. Driving up the hill prevented him going even faster otherwise he would never have made it. He pulled up outside the guardhouse and showed his identity card, aware he'd gotten back by the skin of his teeth.

Back in his room, Alex poured himself another whisky and quickly downed it. A second followed before he had the sense to put the bottle out of sight. He knew if he were caught with it in his room he'd be court-martialled. His head was reeling when he lay on his bed and closed his eyes. The room spun for a few seconds and he gripped each side of his bed. Nothing made any sense. Let go, he told himself. He passed out, still holding on tight.

A banging on his door woke him from a troubled sleep. After a few moments he called out, 'What's the matter?'

'It's me, Ginger. We take off in fifty minutes. Unlock the door and let's have tea before we go.'

'I'll see you in the mess.'

'Are you all right?'

'Yes. Why shouldn't I be?' he asked more harshly than he'd intended.

'All right, keep your hair on. Just hurry it up, old lad.'

Groaning, Alex climbed to his feet and staggered over to the basin. The eyes staring disdainfully back at him were red-rimmed. After brushing his teeth and washing his face he felt almost human again. Donning his flying gear he made to leave the room. He paused by the drawer where the whisky was hidden. It seemed to be calling to him. Suddenly he turned away, striding purposefully through the door.

In the dispersal hut, Squadron Leader Cutler gave the briefing. 'Our information is that Jerry is planning a big surprise. We don't know when for sure but sometime in the next three days.'

'What sort of surprise?' Alex asked.

Cutler scowled at him. 'A big attack, that's all we know. So, full alert for the next two nights. We start at eighteen hundred. Half the squadron at immediate readiness, the other half at fifteen minutes. That's all.'

Ginger grinned at Alex. 'I'm your Number Two.'

Alex nodded. 'I know. I got the call signs.' Rubbing a weary hand across his face he added, 'Let's hope it's not tonight.'

It was 20.30 when the call came through. Alex was huddled in his Irvin jacket, the upper half of a two-part thermally heated insulated flying jacket, designed for cold conditions and open-cockpit flying. The IO took the call. When he heard the message he reached behind and switched on the loudspeaker.

'All scramble. Heavy force crossing the Channel and expected over London in thirty minutes. Bombers and snappers.'

The pilots ran for their machines. If they were afraid none showed it, though each man knew there was a good chance he was going to his death. With every flight Alex was aware of how the odds against him were now stacking up. He had lived longer than almost any other pilot in a front-line Spitfire squadron.

Merlin engines burst into throaty life and the little planes formed up on the field. Pre-flight checks were quickly finished and then they were taxiing. The planes lifted into the sky, anti-collision lights flashing. Alex's eyes were never still, first flicking over his instruments and then over the night sky and the other Spitfires around him.

He flew in a daze. He had been tired before he took off but felt lethargy eating at him as he piloted the plane towards the Germans. Vectors were given and bogey estimates continued to rise.

They engaged the enemy to the north of Margate.

Alex flew and fought like a madman. He felt his plane taking a pounding but ignored it. He quickly lost Ginger Robarts in the mêlée. It was every man for himself.

That night over 10,000 firebombs dropped on the City of London. Water mains were burst at the start of the attack by high explosive parachute mines. The tide in the Thames was at its lowest point and very little water was available for the fire-fighters. When water finally came on again from distant mains supplies, the exhaust pipes of fire engines turned red hot as 20,000 firemen fought to contain the fires.

The Luftwaffe was winning when suddenly the enemy planes turned away and sped towards the coast. Alex and the other surviving pilots chased the Germans all the way, enraged at the damage that had been inflicted.

Wearily, Alex turned back to Biggin Hill, the adrenaline that had sustained him leaving him abruptly. He landed with a heavy bump and turned off to dispersal. When the engine stopped he sat with his head resting against the back of his seat, fighting an overwhelming urge to sleep where he was. The arrival of his fitter and rigger roused him and he dragged himself out of the cockpit to report to the IO.

Pausing outside the hut he suddenly thought, what *had* happened? Christ, he couldn't remember any of the details! One plane. Yes, he'd hit one and followed it down. Suddenly, like a switch going on in his head, he remembered. A Junker 88A-1. He'd hit the starboard engine and the plane dived to port, losing height. He'd gone after it, sticking like glue to its tail. He'd kept firing, hitting the Junker's fuselage. Then the fire had started and he's seen the plane spiral into the water. What next? He'd gone to angels 25 and gone in again by which time they were over London. His Spit had taken some serious pounding but had flown on gamely.

He stopped at the door to the hut and turned to go back to the plane. What the hell! He'd know soon enough how bad it was.

The de-briefing over, he left to go to his room. Outside, Sergeant Simpson, his fitter was waiting for him. 'Sorry to trouble you, sir,' he began.

Alex nodded wearily. 'Hullo, sergeant, what can I do you for?'

'Thought you'd like to know, sir, we counted fifty-six holes in Harry. This is for you.' He held out his hand with a spent bullet in it. 'It was lodged in the back of your seat, sir. You was bloody lucky. Beg pardon, sir.'

'That's all right, sergeant. Thanks.' His hand curled tightly around the misshapen bullet and he walked away. His first reaction had rattled him. If only it hadn't been stopped!

The 6th of January brought news of Amy Johnson's death. The famous pilot, who had flown solo to Australia, had spent the previous six months delivering new aircraft from factories to RAF bases. They were told her engine had cut out, plunging her plane into the sea. Her death greatly saddened the fighting pilots of the RAF, who had seen her as something of a good luck charm. Alex had met her a few times and her demise hit him hard.

The war in North Africa had been going the way of the Allies, the Italian troops surrendering or retreating as fast as they could raise their hands or run. Then in the middle of February General Erwin Rommel arrived with his desert warfare panzer divisions supported by the Luftwaffe. The German resolve helped to stiffen the resistance of the Italians. The war in Africa was no longer a pushover.

A month later a bill to mobilise women into factories was laid before parliament and passed. All twenty and twenty-one year old women were required to report for work at various factories, particularly those filling shells. The work was to be carried out twenty-four hours a day, seven days a week. Childcare with day and night nurseries was established. Males above the age of forty were also to be called-up into the factories to do the same work. Wages were set as £3.0s.6d for men, £1.18s for women.

Throughout this time Alex somehow managed to hold it together. Sleep was elusive, usually brought on by a large dose of whisky each night, but even so he rested badly. He became edgy, snapping at the other pilots, alienating his friends, including Ginger.

Yet somehow, he kept going. Cutler was always on his back, giving him a hard time. Though it almost killed him, Alex nodded, smiled and walked away every time. Occasionally the man's attitude towards him made him boiling mad, usually he couldn't care less.

The one place he operated with control was in the Spitfire. So far his drinking hadn't affected his reactions too much and his professionalism, coupled with his natural ability, stood him in good stead. But he was becoming more reckless. As a result his confirmed kills and probables continued to rise. He was long overdue for a bar to his DFC.

Squadron Leader Cutler approached him in the mess at the end of March. 'I want you on dawn patrol, Griffiths. Sunrise is at six forty eight.'

He and Alex were alone in the bar, the stewards away getting their supper before returning to duty. Something snapped inside him and Alex stood looking down at his superior officer with barely concealed contempt.

Cutler scowled back at him, a vein throbbing in the side of his forehead.

Though he knew he should, Alex couldn't break eye contact. He wanted, more than anything, to punch the man in his face. Instead he asked, 'What's your problem, Cutler?'

Taking half a step back Cutler bristled with anger. 'Don't you dare speak to me like that, Griffiths. I'll have you court-martialled. It's sir when you address me.'

Alex took a pace forward and put his nose close to the Squadron Leader's. 'Hugo Wakefield was sir, you little shit. You aren't fit to clean his shoes. The idea that you're a squadron leader would be farcical if it wasn't true. Take a look around you. There's nobody here except you and me. So if I take a swing at you there'll be no witnesses.' He prodded the other man in the midriff with his forefinger, hard. As the breath was expelled from Cutler's body, Alex knew he'd gone too far, but couldn't stop. 'You've picked on me ever since you got here. What's your problem?'

Cutler was so livid he was spluttering. 'I'll have your guts for garters for this Griffiths. Striking a senior officer will get you shot.'

Alex smiled, his emotions back in control once again. 'I never laid a finger on you. And if you think you can make a charge stick then try it. My family will have you out of here before you can blink.'

Alex had never used his family name to threaten or persuade before.

He wanted his own success, needed to make his own way in his life. Using his family as a fall back position would never have occurred to him until today. What the hell was going on with him?

'Your family,' sneered Cutler. 'You make me sick. You and all your kind, with your wealth and connections. You think you can get away with anything you like. Well you can't. I've seen your sort before. Spoiling a man's career. Men like me get held back for promotion, watching lesser men rise above them just because of "family connections". I loathe you all.' Cutler had spittle forming at the side of his mouth.

Alex was watching the other man with utter fascination. What the hell had happened to make Cutler react like that? He'd have to find out. 'The reason you haven't been promoted, *sir*,' he spoke the word with contempt, 'is because you weren't good enough. And never will be. Why don't you fly, eh? Everyone is sick of your excuses. Bad nerves, is it, *sir*? Is that it? Are you afraid?'

Cutler flinched. 'I'll have you, you little bastard. See if I don't.' With that he swung on his heels and marched out of the room.

Alex watched him go. *He's frightened*, he thought. *He's scared witless!* Realisation gave way to sadness and he shook his head. *Well, I can't say I blame him. We all are at one time or another.* Not showing your fear was what mattered. Alex was at least honest enough with himself to acknowledge he needed his whisky to help him through the long nights.

The scar on the back of his neck and shoulder itched, a reminder of the close shave he'd had. Irritably he scratched it before following Cutler from the room.

The Squadron Leader continued to pick on Alex, riling him, but never going far enough to give Alex grounds to officially complain. Most of the time Alex rose above it, though occasionally he'd snap back at his superior officer. When he did Cutler took great delight in belittling him in front of the other pilots.

After one such confrontation Ginger asked Alex, 'What the hell's the matter with him? He's always on your back.'

Alex smiled and shrugged. 'He doesn't like who I am. He thinks because of my family I've got a golden tit in my mouth and I keep sucking on it.'

'That's ludicrous. Family can't protect you when you're in a dogfight.'

Alex held up his hand. 'It's okay, Ginger. We both know that. I think it's time I fought back. I've had about enough of his nonsense.' But the question was – how to get Cutler off his back without being court-martialled?

Finally he had a weekend off that even Cutler couldn't prevent. Ensuring his uncle was at *Fairweather* he set off for the south coast. He was conscious too of the fact that Connie would also be at the house. Would she still behave as if he didn't exist?

He took his time, weaving through the country lanes, passing small towns and villages, some showing damage, a constant reminder of the war, if anyone needed reminding. Spring was well advanced with a hint of a glorious summer ahead. Alex couldn't help but be aware of the blossoming hedgerows and the trees beginning to leaf. He stopped for a pie and a pint of ale at a small country pub and sat outside to listen to the birds. Black specks high in the sky disturbed his tranquillity. He saw a squadron of Griffins winging their way towards the coast. The Hun was obviously making another sortie into England. Sighing, he contemplated buying a large whisky and soda but reluctantly dismissed the thought. He'd wait until later to have a good drink.

He arrived at Ovingdean in the middle of the afternoon. The damaged wing of the house had been repaired and was in use again. Alex wandered around looking for familiar faces but saw none. Finally he found Gibbs in his pantry. The butler greeted Alex warmly.

'You're in Number Five bedroom, sir.'

'Number Five?' Alex repeated. 'What happened to the lilac suite?'

'The old names were proving too difficult for some of the children to remember, sir, so all the rooms have been numbered. It makes life much easier.'

'Well, thank you, Gibbs. And where's my uncle?'

'He's gone riding, sir. He said he'll be back in time for tea.'

'I'll see him then. Thanks again.'

Alex found his room, dumped his bag and went along to his uncle's study. Inside he helped himself to a large whisky and soda, filled his hip flask and went back to his room. Standing at the window, looking down towards the Channel, he sipped his drink. After a few minutes he was surprised to find his glass empty and refilled it from the flask. In the distance he could see the sleek hull of a Daring class destroyer heading towards the North Sea, followed in line astern by another two. He raised his glass in salute to them, drained the whisky in a gulp and lay down on his bed. The alcohol had the desired effect and he drifted off to sleep.

When he awoke he had a sour taste in his mouth and a headache that started somewhere behind his left eye. He checked the time. Just after 6pm. With a groan he climbed off the bed. By the time he had dressed in slacks and blazer with an open-necked shirt he was feeling human again. He found his uncle in his study.

'Alex, wonderful to see you. Can I give you a drink?'

'Thanks, Uncle David. A whisky and soda, please.'

His uncle poured a large malt and added a dash of soda. 'This is a great pleasure. You're lucky to find me here. I nearly had to stay in London.'

'I'm glad you're here – I want to ask a favour.'

'Fire away. If I can help I will.'

Alex told him about the row he'd had with his squadron leader and how Cutler was picking on him. David was incensed. When it came to family, his loyalty knew no bounds. An attack on one, as far as he was concerned, was an attack on them all.

'Leave him to me, Alex, I'll take care of it.'

'No, it's all right, Uncle David. I just want to find out the man's history. To have some ammunition I can use against him if need be.'

His uncle looked at him through narrowed eyes. After a few moments he nodded. 'Fair enough. But if you can't control him let me know. He'll be running a sea rescue post in Orkney, if he's lucky.' The door opened and he smiled over his nephew's shoulder. 'Susan, my dear, come in.'

'Hullo, Susan,' Alex hugged his cousin, a smile plastered on his face. 'How's the sprog?'

'John's fine. Connie's is giving him his bath. He'll be down shortly to play. He knows you're here and is impatient to see you.'

Alex grinned and tapped his pocket. The precious chocolate was there.

Susan helped herself to a gin and tonic and refreshed the glasses of the two men. The talk turned as always to the war.

'It's a damnable show,' said David. 'Yugoslavia's fallen and now Athens.'

'Sometimes it feels like they're an invincible tide,' said Susan, 'sweeping away anything in their path.'

'We'll beat them in the end,' said her father with conviction. 'We must believe that. It's that certainty that keeps us going. As far as I can see, we need two things to happen.' David lifted his drink and sipped, savouring the peaty taste.

'Go on,' Alex said, taking a mouthful, not even noticing the quality of the drink.

'We need the Americans to enter the war and, more importantly, we need the Germans to attack the Russians. A second front would drain men and resources from the west. That would give us an opportunity to hurt the Hun.'

'It sounds like a long drawn-out business,' said Alex, finishing his drink and going over to the bar to top up his glass. He waved the bottle at his uncle who shook his head.

'It will be. It's almost May. I predict we won't be ready to retake Europe for at least three years. And even then it will be a slog.' The door opened and his grandson came bounding in, making a beeline for his Uncle Alex.

Delighted to see the child, Alex picked him up and carried him outside on his shoulders.

At dinner they were four – David, Alex, Susan and Connie. Madelaine had been due at the house but something had come up preventing her leaving London. To Alex, Connie looked as captivating as ever. Susan's admonition to be patient made sense, but he felt his entire being quicken every time he looked at her. Most of the time she avoided eye contact with him. By the end of the main course, Alex had decided she was being cruel, ignoring him so. He drank too much red wine with the meal and too much port with the Stilton.

His head was buzzing by the time it came to say goodnight. He went to his room and sat quietly at the open window, looking out onto a moonlit lawn. His thoughts were filled with Connie. Angrily he used his hip flask to top up the whisky he'd brought with him from the study. The grain on top of the grape hit his stomach and head and he felt the room sway. Controlling the rush of nausea he was feeling he sat in utter misery. *This was ludicrous,* he told himself. *I'm going to have it out with her now.*

Connie's room was at the end of the wing they were in, next to the nursery. He staggered along the corridor to her room and knocked on the door. It opened almost immediately.

'Connie . . . Let me in, please. We have to talk.'

220

'Go away, Alex. Leave me alone.'

Her casual dismissal enraged him and he roughly pushed the door open. She staggered back and sat on the bed. Alex followed. Awkwardly he grabbed at her, feeling the thin nightdress beneath his fingers. He was inflamed by her nearness, wanted her more than anything in the world. His fingers clutched at her neckline and he tugged, ripping the thin cotton. Connie pulled away, tears dampening her cheeks but Alex didn't notice.

The harder he tried to embrace her the harder she struggled. It was a battle fought in complete silence.

21

ALEX TRIED MURMURING reassurances into Connie's hair, urging her to relax, waiting for her body to soften against his. Suddenly he realised she was trembling, not with anger but with fear. The realisation penetrated his alcohol-befuddled brain and he moved away from her, the maelstrom of passion he had felt spiralling down into total self-disgust.

She was looking at him as if he were a wild beast. Whatever enchantment he found in her as a woman, he realised, Connie found no such attraction in him. She was cowering away from him as if in fear of her life. Wide-eyed she stared at him in silent accusation. How could he have grabbed her so fiercely? Behaved so savagely? She must have thought he was about to attack her, to rape her. The thought left him filled with horror. He peered through the darkness at her. The spring night was chill, but he could smell her perfume, feel the warmth of her. Her dark hair fell around her shoulders as she sat, poised for flight, for all the world like an animal waiting to see which way the hunter would move. And then he realised – it wasn't him Connie feared, it was any man.

'You've been raped, haven't you?'

It was as if a spell had been broken. They spent the night talking. Or rather, Connie talked and he listened. Knowing her story it was easy to understand her terror of intimacy, her need to make herself safe. He held her, soothing her when she wept, kissing her when the memories became too much. Finally, they fell asleep in each other's arms.

At breakfast Alex and Connie were animated, openly affectionate. Susan glanced at Connie and saw her blush. Something had happened between her cousin and her best friend, Susan realised. Her father saw none of it. Not even the glare Connie gave her friend to stop her saying anything.

Breakfast couldn't end quickly enough for Susan. She grabbed

Connie by the arm and dragged her outside, leaving her father and Alex to linger over their coffee.

'What was all that about?' David asked.

'I've no idea,' Alex blushed, wondering what Connie was telling Susan.

Alex went to the library, to read a book. Having read the same paragraph three times and not understood a word he was on the point of giving up when Susan found him.

'Alex, I'd like a word, please.'

Raising a quizzical eyebrow Alex wondered what was coming.

'I trust you will be kind to Connie. She deserves and needs looking after.'

'I love her. I'll do anything I can to make her happy.'

Susan's austere look blossomed into a radiant smile. 'I know you will, dear Alex. Just go slowly, that's all.'

That night, Alex and Connie sat together in her room, talking and kissing. He was afraid to go any further, waiting for her to give a sign that she was prepared for more. It never came but Alex knew he could wait – forever if need be, he told himself.

Dawn was breaking when he left the house to hurry back to Biggin Hill. He drove like a maniac but still arrived late. At the guardhouse he received the unwelcome news that Squadron Leader Cutler wanted to see him as soon as he arrived back.

'You're on a charge, Griffiths,' Cutler greeted Alex when he entered his CO's office.

Alex nodded, saying nothing.

The silence unnerved the Squadron Leader. 'Did you hear me?'

Alex frowned as though puzzled by the question. 'There's nothing wrong with my hearing.'

'You insolent young swine, don't you dare speak to me like that!' White spots of anger showed on Cutler's cheeks as he struggled for control of his temper.

Alex shrugged. 'I really couldn't care less what you do, *sir*.' He infused utter contempt into the last word. 'I'm needed to fly for my country. You can stop my leave and that's about it. Or, I suppose,' he added as an afterthought, 'you can give me some onerous duty or other. I'm thirty-five minutes late. Anybody else would have been let off with a "Do better next time". But not me. All right, I was delayed when a bomb blew out a bridge and I had to take a detour.'

Cutler glared at Alex. 'That's a lie.'

'Prove it,' said Alex angrily, getting fed up with the conversation. 'Get off my back, *sir*,' he hissed, 'or you'll regret it.'

'Are you threatening me, Griffiths?'

Alex sighed, the good mood he'd been in now completely evaporated. 'This weekend my uncle offered to have you removed and put in charge of an air-sea rescue post in the Orkneys. I'm warning you, don't make me phone him. He's very well connected; in fact he's on first name terms with the Prime Minister. Try us. I know what he can do. You can only guess.'

'Get out! You little swine! Get out! I'll have you, Griffiths. As sure as God made little green apples, I'll have you.'

Alex was appalled at the look on his superior officer's face. It was now chalk white with sweat beading his forehead. The man's anger was so great his hands were shaking and for a second Alex wondered if he was going to attack him. Pretending a nonchalance he wasn't feeling, Alex sauntered from the room, leaving the door open behind him. He didn't turn when it was slammed shut.

His petty quarrel with Cutler was soon put into perspective. May 11th was a bright moonlit night. Five hundred and fifty German bombers indiscriminately attacked London, dropping a hundred thousand incendiaries in a few hours. The House of Commons was reduced to rubble and Big Ben was scarred though the clock kept accurate time. Westminster Abbey and St Paul's Cathedral were hit though both survived. That night over twenty thousand civilians were killed and a further twenty-five thousand injured. The moonlight helped the Germans, but it also gave the RAF a chance to retaliate.

The Spitfires, Hurricanes and Griffins were piloted by madmen. Angered beyond words, each warrior pressed an attack at every opportunity. The devastation of London was horrendous. The price paid by the Germans was low – twenty-nine bombers shot down by the RAF and four by anti-aircraft guns. It was a poor rate of return for so many deaths and injuries.

Alex claimed a possible although he had attacked at least six different targets. Back at Biggin Hill he went to bed sober for the fourteenth night in a row. His thoughts were filled with Connie. He was hoping to see her on his next day off – if Cutler didn't scupper his plans again.

Alex was eating breakfast, powdered eggs and toast, when Cutler appeared. 'Flight Lieutenant Griffiths,' said Squadron Leader Cutler, 'I have a task for you.'

Alex paused with a fork of the watery yellow substance halfway to his mouth and looked at his senior officer. Others in the mess watched them, aware of the animosity that existed between them. Cutler waited for Alex to respond in some way. A courteous "Sir" would have been normal. Instead Alex kept silent.

'See me in my office in five.' Not waiting for a reply Cutler stalked out of the room, his back rigid with anger.

Alex nonchalantly finished his eggs, ordered more toast from the steward and loitered over a cup of coffee. It was over twenty minutes before he arose and walked out to the foyer to get his hat. Even then he paused in the doorway to look at the bright morning and feel the warmth of the sun on his face. He knew he was pushing it, but certain information had come his way that gave him an edge over Cutler. According to his uncle's sources, the squadron leader had very nearly been drummed out of the RAF for cowardice in 1939. He had no details at present but the scandal centred on the town of Amiens. Alex hoped that would be enough information to make Cutler back off.

Alex wandered over to Cutler's office. His reception was what he'd been expecting.

'I expected you half an hour ago. Where have you been?' Cutler was sitting in his cluttered office, behind a desk covered in piles of papers and files. It was, Alex knew, not the way the RAF dealt with its paperwork.

Alex didn't reply. Instead he insolently drew himself to attention and saluted.

Cutler didn't move, staring at Alex with naked hostility in his eyes. After a few seconds he said, 'Answer me, damn you!'

Alex stayed silent, aware that he was exacerbating the situation. Cutler hit his palm hard on the desk, his face mottled in anger. 'Damn you, Griffiths, I gave you an order.'

'I have just saluted, *sir*, and I am waiting for you to do me the courtesy of returning my salute.'

Cutler looked as though he was about to explode. His fists were opening and closing in a frenzied clenching motion. For the first time Alex wondered if his senior officer was unbalanced.

'Hell will freeze over, Griffiths, before I salute you.'

'As you wish.' Alex relaxed and sat in the hard-backed chair facing the desk.

'Stand up, Griffiths. I haven't given you permission to sit.'

Looking at Cutler, Alex wondered how far he could push the man. 'What happened over in Amiens?' Alex spoke in a soft voice, watching Cutler intently.

The Squadron Leader went rigid and looked at Alex as though he'd been pole-axed. 'What . . . What did you say?' His voice was barely above a whisper.

'Amiens. Want to talk about it? The inquiry? Or was it a court-martial?'

Cutler's voice continued in a whisper. 'How did you find out?'

Alex shrugged. 'It wasn't difficult. We've already discussed my family connections. I've come to warn you, *sir*, leave me alone. Let me get on with my job. If you persist in hounding me I'll get the details and tell the entire squadron. Do I make myself understood?'

Cutler couldn't bring himself to look at him. 'Get out!' he breathed. His voice rallied and he yelled, 'Get out, I say!'

Alex got to his feet and left the room, unaware that he had just made the biggest mistake of his life.

Cutler left Alex alone. Occasionally he found the squadron leader looking at him strangely but gave it no thought. At the end of May the Allies were given a boost when Germany's newest and fastest battleship, the 45,000 ton Bismarck was sunk. It took the Royal Navy three days and around one hundred British vessels to achieve their objective, but it was sweet revenge for the sinking of HMS *Hood* a few days earlier.

Alex and Ginger flew often. With the coming of summer and the long days, the attacks by the Hun were regular and devastating. Hitler was trying to pound the British into submission. But the more damage and deaths he inflicted the more determined and bloody-minded the people of Britain became. Their efforts doubled, their numbers swollen by the tens of thousands who came from the Empire, "to fight for the mother country". Those who had escaped occupied Europe pitched in to add their weight to the war effort.

The death rate amongst the pilots was horrendous, many "Aces" dying as the attrition continued. As Ginger put it, 'Your time runs out. It's as simple as that. You can't keep going and hope to survive. The odds won't allow it.'

Alex nodded agreement but he had reason to live now. Connie. At her urging he had stopped drinking. He was sleeping better and looked forward to receiving Connie's regular letters. They were usually misspelled and sometimes difficult to read, but he loved getting them. He wasn't so punctilious at replying but would write a few sentences when waiting to scramble.

They had met several times – always at a small country hotel near Biggin Hill. Alex treated her with such gentle respect, Connie could scarcely believe how happy she felt in his company. She wanted, she said, to escape the past. Alex was prepared to woo her and wait – until she was finally ready to give freely of herself. Although they shared the same bed, they had yet to make love.

The months passed in a blur. He lived for his moments with Connie. When they finally made love he was as considerate as he knew how but even so neither of them were properly satisfied. But each time got better. Connie's passionate nature began slowly to reassert itself and the pain and horror of her past faded away in her love for him.

Even Cutler left him alone. An uneasy truce descended between them. Alex stayed clear of the Squadron Leader who spent a good deal of his time in his office, away from the rest of the pilots. December promised to be the bleakest month of the war yet. Then on the 7th of the month everything changed. Japan attacked America at Pearl Harbour in Hawaii. All the talk was about what the Americans would do now.

Christmas was lost to Alex. He stayed in the mess and had a thoroughly rotten time in spite of the gifts sent from home. He particularly liked the drawing by John Phillipe of Connie. Apart from the mass of black hair she was unrecognisable but he cherished it nonetheless.

The war in Europe was being over-shadowed by the fight against the Japanese in the Far East. The first sign that America was fully committed to the war against fascism was the arrival of American troops in Northern Ireland on 26th. January. That was the start of Britain's invasion by the Americans. An invasion welcomed on one level, resented on another.

In the air the battle continued unabated. It was not as intense as the hellish days of 1940 and 41 but brutal for all that. For Alex, as for so many of them, staying alive was the priority. In June Major-General Dwight Eisenhower was given command of the United States forces in Europe, headquartered in London. At the end of that month the Polish underground sent a report to Jewish leaders in London. The Nazis had killed one million Jews, either in gas chambers or from disease and starvation.

That August the biggest assault on Hitler's Fortress Europe took place at Dieppe. Thousands of Allied troops were involved. Alex's squadron played a vital role supplying air cover. The Germans lost 82 planes that day and another 100 were chalked up as probables. The Allies lost 95 planes, including three from Alex's squadron.

Back at the field Ginger and Alex were walking to the debriefing hut. Both were saturated in sweat. Neither man spoke. The relief at the other man being alive said it all. Theirs was a friendship that was tempered in war and adversity. It knew no bounds.

Later in the mess, over a pint of watery beer, Ginger said, 'I'm up for a gong.'

'About time too,' said Alex, with a smile, raising his glass in salute. 'So you should be. You would have had it yonks ago if it hadn't been for me.'

'You?' Ginger was startled.

'Yes. Because we're friends Cutler's had it in for you.'

'Sod Cutler. He's as peculiar as they make them. How the hell he's kept this job is beyond me.'

'That goes for the rest of us as well. The sooner he's moved the better.'

At the end of September the new day started hazy, with the promise of being warm, even sultry. The squadron had been up once already and they were lounging outside the dispersal hut, dozing in deckchairs or sitting comfortably in ancient armchairs, good only for the scrap heap or bonfire. Alex was scribbling a few lines to Connie, memories of the weekend still vivid in his mind, when the phone rang, bringing everyone alert. Seconds later the order to scramble was given over the tannoy; bandits approaching from the southeast.

Alex ran for his plane, lifted his parachute off the wing where he had hung it and shucked it on. Clambering inside the cockpit, he was indicating start-up to the fitter before he was aware of his actions. On his wing was Red Harris, only one kill short of being "Aced" but with over a dozen probables and possibles to his name.

The planes lifted into a clear blue sky. Once airborne they formed up into a single V with Squadron Leader Cutler in the lead. Sapper ordered them onto a heading of 225 degrees and advised that bombers were at Angels 12. The snappers were at Angels 20. Their targets were the bombers. Other squadrons would take care of the fighters.

Within minutes the Germans were spotted and the cry, 'Tally-ho,' came over the R/T.

'White Two,' said Alex over his wireless, 'stick with me.'

'Wilco, White One,' said Harris.

The bombers were Heinkel He 111s and Alex counted about fifty of them. They were already weaving as the Spits pounced.

Typically for the time of year, black clouds were gathering and a thunderstorm was forming over the South Downs. Its anvil shaped head was already turning black and brought with it the promise of a deluge. The planes were at least fifty miles away but, thought Alex, the cloud cover was somewhere to run and hide if necessary.

The target grew large in his sights and as the crosshairs settled on the cockpit he opened fire with a short burst of two seconds. He saw bits fly off the plane and adjusted his aim just as the He 111 dived. He followed it down, getting off another two short bursts before he was too close and had to pull away in a tight turn. Red Harris was just behind and had slowed down. He took over and let loose with one long burst of the Spit's eight .303in machine guns. Chunks of the tail broke away and Harris walked the bullets along the fuselage. The Heinkel's aspect steepened and the plane dived towards the fields below, smoke pouring from the starboard engine.

Alex had already turned and was now flying high and behind Harris when he saw the Me109 pounce.

'Break Red! Break left!'

Harris didn't question the order. He threw the Spit into a hard roll to port and sent the plane diving towards the earth. The Me109 opened fire and the bullets flew past the Spit's tail, missing it by inches. The German dived after Harris, unaware that Alex was lining his sights on the Me109's belly as the planes crossed. Alex opened fire in a long burst and watched the German plane burst into flame as its fuel lines were smashed. Alex took his Spit into a vertical loop and at the top, with the plane upside down, flipped the right way up. He looked down to see the German pilot jump clear of the plane and parachute to safety.

Glancing over his shoulder he saw that the thunderclouds had gathered depth, height and momentum and the first squalls were beginning to make themselves felt. He searched the sky but saw no other planes. Looking down he could see the German's parachute drifting lazily about two thousand feet above the ground. He wasn't aware of the Spit skimming the earth until it suddenly rose up and opened fire on the helpless man hanging from the shrouds of the parachute. Bile erupted in his stomach as he saw the body jerk and then the white canopy shred and collapse.

What the hell! 'Sapper this is White One, a Spitfire just attacked a German parachutist.'

'This is Sapper, say again, White One.'

Alex repeated his message even as he dived after the absconding plane. He was in time to see it enter the wall of cloud that was now towering over the landscape. Without giving it another thought he went in after it, his blood boiling. He had just witnessed a murder. It was an unwritten code for fighter pilots, helpless men wouldn't be shot at. *Who the hell was that cruel bastard?*

His world went from open country and bright light almost immediately into an opaque hell. Alex had entered the cloud at roughly the spot he had seen the Spit go in and on about the same heading. Once inside he realised that his quest was hopeless. Huge winds were buffeting the small plane, lifting it in gut-swooping wrenches and dropping it just as fast. Rain beat down, blinding him to everything outside, as he struggled to retain some semblance of control. His mouth went dry with fear when he looked at his compass and saw it yawing through an arc of over ninety degrees. He was effectively lost.

A quick glance at his fuel gauge showed he had about an hour's flying time left. Not knowing whether to go left or right to get out of the clouds and unable to steer a steady course he did the only thing he could. He went up.

The cloud changed from grey to black as the storm-tossed fighter clawed for the sky. Rain came down in a solid wall of water and he heard the engine misfire for a second as the air intakes choked before the sturdy plane picked up and continued with its lusty roar as it burst into a quiet patch of sky. Around him the dark clouds reared high above, forming a ceiling over the quiet, almost tranquil spot he'd flown into.

The wall of cloud was about five hundred yards away. Half way across he thought hailstones were hitting the aircraft. With a sense of shock he watched holes appear in his starboard wing, seconds passing before his mind registered them as bullet holes. Instinctively he dived towards the bank of cloud. He glanced up and saw the unmistakable outline of a Spitfire, partly obscured by wisps of cloud, heading away from him.

He had no time to think as his plane plunged back into the maelstrom. It kicked and bucked, swooping high and low in gut aching movements that threatened to tear the wings off the plane. He had his oxygen on at full flow as the Spit passed through 35,000 feet and hit less turbulent air. He tried his wireless but could raise nobody. He was hopelessly lost. A glance at his fuel gauge showed he'd been in the storm for less than ten minutes, although it felt like a lifetime. A glimpse of the sun sent him hurtling west, straining his eyes to see some sort of feature below that he could identify.

Suddenly the wall of cloud was behind him and he burst into clear air. Below was the sea, and in the distance and behind, he could see the white cliffs of Dover. He was over a hundred miles away from where he thought he was. The Spit was labouring at that altitude and he put it into a shallow dive and headed towards Biggin Hill. Now that the immediate danger was past he was able to think more clearly and wonder about what had happened. The plane that had attacked him, was it the same one that had killed the helpless German? A Spit was unmistakable, like no other plane. Nobody, especially a fighter pilot, could mistake one for anything else. So who had fired on him and why?

The controller at Biggin Hill told him to line up behind P for Papa and he followed Squadron Leader Cutler onto the ground. After taxiing to dispersal he climbed wearily out of the cockpit, glad to have his feet on firm ground once again.

'Blimey, sir,' said the rigger, 'you took a battering.'

Alex walked around the aircraft, examining the holes in the starboard wing and fuselage. He was as certain as he could be that the plane which had fired at him had been the same one that had killed the German pilot.

In the Intelligence "Shed", he asked the IO, 'Are there any other Spits in the air?'

'Not from here,' said Flying Officer Edge. 'I'd think most, if not all, planes are down. The threat's gone, so apart from the normal patrols there's no activity. There's a heap of bad weather going down over Europe right now. So we've got a respite. Why?'

Alex explained what had happened to the German pilot and the attack he'd been subjected to. Edge looked suitably shocked.

'I say, old man, that's appalling. Are you sure you've got your facts right?'

'Positive. The Spit killed the German and beetled off into the cloud. I followed. When I was attacked I could clearly see the other plane. Hence, he must have seen me!'

'Did you get its number? '

Alex shook his head. 'No. I was too busy escaping and evading. Are you sure there are no planes left flying?'

'Positive but I can check. You and the Squadron Leader were the last two down.'

It was like an electric shock passing through him. Cutler! Of course. He had the opportunity and the motive. Cutler couldn't trust Alex not to say anything to any of the others about Amiens. He felt in his bones that he was right. He had no proof but it was the only logical explanation.

'Are you all right, Alex? You look ghastly.'

'What?' Alex was brought back to earth with a bump.

'I'll let the powers-that-be know about the incident. Someone may want to talk to you.'

'Okay, Gavin, thanks. I'll see you in the mess later. Is everybody back?'

'Yes. Thank God. For once.'

On that cheery note Alex left the hut and made his way towards the mess. If he was a target he needed to protect himself.

22

FOR THE NEXT week Cutler had one reason or another not to fly. His excuses varied from a problem with his Spitfire to blocked sinuses and shooting pains across his nose and forehead. As that was a common problem, particularly after colds, it was accepted.

But when the squadron was called for a special operation every man was needed in the air. The CO, Group Captain Fox, gave the briefing.

'The target for the bombers is the complex at Le Havre. We must stop the fast patrol boats before they become too much of a problem. They speed across the Channel, shoot up any shipping they see and scoot back across the water. They're damned difficult to strafe and bloody impossible to bomb. In Le Havre the boats enter the outer harbour and then go through here,' he pointed at a map pinned to the wall, 'past the inner wall. Below these cliffs there are two entrances, which lead into underground caverns. This is where the patrol boats hide. Our best bet for taking them out is to bomb the entrances when the boats are safely inside. Any questions? Yes, Ginger?'

'How can we be sure they'll be there, sir?'

'The French resistance will let us know. They have a man on the inside. Our information is that the boats will be buttoned up tonight and not expected out until dawn tomorrow. That's when we go in. In the half-light before sunrise. The bombers will be Halifaxes and you're riding cover. You all know the main problem. The Boys from Abbeville will be all over us like a rash.' The crack German squadron had earned their reputation the hard way. Brave and audacious flyers, they were a thorn in the side of Bomber Command. 'We are hoping for a quick in and out. The bombers are flying to Cherbourg as though the base there is the target. Two of their flight will attack and RTB as soon as they've dropped their loads. The other four will turn south east and head for Caen. As they near the city they will turn north east for Le Havre. Flying time is six minutes. The Halifaxes should be in and out before Abbeville knows what's happening.'

'What about flack?' Alex asked.

'Around the harbour mouth it's heavy. Back here it's not so bad. However, there are gun emplacements on the top of the cliff. The bombers will be going in low and we understand the guns can't fire more than a few degrees below the horizontal. The planes will be in danger only after the bombs are away and they are clawing for the sky. That's a risk the crews have to take. We've no option. This operation comes from the top. Its success is imperative. Any more questions?'

A few queries were raised and dealt with and then the briefing was handed over to the Met Officer. He promised fair weather with virtually no cloud cover.

Group Captain Fox finished the briefing. 'You will be led by Squadron Leader Cutler. Take-off is at zero three forty. Nothing else? Good. Good luck to you all.' Pausing, Fox looked at the pilots as they trooped out. He called Cutler back. 'A word, James.'

Alex paused in the doorway to listen. If his life was at risk he needed every advantage.

'James, I don't want any excuse why you can't fly. If you don't go I'll have your guts for garters.'

'I'm . . . I'm sorry, sir. I fail to understand you.' Cutler had lost what colour he had in his cheeks and was nervously clenching and unclenching his hands.

'I think you do. Make sure you lead the squadron. Understood?'

'Yes, sir.'

Alex made the error of looking at Cutler who had turned and caught Alex's eye. It was clear to the Squadron Leader that Alex had heard the exchange and he looked furious, marching stiffly from the room and brushing past Alex.

The pilots were woken at three o'clock. After tea and toast they were ready to man their Spitfires. The squadron lined up as a hint of daybreak appeared far in the east. Alex looked up at the sky, recognising Vega and Capella and then identified Venus. *A good day to die*, he thought and then shook himself. *Buck up and concentrate on living through the next few hours*, he told himself. Thoughts of Cutler muscled in on his reverie but he dismissed those too.

Ginger was flying on his wing, call sign Green Two. The twelve planes lifted gracefully into the sky, bringing on the dawn as they gained height. Squadron Leader Cutler piloted the lead plane.

They formed up and headed south-by-south west. The Isle of Wight was a dark blob, almost indiscernible from the flat calm of the Solent. A sliver of moon reflected off the water and the island showed up in the murk.

Air traffic control confirmed there were no other planes in the air apart from the bombers from 192 Squadron, Foulsham, northwest of Norwich. With the bombers at 16,000ft, the Spitfires took station at 30,000ft. Like hawks, they were ready to pounce.

From their height they could see the sun begin to chisel open the sky like an oyster, casting a pearly white and orange glow, while far beneath them, the world was still black. This was Alex's first flight with Cutler since the attack and he was alert to what the next few hours could bring.

Sapper continued to advise clear skies as they moved south towards the French coast. North of Cherbourg four of the bombers turned eastwards while two pressed on towards Le Havre. The area was lit up with search lights and ack-ack fire as the two Halifaxes dropped their bombs on the port and high-tailed it back to England. Now they were flying over the Baie de la Seine and turned twenty degrees south for Caen. Still no enemy aircraft. The operation was going exactly to plan. Alex knew, as did the others, that their luck wouldn't, couldn't, hold.

The planes droned on. Alex's eyes flicked across his instruments and out through the canopy. Every gauge was within normal operating range. He turned up the oxygen flow and breathed deeply through his mask. If a dogfight started he wanted to be ready. The journey had been timed to the minute. It was imperative that they arrived over the target as the sun rose above the horizon.

Moments later they were heading due north. The target was now obvious to the meanest intelligence – Le Havre.

As they hit the Seine estuary the bombers turned east, over the port complex. Ack-ack guns opened fire and the sky was alive with bursting shells. The Halifax bomber pilots kept their nerve as they neared the inner harbour, dropping to less than 100ft above sea level. The planes jinked left and right every few seconds as shell after shell exploded around them. One Halifax was hit and its port engine caught fire. The pilot extinguished the flames using carbon dioxide operated by a remote switch in the cockpit. Ahead he could see the cliff face and the two openings, which housed the fast patrol boats. Even as they approached one of the boats was leaving, nosing out of its berth.

By now the Spitfires were strafing the gun emplacements, drawing the fire from the bombers, giving them a chance to succeed. The first Halifax released its bombs and was clawing for the sky, turning to starboard even as Alex found himself attacking the guns on the cliff top. The ack-ack turned on him and his plane was jumping as shells exploded around him. By a miracle neither he nor the plane sustained a mortal hit. With the emplacement in his sights he opened fire, machine-gunning the soldiers manning the twin-barrelled guns.

Even as he turned hard to port and dropped low he saw the lead Halifax and his Number Two escape to the east.

Over the R/T came the announcement, 'Bandits at twelve o'clock. Looks like the boys from Abbeville.'

With Ginger glued to his port wing the two Spits clawed for height, their Merlin engines screaming like banshees as maximum power was applied. Already the squadron was all over the sky as vicious dogfights began. One Me109 passed ahead of Alex and he fired a quick burst that missed. Ginger had the advantage and turned onto the German's tail, firing a long burst into the fuselage and wing of the plane. Trailing smoke, the plane dived towards the earth. Now it was every man for himself, and Alex found he was looking for enemy aircraft while keeping an eye on the other Spitfires, afraid Cutler would pounce and take him unawares. With his attention split, he didn't see the Me109 come up from below and was only aware of the danger when he felt his plane begin to shudder from the impact of bullets. He threw the plane in a frantic series of manoeuvres as he tried to evade the attack.

Bullets hit his port wing and he rolled his aircraft clear, changing the movement into a gut-wrenching swoop towards the ground. Ack-ack opened fire and shells exploded around him, buffeting his plane, causing the controls to vibrate in his hands. The enemy fire scared off the German plane and Alex turned sharply to starboard to avoid any more of the flack.

He could see the other two Halifax bombers going in, releasing their payloads. As the bombs flew free the second Halifax exploded in mid-air and smashed into the cliff. The bombs erupted and huge slabs of cliff face began to slide down into the sea. One fast patrol boat was buried under tons of rock as it tried to nose its way clear. Now the whole cliff face was on the move and the pens that held the FPBs were obliterated under thousands of tons of rock. *It was,* Alex thought, *time to get out of there.*

Already the sky was beginning to clear as planes headed north for Britain, chased by the German fighters. A Spit appeared ahead and Alex had a moment of fear as he wondered if it was Cutler. Then, to his relief, he saw it was Ginger who waggled his aircraft's wings at him. Alex copied the signal and was still smiling as a second Spitfire thundered across his view and opened fire on Ginger's aircraft. The bullets must have hit the fuel tank for the plane erupted in a ball of fire and exploded in front of Alex's horrified eyes.

In a killing rage he turned towards the other aircraft and opened fire, recognising Cutler's number on the fuselage. The other Spit turned sharply, dived, did a loop and a roll and headed straight at Alex. His eyes blurred by tears, Alex opened fire, holding the button down, seeing pieces breaking off the other plane, which was now a hundred yards away and closing at a combined speed of over 600mph. There was no time to evade and the two planes collided in a mighty fireball, raining burning debris down into the Channel, watched by the incredulous eyes of the officers and lookouts onboard HMS *Daring.*

The telegram Sion received was the one he'd been dreading since the start of the war. *We regret to inform you . . .*

Mike's Story

23

Early Winter 1942

NEVER HAD I felt so helpless. News of Alex's death hit me like a body blow; in many ways he had been the son I never had. But watching his family grieve, watching their torment, unable to ease their suffering, that was the hardest thing I've ever had to do.

Flowers and messages of condolence flooded in – platitudes urging them to be proud of the way their son had died, fighting for his country. Looking at Sion, bereft, unable to comprehend the death of his first-born son, I knew that their loss was too great a price for any man or woman to pay. But it was being paid all over Europe – all across the world. But that was never consolation, not when it was *your* child.

Both Paul and Louise did their best for their parents but they had their own lives to live and were rarely at home. When they were, Sion and Kirsty made an effort, but it was unsustainable and they reverted to their despair when the two kids left.

Alex had been so full of life. He'd had such wonderful plans for after the war, which he had shared with me over a scotch or two. I'd loved the boy, so full of fire and enthusiasm. And now he was gone, wiped out like so many others.

Was it anger? Frustration? Looking back it was difficult to tell what compelled me to lie about my age and join up. I was now 44 years of age, and had already fought in the first lot – 'the war to end all wars', when a few moments of insanity had earned me a Victoria Cross.

If pushed, I'd have to say I signed up for love – love of Sion and his family, and gratitude for all the blessings they'd given me over the years.

My full name is Michael Patrick Seamus O'Donnell, but everyone calls me Mike. With a name like that I could only be an Irishman. Unlike many of my fellow countrymen I was an only child, a late baby to my parents, both now dead, God rest their souls. They probably burdened me with so many names believing rightly they'd never have any more sons.

My parents had come to England in 1910 and lived in the back streets of Liverpool, my father getting occasional work down at the docks, mainly loading and unloading ships. As soon as I could I got out of the place. The only escape route was into the British Army. There I trained as a mechanic and not a bad one, even if I do say so myself. It wasn't until the war started that I began to be promoted, reaching the dizzy heights of sergeant major. Mainly because I was the only one still alive after four death-filled years.

I won the VC in 1918, just before the war ended. Like all the others distinguished for their service, I had been terrified out of my wits, too tired and too sick to care whether I lived or died. Too angry as well. Pinned down by enemy machine gun nests, my men were being cut to pieces every time they moved. Unable to stand the slaughter any longer, I wormed my way through the mud and threw a hand grenade at the nearest emplacement. It landed on top of the Boche's machine-gun and exploded. I followed and worked my way from nest to nest, wiping out three of them. The press exaggerated my exploits a little; the next thing I knew I was up for a gong. For all my cynicism I was proud to meet the King and receive the award. I'd only wished my parents could have been there to see it.

When the war ended I was de-mobbed without so much as a by-your-leave. One day I was a hero and the next I was nobody. I was literally in the gutter when I first came in contact with the Griffiths family. That day would change my life. I ended up working with Sion, first as a mechanic at his airplane factory and then as sales manager. Eventually I learned how to fly and, somehow, as the years passed, became Sion's best friend and right hand.

When the war started in '39 I was working in David's factory in South Wales. I had just married my darling Betty, who had previously been married to one of David's first cousins. She was, in effect, family by marriage but was very much treated as a Griffiths. There was nothing they wouldn't do to help her. And she had proven herself worthy of their trust. The factory Betty managed for David made wirelesses, for use in homes and offices. With the war came the requirement for radio transmitters in planes, and between army and naval units. We expanded. Betty and I became joint-managing directors, she running the wireless division while I oversaw the military end. We opened a third section, in research and development, where we endeavoured to make the R/Ts smaller and more efficient.

Although I knew it was important work, Alex's death brought forth in me a need to contribute, to be in the thick of things. As they say, there's no fool like an old fool. My original intention had been to go to the nearest call-up station and sign on the dotted line. But after a little reflection I realised that would be ludicrous. There was no way I was going to become a squaddie at some junior officer's or NCO's beck and call. So I did the sensible thing. I used the family connections and went to London to Whitehall. David pulled strings for me. I was given the rank of lieutenant commander, Royal Naval Volunteer Reserve and sent to HMS *Vernon*. I was to become a member of Coastal Forces.

I was sent on a course to render safe mines, laid either at sea or dropped by parachute, and bombs found below the high waterline. Why that was the demarcation line I was never sure, but the Army dealt with those bombs found above the waterline. The decision to put me in mine and bomb clearance was made on the dubious grounds of my knowledge of radios and electrical circuitry.

When I told Betty of my decision to enlist we had our first real argument. However, she accepted my need to do my bit, albeit with a good deal of bad grace. She even went so far as to sew my medal ribbons onto my uniform. The crimson VC was like a dash of blood on my chest, while the campaign medals from 1914 to 1918 seemed incongruous by comparison.

After the course I had a week's leave before taking up my first appointment. On the morning of my departure to Portsmouth we stood in our house, *Anghorfa*, in the village of Efail Isaf, my arms around her waist, as she made a pretence of straightening my tie.

'I'll miss you, boyo,' she said, trying to smile.

I nodded. 'The same goes for me, *acushla*. But you'll manage. You've plenty of help.'

'That's not what I meant and you know it, *cariad*.'

I nodded. I loved her with all my heart. Something I hoped she knew. 'I have to go,' I said. 'I can't bear it any more, sitting round on my bloody arse watching others fight.'

She nodded her understanding. 'Take care.'

I summoned a smile from somewhere. 'You know me. I've nine lives.'

'Yes, and you've used up most of them. What exactly will you be doing in Coastal Forces anyway? No chance of a nice, safe desk job, I suppose?'

'I'm on small ships mainly. Their Lordships thought it appropriate because of my sailing and boating experience.' I hadn't told her about the bomb and mine disposal work I'd be doing. She had enough to contend with as it was. She thought the course I'd done was for general duties at sea.

'What tosh!' Betty allowed her anger to show. 'You know more about planes than boats. They really are fools.'

'Betty love, that's no way to speak of the good and the great,' I chided her gently.

'It's too late now anyway.' She kissed my cheek, her lips soft and warm.

Pulling her close I whispered. 'We've still time.'

Wriggling out of my arms she pushed me away. 'You'll have to wait for your next leave. Now be off with you. The train will be along in twenty minutes.'

She was right. With a sigh I picked up my tan-coloured canvas grip and hefted it in my hand. 'Take care. I'll write every day.'

I hurried out the back door, down the garden and across the orchard. Through the hedge was the railway track and I turned right towards the station, half a mile away. My train arrived on time. It had travelled from Merthyr Tydfil, stopping at all the small stations, picking up service men, taking them back to their units, back to the war.

I sat in a first class compartment, between two army officers, acutely aware of the shine on my new stripes and the tarnished and worn look of their khaki uniforms. The wavy stripes proclaimed me as a volunteer reservist, the crimson ribbon a veteran of the last war. They were a contradiction, anomalies in a world that was full of them. Like the fact that our Allies against the fascists were our enemies, the communists, while Germany's Spanish friends stayed on the sidelines. Japan had sided with Germany. And America – at long last – had sided with us.

I watched the countryside roll slowly past, thinking about Alex. After his death some ugly rumours had emerged. Could it be true that Alex had died in a dogfight with his senior officer? A Hurricane pilot, flying over the scene had seen the attack. So had a lookout onboard the destroyer HMS *Daring*, heading up Channel. The RAF had believed neither man. But I believed them. Alex had sent me a letter detailing his problems with Cutler and outlining the enmity that existed between them. I had been in two minds whether to show it to Sion. But what was the point in adding to his suffering? In the end I told David. He told me to leave it with him. He'd make enquiries.

He had promised he would keep me updated on his progress, or lack of it. The RAF had closed ranks and refused to acknowledge the situation. But David was persistent and kept burrowing, pulling in favours, making demands, using his office and the name of Churchill. A picture was emerging which he hoped he could tell me about soon. I was still brooding on the situation, waiting to hear.

It wasn't long before we reached the outskirts of Cardiff and the train picked its way past bombed buildings and derelict houses. Cardiff Central Station was bedlam. Thousands of men and dozens of women, nearly all in uniform, were on the move. I shouldered my way through the throng until I got to the right platform and waited impatiently for my connection.

Standing there I was finally honest with myself. I was eager to get to Portsmouth and get on with my job, of course. But I was also anxious to get away. I was well aware that I'd joined up not to go to something but to get away from Sion and the constant reminder of Alex's death. Kirsty was finding it hard to deal with, but Sion was being eaten alive. I couldn't sit and watch his pain. And so I had run away. A coward with a VC, just another contradiction in a world gone mad.

The train jerked and shuddered all the way to Bristol Temple Meads. I changed again and this time found myself on a train so crowded that I was forced to spend the journey in the corridor, sitting on my bag. The heating wasn't working so I wore my greatcoat and gloves. Somebody produced a bottle of Scotch and passed it round. It warmed the cockles of my heart.

Conversation was desultory, each man busy with his own thoughts. Two petty officers were returning to their destroyer, HMS *Diamond*, and one was joining the gunnery school at *Excellent*, as an instructor.

'You just in for the duration, sir, are you?' one of the PO's asked.

'That's it. Just joined.'

'What you been doing for the last three years then?'

'I was working at an airplane factory and then a wireless manufacturers. I joined up a few months back. Done my basic training and then got sent to Coastal Forces.'

'Crikey, you with that lot?' The PO paused with the bottle at his lips.

'Fraid so,' I nodded.

'You must have a death wish, mate, that's all I can say.'

'You a regular?' I asked.

'Yep. Nineteen years, man and boy. I get my buttons in two weeks.'

'Only if you ain't put back in your square rig,' said his friend. Seeing the puzzled expression on my face, he added, 'Back to leading hand. But I reckon he's safe this time. There's not many with our experience in the mob nowadays. They're all gone,' he spoke with a melancholy sigh. 'Aye, all gone now.'

They began to reminisce. Names and places brought back my own memories of the Great War. Memories I had long ago buried, too painful to be aired. At least, I thought, this war was different. No mass murder of troops for a few lousy yards of mud.

I must have dozed. Next thing I knew yells of "All change" were echoing through the train. We had arrived at Portsmouth.

At six feet, with broad shoulders to match, I was able to manoeuvre my way out of the crowded station and along to the taxi rank. Only officers queued for taxis. Even so there were a good dozen men waiting. A taxi drew up and an officer about to enter looked over his shoulder and called, 'Anyone for *Vernon*?'

'Me!' I went to the head of the line and joined him.

'Go halves? All right with you?'

'Sure,' I replied. The shoulder boards on his great coat proclaimed him to be a regular lieutenant, the tarnished gold evidence of his time served.

We settled into the car and it pulled away. My fellow passenger held out his hand. 'Andy Drysdale.'

'Mike O'Donnell.'

'Nice to meet you, Mike. What are you doing at *Vernon*?

'Coastal Forces. Mine and bomb disposal. You?'

'CO of a minesweeper. A converted trawler. Another six weeks and then I'm away. Back to destroyers.'

The taxi drew up at the main gate and we climbed out. We showed our passes to the sentry, returned the man's salute, and went past the guardhouse. A thin layer of snow lay upon the ground and a stiff wind was blowing from the north. The sun was setting, though the clouds brought on an early dusk.

'Fancy a drink?' I asked.

'Why not? My Number One can hold the fort for a bit longer.'

Having signed in with the head porter, I was given a room key and dumped my pack in the cloakroom. Andy and I shucked our greatcoats and went into the bar. It was already busy, the air thick with smoke and raucous laughter, some of it sounding forced to my ear.

Along with my key the hall porter had given me my mess number and I used it to sign for a couple of large whiskies. Drysdale and I raised our glasses to one another before drinking. He paused with the glass to his mouth and stared at my left breast. I knew he was looking at the piece of crimson ribbon and grimaced.

'Jesus H. When did you get that?'

'The last lot.'

'I'd better treat you with a bit more respect then, hadn't I?'

I shook my head. 'It changes nothing.'

Grinning, he held out his hand to me. 'There was I thinking you were one of those death or glory boys and instead I find a real live hero.'

'I'm here because I hope to make a difference. I also mean to live through it.'

'Let me get the next one.' Andy drained his glass.

I followed suit. A number of other officers came over and introduced themselves, though none remarked on the medal, thank goodness. I was beginning to wonder whether or not I should have worn it. Then I thought, why the hell not? I'd been given the bloody thing after all.

The base commander, Phillip Norris, DSO and bar, joined us. He was a regular officer, apparently passed over as a lieutenant commander at the outbreak of hostilities but since promoted. I'd first met him when I'd been doing my training. Friendly buffoon was the first description that came to mind, what with his slow way of talking and shambling gait. However, his DSO had been earned during an affray in the Indian Ocean and the bar when he had been fighting at Dunkirk. So maybe he wasn't such a buffoon after all.

'Mike,' Norris shook my hand, 'glad you're back.' He held onto my hand and nodded at my shoulder. 'You weren't wearing that when you were training.'

'No. My wife insisted I put it on.'

His scowl turned to a friendly grin. 'Good. She has excellent sense. If you've got it flaunt it.' He clapped me on the shoulder. 'It's good for morale. Trust me, I know.'

A short while later Drysdale left and I went up to my cabin to unpack. The room was small, the bed covered with a blanket embroidered with the fouled anchor of the Royal Navy. I felt like a fish out of water. Brushing my teeth I looked at myself in the mirror. *You bloody fool*, I told my forty-four year old reflection.

The following morning I made my way past the new squash courts, the pride of *Vernon*, and along to the offices of Coastal Forces. I reported to Commander Alan "Tam" McVey, a man I'd already met and liked. He had been a regular officer who had left prior to hostilities for a job in the City. As soon as war had broken out he had quit and re-joined with his original rank, though he had lost his seniority. He was a natural to head up our small command, having spent years in coastal minesweepers. He had been CO of the minelayer, HMS *Teviot Bank*. We'd become friendly during training. His stint in the City had made him aware of the Griffiths family and my connection with them. As a result we had become quite close, albeit restrained by the difference of rank, still a factor within the Royal Navy. I'd come a long way from my days as an ignorant Mick, thanks to Sion and David, and so I could hold my own with the best of them.

I opened the door to the outer office. 'Morning,' I greeted the Wren sitting at the desk just inside the door, a covered typewriter in front of her.

'Morning, sir. Can I help?'

'Name's O'Donnell.'

A smile widened her pretty features and dimpled her cheeks. I saw she was a leading Wren writer. 'We've been expecting you. Go right in, he's waiting for you.'

I crossed the room and knocked on the wooden door.

'Enter.'

I went into a room filled with pipe and cigarette smoke. 'Mike, glad to see you.' McVey spoke in a Scots accent, curtsey of a boarding school in Edinburgh. His voice could have been heard across two parade grounds and that was when he was whispering. In his forties, he was thickset, with grey hair swept back from a high forehead. His eyes were hawk-like and his nose hooked, adding to the bird-like impression, but his thin lips were often wreathed in a smile, removing the harshness from a hard face.

'Mike, I'd like you to meet Paul Geddes and Tom Boycroft. They'll be working in your section.'

We shook hands. Both men were RNVR sub-lieutenants. They had graduated from universities that year and had joined as soon as they'd received their degrees. Both were engineers, Geddes in electronics and Boycroft in mechanics. Seeing their fresh, eager faces made me feel old.

'Mike, we were discussing a new development in German mines. Take a seat while I get us some coffee.' Raising his voice Tam called, 'Hazel, coffees please.'

He neither expected nor received a reply. While we waited, Tam puffed on his pipe while Boycroft drew furiously on a "Blue Liner", the strong cigarettes issued by the navy. Geddes sat twiddling his fingers, his eyes screwed up against the fog of smoke.

'Mind if I open a window, sir? I need some air,' I said.

'What? Of course not. Sorry. I'm apt to forget sometimes.'

Opening the window let in a blast of cold air and after only a few seconds I said, 'Perhaps not. I'd rather suffocate than freeze.'

McVey's broad grin showed he'd been expecting such a reaction. Coffee appeared and we got down to the briefing.

'Mike, you should know one of our men, Lt. Chippings, was killed last week. He was a good man. One of the best, followed procedure precisely.'

'What was he working on?' I asked.

'A magnetic mine. It was meant to land in the middle of the Solent but instead hit shallow water and got stuck in the mud banks. Chippings talked his way through each part of the procedure and all appeared to be going well.' He paused.

'What happened, sir?' Geddes asked.

McVey shook his head, a frown on his face, his fingers fiddling with his dead pipe. 'We don't know for sure. The last thing his assistant heard him say was, *'The diabolical bastards.'* Then it went up.'

'Have we any ideas?' I asked. 'Any at all?'

Shaking his head, McVey said, 'All sorts of theories but none that we can put forward with any conviction. Obviously another booby-trap has been put in the mechanism but God and the Germans alone know what it is.'

Booby traps aimed at disposal experts were an on-going problem. No sooner had we found one booby-trap than the Germans set another. Which was why we worked in teams of two. The officer at the mine, the other on the end of the phone cable writing down everything the officer saw and did. Such work frequently cost the life of an officer – highly trained and irreplaceable for the most part.

'You're all new to this, but you're as well trained as we can make you.' McVey continued, 'As from today any one of you can and will be called out. I've assigned your assistants. Their 264s are with Hazel. You can collect them and read them later.' A 264 followed a rating throughout his career. The navy, even in war, ran on its paperwork.

'The three of you are up to speed with all we know right now, but you'll only get good at the job after a few live ones.' He had no need to add, provided you live. We were all aware of the caveat. The phone on his desk rang and Tam answered it. Acknowledging the call, he replaced the receiver and looked at me. 'It's your shout, Mike. Chesil Beach, Portland. Your driver knows the way.'

I stood up with a nod, my mouth suddenly dry. 'I'll see you all later.' I jammed my hat on and walked out. As I approached the outer door, the leading Wren called after me.

'Sir, you forgot this.' She held out a buff coloured folder and I took it from her with an automatic thanks.

I glanced at the name on the front cover. PO Clive Butterworth. It was too late to read it now. I'd know what he was like soon enough, without the prejudice of his previous officers.

Outside the door a cold, biting wind was blowing and I shivered. I was wearing navy blue battle dress and needed to wear something a damn sight warmer if I was going to tackle a mine. It was one thing, I thought with a savage grin, to shake with fear. It was quite another to shake with cold.

24

WEARING MY BURBERRY and gloves, I stood outside the wardroom waiting for the car. An old Austin drew up and a young Wren climbed out and saluted. She opened the back door. I could see a figure sitting in the front, through the misting windows.

Climbing into the car I said, 'Are you PO Butterworth?'

'Yes, sir. Clive Butterworth. I've got the bag and all the gear in the back. This is Wren Johnson. We all call her Johno and she's our regular driver.'

'Pleased to meet you both. You know where we're going?'

'Yes, sir.' Johno had a pleasant voice, with the dulcet tones of Devonshire. She was a pretty young thing and I was surprised to find she was a driver. She couldn't have been much more than eighteen or nineteen. On impulse I asked, 'How old are you Johno?'

Startled, she squinted at me through the rear view mirror. 'Twenty-four, sir.'

I smiled and shook my head. 'I'd put you down as much younger. Sorry to be rude. No offence meant.'

'That's all right, sir. None taken.'

I wondered if they both realised that I was talking to hide my nervousness. All I prayed was that I didn't cock-up the job.

'First job, sir?' Butterworth asked.

'Yes,' I bridled and then realised that I was being unreasonable. Trying to relax I added, 'Does it show?'

Butterworth smiled and looked over his shoulder. 'Not really, sir. But we all have to start somewhere. This is my eighteenth.'

I looked him in the eyes and waited for him to continue. He cleared his throat and said, 'You're the third officer I've worked with.'

'Thanks for that.' I didn't pursue it, a sudden attack of superstition preventing me from asking how long each of the others had survived. However, the PO was keen to supply the information anyway.

'My second officer died four days ago, sir. Lt. Chippings.'

'Ah, I'd heard. I didn't know you'd been with him.'

'The navy's idea is that when you fall off a horse, you get right back on.'

'I've never fallen off a horse,' I said with a smile.

We settled into silence, the heater in the car fighting a losing battle against the insidious cold. A few snowflakes soon disappeared and the remainder of the journey passed under a cloudless, pale blue sky. All too soon we were at Weymouth and heading out towards the Bill. As the promontory narrowed, we saw a barrier ahead, manned by a contingent of three policemen. We stopped.

'Road's closed. You'll have to go back and wait until it's cleared.'

'I know,' I said. 'We're here to clear it.'

'Sorry, sir. I didn't know. Go ahead about three hundred yards and you'll see a bucket of sand on the side of the road. The mine is on your right, next to the bucket.'

Standard procedure, showing us where to go without endangering anyone's life any further. The Wren stopped where she was and we climbed out.

The wind had dropped to a mere whisper and the sun gave a semblance of warmth. I took it as a good omen. Butterworth and I got our bags from the boot and walked towards the marker. When we got there we stood and looked at the offending beast. I had no choice but still I hesitated. If it exploded it would take away the road and cut off the naval base at Portland.

'It's German contact,' Butterworth said. 'The fuse is at right angles to the lifting eye. Contact pushes the horn in and makes the impact switch. That in turn triggers the firing condenser, the arming resistor and the capacitor. You've anything between two and sixteen seconds after that.'

'Thanks, Clive.' I was truly grateful to him. For a second my mind had gone blank when I looked at the black monstrosity. His words had brought back all I needed to know. 'You set up on the other side of the road.'

Armed with a pencil and notepad and carrying the telephone cable reel, Butterworth walked across the narrow road and stood there, watching me climb down the steep, shingle-covered embankment towards the mine. As I did, he unrolled the reel so that the earphones around my neck didn't get snagged.

Above me the seabirds were making their raucous call, but my focus was on the black obscenity and I had neither eyes nor ears for what was around me. The mine was lying completely uncovered on the shingle. I walked around it, looking at the horns. Only one was touching the ground and as far as I could tell the brass tip had not been pushed in at all. That was good news.

'Right, Clive, I'm at the mine. I'm placing my bag next to it. I'm taking the spanner and putting it in place.' The tool was specially constructed of non-magnetic metal. The centre hole fitted over the fuse cover and between the two, small, opposing lugs. Its handle protruded either side, allowing me a good purchase.

'Sir, before you try the fuse, check the mine for wobble.'

I stopped what I was doing. Damn! He was right. I was too keen to get blown up. I gently pushed the mine and to my horror felt it move slightly. I stopped what I was doing, sweat beading my brow in spite of the cold.

'I'm bracing the mine.' Using rocks I placed them carefully around the mine, creating a bed, ensuring none were near a horn. It took a few minutes which seemed to last a lifetime.

'Turning the spanner.' Gripping it at either end I slowly turned the handles in an anti-clockwise direction. Three complete turns and it was open. 'Taking off the cover.' All my senses were trained on the mine. I was listening hard but praying harder. The cover came away and I looked inside, using a small torch. I could see the fuse a few inches under the plate, mocking me. Licking dry lips I used a screwdriver to remove the three holding screws and reached tentatively inside. Each time I told Clive exactly what I was doing. Slowly but surely I removed the fuse and once I had it outside the casing I cut the wires at the bottom. I gave a sigh of relief and told Clive what I'd done.

'The beers are on you, sir,' he said, with a smile in his voice.

'Holy Mother of God, they are that,' I said, my heritage Irish coming out under the stress. Collecting my gear together I climbed back onto the road. Butterworth and I trudged back towards the car in silence.

Arriving at the car I said, 'It's all right now. You can open the road again. We'll go up to the base and arrange a boat to tow the mine away and blow it up.'

The constable saluted. 'Yes, sir. Thank you, sir.'

It took only a few minutes at the base to explain the position and start back towards Portsmouth. We arrived as the sun was setting. I felt exhausted – as if I'd climbed Mt. Everest in a diver's suit. What a way to earn a living!

We stopped at the Keppel's Head, one of the few pubs which hadn't been bombed. We persuaded our Wren driver to join us and I bought two pints of watery ale and a dry sherry. My glass was empty before I knew it. I got myself a second.

'The first one gets you like that, sir,' said Butterworth. 'I know it did me.'

'We're off duty now, Clive, so call me Mike. What's your first name, Wren Johnson?'

'Daisy, sir.'

'The same goes for you as well. Off duty it's Mike. I don't stand on ceremony. How long have you been in?'

'Two years, sir. I mean . . . Mike. I joined up after my fiancé was killed. I had a driving licence and ended up here. I think it's useful work and so I feel like I'm contributing. How come you've joined?' She asked with a mischievous smile. 'Wanting to get away from the wife?'

I laughed. 'Quite the opposite. Truth is, I'm very happily married. Only tied the knot a couple of years ago. No, I volunteered.'

'What were you doing?' Butterworth asked.

'I ran a wireless factory in South Wales, with my wife. A lot of the R/T sets you find in planes nowadays come from us.' I pointed behind the bar. 'See that set? That's one of ours.'

They both looked suitably impressed. 'You make those?' Butterworth asked. 'I've got one at home.'

'We've got one in the mess,' said Daisy. 'They're everywhere.'

I nodded. 'We like to think so.'

'Do you *own* the company?' she asked in awe.

'No. Though I've got shares in it. I've worked for twenty years for a remarkable family called Griffiths. They make the Griffin fighters and bombers.'

'Crikey,' Daisy took a gulp of her sherry and gasped. Coughing, she added, 'Sorry, that went down the wrong way.'

'I'll get another one.' I shouldered my way to the busy bar and managed to attract the barman's attention. I got another sherry, a large rum for Butterworth and a double whisky for myself. I'd had enough of weak beer. Back at the table they wanted to hear some more about the Griffithses. I began to entertain them with some of the exploits I'd had with Sion. After a short while I realised that I sounded as though I was boasting and shut up.

'You must like them a great deal,' said Daisy with insight.

I nodded. I was aware I'd said too much. Partly, I knew, because of the tension I'd been through. Nothing like facing your first unexploded mine to get an attack of verbal diarrhoea, it seemed. Sion and I, after being in a harrowing situation, and there'd been a few in our time, liked to sit and demolish a bottle of whisky and talk profound drivel. Talking helped. We hadn't done much talking since Alex's death, I realised.

'Time to get back,' I announced. We returned to *Vernon* and the car dropped us at the workshops where we kept the gear. After checking it in, we walked towards the senior rates' mess on our way to the wardroom. At the door I held my hand out to Butterworth. 'Thanks for what you did today. I appreciate it.'

'Appreciate what, sir?'

'You know damn well what. When we were standing looking at that beast my mind went completely blank. Your litany made my brain function again.'

Butterworth nodded. 'I've seen it before, sir. But I knew you'd be all right once you got started.'

'Thanks for the vote of confidence.'

'My pleasure, sir. Now, if you'll excuse me, I'm going in for my tot.'

I walked back to the wardroom in time to change out of my working rig and into evening wear. There might be a war on but the navy still maintained its standards.

That week I dismantled a second mine and blew up a third. Before we knew it, Christmas was upon us and I was given some leave. Four whole days.

I arrived back in Cardiff to hail and sleet. The train had been packed with servicemen and women, all enduring various degrees of discomfort, either standing in the corridors or crammed into seats. Woe betide anyone who wanted to use the toilet. The journey was made worse by the trains being over-heated, stuffy and subject to numerous and unexplained delays. I climbed out at Cardiff with a sigh of relief.

Betty was waiting impatiently for me, stamping up and down the platform, her old fur coat and hat helping to keep out the cold.

Her smile when she saw me pushing through the crowd was enough to warm me to my soul.

Betty had a daughter from a previous marriage, who was now eighteen. Myfanwy had started at Cardiff University that autumn, reading mathematics. She wasn't especially pretty but her personality more than made up for it – she was vivacious, blessed with a zest for life matched with a cutting wit. I can say truthfully that I loved her as my own. I was thrilled to see her sitting at the wheel of the car outside the station; and slightly less thrilled to hear she'd passed her driving test only the day before.

'Hi, Mike,' she smiled at me as I opened the door.

'Hullo, Myfanwy, my darling, how's university?'

'Wonderful. Simply wonderful.'

Betty and I sat in the back, Betty snuggling against my arm as we pulled away with a sharp grating of the gears that made me wince.

'Isn't this fun?' Myfanwy laughed, looking over her shoulder at me.

'I'd rather you watched the road, my girl,' I said with sincere severity.

She laughed again. 'For a VC holder you're a terrible coward.'

'We've a Christmas tree up, and decorations in the lounge,' said Betty. 'And I lied and cheated and got us some extra food coupons so we'll have a decent meal.'

'I told Mother it was wrong but she wouldn't listen.' Myfanwy displayed all the honesty and outrage of youth. I grinned at the holier-than-thou tone in her voice.

'Mother?' I asked. 'What happened to Mam?'

'That's far too *plebeian*,' she announced.

I suppressed a grin and looked at Betty who raised an eyebrow and a smile. 'It's wonderful what a university education will do for you,' she said.

'Such as?' Now I was suppressing the urge to laugh.

'You learn to use such words as *plebeian*,' Betty spluttered, wanting to laugh as well. 'You've lost weight, *gwas*,' Betty said, using the Welsh for lad or servant.

'You'll have to help me put it back on then, won't you, my lady?'

Dusk had fallen and we were driving slowly through what was now a light snowfall, our covered lights barely making an impression on the visibility. Like the other vehicles on the street we were driving slowly, fearful of hitting anything or anyone. As it was Christmas Eve we were fairly certain there would be no air raid that night. The weather ensured it.

Once we were out of the dark city we hit countryside and the snow began to fall in thickening flakes, beginning to lie on the cold slush. Red Lava hospital loomed on the hill on our right and we turned off the main road towards Creigiau. The high hedges kept some of the snow away and the road was relatively free. Even so my heart was in my mouth when Myfanwy took us up to 30mph. I asked her to slow down, which she did, with a laugh and a glance over her shoulder.

The road deteriorated into a small country lane and we finally arrived at the steep hill leading to our village, Efail Isaf. Here was open country and the snow was beginning to pile up on the road. No other cars had passed and the road lay virgin white ahead of us.

'Take it slow and steady, don't accelerate and don't brake, even if the back of the car begins to slide from under,' I said, fairly certain we wouldn't make it. Luckily there were no ditches, only hedgerows on either side.

Myfanwy took a deep breath, moved into second and we travelled along at a steady ten to fifteen miles per hour. Then, halfway up the hill, the back wheels pushed and the front lost their grip. The car began to turn. Myfanwy panicked, took her foot off the accelerator and braked. The car came to a halt and began to slide sideways down the hill.

'What shall I do? What shall I do?' Myfanwy cried in panic.

'Nothing. Don't worry. Let the front of the car touch the bank and we'll spin round,' I said. The car touched, the front slowed and the rear slid back. 'We'll go all the way to the bottom and start again.' We continued sliding, with Myfanwy looking over her shoulder, steering, worry etched into her face. At the bottom we came to a halt.

'Right, that's it! You can drive,' Myfanwy threw at me.

'Nope, my darling, *you* can drive. We'll start again. Go into first gear, build up to ten miles per hour and go into second. Keep it steady, follow our tracks. Don't brake but slow down if you have to by taking your foot off the accelerator.'

'I can't. I'm hopeless,' she wailed.

'No you're not.' I said sharply. 'You can do it. And if we fail again you can have a third try and a fourth. Now let's go.'

She put the car into gear, this time without the loud grinding noise, and moved off slowly, picking up speed and then changing gently into second. In the dim headlights, I could see the tracks we had made earlier beginning to fill with snow as I leaned forward and encouraged her.

'That's it. Good girl. Nice and steady.'

We reached the point we'd been at earlier, passed it and were almost at the summit. In her eagerness to reach the top, Myfanwy pressed too hard on the accelerator and the back kicked out again. We stopped at right angles, the car juddered to a halt and the engine cut.

'See! See I told you I couldn't do it!'

'Myfanwy, calm down,' I said soothingly. 'In the overall scale of things, what does it matter? I'll get out and push the front of the car so it is pointing downhill. Start the engine and put the car into reverse and drive the last bit backwards.'

I got out. The wind had died away and the snow was falling gently but thickly. There was a peaceful feel to the night, warmer than when we'd been in Cardiff. 'Turn the wheel hard to the left and I'll push.' The nose of the car slid round and the car came to a halt, facing down hill. 'Start the engine and go backwards,' I called. 'Don't over-rev it! Nice and steady when I say.' I stood in front of the car and pushed on the bonnet. 'Now!'

The back tyres scrabbled at the snow and I pushed with all my might. The car didn't move. I strained harder, heard the car door slam and then Betty was beside me, pushing. The wheels gripped, the car moved and she and I fell flat on our faces as the car went over the brow.

I looked at Betty, with her hat to one side and snow on her face and laughed out loud. She looked askance for a moment and then burst out laughing too. I gave her a resounding kiss. A few seconds later Myfanwy called to us and we climbed to our feet, laughing still.

The remainder of the journey was safe and simple and we arrived at our house, *Anghorfa*, a short while later. The fire in the kitchen stove was alight, though low, and I stoked it up. One thing about living near the Beddau mine, there was plenty of coal to buy if you knew the right person and were prepared to pay the price. To Myfanwy's disapproval, we did.

It was good to be home. The house was the third in a row of three, with a driveway separating it from the next three. Downstairs we had four tidy sized rooms and upstairs three bedrooms and a bathroom. The toilet was outside, next to the coalhouse and shed.

A meal of lamb stew was in the oven. We ate it at the kitchen table, washed down with cups of tea. The conversation was a catch-up on all that had happened while I'd been away, interspersed with events at Cardiff University.

The factory was working flat out. All day, seven days a week, three shifts a day. Production had shifted from wireless sets, still an important and profitable market, to R/T equipment for airplanes and now ships. Our research and development section had doubled, working to reduce the size of the sets, increase their range and their frequencies.

Betty's eagerness to share developments at the factory pleased me greatly. 'We've had to hire new buses to cope with the increase of workers – we're bringing some of them in from as far away as Merthyr, Treherbert and Aberbargoed. Manpower is proving a problem. Or should I call it womanpower? On the assembly line women are far better than men,' she smiled. 'Faster and nimbler. The men are better at operating machinery and humping the heavy boxes.' Her light-hearted talk no doubt hid many obstacles she'd had to overcome – I was so proud of my wife.

I turned to Myfanwy and asked, 'How are your lodgings?'

She rolled her eyes theatrically. 'Rooms, Mike, we call them rooms. On my stairs we have a set of eight. The girls are good fun. We have late night sit-ins, drinking wine and smoking.'

She made it sound like a bacchanalian orgy, but the girls, I suspected, were all from sheltered backgrounds. Drinking wine and smoking was about as hedonistic a life style as they could imagine. I knew it would change all too soon. Soon, no doubt, she'd meet someone. I hoped whoever she met would be kind and gentle to her. I shook my head. I was getting maudlin and I'd only just arrived home.

'Let's go into the lounge,' Betty said. 'Leave the dishes. We can do them later.' I was stunned. Not washing the dishes immediately after eating went against years of Welsh indoctrination.

Before switching on the light we checked the blackout curtains were properly drawn. It was now a habit in every household, done without thought. Betty switched on a sidelight, while Myfanwy turned on the lights decorating the Christmas tree. The bulbs flickered for a few seconds and then burnt brightly. The tree was beautifully dressed in decorations. Under it lay a number of parcels. I reached out for the nearest one only to have my hand slapped by Betty.

'Leave it, *cariad*, until the morning. Let me get you a drink. A whisky and soda.'

A fire was laid in the grate and Myfanwy lit it with a match. I settled into my favourite seat while Betty went to the sideboard where a new bottle of whisky and a soda syphon stood. Myfanwy fiddled with the wireless and got the Proms, now housed in the Royal Albert Hall, playing Shostakovitch's Seventh Symphony. It had been written in Leningrad when the city was under siege by the Germans and smuggled out on microfilm in the diplomatic bag.

Just for a moment God was in his heaven and all was right with the world. I must have been nuts to have joined up. But it was too late now – I was in the system.

25

CHRISTMAS WAS JUST the three of us. In the morning Betty and Myfanwy went to chapel at the top of the village. I walked up the hill with them but stopped halfway, at the Carpenter's Arms. It was my local and I was welcomed back like the prodigal son.

After Betty's delicious turkey dinner we spent the afternoon listening to the wireless, where we were treated to the King's Christmas Message followed by an afternoon play. The evening show, live from London was a joy, with songs like *"White Christmas"* and *"We'll meet again"*. It was later that night, as she lay in my arms, that I finally asked her about Sion.

'I've been so busy, Mike, I haven't seen him for weeks. We've spoken on the phone twice but that's been about business.'

'How did he sound?'

'Tired. But I guess we're all tired.'

'Aye, love, that's for sure. I need to get over to see him. David wrote to me a couple of weeks back with information about Alex's death. His senior officer, Squadron Leader Cutler attacked both planes. It seems he shot down Ginger and then Alex. Alex got him at the same time.'

'My God, that's terrible. Why?'

'I don't really know. Neither does David. It seems Cutler was a coward. He resented Alex, his money and his success as a pilot. He'd been passed over for promotion a few times – Alex had come to symbolise his own twisted failures. Who knows what goes on in the head of someone like that?'

Betty was devastated. 'Poor Sion and Kirsty – my heart goes out to them. What a tragic waste. To be killed by the enemy is one thing . . .' she tailed off, clearly very upset, tears trickling down her cheeks.

'According to David, they're still suffering very badly. I dread seeing them.'

'I know, my love, I know.'

There was no chance of getting to St Athan to see Kirsty and Sion – all of South Wales was snow bound. The war, just for a little while, had come to a stop because of the bad weather. There were blizzards out of the Arctic sweeping the Continent. For me it meant more time at home, for the factory it meant a loss of production, which it could afford but the war couldn't.

I badly wanted to get out to Sion's place. Three days after Christmas I heard a local farmer in the pub, complaining about the weather. I stood next to him with a pint of Hancock's beer in my hand.

'The sheep are half buried under the snow, but at least I've got fodder out to them. All I can do now is wait for the thaw.'

Suddenly I had the solution to my problem. 'Do you have a tractor?'

'Daft question, man, of course I do.'

'Can I borrow it?'

He looked at me suspiciously. 'What for?'

'I need to get to the airfield at St Athan.'

I had lived in the small community for a number of years and everyone knew just about everything there was to know about each other. He thought about it for a few seconds and asked, 'What will you pay me for it?'

'What will you take?'

'One of them new radiograms what you're making in Taff's Well. And ten records.'

The retail value was heavy but the cost to me was well worth it. I didn't want to seem too eager though, so I said, 'The new model but no records.'

A wide smile creased his weather beaten face and he held out his hand. 'Done.'

An hour later I drove up outside the house on the tractor, diesel smoke belching out the back of the exhaust, my hands already frozen to the steering wheel. The tractor had no cab and no heating system. Thankfully the blanket of snow that lay across the country had brought with it calm weather, cold but clear. All I needed was warm clothing and a thick pair of gloves.

Betty's surprise turned to mirth when I told her what I was about.

I packed an overnight bag, put on my battledress uniform and warm winter overcoat, pulled my cap low over my forehead, wrapped a scarf around my ears and throat and finally slipped my hands into a pair of thick mitts, my Christmas present from Myfanwy.

'I must see Sion. I'll be back later tomorrow.'

'I understand, *gwas*, only take care.'

I kissed Myfanwy's cheek, gave Betty a big hug and climbed onto the tractor. Sitting so high I had a good view of the countryside. I engaged the gears and moved away with a jerk, the huge back wheels and deep treads easily gripping in the snow. I had, I knew, more or less ten miles to travel.

I had hoped to enjoy the journey but the truth was it was damned uncomfortable. The steel seat began to hurt after a while, the tractor bucked and jerked under me, the engine often sounding as though it was about to cut out as water in the fuel was sucked through the system. After twenty minutes I began to think I must have been crazy to start the journey and after a further twenty I *knew* I was mad. But I persevered. I'd gone that far so there was no turning back. In truth I didn't want to. I knew it was important to talk to my friend about Alex's death. I owed him that much and a great deal more. In fact, I owed him everything. So I told myself to quit bellyaching and get on with the ride.

The deep snow persisted almost to the coast where it quickly faded away as the salt air had its effect. I saw planes taking off in the distance and knew there wasn't far to go. When I arrived at the gatehouse I was greeted with grins. Stiffly I climbed down off the seat, hardly able to walk until I got my circulation going again. I showed my identity card and explained I was there to see Mr Griffiths. A phone call was made and I was told to go over to the house.

Sion and Kirsty were waiting outside for me when I arrived, wan smiles on their faces. Both were looking gaunt and tired.

Climbing down, I gave Kirsty a hug and Sion a warm handshake. They had both aged since I'd seen them last.

'I've come,' I announced, 'with your Christmas presents.' To the back of the tractor I'd tied a bag with gifts for each of them, as well as for Louise and Paul.

We went inside the house. There were no decorations and it was obvious that Christmas hadn't been celebrated.

Superficially they appeared all right but it was clear they were going through the motions. There was a coldness between them that

I didn't like. One I had never seen before. They were polite to each other, but nothing more. It was as if they were strangers.

Kirsty made tea, which we drank almost in silence. The atmosphere was eerie. How many evenings had passed like this since Alex's death? I knew them to be such a warm, loving couple, yet it was clear that the pain of their loss was driving them apart. When Kirsty cleared the cups away, I decided to confront Sion. Did he realise what was happening to them?

'I figured there was a reason for your visit, Mike. Not that rubbish about Christmas presents. I know you mean well but mind your own business, there's a good chap.'

'What about Alex?' I asked. 'What would he say if he could see you now?'

'Shut up, Mike.' Sion said, his voice quiet, menacing.

I decided to give it to him straight. If someone didn't lance the poison it would eat away at them until it was too late. 'Sion, you are my best friend. After all we've been through together and after all you've done for me there's nothing I wouldn't do to help. And you know it. Alex's death was pointless, a tragedy. But you've got to get out of your self-pity and misery. You are destroying your family.'

'How dare you speak to me like that?' Sion was yelling now. Kirsty came back in to the room, her face chalk white, a hand to her throat. He got to his feet, the chair falling over with a clatter. 'Get out! Get out of my house, you unfeeling bastard.'

I sat where I was, looking at him, trying my best to keep calm, not to lose my temper, which, believe me, was very difficult for a man of my temperament. I reminded myself of my regard, even love for Sion and stayed seated. My stubbornness paid off, for Sion tottered to the next chair and sat down, his head resting in his hands. Kirsty placed a hand on his arm, which he ignored.

'You have to listen to me, Sion. Alex's death was quick and relatively painless. We know that now. Cutler was a piece of scum who should never have held the position he did. Alex and Ginger – their dying was a tragic waste. God alone knows what either of them might have achieved if they'd lived. But men are being killed, either on the battlefield, by accident or heaven forbid, murdered, every day. Alex was plain unlucky, that's all.'

'Unlucky? Unlucky? He was my son, damn it.' Sion hit the table with his fist.

'He was also Kirsty's son and Paul and Louise's brother. And don't you forget it. You have to move on. Put it behind you. Life goes on, Sion. What happened to Christmas here?'

'Christmas,' he said bitterly. 'How could we celebrate Christmas?'

'But what about Louise and Paul? Didn't they deserve to celebrate Christmas? You've got to try, Sion. You owe it to them. You owe it to Kirsty.'

'They stayed away. Made excuses.' Tears sprang to his eyes and I knew my words were hitting home. He knew he was being unreasonable, but some inner wellspring of grief was holding him in its grip and wouldn't let him go. He got unsteadily to his feet and lurched to the cupboard in the corner, opened it and took out a bottle of whisky. His hand was shaking as he opened the top and poured a couple of inches into a glass.

'That's it, Sion,' said Kirsty bitterly. 'Drown your sorrows, why don't you? I never thought . . .' her voice faded.

Sion turned to her with a piercing look. 'Never thought what? That I could be so pathetic? Say it, why don't you?'

She shook her head, tears rolling down her cheeks. 'Please, Sion, come back to me.'

It was one of the saddest things I have ever heard. As she crossed the room to him, Sion snatched up the bottle and smashed it against the wall. In the grim silence that followed we heard the air-raid warning sirens begin to sound, faintly at first but building. The sound of planes grew louder. Next came the ack-ack guns, firing repeatedly. It looked as though the bad weather in Europe had finally abated and Jerry was back in the war. Bombs began to drop, exploding loudly in the distance.

I had taken half a step towards the door when I was blown off my feet as an explosion ripped through the side of the house.

I came to after only a few seconds. Dust was still settling as I looked around me. Kirsty was lying with blood on her face, as still as death, while Sion was sitting up, groaning, his head in his hands.

I crawled over to Kirsty, calling her name. Sion, seeing her, let out a cry of anguish and crawled across the rubble. He called her name, telling her over and over again how sorry he was. Her hand was as cold as ice but I could feel a pulse in her neck.

'Help me get her into the bedroom,' I said.

'If it's still standing.'

Picking her up between us we went along the corridor to their bedroom. It was intact and we placed her gently on the bed. The attack was already fading as the guns and lack of fuel drove the German bombers away.

'Get some warm water and bandages,' Sion ordered.

The warm water washed away the blood to show a deep gash across her forehead. She seemed otherwise unhurt. Sion bandaged her head with strips I tore from Kirsty's cotton sheets. She was breathing steadily and her pulse seemed to be beating strongly.

'Is there a doctor anywhere?'

'No, but we do have a medical orderly and a nurse from the Queen Alexandra lot. They're normally over in the main offices but I suspect they're out around the field checking on any wounded.'

'I'll go and see if I can find one of them.'

He nodded and I left him holding her hand, tears rolling down his cheeks.

I returned with the nurse, a competent-looking woman from the Queen Alexandra's Imperial Nursing Service. She quickly checked Kirsty over, lifted an eyelid and checked her pupil before nodding.

'She'll be all right after a bit of rest. A small concussion I think. There are no other injuries?'

Sion shook his head. 'Not that I can tell.'

'If you gentlemen will leave the room I'll take a look.'

We left her and went back to the kitchen. It was a real mess. One wall was blown out and the two adjoining walls had large cracks in them. Darkness was falling and the wind was picking up, bringing with it a biting cold. The room looked as desolate as Sion's face. I said nothing, waiting for him to speak.

Before he could say a word the nurse appeared. 'I'm sure Mrs. Griffiths will be fine, sir. If you'd like me to fetch the doctor from the village to confirm . . .'

'No, nurse, that's quite all right. I've never known you to be wrong before. Thank you very much. You'd better see to your other duties.'

He looked at me. 'So had I. I'll check the hangars and assembly sheds.'

'I'll come with you.'

First Sion checked on Kirsty before going out into the deepening darkness. The raid had missed most of the buildings but had blown holes in large chunks of the field. A downed Dornier lay smouldering in the middle of the airfield and two Griffins sat broken at their

266

dispersal points. After an hour we established there had been relatively little other damage. But there had been loss of life. Two of the 40mm Bofors emplacements had been wiped out, killing three men and injuring a fourth. Two others had also been hurt but not seriously. The squadron of fighters that normally would have been on the ground had been out on patrol, otherwise casualties would have been heavier. We returned to the house to find Kirsty awake.

I left her and Sion together and went to the room Sion used as a study. Although the house was a pre-fab, he'd now put five of them together, creating offices, work places and living quarters. I knew where another bottle of whisky was kept. I poured a large tot and took a grateful mouthful before lighting the fire, stoking it high, getting some warmth into my bones. I hadn't felt warm since I had started out from Efail Isaf but between the drink and the fire I was beginning to feel human once again.

I looked round the room, my eyes returning to the collection of silver in the corner. I stood up and went to look. I can only describe it as a shrine to Alex. The entire cabinet was filled with photographs and trophies – milestones in Alex's life. The centrepiece was his Distinguished Flying Cross, mounted in a glass-fronted wooden box. Looking at it filled me with emotion for a few seconds and then I turned away. How hard it must have been for them – these few tokens all they had left of their wonderful boy.

Sion was some time. When he finally came into the study his face was still haggard but there was a shift, a gentleness in him that hadn't been there since Alex's death. He walked over to me and held his hand out. I stood, took it in a warm grip and shook it. There was no need for words.

'Welcome back, Sion,' I said, and he knew what I meant.

Nodding, Sion helped himself to a large whisky and soda. Taking a mouthful, he stood looking at the corner, staring at Alex's medal. After a moment Sion lifted the DFC off the wall, stood looking at it for a few moments, wiped the glass with his sleeve and placed it in the top drawer of his desk. Other items followed. Finally he held a picture of his son in flying gear, touched it gently then placed it on the sideboard. It sat alongside a picture of Louise in her nurse's uniform and Paul in blazer and slacks. I thought there were tears in his eyes, but I was finding my eyesight oddly blurred so couldn't be sure.

After a while he said, 'I nearly lost her. Nearly lost everything. But I couldn't see beyond my grief. It had me in such a powerful grip I felt I was drowning.' Taking another mouthful of whisky he summoned up a smile. 'I've neglected things for too long. The nights have been hell.' He looked at me and said, 'I've been waking up, with a wet face, Mike. Tears in the night. Like a baby. I didn't know what to do.' He paused and added. 'You've heard about Paul?'

'No, what?'

'He's some sort of mathematical genius. We knew he was clever at sums but his tutor says he's never seen anything like it. Apparently he's invented some formula which helps to crack codes. Something to do with random access of letters and numbers. He told me about it but to be honest I only understood about one word in three. It seems Bletchley Park are after him.' Sion shook his head.

'Is he signing up?'

Sion shook his head. 'He can't, thank God. His eyesight isn't good enough. Besides which, the boffins want him. David knows all about it. He says Paul's work would be invaluable. Worth a battalion any day.' Sion shrugged. 'In a selfish way I'm just grateful he's not fighting.'

It was ironic that Sion wouldn't hesitate to risk his life whilst fearful that his children did. I supposed it was the nature of parenthood – something I would never know for myself.

'You should be proud. Of them all.' I cast a glance at the photographs of his three children.

'I am.'

Raising my glass in salute I silently thanked God he'd be all right now.

He sat opposite me, on the other side of the fire, staring at the flames. I left him in peace. He had made the first steps. I hoped he had the strength to continue. Of course he would, I consoled myself, he was a Griffiths.

I finally returned to Portsmouth on New Year's Eve. It was 1943 and the country, the world, was gripped by war. There were no taxis and a long queue outside the station so I decided to walk to *Vernon*. Passing the local flea-pit I saw there were two films showing, "*In Which We Serve*", written by and starring Noel Coward, about the sinking of Lord Mountbatten's ship, HMS *Kelly*, and "*Casablanca*", with Humphrey Bogart and Ingrid Bergman. I'd seen neither, but made a mental note to take Betty when I had a chance. She was a big fan of Bogey.

A wet snow started again and I turned up my collar and trudged on, my head down against the wind. As I walked through the gloom of the dark city I thought of Alex. An old poem, "For the Fallen", came to me and I began reciting it to myself.

They shall not grow old, as we that are left grow old.
Age shall not weary them, nor the years condemn.
At the going down of the sun, and in the morning,
We shall remember them.

I had always loved it, but now, more than ever, I treasured it. Laurence Binyon had written it about the soldiers who had fallen during the Great War. The fact that it was still so apt was, to my way of thinking, a terrible indictment against man. Why, despite all the lessons of the past, did we continue to kill each other? I changed my grip to my left hand, hefting the bag, easing the cold in my fingers, and reached into my pocket for my ID card. I was at the gates and back fighting the war my way.

26

THE YEAR STARTED quietly but we had a heavy air raid on Portsmouth during the third week of January. There was nothing for me to do but cower in an air raid shelter and wait for the bombing to stop. The shelter was packed with men and women from various branches of the navy – signallers, cooks, drivers, asdic operators, alongside medics and nurses and chaplains – all squashed in alongside the supply branch and staff from the NAAFI. The bomb and mine disposal units and the diving section were last in. A disparate mass of humanity united in a common grip of fear. Some showed it, others didn't, but we all felt it.

A bomb landed close by and shook the solid concrete roof. Dust descended like a cloud, making us cough. A couple of light bulbs burst.

Someone started the refrain "*It's a long way to Tipperary*" in a deep bass and we all joined in, raising our voices and our hopes. After a while things went quiet and then the all-clear was sounded. As the notes faded and we reluctantly began to disperse, to re-enter the real world, a door opened and a voice yelled, 'Bomb disposal needed. Please hurry.'

The crowd parted like the Red Sea and we walked through as they silently watched us leave. It could only mean one thing.

We went straight to the office. Tam McVey was waiting for us. His face was grim.

'A school was hit during the raid. The kids had stayed behind to watch a rehearsal of "A Midsummer Night's Dream" by the local amateur dramatics society. Some of the children were killed outright, though we don't know how many yet.'

I was still waiting for him to get to the bad news and from the look on PO Butterworth's face, so was he.

270

'Dozens of kids are trapped under the rubble and the Fire Brigade is working to get them out right now.'

I knew he still hadn't got to the bad bit. Then he did. 'An aerial mine landed next to the school. One of the firemen reports that he can hear ticking from inside the mine.' Here was another anomaly about lines of demarcation. The mine was clearly above the high-water mark, but it was a naval weapon. We'd drawn the short straw on this one.

My mouth was suddenly dry and my palms sweating. Butterworth and I exchanged glances.

'As you know,' Tam lectured us, 'we have no idea how long it will be before detonation. The maximum time we have on record is, as near as we can tell, ninety minutes.'

'How long so far?' I asked.

McVey shrugged. 'Between twenty and thirty minutes. Look, you don't *need* to go.' He paused. 'It's a job for volunteers, if anybody. You two are too valuable saving strategic targets, which are our main concern. That goes for all the teams.'

'What are the Fire Brigade doing?'

'Digging through the rubble.'

'Presumably the Home Guard, parents and others are there as well?'

Looking at me he nodded bleakly. He knew where I was going.

'Then the sooner we get there the better. Come on, Clive. Address?'

'Johno knows.'

Grabbing our gear we hurried away. Wren Johnson was already waiting outside with the car, the engine running.

We set off with a jerk and a roar. The barrier at the gate swung open and the sentry saluted as we swept past. It didn't take long, ten minutes at the most to get to Southsea. The old town had taken a battering that night and in the clear skies we could see the glow of fires across the whole area. We came to a stop about three hundred yards from the school.

Butterworth and I walked towards the destroyed building. There we met the fire chief, directing operations from the road.

Briefly shaking hands I asked, 'Where is it?'

He pointed at the corner of the building, which was still intact. The parachute of the aerial mine was caught on the top of the outer wall. Underneath it dangled the unexploded mine, its nose in the rubble, its tail inches from the ground. People were frantically digging

271

within yards of it. Though it looked like there was no order to their efforts I quickly saw that they were tunnelling in two places.

'We can hear the kids. When the raid started they went into the boiler room in the basement. Not all of them made it. So far we've dug out six bodies. I don't need to tell you what'll happen if that thing goes off.'

'When did it land?'

Glancing at his watch he said, 'Approximately thirty minutes ago. We can't be exact, I'm sorry.'

'That's all right. I didn't expect you to be. You know that once the ticking starts the longest the clock runs is ninety minutes?'

'So I've heard.'

'How long do you need?' I asked.

He shrugged. 'At least two hours.'

'Then we've no choice. Hopefully we know enough not to set it off, provided Jerry hasn't come up with any more nasty surprises. If he has . . .' I shrugged. Words were unnecessary.

He stood looking at me, stoically. His lined face showed that he knew the score, that he'd seen it all and some. 'We lose either way. We can't reach the kids in time or . . .' he left the sentence hanging in the air.

'Do you want to call your men and the civilians away?'

'Many of them are digging for their own children. What would you do?'

I nodded. 'Fair enough. We'd better get started.'

Butterworth had already run out the telephone cable. Whatever happened he had to be far enough away to survive the blast.

It was a German Mark III air mine with a castellated parachute holder at one end and a fuse at the other. Four feet wide, one foot in diameter and packed with enough explosives to demolish an area of hundreds of yards. If it went off I wouldn't even know I was dead.

The lifting lug in the centre of the mine was the reference point and we measured degrees around from it. When I approached I saw that the detonator placer was at 270 degrees. The bomb fuse in the nose was resting on a pile of rubble. The contact had started the clock ticking.

I was aware of eyes on my back as I knelt beside the bloody thing and began my monologue to Clive. A stethoscope confirmed the ticking, louder than my heartbeat.

'The nose fuse started the clock. It's got a det placer and so I'll have to remove the whole thing. I've checked over the surface but can't see any light sensitive cells. I'm placing the spanner around the lugs and turning now.'

A sharp blow with a wooden mallet started the spanner turning and I twisted it smoothly. I removed the holding nut and placed it on the ground. In spite of the cold I felt the sweat on my brow. I did my best to ignore the noises around me, concentrating on the task in hand, praying it wouldn't explode. Not now. Not when I was so close. The thought came unwanted into my head. If the ticking stopped I had about two seconds to live.

The plaintive cries of children in distress came to me as I eased off the cover and exposed the detonator placer. I had two nuts and two wires to cut before it was rendered safe. But before I could do that I had to see if there were any surprises inside that could prove "fatal to my health". I grinned to myself, remembering the euphemism used by my instructor only a few months ago.

I shone a thin pencil beam torch inside and looked closely. Everything seemed normal. Taking out the socket spanner set, I fixed the extension, selected the right size and placed it over the first nut. 'Clive, I'm removing the two nuts.' The first twisted cleanly off. I began on the second one but after a few turns I paused. It didn't feel right.

'Clive?'

'Here, boss.'

'As I twist the second one I can feel the pressure remaining on the back of the plate.'

He was silent for a few moments and then said in a subdued voice, 'A pressure switch?'

'That's what I figured.' I licked my lips with a tongue that was drier than the Sahara desert. Luckily the ticking was loud in my ears.

I felt with my fingers around the back of the clock. Gingerly I touched a spring and felt a flat square plate pushing outwards. How far did it need to travel to engage and detonate? Whatever the distance I knew it could be measured in tenths of an inch, if not hundredths. The ticking clock was suddenly louder in my ears and the sweat began to sting my eyes.

I could get my hand behind the placer and I felt for the pressure plate. I took the precaution of tightening the bolt a full turn before removing my hand and reaching into my bag for a thin metal plate about an inch wide. With the utmost care, I slipped it behind the placer and pushed it down. The spring contracted and the plate moved away from the holder. Now came the really tricky bit. I held the spring down while I undid the second bolt, praying there were no further surprises. The second bolt came clear and I slipped the detonator placer off and let it dangle at the end of its wires. Holding the plate in position with one hand I felt in my bag for a pair of wire cutters. Grasping them I placed the cutting edges around the first wire and was just about to cut when I heard the ticking stop. I severed both wires in a slashing motion and threw myself to the ground. I lay there for a few seconds waiting for the bang, for oblivion. Nothing happened. I realised the bomb was silent. Bile rose from my stomach at the thought of how close I'd come.

Climbing to my feet I wiped my mouth with the back of my hand and spoke to Clive. 'You can come in now.'

I needn't have bothered. He was already there.

'You all right?'

I nodded. 'Yeah, I'll live. The bastard thing stopped just as I was about to cut the wires.'

'Jesus. That was close.'

'Call the squad to take this thing away and we'll give these fine people a hand digging out the children. Some honest work will do us good.'

Keeping busy I was able to hide how shaken I was. I had been within a second of death. To lose your life in the heat of battle was one thing, to be obliterated by a bomb quite another.

Digging through the rubble hid the tremor in my hands.

Forty-eight youngsters and three adults came out alive. However, the bodies of seven children and two adults were dug from that collapsed building. Nine lives. Anger coursed through my body as each tiny corpse was retrieved from the ashes – with each casualty my instincts screamed for revenge.

We returned to *Vernon* where we were told that we would not be needed any further that night. I said goodnight to Clive and Daisy – I couldn't think of her as Johno for some reason – and went to the wardroom. A large whisky calmed my nerves and washed the taste of fear from my mouth.

I wondered if it was true what they said about courage – that you only had so much? That once it was used up you were finished? Or did it keep replenishing itself, like a bottomless well, springing from a source deep somewhere within the soul? Jesus Nelly, I was becoming way too introspective for my own liking.

Andy Drysdale appeared, slightly the worse for wear. 'Ah, Mike, have a drink with me. I've now been officially relieved and this is my last day. I'm off to Scapa to join my new ship. Work-up followed by Atlantic convoys. I'm looking forward to it.'

I joined my friend, sitting in the wardroom, drinking too many whisky and beer chasers. When he went tottering down the corridor to his bunk, I went the other way. It was the last time I saw him. Three weeks later he was missing-in-action on the Russian convoys, presumed dead. Of course, we *knew* he was dead. In winter, at that latitude, you froze to death within a few minutes.

As spring approached the war began to turn in our favour. There was no defining moment, just a growing realisation that eventually we would win. Or rather that the Nazis would lose. There would be no winners. Too much had already been sacrificed, in lives and resources. The realisation came to me as I sat in the wardroom listening to news broadcast by the BBC. The Red Army were, at long last, driving the Germans out of Russia and the Americans were pushing Rommel's Afrika Korps out of Tunisia.

I was averaging two call-outs a week. If it was at all possible we blew them up. If not, either for strategic reasons or because the devastation would be too horrific, we dealt with them there and then. Across the UK, one bomb disposal officer was dying per week. It was a sobering thought. Alternatively, I mused as I replenished my glass at the bar, a good reason to have another drink.

Geddes came into the wardroom and joined me. 'Rot your guts that will,' he said with a cheery nod at my glass.

I grinned. 'Lemonade is for women,' I retorted.

Raising his glass in salute he took a healthy mouthful. 'Refreshing though. I've had an idea.'

Patiently I waited for him to continue. He spoke with the relaxed, deliberate drawl of a west countryman and though he sounded slow I knew he was far from it. In fact, when it came to explosives and mines he was brilliant, having designed a number of useful tools already, which we were now employing.

'Do you know what happens if you steam explosives?'

I shrugged. 'No idea.'

'It melts. It also becomes more stable. It's as if the steam has destroyed the instability of the explosive that makes it go off with such a bang.'

I knew he was leading somewhere but I just wished he'd get on with it.

'What if we shoved a steam pipe into a mine and steamed out the high explosive?'

'Suppose it goes off halfway through?'

'Half the bang.'

'Are you certain?'

'Pretty much so. I haven't tested it properly yet. Only tried it on a bucket of HE.'

'What did you do with the explosives afterwards?'

'I burned it. Went up with a nice blue flame and a lot of smoke. I've made a few drawings you might like to look at.'

'Sure. But why are you telling me? Hadn't you better take it to Tam?'

Nodding, he placed a few sheets of paper on the bar in front of us and smoothed them open. 'I thought it would be better coming from you. Chain of command and all that rot.'

I wasn't so sure but I nodded encouragingly to him. 'Explain it to me.'

'This is a simple boiler arrangement. The steam feeds through this flexible metal pipe and out of the nozzle.'

'What's the fuel?'

'Coal or wood.'

'How long does it take to melt a mine load?'

'That's the snag. If the clock's ticking then it's too long. If it isn't then we set the thing going, retire gracefully and let the explosives wash out. A mine takes between four and six hours I reckon.'

I liked the idea and nodded. 'We'd better take this to Tam and see what he has to say. Have you said anything to Tom Boycroft?'

'He's already building the boiler. He had an idea to improve the steam delivery by incorporating water baffles along the hose. He's in the workshop now.'

I eyed my drink and with a sigh placed the glass on the bar. 'We'd better go over and see him. He may need a hand.'

We worked late into the night. Finally, Boycroft announced his satisfaction with the contraption we'd come up with. It was heavy and cumbersome but it worked. The main section was the boiler, an old stove we'd altered to hold water in the top. A fire in the base heated up the water and the steam passed through a hose made of one-inch diameter copper pipe cut into short sections to give flexibility. We lit the fire and watched the steam forming. By the time it reached the end of the hose, a mere ten feet, there was hardly anything left. It had leaked or condensed en route.

'Leave it for now,' I said with a groan. 'I'm shattered. We need a better hose pipe from somewhere.'

Boycroft snapped his fingers. 'And I know just the place. The insulated pipe in a ship's engine room. That'll do the trick.'

'You could be right. But as it is now midnight,' I said, looking at my watch, 'Let's leave it until tomorrow. I suggest you two get some sleep as well. You never know if we will get a shout.'

I was called away at breakfast following an air raid on Southampton. Clive Butterworth and I dealt with a mine that had landed in a dry dock alongside a Flower Class frigate that was in for repairs. As jobs went, it was relatively simple. An hour after arriving we were packing up to leave. It was a calm day and the raid was long past. So the explosion we heard about a mile away was all the more shocking.

Butterworth and I exchanged looks. Which team was that?

We found out when we returned to *Vernon*. Geddes and Petty Officer Barker had been dealing with a parachute mine that had landed in the mud flats next to Whale Island. As they approached the half-buried carcass it had exploded. Barker had been blown flat on his back and Geddes had been hit in the arm by a piece of flying metal. Both men were otherwise unhurt, the blast moving away from them across the open water. Stories abounded of exploding bombs, which stripped people naked but left them uninjured. Tales of blasts which went over officers' heads were well known and documented too. All the stories had a common denominator – luck.

When I arrived back at the wardroom I found Geddes the worse for having got outside most of a bottle of scotch. I couldn't blame him.

The following morning Geddes came in to breakfast looking green around the gills. He took one look at the powdered eggs and bacon slice and rapidly left the table. I finally met up with him around lunchtime. He still looked dreadful but at least, so he claimed, his brain was beginning to work again.

We continued work on the steam machine, this time using insulated engine-room pipe. When we flashed up the boiler and began pumping steam it travelled the twenty feet of the pipe then came out hot. We stuffed the end of the pipe into a bucket of explosives and watched the brittle and unstable compound melt and seep out. In its altered state it could be easily manhandled and burned. That evening we celebrated, Boycott and I with a beer, Geddes with a ginger ale.

The following morning the Prime Minister arrived to discuss a new mine-laying policy with C-in-C Portsmouth. We stood to attention, smartly saluting Churchill as he emerged from his black sedan. I noticed his companion and couldn't stop a huge grin forming on my face. It was David Griffiths.

27

DAVID, IN HIS Colonel's uniform, looked smarter than I'd ever seen him. He came over to me as soon as was decent. 'Mike, I knew I'd find you here. How are you? How's Betty?'

I could feel the wide grin still plastered on my face. David had that effect on me and many others he met. He was, without doubt, the most charismatic man I'd ever known. 'David, what an unexpected pleasure. What brings you here?'

'I'm accompanying Winnie for a day or two.' He lowered his voice and added, 'He's got a bee in his bonnet about mine laying. Come and join us.'

I looked across the room at the gathering of heavily braided officers and pulled a wry face. 'I'm a lowly two-and-a-half reservist, don't forget.'

'Rubbish. Your input will be invaluable. You know about mines.'

I shrugged. 'I'll join in if you tell me why you're really here. Mine warfare is hardly an intelligence matter.'

'There's a report of a German spy ring operating around here.'

I raised my eyebrows. 'I'd have thought that was a job for the police. Besides, there are always reports about spies. Especially around naval bases.'

David shrugged and raised a smile. Discretion was one of David's strengths – one of the many reasons people knew they could rely on him. Somehow I wasn't surprised to see him in such exalted company. His father had laid the foundations to the family's fortune but David had driven it to great heights and taken the Griffiths name to the highest echelons of society. He had access to heads of governments and royalty across Europe. Our own King and Queen appeared to hold him in high regard. When I'd questioned him on the subject he'd merely smiled and replied, 'Services rendered, Mike. Services rendered.' I didn't press him. He could be as silent as the crypt when he wanted to. He was also very persuasive.

I followed him reluctantly to the group of senior officers surrounding Churchill. They parted and let us through when David said, 'Prime Minister, I'd like you to meet one of my oldest friends, Mike O'Donnell.'

'Mr O'Donnell,' Churchill said in his gravely voice, 'and what do you do?'

'Sir.' I nodded nervously, aware of the looks from his entourage. 'I'm in the mine and bomb squad.'

'Dangerous work, O'Donnell.'

'Yes, sir.' What the hell was I to say? I felt like a tongue-tied kid and cursed David for putting me on the spot.

'What Mike won't tell you is that he's an innovative engineer and worked on the wireless sets we use in some of the planes. Especially the Griffin.'

'That so?' Churchill took a gulp from his glass of whisky and, waving his cigar in the air, said, 'We need new devices, O'Donnell, inventions of all sorts. This war will be won through new technology. Bombs, airplanes, subs, ships, guns. You name it we need it. Bigger and better than the Germans. It's our only hope.'

'I agree, sir. In fact we've just come up with a steam machine to wash out explosives. The process makes the explosives more stable, allowing us to burn them.'

Winston had a gleam in his eye. 'Excellent. Excellent. You hear that gentlemen?' He beamed at the others.

The officers made appreciative noises and then the talk became more general. As I eased away from the centre, I realised David was at my side. Taking me by the elbow, he manoeuvred me to the back of the room.

'Mike, I'll come clean. I've been given a new job. Two years ago Winnie tasked Hugh Dalton, the Minister of Economic Warfare, with creating a new organisation called the Special Operations Executive. Ever heard of it?'

I frowned and then shook my head. 'I can't say I have. What is it?'

'It's a part of SIS, the Secret Intelligence Service, intended to co-ordinate all subversion and sabotage against the enemy overseas. It's brief was to set Europe ablaze. Those are Winston's words.'

'I've heard of SIS, of course.' I nodded at David's green background to his crown and two pips on his shoulders. 'You're part of it.'

David nodded. 'The SOE element is top-secret. Very few people know of it's existence.'

'So why are you telling me?'

David's grin widened. 'Because I want you to join us.'

Whatever he'd been about to say, that was the last thing I expected. 'Why me?'

'I gather you're a dab hand with explosives.'

I shrugged uncomfortably. 'Who told you that?'

'Tam McVey. I asked him who his best man was and he unhesitatingly named you. Don't look so surprised, Mike. He has the highest regard for you. Are you in?'

'Just like that? I have to say now?'

David shrugged. ''Fraid so. Then join me on my little jaunt later on.'

I blew out my cheeks and frowned. My initial thought was *What the hell would Betty say*? But then I knew there was only one answer. If anybody else had asked me I'd have told him to take a run and jump. But not David. I owed him too much. Besides, I grinned and held out my hand, it might be fun.

He shook my hand warmly and grinned back. 'Good man, I knew I could rely on you.'

Glancing across the room I saw Churchill watching us. He grinned and waved his cigar before turning back to the crowd.

That evening we drove to the police station in Havant. 'What's this all about?' I asked David as we climbed out of the car.

'I want to meet a Chief Inspector Gill. He's in charge of tonight's little party.'

'Is that why we're wearing mufti?'

'Less conspicuous that way, Mike. But get used to it. You won't be wearing uniform much from now on. We're an informal lot at Baker Street.'

We passed through the blackout curtains and into the lobby of the station. Five men were waiting for us. The tallest, an impressive-looking six-footer, stepped forward to meet us. I guessed he was about thirty-five years old. 'Colonel Griffiths? I'm Robert Gill.'

He and David shook hands warmly. Introductions were made all round and a quick briefing given. At the end David said, 'It's obvious from what you tell me that the suspects are up to no good. We want them alive preferably but we also want code books and anything else they might have. However, don't take any chances. If either of them reaches for a gun shoot him or her. Chief Inspector?'

'Thank you, sir. We'll draw weapons and meet outside in a quarter of an hour.' The men left and Gill turned to us, his dark eyes questioning. 'Are you gentlemen armed?'

'Webleys. Both of us,' said David.

'Good.' There was a few seconds of silence and Gill continued. 'Why are you here? With all due respect, we normally take care of this sort of thing.'

I had to admire him for asking the question. Others might have avoided it for fear of stepping on the wrong toes. But Gill had the air of a man who was comfortable with himself.

'Granted. But you know how it is. Too long behind a desk. Like to see the results of an operation if I can.' David left it at that.

Whatever Gill thought of that he kept to himself. His men joined us and we piled into a couple of cars and drove towards Gosport. The night was wild with heavy rain and thick cloud. It would keep the air raids away, at least. We stopped in a street of terraced houses. Southampton Water was on our right. An ideal location to watch the comings and goings of merchant ships.

Gill immediately took command. 'It's along there. Number 41.'

'How are you going to do this?' David asked.

'It's after midnight. I expect both suspects have gone to bed. We'll go in nice and quiet. If anyone is awake, we'll deal with them.'

'Good. Mike and I'll wait here.'

Gill deployed his men. We watched three of them go down to the end of the street and round the back while he and two others walked up to the front door. We saw him working the lock and door handle. One of the policemen returned along the street and spoke to Gill, who paid a courtesy visit to the car. 'Plan B, it seems they've fitted dead bolts. We'll try taking out the front window. If that doesn't work then we'll smash it and go in hard and fast.'

We sat watching, the rain now a drizzle, steady but not heavy enough to mask the sounds of Gill and his men as they cut out a pane of glass. I saw the upstairs curtains twitch and a white face appear at the window for a second.

Leaping from the car I yelled, 'They're on to us, Gill!'

The words were hardly out of my mouth when something flew through the window upstairs, smashing it. I reached into my pocket for my revolver as someone leaned out through the opening, his arm pointing towards the front door. I didn't hesitate. I fired three rounds in quick succession. The Chief Inspector also looked up, his arm outstretched. He too was firing. I saw a policeman climb through the broken downstairs window, but my attention was on the person upstairs. I saw the body jerk and fall across the broken glass, arms hanging down, lifeless.

Lights were coming on and doors and windows were being opened. Gill yelled, 'Watch the lights, for God's sake. Do you want every German plane targeting this street?'

Lights were hastily extinguished. A few seconds later men appeared in overcoats hastily thrown over pyjamas, carrying rifles. The Home Guard had arrived. Gill quickly disabused them of the notion that the invasion had begun and sent them back to their beds. The remaining suspect was dragged from the house, his hands behind his back. Gill spoke to him briefly before gesturing to his men to take him away. He came back to our car.

'We caught him burning code books. The body is female.'

'Good work, Gill. We'll let you finish. I'll send the car back for you later. I'd like you to come to my hotel in the morning. I'm at the Esplanade. Breakfast at eight sharp. My treat.'

The following afternoon when we left Portsmouth Chief Inspector Robert Gill accompanied us. David now had two new recruits for the SOE.

'What happened to the suspect you arrested?' I asked.

'Won't say a word,' said Gill, 'but he will. The iron fist is being used about now. We're trying to find if there are any others in his network. We don't have much time. As soon as he fails to send in a check report the network will scatter. So it's a matter of hours rather than days.'

'Glad to be out of it?' David asked.

'I wouldn't say that. But I'm looking forward to a new challenge.'

'Good man, that's what I expected.'

Accommodation wasn't a problem in London. Like David, I had been a member of the United Services Club for years and I managed to get a room there, albeit for a few days only. Rooms were being allocated strictly according to rank and as a lowly lieutenant commander I didn't rate very highly. However, staff housing was a problem the SOE had foreseen. Small flats were being made ready for us and any subsequent recruits.

David, Gill and I decided on a nightcap in the bar. David used the time to familiarise us with SOE.

'Like I told you, we're an informal lot. I've been with the outfit for eight months now and though there is a hierarchy, naturally, it's not a yes, sir, no, sir, sort of organisation. We are known as the Inter-Services Research Bureau and are led by a man named Frank Nelson. Sir Frank is an MP and a very successful businessman. He reports to Dalton, who reports directly to Winnie. There's a rumour he's about to take early retirement. If he does, I think Charlie Hambro will take his place. You know Charlie, Mike?'

I nodded. Hambro was a merchant banker and on the Court of the Bank of England as well as Chairman of the Great Western Railway.

'If Charlie gets the job I'll probably be his Number Two,' David continued. 'Dalton is being shuffled to the Board of Trade and Lord Selborne is taking over.'

The information was given without boasting. His tone was quite matter-of-fact. Proof he was one of the insiders of the Establishment.

'If I do get the job I'll take a hand-picked team with me. You two will be the embryo of that team. That suit you?'

Gill and I exchanged delighted looks.

'The way we organise is each team has areas and agents of responsibility. Sealed units with no crossover for security reasons. It's worked for the last few years. That way there's no red tape. We have a free hand to create chaos wherever we can. Security is as tight as a duck's arse, however; networks have code names, as do areas. We now have a French section, known as F section, which operates independently of de Gaulle's parallel RF Section. That's what we call it. It's really the *Bureau Central de Renseignments et d'Action*. We *do not* crossover *or* cross-reference with de Gaulle. That's because we don't trust him. Or more precisely some of his men.'

'Why ever not?' I asked. 'I thought he was our ally.'

'He is. But he only sees the war in terms of liberating France. He will not, or perhaps cannot, see the bigger picture. Nothing other than France matters to him. As a result he's jeopardised some of our operations. So stay clear of him and his merry men.' David beckoned a waiter. While we waited for our glasses to be replenished we exchanged talk about the family.

In answer to Gill's question whether we were related, David answered, 'By marriage. But we go back a long way. To nineteen eighteen or nineteen. So our friendship came long before the family connection. Ah, here are the drinks.'

As the evening unfolded, David gave us some more useful tips about what we could expect, then he and Gill departed. Gill to a hotel, David to his flat. I went upstairs to my room and, with the light off, opened the curtains to look out. Summer was in the air but London was looking tired and worn out.

The following morning I walked to Baker Street and easily found Marks & Spencer, walking briskly through the store to a door marked private. The offices of the SOE had once belonged to the department store, but had expanded so much that it now occupied a further six large buildings in the area. The senior staff was still housed where operations had begun. Through the door I was met by two individuals with sidearms. My ID card was carefully checked, a phone call made and then I was in.

They directed me up some stairs and along a corridor, to a door marked J1. I knocked and entered.

The room was large and jammed with desks, all empty apart from the one nearest the window. Robert Gill was sitting there, a telephone receiver to his ear – he waved a greeting to me. A kettle stood on a table in a corner, on a gas stove, and I went to see what was on offer. I grinned when I recognised David's handiwork. His special coffee was in a jar alongside.

I took the kettle outside and wandered around until I found the heads. After filling it with water I returned to the office to find David had arrived.

'It was confirmed this morning. Charlie Hambro's taken over. I'm being elevated to his inner circle. Our task will be to co-ordinate the different sections across France and Italy. This is absolutely top secret. No paperwork to be left on desks. The cupboard in the corner has a four digit tumbler lock.' David continued to brief us on what he called "the housekeeping".

I listened while making the coffee.

'We'll spend the rest of the week recruiting.' Opening his briefcase he took out a pile of buff folders. 'These are the people I'm most interested in. They come from all the services and include half a dozen women.'

I noticed a message board and strolled over to take a look at the single piece of paper pinned there.

David noticed immediately. 'It was issued by Hitler's headquarters on the eighteenth of October last year and marked top secret. We got a copy three weeks ago.'

Gill joined me and we stood shoulder to shoulder reading it.

I therefore order that from now on, all opponents engaged in so-called commando operations in Europe or Africa, even when it is outwardly a matter of soldiers in uniform or demolition parties with or without weapons, are to be exterminated to the last man in battle or in flight. In these cases, it is immaterial whether they are landed for their operations by ship, or aeroplane, or descent by parachute. Even should these individuals, on being discovered, make as if to surrender, all quarter is to be denied on principle.

'There's more underneath,' said David.
Horrified, I lifted the sheet of paper and continued reading.

I have been compelled to issue strict orders for the destruction of enemy sabotage troops and to declare non-compliance severely punishable . . . It must be made clear to the enemy that all sabotage troops will be exterminated, without exception, to the last man. That means that their chance of escaping with their lives is nil. Under no circumstances should they expect to be treated according to the rules of the Geneva Convention. If it should become necessary for reasons of interrogation to initially spare prisoners, they are to be shot immediately after interrogation. This order is intended for commanders only and must not under any circumstances fall into enemy hands.

'This is outrageous,' I said, turning to David, overwhelming anger surging through me. If we needed confirmation of Hitler's insanity, this was it.

He nodded. 'Events have proven he means it. Now that we're using female agents we had given them commissions in the WAAF or as

FANYs, hoping they'd be treated as prisoners of war, if captured. But it hasn't worked – those two directives explain why.'

The First Aid Nursing Yeomanry, defined as the "First Anywheres" had been active in the Great War. They had driven ambulances and other vehicles and thanks to them I survived a particularly brutal shelling of my trench in 1917. *Christ*, I thought, *the Germans were filthy brutes.*

'We won't be running bods directly . . .'

At Gill's raised eyebrow David interrupted himself.

'It's what we call our agents.'

'Quaint,' he said.

'We have our idiosyncrasies, like every department, but make no mistake, this is the most secret outfit in the war. We take that secrecy and security very seriously indeed. Everything has a code name. You'll soon get used to it. Many lives are at stake, not just *our* bods, but also their contacts in Europe. We have over ten thousand men and women working for SOE and the numbers are increasing.'

I looked at David in utter astonishment. 'That's a lot of personnel – astonishing that nobody knows anything about them.'

David shook his head, smiling. 'SOE is known as the Stately 'Omes of England. We run nearly eighty establishments across England and Scotland. Mainly for training but also as staging, receiving and debriefing places. Sometimes they're needed for the recuperation of a bod as well. Right, let's get on with it. We'll go through the files and see who we want. We need secretaries and clerks as well as staff. Be aware, there are other departments that deal with the Middle East, Far East, Europe and Africa. Our watching brief is to ensure that operations don't overlap or, worse still, clash. Co-operation is the name of the game and bloody hard to achieve. It's why Charlie Hambro wants us up and running. Too many mini-fiefdoms for his liking. Security is one thing, common sense is another. One thing, your ID cards. You'll need new ones for here. I'll see to that. Any questions?'

There were so many I didn't know where to begin. Opposite me Gill merely shrugged and raised a quizzical eyebrow. I smiled back. What had we let ourselves in for?

28

WE WORKED FIFTEEN-HOUR days. There was a great deal to do and much to learn. The complexities of the SOE were considerable; no one person could possibly control it all. It was compartmentalised to an astonishing degree, partly because of the need for secrecy, which in turn led to all sorts of difficulties. Our job became one of co-ordination. I was made responsible for France, and Gill covered North Africa as far as the Gulf.

We had been there about a fortnight when I found the shooting gallery over Baker Street Station. Right in the heart of London the bods learnt to fire revolvers. It was meant for close work, firing down galleys at man-sized metal targets. I carried a Webley .38 Mark IV service revolver. It was two-thirds the weight of the Mark VI and though the bullets were .38 instead of .45 it had as much stopping power. Gill and I worked off our frustrations on that range whenever we had the chance.

David was like a human dynamo. He was everywhere, organising, arranging, implementing. Our team had grown to twenty-five and still we had more to do than we had hours in the day. David pushed us hard but he pushed himself harder, so nobody had the right to complain. Those that did were given a choice – buck up or bugger off. Paranoia was practically rampant. The office walls were plastered with posters extolling us to keep silent and reminding us that we could never be sure who was listening. Friend or a foe? Secrecy ran through the organisation like a river of distrust, the left hand not knowing what the right was doing. Such paranoia resulted more than once in loss of life of agents and members of the Maquis in France. On a day-to-day level it made our jobs more difficult than they needed to be and by God they were difficult enough.

I co-ordinated a number of circuits across France, each using a code name. The group, centred in Marseilles, was called Orange. A second at Dieppe was named Thor and a third in Paris went by the name of Hubris. Knowing Parisians as I did, I thought the Latin for "wanton arrogance" quite apt.

I was scowling at a wireless message when David walked into the office. Communications were vital, and often the source of great frustration.

'Problem, Mike?'

'A message from Aramis in Paris.'

'He operates Hubris?'

'Affirmative. Blanche and he have been having problems with his wireless, some of the crystals aren't quite right. I'll need to get them some replacements.' The crystals were the bane of our communications system. Fixed frequencies, they often gave trouble. They were carried separately from the wireless set itself and prone to damage.

'Who's the operator?'

'George 22.' I was quickly getting the hang of things – all wireless operators working for SOE were named George and known by their number. In the same way that France was known as 27-Land and Spain was 23-Land. Code names were the watchword of the organisation, and took some getting used to. Sometimes we seemed to go to ludicrous lengths but the organisation had suffered horrible setbacks in the past, as well as enjoying significant successes, so the need for secrecy was all too evident. "Setbacks" usually involved betrayal, resulting in agents being arrested, tortured and killed. Each one was a personal blow, felt keenly by all of us in HQ. When it happened we'd re-check our procedures. *Why* had it happened? Was it an accident, sheer luck on the part of the Germans or had their hard work tracking down our men and women paid off? If it was a betrayal, who was the traitor?

Robert Gill and I had decided to share a two-bedroomed flat in Maida Vale. The more I got to know him, the better I liked him. Robert was quiet, conscientious and a calm influence in the office, where tempers often ran high. He was a bachelor and a handsome one at that, who appeared to have the devil's own luck with the ladies. A few times he offered to fix me up with the friend of a friend but I declined, happily admitting that I was a married man.

Instead of spending my evenings in delightful female company I became a Francophile, immersing myself in the culture. I listened to

French records and read French books. I'd learnt the language over the years; it was inevitable if you worked in the aeroplane industry. There was a good deal of collusion between manufacturers across Europe as we tried to develop planes for the twentieth century. This was particularly true between France and Britain. The other main player, Germany, had been considered the enemy from 1920 onwards. Many believed flying was the future of transport. Visionaries like Sion believed that air travel would be as common as travel by roads. Thanks to my work I could speak and understand French although my accent was pretty atrocious. I was working hard on it, so as to be more easily understood by our French agents, although with what success I couldn't tell. It also helped to pass the time and fill the lonely evenings when I had nothing to do but fret.

Now that I was no longer in the front-line, dismantling bombs and mines, my life expectancy had soared. So what was there to fret about? I'm not a worrier by nature, but with Betty in South Wales and me in London, I couldn't help but be anxious. I was worried the factory could be bombed, as it was a prime target on the edge of Cardiff. Intellectually I knew raids tended to be at night when Betty was naturally at home, but the "what ifs" disturbed my equilibrium. Love had come to me late in life – I couldn't bear the thought of anything happening to her.

I poured myself a cup of sugarless tea before settling into an armchair and dragging my mind back to the record I was listening to. I followed the spoken word in a textbook, speaking out loud, concentrating on the sounds of the language. I'd been studying for about eight weeks. It helped to take my mind off problems, particularly relating to work. In mine and bomb disposal you dealt with the job in hand and forgot about it. Life at SOE was very different. With agents all over France, constantly in danger and utterly reliant on us for our support, the worries never abated. They were with you from the moment you woke up until you went to bed. Most days I woke with the lark and by seven was on my way to Baker St. Saturdays and Sundays were no exception.

Some people can say with certainty which was the greatest day of their lives, while others can clearly state which was the worst. For me, Saturday 31 July 1943 was my nadir.

I had been to Baker Street, having blasted off a dozen rounds at the targets in the shooting gallery. Mid-morning I was sifting through paperwork, sipping a cup of coffee. David shamelessly used his influence and connections to get the real stuff and I'd helped myself from the supply he kept in his desk drawer. Robert Gill had just arrived and was similarly occupied. About half the desks were vacant – the lucky ones were enjoying a Saturday in the sunshine. There was even more work than usual – the situation in Europe was precarious. Two weeks earlier we'd invaded Sicily and the battle for Europe had begun. The fallout from the decision was still reverberating around Whitehall. De Gaulle had been insistent that we should invade through France. Nobody in the British War Cabinet or amongst our Allies agreed with him. The argument resulted in an intransigent French ally who practically withdrew his co-operation in the war effort. De Gaulle reminded me of a spoilt child going home with his ball because he hadn't been picked for the football team. However, we at SOE turned up the heat in France, partly to placate de Gaulle.

Every month, for one week either side of a full moon, the night skies were light enough to navigate by. Usually our pilots flew small planes along Europe's great rivers, their still surfaces glinting in the moonlight, easily visible. Some routes were flown so often that we joked about a possible traffic jam in the skies. The truth was, the Germans were stretched so thinly, defending cities and airfields, that they couldn't look out for the small Lysanders, unarmed and highly vulnerable, flying at 150mph, ferrying our agents across Europe.

Our radio room was manned twenty-four hours a day, seven days a week. Regular transmissions were timed to the second and of course the BBC sent many messages by open broadcast but in once-only code. The rest of the time we monitored radio signals for unexpected messages and emergency transmissions. The majority were situation reports, often sent in a matter-of-fact way after an agent had been either arrested or killed. Some had been pleas for help. To my mind our agents were, without doubt, the bravest people on the planet.

I had just checked in with our radio operator, Jim, a quiet young chap, with rather a sober demeanour, and returned to my office when a hand waving frantically from the door to the wireless room caught my attention. I hurried over, weaving between the desks, a knot in my stomach.

'George 22 called. He sent this.'

Taking the proffered signal flimsy I read it with dread.

Aramis shot. 9 or 10 arrested. Blanche on the run. Must . . .

'Is that all?'

'Afraid so. The transmission suddenly stopped. I tried to establish contact again but there was no reply.'

'Mother of God, that's ten percent of the Hubris circuit.'

Jim nodded, his long, mournful face more gloomy than ever. He shrugged his narrow shoulders and said, 'Let's hope he managed to burn the code books.'

'We'll change them immediately. Send the signal through the BBC.'

'Will do. What do you propose?'

I shook my head. 'I'm not sure. If Blanche is on the run I know which way she'll go. We should try and get her out.'

Blanche was the code name for Kitty Westacott, a *tour de force* from County Wexford. Kitty inherited her beauty from her French mother, her passion for revenge from her Irish father. She spoke French like a Parisian and had spent much of her childhood in Paris with her grandparents. She had been holidaying in France, in the town of St. Quentin, when the Germans invaded. Her mother, brother and grandparents had been killed during an air raid. She had survived only because she had been walking in a nearby park at the time. When the sirens sounded she had tried to get home but found her route blocked by a collapsed building. By the time she had found her way around the obstruction and back to the street where her family were staying she was too late.

She didn't even wait to bury her dead, but set off for England immediately with the sole intention of doing one thing in particular – to kill the Hun. She had literally walked into SOE, demanding to be put to work. We took great care in checking out her story, but soon discovered it was true.

I sat at my desk remembering her, a fiery chit of a girl. She was twenty-one, five-feet four inches tall, with a shock of black curls and large blue eyes. She looked the picture of innocence. After wireless training at Special Training School 52, Thame Park, Oxfordshire, Kitty had successfully carried out one low level job in Vichy. After further training she had been sent to Paris. When I had taken over, my main task was to help her build a circuit in the French capital.

We had been successful so far. In fact our success worried me. The circuit was over a hundred strong and growing. I kept telling Kitty to slow down, to consolidate and check out her recruits but she was impatient. I'd warned her of the danger of betrayal but she'd merely laughed. In her turn Kitty would remind me of Churchill's exhortation to the SOE – to set Europe ablaze. And that she was determined to do.

So far Lady Luck had smiled on her. It was amazing what she had done. Trains derailed, sentry boxes blown up, convoys of trucks disrupted and banks robbed to finance their work. She had established a network of safe houses to place agents whenever the need arose. Neither had she shrank from violence. Under her command several collaborators had been hanged and left in public places. Kitty understood that for every collaborator killed dozens of French citizens had lost their lives helping the Allies. She was proving a real asset to SOE. So much so that a price had been placed on her head, one hundred thousand French francs for information leading to her identification and arrest. I had already been toying with the idea of pulling her out of France and sending her elsewhere. But it looked as though I had left it too late.

Damn, damn, damn! Kitty and I had agreed weeks before that should the going get too tough she would leave Paris and head for the South of France. I stood up and walked across the room to the map of France filling one wall. I mentally traced Kitty's route, trying to decide what to do.

'Mike!'

Jim was calling from the radio room. 'This just came in. It's from Blanche. I've checked the code words and they're correct.'

From certain words inserted into a message we could tell whether the transmission was being sent under duress or if it was genuine.

'And?'

'She appears to be all right. I've double checked her reply.'

'Where is she?'

He allowed a smile to crack his long face. 'On a bicycle heading south.'

I nodded. That made sense. The preferred method of travel for all our bods was bicycle. Good. That meant she was heading for Etampes. Kitty had proven herself to be brave and resourceful. It would be disastrous if anything were to happen to her. She had been put up for a CBE but the honour had been reduced to an MBE by the government cheese-parers. She was due to collect her medal when she next returned home. Of one thing I was sure; the country owed her. I was determined that she would collect that honour. In two days she would be at the first possible pick-up point. I was going to be there, waiting for her.

Unfortunately David had other ideas.

'You aren't going and that's final. You're far too valuable, Mike. Besides, you know too much. If the *Gestapo* got their hands on you God alone knows what damage could be done. Look, Mike, I sympathise, I really do, but it's no go. I cannot give you permission. It's more than my job is worth should anything go wrong.'

'Since when is your job worth more than your principles? Kitty's in terrible trouble, David, and I'm responsible.'

'As am I. And for many others besides Kitty. I daren't risk our assets any more than I have to. And you're a major asset. It's the essence of command, Mike.'

We argued back and forth. When it became clear David wouldn't back down I made up my mind that I'd go without permission and hang the consequences.

'All right,' I stood up resignedly, 'We'll see how she does on her own. Thanks for your time.'

As I left the office David was looking more than a little incredulous. As if he had expected a harder fight from me. Well, he could have my resignation on his desk for Monday. By which time it would be too late. Either Kitty would be with me or I'd be dead. I wouldn't be captured alive – of that I was damned positive. So what was my best course? First and foremost I needed a plane. I could requisition a Lysander and get taken from Selsey to the pick-up point in France. But I didn't have the authority. I sat with my hands behind my head pondering the problem. I could forge David's signature. Phone the squadron and explain it was an emergency. That the paperwork would follow. Would anyone there check up? I doubted it.

I was reaching for the telephone when another solution presented itself. I was a competent pilot. I'd been flying for twenty years, albeit in Griffins. So that was the obvious solution. Borrow a Griffin from Sion. He wouldn't hesitate to lend me a plane. It would mean flying and navigating it myself but what the hell. I'd done it often enough in the past.

Within seconds I had the receiver pressed against my ear and was asking Kirsty if I could speak to Sion.

'Hullo, Mike,' he said, 'has there been a change of plan?'

I shook my head. 'Sorry?'

'Changed your mind, have you? Only the plane is ready right now.'

'How on earth did you know I would be wanting a Griffin?'

'David's just off the phone. He wouldn't say what it was for. Just that it would be for the best. It would save you a lot of trouble, he said.'

I was aware of a presence looming over my desk and I looked up into David's rather smug-looking face.

29

'YOU DIDN'T REALLY think you had me fooled, did you? I can't sanction you going after Kitty, but I want you back here in one piece. So I'll do what I can to help. Unofficially.'

I nodded. 'Thanks, David. I appreciate it. What's this?' I added taking the piece of paper he proffered.

'Your three-day leave approved. It starts Monday. I want you back here by Thursday. With or without her. Have you given any thought to your legend?'

Shaking my head, I said, 'I hadn't got that far yet.'

'Stick with the truth as far as possible. You're an Irishman. Not pro-German but anti-British. You've fought the Brits in Eire. There's a price on your head and you're cooling it until things die down around Dublin. If you're picked up and they keep asking tell them you were part of the cell that shot Clive Delaney.'

I nodded. That made sense. Delaney had been killed by the IRA as a traitor for not arguing for the return of the six counties. It was a good cover story.

'Use your own name. It's common enough not to excite attention and we can knock up an Irish ID in five minutes. Anything else?'

'Money.'

'I've thought of that. I'll arrange for you to have funds before you go. We've made a substantial profit on the black market dealing in currency exchange. We have a merchant division tasked to raise funds for clandestine use. I help with my contacts. Last month we made a profit of over a hundred thousand pounds. Mainly in French francs and Italian lira. That way we keep the use of our funds secret. Particularly from Members of Parliament who may say the wrong thing in the house.'

'As is their wont,' I grinned.

David nodded. 'The Griffin is being delivered to Selsey Bill. You can take it from there. I've asked for a weather forecast. It's a bit late in the month but you should be able to navigate okay, provided the cloud cover isn't too thick.'

We spent another twenty minutes discussing the operation. When we were both satisfied, I said, 'I don't know how to thank you.'

He waved a deprecating hand. 'Thanks aren't necessary. Kitty's mine as well as yours. I want her back safe and well too. But you know the rules. So be careful, Mike. And I meant it when I said you mustn't be taken alive. A cursory glance at your papers and a brief cross-examination is one thing. A full interrogation by the *Gestapo* is another.'

He didn't have to spell it out and I nodded. He had been sitting across the desk from me and now he stood and offered me his hand. 'Good luck and take care. Betty will never forgive me if anything happens to you.'

I grinned at him and shook his hand. He never failed to surprise me. I always maintained that if he bothered to fight for leadership of the Conservative Party he could become Prime Minister one day. He was adamant that he wasn't interested, although sometimes I thought he protested too much.

Events moved quickly after that. I packed an overnight bag from the storerooms we had at Baker Street, where we had a motley collection of European-styled clothing. Whenever a bod returned from abroad he or she brought with him clothes bought in that country. Our tailors then set to work replicating them, creating entirely authentic clothing, from suits and dresses to underwear. I requisitioned a wireless set and, as an afterthought, a couple of pounds of explosives and detonators.

Then I drove south, arriving early. Instead of stopping at the airfield I went on to the tip of Selsey Bill in time to watch a glorious sunset. The sun's rays hit the underside of thick, dark clouds, creating a panorama of colour, awesome in its majesty. The peace of the moment was at odds with the world we inhabited. Reluctantly I climbed back into the car and drove to RAF Tangmere, a few miles north.

The airfield was used principally by SOE for sending agents into France. Its proximity to the Continent gave the small planes a greater range and we could send bods as far as Vichy, reaching Marseilles if necessary. I showed my ID at the guardhouse and parked outside the officers' mess. The air was still and warm, laden with that unmistakable smell of all airfields – a mixture of petrol, rubber and burnt oil, the smell of aircraft. I was filled with a mixture of dread and excitement. God alone knew what the next few days would bring. I thought about the brief letter I'd left in my desk for Betty should anything happen to me. Apart from telling her how much I loved her, I couldn't think what else to write. My thoughts were turning distinctly morbid. I was relieved to hear the unmistakable sound of a twin-engined Griffin IIId. The plane was based on the original Griffin III but had been modified and upgraded in the last few years. It was quieter, faster and had a longer range than the Lysander, aircraft of choice for clandestine operations.

The Griffin lined up and landed with a gentle bump. I wondered idly who the ferrying pilot was as the plane trundled across the runway towards the fuel point. The door opened and a hand waved to me, then I saw a cheery grin plastered on the pilot's face. I grinned back. Somehow I wasn't surprised to see Sion.

Thumping his back I asked, 'What are you doing here?'

'I needed some fresh air and this was as good a reason as any to get away.'

As we talked we walked over to the bowser where a soldier was sitting in the cab. He climbed down, threw a sloppy salute and asked for our papers and authorisation for the fuel. I gave him what he wanted and left him to do his job. Sion and I crossed the field to the officers' mess where we were served with tepid, weak coffee. We planted ourselves in a corner, out of the way.

'Thanks for bringing the plane. It's great to see you.' I didn't say how much better he was looking than last time, but the thought hung in the air.

Nodding, Sion gave a lop-sided grin. 'It was my pleasure. Such a lovely evening for flying.'

'The weather forecast says there's cloud over France. Which will suit me as long as it isn't too low. Navigation will be a pig as it is.'

'That's what I figured. Which is why I'll be coming with you.'

For a split second I thought about protesting at his offer. Instead I held out my hand, unable to keep the pleasure and relief out of my voice.

'Once more unto the breach, dear friends . . .'

'For God, King and Winnie,' he finished. 'I've brought charts, though they aren't as up-to-date as I'd have liked.'

I nodded. 'That's always a problem. So much has changed in Europe since the occupation and of course intelligence is pretty poor. I've got a few *Notices to Pilots*, which may help. And I can point out one or two places we should avoid like the plague.'

We discussed the flight plan, checked distances and times and agreed we should depart soon. But we had a few matters to deal with first.

I filled four one-gallon tins with petrol and stuck a small quantity of plastic explosives into the top. Into the PE I inserted one-minute pencil-timers. 'You got the rest of the kit?' I asked.

'A complete outfit in the trunk.'

Knowing Sion as I did, I knew he wouldn't be flying into enemy territory unless he was armed to the teeth. The two seats behind the cockpit had been removed and replaced with a metal trunk containing a motley selection of weapons and explosives. Pre-flight checks took only a few minutes and soon we were accelerating down the runway and lifting gracefully into the rapidly darkening night.

'Like old times,' Sion said to me above the noise of the engines. He was sitting in the left hand seat, while I sat in the right with a chart on my knees.

'Remember Russia?'

'How could I forget! You and I against the scariest, most corrupt officer in the Russian military. That was a close shave. But at least we were getting the hell out of there. To-night we're going in *and* out again.'

'Come left ten degrees and head for the point,' I instructed him. 'We'll be over the coast in ten minutes. Time to hit the deck.'

'Wilco.' The plane's aspect changed into a dive and we headed for the sea, straightening out about one hundred feet above the gently undulating water. The cloud base was at 1,500 feet, thin but thickening. Moonrise was in fifteen minutes and already a faint glow was evident in the south east against the dark land mass. Europe had become an eerie place to fly over as most of the lights were out. The dark and brooding land was only broken up by lakes and the silver ribbons of large rivers. Occasionally a car's headlights could be seen, or an isolated farmhouse, but on the whole it was just vast blackness, which made navigation a nightmare. I was grateful to have Sion beside me.

'Will the agent have an S-phone?'

'I doubt it. She's running, so I don't suppose she'll have anything but the clothes she's standing up in.'

The S-phone enabled a bod on the ground to speak to a pilot. Most of the Lysanders and Griffins used in clandestine work had them fitted. They also carried rebeccas, which received a beam from a transponder on the ground known as a eureka. With that capability agents could guide the planes to their destination. But the eureka was big and heavy and heartily disliked by most agents, who needed to move fast should the occasion arise.

'Kitty must be pretty important for you to risk going to France for her.'

'She is. She's one of the most effective agents we have. Her organ-ising abilities are second to none and she always gets the job done. Whether it's espionage, sabotage or passing people down the line, she's damn good at it. If she has one fault it's that she doesn't suffer fools gladly. She's also suspicious to the point of paranoia.'

'So what went wrong?'

'God knows. Kitty probably doesn't either. We'll find out when we reach her.'

We were wave skimming now, the coast looming dead ahead. Sion raised the plane's nose and we flew over the beaches south of Le Havre, gaining height by a hundred feet. The cloud thinned for a few seconds and moonlight bathed the land below. To our left we could see the river Seine, moving sluggishly towards the sea.

'Come right forty degrees.' I felt the plane bank and turn to star-board. 'It's as black as Hades when the moon disappears. According to my dead reckoning we stay on this course for thirty-two minutes and then turn a further fifteen degrees right.'

'How sure are you the woman will be at Etampes?'

'As sure as I can be. If she isn't there she'll be at the next pick-up point. If Kitty isn't waiting for us, you take off and leave. I'll get a message to David somehow, requesting either you come back here or to another pick-up point. Or else we'll make a run for the Spanish border.'

'Okay. Let's hope she's waiting for us.'

The plane droned on, a backdrop to our companionable silence. Whenever the moon came from behind the ever-thickening cloud I was able to confirm our position, satisfied that my dead reckoning skills hadn't become too rusty.

The lights ahead could only have been Paris, although the city was nowhere near as brightly illuminated as during peacetime. Another flight adjustment and Paris was on our port side. It was now a straight run into Etampes.

'That's the hillock that marks the town. Dead ahead. Come left a few degrees and drop two hundred feet.'

Sion did as I said while I peered anxiously through the windscreen. Glancing up at the sky, I added, 'Throttle back a few knots, Sion, I think the moon is about to make a timely appearance.'

He did as I asked and, sure enough, moonlight bathed the area a few moments later. 'Good. We can go lower. See that copse of trees? Leave them to port and head in. There's flat land just to the side. We ought to see two vertical lights, if Kitty's there.'

'See anything?' Sion asked as we approached to land.

'Not a thing. There's the railway line! Land with it on our right. The ground is hard, mainly packed earth and stone.'

Sion throttled right back and let the plane glide, a superb characteristic of the Griffin.

'See the landing place?'

'I see it. Piece of cake. As soon as I stop you get out. I'll have to turn if we want to head into wind for take-off.'

'I'll make for that copse over the other side of the tracks. If she's anywhere that's where she'll be.' I looked at Sion, 'Any problems get the hell out and come back later.'

'We'll see,' he said. 'Any problems, run like a nun with a rapist after her and get back here. Here we go.'

The Griffin glided in with occasional touches of power, which kept the engine noise down to a minimum. The plane touched, bounced and landed foursquare. Sion applied the brakes and brought us to a rapid halt. I slung my Sten Mk IIS over one shoulder, my knapsack over the other and dropped to the ground.

Feeling strangely calm, I hurried across the railway lines. Behind me I heard the engines revving as Sion turned the plane to take off into the wind. The gravel crunched under my feet before I reached a slight grass-covered embankment and the noise ceased. The trees were about a hundred yards away when I tripped and fell headlong. In that very second a machine-gun opened fire, the bullets fanning the air over my head like angry wasps.

A mortar sounded and exploded behind me. I looked back to see the plane lit up by a bright flash. A second exploded on the other side and I saw the Griffin's wings rock. The plane was bracketed! Sion accelerated just as a third mortar round hit the ground where the tail had been milli-seconds earlier.

Machine-guns opened fire from all round the perimeter, striking the Griffin as the plane leapt into the air, banked and flew away. I listened to the engines. Three short growls, two longer growls. Silence for a few seconds and then three short and two long growls. The land dipped away and the plane swooped down and out of sight. Even as I lay there gathering my wits I saw a flash of light and an explosion where the Griffin would have been.

I turned away, suppressing a grin, very aware that my situation was dire. As far as I could see there were gun emplacements all around me.

Cautiously I crawled through the grass, keeping low, expecting more fire to heap down around my head at any second. I fell into a water drainage ditch, dry and bramble covered. Immediately I felt a thorn digging into my cheek then blood dripping from my chin, like sweat after a hard day's work. Or when fear has its grasp on your bowels.

I unslung the Sten and cocked it. The gun had been in production for only a few weeks. It had a built-in silencer and the barrel was wrapped in a canvas sleeve to prevent the user's hand being burnt. I pushed the fire selection switch from right to left and fully automatic. Firing the weapon on automatic was not recommended except in a dire emergency, due to the build up of heat and a propensity for the gun to jam. I figured this qualified. Easing two grenades out of my bag I placed them at the ready. If I created enough confusion, with luck, I might be able to slip through the lines.

I listened intently to the sounds around me. German voices were shouting commands. Replies came from various set positions. I understood enough to know they were coming for me. Torchlight appeared from the other side of the railway track, strung out in a long line. I caught glimpses of heads against the skyline and guessed every fifth or sixth man held a torch. They smelled blood.

To either side I saw more men and torches. Ahead was the copse of trees, suddenly lit by more torches. The ditch I was in ran roughly towards the trees and I began crawling on my hands and knees. The further I could travel the better. I was making a devil of a racket as

I pushed through the undergrowth, but I ignored it and prayed to God the Germans didn't hear me. I'd gone about fifty yards when I hit an impenetrable mass of undergrowth. The only way was over the top.

30

LOOKING OVER THE edge of the ditch I could see a German machine-gun emplacement about thirty yards away, directly where I wanted to go. To the left and right were men, torches in hand, moving slowly towards me. I aimed my Sten at a man on the left of the emplacement, carrying a light. I fired, the sound a loud burp in the night. I was gratified to hear him cry out, his torch drop to the ground. I fired a second shot at the next torch carrier and hit him too. There were yells of consternation and the other torches were suddenly extinguished. Seizing my advantage I threw two grenades in quick succession.

As they exploded I scrambled from the ditch and ran, bent over, towards the emplacement. Other explosions followed on my left then I heard the aircraft's engines.

Sion had returned. From the ground the explosion from the petrol can he'd dropped would have been enough to convince the Germans the plane had gone down. Having gained enough height, he glided back. As he returned he dropped a second petrol can and a huge fire-ball lit up the landscape. The troops began firing into the air, aiming at the Griffin, their attention torn away from the ground.

Two soldiers were less than ten yards away, firing machine-guns at Sion. I shot them both, my silenced gun unheeded in the cacophony of their continuous fire. Almost without stopping, I darted forward, through the ring of Germans, just as another bomb exploded behind me.

Now I was in the copse, darting between trees, ducking behind bushes, putting a screen and distance between the German soldiers and me. I wondered briefly if they had tracker dogs but then dismissed it from my mind. With all the other scents in the area, it would be impossible for a dog to pick out my smell.

The snicker of a gun bolt being drawn back brought me up cold.

I was about to throw myself onto the ground, away from the gunman when a low voice spoke.

'Don't move or I'll kill you.'

The words were English, but the accent was as Irish as my own.

'Kitty, it's me, Mike.'

'O'Donnell? Jesus, Mike, I was just about to shoot first and ask questions later. What on earth are you doing here?'

'Looking for you. Come on, we'd better move. Now the plane's gone they'll be searching for us.'

'Follow me.'

She was like a will-o'-the-wisp, flitting through the trees while I blundered along behind her. We came out onto a track, which she crossed then went unerringly to a spot a few yards away where she had hidden her bicycle.

'Give me your rucksack and gun. I'll ride the bike while you run beside me.'

I did as she said and we started moving quickly up a gentle incline. After a few hundred yards I was puffing like a steam engine building up pressure. I was sorely out of condition and it showed but I wasn't going to give up. Not yet anyhow. I stumbled a number of times but kept running. Fading into the distance behind I heard the sound of whistles being blown. By now my breath was coming in ragged gasps. My legs ached and I was on the point of collapsing.

Kitty was drawing ahead of me when she stopped and looked back, silhouetted against the night sky. As the moon appeared I saw the smile on her face. I caught up with her and bent, gasping, my hands on my knees.

'Feeling your age, O'Donnell?'

'Fun . . . Funny,' I managed to gasp.

'Come on. Hop up behind. It's downhill for the next few kilometres.'

I climbed onto the saddle and she pushed off, standing on the pedals as we freewheeled down the track. After a while my breathing returned to something near normal and my heart stopped pounding. I was too old for these shenanigans.

Looking over her shoulder the breeze rapidly dried the sweat on my face. I could feel the warmth of her body and was aware of her breasts just above my hands. God forgive me, I couldn't stop my right hand moving about half an inch upwards.

'Don't even think about it,' she called out, the bike wobbling slightly.

I grinned. She was a feisty one and no mistake.

Kitty had been braking, slowing us down, as we felt our way through the darkness. It was too risky to put on a light, assuming the bike was fitted with one. At any moment I expected us to come a cropper. But apart from the rattle and bounce as we went over the track nothing untoward happened. We finally came to a halt.

Hopping off the bike, Kitty said, 'There's a road up ahead. There may be a patrol out or a roadblock. We'd better go carefully.'

I unslung my Sten from my shoulder. Kitty took her Sten from the basket on the front of the handlebars and cocked it.

We were about a hundred metres from the road with hedgerows on both sides. Treetops stretched away into the distance. Slowly I advanced along the track, listening intently. On such a night my ears and nose would warn me of an enemy well before my eyes saw anyone. Sure enough I soon heard the unmistakable sound of metal striking metal. I froze, turning my head slightly to catch the noise, which appeared to come from ahead. There it was again. Carefully I inched my way forward, peering into the night, feeling oddly calm.

I heard a cough followed by the noise of hawking. Then I could clearly distinguish German voices. Slowly and cautiously I retreated. Reaching Kitty I put my mouth close to her ear. 'Germans at the road. At least two. Possibly more.'

'Right,' she whispered. 'We go back about fifty metres – there's a stile and a path. Come on.'

I followed her as we made our way back along the track. The stile was on our right and after she climbed over it I passed the bicycle to her. The path meandered into the woods. This time I led. It wasn't quite pitch dark but, for all that, it was as black as a coalminer's armpit. I walked with one hand stretched out in front of me, feeling for gaps in the undergrowth. The path was about two feet wide and wove like a sidewinder. We stumbled a good deal, making more noise than I cared for. I hadn't checked the time when we entered the woods and I lost all sense of how long we were in there but it felt like an eternity. I thought the blasted trees would never end, then suddenly we were out of it and standing in the open. Another pace forward and I was standing on a tarmac road. The front wheel of the bike hit my leg and Kitty stood beside me.

'What time is it?' She spoke softly.

'I can't see my watch.' I looked up at the sky. Orion's Belt was low down and I knew dawn couldn't be far away. We'd passed most of the night stumbling through that damned wood. 'It'll be light soon. We'd better make tracks. Here, you sit behind while I pedal.'

After a wobbly start we picked up speed and settled onto a straight course. The road was flat and I could see the trees either side without any difficulty. The tyres hummed beneath us, a soporific sound dulling my senses. Soon I was bone tired, peddling and steering like an automaton, intent on putting as much distance between us and the Germans as possible. I became dimly aware that what had been only shades of black were turning grey. The light hardened and dawn crept ever closer, bringing with it the dangers of a new day.

'We'd better stop,' said Kitty. 'Hole up for a few hours and get some rest. It's madness to keep going. You said often enough that tiredness kills more than anything.'

I nodded but kept peddling. 'Soon.' She was right of course. Tiredness clouded your judgement, made you foolhardy. It distorted your perception of risk and reward and lead too often to arrest or death. It was an agent's greatest enemy in occupied territory.

Kitty thumped my shoulder. 'Stop, Mike! There's a barn over there. Let's get off the road before anyone sees us.'

That made sense and with a sigh of relief I stopped peddling. Awkwardly, with every muscle in my body aching, I climbed off the bike. The sun still hadn't risen but in the strengthening light we could see that the wooden structure was dilapidated. The only noises were the sounds of birds beginning their dawn chorus.

Half the roof had fallen in, a wall had collapsed and the rest looked as though a good wind would blow it over. We picked our way into the gloomy interior, me with the bike raised above my head. We heard scuttling and loud squeaks as the rats took off for their cubby-holes in the packed earth floor. Rotten straw bales were stacked along one wall and a pile of empty sacks lay in a corner. On closer examination I saw they were used for picking potatoes.

'All the comforts of home,' I said cheerily.

'Hardly,' said Kitty. 'But it'll do while we rest and plan our next move.'

'I'll take the first watch. You get some sleep.'

'We'll toss for it. This is no place for chivalry.' She took a coin out of her pocket and tossed it into the air. 'Heads or tails?'

I snatched the coin out of the air. 'Heads.' Without looking I added, 'Nope, it's tails. I win. You sleep. And that's an order.'

She was about to argue but then thought better of it. Shrugging, she pulled small piles of the sacks onto the floor, using her bag for a pillow. She checked her Sten, smiled at me briefly and promptly fell asleep.

I wandered around the barn. It was open countryside as far as I could see with not another building in sight. The land was undulating and cultivated. One field I saw was wheat while another appeared to be potatoes. In the distance, in a fold between low hills, I saw smoke begin to rise. I guessed there was a farmhouse. Satisfied no one was around I sat on one of the bales for a few seconds. Suddenly I jerked awake with a dry mouth and a hammering heart. I staggered to my feet, berating myself for not staying awake. I couldn't have dozed off for long as the sun was only beginning to rise above the horizon. I walked around the barn, taking a closer look at what was there. A rusty plough lay in one corner while in another I found a tap. Turning it on I was rewarded was a gurgle and hiss followed by clean-looking water.

Using my cupped hand I washed my face and drank a bellyful. It tasted as good as a cold, dark stout on a warm summer's day. More to the point it refreshed me and woke me up for a few minutes. While shadows were still stalking the land I decided to go outside and see if there were indeed potatoes growing about twenty yards away. Keeping low I crossed to the field and sure enough found rows of summer potatoes. I pulled a few plants and returned to the relative safety of the barn. Using a knife, I peeled the largest and ate it raw. Then I promptly wished I hadn't as it sat heavily in my stomach.

I stayed on my feet and paced around, looking through one gap in the wall after another. By nine o'clock I'd had it. I woke Kitty, mumbled to her that I needed my beauty sleep and promptly fell into a comatose state on the sacking she'd been using.

I was awake by midday. With my eyes shut, I lay listening to the silence of the day, aware of Kitty's movements as she patrolled the walls, peering out. Sitting up I stretched and yawned. 'I feel a lot better for that.'

'Good. All's quiet. I've got some potatoes in a fire. They'll be ready to eat in about ten minutes.'

A small, smokeless fire was burning under the hole in the roof. I lumbered to my feet and went across to the tap. A quick wash and drink and I felt one hundred percent once more.

'We need to decide what to do.'

I nodded, looking at her squarely. Even in the bizarre situation we found ourselves in, I couldn't help but be struck by her sheer beauty. Her wavy dark hair fell across her face as she leant to check on our rustic meal. Who would believe that her blue-eyed innocence belied such controlled power?

'Do you have any contacts you can trust?'

'If you'd asked me that a few days ago I'd have said plenty. As it stands, any one of them could be the traitor.'

'You were lucky to get out when you did.'

'Damn lucky.' Kitty began to walk agitatedly around the floor. 'My apartment was a garret with a shared lavatory on the floor below. I was actually in there when I heard the Germans' jackboots thundering up the stairs. As soon as the last man was out of sight I legged it.'

'There was nobody downstairs waiting?'

'One officer. *Gestapo*.'

'What happened to him?'

'I shot him. In the face. I had no choice. I'd already lost bods and I thought my place was the safest. Yet they still found me. When I checked on three others in my circuit I found they'd been lifted as well. So I decided to run. Alone.'

'It was the right decision. What papers do you have?'

'Only my original ones. In the name of Michelle Delours.'

'I've brought you new ones. In the name of Kitty O'Donnell. We're a couple of Fenians. Not pro-German, just anti-English.'

'O'Donnell? So I'm your daughter?'

I grimaced. 'My wife, you cheeky pup.' Seeing the look on her face I added, 'Don't worry. Everything will be strictly above board.'

'As long as it stays above the navel, O'Donnell. That's my biggest concern.'

'Avoiding the Germans should be your biggest concern, my girl.'

Kitty smiled, illuminating her whole face. 'I'll leave that to you, husband dearest.'

'In that case, wifey, how about those potatoes?'

The skins were black but the insides were cooked to perfection. A smidgen of salt wouldn't have gone amiss. But then, sure, you can't have everything.

'Who do you think is the traitor?' I asked when I'd eaten enough.

Sadly she shook her head. 'I've thought of nothing else but the fact is, I've no idea. The last man standing, I suppose.'

'With the Germans wanting you for murder we've no choice now but to run for it. Is there anyone *at all* we can trust?'

'Not with any certainty. Besides, most of my circuit were in Paris. I have a few contacts in Amiens but nothing we can work with. Not yet, at any rate.'

'It looks like we head for Vichy and then the Spanish border.'

'It's a long way.'

'Any better ideas?'

'None at present.'

'What about a wireless set? Do you know of one we can get our hands on?'

Kitty shook her head. 'I had three in Paris along with two *Georges*. I presume both operators were taken and the sets either destroyed or captured. Don't you know where to find one?'

I shook my head. 'I run two other circuits but none near here. I do have a name, though, once we get closer to the border. A guide. I've got a price as well.'

'How much?'

'Twenty-thousand francs each. I've got plenty of money.'

'Good. We'll need it. Once we leave here it's bluff all the way. We can't fight our way across France.'

'Did you have a back-up plan if things had gone wrong at the pick-up?'

'Naturally. If you hadn't arrived or, as things are now, I intended making for the station at Chartres.'

'That's what? Forty miles?'

'A bit more. A bus leaves about three miles from here. The danger is from random checks. Once on the bus we've nowhere to hide.' While she was speaking she was rummaging in her pannier basket. She withdrew a pair of nail scissors. 'Here, you'd better cut my hair. Short. I'll tell you what to do and where to cut.'

I did as she said. It took a good twenty minutes but in the end she looked a different woman. 'That's better,' she announced, looking at her reflection in a small hand mirror.

'What about your identity card?'

'I have one with my hair like this. I'll burn the other.' So saying

310

she reached into a pocket, removed her *Carte d'Identité* and dropped it onto the fire. I watched as the black and white picture of her in profile curled, browned and burst into flame. 'Give me your other card. I'll take the photograph and replace the one on the papers I brought with me. I've got a complete set of stamps and ink to do the job.'

While I set to work on Kitty's new ID I asked, 'Do you know the countryside around here?'

'No. I can find my way along the road to the bus stop but I don't think I'll manage if we cut across country, if that's what you're thinking.'

'In that case our best bet is to start out now. If we run into a patrol we just have to hope our papers withstand scrutiny.'

Picking up the ID she looked critically at my handiwork. 'It'll do.' It was as close as she came to giving a compliment.

By now it was after 3pm. 'We'll bury the Stens here. I'll keep the pistol with me. It's a German Mauser. If anybody stops and looks at it I'll tell them Goering gave it to me.'

'Do you expect them to fall for that?'

'That's what it says on the engraving next to the safety. Here, look.'

I passed the gun to her and watched the astonished look that flickered across her face.

'It's not real. But would a German soldier question it?' It was one of David's ideas and had been done at the last minute. *To Herr M. O'Donnell, aus Dankbarkeit, H. Goering.*

'And if they ask in gratitude for what?'

'I shall tap the side of my nose and tell them it's a state secret.'

'Suppose they check?'

'How? Phone Fat Herman in his office? It's hardly likely.'

'What if they don't believe it?'

'Would you risk it? Suppose it's true? You're in deep trouble. And if it's not? No one is any the wiser as we are allowed to travel on our way. It is, as David says, a bit of bullshit baffling brains.'

'Who's this David you keep mentioning?'

'Your boss. And one of the brightest men I know. Right, let's get going.'

We doused the fire and left the old barn. Quickly we retraced our steps. Once on the road Kitty climbed onto the seat of the bicycle while I took up position on the pedals once more. As soon as we'd picked up a little speed we stopped wobbling and I settled down to an easy rhythm, the bike eating up the miles.

We reached the *arrêt d'autobus* without mishap and ditched the bike behind a hedge. According to the timetable pinned to the post, a bus would be along at 18.10. We had forty-five minutes to wait.

'Perhaps we'd better get out of sight,' I suggested. 'Better safe than sorry.'

It was just as well that we did. Ten minutes later two people arrived at the bus stop. Five minutes after that a German patrol turned up. The soldiers demanded to see papers. An argument followed and then the sound of a door opening and slamming. One of the men had been taken away for further questioning.

From where we were hidden we watched for the bus. Sure enough, it turned up only a few minutes late, belching diesel smoke and rattling like the heap it was. We climbed through the hedge as it stopped and went on board. It was half full. Dull-eyed locals avoided looking at us, immersed in their own concerns. For that I didn't blame them, in fact I was grateful. The less notice taken of us the better.

The old bus chugged along, dropping off and picking up passengers every few miles. I sat there like a coiled spring, my nerves near to breaking as I waited for the next German patrol to arrive and arrest us. Kitty, God bless her, looked utterly sanguine. Eventually we arrived at the outskirts of Chartres. Here the embarking and disembarking became more frequent as we headed towards the centre of the town. The *gare routière* was next to the train station, where we finally alighted at a few minutes to nine o'clock.

The place was teeming with people in spite of the relatively late hour. Many of them were Germans in uniform, enjoying an evening out. Some carried rifles slung over their shoulders and were obviously on duty. Civilians were being continually harassed and asked to show their IDs. After three years of occupation many of the French were prepared to argue, particularly if it concerned some minor infringement of the rules. Arguments often resulted in an arrest, amidst much protest. These scuffles caused a good deal of confusion and occupied many of the Germans on duty. We weaved our way through the crowds, avoiding anyone in uniform as best we could.

Finally we made it on to the concourse and across to the booking hall. There was a train at 22.10 for Toulouse. I let Kitty buy the tickets. Returns. If we were asked, we'd say we were visiting the city for its culture. I bought a guidebook, in French, about the area.

By now my stomach thought my throat was cut. We made another beeline through the crowd, this time towards the buffet. I elbowed my way to the bar, ordered cheese sandwiches that looked as though they'd been cut in the early hours of that morning, four coffees and two large brandies. The barman was good enough to give me a tray in exchange for a five franc tip and I forced my way back outside where Kitty was waiting. We were in luck. As I arrived two people left one of the tables right out on the concourse. The sandwiches tasted as bad as they looked, but we forced them down. The coffee was excellent as only French coffee is, even in time of war, and the brandy gave me a pick-me-up I was in sore need of. A glance at my watch told me we had twenty minutes to wait. As I looked to Kitty to confirm, she mouthed one word to me, '*Gestapo.*' Two men, dressed in black suits and wearing fedora hats had arrived and were demanding papers from other patrons. They would be with us in a few minutes.

'Let's go. Use the toilets at the back of the restaurant.'

Unhurriedly we stood up and walked back into the throng, through the fetid, smoke filled air of the restaurant. Guttural German voices mingled with lilting French accents. Kitty and I headed for the door marked "*Toilettes*".

The *pissoir* reflected the general French attitude to hygiene and I wrinkled my nose at the smell. At the latrine I stood shoulder to shoulder with a German soldier, his lapel insignia suggesting he was an infantryman. It was the oddest feeling in the world, to be so close to the enemy doing something so natural and innocuous.

To delay my return to the restaurant I spent a long time washing my hands under a cold-water tap. Ignoring the filthy piece of towel I rubbed my hands on my trouser legs before adjusting the knapsack on my shoulder. Yet another argument over papers was taking place by the entrance between the *Gestapo* officers and a man in rough civilian clothes, who appeared the worse for drink. He stood up and threw a punch at one of the Germans. It connected with a solid thump and the officer went down like a ton of bricks, knocking over the other German.

The man who had thrown the punch was suddenly sober and he and his companion took to their heels and ran. To my astonishment the crowd, including the German soldiers, parted to let them through and then closed ranks behind them. The two *Gestapo* were left to get to their feet, ignored by everyone. One took out a whistle, blew it loudly then both officers rushed off in the Frenchmen's wake.

I was aware of Kitty by my side. 'Did you see that? Why didn't the soldiers help them?'

'They hate the *Gestapo* almost as much as the French.'

I smiled. 'Good. Perhaps they aren't all bad. Come on, we'd better get going.'

We worked our way towards the platform where our train was building up steam, flexing its mechanical muscle, eager to go. But there was another obstàcle for us to overcome. At the ticket barrier were three men, one in railway livery and the other two in the ubiquitous black suits and fedoras of the *Gestapo*. They weren't stopping everyone, but watching as each person presented their ticket for inspection. One of the men asked an occasional question, nodding when satisfied with the answer.

We were now in the queue and slowly getting nearer; soon we were two people away and then it was too late.

Showing our tickets to the ticket collector we walked past. We'd gone perhaps two paces when a voice said, '*Ein Moment, bitte. Ihre Papiere.*'

31

I IGNORED HIS instruction and continued walking, my left hand holding Kitty's right upper arm. Within seconds I was grabbed roughly, by the shoulder. I swung around angrily.

'Touch me like that again and I'll break your arm,' I said in English. I wasn't going to pass muster as a Frenchman or a German, so I used my real persona – that of bloody-minded Irishman.

The officer looked at me in surprise and exclaimed, '*Herrgott, ein Engländer.*'

'Call me an Englishman,' I said in German, 'and I *will* knock your block off. I'm Irish.'

The two *Gestapo* were now menacingly close. The younger man, somewhere in his mid-twenties, spoke excellent English. 'You will come with us. You are under arrest.'

'I don't think so.' I narrowed my eyes and spoke through a clenched mouth. 'Check our papers. They are in order. If we miss this train you will find yourself on the Eastern Front within a week.'

Clearly unused to being contradicted the young German's face mottled with anger, but some instinct held him back. His taller, grey-haired, more senior colleague swivelled round to him and he translated. Though my German wasn't fluent I understood the older man's reply. 'Tread carefully. I don't like the look of the man.'

I didn't wait to be asked any more questions, figuring it was time to be co-operative. 'Here. You can see that I am Irish. My papers are fully in order.'

The *Gestapo* scrutinised them and then passed them to the older man. 'And you?' he asked Kitty.

'This is my wife. You may see her papers too, if you wish.'

Kitty handed over her ID and stood by my side, clearly nervous – a natural reaction when all was said and done. The power of these

315

men was legion. And they weren't afraid to use it. But like all bullies I figured they were also cowards, otherwise they'd have been in uniform and fighting the war like soldiers. The train was about to depart and I intended being on it, one way or another. I reached into my pocket for a pack of cigarettes, lifted a cigarette to my mouth and reached back inside for my lighter. I left my hand there, clasped around the butt of my pistol. Nonchalantly I removed the cigarette from my mouth and waited for the *Gestapo* to make the next move.

'*Alles in Ordnung, danke.*' He returned the papers to us and I nodded my thanks, turning away. '*Ein Moment.*'

I turned back, wondering what the hell he wanted now. He reached into his pocket and for a second I thought my bluff had failed and he was about to draw a gun. Instead he brought out a lighter and offered me the flame. I lit my cigarette, nodding my thanks and managing a half-hearted smile.

I didn't smoke, hadn't had a cigarette since leaving the trenches in 1918. Carrying them was an excuse to put my hands in my pockets. Somehow I managed not to cough my guts up and we continued along the platform.

Amidst the usual whistles and yells we climbed onto the train only seconds before it departed. As I closed the door I looked back but the two *Gestapo* had already moved on.

It was a corridor train with eight-seat compartments. We were travelling first class and had to walk most of the length of the train to the front car to find our seats. The whole train was packed, mainly with civilians but with a fair scattering of German soldiers too: I wondered where they were all headed. Passing through the restaurant car, I tipped the headwaiter and booked a table for the first sitting. The next car along we found our compartment and seats. Thankfully it was empty.

'That was close,' said Kitty as we entered and I closed the door behind us. 'What were you going to do? Shoot them?'

I grinned. 'No. Show them the inscription from Herman and threaten them with my connections. If that hadn't worked, *then* I'd have shot them.'

'That might have spoiled your appetite, Mike. Aren't you the brave one booking dinner?'

'We can skulk in here or we can be as brazen as two innocents abroad. We know our tickets and papers will be checked again so we may as well be open about it. What time do we arrive in Toulouse?'

'Six o'clock. All being well. We can stretch out later on and get some sleep.'

'I think we'd better take it in turns. So we aren't woken unexpectedly.'

Kitty nodded, laid her head back and closed her eyes. 'Wake me in time for dinner.'

Pulling down the roller blinds, I sealed off our compartment from prying eyes and went into the corridor. I walked forward, glancing in where blinds hadn't been closed. Most compartments had one or two occupants. The end of the corridor led to a second First Class carriage. I didn't stay long. It was full of German officers, loud, raucous and drinking heavily. I guessed they were going on a spot of leave. Lord God Almighty, whatever happened we wouldn't be able to shoot our way out of trouble.

A bell rang in the corridor for first sitting for dinner. I woke Kitty from a sound sleep then went ahead while she used the *cabinet de toilette* to freshen up. Shown to a table set for four, I reminded the headwaiter I'd paid for a table *pour deux*.

'I apologise, *monsieur*, but we are full.' He lowered his voice. 'The train, as you can see, is full of Germans.'

I nodded my understanding. From my work at SOE I knew that many of the staff of the French railway were either Maquis or saboteurs. They had damaged or destroyed more trains and lines than the whole of bomber command to date. It was one reason the *Gestapo* often travelled the trains. They couldn't trust the French but they couldn't operate the railways without them.

Kitty arrived and we ordered two aperitifs. A brandy and soda for her, a pastis for me. With the drinks arrived two German majors.

Very punctiliously they wished us a good day and took their seats beside us.

I replied in English, 'Good evening.'

Both men turned to me immediately. 'English?'

'Irish.'

The major by the window seat said in perfect English, 'Then you are here to fight with us?'

'No. I am here to fight against the English.'

He shrugged. 'Your reasons are of no consequence. The result is the same.'

I inclined my head in apparent agreement and beckoned the waiter. 'Bring these gentlemen a drink and put it on my bill.'

'That is too kind of you. And not necessary . . .'

'It is my pleasure. Please.'

The blinds were tightly drawn, to avoid a potential attack by British bombers, and so we had no choice other than to look into the carriage, at the other diners, to observe and be observed. The buffet car was full. At least half the tables were taken up by German officers, the others by men travelling singly or in pairs, salesmen for the most part. Commerce never ended, not even in time of war.

A second round of drinks came before we ordered our meal. By that time we were in conversation with the two officers. They had introduced themselves as Marcus and Axel. After two years on the Russian Front, they counted themselves lucky to be alive.

'Are you on leave?' Kitty asked.

'*Ja*,' replied Marcus. 'For a few days. And then we join our regiment in Italy.'

'Marcus,' hissed Axel, 'you should not say where we are going.'

'Herr O'Donnell is no friend of the English, is that not so? We are amongst friends, Axel, relax.'

Both were hard-bitten veterans. They wore Iron Crosses around their necks, two rows of medal ribbons on their chests and possessed a toughness that came only when you'd survived a living hell and gotten out before it destroyed your spirit. I recognised it, for I had been there.

They were chalk and cheese. Marcus was tall, blond and typically Aryan whilst Axel was slight, dark and intense, with unhappy brown eyes staring out from an intelligent face. We learnt that they had been at university together and had degrees in German literature and philosophy. Both had spent a year in England which accounted for their fluency. At the outbreak of war they had been called up and shoved unceremoniously into officer school. Promotion had been rapid on the Eastern Front due to the attrition of the troops.

Our meal started with a watery cress soup, followed by tough horse steak with over-cooked vegetables. Two bottles of exceptionally good wine counter-balanced the cuisine, though I was careful to pour most of it for our new friends. The freely flowing alcohol helped build a rapport.

Sitting at the far end of the carriage beside the bar, I was well placed to watch the far door. As the head waiter served our cheese and coffee, I watched as the ticket collector, accompanied by two men in black suits, entered the buffet car and began to check everyone's papers. Even without their hats they were clearly *Gestapo*.

I looked over my shoulder at the waiter and attracted his attention. 'Glasses of port, please. Large ones.'

'No, no, Herr O'Donnell, I must protest.' Axel spoke without conviction and I merely smiled.

'You are my guests for this evening. And *I* insist.' The drinks arrived and I said, 'Let me propose a toast. An end to the war. Victory over the English.'

By the time the ticket collector reached our table we were on a second round. A perfunctory glance, and he moved on. The two *Gestapo* officers held out their hands for our papers.

'*Ausweise*,' snapped the first man.

Marcus looked at him with something akin to hatred and leant back in his chair. 'You will address me as *Herr Major*. Stand up straight when you speak to a senior officer.'

The reprimand had little effect. 'I have no time for this nonsense. Show me your papers *Herr Major* or it will be the worse for you.'

'You dare to threaten me, *Sie kleines Miststück*?' Marcus lurched to his feet and grabbed the man by his throat. A good head taller, he snarled down at the man. 'You are a disgrace to Germany. Speak to me civilly or I will break your neck.'

I had to hand it to the little *Gestapo* runt, he showed a modicum of spunk.

'You wouldn't dare. You will be arrested for murder.'

Marcus laughed out loud and called out, 'Do you hear that lads? I wouldn't dare. What do you think?'

The other officers laughed and cheered. It was only then that I realised they were all from the same regiment.

One soldier called out, 'Break it anyway, Marcus, he deserves it.'

Now the little man showed real fear – his eyes bulged as Marcus squeezed before letting him go, shoving him away. He staggered backwards, rubbing his neck.

'My name is Marcus von Kleinhoff. I am on leave with my fellow officers. Are you suggesting that all of us are spies? Or that we are an English regiment which has somehow secreted itself on this train?'

'No . . . No, of course not, *Herr Major*. Understand, please, it is my duty to check everyone's papers.'

'To make sure we are not deserters? Do you intend to send us back to the Eastern Front to die? Or put us in front of a firing squad as an example to others? You miserable worm. Get out of my sight.'

'Please, *Herr Major*, I must check the papers of these other passengers.' The *Gestapo* officer gestured at Kitty and me.

'These people are my friends. Now go, *verdammt noch mal.*'

I had to hand it to the little swine, he wasn't giving in easily. 'I . . . I shall have to report your interference in my duties. It is most irregular.'

'Then report it. Allow me to spell my name and regiment.' Marcus did so.

The *Gestapo* wrote it in his little black book before turning to leave. Three other officers blocked his way.

The tallest one reached across and snatched the notebook from his hands. 'This officer is a hero of the Fatherland. He won an Iron Cross at Stalingrad and a second at the gates of Moscow. The Führer himself pinned the second cross on him. Now, you can either walk on or we will throw you off the train. Which is it to be?'

The two *Gestapo* scuttled back the way they had come to jeers and laughter from the soldiers. I'd heard of von Kleinhoff and Kitty and I looked at him with new respect. 'I had no idea we were in such august company.'

He looked at me in surprise. 'You've heard of me?'

'Yes. And of your exploits.'

'Exaggerated by the newspapers,' he said disarmingly.

'Do not believe him,' said Axel. 'If it hadn't been for him we would have all died at Moscow. Those stupid clods in their Panzers, and us following like cattle to the slaughter.' Axel stopped and looked at me, 'You wonder why we hate the *Gestapo* so much. Outside Moscow we were taking a hell of a beating. The Russians were dying ten to our one but they fought like tigers with antiquated tanks and weapons. They would not give in. We were ordered to attack. Our Commanding Officer, a truly great man, argued it would be in vain. The *Gestapo* took him out and summarily executed him.'

'My God,' said Kitty, 'that's barbaric. What did you do?'

'Marcus shot the men from the *Gestapo* and we pulled back to fight another day. It was a strategic decision, agreed by our High Command.'

'If it hadn't been, Axel, *I'd* have been shot,' and Marcus let out a roar of a laugh.

He was my enemy and yet I liked him tremendously.

'I've had enough of port. Waiter,' Marcus beckoned, 'get us some schnapps.'

A bottle and four small glasses appeared. For Kitty there was no difficulty refusing. Women weren't expected to be big drinkers. I tried hard not to drink too much. Finally we were asked to vacate the table as there was another sitting due. We staggered to our feet. I insisted on paying the bill and stuffed a handful of notes into the headwaiter's hands. We lurched back to our compartments, bade the Germans goodnight and sank thankfully into our seats.

'My God,' said Kitty, 'what an evening. One to tell the grandchildren about. Who'd have believed it?'

'Not me, that's for sure. We'd better get some sleep. You want to go first?'

She looked at me and said, 'I think you'd better go first. You look like death warmed up.'

'Too much schnapps. Those Germans have hard heads.'

'I thought the Irish did as well.'

'We do, but we aren't in the same league. Wake me in two hours.'

Kitty switched off the light. I pulled off my shoes and, with the armrests stowed away, lay across the seat. I fell fast asleep immediately. When I awoke the compartment had turned from pitch black to grey. Kitty was fast asleep on the other seat. My mouth felt like the bottom of a birdcage and there was a throbbing behind my right eye. I peered out from behind the blind. The sun was almost up. I was looking out on to the wide, open spaces of the countryside.

Grabbing my toilet bag I eased open the door not to disturb Kitty. A shave, wash and brush-up left me feeling more or less human again. Back in the compartment, I sat quietly in a corner and dozed off for a while. The next thing I knew we were pulling into a station. Peering out once more I caught a glimpse of the name, Montauban. I'd never heard of it but as it was approaching 05.15 I figured we weren't too far from Toulouse. We'd been travelling for another ten minutes when our compartment door was unceremoniously thrown open.

Framed in the doorway was our little friend from the *Gestapo*. 'Your papers!'

Rummaging in my jacket pocket I handed them over. He thanked us then stepped outside to examine them. Realising he had spoken English I wondered how the hell he had known we spoke little German. It was some time before he returned, with a satisfied smirk on his face.

'As I thought, these are forgeries. I am always suspicious when such kindness is shown to our soldiers, even ones as distinguished as your guests last night. I made enquiries of the headwaiter. A very accommodating man when threatened.'

'You can see from our papers that we are Irish – citizens of a neutral country. I can assure you, you're making a big mistake.'

'Somehow I doubt that. But if I am,' he shrugged, 'I shall apologise profusely and ask that you forgive me. We will be stopping in a few minutes. Get your coats and bags and come with me.'

Used to instilling fear in those he confronted, he was sure we would do as he said. I grabbed my bag and stepped into the corridor while Kitty stayed where she was.

'*Kommen Sie, schnell.*'

'No! No! I'm afraid.' Kitty sat with her back against the wall, cowering away from the door. Exasperated, he stepped past me and inside. That advantage was all I needed. I stepped up behind him, put my right forearm across his throat, my left arm across the back of his neck, gripped my own arm and jerked. His neck broke with the sound of a dry twig.

'What now?' Kitty whispered.

'Now,' I said, 'we shove the body onto the luggage rack. It could be there for a while, until someone comes in and tries to put a case up there.'

Between us we manhandled his body up on the deep wooden rack where it slid to the back. His coat hung over the edge and I tucked it away. Unless you stood on the seat you would never know he was there.

The train began to slow down. We were entering the station at Toulouse.

'Time to get off. Too dangerous to hang around the station for another train. We'd better find another way.'

The train came to a halt and its passengers poured off. As we alighted, I spotted the second *Gestapo* man looking around, obviously wondering where his companion had disappeared to. Keeping our heads down we hurried away. Not a moment too soon. We had hardly reached the exit when we heard police whistles sounding behind us.

32

THE GUIDEBOOK I'D bought in Chartres proved useful. From the Gare Matabiau we crossed Boulevard André Sémard and hurried along Rue Bayard. Every second took us further from the commotion back at the station but it wouldn't be long before the *Gestapo* organised city-wide stop and searches. Demands to see ID cards would be followed by wholesale arrests and interrogations. How the hell had they come to find the body so quickly?

We crossed the river Garonne with seconds to spare. Lorries and jeeps screeched past us, slamming to a halt. Disgorging troops quickly set up road barriers, directly behind us.

'We'd better slow down,' I said. 'Walk arm-in-arm, a couple without a care in the world. Enjoying the sights of this beautiful city.' I hefted my travel bag in my left hand.

Kitty tucked her arm through mine and smiled up at me coquettishly. 'It's a pity you're already taken, Mike O'Donnell.'

I licked dry lips and nodded. 'Probably just as well.' Maybe the croak in my voice was because of her smile. Or maybe being thrown together had brought out my protective instinct. Whichever it was, she was clearly enjoying my discomfort. I'm happily married, I kept reminding myself.

'It'll be hours before any buses are able to get out of the city. We'd better walk a bit further and find where they stop.'

Kitty nodded. 'How far to the border?'

'Just under a hundred miles, I think.'

'We could walk it in a week.'

'I've already considered it.' Further south there were fewer German troops about. And those troops tended to stick to the cities and towns. It was too dangerous for them to be out and about otherwise. There was a strong Maquis presence all across the area. Ambushes were frequent and deadly.

We had been walking steadily away from the city. Once we were in the outskirts we were highly conspicuous. It gave me an uncomfortable feeling between my shoulder blades. At the very edge of the city we found a small hotel and were quickly served with fresh coffee, bread and cheese. I was ravenous and from the way Kitty tucked into the food I guessed she was as well.

'According to my guide we need to get to Pamiers. We'd better ask the girl behind the counter if she knows when the next bus is due.'

'This coffee,' said Kitty, ignoring me, 'is delicious. We had nothing as good in Paris.'

'It's smuggled in from Spain. There's a vast trade in contraband between the two countries.'

'Not only goods. People smuggling as well,' said Kitty thoughtfully.

I nodded. 'Exactly. It would be easier and quicker to get across the mountains to Spain if we had a guide. I've enough money to bribe someone.'

'Good . . . Damn. Don't look round, Mike. Two German soldiers have just come in.'

We had elected to sit by a back door, as unobtrusively as possible, hoping to be ignored should a patrol come in.

'What are they doing?'

'Looking around. They've taken a seat by the main door. They're ordering something to drink.' Kitty let out a sigh and smiled radiantly at me. 'Officers. Lieutenants, I think.' Kitty watched for a few more moments. 'It's all right. They're deep in conversation.'

'This is bloody nerve-wracking. Let's get out of here.'

I waited outside while Kitty checked the route with the girl behind the counter. The day was warm, a pleasant breeze blowing from the south. A small Peugeot was parked in the courtyard and I assumed it belonged to the Germans. Kitty joined me and nodded at the direction we'd been heading.

'Pamiers is straight down that road. There'll be a bus in the middle of the afternoon.'

'I don't think we should wait around here. I feel too exposed.'

'There's another stop about four kilometres away. In the middle of nowhere. It serves the farm workers in the area.'

I moved the rucksack to a more comfortable position on my back and we set off. It was the oddest of feelings, to be strolling through enemy held territory as though we hadn't a care in the world. The day was so peaceful it was easy to forget how precarious our situation was. Complacency, I knew from bods I'd debriefed, was one of the main reasons agents were arrested or killed. Blasé contentment lulled you into a false sense of security until it was too late. We'd preached constantly about the risk, but now that I was experiencing the feeling myself I had a clearer understanding of how potent it could be.

'Let's get off the road,' I said. 'Over this gate. There's a path following the edge of the field which we can use.'

'Good idea. It's too quiet for my liking. Too peaceful. Besides, the back of my neck is itching.'

Many of the bods had superstitions and quirks they relied on – ninety-nine times out of a hundred they were wrong, but who was to say it wouldn't save their life at some time?

I helped her over the gate. The path meandered alongside the road on the other side of a tall, thick hedgerow. A few times we heard a vehicle passing. Twice it sounded like a lorry, moving rapidly. Was it Germans, racing to set another roadblock?

We stopped a short while later, by the side of a brook. The water was cool and fresh and we made ourselves comfortable, the water energising and relaxing us at the same time.

'We'd better not stay too long,' I said, more to myself than Kitty

She had fallen back and closed her eyes. A faint snore told me she'd fallen asleep. We had plenty of time so I left her to rest. I wasn't so certain that the bus would be a good move after all. I took out my travel guide and read a few more pages about the area, my eyes drooping and my head jerking as I fought to stay awake. A fly buzzed around my head and I made a feeble attempt to swat it. If I didn't move soon I knew I'd doze off as well. Reluctantly I stood up.

I was now fully alert and flicked through the pages of the book, learning what I could. There was a canal to the Mediterranean but it would take us too far east for my liking. A waste of travel time, when we wanted to go directly south. Another canal went south-southwest to a place called St Gaudens, which was nearer the border than Pamiers. It set me thinking.

I let Kitty sleep for a while longer and then woke her with a gentle shake of the shoulder. She came wide-awake instantly, sitting up with a quick motion. 'How long did I sleep?'

'About forty minutes. I've had an idea. We're only a few kilometres from this canal,' I showed her in my guide. 'There's a hire place for boats just by this village called Cugnaux. We could hire a boat and go along the canal. It's the last place the Germans will expect us to choose, as we'll be travelling so slowly. But a day's journey will take us half way to the Spanish border.'

'Makes sense. I doubt the Germans will have patrols on the canal.'

We had ten kilometres to go across country. By late afternoon we'd arrived at Cugnaux. We holed up for a while, reconnoitring the village. It seemed quiet enough.

'Let's find a shop,' said Kitty. 'Buy provisions. The boat hire place is half a kilometre away, on the other side of the village.'

'Agreed. If we're asked we'll stick to our story about a short sight-seeing holiday. What could be nicer than a few days on the water?'

We stocked up with enough food to last a couple of days before walking down to the canal and along the bank. It wasn't far to the place we wanted. The owner didn't exactly receive us with open arms; I couldn't tell if it was French arrogance or my paranoia, but he was certainly suspicious.

They had narrow boats for hire, ten metres long, two wide, clean and prettily decorated. We negotiated the hire of one and paid a deposit equivalent to a week's rental. There might have been a war on but they still had a nose for a handsome profit.

The owner checked the fuel, showed me where to fill the tank, check the oil and top-up with fresh water. It didn't take long before we were casting-off. I stood with the tiller in my right hand and looked back at the Frenchman, standing, watching us depart. I waved goodbye but he ignored me. A curious attitude for a businessman eager for trade, I thought wryly.

Kitty scratched the back of her neck before announcing, 'I'll get us something to eat.'

I could hear her pottering around down below while I throttled back, put the gear lever into neutral, then astern and then increased the revs. The boat stopped in just over its own length. Good. The last thing I wanted was to cause an accident.

The waterway was relatively busy, with barges plying their trade in both directions. The owner had given me a short briefing on the rule-of-the-road for the canal and I kept to the right, allowing other boats to overtake and pass us down our port side. Kitty appeared with a plate of bread, cheese and paté and a dish of olives. A glass of red wine went down a treat, as we chugged along at 6 km per hour.

'There was something odd about our friend back there,' I said once we'd finished eating.

'You noticed it too?'

I nodded. 'His attitude was peculiar to say the least. David always says it's far, far better to look foolish than to be sorry. I've no intention of stopping at Lherm, as we told him. We'll go on a bit further and find a quiet spot. Here's the first lock.'

Every five kilometres or so we had to wait for the big cargo barges to enter a lock before we were squeezed in, like an afterthought. The other bargees were a sociable lot, as we soon discovered. They didn't appear to know there was a war on. Glasses of wine were handed around while we waited for the locks to fill with water.

For the men and women on the barges it was a way of life. They enjoyed freedom and independence that nothing, not even war, would be allowed to spoil. By the time we motored out of the third lock, with Lherm three kilometres behind, I was beginning to envy them.

A short distance along, the canal had been widened to allow berthing for the night. We tied up and I cut the engine. A blessed relief descended over us like a mantle. I hadn't realised how intrusive the sound of the engine had been, throbbing through the soles of my feet.

We sat in companionable silence. The pressures and demands of our situation seemed a long way away. I admired Kitty immensely for being able to withstand them. 'Tell me, Kitty, me darling, why is there no man in your life?'

She was silent for a moment or two and then lifted her chin a notch. 'There was. The *Gestapo* took him six months ago. They shot him as he tried to escape from the local Gendarmerie less than two hours later.'

'I'm sorry.'

I sensed her shrugging. 'In war we don't have the luxury of permanent attachments. It's better that way. Enjoy life while you can, for tomorrow we may die.'

'I'm still feeling uneasy,' I said. 'I think we should take a few precautions. Now it's dark we can't go any further. If we split the watch, we can catch up on our sleep during the day. I stopped here because of the copse of trees over there.' Silhouetted against the night sky were the branches of tall elms, about twenty yards away. 'That's where we set our watch. In the toolbox I found this ball of twine.' I explained my idea to Kitty.

'Who takes the first watch?'

'You do. Wake me at two.'

Kitty smiled. 'Because if anybody's coming it'll be in the early hours of the morning.'

'That and the fact I'm knackered.'

It was a warm night and so we put a mattress in the well at the stern where there was just enough room to lie out straight. Kitty took the pistol, and before she headed off for the copse we ran out the twine, which I tied around my wrist. Knowing she could tug on it to signal me, I lay down, gazing up at the heavens. A comet blazed briefly and I closed my eyes. The next thing I knew Kitty was shaking my shoulder.

Dawn was breaking as I started the engine. Throughout the day we worked our way through seven locks, losing more time than I'd expected. When dusk fell we were still about fifteen kilometres from St Gaudens.

Kitty had been reading the guide. 'It makes more sense if we abandon the boat at St Martory. Look at the roads. There's a track that cuts over the hills to Aspet. This is where the mountains really begin. Look at the track.' She traced her finger along the page. She was right. It did make sense.

'It's too dark to start out now. We run the risk of spraining an ankle or worse. We can leave at first light. From now on it'll be a slog.'

We took the same precautions with the twine as we'd done the previous night. Which was just as well. Around 03.30, the darkest hour before the dawn, we had visitors.

This time there was no convenient copse, just a low hedgerow about twenty yards from the canal bank. I lay hidden by a combination of long grass and the overhang of the hedge, wrapped in a blanket. I'd been kept awake by the cold and my efforts to subdue amorous thoughts about Kitty.

It was a still night. So when I heard rustling I knew it was either some nocturnal animal or we were about to have unwelcome company. A loud whisper confirmed what I wanted to know and I pulled the string to wake up Kitty.

Almost immediately she gave me a tug back. The snicker of a bolt being pulled back and released convinced me it was time for Kitty to abandon ship. I gave a series of tugs and she replied. Try as I might I heard no splash, no indication she'd gone into the water. I prayed she'd made it.

There were three of them, stalking across open ground about fifteen yards from me. Not one of them so much as glanced in my direction.

The half moon gave enough light to distinguish shapes and I could see that two of the men were armed. One had a long-barrelled rifle slung over his shoulder, the other a machine-gun of some sort. The third man was carrying what appeared to be a stave similar to the one I'd cut only hours earlier.

They stopped about five paces away from me and looked over the hedge at the boat. One of them said, 'That's her. Quietly does it. André, you go round to the right, Marcel, to the left. I'll step over here. Quiet now!'

One of the men passed so close to me I could have reached out and touched him. I smelled his stale cigarette smoke and the rancid stench of his wine-sodden breath. The hedge curved inwards towards the canal in both directions. Very soon the two men were out of sight, leaving the third man in the middle. He began to climb cautiously over the hedge. I waited until he was half way over.

Crawling out from under the blanket I hefted the stave in my hand. I was about a pace away when some instinct caused the man to look my way. It was no contest. I brained him with a solid smack across his head.

Dragging him back over the hedge I checked his pulse. It was still beating soundly. I checked his gun – a Sten. Were they thieves or Maquis?

I started as a figure appeared beside me. 'Kitty!' I whispered. 'Are you all right?'

'Yes,' she whispered back. 'I swam about a hundred yards before coming ashore. Who else is here?'

'Another two of them. One each side of the barge.'

The two men were approaching from opposite ends. I slung the Sten over my shoulder and stepped over the hedge. Ducking down, my head bent, I crossed to the water's edge. The two men, their attention on the boat, moved closer. The one armed with the rifle now held it in his hands, while the second held his stave up to his shoulder, as though he was about to swing it. Two paces and I was alongside the man with the rifle, shoving the end of the Sten into his side.

'Drop it!' I said harshly. 'Or you're dead.'

He looked at me stupidly. Obviously I needed to be more persuasive.

I smashed the end of the Sten across his fingers and the rifle clattered to the ground. Stepping back I shouted to his comrade, 'Drop it. Now!'

Immediately his hands were in the air.

I called to Kitty to join me.

'Sorry, Mike, but I've got a small problem.'

I glanced over in her direction. Kitty was standing with her hands on her head, surrounded by heavily armed men.

33

CHOOSE YOUR BATTLES wisely – that was another piece of wisdom I'd learned in the forces. I put the machine-gun catch to safe and handed over the weapon.

An altercation in idiomatic French took place, of which I understood not a word. As the men surrounded us, I recognised the owner of the barge hire company.

'Is this how you do business?' I asked, seething with anger.

'I regret, *monsieur*, this intrusion. We had heard about the dead *Gestapo* officer on the train. The Germans are looking for a man and a woman who fit your description. We have been following your progress, getting regular updates on your journey from the other barge owners. We have a superb spy network across the whole area, thanks to the canals.'

'So what do you want us for? To hand us over to the Germans?'

'Help the Boche?' He was scandalised. 'If you are SOE, as I believe, we may be able to help you, in return for, shall we say, certain favours? We want to establish contact with England. We need guns, explosives. A wireless, if possible. And money, of course.'

'We may be able to help,' I said cautiously. 'Though you seem well enough armed.'

'About six months ago we helped an agent to escape to Spain. He left the Sten with us. Unfortunately we are now very short of bullets. In fact we have only half a magazine left.'

My mind was buzzing. There were few Germans in the area, which meant it had little or no strategic value. Supporting any Maquis would be a bitch because of the length of the supply chain. On the other hand . . . The clarity of my thought was breathtaking. I looked at the cut-throat mob standing in front of me with a heightening sense of excitement.

Precisely because there were so few Germans, a heavily armed and motivated Maquis could create havoc. Pick soft targets. Kill German soldiers, force more to come south. Bloody hell, why hadn't anybody else thought of it?

'We need to contact London. Get a wireless set dropped along with some gear. Let's get on the boat. We've plans to make. How's the man I hit?'

'He'll be all right. Michel has a thick skull,' came the callous reply.

The barge owner, Martin Boucher, was about my age, small and wiry, with a hooked nose and narrow-set eyes. He was the group's spokesman. I learned that on three previous occasions they had helped agents escape across the Pyrenees, having been promised help and equipment. Nothing had happened. Boucher was determined to take no more chances.

'We will send André with a message. Give him details of whom to contact and how. Arrange a plane to drop us supplies.'

'We need bods as well,' said Kitty. 'A couple of officers to organise and plan.'

'We can do that,' said Boucher, tapping his chest.

'It doesn't work that way,' I replied. 'Wireless operators have to be trained. Procedures have to be explained and followed. A complete *organisation* has to be created. How many men do you have?'

'We can call on thirty, maybe forty.'

'That's a start. We require a network of at least ten times that number. Even more. Which is why I need to return to England. With Kitty,' I emphasised.

'That is not possible. I told you. We have been promised help in the past. So you stay here, both of you, until we get our demands.'

'But that's absurd,' I protested. 'I came to France to get Kitty out. Her life's in danger.'

'All our lives are in danger,' was the succinct riposte. 'She will be safe on the boat. For a few days at least. No Germans come this way. When we get word through – no promises, firm commitments – we will escort you over the mountains and into Spain. Do not consider leaving on your own. You would never make it.'

On our own I knew we had little chance. I shrugged. 'All right, there's a lot to do. How soon can we get a message to London?'

Agreeing our plans took what remained of the night. In their excitement they often lapsed into their local patois, which slowed us down.

With the sun the Frenchmen departed. Boucher had advised us to travel another couple of kilometres to a small inlet where we could berth away from the main canal. Four days of total inactivity followed. I was driven to distraction. On the evening of the fourth day Boucher returned with news.

'We can expect a drop at midnight tomorrow. As you suggested, five fires lit in the form of a T will be the signal.'

'I also told you the difficulties a pilot has navigating in the dark. If there is any cloud he won't come.'

Boucher nodded. 'We wait for three nights. If the weather is too bad then we will have to wait for another ten days for sufficient moonlight.'

'All right. Have you thought about targets?'

'The railway south of Toulouse, a small German garrison at Castres and the airfield outside Toulouse.'

'How many in the garrison?' I asked.

'Twenty, maybe thirty,' Boucher shrugged.

Shaking my head I said, 'Monsieur Boucher, you never, *ever* attack unless you know exactly what you're up against. Twenty or thirty can mean the difference between success and failure. Between living or dying. We hit hard and run away to fight another day. What about the airfield?'

No intelligence worth a penny. 'That leaves the railway.' I knew the efforts of the railway staff were invaluable in the war against the Germans. 'We don't want to kill any of the workers if possible.'

Boucher nodded. 'What do you propose?'

'We stop the train first and then wreck it. Every train has at least two, sometimes three soldiers onboard. They'll have to be taken care of, which shouldn't be too difficult. Check times, routes both in and out, and decide what target to go for. Our primary task is to damage the engine, put it out of commission for good if possible.'

The night of the drop was so overcast there was no point in even setting up a welcoming committee. This was confirmed by the BBC when they broadcast their nightly list of instructions to circuits and agents all across Europe. Our code – *twenty francs was not enough, one more was needed* – meant they'd try again the following night. So we set out to attack a train instead.

Twenty kilometres southeast of Toulouse was the village of Baziege. Through it ran a major railway line, connecting Bordeaux near the Atlantic with Narbonne on the Mediterranean. Outside the village a steep incline meant the trains slowed down considerably. At the top of the incline the railway levelled out for about a hundred metres before dropping gently down towards the coastal plain and picking up speed. We had no explosives but we had other means to sabotage the line.

Boucher and twelve others drove to the designated spot. I went along as a witness. It was pitch dark and the weather was blustery. Around 02.45 we could expect a goods train to arrive, heading for Narbonne. From there the cargo was destined for North Africa, equipment and food for Rommel's men.

I wondered how they intended stopping the train. It was simple. Unloading two long-armed, "T" spanners, they removed all the bolts of the metal track at the start of a bend, just as the decline started. The rail was shifted to one side.

We took up positions about fifty metres from the line and twenty metres higher. The train would be travelling from our left to right. On the other side of the tracks a steep bank ran down to the Garonne, now little more than a stream.

We couldn't see the train but one of the men had lay on the track listening to the rail and was able to give us plenty of notice. A Cyclops light emerged in the distance, drawing slowly nearer. On such an overcast night they knew there was no chance of an attack by the RAF.

The train breasted the rise and began to pick up speed. We could see that every third carriage had a machine-gun on top of it, manned by German soldiers. It could only mean one thing. It was a troop train! *Mary, Mother of God*, I thought, *if this didn't work we'd be in deep trouble.* The light hit the spot where we'd shifted the rail and the brakes came on, in a shower of sparks.

We opened up with the few guns we had at our disposal, firing at the engine, distracting the driver. Before the machine-guns on the carriage roofs could shoot back the engine hit the break in the track and slowly toppled to the left, still moving, its wheels driving it closer to the edge of the bank.

The driver and two other men leapt clear of the cab as the engine completed its fall and crashed onto its side. The carriages followed, almost in slow motion, soldiers on the roofs leaping to safety, their screams filling the night air.

'Let's go,' I said, 'before the bastards come after us.'

The men needed no encouragement and we moved quickly towards our dilapidated cars and vans. They were in high spirits and I couldn't say I blamed them. We'd probably left many dead and injured back at the track, as well as virtually destroying a train engine and a string of carriages. The RAF couldn't have done more with a squadron of bombers.

The following night our luck held. The sky was clear, not a cloud to be seen and the quarter moon cast a dim glow over the landscape. I hoped it would be enough for the pilot to find his way. Shortly after midnight we could hear the faint sound of an aircraft's engines in the distance. It was droning nearer then receding again as it quartered the land, looking for our signal. We lit the fires but still it came no closer, continuing its search pattern some way from us.

We were miles from the nearest road and at least ten miles from the canal. I had taken the precaution of having a very large bonfire built, just in case. Normally, we wouldn't be able to light one but out here in the sticks I figured there was very little risk. When the plane's engines were loudest I threw a burning rag onto a petrol-soaked heap of wood and ran back as it erupted in a huge blaze.

Minutes later we saw white parachute canopies opening like mushrooms and fluttering down to earth. Already the fires were being torn apart and extinguished as we waited to collect whatever London had sent.

Two agents dropped first. A second pass by the plane followed. Now we had three containers. I recognised two Cs and an H type. The C containers, made entirely of metal, consisted of three bins encased in an outer shell. They carried 68–72 kilos of gear and, in this case, were packed with explosives and ancillary equipment. The H type, also 1.6 metres long, and with the same payload, consisted of five bins held together by steel strips and locking devices. In it we found guns and ammunition.

The plane made a third pass and another parachute opened. Against the star-studded sky I saw a flicker of movement and realised that the parachute had candled. The container slung under it was plummeting to earth. Before I could do more than yell it hit the ground with an almighty crash and burst open. By now the containers had been collected, their contents distributed to the men. The empty containers were buried in a ditch already prepared for the purpose.

We searched the ground for the contents of the burst container. For protection, each item was wrapped in Hair-loch, a mixture of horse-hair and rubber. Some items were broken, including a wireless set. We gathered what we could and started the long trudge back to the lorries and vans.

One of the two men who had parachuted in was a wireless operator. The other was there to establish the new circuit, code-named Ulysses. Kitty and I were free to leave.

Back at the barge Boucher climbed out of his battered Citröen van and solemnly shook my hand. He kissed Kitty on both cheeks.

'I want to thank you for your help. Now we can begin to make a difference. We will draw many Germans into our web and squash them like flies. Tomorrow someone will take you over the mountains. His name is Claude Dubois . . .'

Kitty gasped. 'Claude Dubois? From Paris?'

'Why, yes. Claude's originally from this area but went to Paris three years ago. Do you know him?'

'I thought he was dead. Martin, Claude is a great friend, please don't tell him I'm here. I want it to be a surprise.'

'Certainly, Mademoiselle Kitty. Be careful tomorrow. The route you will be taking is dangerous. The Germans know we use it and have stationed a small garrison in an old farmhouse near the track. Claude is aware of the place.'

He bade us *bonne nuit* and departed in his rattling van, its exhaust belching smoke.

'Are you all right, Kitty? You look like you've seen a ghost.'

'Good analogy, Mike. I was told that Claude Dubois had been arrested and killed while trying to escape.'

'When was that?'

'About four weeks ago. Not long before my circuit collapsed.'

'Was Claude one of yours?'

'One of my best. He was invaluable. A good organiser and he'd been trained as a wireless operator.' She paused. 'Claude was one of the few people who knew almost as much about Hubris as I did. It makes no sense.' She fell silent and then added, 'Unless . . .'

'. . . he was the traitor,' I finished for her.

'I just can't believe it. Not Claude. It's impossible.'

From the tone of her voice she thought it was all *too* possible. Operating in enemy held territory, the agents who survived were those who trusted no one until proven otherwise. But at some point you had to begin to trust and your safety passed into someone else's hands.

'What do you want to do?'

'Surprise him. Gauge his reaction when he sees me. We'll have to be on our guard. I pray I'm wrong, that he has an explanation for what happened.'

I nodded. Amidst all the horror, the abominations of war, such miracles did occur. What caused them? Divine intervention? Random luck?

People were released from prison because of a clerical error, bribery or threats or because a policeman was a Maquis. With so many arrests taking place across Europe it was inevitable. I knew of numerous incidents when men and women had walked free, only to be accused and condemned by their own side for allegedly collaborating with the enemy. Their fate had been fast and brutal. Such mistakes couldn't be rectified. We'd lost some very good people as a result.

We prepared for the journey across the border. It would be long and difficult, yet we needed to take the minimum required to stay alive. We had stout shoes and suitable clothing. Our rucksacks contained spare clothes, blankets and food we could eat cold or on the march. Water we'd get from streams. A small tin of coffee was carefully stowed away, a small treat if we got the opportunity to light a fire.

We completed our preparations in the chill of a heavily dewed dawn. When Dubois arrived at the barge he had a companion with him. Alarm bells rang in my head. I stood with my Sten in hand, cocked and pointing nonchalantly at the ground.

From Kitty I knew Dubois to be in his mid thirties, unmarried, apparently disinterested in women. He was short, stocky, his complexion swarthy. The other man he introduced as Emile Chirac. He was in his early twenties, I guessed, tall and thin, with a long, unsmiling face. I didn't like the look of him, but then, I didn't exactly have a wide grin plastered on my face either. It was too early and, more importantly, too dangerous.

'Where's the woman with you?' Dubois asked.

'Hullo, Claude,' said Kitty, stepping through the hatchway onto the deck.

'Blanche? Is that you? Really you?' He hurried forward, grabbed her in a bear hug and swung her off her feet. 'I cannot believe it. I just cannot believe it,' he repeated, a huge smile on his face. Was it real, or fake? I couldn't tell. He could have been a consummate actor for all I knew. One thing I did know for sure. His gun, a Sten, was slung across his shoulder out of harm's way. As was Chirac's, who was looking on with some surprise.

34

WE SET OUT just as the sun's rays broke over the horizon, crammed into the back of the Citröen with Martin Boucher driving. Soon we were bouncing over small tracks, the engine wheezing asthmatically, the stench of exhaust fumes acrid in my nostrils.

'We will stay away from the roads, my friends,' Boucher called over his shoulder, 'it is safer. I can take you as far as Aspet. I have a cousin who lives there, so I have a reason for my journey, should I be stopped on the way back.'

'And on the way there?' I yelled.

He laughed. 'We kill Germans!' And he laughed again.

It took four uncomfortable, backside-numbing hours before we finally stopped. Stiffly we climbed down out of the van and stood in a small group. Boucher shook our hands, kissed Kitty on both cheeks and waved farewell. Silence descended as he vanished from sight.

We stood at the foot of the mountains. The air was cooler, in spite of the brilliant sunshine. There wasn't a breath of wind. Only our breathing broke the silence.

A footpath led higher into the hills, the mountains in the distance like a barrier to Spain and safety. I wondered briefly if we'd get to the other side.

When we had climbed out of the van I had passed the bags and guns to the others. I took the chance to switch my own Sten with Dubois' gun. He didn't seem to have noticed but then there was no reason why he should. One Sten looks much like another, especially in the murky half-light of early morning.

We set off at a reasonable pace. Dubois led, Kitty followed, then Chirac. I brought up the rear. It was easy going underfoot but my mind was on other things. Was Dubois a traitor? I determined to question him later, when we stopped for the night.

I'd spent four years in the trenches during the Great War. And over twenty years flying aircraft and navigating, using the stars at night, the position of the sun, and the direction of the prevailing wind. It had given me an instinctive knowledge of where I was heading. Claude was leading us the right way. But would it last?

Soon we were climbing upwards. My breath became more laboured but my thoughts ran as fast as ever. I had a bad feeling but was it merely paranoia? Uncertainty was normal when operating behind enemy lines. I realised I wasn't trained to deal with my fear, but then, in the end, who really was? My respect for our agents moved up several more levels.

In the middle of the afternoon our track veered right. Not drastically, but enough to give me cause for thought. There were goat paths all over the mountainside. Only someone with an intimate knowledge of the area would have known which to take. I was disconcerted enough to ask, 'Are you sure this is the right way?'

'Trust me, I know just where I'm going.'

Of that I had no doubt. But did Dubois mean to Spain or somewhere else?

Throughout the war, German intelligence had benefited greatly from spies or operatives who had turned, either out of fear or conviction. Someone like Claude, who had disappeared from his circuit, would have been invaluable. Had he betrayed Kitty? And if so what information had he given? Who had he sacrificed? What secrets did he still possess?

When we stopped later that evening Kitty said, 'So what happened in Paris, Claude? How did you escape?' Her eyes shone blue and clear, her expression betraying nothing but concern and curiosity.

He smiled disarmingly. 'It was the usual cock-up. I was taken to the police station on the Avenue de Breteuil, behind the Military Academy.'

'I know it,' said Kitty, nodding for him to continue.

'For seven days nobody came except the police to give me food and drink. After a few days I was demanding to be let out. I could hear the traffic outside. The street was right there!' He spoke excitedly. 'I could *feel* the freedom!'

'So what happened?'

'After one week an Inspector opened the cell door and told me to leave. By law he was unable to hold me longer than seven days. No one had come to interrogate me; I was free to go. I didn't hang around. I got out as fast as I could. Paris was too hot.'

I'd heard many similar stories in the past. The French police did precisely what the Germans ordered but no more, acting within the strict letter of the law. Their attitude had frequently benefited members of the Maquis as well as our own agents.

'I left you a message, Blanche. Did you get it?'

'No. I escaped by the skin of my teeth three days after you were taken. To the best of my knowledge you and I are the only two Hubris members left alive.'

Dubois' head shot up. 'There *must* be at least one other alive.'

Kitty frowned at him, not understanding.

'The traitor of course. One day I'll find out who it was and take care of him.' Dubois' story sounded sincere but for some reason I didn't believe him. I sighed as we climbed back to our feet and started out again.

It was fully dark when we stopped. We lit a small fire and boiled water for a cup of coffee to wash down our diet of dried meat, cheese and hardening bread. Agreeing to share the night in four watches, we drew straws for it and I got the shortest. I had the morning watch.

Lying on the ground, rolled up in my blanket, I looked up at the stars and quickly identified the ones I knew. I could only see three of the Plough, pointing to the North Star, which was still below the horizon. But it was enough to know we were walking in the wrong direction.

We were headed west. Of course, there could be a good explanation. Like avoiding difficult terrain, or heading for a certain pass before heading south again. It wasn't possible to walk in a straight line through a range of mountains. That was why we needed guides. Guides we could trust.

I let the thought take me to sleep.

My watch passed without incident. The sun was still hidden behind the mountains when we set off, casting deep shadows. The going was slow if we were to avoid a twisted ankle or worse.

We passed what looked to me like a suitable route south. I called to Dubois, asking why we continued westwards. Couldn't we use this route?

'All dead ends,' he replied cheerfully. 'We need to head west before we can go south again.'

Kitty fell back and walked alongside me. She spoke in a quiet voice. 'What did you think of his story?'

I looked down at her frowning face and shrugged. 'It's all very plausible. Only . . .' I let the word hang between us.

'Only I don't believe him either.'

'What shall we do? Put a bullet in his back when we reach Spain?'

'He might be innocent, Mike.'

'Precisely. We need proof and I don't see how we'll get it.'

She was silent for a few minutes, looking at the ground, watching where we placed our feet. 'I could goad him. Tell him my suspicions. It might push him into trying something.'

'Like killing you, you mean?'

'At least then we'd know. If he is a traitor, think of the damage he can do to Boucher and his new circuit. You know what they say. Once a traitor, always a traitor. There's no going back once you've started down that road.'

'Now he's out of Paris he may have switched back permanently. He may have turned you in under torture, Kitty.'

'Can we risk that?'

I shook my head. 'No, we need to know, *somehow.*'

We were now climbing steeply. Despite the warm sun there was a chill in the air and I knew we were probably as high as two even three thousand feet. We were still going west.

Every hour we stopped for a rest. The previous day it had been for five minutes, today it was ten. During the trek we had seen a number of goats and sheep, which ran wild in the area. They were shy creatures, and kept their distance. Towards evening on the second day we stumbled across a lamb that had slipped down a ravine and broken its leg. It was still alive when I scrambled down to it and cut its throat, putting it out of its misery.

Chirac now came into his own. He skinned and dissected the carcass while we lit a small fire surrounded by rocks and barbecued the cuts of meat. It was delicious and we ate with gusto, as though we hadn't had a hot meal in weeks. With mugs of coffee in our hands Kitty cross-examined Dubois some more. She was skilful with her questioning but after a few minutes it was clear she didn't believe his answers, each time sounding more sceptical.

Finally Dubois had had enough. 'Blanche! You don't believe me! I am devastated!'

I had my eyes on Chirac. He was looking from Kitty to me in a nervous manner, licking his lips and rubbing his right hand on his thigh. His gun was on the ground while Dubois had his Sten across his knees. But then, so did I.

'What are you saying, Blanche? Are you calling me a liar?'

For a few seconds the tension was unbearable – something had to give. It did. Dubois burst out laughing.

'Blanche, Blanche, *ma petite puce*, no wonder you've survived so long.' He shook his head, highly amused at the notion. 'I'm no traitor. And I'll prove it, by getting you both safely out of France. By this time tomorrow you'll be in Spain.'

The tension eased and Kitty nodded as though satisfied.

'I'll go first watch,' Dubois smiled. 'I am not tired just yet.'

Heavy dew was falling as I wearily arranged my blankets, using my bag for a pillow. My Sten would act as a comforter down one side. Tricky guns, Stens. They could go off just by being dropped onto a hard surface. It was safest to have the weapon uncocked and the safety on. I compromised. When I left the camp to do my ablutions I took the gun with me and returned with it cocked, the safety on. I settled down on my makeshift bed, with no intention of sleeping.

I lay awake for some time but at some point I was betrayed by my tiredness. The next thing I knew I was being shaken roughly by the shoulder.

'Your watch,' said Dubois.

I came wide-awake, mentally berating myself for a fool and climbed to my feet. Dubois was already settling down to sleep and I walked away from the camp, my blanket around my shoulders, to a vantage point a few metres away. The night was quiet in spite of the wind that had picked up from the west. Clouds scudded across the sky, the stars only visible intermittently. I checked the positions of the friendly ones and confirmed my suspicions. We'd been travelling west since the previous noon or thereabouts.

An hour into my watch I was startled by the sudden appearance of Kitty by my side. She sat close to me and whispered, 'Dubois left the camp.'

'What?'

'He was away for about an hour. It proves once and for all that we can't trust him. I say we put a bullet into him now.'

'And what about Chirac? Do we put a bullet into him as well? You

343

can't go round shooting someone just because you *think* he's a traitor.'

'It wouldn't be the first time.'

How often had the *Maquis* held kangaroo courts, found the person guilty and executed them within hours, sometimes minutes? Sometimes errors came to light, when it was too late. I looked into Kitty's tired face. 'Yes, but not like this. All we can do is stay vigilant.'

When Kitty returned to her blanket I sat there with my uneasy thoughts. What the hell had Dubois been up to? He could have been scouting the area, I supposed, but that didn't make any sense. It was far too dangerous to go wandering around at night, especially alone. One slip and you could break a leg and never be found alive. Even someone who knew the area well was at risk.

I spent the rest of the watch moving around close to the camp, more to keep warm than anything. I let Kitty sleep a while longer than I should have and then handed the watch over to her. In spite of my disquiet I fell asleep as soon as I lay down. When I awoke it was to a grey and misty dawn, the mountains wreathed in low cloud, rain in the air. As I turned on my side I saw Kitty and the two others, frozen in a confusing tableau – Dubois' gun pointed directly at Kitty, Chirac training a small revolver on me.

'Tell me,' Kitty spat out. 'Tell me why you betrayed us. Go on!'

Dubois said nothing, merely shrugged. I moved my hand until I felt the comforting hardness of the Sten's trigger guard.

'Tell me, you murderous traitor. You yellow piece of scum!' Kitty hissed in fury. 'What earthly reason could you have had?'

'There were two reasons, Blanche,' said Dubois in a steady voice. 'The first was money. The Germans paid me a good deal to betray the circuit. The second I am less proud of. I have no tolerance of pain. Even as a child, if I so much as grazed my leg I'd pass out. So I had a choice. To suffer torture or be paid a good deal of money. For me it was an easy choice to make.'

'You bastard!' Kitty was shaking with fury. 'You callous swine. You sent good men and women to their deaths for money!'

'I just told you. I was not going to let the *Gestapo* work on me. Now sit down. My German friends will be here shortly. There's a main road about three hundred metres from here.'

'How do they know where to find us?'

I let Kitty do the talking, distracting them, giving me an opportunity to slide my legs around and move the Sten. They were standing

344

about five yards away, Kitty on the left, the two men to the right. Dubois was nearest, while Chirac stood next to his shoulder.

'There's a garrison not far away. The commanding officer is very eager to meet you. Apparently the *Gestapo* wants you dead or alive. You have a sizeable bounty on your head for killing one of their officers.'

'I hope the money is worth it, Judas,' she spat at him.

'One hundred thousand francs? Oh yes, I think so.'

The light was strengthening. In the distance a whistle blew. I knew it was now or never. Dubois smiled and took a pace forward.

'Goodbye, Blanche.'

He pulled his trigger but nothing happened. 'What the hell . . .'

I swung my Sten into line and opened fire, the chattering machine-gun devastatingly loud in the morning air. Bullets stitched across Dubois' stomach and he collapsed. A bullet hit Chirac but he was tougher than he looked. As I corrected my aim and pulled the trigger again he fired at me, hitting me in my left thigh. I shot him in the chest and sent him flying backwards. Through the excruciating pain I could hear whistles being blown frantically.

35

KITTY KNELT BY my side, tying a tourniquet around the top of my thigh. Chirac's bullet had taken a chunk of flesh out of my buttock, missing a main artery by fractions of an inch.

'Half an inch further and you'd be singing soprano,' she joked.

Through clenched teeth I replied, 'Hurry it up, *acushla*, we need to go. Those bloody whistles are getting closer.'

She busied herself for a second, pulling the tourniquet tighter. 'Right, that's finished. Let's go. Can you stand?'

'Sure.' I awkwardly climbed to my feet but would have fallen if Kitty hadn't grabbed my arm. A wave of dizziness swept through me and I had to wait a second for my vision to clear. 'Okay. Let's go.'

Chirac and Dubois lay dead where they had fallen. The sound of the Germans was closer than ever and we hurried as quickly as we could in the opposite direction. About half a mile back the way we'd come I'd seen a path cutting through the mountain towards the south and that was where we were headed. Gradually the sound of the whistles faded behind us. My left side throbbed in time with my heartbeat, which doubled each time I put my left foot on the ground. I gritted my teeth and followed as Kitty's lead opened.

We reached the path, which cut into a narrow defile and headed along it. The sides were steep and covered in scree but the path was level and firm enough. I guessed we were walking along a dried-up water-course. Kitty stopped and waited for me to catch up. I had alternating red and black spots floating before my eyes and dropped to the ground when I reached her.

'Let me take a look,' she said. 'Damnation. You've lost a lot of blood. We'll rest for a few minutes while I check this bandage.' Despite my attempts at preserving my modesty, she managed to pull the bandage tighter. 'There, that's better. Now I know why your wife married you.' She grinned while I tried to pull my underpants back up. She gave me a hand and then buttoned up my trousers.

'Have you no shame, Kitty Westacott?'

'None,' she said tartly. 'Can you get up?'

'With your help.'

She hauled me to my feet and we started once more, slower than ever. The sides of the defile were high with an occasional stunted bush or small tree growing precariously out of the thin soil. Some had fallen and lay rotting in our path. One piece I saw was as thick as my arm, long, with a fork at the top. A few minutes with my knife and I had a make-shift crutch. I tucked it under my left armpit, confident I could swing along at a reasonable speed. It took all my concentration not to fall over but I managed to stay in Kitty's wake as she forged ahead.

We reached a dead-end. The defile towered high above us, obviously a waterfall in the far distant past.

'What now?'

'We climb to the top.'

'How?' Kitty asked, sitting down on a large rock.

'Up the side. This left hand one is too steep so we'll go up the other.'

'Can you manage?' In the distance we clearly heard the blast of a whistle.

'Somehow, Kitty dear, I don't think I have any choice. They're closing in.'

We began scrambling up the steep side, dislodging small, flat rocks that slid beneath us, threatening an avalanche. Soon we were on our hands and knees, literally crawling up.

It was agony. It felt like a red-hot poker searing my thigh each time I lifted my knee. I wasn't sure if the moisture down my leg was sweat or blood but it didn't matter. I had no choice other than to keep going.

The slope suddenly flattened out and we found ourselves on a narrow path about two feet wide. We lay there panting, getting our breath back – and me my strength.

Kitty checked the bandage again. 'There's blood seeping through but not much. Ready to go?'

I nodded, saving my breath.

'We'll go along this ledge and see where it leads.'

I followed Kitty. Our luck was in. The path bent round a corner and lead in a gentle incline to the top, cutting in from the defile. We stood on the top of a windswept col, two mountains rising up on either side of us, grinning at each other like delighted children. But our happiness soon vanished when we heard the sound of an engine. Before we could move a spotter plane with the ignoble swastika painted on its wings swept over us.

I lifted my Sten to fire but it stayed out of range. All it needed to do was hang around and radio our movements to the troops below.

'We need to cut and run,' said Kitty.

'You run, I'll hobble,' I replied. I'd had the sense to tie my makeshift crutch to my backpack and now jammed it under my arm. 'Let's go.'

I got into a kind of swing, taking most of the weight on the crutch. We were heading south but I guessed we had a long way to go. Longer than I cared to think about. Our running was a gesture, albeit a futile one, but neither of us intended surrendering. We'd carry on to the bitter end.

We kept going as the plane circled overhead. Suddenly I was aware that it was no longer there and looked up in time to see it vanishing behind a ridge. We stopped in bewilderment.

'Either she's low on fuel or else the troops know where we are and are closing in on us.'

Kitty nodded. 'That's what I thought. It's getting cold,' she shivered.

The wind had dropped but we found ourselves in an intermittent mist, swirling in little eddies around the floor of the shallow valley. We kept on, alert for any sounds, especially of the plane's return, until we found ourselves on a flat, grassy piece of land. Finally, around noon, we stopped for a rest and something to eat. No one, not even the ablest bodied, could keep going at the rate we had travelled. I was utterly exhausted.

'Kitty, it's time to be sensible. You go on. This valley seems to be leading straight into Spain. There's no point in both of us being caught.'

'Forget it, Mike. Either we both get out or . . .' she shrugged.

I could see there was no point in arguing and merely nodded. 'In that case we'd better get going.'

She helped me to my feet and we set off, more slowly this time. I had a raging thirst. When we finally found a stream we collapsed by its bank and eagerly drank our fill.

The land lifted gently and fell in a gradual decline. We could see ahead of us another bank of cliffs and for a heart stopping moment I wondered if it was a dead end. Soon, though, I realised I needn't have worried as we'd never find out. A line of German troops appeared about half a mile behind us, strung out across the valley, converging on our position. Whistles blasted the air. We turned and ran. At least, Kitty ran, while I hobbled and swung along as best I could. She pulled ahead as the Germans got closer.

We made it across to the other side then came to a stop. In front of us was a tarn, how deep it was impossible to say. Across the water was a cliff, towering perhaps a hundred feet straight up. The walls of the valley had closed in to perhaps sixty or seventy feet across and boulders lay all around, washed down by eons of storms.

'It looks like this is where we make our last stand,' Kitty said.

'Do you think I've come all this way for nothing, Kitty? I'll stay here. You go around the side of the lake and stay down. I'll draw them this way. Once they're past, you get the hell out, while I try and keep them busy.'

Seeing her face, I cut her off. 'Kitty, that's a bloody order. Now do as you're told. We've a war to fight. I don't believe in wasting lives. You're needed where you can do a bit of good. There's no point in us both dying. Now for Christ's sake go!'

Nodding she kissed my cheek. 'Anybody tell you that you're one of the best?'

She disappeared to my left while I found a suitable boulder as cover. I bided my time. I was in no hurry to die, even though I knew that would be the outcome. I looked up at a cloud-filled sky, a wind picking up again. How many times had I gone over the top in the last war and not expected to return, yet return I did? God had smiled on me long enough. There is only so much luck in life and I'd used all mine up. Now I needed to make sure Kitty had every chance to escape.

From my vantage point I counted twenty Germans headed my way. I'd take a few with me at any rate. I waited patiently. Behind me lay another thirty or forty feet of boulder-strewn ground that I could retreat into before my back was to the water. I intended making as much use of it as possible. I had three spare magazines for the Sten and two hand grenades. I also had Irish cunning.

I took one of the grenades and jammed it amongst some rock. From my trusty twine I cut a section and tied it to the safety pin. Next I placed my blanket inside my coat and laid a brown stone at its head. Close to, it looked what it was. I just hoped it would fool the Germans for a little while.

At a hundred yards the Germans had bunched in a little. They were advancing cautiously, looking behind the rocks and boulders as they grew closer. At any minute I expected one of them to spot Kitty. I dared not wait any longer. I took aim and opened fire, spraying the three men in the centre, hitting all three.

The remainder dived for cover and were out of sight before I could change aim. Discretion being the better part of valour I retreated halfway towards the cliff, lucky not to draw any fire. I settled down again. This time I had the twine in my hand. After a few minutes I discerned movement and a couple of the troops came into sight. Suddenly the air was rent with the staccato sound of machine guns firing and I saw bullets strike my coat and the boulder where my head should have been. I waited, willing them on.

After a few minutes two of them suddenly appeared next to my coat. Where the hell they had come from I had no idea but I didn't wait to work it out. I pulled the twine and six seconds later the grenade erupted, blasting stone and metal into the air. Two of the troops standing nearest the blast were blown to smithereens while another was badly wounded.

Movement further down the valley caught my eye and I looked across to the far end. My heart sank. Another string of soldiers had appeared and was making its way purposefully towards me.

I heard the noise of a plane's engine. The spotter plane was back. Then the sound changed and a second, twin-engined plane sped across the sky. A bomber. My luck had really given out this time.

There was no point in prolonging the inevitable. I took aim at the nearest German now about seventy yards away. I opened fire and saw him fall back as the magazine clicked empty. I changed mags and fired again, shooting at anything that moved, often missing the targets but ensuring they kept their heads down. Bombs began to explode and then I heard the sound of a plane's machine-guns strafing the ground.

I couldn't understand why none of the bombs landed near me. The noise of the engines finally penetrated my thick skull and I stopped shooting long enough to look at the plane. A Griffin? For a second I thought I was dreaming.

The plane zoomed overhead and went into a steep climb to miss the cliff face. It turned on its side and came screaming in again, dropping a stick of bombs along the Germans' position. I needed no encouragement. I went towards the bastards, keeping down, looking for targets.

The Germans were too busy shooting at the sky to take any notice of me. I managed to get within twenty yards of two of them. I threw my last grenade and had the grim satisfaction of seeing them die.

I became aware that there was no more shooting or bombs dropping around me. The plane had switched targets to the other troops at the far end of the valley. Cautiously I moved out from behind my hiding place.

'Mike! Mike! Over here.'

I followed Kitty's voice and found her about a hundred yards way. She'd killed three Germans, shooting them in the back. 'When I saw the Griffin I came back to help,' she explained. 'They weren't expecting me. What now?'

'I don't know. It depends on what the Griffin does. God knows where it came from but it can't possibly hang around for long. Besides, I counted the bombs. It can't have any left. My God,' I pointed, 'the mad fool is landing on the tarn.'

Sure enough, the Griffin had strafed the troops at the far end and was coming in to land. I marvelled at the courage, or reckless stupidity, the landing required. The pilot had no idea how deep the water was and could easily hit a rock or other obstruction.

In a flurry of spray the Griffin landed safely and slowed rapidly. We started towards the water, Kitty with her shoulder under my arm. The side door opened and a figure appeared.

'Come on, Mike, get a bloody move on. You'll have to swim for it!'

I gasped in complete astonishment. Robert Gill was standing there waving to us. We waded into the water. It was icy cold and we both gasped from the shock. Almost immediately we were swimming for it, Kitty pulling ahead of me in a fast crawl. The plane had already turned into the wind and was ready to taxi. Gill grabbed Kitty by the collar of her jacket and dragged her inside. I was seconds behind her. Reaching up, I gripped Gill's hand and was hauled unceremoniously into the cabin.

I collapsed gasping onto the floor as the plane accelerated and soared into the air. When I saw the pilot glance over her shoulder at me, I knew I must be dreaming.

'Hi, Mike,' Susan said with a beaming smile.

'What the hell,' I asked, 'are you doing here?' It was then I noticed Sion in the other seat. My dear old friend wasn't looking too well.

Susan glanced at her uncle and said, 'It all started two days ago.'

Susan's Story

36

Two days earlier, 7 August 1943

'STILL NO WORD from Mike?' Susan demanded.

'Nothing. I've just been on to your father at SOE. He's heard nothing either. All we can do is wait and hope for the best.'

Patience had never been Susan's forte. Silently she paced the cramped office. 'There must be something we can do, Uncle Sion.'

'SOE is doing all it can. We know Mike's alive because of the drop he organised. If we can go in to get him out we will. If we can't we leave him to walk into Spain.'

'At least we could be in Spain waiting for him.'

'I've thought of that. We've access to a landing place to the east of San Sebastián Donostia, next to the border with France. I'll be as close as I can get. Less than two hours flying time from the area Mike'll be in.'

'What's with the "I", Uncle Sion? I'm coming with you.'

'I know how fond you are of Mike, but I won't allow it, Susan. Your life was endangered under Franco. You're still *persona non grata* in Spain. They're liable to shoot you first and apologise afterwards. Five years isn't so long and the Spanish fascists have long memories.'

'Uncle Sion, I can look after myself. And I owe Mike so much. We've already lost Alex and I couldn't bear it if something were to happen to Mike too.'

'Your father has expressly forbidden me to take you, so that's the end of the matter.'

Susan crossed her arms and looked balefully at Sion.

'It's no good, Susan, you aren't coming and that's that!'

'All right,' she gave in with bad grace. 'When are you leaving?'

'In the morning; the forecast is good and even with a full payload I can carry enough fuel to get me there.'

'Who's flying with you?'

'David's sending a fellow from the SOE by the name of Robert Gill. An ex-policeman. He's a friend of Mike's and officially on leave, but he's fully briefed. When it was put to him he didn't hesitate. Sounds like a good man.'

The phone rang and Sion lifted the receiver. 'Hullo, David. I was just filling Susan in on our trip to Spain and I've passed on your instructions that she is to stay put this time.'

Leaving the office quietly, Susan went out to the aircraft that had been modified for the flight to Spain. Twin-engined, all seats had been removed apart from two in the back. The bomb bays which had been fitted made the Griffin a formidable plane. With retractable floats for water landings she was also highly versatile.

After prowling around for several minutes Susan left with a smile.

Robert Gill arrived from London that evening. Kirsty directed him to the nearest hangar. In the gloom he spotted a mechanic in a dirty overall leaning over an engine port.

Gill tapped him on the shoulder and was taken aback by the mechanic's very feminine screech.

'Oh my God, you startled me.' Removing her borrowed cap, Susan rounded on Gill, intent on giving him a piece of her mind. Her reproach died on her lips. Who was this divine man standing in front of her?

Gill apologised and introduced himself, asking if she knew where he could find Sion. 'He's poring over charts of the Pyrenees.'

'Thanks.' Gill smiled and walked away. *What a looker*, he thought. *Pity she's covered in oil.*

Normally extremely thorough, Susan couldn't finish the repair quickly enough before rushing back to the house. In the bathroom she looked at herself in the mirror with dismay. Her cheek and nose had stains on them, her face was bereft of make-up and the cap made her look ridiculous. Her fingernails were caked in oil and a knuckle was scraped where she'd knocked it. She began to repair the damage; halfway through her bath she had a horrible thought. *What if he's married?*

She was very thoughtful going in to dinner.

'Susan, dear, come and meet Robert Gill,' said Sion.

'We've already met,' replied Susan.

'Good Lord! The mechanic.'

Susan smiled, 'Only in my spare time.' They shook hands and Susan was quick to notice he had no ring on his left hand. Still, that didn't mean anything. Her second impression was as good as her first. She liked his smile, the set of his shoulders and the way his hair curled over the back of his collar.

Thanks to adroit questioning by her aunt, Susan learned he was two years older than she and unmarried. More casual conversation established that he'd been engaged but had called it off when he'd found his fiancée was having an affair with someone else. Kirsty saw Susan hide a smile behind her napkin at that particular piece of information.

After dinner Sion and Kirsty left the two of them to chat, going into the study to discuss any problems that might arise at St Athan while Sion was away.

'Now, Susan,' smiled Gill, his dark brown eyes crinkling at the corners, 'your aunt has spent the last hour or so cross-examining me about my private life and now I'd like to hear about yours.'

Susan had the good grace to blush.

Gill burst out laughing. 'Until I joined your father I was a detective chief inspector in Portsmouth. I know an interrogation when I hear one. Even one as skilfully conducted as Kirsty's.'

'Drink?' Susan asked, getting to her feet, giving herself time to think.

'A whisky, please, if there is one. With a dash of soda.'

'I'm sure there is.' She opened a cupboard. A bottle of Glenmorangie came to hand and she busied herself pouring. She should she tell him about her son, she thought. She wouldn't lie. How could she deny John Phillipe?

She handed Robert his drink and took a glass of port for herself. 'So you want to hear my life story? I didn't have what you'd call a conventional upbringing. I saw my mother killed when I was living in America. My stepmother, Madelaine, took me in. She's been like a mother to me. We're a strong family – Uncle Sion taught me to fly. I'm pretty good at it, even if I do say so myself. After university I went to Spain and fought in the civil war. That's where my story becomes a little . . . complicated. I'll tell you about it sometime. The most important thing to come from my time in Spain is my son. I have a five year old, John Phillipe. He's the love of my life.' Susan sat back and waited for his reaction.

'The child's father?'

'Killed by the fascists.' Susan thumbed the rim of the glass. 'After he died my only thoughts were of revenge. I was determined to kill as many of Franco's men as I could – and spent the next two years doing precisely that. In the end I found myself in front of a firing squad.'

As if afraid to interrupt, Gill asked gently. 'But you escaped. How?'

'Thanks to my father and Mike O'Donnell. I owe him my life, Mr Gill, and I'd do anything to save him.'

Sion lined up the Griffin for take-off. Gill sat in the seat next to him, a chart on his knees. Normally a confident man, he felt strangely ill at ease. This was all new to him. Identifying landmarks against a map was difficult at the best of times, from the air, nearly impossible.

The plane accelerated and eased gently into the air.

'Did you say goodbye to Susan?' Sion asked, his curiosity piqued by Kirsty's observation of a budding romance. Since Alex's death she had known little happiness. Kirsty had been so thrilled at the possibility of Susan finally finding a suitable man. He'd been slightly more circumspect, but looking at Gill out of the corner of his eye he had to acknowledge that Susan could do a lot worse. 'I looked for her but I couldn't find her anywhere.'

'Neither could I.'

'I don't trust that young lady.' Sion looked over his shoulder as though expecting to see Susan standing behind him. All he saw was the modified bomb bay and an old wicker hamper secured behind the seats.

Sion turned round to concentrate on his navigation. It was vital he left England with a clear position of departure and a course to steer, otherwise they'd never land at the right destination. An hour later England was behind them and they were over the open sea.

'There's a bit of a head wind,' said a voice behind him.

Gill jumped liked he'd been prodded with a hot iron while Sion just sighed.

'Get the coffee, while you're there,' he ordered, not looking round.

'Yes, Uncle Dearest.'

'Don't "Uncle Dearest" me. Your father is going to kill me when he finds out you smuggled yourself aboard.'

'Where the hell was she?' Gill asked.

'In the wicker basket,' Sion replied. 'I thought it was SOE property.'

Gill laughed. 'And I thought it had something to do with the aircraft.'

Susan smiled at both men. 'And I thought you'd be typical men and not ask each other.'

Gill thanked Susan for the coffee, looking at her with more then a modicum of admiration. He'd learnt more about Susan's adventures from Sion, after she had gone to bed. She'd had one hell of a life so far, and obviously it was still a roller coaster of a ride. How many other women would be prepared to flaunt convention and risk their lives?

Female SOE bods, of course. But even their adventures paled in significance to what Susan had been through. What an amazing woman, he thought, and so beautiful. His heart sank. She was also extremely rich. Out of his league as an ex-copper. He told himself to forget it and turned to look back through the cockpit window.

Susan's eyes were darting over the dials. Excusing herself, she took the chart off Gill's knees, ran a course, wind speed and direction calculation then said, 'Come left fifteen degrees.'

Sion didn't question it and the plane turned to port.

Gill, realising he was out of his depth, undid his seatbelt and stood up. 'You'd better sit here. I'll sit behind.'

Susan nodded. She wouldn't have suggested it but it made the most sense. Dead reckoning was an art as well as a skill and she had an instinct honed by years of practice.

The flight passed uneventfully. The mountains of the Pyrenees, a natural barrier between Spain and France, could be seen shrouded in mist, long before they could see the land.

'Right on the nose,' Sion smiled to his niece.

Susan shrugged modestly, pleased with her success. It was, they both knew, a remarkable piece of navigation.

'There's the farmhouse, the white building down the valley. And there's a windsock. They're organised.'

Gill pointed out the landmarks he knew of, and then leant on the back of Susan's seat. 'We use them regularly once we get our agents over the border. They've been very helpful in the past, even if they are expensive.'

'You mean they don't help out of love of for their fellow man?'

Susan looked over her shoulder into his deep-set eyes, a small smile on her face.

Gill shrugged and turned away, perturbed by her nearness.

They landed on a well-marked track and trundled over a field towards a dilapidated barn. Sion flexed his fingers and legs, undid his seatbelt and climbed out of his seat. An elderly Spaniard came out to greet them. Later Sion wasn't sure what had been most surprising – his vigour or his accent.

'Good flight, old boy?' he greeted Sion, extending his hand.

'Yes, thanks. No problems at all,' Sion smiled. 'Have you fuel for us?'

'Yes. Cost a fortune as usual. As long as we keep the bribes going we're okay. How do you do, young lady?' Their host greeted Susan with a smile. 'Wing Commander Beresford Green at your service.'

'A wing commander? What on earth are you doing here?'

'I'm doing my bit, dear girl. I'm a damn sight more useful here than back in Blighty.'

Green bent down and tapped his left leg. 'Wooden. Lost it during the Battle of Britain. Came here with SOE over a year ago, to organise a major part of the escape route out of France. I've got some hot food ready and some coffee. Come along in.'

'I'd like to refuel first,' said Sion.

'Of course, old boy. Let's get to it.'

They manhandled drums of fuel into position and a hand pump was placed in the first one. It was primed and the fuelling began. Susan stood with a cup of coffee in one hand, the pump handle in the other, listening to the slosh of petrol each time she pushed the handle.

Something told her this was as far as she would be going. Her uncle wouldn't take her with him and there was no way she could pull the same stunt again.

'Look out!'

Susan heard a yell behind her and spun around, rushing into the barn where the howl of pain had come from. Sion was lying on the ground, clutching his leg. A drum of fuel had rolled into a corner.

'Are you all right, Uncle Sion?' Susan rushed to his side.

'Christ, no. I think it's broken,' he gasped.

'What happened?' She knelt by his side as Gill appeared in the doorway. 'Get the first aid bag out of the pocket behind the pilot's seat,' she called to him. 'Let me take a look.'

Gingerly she rolled up his left trouser leg. Already the leg was turning blue, the skin stripped to the bone down the shin. Tenderly she felt along the tibia, Sion grimacing and holding his breath.

'I don't think it's broken. But it's a hell of a mess.'

Gill returned and knelt alongside her. 'Here, let me take a look.' He gently manipulated Sion's leg before saying, 'It's a greenstick fracture. If you're careful you can feel small bumps along the shinbone. I used to play rugby. It happened to me twice. It's painful and debilitating, but heals quickly thankfully.'

Susan set to work with the bandages. She did a good job and then helped her uncle to his feet. He took one step and would have fallen if Gill hadn't been there to catch him.

Gasping and sweating, Sion accepted Gill's help across the barn and onto a bale of hay. 'Bloody hell, it hurts like buggery.'

Just then the wing commander appeared. 'What on earth's happened?'

Sion groaned, 'I tried shifting a drum by myself. It toppled onto my leg.'

'Can you fly?' Green asked.

'I have to,' Sion replied harshly. 'I'm not leaving Mike.'

'I'll fly,' said Susan, 'you navigate.'

'Susan . . .' Sion began.

'Face it, Uncle Sion, and be honest. I'm at least as good a pilot as you are. And that's when you have two good legs. Look at you. You'll crash ten minutes after take-off.'

Sion was about to protest when he saw the determined look on her face. Reluctantly he nodded. 'You're right. Though God alone knows what your father will say about all this.'

'He'll say we made the right decision. He's no fool. And he knows how good I am.'

That was true. His brother had often commented proudly on his daughter's accomplishments. And her failings, Sion thought. Like pride and pigheadedness like all the Griffithses.

An hour later they were in the air. Thanks to Martin Boucher they had a rough idea where to look for Mike and Kitty. Susan was piloting the plane, Sion navigating. Gill stood behind their seats, scanning the horizon with a pair of binoculars.

Two hours later all three of them were utterly dispirited, thinking they'd never find them.

Sion was in great discomfort in spite of swallowing Aspirins like

361

sweets. Gill's back was aching and his eyes smarted while Susan was continually flexing her hands and feet, getting the circulation back. She was weary from such lengthy concentration and continual alterations of course and height. Flying over mountainous terrain was difficult. Updrafts and downdrafts threw the plane all over the place at the heights they were trying to maintain.

'How much longer do we have?' Gill asked.

'Two hours before we have to return,' Sion replied. 'But that's not the problem. This is like searching for a needle in a haystack.'

'Any better ideas?' Susan asked.

'None. We keep looking. I've double-checked the information given to us from SOE. They must be in this area somewhere.'

'Perhaps he thinks we're the enemy and is hiding,' suggested Gill.

Sion actually laughed. 'Mike knows the sound of a Griffin's engines better than anybody alive. That's why we're quartering the sky as we are. Nice and low, he may hear us.'

They continued for a further dispiriting hour, the search area being slowly expanded towards the east.

'What's that?' Gill suddenly asked.

Sion sat up straighter, peering ahead of the plane instead of below.

'To the right. Something's moving. My God, it's a plane.'

'Here, let me look.' Sion reached behind and unceremoniously grabbed the binoculars out of Gill's hands. 'He's right! It's a bi-plane – a Fokker. It's used as a spotter because it can fly so slowly. Head towards it, Susan. Better take a seat, Robert.'

The Griffin banked and swooped higher before taking up position in the sun and pouncing like a hawk.

'I can see troops on the ground. They're attacking somebody. It's got to be Mike. Susan, shoot that damn plane down and bomb the hell out of those Germans,' Sion ordered.

As the plane's machine-guns opened fire, blasting the spotter aircraft to bits, Sion yelled over his shoulder. 'Robert, see if you can make sense of what's happening below.'

Gill peered out of the side window, trying to get a glimpse of the ground. 'There's a line of soldiers moving towards the top of that valley. It looks like a dead-end. They're firing at somebody but it's impossible to see who it is.'

'I'm sure it's Mike,' Susan said. 'But whoever it is, they're on our side so we'll give them a hand. Tally ho!'

First she dropped the bombs and then steadily and systematically she began to strafe the troops.

'There's another wave of soldiers coming over the far ridge,' Gill called out.

'I see them. I'll encourage them to keep their heads down and then we'll go in.'

Another strafing run was followed by a sharp turn back into the valley, floats and flaps going down simultaneously. Neither Sion nor Susan needed to say how dangerous the manoeuvre was. The slightest mistake could be their undoing. A rock or log could hole a float or send the nose plunging and the propellers digging into the water. Either way they'd have bought it.

The floats touched, bounced and settled. The water's drag quickly brought the plane to a halt. Gill had the side door open and was yelling at the top of his voice.

As the SOE agent was dragged onboard Susan noticed immediately how pretty Kitty was. She had better keep an eye on Mr Gill.

37

Susan banked the Griffin X and lined up to land. The two-seater fighter/bomber was superb to handle, responding to her touch like the thoroughbred she was. The new Merlin Rolls-Royce engine and the slightly swept-back wings made her one of the fastest aircraft in the sky.

She had left St Athan early that morning to deliver the plane to Biggin Hill. Women now made up the majority of delivery pilots working around the UK, with retired and older pilots adding to the numbers. She'd recently flown from Canada in command of a four-engined bomber and now here she was in a single-engine fighter. Susan grinned to herself. Like going from a juggernaut to a sports car.

Behind her head, strapped into the navigator/bomb aimer's seat, was her overnight case. It contained everything necessary, she hoped, for a subtle seduction. Or perhaps not so subtle.

Her relationship with Robert Gill had come to a frustrating stand-still after their trip to Spain. She *knew* he liked her, had often noticed him looking at her, but the damn man seemed reluctant to take things any further. She intended to change that. Robert was the most wonderful man she'd met in years – handsome, intelligent, and thoughtful. He had integrity, courage and when she was with him . . . well, she felt emotions she'd thought she would never feel again. She was deter-mined to find out if he felt the same way. After tonight she would know.

Before then, however, duty called. She landed the plane, touching down as lightly as a feather. After taxiing to the main hangar she presented her paperwork for signature and went to the officer's mess for a cup of tea. A Second Officer in the Air Transport Auxiliary, her relatively low rank rankled with her. As did her salary of £260 per annum, 20% lower than her male colleagues as per Treasury Department instructions. She had well over the 500 hours flying time and the multi-engined experience required for promotion. Like her father and grandfather before that, she had the predominant Griffiths character trait – a burning ambition. She knew how single-minded she could be and what she wanted she usually got, no matter what it took. Which was why she'd made some dreadful mistakes in her life. She just hoped this evening wasn't going to be one of them.

She'd heard nothing from Gill, after he'd gone back to London. Within days of him leaving she wondered when he'd contact her. Two weeks later she was furious at him and after a month decided to take matters into her own hands. Her telephone call to him earlier had obviously come as a complete surprise. It rankled that while she had been mooning over him he had contrived to forget about her completely. Or had he? He had agreed enthusiastically to her suggestion of dinner and a show and had behaved like the perfect gentleman – too perfect, too much the gentleman.

She hadn't been looking for anyone, had been quite happy with her son and her work. But since meeting Robert old feelings had come awake. She craved passion and excitement and now, with the war stretching ahead of them for years possibly, she intended having both. Ferrying aircraft was a bore. Tedious, dull, undemanding, requiring little ability and less flair. She'd thought that after Spain's civil war she wanted peace and quiet. But now she knew it wasn't true. Love had been missing in her life for too long and now she wanted it back.

Finishing her tea, she reported to the Officer Commanding the airfield, Group Captain Brian Ogilvie. Having made up her mind about Robert, she intended not to waste any more time delivering planes either.

If Ogilvie was surprised he didn't show it. Susan liked him. The group captain was in his early forties with prematurely grey hair and craggy good looks that, it was rumoured, had got him into trouble when he was a junior officer. And not so junior, either, thought Susan, if the other rumours are only half true. 'What can I do for you?'

Whatever he'd been expecting it wasn't her next sentence. 'Brian, I'd like to join an operational squadron.'

'What?' He sat up straight in his chair. 'You can't be serious.'

'Deadly serious. I'm fed up ferrying planes around. I've brought my flying logs to show you. I even kept a log when I was in Spain in '38 and '39. Take a look. I'll wager my experience against three-quarters of the pilots you have on this station.'

'I've no doubt you're extremely experienced,' he said dryly, 'but it's not on.'

'Why not?' Susan felt her face flushing, her anger bubbling up. 'Bloody chauvinism, that's what it is. It's ludicrous. I'll pit myself against your best man in a dog-fight and I bet I'd win.'

'That's as maybe, but women do not fight. It's as simple as that. There's no doubting your ability Susan, but government guidelines don't allow it. It has to do with the treatment of prisoners of war. At present, women captured by the German are treated . . . a certain way. If you were flying operationally we don't know what would happen to you.'

Susan leant forward in her seat. 'Brian, a month ago I returned from Spain after picking up two SOE operatives. A man and a woman. I learned first-hand what happens to women if they fall into the hands of the Germans or the *Gestapo*. They aren't treated humanely. Quite the reverse. Many are tortured and shot in front of a firing squad. They risk their lives every minute of every day. Fighting *our* war while we stay safely in Britain. Look at my record. Read my logs. Consider how much action I've seen. I've survived situations you could only dream of, Brian.'

Ogilvie sat in silence for a few seconds before sighing and reaching out his hand. 'I'll read your logs. I've an idea, Susan, but I don't guarantee anything.'

'Tell me.' Susan tried hard to keep the excitement out of her voice.

'What did you have in mind when you walked in here?'

She thought about her reply and smiled. 'I'd heard rumours you were going to run One-Six-One Squadron for SOE. Using converted Halifaxes.'

'All right. Leave it with me. But I warn you. I'm not promising anything.'

'Thanks, Brian, I appreciate it.'

A staff car deposited her at the railway station and a train took her to London. She booked herself into the luxurious Canterbury Hotel off Park Lane and telephoned the offices of SOE. After much cajoling she finally got through to Gill.

'Robert? It's Susan. I'm in London, at the Canterbury.'

There was evident pleasure and warmth in Gill's voice, but work, he said, was crazy. 'I'll be at least an hour. Can we meet for a drink? The United Services Club?'

'No fear. I'm likely to bump into my father or Madelaine if we go there. What about the Crown and Thistle in the West End? Eight o'clock? Then the theatre and supper?'

'I wasn't sure what time you'd get here and so haven't booked a table anywhere,' he apologised.

'That's all right. Leave it to me. See you later.' She hung up, rang room service and gave explicit orders to an attentive manager.

Susan dressed carefully in a black velvet dress she'd had copied from a magazine and was assured was all the rage. Sitting at the dressing table mirror, she swept her hair up. For so long she hadn't worried what she looked like. There had been no one she had wanted to look pretty for. She was feeling quite sick with nerves at what she planned. What if he didn't want her? What if he didn't find her attractive? She was so bossy and forthright – what if he didn't like assertive women? Stop worrying, she told herself. This evening she would have her answer.

She considered wearing the diamond bracelet her father had given her for her twenty-first birthday but then thought better of it. Instead she wore a plain, gold watch and a necklace of pearls. Dabbing French perfume behind her wrists, neck and near her cleavage she looked at herself critically. *Not bad, considering the wear and tear. If this doesn't set your pulse racing, Mr Gill, nothing will.*

The evening was warm and she went out wearing a thin silk coat over her dress. A taxi was waiting and, a respectable ten minutes late, she arrived at the pub. Gill was waiting for her. He was wearing the suit he'd worn all day and stood self-consciously when she walked over to his table.

Eyes other than his followed her across the room and murmurs of "lucky swine" and "lucky bastard" made him smile. *God*, he thought, *she's lovely.*

'If I'd known I'd have gone home and got changed. You look gorgeous.'

'Why, thank you, kind sir. And you'll do as you are.'

'What would you like to drink?'

'A gin and it, please.'

'Barman, a gin and it for the lady and I'll have another pint of ale.'

They settled down to talk about the war and the people they now had in common. Robert also told her a little of his childhood. He had been born and brought up in Portsmouth. His father had died of a heart attack at age fifty-eight.

'Your mother still lives there?'

'Mmm. I keep telling her to move and go and stay with her sister in Chichester where it's safer, but she won't listen. She's very active. Has her church. God knows how many committees she's on; I don't think she knows herself half the time. And there's a local widower who's taking an unhealthy interest in her.'

'You don't mind?'

'She's lonely since my father died. I wish her well.'

'What did your father do?'

'He was a teacher in the local grammar school. He also wrote several books about Napoleon and Nelson. He did quite well out of the royalties, although we were never rich or anything like that. History was his great love, though. You mustn't tell another living soul but my middle name is Horatio.'

Susan smiled, assuring him of her discretion and made a mental note to get hold of his father's books.

'We'd better go. The curtain goes up in fifteen minutes. We still haven't sorted out anywhere for supper.'

Susan smiled. 'I told you to leave it to me. It's all sorted.'

They went to a revue in the Palladium where they listened to Gracie Fields, George Formby and the Glen Miller Band. The sketches were hilarious, especially the lampooning of Hitler, which brought the house down.

Outside there was a scramble for a taxi but Gill managed to shoulder another man out of the way and handed Susan in.

'Where to, Gov?' The cab driver asked.

'The Canterbury Hotel,' replied Susan.

Susan settled back and snuggled up against Gill's arm. She caught him frowning at her. 'What's wrong?'

'The Canterbury? But that's where you're staying.'

'I couldn't find anywhere else,' she lied.

As the taxi pulled up outside the hotel, a uniformed doorman stepped forward and opened the door, saluting.

Gill paid the taxi fare and they went inside. The Canterbury was known only to a select few. It was the sort of place where, as it was said, if you had to ask how much it cost, you couldn't afford it.

Susan strolled across to the desk and claimed her key. 'Any messages?'

'No, miss.'

'Thank you.' Smiling, she lead the way to the lift. Gill followed. If he was impressed by the sheer opulence of the place he wasn't showing it. Their shoes echoed on the marble floor. Standing waiting for the lift, Gill caught the signature on a painting hanging on the wall.

'Is that real?'

'What's that? Oh, the Picasso. I should think so. Unless it's a copy put there for the duration. You know many of our country's great paintings have been stored for safe keeping.' She peered more closely. 'Not this one. I'm pretty sure it's genuine.'

The lift arrived. The attendant who bade them enter didn't need to ask which floor and the lift rose smoothly to the top.

Susan lead the way to her room, nervous beyond belief. She tried to think of something to say but couldn't. She fumbled the key until Gill gently took it in his hand and opened it for her. She smiled at him, suddenly completely unsure about what she was doing. She'd been mad, she thought. What if he didn't feel the same way about her? It was too late. The door was open and they'd gone inside.

Champagne stood in an ice bucket. Oysters on the half-shell sat on a bed of ice. Candles had been lit at intervals around the room. It was the perfect seduction scene. Susan stood in the middle of the room, suddenly horrified, seeing herself through his eyes. Cheap and tawdry, throwing herself at him. She wished with all her heart she could disappear.

As if sensing her mood, Robert came to her and put his arms around her waist. Tightening the embrace he whispered against her lips. 'I hadn't dared hope.'

Susan saw Gill at every opportunity. She knew she was in love with him and though she tried to rein in her feelings she couldn't. Her emotions were too powerful. He never spoke of how he felt though he was very loving towards her. There was, she knew in her heart, something holding him back, stopping him from declaring himself. Could it be because she already had a child? It might break her heart but she'd never be able to stay with him if he couldn't accept her son.

On the two occasions she'd taken Robert to Wales to meet John Phillipe, they'd had fun together, or so it had seemed to her. But there was something wrong and she couldn't figure it out.

There was only one thing for it. She phoned SOE. 'Mike? It's Susan. Can we meet for a drink? I need to talk to you in private.'

An hour later Susan waited impatiently in the ladies' bar at the United Services Club, an untasted dry sherry at her elbow. Mike O'Donnell entered the room with the barest of limps and crossed to where she was sitting, a beaming smile plastered his face.

'How's the leg?' Susan greeted him.

'Fine. It's left a scar but even that'll fade in time. Betty spoilt me rotten.' After a pause, he said, 'I suppose this is about Robert?'

Startled, Susan picked up her glass and took a mouthful, giving herself time to reply. 'Why do you say that?'

'It's obvious. I know you two have been seeing each other for the best part of two months now and I'm delighted for you. He's a hell of a guy. You'd find it hard to do better.'

'That's what I think too. But he's holding back on me. He's . . . Oh, I can't explain it, Mike, but there's something. Some sort of barrier between us. I'm beginning to wonder whether or not he's married.'

O'Donnell, a large whisky in his hand, shook his head. 'He's definitely not married. Or ever been married. There are no skeletons in his cupboard, I can assure you. Our positive vetting procedures make sure of that.'

'Then what is it?' The anguish was clear in her voice.

O'Donnell looked at his glass, looked at Susan, placed the glass on the table in front of him and sighed.

'Come on, Mike. You know something.'

'Only conjecture. From a few things he's said.'

'What, is it, for God's sake?'

'Money. *Your* money.

'What the hell has money got to do with love?'

'It's hard for him, Susan, he's a proud man. It's difficult for anyone to come into your world if they aren't used to it.'

'But that's ridiculous. *You* did.'

O'Donnell shook his head. 'Not true. I was working with your father and Sion. We made money together. I contributed my share to the work and the risk and was rewarded for it. I've invested with your father and Sion ever since. Your father's rich, Sion is comfortable and I'm not doing too badly. Robert only has his salary, Susan – and a civil servant's salary at that. He can't just step into a life where money is no object. Where you can have whatever it is you want just by snapping your fingers.'

'But you know it's not like that,' Susan protested. 'Look at the life I lead. I take nothing for granted, not even the fact that I'll still be alive tomorrow.'

'I know it and you know it. It's Robert you have to convince.'

'What should I do?'

'Short of giving up your money and living on his salary I don't rightly know.'

'I'm not about to do that. We've earned what we have and we have the right to enjoy it.'

'As I said, I agree with you. But you still have to convince Robert.'

'I'll have it out with him,' Susan spoke with spirit. 'Point out how unreasonable he's being. Explain to him that my money can be used to our benefit.'

'Hold it right there, Susan. You just said the wrong thing.'

'What?' She looked at him in bewilderment.

'*My money,* you said. It'll always be your money.'

'Get me another drink, Mike, I need to think.' He sat there unmoving, an eyebrow raised until she noticed. 'Please.'

'That's better,' he grinned at her. 'I'll do what I can to help but as obstacles go, it's a big one.'

She left the club in a thoughtful mood. Mike's bombshell had rather put a dampener on her big news. Her posting had come through – Special Operations Executive's Squadron 161, flying Halifaxes into Europe.

38

THIS WAS HER third operation in ten days, a straightforward run to an area behind Dieppe. The Halifax BII (SOE) she flew had increased tankerage, lower drag engine nacelles and a streamlined nose called a Tempsford, instead of a turret. Armament was at a minimum. Speed and range were considered more important than firepower. The mid-upper turrets and under-wing fuel jettison pipes had been removed in order to reduce drag and the flame-damping exhaust shrouds were replaced with heat-resistant paint. Her aircraft, known as P for Peter, had a retractable tailwheel as well as a streamlined exit cone fitted around the paratroop door. Susan felt highly vulnerable relying so heavily on speed and manoeuvrability – it meant her crew relied entirely on her skill.

It hadn't been easy transitioning to an operational squadron. In the air she was the commander, in charge of the aircraft and a crew of four – flight engineer, wireless operator, navigator and tail-gunner – the only "sting" carried by the plane was shooting while running away. There had been a good deal of resentment at the idea of taking orders from a woman. Other members of the squadron had ridiculed the crew, a state of affairs Brian Ogilvie had warned her about. However, she'd been prepared to accept whatever was thrown at her, her quick wit and intelligence often winning in a verbal spat with other squadron members.

What had convinced them was that she had proven herself to be such a superb pilot. The squadron, professional to their fingertips, acknowledged the fact amongst themselves, though never to her.

She settled her parachute covered rump into the bucket seat and went through her check-off list. Flight engineer, Tony Scabbard – known to all as Scabby – stood behind her, checking his own panel. From there he controlled the engines and fine-tuned the fuel when the throttles had been adjusted by Susan.

Bill Shore, known as Sandy, sat below and in front of her at the wireless console. He finished his internal and external communications checks quickly and sat bored, ready for the take-off.

In front of him was the navigator, Leo "Fish" Salmond. He checked his instruments and charts carefully. Meticulous in all that he did, Fish was an excellent navigator, often guiding P for Peter back to base in the most atrocious weather conditions. Born and brought up within the sound of Bow Bells, when complimented on his skill he'd merely smile and say, 'I've got the homing instincts of a blooming pigeon.' The longest serving member of the crew, he was offered a transfer when the previous pilot had returned to bomber command. He'd refused and by the time he learned he was to have a woman pilot it was too late.

The gunner, Fred Barclay, was known as Dog, for no fathomable reason. His was the loneliest position in the plane, at the far end, away from the others. He had nothing to do until after take-off when he'd test fire the four 0.303in Browning machine guns, fitted to the Boulton Paul E type turret.

As well as the crew, they also carried human cargo, two agents who were to be dropped into enemy territory.

Susan was well aware of her nickname – Miss Petticoat – used disparagingly, but never to her face. She had just finished checking the massive throttle quadrant on her right, operating each of the eight levers, one for pitch and one for power – two per engine, in turn. She set the compasses and altimeter, checked the barometric pressure and anemometer, adjusted the artificial horizon bar and set the clock, which gained two minutes in twenty-four hours.

The order came to start up engines and she and Scabby went through the routine quickly. She adjusted the throttles to idle, Scabby fine-tuned the fuel flow, a final internal comms check was completed and then they were rolling. Before leaving the ground Susan checked her two passengers were strapped in and then announced, 'Up we go.'

The plane lifted into the air like a wallowing pig. However, once the wheels were up, P for Peter became almost graceful, more at ease in her unnatural environment. They settled into their flying routine. Every member of the crew was busy. For Scabby engines had to be checked continuously – temperature, fuel richness, and obversely, oxygen starvation, as well as fuel remaining, to calculate range. Susan and Fish needed that information on a regular basis.

Sandy Shore had modified his headset so that he could walk about whilst still plugged in to his console. The modification enabled him to stand beside the engineer and search the skies. Their greatest fear was of being jumped by an enemy fighter. In the tail, Dog calmly looked around, occasionally glancing inside to focus his eyesight before searching again. Should a German pounce, he would attack from the front and above. Still, he wasn't taking any chances.

In the cockpit, Susan was constantly busy, continually being given course and height adjustments by Fish, keeping to the planned track, following the narrow flight path where there were no known dangers, ack-ack batteries or airfields with fighters ready to be hurled at them.

Today's flight was known as a "Milkrun", an innocuous sounding name. Many planes had been damaged or destroyed, with injuries and deaths sustained by the crew, due to a lack of vigilance because of the misnomer. Susan swore she would never make that mistake.

They hit the French coast, dropped below three hundred feet and raced for the target. Susan had so many variables to consider; fair weather, good visibility, a half to full moon plus the need to stay hidden; the balance was a delicate one, not achieved easily.

'I have contact,' said Sandy. 'They hear us. I've exchanged ID's and all seems okay.'

'Right. Go aft. Tell them to standby. Scabby, give a hand with the equipment.' The plane went up to 500ft. The red light inside the fuselage turned to amber and the parachute door was opened. Susan confirmed with Fish they were at the exact spot and the two SOE operatives they were carrying jumped. P for Peter went round again. Five packages followed. Susan dropped the plane back to the deck and hared for home.

They landed at the base just after midnight, as the waxing half moon sank below the horizon. It had been a milk run after all.

Their debrief took no time at all and she was soon in her room, trying to relax, sleep elusive. She knew the others would be in the mess having a drink, unwinding, perhaps talking about the mission, or at least thanking their lucky stars that it had been so uneventful. She was tempted to join them but then thought better of it. She would only put a damper on things. Thoughts of Robert filled her mind. Their love making had been intense yet tender. Mike O'Donnell's words kept haunting her. Could money really come between them?

Robert seemed to accept all her many character traits, her stubbornness, her feminist leanings. Why couldn't he accept the fact that she had money? She wasn't flashy with her wealth, merely accepted it gratefully. She'd grown up hearing her grandmother's stories of poverty and what it meant. *And* she had painful memories of the squalor of her own childhood. It was a world Susan had no intention of inhabiting again.

The following morning the crew of P for Peter assembled in the briefing room.

Intelligence Officer Joseph Grant had been a chemistry master at a prep school before the outbreak of hostilities. As soon as war had been declared he'd signed up.

'Well done last night,' he congratulated them.

'It was a doddle,' said Fish.

'Good. Unfortunately, tonight's run won't be. You're dropping a *George* at a position twenty miles to the east of Paris. I'll give you the exact co-ordinates later. There are fifteen packages to drop, including a wireless. Weather permitting, take-off will be at 22.30.'

Scabby sat in the foldaway seat alongside Susan for take-off. Once in the air he would shift to a position behind her where his panel was situated. All checks had been completed and they lined-up on the runway. Scabby glanced at Susan, her face hidden behind her oxygen mask. The more he flew with her the more impressed he was. She'd flown lower and faster than any other pilot he'd been with. She seemed to have an instinct, a natural ability that somehow made her as one with the controls she manipulated. If only she knew what the others said about her. Not her own crew, but the rest of the squadron. Sleeping with the boss was the least of it. Still, they had yet to see her in real action, although if the rumours were correct, she'd seen a ton of it in Spain, long before this lot had blown up. Scabby's eyes flicked across the dials and outside to the four big Merlin XX engines. Everything was in order.

The plane was only halfway along the concrete when the front wheels began to lift. Then they were up and banking to port. Immediately his ears told him something was wrong. There was a rough noise coming from the port side. Dials and indicators all okay. He stood up to have a better look. Even as he saw the first flicker of flame the warning bells began.

'Fire! Fire in the port engine,' he announced, his hands already cutting fuel, pressing the button to the carbon dioxide extinguisher, feathering the prop, starving the fire of oxygen.

Susan calmly took the plane round in a low circle, called up flight control, received permission to land and within six or seven minutes was already touching down again. Evacuation was orderly and unhurried. There was no sign of the flames and with luck any damage would have been kept to a minimum.

Susan waited with the fitters as they examined the damage. After half an hour a sergeant reported to her. 'Appears all right, Ma'am. No structural damage. Only the engine. Have it out and stripped in twenty-four. Leave it to us.'

'Thank you, Sergeant Samson.' She smiled and went to her room. Having changed out of flying clothes she wondered what to do. It was only just after 23.30 and she was too wound up to go to bed. In an emergency situation, even one where very little had happened, adrenaline left a high she would have to come down from before going to bed. Although she avoided the bar as often as possible she decided to go across for a drink. She was in the right mood to confront anyone who said the wrong thing to her. By now she felt she'd proven herself often enough as a pilot and it was time she was accepted for what she was, not who she was.

She examined herself critically in a mirror. Crows' feet a bit deeper than she'd like, hair okay, eyes tired. About normal, she decided.

At the bar she ordered a dry sherry from the mess man. She stood with her back to the room, imagining the comments being made about her. Of her crew only Fish and Sandy were commissioned officers. Scabby and Dog were both sergeants and had their own bar. The room was half full and the cigarette smoke was thick in the air, an open window failing to help because of the blackout curtains. There were half a dozen WAAF officers present, all with important ground jobs, whether in administration or helping to control the plot during flight operations. The aborted flight had meant a rare evening off for them as well.

In the time she had been at the base she had tried to strike up a friendship with a couple of them but it was as if there was an invisible barrier. She flew. She was one of the Gods. On a pedestal with the rest of them. The women couldn't accept the fact that she'd broken into the male preserve of operational flying. And ironically the men didn't want her there because she was damned good.

Another sherry and I'm out of here, she thought.

'Hullo, Susan, can I buy you a drink?'

Startled out of her reverie she looked at the tall, thin squadron leader who appeared at her elbow. 'No thanks, Charles. You know the rules.'

'Rules,' he smiled at her, 'are for the guidance of wise men and the obedience of fools.'

'Even so, I'll buy my own.' Charles Albright had film-star good looks, complete with a dimpled chin, blue eyes and a hank of hair that fell appealingly over his right eye. He considered himself God's gift to women and had, she was sure, slept with half the women, officers and non-comms, on the base. He was, to put it politely, a rake.

'Don't be like that. Come on. I won't bite.'

To take the sting out of her words she summoned up a smile. 'That's not what I've heard.'

'Don't believe everything they tell you.'

'Charles, if I believed ten percent it would be too much. So the answer is still no. I'll buy my own.'

A smile on his face, Albright leaned forward. The smile vanished and he whispered, 'You really are a stuck-up cow, aren't you, Susan? But I'll have you. Just wait and see.'

The ugly scowl was replaced by another smile as he turned back to the room and went to rejoin a group in the corner. Susan was so taken aback that she stood in shock for a few moments. Then her temper flared and she stalked across the room.

The seven or eight men and women sitting around his table looked up as Susan came to a stop by Albright. She had a glass of sherry in her hand and, not stopping to think, threw its contents in his face. Albright leapt to his feet and raised his hand to her.

'Go on,' she spoke with suppressed fury. 'Try it. You speak to me like that again and I'll report you, you animal.'

The rest of the mess fell silent, watching the drama unfolding. Albright's navigating officer leapt to his feet, drew a handkerchief from his pocket and offered it. 'Come on, Charles, ignore the silly bitch. She's not worth it.'

Susan's eyes were locked on Albright's, which had narrowed with distaste. 'Perhaps you'd both like to repeat the comments you made to Captain Ogilvie?'

'No. Sorry. Come on, Charles, let's go.'

Both men left the room. The noise level had picked up again. This time the excited chatter had a focus. Susan felt the fight go out of her and her shoulders slumped. She knew she had acted badly. She should have ignored it. Played the game. Boys will be boys. But nobody, she thought, speaks to her like that. Her eyes caught those of Fish, who looked away, embarrassed. Well sod him too, she thought.

She went back to the bar. 'A whisky. Make it a double.' She had no flying duties the following day. A whisky or two wouldn't do any harm. She stood with her back to the room, aware they were talking about her. As the colour in her cheeks gradually subdued she became aware of somebody standing beside her. She looked across at the pretty features of Sarah Golding, a WAAF lieutenant in the plotting section.

'I came over to say well done.'

Whatever she'd been expecting it hadn't been that. Susan looked at Sarah in some surprise.

'Albright's a despicable cad. I wanted you to know that you aren't alone. The rest of us just don't have the nerve to stand up for ourselves – but you're different from us. Tonight only confirmed it, I suppose.'

'Not so different,' Susan began.

'Oh, but you are! Look at what you just did.'

Susan smiled wryly. 'Made an ass of myself you mean?'

'You'll have risen even more in the girls' estimation now. I know we've all been a bit catty to you, and about you, but I think,' Sarah smiled, a wide beaming smile, 'that'll change from now on.'

'Thank you.' Susan was at a loss for words. 'I know it's against mess rules but can I buy you a drink?'

'Better not. But I will get one though and stay and chat for a while.'

When Susan left for her bed she had made a firm friend. When her head hit her pillow she felt the room swaying and closed her eyes. Too much alcohol when she wasn't used to it wasn't good. She fell into a deep and dreamless sleep to be woken by the steward knocking on her door, depositing her early morning cup of tea outside.

A little later another knock brought the cheery face of a messman. 'Group Captain's compliments, Ma'am, but he'd like to see you immediately.'

'Thank you. I'll be right there.' *I wonder what he wants*, she thought.

When she was shown into his room she knew she was in trouble from the thunderous look on his face. Without preamble he said, 'What on earth possessed you to behave like that in the mess last night? I heard about it at breakfast and I've spent the last hour getting to the bottom of it. What on earth were you thinking?'

Susan shrugged. 'I wasn't thinking. I'm sorry, Brian. It won't happen again.'

'You're right it won't happen again. If it does you'll be off the station quicker than you can believe.'

'That's not fair,' Susan protested. 'You didn't hear what he said to me.'

'It doesn't matter. I know about Albright's reputation but he's a damn good pilot. One of our best.'

'And that excuses him, does it?'

Ogilvie had the grace to look away. 'I won't allow conduct unbecoming on my station. Watch your temper in future. That'll be all, Susan.'

She turned to go.

'One more thing. I read the report about last night's emergency. Good work. The operation has been rescheduled for tomorrow.'

'Yes, sir. Thank you.' She reached the door and had her hand on the knob.

'Susan, a word of warning – watch out for Albright. Underneath those boyish charms lurks a rather unpleasant man.'

Susan looked at Ogilvie in surprise. The group captain's admission meant a lot to her. He grimaced. 'I'm not a complete moron, you know.'

'Yes, sir. I mean, no, sir.' In some confusion she went out, heaving a deep sigh of relief. She'd better watch herself in future. There was no way she wanted to go back to ferrying aircraft around Britain after SOE.

This time P for Peter behaved. They lined up for the Channel, completed their post take-off checks and headed south east. Over the Channel they dropped to one hundred feet and sped towards occupied France. Beneath her cool exterior Susan felt her pulse race. God, she loved this! *Maybe I should have been born a man*, she thought. No! Better to be a woman. This way she had the best of both worlds. *Now concentrate, you daft sod.*

'Coastline coming up,' Fish spoke in her earphones.

'Got it. Looks like Dieppe.'

'It had better be. Come right twenty degrees. Over Rouen in six minutes.'

The dead reckoning navigation continued, confirmed by sightings of towns, hills and rivers. Then came the Seine and the plane followed the course of the river directly towards Paris.

'Come left forty degrees. There's a battery reported about a mile south of here.'

'Searchlights have come on. They're looking. I'll go lower.'

Susan had the plane down on the deck and opened up the throttles still further. The fingers of light passed safely to starboard and they were flying once more across a featureless landscape.

'Drop point in ten.'

'Okay. Tell the passenger to stand by.'

The agent jumped and P for Peter went round again to discharge the packages. That was when all hell broke loose.

Searchlights suddenly lit up the sky and pinned the Halifax like a butterfly on a specimen board.

39

Susan's reactions were automatic, so fast that she had taken action before conscious thought had taken hold. Her reflexes saved them in the beginning. Ack-ack guns opened up, exploding all around them, lifting the plane, peppering it with metal. She was jinking hard left and right, diving down, trying to get below the guns' elevation.

Even with her hands full she was able to ask, 'Everybody all right?'

A chorus of affirmatives helped to settle her fear. 'Dog, if possible, shoot out any lights you can. It's like daylight up here.'

Beams of light followed them relentlessly across the sky. Whoever had set the trap had known what he was doing. Not only had there been a welcoming committee at the drop point but now there were outer perimeter rings of lights and guns. The Germans were determined to shoot them out of the sky. And all they could do was run for it.

Thoughts of the parachuting agent fleetingly passed through her mind but were swept away as another shell exploded directly underneath the cockpit. The plane jarred and leapt in her hands. Searing pain struck her right leg but passed almost instantly. In its place she could feel a warm trickle down her calf and an ache when she tried to move the pedals under her feet.

'We're going round again.' Her anger was up and she was in a reckless mood. 'We'll go in low, Dog, shoot the hell out of them. Perhaps the bod will get a chance to escape.'

'If he's still alive,' said Fish. 'Let's do it.'

The plane was so low, Susan heard the tops of the trees scraping across the underbelly.

The Germans hadn't been expecting them to return. Dog opened fire as they flew over each searchlight and ack-ack emplacement. He had the satisfaction of seeing two explosions as his bullets set off a pile of anti-aircraft shells. Searchlights went dark and soldiers died, though how many he had no idea. Another round went off under the plane, causing it to buck and twist in the air.

'Fire!' Sandy shouted over the intercom.

'Deal with it,' Susan ordered grimly. 'Tally-ho.'

They'd passed the outer perimeter of the lights and guns and were going round for a third time.

'You ready, Dog?'

'Ready and able. Let's get the bastards.'

'Fire's out,' Sandy confirmed.

'Good. Here we go.'

The searchlights came on again, vainly trying to find the plane. Shells were exploding overhead, their fuses set too late for the altitude Susan held the Halifax at. One shell hit the starboard inner engine and knocked it out though there was no fire. As quick as lightning she corrected for the damage while Scabby feathered the engine and ensured there was no blaze.

Dog fired continuously, spraying the ground, barely aiming, hosing the area, causing untold damage.

They passed once more out of the circle of fire and light. 'Right, that's enough for one night. Time to get the hell out of here. Fish, course to steer?'

'Continue left to three four zero. Our height is one hundred feet above ground with the land rising gradually. Start gaining height now. Speed two five-five. Alter course in three minutes . . .'

His quiet, firm voice continued giving directions. Landmarks appeared when they were meant to and the return journey flashed by in relative peace, each member of the crew busy with his and her own thoughts. It had been a near thing. What had happened to the agent who had jumped? Had he been killed or captured?

In the moonlight they could see the Channel, a big, beautiful barrier between Britain and the rest of Europe. A line of destroyers flashed by underneath, though whether they were British or German Susan couldn't tell.

Her leg was aching like hell and she was beginning to feel light-headed. She slipped off her oxygen mask and slapped her face, trying to stay awake.

'Speak to me, Fish. Tell me distances, heights, courses.'

'Susan, are you all right?'

'Sure. Nothing wrong. Just a flesh wound. Just talk to me.'

Scabby stood next to her, the first-aid kit in his hand. 'Where are you hit?'

'Right leg. It's okay I tell you.'

'Let me take a look and I'll be the judge.'

'Can't take my foot off the pedal.'

'I'll get down and have a look.' Flashlight in hand, Scabby knelt on the deck and examined her leg. Blood was trickling from a deep wound in the calf. A pool of blood was at her feet and her trousers were soaked. 'Stay still. I'm going to whip a bandage on and stop the bleeding.'

Deftly he began to wrap a bandage around the wound.

'Jesus, Scabby, that hurts.'

'Sorry. It's the best I can do. Can you manage?'

'I . . . I think so. Fish, distance?'

'Eight minutes, Susan. Hang in there.'

It seemed to last forever. Her vision was beginning to go, blurring in and out. Concentration was proving difficult and she strapped the oxygen mask back on, opening the flow valve to full. For a few seconds she felt revived though she knew it wouldn't last.

'Come left five degrees. Airfield's dead ahead. Drop flaps. Come on, Susan, keep your wits about you.'

'Sure, sure, no problem.' It came out in a mumble.

'Wheels, Susan! Wheels!' Scabby's yell brought her back to life.

Her heart thumping, in control again, she went through the landing checks. 'Okay, going in.'

P for Peter landed with an uncustomary thump and began to slow down as she applied the brakes. The pressure opened up her wound and blood trickled down her leg. They came to a halt near the end of the runway. That was when she passed out.

'Hullo, Brian. It's good of you to come and visit.'

Group Captain Ogilvie smiled at her. 'You're a very lucky woman.'

'I am? Then why don't I feel lucky?'

'Because you don't know the facts.' Ogilvie sat down beside her hospital bed and asked, 'They treating you all right?'

'Can't complain. Be out in two days. The wound's healing nicely. At worst I'll have a small scar.'

'Good. You'll be pleased to know you're coming back to us.'

Susan nodded. 'Thanks.'

'It was a close call, Susan. I didn't know whether to court martial you or give you a medal.'

'Sorry to give you such a dilemma.' There was no sarcasm in her voice.

'You know that once clear you should have kept going. Got out of there. Left the agent to his own devices.'

'I know. It won't happen again, Brian, I promise.'

'Don't make promises you can't keep. It so happens that thanks to your action the SOE operative got away in the confusion. SOE are delighted. So instead of a court martial you get a DFC.'

She sat up in bed, wincing at the sudden stab of pain in her leg.

'I thought that might get your attention. It's all arranged. As soon as you can walk you'll go to the Palace to receive it.'

'What about the others? Scabby and Dog, Fish and Sandy?'

'DSMs for Sandy and Fish, DFMs for your gunner and flight engineer. It's unusual, I know, but they're intending to play up the woman pilot angle a bit. Make a heroine out of you. You normally have to have eight aerial victories for a Distinguished Flying Cross but they're making an exception for you.'

She sank back on her pillows and said, 'I don't deserve it.'

'You're probably right, but you're getting one. Susan, you were damned lucky. And I believe in luck. But don't use it all up too quickly. You'll live longer that way.'

'Thanks, Brian.'

'That's okay. When you get out of here you've got two weeks leave. Recuperation.'

'What about the others? Are they okay?'

'Yes. Basking in the reflected glory. Your nickname's been changed by the way.'

'What nickname?' she asked innocently.

Ogilvie looked at her in surprise for a second and then realised she knew only too well. 'Miss Petticoat. It's been changed. I don't say it's an improvement but apparently you're now known as "Hen" because of the way you fuss over your brood and protect your charges.'

Susan looked at Brian in complete surprise and burst out laughing. 'Hen! That's ridiculous.'

'It's a ridiculous time of our lives. Personally I think they should have chosen "Death-wish Daisy".' On that note he left her.

Word of the medal got around the hospital and all day other patients came to the ward to have a peek at her. After a very short while it began to irritate her and she asked to be moved to a private ward. Her request was denied and she suffered another two days before she was discharged.

She was wheeled out of the hospital not to an ambulance but a Rolls Royce, driven by her father.

'Hullo, my dear. I thought we'd get you home in style.'

'Thanks, Dad.' She was glad to see him, though part of her wondered where Robert was.

As if in answer to her thoughts, he said, 'Robert sends his love. We're going to town. Our flat is empty so you can have it for as long as you like. Unless you'd prefer to go to Wales or even *Fairweather*.'

'I don't want John Phillipe to see me like this. I'll travel down to Wales when I can walk without a crutch or a stick. The flat will be great.'

'I've given Robert a four-day pass. He can look after you.'

She smiled. 'Thanks again, Dad. That's very thoughtful of you.'

David shrugged. 'It's nothing. He may help you to mend quicker. Everyone sends their love. Madelaine is in Portsmouth so can't be here but has asked if she can go to the Palace with you.'

'Of course! That'll be lovely. You'll be there as well, I take it?'

'Wild horses wouldn't keep me away. We're all very proud of you, Susan. I've seen the report, naturally.' David sighed, 'You were damned lucky. Just stop pushing so hard, my girl.'

Her father helped her up to the small flat. He had thought of everything. There was food in the cupboards, drink on the sideboard, and fresh linen on the bed. A bowl of flowers had been placed next to the new combined wireless and record player, and a bottle of champagne stood ready to be immersed in an ice bucket.

'Do you have everything you need? If so, I'll be off.' David looked at his watch. 'Duty calls. I've a Head of Departments meeting in an hour. It's a three-line whip so I have to be there. Robert shouldn't be long.'

Susan put her arms around her father, hugged him tightly and kissed his cheek. 'I don't know how to thank you.'

He stared into her eyes. 'By staying alive, my dearest girl. Be more careful.'

'I will. I mean it when I say I'll take fewer risks.'

385

'Enough said. We can suggest, even counsel, but you young people rarely listen to advice, particularly from your parents.' David grinned. 'Which may be just as well.'

On that philosophical note he left. Susan hobbled into the bathroom where she ran a bath, taking the last of the hot water before awkwardly climbing in. She kept her leg hanging over the side, to keep the bandage dry. It was beginning to itch like mad and she had to resist the urge to scratch it.

When the water had gone tepid she climbed out of the bath, having washed the stench of the hospital away. She selected a becoming suit with a low blouse and a light jacket, its dark blue setting off the colour of her eyes to perfection.

She couldn't wait to see him. The letters she'd written Robert with such an outpouring of passion had remained only in her head. What she'd actually sent him had been anodyne, tame. Maybe she should have written how she really felt. Easier, she thought, than saying it. Perhaps he wouldn't come. He was late. The hundredth scenario possible had passed through her head before the phone rang.

Awkwardly she got to her feet and used her crutches to swing to the entry phone. 'Hullo?' It came out like a squeak. She cleared her throat and said again, 'Hullo.'

'Hullo, Susan, it's me.'

'Come on up, Robert.' A few seconds later there was a knock on the door and she swung it open, standing back a little bit, watching him enter.

He stopped and stared at her. They smiled shyly at each other, then he cupped her face in his hands. 'My God, but you're beautiful.'

'Oh, Robert,' was all she managed as he took her in his arms and kissed her.

'I was so worried about you,' he said. 'I would have come to see you but by the time we knew what had happened your father got the message you were leaving the hospital. Are you all right?'

'There's a rumour that I'll live.'

'Thank God for that.' He was grinning inanely at her, his joy evident.

Her heart was soaring. *It's going to be all right*, she thought. 'Champagne?' She gestured at the sideboard.

'Lovely. I'll get it.'

'What's in the bag?'

'A bottle of wine. I managed to get it from the pub round the corner. It cost a fortune, though what it'll taste like God alone knows.'

'We can have it with dinner. Come and sit down and tell me what's been happening. How's Mike?'

'Fine. Sends his love.'

'That's nice of him. What's been going on at SOE?'

'It's all very hush-hush,' he said smiling, taking the sting out of his words. 'But Mike said to tell you that Kitty is already back in France. Marseilles this time. A new circuit. She said that she'd learnt too much from the last débâcle to allow her knowledge to go to waste. So she went in two nights ago.' He looked at her thoughtfully, 'I'm more interested in what happened with you.'

'The Germans were waiting.' She shuddered. 'It was hellish. All I could think of was that I'd dropped a young man to his probable death and got so angry. I ended up endangering the aircraft and crew, but I wanted to protect him.' She took a sip of champagne and looked at Robert. 'Is that so wrong?'

'No. But not very professional.'

'That's what my Group Captain said.'

'He's right, but passion is important.

'Is it?' She looked at him tenderly. She loved the way his hair curled over his left ear but not his right. His sideburns had a hint of grey in them that she found very endearing. His steady brown eyes looked into hers. He leaned forward and kissed her. Supper was late, the wine was corked and undrinkable and the night was utterly wonderful.

Breakfast was hard-boiled eggs and burnt toast in bed, courtesy of Robert.

'I'm a lousy cook,' he told her.

'Then, my darling, we have problems. I can fly a plane but I can't cook for toffee. We'll have to hire someone.'

She knew she'd said the wrong thing by his sudden change in mood. 'What's the matter?'

'Nothing.'

'Yes, there is. You've gone all cold on me.'

'It's nothing, I promise you.'

She knew what the problem was. But she chose to ignore it. Otherwise they'd quarrel and their time together would be ruined and she was determined that wasn't going to happen. So instead she said, 'What shall we do today?'

He immediately switched moods too and said, 'I've an idea. Why don't we stay in and take it easy? You rest, read a book or a newspaper or two. What do the Americans call it? Chilling out?'

Susan laughed. 'Chilling out? How quaint! Where on earth did you learn that?'

'I like American pictures. That's an idea! Why don't we go to the cinema?'

Gill was back in minutes, having found a newspaper vendor on the corner. 'Here we are. The Apollo is showing *Gone With the Wind.*'

Susan groaned. 'I saw that ages ago. Is there nothing more recent?'

'Leslie Howard in *The First of the Few.*'

Another groan. 'I'm sorry he died in the plane crash but, please, I couldn't bear a film about developing the Spitfire.'

'Greer Garson in *Mrs Miniver*? Wait a minute. Humphrey Bogart in *The Maltese Falcon*?'

'Perfect. Where is it?'

'The Carlton in Hammersmith.'

'Goodie! And let's go out for dinner. The Ritz.'

Inwardly Robert winced. It would cost a week's pay but Susan deserved it, he decided. Outwardly he put on a smile. 'Great idea. Shall we eat first or afterwards?'

'I'll phone for a reservation,' said Gill. He lifted the receiver and was put through to the dining room of the Ritz. 'No places? Are you sure? All right, thank you.' He turned to Susan. 'We'll have to go elsewhere.'

Susan laughed. 'Darling, you're hopeless. Listen and learn.' She took the receiver from his hand. 'Merriweather? This is Susan Griffiths. I would like a table for two at nine o'clock, please. Yes. Secluded. Thank you.' She replaced the receiver and smiled at Gill. 'You see? They keep a few seats in reserve, for latecomers. The in-crowd as we say. This world is *who* you know, not what.'

Feeling wrong footed, Gill said, 'It shouldn't be like that. If you want a table you ought to be able to get one.'

'Oh, I agree, darling, I surely do. But the world doesn't quite work like that. Not yet, thank God. There have to be certain privileges to rank and status.'

'Money, you mean.'

'Well, maybe I do. Come on. Let's not spoil the day. We've the whole afternoon ahead of us. What shall we do? Chill out?'

'I have a little surprise for you.' Taking the phone Gill rang down to the concierge. 'Bring it up, Bill.'

Susan looked at him in delight. 'I love surprises. What is it?'

'Wait and see. Here we are.' There was knock on the door which Gill opened.

'How lovely!' Susan clapped her hands when the doorman pushed a wheelchair into the room. 'Where on earth did you get it?'

'Guy's hospital.' Gill grinned. 'When I told them it was for a real heroine, Miss Susan Griffiths, they were only too willing to lend it to me. Let's go for a walk in the park.'

They spent the afternoon in Hyde Park, feeding the ducks and enjoying the autumn weather. Nothing happened to spoil their time together. No air raids, no false alarms – almost as big a bane on Londoners' lives as the real thing – and no friction between them, for which Susan was grateful. She had to find a way to get Robert to accept the fact that she was wealthy. More than anything she wanted to be with him. Should they marry, the thought of living on his salary was less than appealing. Banishing her gloomy thoughts she pointed at a red setter that had just leapt into the lake and was barking at the ducks. Suddenly a swan appeared, raised itself out of the water in a great flurry of its wings and sent the dog packing.

Susan laughed joyously. 'Serve it right.'

A band was playing in the stand, thumping out military two-steps, foxtrots and waltzes.

'I wish I could dance,' said Susan. I hate the feeling of dependency. Silly isn't it, when so many people have far worse injuries than me? What about tea?'

'Where shall we go?'

'The other side of the park. There's a teahouse that sells scrumptious scones. Or it did before the war.'

They made their way across.

'Oh, no!' Susan said as they stopped in horror. The wooden structure had been bombed and burnt. All that was left were jagged and blackened timbers pointing at the sky, a forlorn reminder of happier times.

'Where now?'

She shrugged. 'Somehow I've lost my appetite. How about back to the flat?'

'Your wish is my command,' Gill replied gaily and wheeled her about. He picked up his pace and was soon running, both of them yelling and laughing with the sheer joy of being alive.

They spent the next few hours in bed. Afterwards they bathed and changed and Gill phoned down to the concierge to order a taxi.

The cinema was packed as the lights dimmed and the projector came on, cutting a white light through the thick cigarette smoke curling up to the ceiling. An expectant hush fell over the audience, broken by the crowing of the Pathé news cockerel. The film counted from five down to one on the screen and the programme started. After three years of searching the world for good news to tell its audience, Pathé now had plenty to choose from. The newscast began with the routing of the Germans from the flat corn-lands around Kursk, south of Moscow, the scene of the biggest tank battle in history. Footage followed of American soldiers landing on Sicily and capturing Palermo, to cheers from the Yanks in the audience. The next scene showed the surrender of Messina and Sicily, now in Allied hands once more. Film from September 8th showed the signing of the armistice between the Allies and Italy and the official declaration that the war in Italy was over.

Finally there was an announcement that Italy, completing her military about-face, had declared war on Germany. In response German soldiers had looted the art treasures of Naples, Rome and other cities.

The news finished with a montage of clips showing victorious soldiers of the Allies, raising their thumbs to the camera, smiling and waving and the announcement, '*Right lads, next stop Berlin and Mr Hitler's bunker.*'

Afterwards they pushed their way out of the crowded cinema, Gill shouldering people away from Susan if there was any chance of her being jostled as she swung on her crutches.

'We've been lucky,' said Susan, 'that there was no air raid.'

'Here we go!' A taxi swung into the curb and Gill reached for the door. Another man tried to grab it but Gill said, 'Mine, I think.'

'Here, bud, I don't think so somehow.'

Robert Gill raised himself to his full height. Broad shouldered and tall, he looked at the other man and said softly, 'Oh, I think it is, somehow. Now step aside, Yank, for the lady.'

He handed Susan into the taxi and helped her with her crutches. 'The Ritz, please.'

As the taxi was about to pull away they heard the American say in a loud voice, 'Mr Bigshot, huh? Why wasn't he in uniform, I'd like to know?'

Gill stiffened. Susan put her hand on his arm and squeezed. 'Take no notice. If they only knew.'

'Usually it doesn't bother me. I know how important our work in the SOE is, it's just a bit galling sometimes. And now, somehow it's worse, Susan; I'm sitting safely behind a desk while you are flying over France risking your life every day.'

'Your courage isn't in any doubt, Robert. So forget about it.' Susan smiled. 'Come on, darling, don't let one loud-mouthed American spoil our evening.'

The taxi drew up outside the Ritz hotel and a liveried doorman stepped forward with alacrity. Susan was helped out. With the crutches under her arms she swung quickly across the pavement. Gill was walking alongside her when she slipped and he just managed to catch her before she fell.

'Careful,' he warned.

'Thanks. I'll go more slowly. My dignity nearly took a tumble.'

'It could have been more than your dignity. Here's the maitre d'.'

'Good evening, Miss Griffiths.'

'Good evening, Merriweather. I hope you've got us a nice table.'

'Certainly, Miss. On the far side. You can see without being too obvious.'

'Thank you, Merriweather. That's very kind of you.'

'My pleasure, Miss. Sir.' He nodded coolly to Gill and left them at their table.

'He certainly put me in my place.'

'Take no notice of him. He's a snob. It's only because he knows my father has a title that's he's so nice to me.'

'A knighthood?'

'That too, but dad inherited a baronetcy from my grandmother's second husband, John Buchanan, the Baron of Guildford. He won't use it. It's in trust or something for Richard should he want it when he's older. Though I doubt he will.'

'Why not?' Gill was intrigued in spite of himself.

'Our Richard is a bit of a champagne socialist. Likes the idea of equality but doesn't mind the inherited wealth bit. I was exactly the same when I was younger but I grew up soon enough. Here's the menu.'

In spite of wartime rationing and the huge problems in getting the basic foodstuffs there was a thriving and valuable black market in the sort of food eaten at the more expensive restaurants. The menu included oysters and lobsters, quails eggs and liver paté, venison and pheasant, now that the season had started.

'There are no prices on the menu,' Gill observed.

'Don't worry about it. It's not as expensive as you think. Just order what you want. I'm going to the powder room. Help me up a second, darling, please.'

She left the room. 'Merriweather?'

'Miss Griffiths?'

'When you bring the bill put half of it on my father's account. Only don't make it obvious.'

'Yes, Miss.' He expertly palmed the pound note she slipped him.

'And send a bottle of Lafitte Rothschild across. Is there any of the thirty-seven left?'

'I'll do what I can, miss.'

'I'm sure you will, Merriweather. I knew I could rely on you.'

It was only as she returned to their table, seeing his dark head poring over his wallet, that she knew how badly she had compromised both Robert and herself.

40

THEIR ROW WAS inevitable and, of course, it was about the usual subject – money. Susan had wanted to go to see a Noël Coward production in Drury Lane.

'Not only can I not get any more time off,' said Gill, 'but I can't afford it.'

'I'll pay,' said Susan and wished immediately she hadn't.

'I pay when I take a woman out Susan. Not the other way around. It's a man's duty to pay. That's the way things are done. Where I come from the man goes out to work and supports his family.'

'While the little woman stays at home cooking and rearing children, is that it?'

She knew she was pushing him into a corner but she couldn't help it. She wanted the problem aired, to have it sorted. Damn it! She felt her anger rising. 'This war has changed everything once and for all. Women will *not* be content to go back to the way things were. We're used to our own lives, our own jobs and yes, our own money.'

'Money! It always comes down to money with you.'

'That's your problem, Robert, not mine. I have the stuff. Oodles of it.'

'Yes, from your father.'

Susan laughed, a shrill sound that was unpleasant even to her own ears. 'Dad doesn't give me any money. I inherited it from my grandmother. A wonderful, brave woman who fought the conventions and won. She was born dirt poor in a South Wales mining village as was my grandfather. They fought their way up from the very bottom. And though they left poverty behind they never forgot where they came from. There's no dignity in grubbing for a living. There *is* dignity in achieving status and financial independence and then giving back to your community and your country.'

'What? Like Lady Bountiful?' He was sneering at her and she found her temper flying out the window.

'We paid one hell of a price for what we've achieved. Nothing's for nothing. The first ten years of my life I lived in a log cabin where I was treated almost like a slave. My mother was married to a cruel man who treated her abominably and me not much better.

'He killed my grandfather, Robert. So we know about paying the price. *Everything* has a price and often it is too high. My grandmother often said that she would happily give up everything to have just one more day with my grandfather. And she meant it. Money meant nothing to her and it doesn't to me. It's a means to an end. It frees us from drudgery to allow us . . . some of us . . . to achieve things in life. Look at my family. Not one of us is a waster. Nobody's living a hedonistic, useless life. Not only do we provide opportunities for thousands but we fight for the family and by God, we fight for our country.'

'That's as may be, Susan, but I can't live like that. I need to provide for my wife and family. Me! Not somebody else.'

'Then what do you suggest? We live in a suburban semi, me at home while you go to work?'

'Yes! If need be.'

'But it needn't be like that. We can do anything, go anywhere.'

'We live in different worlds, Susan. This isn't going to work.'

Her stiff-necked pride reared its ugly head. 'You're probably right. My family may have come from humble beginnings but we've changed and adapted. You seem unable.'

'I've nothing to be ashamed of, Susan. I've worked hard to get where I am. When I got into the police I was determined to be a success. Chief Inspector by the age of thirty-one, that's an achievement. My father was so proud. Before he died he used to boast about me to his neighbours.'

'What you're talking about is exactly the same ambition that has driven my family.' She stopped. She could see her words were not getting through to him. It was as if he didn't want to understand. Maybe that was it. Perhaps this was his way of getting out of their relationship. Well, damnit, she'd make it easy for him. 'You'd better go, Robert. We can call each other when we've both calmed down a bit.'

He looked at her and then nodded.

She held back her tears until the door had closed behind him.

She woke to a grey dawn and a feeling of emptiness, lying in bed until restlessness forced her to get up. In the bathroom she examined her wound. It was healing well, the stitches a neat line along the bottom of her calf. She'd been lucky not to sever an artery.

The day passed slowly – with no word from Robert. She phoned Connie in Wales for news of John Phillipe and found herself pouring her heart out to her friend.

Since Alex's death Connie had been very subdued, though she had confessed to Susan how grateful she felt for the time they had spent together. Alex's love had healed her fears, she said. What could Susan do to heal the fears Robert felt?

But Connie had reckoned without Susan's stubborn pride. She was unable to back down.

By the end of the week she was able to get around using a walking stick. The stitches were removed. The doctor told her the livid scar would all but vanish, leaving only a thin white line after a few months.

The morning arrived when she was due at Buckingham Palace. Madelaine and her father came to collect her. If they knew about her argument with Robert they made no comment.

'How do I look?' Susan asked, standing in front of them in her number one uniform.

'Very smart,' said Madelaine.

'Beautiful,' said her father. 'You aren't nervous are you?'

She smiled. 'Very. This is worse than crossing into France. Shall we go?' She led the way, her back straight, hardly using the stick, a surge of anticipation sweeping through her.

At the Palace she found herself with hundreds of others, milling around, unsure where to stand. Her father and Madelaine had gone into the large reception room with the other visitors, to line the walls and wait for the King. The medal recipients were finally placed in order of merit. At the head of the queue was a captain of an infantry battalion who was to receive the Victoria Cross. Susan was seventh in line. They were told what to expect. It would be mercifully brief.

The King and Queen entered the room to warm applause and the ceremony began. In a daze Susan shook the King's hand, smiled, exchanged a few polite words and moved on. Within minutes she found herself being led outside, David and Madelaine beside her. A press photographer was there and took a number of snaps of her before she was allowed to leave. A short while later they sat down to lunch at the Ritz.

'What a load of palaver over nothing,' Susan finally acknowledged, after a celebratory sip of champagne.

'Don't denigrate such an honour,' said David. 'The DFC is only given to those who deserve it. And you deserved it. Make no mistake about it.'

'I'm just lucky to be alive.' She held the silver cross with its purple and white diagonally striped ribbon in her hand. 'It's a bauble.' She placed it back in its case and closed the lid. Without Robert there, everything seemed so empty. She knew she needed to share the experience with somebody. And that somebody was Robert Gill. Damn him!

After lunch they returned to the flat. 'You can finally have this place back, Madelaine. I'm going to Wales. To spend time with John-Phillipe, I've missed him terribly.'

'He'll be glad to see his mum too,' said Madelaine shrewdly. 'But you made the right decision, you know. Sitting at home knitting socks would have made you miserable. Your son is a fine boy and a credit to you. And what a comfort he has been to poor Connie. When are you going down?'

'I thought about catching the five o'clock from Paddington. I can telegram Connie my arrival time and someone will meet me at Cardiff, I'm sure.'

'I'll organise that,' said Madelaine, 'you go and pack.'

Susan went in to the bedroom with David behind her. 'Can I help?'

'Lift my case down from the wardrobe, Dad, please.'

He did as she asked and threw the lid open. 'I know it's none of my business but whatever happened between you and Robert – you should try and put it right.'

Susan, in the act of putting a handful of clothes into the case stopped and smiled at her father. 'It seems that the only way we can be together is if I jettison my worldly goods. The man is a chauvinist dinosaur.'

David raised a cynical eyebrow.

'And I love him more than ever,' Susan sighed. 'I've decided to give him time to think. Hopefully, he'll miss me and finally see sense.'

'Well, you know where we are if you want to talk about it. When do you return to duty?'

'Another week.'

'But you won't be flying?'

'Good Lord, no. Light duties for at least a month, followed by a medical examination and then if I'm passed fit I'll be able to fly.'

'Good. That gives me nearly six weeks of not having to worry about you.'

'How's Richard doing at Eton?'

'Fine. Still desperate to get into the war. I keep telling him he's got plenty of time, but he won't have it. Wants to do his bit.'

'Keep him out for as long as possible.'

A taxi took her to the station to catch her train. Unusually, with so much happening to the rail network, the train was due to depart on time. A porter ensconced her in a corner seat of a first class compartment.

Whistles sounded, steam belched out of the underside of the engine, and with a jolt the train moved out of the station. A number of other people entered the carriage but Susan ignored them, wrapped up in her own world, watching as the grubby station faded behind.

'Excuse me.'

Susan registered the jowly, middle-aged man who was sitting opposite and peering intently at her.

'Aren't you that woman who got the medal today from the King?'

Startled, she said, 'Why do you ask?'

He took an early edition of the London Evening Standard out of his pocket and pointed at the picture of her on the third page. 'Looks just like you!'

Susan laughed. 'My *Doppelgänger*, I expect.'

'Well, she's a very brave woman, is all I can say,' said the man's wife.

'She should leave the fighting to the men,' said her husband. 'I don't own with women being in the front-line.'

Susan was about to argue but decided against it. She would be wasting her breath. The train jerked, slowed and came to a halt, less than fifteen minutes out of the station. Leaving on time had been too good to be true, she decided. Standing up, she was about to reach for her walking stick, which she'd placed on the overhead rack with her case, when she thought better of it. She'd give her identity away if she did. Doing her best not to limp she left the compartment and made her way along to the restaurant car and bar. She needed a drink.

She sat with a dry sherry, toying with the stem of the glass. Her thoughts turned to her son. Being parted from him she had suffered terrible pangs of guilt, wondering what sort of mother could leave her child in someone else's charge. She and Connie had had a long, honest discussion before she signed up. Susan knew she could never have left him with anyone else. Connie made her job possible and she'd never be able to thank her enough.

With a sigh, she took a Leslie Charteris paperback from her bag and settled down to read about the daring exploits of that loveable rascal Simon Templar, alias the Saint.

She alighted at Cardiff Central Station. It was dark, low beam lights showing the way to the exit, a precaution against a possible air raid. Outside she stood irresolutely for a few moments until she heard her name being called.

'Connie! How lovely!' The two women hugged warmly, keenly aware how precious their time together was. In the car the first thing she asked was, 'How's John Phillipe?'

'Fine. He loves school so much. Sets off every day with his satchel and marches along the village with the others. He's even learnt a few words of Welsh. He's so cute to watch.'

Susan held back a sigh. So cute to watch and she was missing it. Like so many other men and women all over the world, fighting in this damned war. At least, she thought, I've got another chance of seeing him. It had been a near thing.

Connie had moved them away from the airfield, to the village of Llantwit Major. She'd rented a three-bedroomed house, with a garden front and back. The house was lovely, more than adequate for their needs, Connie said.

'Who's with John Phillipe this evening?'

'A local girl who baby-sits when I need her. Are you all right?'

'Yes, fine.'

'How's the leg?'

'Mending.'

'I'll take a look when we get home. Any word from Robert?'

Susan sighed and began to share her anxieties and doubts. Connie drove slowly, the narrow beams of the car's headlights barely sufficient in the dark city. As always it was eerie to drive along unlit streets, past darkened houses, with people still going about their business regardless.

Susan was soon lost in a maze of small country roads but Connie knew where she was going and half an hour later they were home. John Phillipe was asleep as Susan crept into his bedroom to look down at his curly head. So like his father she thought, remembering the man she had loved over six years go. Phillipe would have wanted her to love again, she knew. And now Susan had lost her heart to a man who loved his pride more than her.

Connie comforted her over supper, lamb stew washed down by glasses of stout, the only drink Connie could get at the local pub. She laughed, 'You would not believe it, Susan. When I asked if they had any wine they thought I was mad. England is backward enough, but here! It is like being in the dark ages.'

After the meal Connie insisted on looking at Susan's wound. She pronounced herself satisfied. 'It is healing well. You will have only the slightest of scars eventually. Not like the one you have on your belly.'

Susan shrugged, remembering the air attack in Spain, which had almost killed her. 'That one healed pretty well.'

'You use up too many of your nine lives, Susan. You should stop what you are doing and go back to ferrying aircraft. It is much safer.'

'The risks the SOE women take are far greater than anything I do. So I *must* continue. It's only fair.'

'Don't forget your son, Susan. He needs a mother.'

It was the first time Connie had ever criticised what she was doing. Was she being selfish, taking such risks? Was her stubbornness hurting the people around her? For a few moments she feared the answer was yes.

41

THE MAIN UNDERCARRIAGE lifted and P for Peter trundled into the air. Susan had been back on operational duty for a month. During that time she had flown ten sorties into Europe, stretching from Southern France, which had been a milk run, to Holland, where heavy flak had been a nightmare. This sortie was expected to be somewhere in between. The plane was stuffed to the roof with packages as well as four bods. Two handlers had been added to the crew to help with the drops. There would be one south of Antwerp in Belgium and the other to the west of Douai in Northern France.

'On track,' said Fish. 'Time to Channel twenty minutes.'

'Hen, we've got a raid coming in from the east. Destination unknown.'

'Thanks, Sandy. I'll go right twenty degrees. We want to stay away just in case.' It wasn't unknown in the heat of battle for a fighter pilot to mistake a Halifax for a German bomber with disastrous and sometimes tragic consequences. They were at 10,000ft. Susan said, 'I'll drop to one thousand feet and stay below the clouds.'

'Make it one and a half,' said Fish. 'The Chilterns are coming up.'

They were all in their usual places, nerves taut. Instruments were scanned and the sky searched constantly for enemy aircraft. Far over to the left they could see the searchlights coming on and then flashes of gunfire.

'That looks like London,' said Susan.

'Correct,' said Fish. 'Fighter Command have just confirmed engagement.'

'It looks like it's a busy night,' said Scabby. 'Poor bastards.'

'Channel in five.'

'I see it. I'll go low as soon as we get there.' As P for Peter left the land behind them Susan took the plane down to 150ft. December had brought calm air and cold sunshine.

A full moon burst over the horizon to the south and bathed the undulating water of the English Channel in white light.

'Clouds clearing,' said Susan. 'I think we'll be okay going in but coming out could be a different story. We'll have the German bombers and their escorts returning.'

'At least they'll be low on fuel,' said Scabby.

'Hen, come left to zero nine zero. France in eleven.'

'Thanks, Fish.' Susan smiled, her oxygen mask dangling under her chin. It was funny how she'd taken so easily to the nickname. She wondered which of them had thought it up. 'Land ahead.'

'You should have Calais dead ahead.'

'Certainly looks like it. I'll confirm in a moment.'

The plane skimmed the waves with France now on their starboard side. By the light of the moon it was possible to distinguish between beaches and towns as Calais gave way to Dunkirk and then Ostend.

'Come to one zero five on my mark. Now. Keep the river on the left all the way to Brugge.'

Then came Gent and another alteration of course. In spite of the cold, Susan was perspiring. She'd been flying low for what seemed like hours and they still had to reach their first drop point. The scar on her leg was itching and she had an overwhelming desire to scratch it.

She had taken the safest route at the safest height, which demanded the most of her flying abilities. The level of concentration required was intense but she figured it was worth it. They passed over searchlight batteries that briefly lit up, too late to pin the plane in their white grip and far too late for the ack-ack batteries to open fire, although one or two of them did get off a round or two, more in hope than expectation.

'I've picked up the Eureka signal,' said Sandy. 'I'll try the S-phone.' After a few moments he reported, 'Hen, I got them. The password's correct as well as the confirmation phrase.' The confirmation phrase was broadcast by the BBC every night in a long string of messages aimed at the resistance groups across Europe. From Norway to Greece, men and women listened avidly for their instructions and their code words, much to the chagrin and fury of the Germans. They heard the same messages but could make neither head nor tail of them unless they'd captured key members of the circuit the message was aimed at.

'Good. We don't want another mess like last time. Time to drop?'

'Six minutes.'

'Tell them to stand by. Agents first then we'll go round again.'

The second drop would be made at 500ft above the ground and would cover a large area as over twenty loads of equipment had to be pushed out. But that was the easy part. The men and women on the ground then had to break the packages down and handcart them away. It was the most dangerous period for the Maquis and one the Germans were quick to exploit if they could. There were mobile listening posts all over France, trying to pinpoint where a drop was taking place. Sometimes the Germans got lucky.

'That's the last away,' said one of the handlers.

'Okay. Course to steer, Fish?'

'Two seven zero until we clear the area. I'll tell you when to come left.'

They all hated double drops. Their vulnerability didn't double, it quadrupled. They were pushing their luck and they all knew it. The crew's anxiety went up a few notches.

Fish continued giving direction and soon they were approaching the drop point.

'Looks quiet. Any contact?'

'Sorry, Hen, nothing,' said Sandy.

'I've got a light,' said Susan. 'Sandy, can you see it?'

'Answering now.' Sandy Shore used the switch at his console to operate the signal lamp fitted to the nose of the plane. He sent ZZI and received IJK back. 'That's the right signal.'

'I don't like it,' said Susan. 'Send William Yorker Oboe.' These were the phonetic letters WYO.

'Will do, Hen, only Yorker is now Yoke.'

'Since when?'

'Since last week. There's been a bunch of changes. I'll show you when we get back.' The phonetic alphabet was changed from time to time in an effort to make it shorter and clearer. So far all the changes had done was add to the confusion.

'Damn!'

'What is it, Sandy?'

'They sent the wrong signal.'

'That's good enough for me. Let's get the hell out of here.' Susan had taken the plane up to 500ft for the drop but now she put the nose down and dived for the ground. As she did, searchlights came on and began weaving across the sky looking for them. Ack-ack guns opened fire, though none of the shells came near enough to do any damage. But then they were pinned by one light and the guns began to get more accurate.

'Can you shoot out that light, Dog?'

'Any second, Hen.'

She felt a slight judder pass through the aircraft as Dog opened fire. The searchlight was suddenly extinguished and the exploding shells began to fade behind them. They were down on the deck now, the throttles wide open, the engines racing. Just in time she saw trees outlined on a low hill ahead and pulled up on the wheel. 'Come on Peter, come on. Up we go.'

For a second she thought they wouldn't make it but then they were over and past, the searchlights and guns fading behind them.

Before she could ask, Fish said, 'Head three two five. It's the quickest route for the coast. Every searchlight battery and ack-ack gun emplacement will be looking for us so the sooner we're over the Channel the better.'

'Agreed.' The moon suddenly went behind a thick cloud and it was like going into a darkened room. Susan switched her concentration to her instruments, her lips dry, hating not being able to see at least *something*!

Instinctively she flew higher, adding a hundred feet to their height above ground. It was so easy to make an error and hit the land. It happened to a lot of pilots at times like these.

'Hen, come right ten degrees. According to Intel reports there's a large battery north of Bethune.'

'I see it. The lights are on.' Beams of light were reaching into the sky, looking for them. They passed them clear to the left and then turned back towards the coast.

After a few minutes Fish said, 'Calais in four.'

'Fish, we have a problem.'

'Don't tell me. The returning German squadrons.'

'Correct. They are all over the sky. I can make them out, just. There's bound to be a few fighters amongst them.'

'Sorry, Hen, we've nowhere to go. We haven't enough fuel to divert.'

'Listen up. Keep your eyes peeled. I'm going as low and as fast as I dare. The batteries will leave us alone because of the other aircraft as they can't be sure who they're aiming at, but we can easily be jumped. You got that, Dog?'

'Sure, Hen but I can't see anything yet.'

'They're about five miles directly ahead, so you won't. I'll let you know when we're amongst them.'

The Germans planes were flying at 1,000ft or more. Having been driven out of England they were dispersed across the sky and running for their bases, harassed every foot of the way by squadrons of Hurricanes, Spitfires and Griffins.

'There's the coast,' said Susan.

'All clear so far?'

'Nothing, Hen. We're being ignored,' said Scabby.

'The W/T is full of chatter,' said Sandy Shore. 'The usual at this time.' He heard yells of "Break left", "Dive, Jimmy, for Christ's sake", "Hang on, Max, I'm coming" as pilots fought for their lives across the skies of France.

'Dive, Hen! Dive!' Dog yelled, opening fire at a German fighter who had appeared from nowhere.

Susan didn't even think about it. Already flying at only three hundred feet as they crossed the coast she went straight down to the water, pulling P for Peter up at the last possible second. She could feel the shudder as the guns fired at the enemy and then the plane shook as bullets struck the tail.

The firing stopped.

'Are you all right, Dog?'

'Yes! I'm fine. He went straight into the drink. I don't think I hit him. He just flew straight in.'

'Target paralysis,' said Susan. The pilot had become so focused on the target he forgot where he was and what he was doing. Not an uncommon occurrence.

Susan had the plane at fifty feet. The slightest downdraft could spell disaster and she flew with every fibre of her being concentrated on her instruments. A flicker of the altimeter would be her first intimation of loss of height and possible disaster. To look out of the window, at the sea, would be suicidal. She *had* to trust and believe her gauges.

'Hen,' said Scabby, standing next to her, 'there's a ship dead ahead. A frigate. It looks like a Flower Class.'

Susan took the plane up thirty feet and skimmed over the top of the ship's masts.

'It's behind.'

Down she went again.

'Three minutes to Blighty,' said Fish Salmond in his steady voice.

The crew knew what she was doing. In this type of flying no one could equal Susan. Very low, very fast, like no other pilot they'd ever flown with. It was, apart from the flying dangers, the safest way through a circus of enemy fighters. None dared come down to attack as they would simply fly straight out of the sky.

'Cliffs ahead,' said Scabby. 'No other planes in sight.'

P for Peter gained two hundred feet of height.

'I've contacted Bomber Command. They know we're in-bound. Skies are clear. All enemy aircraft have departed these shores.'

P for Peter swooped high in the sky to 10,000ft and Susan hauled back the throttles for optimum cruising. Scabby adjusted his controls and checked the settings.

'We're going in on fumes,' he said.

'Will we get there or do we divert?'

'We'll get there, don't worry.'

'Scabby, with you to look after me I *never* worry,' said Susan with a smile.

Landing was a piece of cake and the plane set down gently on the runway. After taxiing to dispersal and turning off the engines Susan leant back in her seat, completely drained. She just wanted to stay where she was and fall asleep. Instead she undid her seatbelt and dragged her bone-weary body out of the aircraft. A debriefing was called for, along with an explanation of why the second drop hadn't taken place. Well that was easy. The bloody Germans had been waiting for them!

In spite of her exhaustion Susan lay awake for some time, thinking about her son and about Robert. A feeling of loneliness washed through her before she finally fell into a deep but troubled sleep. She awoke jaded and out of sorts.

With operations taking place at the oddest times of the day and night, food was available in the messes virtually twenty-four hours. Susan sat down to a late breakfast of powdered eggs, sausages and toast. The coffee was barely drinkable and the eggs tasteless.

The room held over twenty tables, flimsy affairs that sat four people in a square. Most of them were empty. Only those who'd been on night ops breakfasted at that time of the day. As was customary in officers' messes throughout the armed forces, newspapers and periodicals were read at the table. Susan had propped up a day old copy of the *Daily Mail* in front of her. Although she read the words she didn't take in any of the story.

Feeling eyes on her, she looked up to another table and caught Charles Albright staring at her. He had the good grace to look away but not before she saw the flash of anger in his eyes. She wondered what she'd done to upset him this time. She'd hardly seen him since the incident in the bar. Their independent flying duties meant that the crews passed each other like ships in the night. Dismissing him from her mind she concentrated on the newspaper, this time reading and taking in some innocuous story about the King and Queen's visit to the East End of London.

Outside the dining room were pigeonholes where messages and mail were left. She checked hers and lifted out three envelopes. One was from her outfitters' Gieves, the second from her bank and the third from Connie. Again disappointment claimed her – why didn't Robert write? Damn him, she thought. But then, she hadn't written to him either.

Again she was aware of a presence next to her and she looked up to find Albright standing next to her, looking through his mail.

Glancing down at her he said softly, 'No love letters, Susan? Must do something about that, mustn't we? You and I have some unfinished business.'

Before she could say a word he turned on his heels and walked away. She was about to rush after him and face him but thought better of it. Any scene would merely be embarrassing for her. The man made her skin crawl. Why were some people determined to make enemies when they had a common foe to fight? Egocentric bastard!

In her room she went through her paperwork, the bane of any officer in any force anywhere in the world. But she couldn't concentrate, thinking about Albright's words to her and so she gave up. Deciding to go for a walk, she put on her winter warm – the thick, doe-skin officer's coat she'd bought from Gieves and the subject of their latest correspondence. Throwing off her black mood she went out into the cold, fresh air.

Passing the offices of the Officer Commanding she was hailed by the adjutant. 'I was about to send for you, Susan. Brian wants you.'

She entered the stuffy office, warmed by a wood-burning stove that threw out a lot of heat. 'What am I in for this time?'

He smiled, winked and said, 'You'd better go in.'

When she entered Ogilvie's office he surveyed her from top to toe, his manner disapproving. 'Susan, take a seat.'

'Thank you.' She was alarmed. What on earth did he want?

'Why are you incorrectly dressed?'

'I'm sorry?' She looked down at her coat, checked her shoes and her hat. 'I wasn't aware that I was.'

Suddenly Ogilvie smiled. 'Well you are, First Officer. Congratulations, Susan.'

It took a second or two to sink in but then she smiled, feeling suddenly elated. 'Thank you. Thank you very much.'

'Here you are. This signal came in ten minutes ago.'

Taking it, she saw her name in a long list of others.

'You're off flying for forty-eight hours. I suggest you get the RPC out of the way.' Invitations by signal to a party were abbreviated to RPC – Request the Pleasure of your Company.

'I will. Tonight suit? And please tell Maureen to come.'

'Thank you. She'll be delighted.' Maureen was Ogilvie's long-suffering wife. They'd been married for twenty years and she had been a stalwart in helping her husband in his RAF career, following him around from airfield to airfield. Uncomplaining, she was often regarded as the power behind the throne, determined to see Ogilvie make flag rank, something he didn't particularly wish for.

Her next stop was the clothing store where she was able to purchase the relevant stripes for her uniforms. Then she made a quick trip to the mess to put up a notice inviting everyone who was in the mess after 18.30 to join her in a drink to celebrate. Then back to her room to do a lot of sewing. It was a chore she didn't mind on this occasion.

Since joining the squadron Susan had attended several RPCs. She knew the form. She would pay for the first drink of those who attended, any more they paid for themselves.

The bar was filled. Cigarette smoke had created a haze across the room. Someone was tinkling at a piano and the chatter was loud. For just a short while they were able to forget the war.

'Congratulations, Susan,' said Sarah Golding, raising her glass of Horse's Neck in salutation.

'Thanks, Sarah. Everyone seems to be having a good time.'

'You know this lot. Any excuse for a party. Luckily the squadron's stood down for twenty-four hours.'

'I didn't know. Since when?'

'Signal came in half an hour ago. It's going to be an expensive bash.'

'I don't mind. The more the merrier.'

'Does that include Lover Boy over there?'

Susan looked to where Sarah had nodded. Charles Albright was just finishing a drink and reaching for another.

'He doesn't look too happy,' said Sarah.

'Tough. What's his problem, do you know?'

'I'm not one to gossip . . .' She let the word hang tantalisingly in the air.

'Do tell. I love a good story, especially if it's the juicy kind.'

Sarah laughed, dimples of pleasure evidence of her good humour. 'I heard that he was in the village, caught red-handed so to speak, by the husband. You know the barmaid at the Barley Mo?'

'Not really. I hardly ever go.'

'Her husband's a petty officer. He wasn't due back for a fortnight but his ship was badly damaged and they came back early. He got home to find dear Charles actually in bed with the woman. There was a hell of a barney. I think a complaint's been made to Brian.'

'What's it got to do with him?

'Prejudicial to good order and all that. Especially with another rank's wife.'

'If it had been an officer's wife it would have been all right?' Susan couldn't help smiling. Albright, it seemed, was about to get his come-uppance.

'That, I wouldn't know. But it does serve him right.'

'Serve who right?'

'Oh, hello Charles, I didn't see you there.' Sarah blushed guiltily.

'Talking about me, were you?' Albright was looking belligerently from face to face, obviously three sheets to the wind.

'We have better things to do,' said Susan, recovering quickly, 'than talk about you.'

'I bet. Just watch it, that's all.' Albright turned and walked away, his back stiff with anger.

'Was that a threat?' Susan asked.

'It sounded like one. Ignore him. He's a loudmouth. Listen, Janet's having a little soirée later on in her room. It's her birthday. We wondered if you'd like to come. She only decided a few minutes ago because ops have been cancelled. It's just a few of the girls. Bring a bottle if you can.'

Susan smiled. 'I'd love to.'

The party in the mess was becoming more boisterous and Brian Ogilvie and his wife came over to speak to Susan. 'We're just going,' said Ogilvie, 'before it all gets too rowdy. What I don't know can't hurt,' he said, tapping the side of his nose.

Susan nodded. Reputations and good order were more easily protected if a Nelsonian eye was turned to any high jinx. It had been the way of the services for hundreds of years.

'Congratulations on your promotion, Susan,' said Maureen, 'it's well deserved. I was just saying to Brian we ought to have you over to dinner one evening soon. I'll make arrangements.'

'Ah, yes, thank you. That'll be very nice.' She ignored the startled look on Group Captain Ogilvie's face – the invitation was obviously news to him – and held back a smile.

After they left Sarah came across and indicated they were leaving. Susan slipped back to her room and took out a half empty bottle of gin from her underwear drawer where she kept it hidden. Drinking outside the mess was strictly forbidden but just occasionally she enjoyed a quiet nightcap, especially after a rough operation.

The room the girls were meeting in was at the end of the corridor. It was a corner room and the biggest in the block. Fitting, as the occupant, Squadron Officer Janet Shotley, was the senior WAAF officer on the station and the longest serving. The girls held her in a mixture of awe and affection in her section, the Operations Plot, which she ran with a rod of iron.

'Ah, replenishments,' a voice greeted Susan.

Drinks were passed round and the eight women settled down to swapping gossip and talking about their families, husbands and boyfriends. As was often the case in wartime, sometimes the line between the two became a little blurred.

'I hear you're being invited to Maureen's for dinner,' said Janet.

Susan looked at her in surprise. 'How on earth did you know?'

Janet laughed. She was a vivacious bottle blonde in her late thir-ties, married, with two sons in public school and a husband who was a civil servant in Whitehall. 'I knew she would, as soon as she found out about your family.'

'What on earth do you mean?'

'When she found out how well connected you are, I knew she'd ask. She'll butter up to anybody to further Brian's career.'

'It's no good buttering me up, I'll do her no good.'

Janet laughed again. 'It doesn't work like that. She'll drop into letters, phone calls and conversations that Sir David Griffiths' daughter has been at her house for dinner. And how she looks after you and is a mother confessor etcetera, etcetera. I've heard it all before.'

Susan looked at Janet askance. 'You're joking.'

Janet shook her head. 'No, I'm not. But it's harmless. Let her have her fun. It may help to make Brian a flag officer and if it does, good luck to him. He deserves it.'

'Hear, hear,' said one of the others. 'A toast. To Brian.'

They all joined in, the first toast of many that evening. When Susan came to leave she was feeling a little the worse for wear and decided to step outside for a breath of fresh air.

It was pitch dark, the night overcast. When she heard a sound behind her she turned to look, thinking it was one of the others.

'Who's there?'

'Who do you think, you bitch?'

42

BACK IN HER room Susan stood in front of the mirror and laughed until she felt the tears running down her cheeks. Hysteria was bubbling just under the surface and she knew it. Poor pathetic Charles Albright. Too drunk to be able to manage it. Too incapacitated to carry out the rape he had planned. She sat down wearily on the edge of her bed and put her head in her hands and laughter turned to tears. She may have drunk too much but nothing like the quantities Albright must have had. She also possessed the notoriously hard head of the Griffiths clan. Thank God.

When he'd reached for her all she had needed to do was knee him in the groin. He had collapsed like a ton of bricks. She'd left him crying. Crying, for God's sake. How pathetic was that? Her hands began to shake as reaction set in. If he'd been sober it might have been a different story. If he'd been sober, she corrected herself, it probably wouldn't have happened in the first place.

What the hell should she do about it? If she reported it his enmity would deepen and she'd have to spend all her time watching out for him. Besides, nobody would believe her. He'd deny it outright; ask why he would bother? Everybody knew he could have most women when he liked. Rape the high and mighty Susan Griffiths? It sounded ridiculous, even to her. She told herself to forget it.

She didn't hear the news until she was sitting at breakfast the next morning. When she saw the Chaplain talking to a group of fellow officers she realised something was wrong.

Coffee in hand she walked over. 'What's going on?'

'You haven't heard?' asked the Chaplain. 'Charles Albright hanged himself last night.'

Susan was rocked to her core. 'Does any one know why? Did he leave a note or anything?'

'No, nothing. What a tragic waste. Well, I'd better see about his next of kin.'

Susan examined her feelings. As always, she was brutally honest with herself, and discovered she felt no guilt. Nor was she prepared to think the better of Albright just because he was dead.

The body was being sent back to his parents' for burial. It wasn't until the middle of the afternoon that the stories about why he'd hanged himself began to circulate. They were eventually confirmed in the mess that evening. Albright had been diagnosed with syphilis three months back. A letter from a London clinic had been found amongst his papers.

Susan shuddered at the thoughts that were teeming through her mind. To have been raped was one thing, to have been given a foul disease like syphilis didn't bear thinking about. She knew she had had a lucky escape. *Another one*, she thought.

The run up to Christmas brought a series of milk runs that went without a hitch. In keeping with the times, married personnel were allowed home on leave over Christmas, the "weight" being taken by those who were single. Susan had no choice other than to stay. Nobody on the base knew about her son, John Phillipe. She had questioned her reluctance to talk about him and decided it was nobody's business but her own. It was hard enough being away from him without being asked about him all the time. Explanations would be too tedious and so she said nothing.

Christmas Day morning was cold and frosty. On base nothing stirred apart from the guard. Susan put her nose outside the blankets, shivered and settled back for a further doze. Finally she was forced out by the pressure in her bladder. With her dressing gown wrapped tightly around her she made her way to the bathroom. The heating wasn't working and the water was tepid. By the time she put on her great coat, known as a winter warm, to walk across to the mess, she was beginning to feel a little of the Christmas spirit. The mess was warm and strangely welcoming. Saturday, 25 December 1943, the world gripped in war, shortages of just about everything needed to make life tolerable and they're playing Christmas carols on the radio. What a ludicrous world, she thought.

At least an effort had been made with the catering. Real eggs and bacon for a change and a promise of a proper Christmas lunch later. Better than nothing, she supposed. She sat in the mess reading a book, wondering what she would do with the day when she was called to the phone.

'Susan? It's Sarah. I was told to tell you to go outside and look west.'

'What on earth are you on about? Sarah, have you been at the gin already?'

'No, silly, of course not. I'm in ops. They took a radio message and I'm passing it on.'

Intrigued and puzzled, Susan went out into the cold, clear air. A thin layer of snow lay on the ground. It was picturesque without hindering any aircraft from landing or taking off. She shivered inside her great coat and peered into the blue sky. A black dot steadily grew stronger and she soon recognised the twin-engined Griffin that was closing on the field.

'Who is it?' asked Sarah materialising alongside her. 'I had to come and see.'

Susan laughed and waved gaily at the plane. 'My family! It has to be!'

'Your family? Bloody hell, Susan, you're joking.'

'If you knew my father you wouldn't even ask. He's a great subscriber to the Mohammed to the mountain theory of life. Look! Uncle Sion is piloting it.' Other faces appeared at the round cabin windows, still too indistinct for Susan to make out.

The plane landed and taxied off the runway. Susan and Sarah hurried across the hard ground towards it, the snow crunching underfoot. The main cabin door opened and a small body appeared, waving excitedly. Susan felt the tears well up as she hurried to greet her darling boy.

'Who's that?' Sarah asked, trying to stay up with her.

'My son.'

Sarah looked at Susan in total astonishment. 'Your son? I didn't know . . .'

'It's a long story. John Phillipe, darling, what a wonderful surprise. Connie, Dad! This is so . . . so . . .' Susan gave free rein to the tears she had been holding back.

She lifted John Phillipe into her arms and showered him with kisses while her father gave her a hug. 'Merry Christmas, sweetheart.'

'Dad, what on earth are you doing here?'

'Come to spend Christmas with my favourite girl. We were at your uncle Sion's last night debating how to spend the day and I said it was a great pity you weren't there and Madelaine made the suggestion that we come here.'

'Madelaine! Thank you so much.'

'It's my pleasure, my dear. We've brought the whole tribe.'

From the plane they disembarked one by one – Mike, Betty and Myfanwy, Sion, Kirsty, even Paul and Louise, then Connie and finally Richard, now only a month shy of his nineteenth birthday.

'Hi, sis.'

'Richard!' Susan clapped her hands in joy.

Susan introduced them to Sarah and as they walked back towards the mess she said, 'I don't know what we're going to do about food.'

Her father laughed. 'All arranged. I spoke to Brian Ogilvie first thing this morning. We have provisions aplenty. Look.'

Large wicker baskets were being lifted down out of the hold.

'We brought our dinner with us,' David explained.

Maureen and Brian Ogilvie met them at the door of the mess. Further introductions were made and Maureen, Madelaine and Betty went off to speak to the kitchen staff. The catering officer had been warned and though he hadn't liked it, he was prepared to go along with the arrangements. Any bad feeling amongst the remainder of the ten officers still on station was quickly dispelled when they learnt there was enough food for them all and that the bar would be complimentary all day. Ogilvie and David had agreed the arrangements.

John Phillipe was a little shy at first but the other officers soon put him at his ease. A Christmas tree had been erected in the mess and lit with fairy lights, the bright splashes of colour a welcome respite in the drab surroundings of an RAF officers' mess.

They weren't sure if it was a late lunch or an early dinner, but the meal was very tasty given the restrictions the cooks had to work under. Fish soup supplied by the base, enough goose to go around – cooked in Wales and reheated in a sauce – and Christmas pudding to finish. Wine and port were supplied by Sion, courtesy, he said, of his cellar, now sorely depleted.

As always the talk was about the war. No matter how people tried to avoid the subject, it inevitably monopolised any gathering.

'Sir David, what do you think of Ernest Bevin's proposal to send one out of every ten men between the age of eighteen and twenty-five who have been called up down the coal mines?' Ogilvie asked.

David shrugged. 'So many miners volunteered for the services to get away from the mines that sending unskilled men down them could lead to trouble. I know the miners' leaders aren't happy about it.'

'What about the notion that, as it will be done by ballot, we'll have all classes mixing together? According to the government it'll be good for democracy.'

'It's a good thought, Brian, but I doubt it somehow. Attitudes are ingrained. Bevin Boys, as they are dubbed, could find an unfriendly welcome in the valleys. I hope I'm wrong.'

'David,' said Mike, 'what about Ike being the Supreme Allied Commander for the invasion?'

'Well, he did a good job in North Africa last year. And considering that was the first time he'd ever heard a shot fired in anger or held a field command I guess he'll be all right. Monty will be his field commander and he knows his stuff.'

'He strikes me as being too cocksure,' said Sion.

'I hope that's just his manner,' said David.

'Air Chief Marshal Sir Arthur Tedder will be Ike's deputy,' said Ogilvie. 'That's the army and RAF covered. What about the navy?'

David shook his head. 'They have only one task and that's to get the army onto mainland Europe. Once that's done they'll be out of it. They'll have the task of keeping the supply chain open, mainly across the Atlantic, and so it's not appropriate for the navy to be involved with the High Command.'

'Dad, that seems unfair,' protested Richard. 'The navy does its bit.'

'Oh, more than that, son. We owe our freedom to the RN and merchant navy. Without them we'd have been starved into submission long ago. No, all I'm saying is it's not appropriate for invading Europe. They'll still have plenty to do. Look at the Pacific and what's happening there.'

The conversation turned to that other sphere of war and its implications for the world. Then it came back to Europe and a pall fell across the company when Betty asked, 'What's this I hear about gas ovens? Is it true? Or is it government propaganda?'

David nodded sombrely, all eyes on him. 'It's true and horrific. Jews and other so-called *Untermenschen* are being exterminated at a rate too horrendous to contemplate.' With those words the laughter went out of the gathering.

'But why is it being allowed to happen?' Betty persisted.

'I've no idea. Who can understand the mind-set of the Nazis?' David said. 'They are committing vast resources of men and material to murdering innocent men, women and children. On one scale it is ludicrous folly, on another it's a blasphemous obscenity.'

'Is there nothing to be done?' Paul asked, gazing myopically through his thick glasses.

'Short of winning the war, no,' came the sober reply.

After the Loyal Toast the company broke up into smaller groups, with Susan going to play with John Phillipe for the time they had left together.

In the meantime Brian Ogilvie, David, Sion and Mike sat in a corner talking about the implications for Britain *after* the war.

'I haven't been able to think that far ahead,' said Ogilvie.

'Most people haven't,' said David, 'but we do discuss it. It's going to be a very different world. With America no longer isolationist I suspect it will become the dominant world power, along with Russia.'

'What about us?' Sion asked.

'We'll fade into history,' said his brother with a sigh. 'The Empire will break up and all its countries will be given full independence. Those that want it anyway. No, it will be a very different world. I doubt we will be boasting that the sun never sets on the British Empire for much longer. Mark my words. Drink, Sion?'

'Not for me. I still have to pilot us back to Wales.'

'You can have beds for the night, if you wish,' offered Ogilvie.

'That's very kind of you but we'd better not. Your staff have enough to do as it is.' If David saw the relief in the other man's eyes he chose to ignore it. He was aware that they had imposed upon the base long enough and anything else would be an abuse.

The time came for the party to break up. Farewells were tearful, though luckily John Phillipe was too sleepy to take much notice. Susan watched as the plane headed west, into the dark, eventually visible only because the stars flickered behind it. Then it disappeared.

The next morning brought great rejoicing in the mess. A wireless announcement confirmed that the great German battleship *Scharnhorst* had been sunk, after an attack on an Allied convoy heading for Russia had gone badly wrong.

Signals from Admiralty and the RAF pieced together the picture of what had occurred. The *Scharnhorst* had put to sea late on Christmas day with instructions to attack a 22 ship convoy, JW55B, headed for Russia. The weather was bad, with southerly gales force 8–9 and a sea state 6–7. The six escorting German destroyers couldn't cope with the bad weather and Admiral Bey on the *Scharnhorst* ordered them back to base. At that time of the year, between Bear Island and North Cape there was only an hour of daylight suitable for gunfire, the Arctic twilight supplying the merest paling of the horizon from mid-morning to mid-afternoon.

Thanks to the top-secret Ultra decrypts Admiral Fraser was fully aware of what was happening with the battleship and deployed his forces accordingly. The *Scharnhorst* was spotted by a cruiser squadron and was hit once by a shell from HMS *Norfolk* before the German battleship turned tail and ran, out-distancing the RN with a speed advantage of 6 knots.

Then, with the British no longer in sight, Bey turned north again to go after the convoy. He ran slap into the cruisers, which engaged him at a range of 11,000 yards. The *Scharnhorst* turned south again, straight into the trap laid by Admiral Fraser. The *Duke of York* attacked the German ship with 14-inch shells, scoring thirteen direct hits. Yet still the battleship fought on. At 18.30 the *Scharnhorst* stopped returning fire, yet was still able to float and steam. At last the Allied destroyers caught up with the battleship and opened fire with their torpedoes. HMS *Scorpion* and the Norwegian destroyer *Stord* both scored hits. Twelve torpedoes were fired, of which three hit home. The *Scharnhorst's* speed was down to five knots and she became a sitting duck. Torpedoes, 8-inch and 6-inch salvoes from the cruisers and 14-inch salvoes from the *Duke of York*, struck home. More torpedoes struck and finally the great ship sank. Of the two thousand crew only thirty-six were plucked from the icy sea.

The mess rejoiced at the victory, but were greatly saddened by the waste of life. The same dichotomy of thought and feeling was felt across Europe.

On the last day of the year Susan was again in action. This time she was flying to northern Italy. It meant a long round trip via Gibraltar and Sicily to drop almost three tons of equipment and two agents near La Spezia, the large seaport on the north-western coast.

Although Italy was now on the side of the Allies there was still a large and strong concentration of Germans troops in the Alpine regions. Harassment by resistance fighters, overseen by SOE, meant pinning down thousands of tough German soldiers who were desperately trying to stop the Allies reaching Austria and Germany and extracting their revenge for the past four-and-a-half years. A dozen men, fighting with hit-and-run tactics, could keep whole garrisons busy.

The order to shoot and kill all Resistance and SOE operatives had been issued months earlier. It was now being applied in earnest, as the wounded animal that was the German army fought with a ferocity and viciousness never seen before.

'A new barbarity,' said Winston Churchill, in a radio broadcast, 'has opened across Europe. But it will do the German people no good. We will prevail as surely as good *must* prevail over evil. It is the only hope for mankind.' Sarah and Susan sat, nodding in agreement as the PM continued in similar vein.

'When will the invasion come, do you think?' Sarah asked Susan.

Susan shrugged. 'Your guess is as good as mine but it's all we're talking about. Soon, I hope.'

'I hate this war. I hate what it's done and what it's doing. I hate everything about it. I just want to go back to normality and live an ordinary and boring, yes *boring*, life.'

Susan smiled. 'I know what you mean, Sarah and I agree. I've had enough. I just want to go home and do ordinary things.' She stood up. 'But it won't be today. I need to go.'

'Have a good flight.'

Take-off was smooth and easy. P for Peter settled at 14,000ft and droned south. No enemy activity was reported anywhere that afternoon and they were looking forward to an incident free flight. The four engines were set to maximum range, with just enough fuel to reach their destination. They were over the Bay of Biscay when they'd passed the point of no return.

At last they were setting down on to the short Gibraltarian runway, Susan hitting the brakes, practically standing on them to stop the plane before they ran out of concrete. They came to rest with only yards to spare.

It was midnight and they arrived at the mess in HMS *Rook* to find 1944 was being welcomed in with a raucous party. Susan was in no mood to join in and went to her bed. They would be departing mid-morning for Sicily.

Again the flight went smoothly. The Mediterranean was now firmly under the control of the Allies and no German planes or ships were spotted. In Sicily instructions were waiting for them; the mission was to go ahead as planned.

They needed to be over the drop zone at 02.00, when there would be a full moon to light their way. Cloudless skies had turned overcast and the forecast was for snow in the region of the drop. They flew the length of Italy, the land to starboard, the Adriatic to port. Radio contact was made at the drop, passwords exchanged and the equipment and agents parachuted down.

The Halifax didn't carry enough fuel to return to Sicily. They were scheduled to land at a small airfield on the east coast of Italy, south of Rimini, where the Germans had dug in. The area had recently been liberated by the British army who, with the Americans, were racing up the spine of Italy. The crew landed in the middle of a snowstorm, with winds howling from the north, bringing bitterly cold weather.

Wearing foul-weather clothing, their hoods pulled up against the elements, the five of them collected their bags and followed an American sergeant to a small hut. Inside a group of officers were standing around a table looking at a large-scale map of the area.

'Here's the crew now, sir,' said one of the officers seeing them enter.

'Who's the pilot?' a pugnacious looking American colonel asked, the ubiquitous half-smoked cigar clamped in one side of his mouth.

'I am,' said Susan, pushing her hood clear and shaking her hair out. It was plastered to her head after being encased in her flying helmet and she pushed a hand through it, lifting it away from her face.

The men looked at her in surprise. 'You're a Goddam dame,' said the colonel.

Seeing the effect she'd had on the men Susan did her best to stifle a grin. 'I was the last time I looked. And congratulations by the way.' She didn't expand but let her words hang in the air. She got the response she expected.

'For what?'

'Still recognising a member of the opposite sex, Colonel, in spite of the long period you've undoubtedly had without female company.'

'Sassy, eh? Do you fly as good as you talk?'

Before she could answer, Sandy said, 'Better. She's one of the best pilots in SOE.'

'That so? Good. Then I've a little job for you.'

419

Susan was immediately on her guard. 'Sorry, Colonel, I don't come under your command. My orders are to re-fuel and return to Sicily. And then back to Blighty.'

'Yep, I know. Only I'm changing your orders. And as I'm in command around here you'll do as I tell you. Savvy?' The colonel took his cigar from his mouth, looked at the end in some surprise as though it being unlit was something new and reached into a pocket for a Zippo lighter.

Susan looked at the American through narrowed eyes. She thought about protesting but figured rightly it wouldn't get her anywhere. 'What's the job?'

'Good girl. I like a woman who gives in quickly.'

'Don't patronise me, Colonel.' Susan spoke with vehemence. 'I don't like it and I won't accept it. You explain what you want done and I'll tell you if we can help. If we can, all well and good. If we can't, then tough. I'm out of here and I'll report you to whoever it takes to get you reprimanded.'

'I do believe you might just mean that.'

'You'd better believe it, Colonel,' said Fish. 'Hen here takes no prisoners.'

'Hen?' The colonel smiled at the nickname. 'Appropriate, I'm sure.'

Just then an explosion came from outside, followed immediately by a second.

'That's the problem,' said a British major. 'There's a contingent of Germans holed up about ten miles north of here. They're well armed and we can't winkle them out.'

'Why not send in a plane or two and sort them?' Scabby asked.

'There aren't any,' said the Colonel. 'At least, none for this little job. They're too busy north and west of here. This is a mopping up exercise. One of hundreds that have been going on since we landed in this God-forsaken country. And to think my ancestors came from these parts.' He paused and then said, 'Look, I'll level with you. I have to go in and get these Germans. We've tried three times and lost a lot of good men trying. I don't want to lose any more. I asked for air support and was told there was none. Then we heard you were coming and it seemed like an answer to a prayer. Will you help?'

Susan nodded. 'Of course. All you had to do was ask. After all, the last time I looked, we were on the same side. So what's the plan?'

'Come look at this map.'

The five officers moved and gave Susan and Fish space around the table. The major pointed with his finger. 'This is a long, wooded valley. It ends here. We're here, about five miles down where the plain opens out. The Germans control this point, this one and this one over here. They have Howitzers, heavy machine guns and mortars.'

'How many are there?' Susan asked.

'We figure,' said the Colonel, chewing on his cigar, 'about thirty to thirty-five in each group. If we go in again we'll lose a lot of men and I don't want that. I'd like to get this little bitty war over and get me and my boys back to St Louis. Or at least as many as I can keep alive.'

'You boys are from St Louis?'

'Born and raised. Why, you know it?'

Susan nodded. 'I was born there.'

It was the best thing she could have said. The atmosphere lightened even more as they laid plans for the attack. The concern that they carried no bombs and little armament was soon over-ridden by the colonel.

'We've got a platoon of Pioneers with us. Know what they are?'

'Certainly. Engineers and the like. They build roads and runways,' said Susan.

'Precisely. They made the one you landed on. They've got some stuff we can use.'

The only limiting criterion was the weather. It needed to stop snowing. Instead the wind dropped and the snow fell steadily for the next three days, cutting them off, isolating them from the rest of the war, forcing them to rest. Susan champed at the bit, eager to get the attack over with and return to England. Her four crewmen took it in their stride and relaxed, as far as they could. They learned to play poker, Susan learned patience. The crew were the better students.

43

THE ATTACK WAS scheduled for the afternoon of the fourth day. By then the snow had stopped and the wind had changed to the south bringing with it warm air from Africa. The thick, white covering was already turning to slush and melting. As plans were finalised, the runway was cleared.

'You know what you're doing?' the colonel asked for the third time that morning.

'Trust me, I know precisely what I'm about.'

'Sorry, force of habit. I've already lost a lot of good men and I don't want to lose any more.'

'You attitude does you credit, colonel.'

He nodded acceptance of the compliment. 'I've been asking about you, amongst your crew. They like you a lot, Susan. Told me about you.'

'You listen to too much gossip. And you shouldn't believe half of what you hear.'

'Half will do me. Well, good luck. We're moving out. Do your thing and then you can high-tail it out of here to Sicily.'

'Good luck, colonel. We'll do our best.'

The hour dragged but at last it was time to go. Checks were completed, the engines started and then P for Peter was taxiing for take-off. Once in the air Susan headed up the valley, the parachute door open, Scabby and Fish standing by.

'I see them. Tally-ho,' Susan announced to the others. 'Any second now.'

The home-made-bombs of dynamite surrounded by lumps of heavy metal were pushed out once the fuses were lit – three to each bomb. The troops on the ground were firing at the plane with small arms, a hindrance rather than a serious threat. A lucky shot could hit the plane but the chances of it doing any real damage were remote.

Over each of the three targets they dropped four make-shift bombs. They couldn't see the effect the explosives were having but the Pioneers had done their job well. The dynamite caused huge blasts, sending shredded metal through the bodies of the German troops, killing and maiming indiscriminately. With their attention on the plane the Germans were unable to defend themselves against the Allied soldiers who were now advancing. Soon each target was over-run. Dog helped by hosing down the German positions from the air. At the final tally one hundred and sixteen Germans were killed, eight wounded and seven made prisoners of war. On the Allied side three were killed and ten wounded, none seriously.

P for Peter's arrival back in Sicily was considered miraculous. The plane and crew had been posted missing, presumed POWs or killed. Signals were immediately sent to England, correcting the error. Luckily next-of-kin had not yet been informed due to the pressure of work at the airfield.

Not even SOE had known and so David had been spared the thought that his only daughter had been lost.

In Sicily there was no hold up. The crew managed a few hours sleep while the plane was checked and refuelled and then they departed for Gibraltar. Landing was a repetition of the journey out, the plane stopping at the very end of the runway. They lay over for twenty-four hours as they were expecting passengers. When they finally arrived and Peter took off, it was three hours later than planned. Onboard were senior officers from five different armies – British, American, French, Dutch and Canadian.

Once past the southern tip of Portugal Susan turned to starboard and headed in a straight line for the Scilly Isles. It was a long, boring trip, thankfully uneventful, but finally, in the gathering dusk, they could make out the islands, with Cornwall a thin line to the north-east. The plane had been battling headwinds all the way and Scabby announced they hadn't enough fuel to make base. They'd have to set down somewhere in Devon or Cornwall. Susan checked her gauges and distances to go with her navigator.

Smiling, she announced, 'We'll land at St Athan.'

After landing, totally exhausted, she taxied the Halifax to dispersal. The officers she'd flown in were insisting she take them on to Tempsford as soon as refuelling was completed. She refused point blank.

'I'm exhausted,' she told them simply. 'I intend getting some sleep and leaving in the morning. You don't like it, report me. Quite frankly, I couldn't give a damn.'

She walked away across the airfield, oblivious to the indignant threats. She didn't bother knocking but walked into Kirsty's kitchen to be met with a joyous yell and a hug from her uncle and aunt.

'You'll stay here overnight?' Kirsty asked.

Susan nodded.

Her cousin, Louise, entered the kitchen to see what the noise was about and hugged Susan warmly. 'I'm was about to leave for the hospital but I can stay for another hour. Are you going to see John Phillipe?'

'I had thought about it but it's too late and he'll be in bed. And I have to leave first thing in the morning so even if I did see him it would only be for a few minutes. That would just upset him and me so I think it would be better not to go over there.'

'Probably wisest,' said Sion. 'When was the last time you spoke to your dad?'

'Over a week ago.'

'Then you haven't heard about your brother?' Louise asked.

'Richard? Why? What's he done?'

'Only gone and joined up,' said Kirsty.

'Joined what? The RAF? Army?' She was anxious for Richard, but somehow not surprised.

'He's joined the Royal Navy,' said Sion.

'The RN! Good grief!' Susan made it sound as though he'd committed a sin. 'When did this happen?'

'Last week,' Kirsty replied. 'He and a friend went into a recruiting office and signed up. He's now in *Raleigh*, I think it's called.'

'*Raleigh*! You mean he hasn't gone in as an officer?'

'No,' said Sion, 'a boy seaman. Four months training and he joins his first ship as an ordinary seaman.'

'What did Madelaine say about it all?'

'She was livid. She wanted David to use his influence to get him discharged and sent home. But, surprisingly, he refused.'

'Dad refused? Why?'

'Said he was a big boy now and he should make his own decisions. If he wanted to join the navy on the lower deck then it was up to him. He wasn't going to pull his chestnuts from the fire. Besides which, your dad thinks it might do him a bit of good.'

Susan sat back in her chair in a mild state of shock. 'The idiot! He should have gone to Dartmouth. Done the job properly.'

'The training is too long,' said Sion. 'Richard was afraid the war would be over before he could join a ship.'

Susan nodded. 'He's probably right. Well, good for him. Though he's going to find it tough on the mess decks. His accent will set him apart and then with his background . . .' She shuddered. 'I hope to hell he'll be okay.'

Susan went to bed shortly afterwards, too tired to stay up any longer.

Following an early departure, they arrived back in Tempsford in the middle of the morning to a grey, overcast day, threatening rain or snow. She reported to the ops centre to be told that the base commander wanted to see her.

'You sent for me, sir?'

'Sit down, Susan. Two things. I have a complaint here from one of the officers you flew in this morning. He accuses you of insubordination and a few other things besides.'

'Brian, I was too tired to fly any further. It would have been dangerous.'

Ogilvie smiled at her and held the paper in front of him. He deliberately tore it in half and dropped the pieces into a wastepaper bin. 'That's what I told him. The pompous ass.'

'The other thing?'

'We had a signal from some colonel in Italy. He suggests we give you a medal for some job you did out there. Seems you helped to save a lot of lives. What happened?'

Susan told her story, while Ogilvie listened attentively, occasionally asking a pertinent question.

'That more or less confirms what we know. I have another signal here from Bomber Command. Subject to my confirmation you've been recommended for a DFC. It means a bar to your existing medal. I'll approve it straight away.' Ogilvie smiled. 'Congratulations, Susan.'

'Good Lord. I hardly expected this. What about the rest of the crew? Don't they deserve something too?'

'Probably. But you know how these things work. You accept the honour on behalf of your crew. Buy them each a drink or two to celebrate. There is just one thing. There will be a lot of publicity surrounding the award. You'll be expected to give interviews to the press and so on.'

'You're joking!'

'No!' Ogilvie shook his head. 'It's all about boosting morale. A good news story.'

'There are plenty of those.'

'War stories, yes. But what they call human interest stories are few and far between. Now they'll have a real live heroine to write about.'

'I don't want to be the centre of attention. Keep the medal.'

Ogilvie shook his head. 'It's too late, even if I wanted to. You get the medal and the War Office gets the good press. Newsreels and newspapers. Quite a combination.'

Susan looked at Ogilvie aghast. 'You mean, Pathé news and all that?'

Ogilvie nodded and laughed out loud. 'You should see your face. It's a picture. It will probably mean losing you, unfortunately.'

'What do you mean, losing me?'

'Susan, you'll be big news. You'll be invited to special events, meeting the troops, launching ships.'

'No!' Her cry was from the heart. 'I don't want that! Please Brian! I'm serious! I'm not accepting the award.' She pleaded for a solid hour, but to no avail.

When she left Ogilvie's office she was, to say the least, displeased with events. She would have been utterly furious if she'd heard the conversation that took place between Brian Ogilvie and her father a short while later.

'It worked. She'll do it because she has no choice.'

'Thanks, Brian. I owe you and I won't let you down. Now, regarding your promotion – that is what you want?'

'Not for myself, but for Maureen. So the answer is, yes.'

'Leave it with me. Will Easter suit you?'

'Sir David, are you serious? Can you do that?'

'Let's just say I'm owed a great number of favours. I can pull strings to a certain extent. I have, not to put too fine a point on it, the ear of the PM. So yes, I can get you promoted to flag rank. What I cannot do is guarantee the job you'll get. Although I'll do my best to ensure it's not a dead-end one. Will that do you?'

'Thank you, sir. I'm glad, by the way, that Susan will be out of it. She's done more than her fair share.'

'Yes, she has. Thanks again, Brian. I'll see you one of these days.'

David Griffiths hung up the receiver and put his hands behind his head and leaned back in his chair. With luck his child would now survive the war. She could spend the next few months "meeting and greeting". A promotion to Deputy Commander would also help. He'd already seen to that. There was no point having influence unless it was used. Now all he had to do was pull strings on behalf of Richard. The bloody fool. If only he'd waited or gone in as an officer.

Deep down another part of him was proud of his son. Richard was determined to do his part and so that was precisely what he would do, come hell or high water. He would contact Peter Carbonne and see what he had to suggest. Now a full Admiral, maybe Carbonne could have Richard assigned to his staff, or something. Whatever he did, it would have to be done in total secrecy. Not even Madelaine could know what he was up to, just in case either Susan or Richard inadvertently found out. They would never forgive him. So *nobody* would ever know. That was the true meaning of power, of course. And a privilege not to be abused.

Susan bought her crew as many drinks as they could consume and drank far too much herself. The bash was held at the local pub where officers and other ranks were free to mingle with each other. It came as a shock to learn that she was to be re-assigned after the medal was awarded in ten days time. An even greater shock was her promotion, although the crew of P for Peter all rejoiced in it.

Slurring in a sweet but very drunken fashion, Scabby said, 'You're the best pilot I've ever flown with, Hen, and that's the truth.' He waved an inebriated hand about him, 'And the others all think the same.'

'Thanks, Scabby, that's very kind of you.' Susan hiccuped and put her hand over her mouth. 'I think I've drunk too much.'

'Nonsense,' said Sandy, swaying on his feet, 'I'll get you another one.'

'Better not.'

'No flying for thirty-six hours,' said Fish, 'so another is definitely called for. Barman! Barman! Same again, please.' With drinks in their hands, Fish chimed in. 'Hen, we're going to miss you. I'm the first to say that I wasn't happy about flying with a woman pilot but you proved us all wrong. Do you know where you're going?'

Susan shook her head, she didn't want to leave them. They were wonderful. The salt of the earth. She'd miss them dreadfully. Oh, God . . . She was becoming maudlin and at any moment would burst into tears, which would never do. With an effort she got her emotions under control and ordered yet another round of drinks. How she got to her bed she would probably never know.

The next three operations were milk runs – one to France, a second to Norway and a third to Holland. And suddenly it was over.

Her departure was subdued. They'd already said everything there was to say nearly two weeks earlier in the pub. Quick hugs, bright eyes all around and she was off in her car, headed for London and the flat.

This time when she went to Buckingham Palace it was to a private audience with the King. Private that was, if you ignored the newspaper reporters and photographers and the Pathé News cameras. Much to her surprise, Susan found she was enjoying the attention. But after nearly an hour of posing, answering questions and being asked to repeat the same actions time and again she became fed up with it. The King had only stayed for the first few minutes and when he had left Susan heard the sigh of relief he had given. Now she knew how he felt.

Her father appeared from nowhere to spirit her away. David brought the proceedings to a halt, placated those who wanted more of her story and yet more pictures and got her away via a side entrance.

'If I'd known it would be as bad as that I wouldn't have agreed,' Susan said with a sigh, settling back in the car.

David smiled at her. 'That's the worst. Only the BBC interview to go.'

'What BBC interview?' She sat up with a jerk.

'We're on our way there now. Gilbert Harding is going to interview you. It'll be live. The broadcast is for six o'clock. So we've plenty of time.'

'Damn, Dad, I don't want to!'

'Too bad, because it's all arranged. Afterwards we'll go to the Ritz for dinner. Madelaine will join us with a few friends.'

The interview was low key and pleasant. The questioning was innocuous and Susan fended each one with wit and charm. Suddenly it was over and she was saying goodnight to Harding and goodnight to those who were listening. Minutes later she was in the car and heading for the hotel.

A table had been set for them in one corner. She was startled to find herself seated next to Winston Churchill but even more startled by the man who was seated opposite her. Robert Gill.

44

ALMOST OF THEIR own volition it seemed her eyes kept locking with his. Each time he appeared to sense her annoyance and smile back at her. Damn him! What was he doing here?

She realised that the PM had said something and was waiting for a reply. She dragged her thoughts back from Robert. 'I'm . . . I'm sorry, Prime Minister. What did you say?'

Churchill chuckled, evidently in a good mood. 'I was asking if you had any hobbies. Something which helps you relax and forget about the cares of the day.'

'I enjoy reading but that's about it.'

'You should find some creative outlet, my dear, I highly recommend it. Me, I like to paint. I can forget about the cares of state for just a little as I daub. You should try it someday.'

'Me? Paint?' Susan laughed out loud. 'Oh, no! I have absolutely no talent for it at all. Perhaps I should take up embroidery, what do you think?'

Across the table, Robert Gill almost choked on his dessert.

Churchill smiled indulgently. 'I suggest you find something, my dear, it helps to keep you sane. Griffiths,' he turned to David, 'an excellent dinner. I fear I have to leave as I have another pressing engagement.' Churchill departed with very little fuss.

Dance music started in the ballroom next door and Mike asked her to jitterbug. She acquiesced with a smile. 'What's Robert doing here?' she hissed as soon as they'd left the room.

Mike smiled down at her and patted her hand, which was linked through his arm. 'I dragged him along.'

'Why?'

'Because this nonsense has gone on long enough. You told me you loved him.'

'That conceited, self-centred oaf?'

'Ah, so you do.'

'Mike, don't be absurd. We had a . . . disagreement.'

'I know, he told me all about it.'

'He had no right. It was private, between him and me.'

'To be sure, but when you're as drunk as he was you don't know what you're saying. Only that you speak from the heart. And I'm telling you, Susan, he loves you. So listen to old Mike. Talk to him. Sort it out. Life's too short to be unhappy.'

'Mike, you're an interfering, Irish . . .' she was lost for words.

Mike laughed delightedly. 'I know I am. But I've known you far too long and I love you far too much *not* to interfere. Susan, you're as head-strong and as stiff-necked as he is. God help any children you have.'

'Children?' she spluttered. 'You have us with children and I'm not even talking to him! You are incorrigible.'

The jitterbug ended and was followed by a jive, the latest dance craze. Mike professed it was beyond him and escorted Susan back to their table. Some of the others had gone up to dance and Susan sat by David and Madelaine.

'Any more news on Richard?'

'He won't be leaving basic training for another fourteen weeks,' said her father.

'Thank God!' said Madelaine. 'The little idiot. I'm worried sick. He should have gone to Dartmouth and gone in as an officer.'

David shook his head. 'We should be proud of him. We can only hope and pray he survives and once this mess is over he can either become an officer or try something else.'

'We should have made him leave,' said Madelaine. 'I pleaded with you to use your influence.'

David shook his head. 'It wasn't on, darling. Richard told me that if I did he would never speak to us again.'

'At least he would have been alive.' There was no mistaking the bitterness in Madelaine's voice.

David sighed. 'But we'd still have lost him forever. This way, there's a chance we get him back.'

Her father and Madelaine were such a close couple that it was unusual to hear them argue. Susan was worried about Richard. How much more difficult it must be for them! As she turned away to afford them a little privacy she felt a hand on her shoulder.

'Will you dance?'

She found herself saying, 'Yes'. Before she'd thought through a proper, cutting reply, it was too late and in something of a daze she followed Robert across the room. A dozen replies leapt to mind, each funnier and more devastating than the one before but then she was in his arms and they were waltzing around the grand ballroom and it felt so damned wonderful!

Just looking into his deep brown eyes brought a flutter to her mid-section and she sighed.

'Something wrong?'

Susan shook her head and smiled at him. 'Nothing. Nothing at all.'

Catching her mood, he held her a little closer. Susan allowed herself to be held, as they whirled and turned to a quickstep. They continued dancing for several minutes, not talking. One word described how she felt. Whole.

Taking her by the hand, Robert led Susan outside to the terrace. In a secluded corner he pulled her into his arms. 'I've missed you. Can you ever forgive me?'

With those words the emptiness she had been feeling was banished. Before she could say a word he murmured, 'Never leave me again.'

'I won't, darling. I won't!' she promised and returned his kiss.

After several moments they stood, just holding each other and began to talk, to catch up. It rapidly became clear that Gill knew a good deal about the operations she had been on.

'Mike and your father always wanted to know where you were. It became a habit that one of us would check up on the safe return of the plane and tell the others. And if you were on a mission your father always stayed in the office.' Gill laughed. 'We all did. We put up camp beds. The Ops Controller at Tempsford had strict instructions to phone us as soon as you'd landed safely.'

Susan smiled. 'It's as if I had three fairy godfathers watching over me.'

Gill laughed. 'Something like that. Though there was nothing we could have done except pray. Thank God it's over. At least for now. I heard you on the wireless being interviewed. You were very good, Susan. Very natural. I suspect there'll be a few more interviews like that.'

'God, I hope not. I was a bag of nerves.'

Silence fell between them as they both wondered how to approach the subject that had spilt them apart in the first place.

'Robert, I . . .'

'Susan, I . . .'

'You first,' said Susan.

'You know I love you. But I haven't changed my mind about the money.'

Sadly Susan nodded. 'Ditto for me. I refuse to live in a small house. I've been there and done that and quite frankly I like the life I have. But things are changing, my love. I suspect after this war is over life will be radically different for everybody. There won't be any more deferential maids and butlers prepared to work for a pittance of a wage. But I'll still want a big house and an expensive car.'

'I understand that. And I'll want to continue in my work as a policeman. I've thought about it a lot. Crime won't go away. Ever. So we compromise.'

'Compromise? What a wonderful idea.' She paused. 'Did Mike put you up to this?'

Gill looked a little sheepish. 'He's been bending my ear at every opportunity. Making me see the error of my ways, so to speak.'

Susan laughed out loud. 'That sounds just like Mike. Thank God one of us has some sense.'

Gill leaned forward and kissed the base of her neck.

A cough made them both look up with a start. 'Here you are,' said her father. 'About time you pair made it up. I take it you have?'

They exchanged glances and happy nods.

'Good. Robert here's your forty-eight hour pass. You, young lady, will start a tour of Britain on Tuesday. I have the itinerary in my office. It's all been arranged. I don't expect to see either of you before 08.00. All right? By the way, I've organised rooms for you here. Mike will send Robert's bag over from the office. Now I must get Madelaine home – goodnight.'

They watched the tall, upright figure walk away. 'He never ceases to amaze me,' said Gill.

'He's *my* father and he amazes me. Are you tired?'

'No. But I still think it's time for bed, don't you?'

On the evening of the second day there was an air raid, with the docks taking another pasting, although the Germans were far from getting it all their own way. Bomber after bomber was shot down, the attrition rate more than the Germans could sustain. Susan and

Gill sat it out in the underground at Hyde Park, wrapped in blankets, waiting for the all clear. When it finally came they joined an orderly line and followed the hundreds of others who had taken shelter. Fires were raging away to the east and a heavy pall of smoke hung over the docks.

They were walking back towards the hotel when Gill suddenly said, 'Will you marry me?'

'Yes.'

They both stopped walking and looked at each other in amazement.

'You did just ask me to marry you, didn't you?'

Gill nodded. 'And you did say yes?'

'I did.'

He swept her up into his arms and kissed her. 'I haven't even got a ring. I'll buy one tomorrow.'

'I'll come with you. I want a simple one. Nothing fancy.'

'Just as well on my salary.'

'Robert . . .'

'Only joking. Honest. Come on, we'd better see if we can get a bottle of bubbly out of the hotel.'

'That,' said Susan, with a determined look in her eye, 'will not be difficult.'

They arrived at the offices of SOE late. Susan had telephoned her father to give him the good news. He made it clear that he was delighted.

In David's office, after congratulations and handshakes, Gill turned to go to his desk. 'I might be marrying the boss's daughter, but I've still got two circuits to run.'

'When will I see you?' Susan asked.

'Sir?' Gill asked David.

'It'll be at least a week, Susan. I have your itinerary here. You're travelling Britain. There'll be interviews with local newspapers. A new factory to open in Leeds. Two hospitals you're to visit. Plus a burns unit for downed flyers. It's all here in this file. You're going to be busy.'

'Is this really necessary, Dad?'

'Susan, don't underestimate the good you'll do or the contribution you'll be making. The country is tired. We're all sick to death of this blasted war. You, my girl, are a real live heroine to millions of people.

An inspiration. The King and Queen have a tremendous effect on morale. After they visit a place there is a lightening of mood. You have that ability too. The ability to be pleasant at all times, smile and say encouraging things to the people you meet.'

Susan nodded. 'I suppose so.'

'And don't forget, this war won't last forever. What are you going to do with your life once it's over?'

Susan recognised the glint in her father's eye. 'What are you getting at, Dad? I'm going to marry Robert. Be a wife and mother.'

'That won't be enough for you, dearest daughter. I know you too well. You're young, vital, someone people respect – and you're passionate, Susan. And passion gets votes.' He smiled as comprehension dawned in Susan's eyes. 'I see the penny's dropped at last. Robert wishes to rejoin the police so he can go to Scotland Yard. You could, if you wish, get a safe seat and enter the House. Just think about it.'

'Winnie knows all this, doesn't he?'

For a few seconds her father looked at her before nodding. 'It was his idea. The war is moving inexorably to a close. We can't say when the end will come but it will be within a year or two. Already plans are being forged for the future. One thing we are sure of, Susan, the world will be changed forever. The Empire will be gone. A Commonwealth will take its place, with our King and Queen at its head. Russia will become a global power and America will flex its muscles worldwide. Susan think about it. But we need your answer soon. And if it's yes, we will need to make plans. Trust me, I know what I'm talking about. In the meantime, think of this trip of yours as a precursor.'

'To what?'

'Your election campaign.'

The file she had been given was detailed and had been meticulously drawn up. It stated whom she would see, which newspaper reporters she would meet and what was expected of her. She had been assigned a car and a driver. Three days later she arrived in Leeds. So far she had appeared at thirteen different events. Each time she had been made very welcome. Not, she admitted to herself, by large crowds, but enough so that she didn't feel let down. The press were there, interviews were given, and a camera crew from Pathé followed her everywhere.

It was in Leeds that she was first asked the question, 'Susan, do you have any political ambitions?'

She had been thinking of little else since she had left London, yet the question startled her by its astuteness. Then she rallied herself. 'We've a war to win first, before I can think of anything else.' She held up her hand with the single diamond on a gold band and said, 'And a wedding to organise.' That got her a laugh and the subject was changed.

In her hotel room that night she lay in bed and thought more about her situation. Robert and she had discussed the idea *ad nauseum*. He had offered her his total support, convinced that she could represent the people's desires, ambitions and dreams of a better future. But Susan wasn't so sure. She felt things so passionately. Wouldn't her temper, her hot-headedness, get the better of her? Parliament was for reasoned debate, listening to the arguments and making sober decisions as a result. Did she have the patience to do the job? The perseverance? Robert said yes; she wasn't so sure.

In Liverpool the welcome was greater than ever, due to the publicity already garnered. As always she was dressed in her best uniform, her campaign medal ribbons and DFC ribbon gleaming above her left breast. Her new stripes showed she had earned her promotion the hard way. She was due to stay a second day in the city, a Sunday, for a day of rest, before travelling all the way to Glasgow. The phone call came after dinner.

'Miss Griffiths? My name is Edmund Carfax. It'll mean nothing to you but I am the managing director of Harland Shipbuilders.'

'I know the company.'

'The King was due here tomorrow to launch our new destroyer. He was tying it in with other duties, you understand.'

'Yes. I knew he was coming. It was in the papers.'

'Unfortunately he has had to cancel due to a bout of influenza. We were wondering if you would do us the honour, therefore . . .'

Susan still hadn't understood his request and so said, 'I'm afraid I leave tomorrow for Glasgow.'

'Yes, we know. But we can bring the ceremony forward by say two hours.'

'You mean,' she suddenly realised what Carfax was asking of her, 'you want *me* to launch the new ship? Instead of the King? Isn't that . . . I mean . . . Isn't that somewhat presumptuous? I can't take the King's place.'

'Indeed, indeed. But you understand, we must launch and it struck me that you're the person to do it. Otherwise we'll have to ask the mayor's wife and let me say, we'd rather have you.'

'You do me a great honour and of course, I accept. What time and where?'

'The Rolls will pick you up at your hotel at a quarter to eleven. Will that suit you?'

'Yes, of course. I look forward to it.'

She tried to place a call to Robert at SOE but, after half an hour of trying, she gave up. The call couldn't be routed all the way through.

The following morning she was taken to the shipyard where she was met by a huge crowd of dock workers and their families. The launching of a new ship was always a great event, even when the vessel was a lowly destroyer. If the crowds were disappointed it wasn't the King, they didn't show it.

The specially weakened bottle of Champagne was ready. To loud cheers Susan announced, 'I name this ship HMS *Antrim*. God bless her and all those who sail in her.'

The bottle swung against the hull, smashed and set the ship rolling into the water. There were tremendous cheers and naturally Pathé News recorded the event for posterity. By Friday it would be showing in picture houses across the land.

Susan was becoming famous.

45

GLASGOW WAS COLD and wet. She visited the Western Infirmary Hospital and a new factory that made torpedoes. During the tour she learned more about torpedoes than she wanted to know, but she listened intently and asked intelligent questions about range and speed. Such information was secret she was told, but was assured the new weapon was an improvement on the old.

By now she had been away for two weeks. Not only was she missing John-Phillipe and Robert, she was disenchanted with the whole rigmarole. And it still wasn't over. She had yet to visit Newcastle and then Hull before she could return to London.

In Newcastle she visited a school, a hospital and a factory making spare parts for tanks. Each visit was spent chatting to people, smiling for the cameras, waving, being *interested*, which, truth be told, she found no hardship. The human stories often touched her. The hardships faced and stoicism shown by ordinary people amazed her. In spite of the life she had lead, hers had been a sheltered upbringing of wealth and privilege. Yes, she'd seen deprivation and horror in the Spanish Civil War at first hand but . . . somehow seeing it here at home was so much worse. She was seeing her country through the eyes of ordinary people for the first time. The tour had another effect; it helped her to understand Robert's point of view about inherited wealth. With this realisation came a hardening desire. She wanted to help. And the best place to do that, she realised, was in Parliament.

She thought about her father and Churchill. They saw her as a true blue Tory. But ever since university she'd had socialist leanings. How far could conservatism go hand-in-hand with helping people like those she had met on tour?

Hull had been bombed so often it was like visiting a vast building site. The Pathé News of the *Antrim* had been showing all week. As a result her itinerary was changed. She was asked to perform a small ceremony for the rededication of a refitted cruiser, HMS *Cardiff*, which had been in repair in dry dock for over six months following a sea engagement off the Hook of Holland.

When this new footage was shown in cinemas across the land it began, *'Flying Ace Susan Griffiths is the most famous woman in Britain, after our beloved Queen, of course. And here she is . . .'*

She was thankful when she finally arrived back in London, nineteen days after departing. Her reunion with Robert was all she could have wished for. She was so excited by what she had seen and learned, she was desperate to share her thoughts. Robert recognised the change in her and listened avidly as she recounted her adventures. He smiled. He knew this was just the beginning.

'The sheer strength and resilience of the people I met and spoke to . . . it was just incredible. Children with incurable cancers, smiling and joking, comforting their parents, instead of the other way round. Women whose husbands had been killed bringing up four, five, even more children in slums in Liverpool and Glasgow but getting on with their lives. It was a real eye-opener.'

They were lying in bed, in a small, anonymous hotel in Bayswater. Gill had his head propped on his arm and was drawing concentric circles on her stomach.

'Are you listening to me?' She asked, grabbing his hand.

'Of course. I'm just waiting for you to tell me your decision.'

She looked at him in surprise and then smiled. 'Hmm, you do know me rather well, Mister Clever Clogs.'

'It's settled then? You're going up for election after the war?'

'You don't mind?'

'Mind?' He looked at her in amazement. 'Why should I mind?'

'It'll mean long hours in the House. Late night sittings, canvassing to get elected, ward work. It won't be easy.'

'I can't think of anyone better to take on the job, sweetheart. Parliament won't know what's hit it. You'll turn the place on its head.'

'But what about you? What do you really want to do after hostilities are over?'

'Your father has been talking to me, sounding me out. Once this lot is over we'll still need SOE to look after Britain's interests. Some sort of intelligence gathering organisation. He suggests I give it some thought – he'd like me onboard. We'll see. I find it hard to think beyond the next few days and weeks, never mind the end of the war. Christ, we can't be sure we'll survive!'

Susan sighed. 'You're right. But we all need dreams, even at times like these.'

'Especially at times like these. Want to hear about my dreams?' he whispered, his hand moving lower.

Being so well known had distinct disadvantages Susan discovered. After her gruelling tour of Britain the next few days were an anti-climax. She made a number of appearances in and around London but these were called to a sudden halt.

'Why am I stopping now?' she asked her father when they met at the London flat.

'There is such a thing as over-exposure. Right now you're the darling of the people. But they'll soon tire of you. We intend to drip-feed stories to the press, keep you alive in the minds of the people but without boring them. Trust me, I know what I'm doing. Besides, I've got details about your next posting.'

'Why hasn't it come through proper channels?'

David shrugged. 'Because I have some say in the matter.'

'Your influence doesn't extend to the RAF, surely?'

'Not directly. That's not the way to use influence.' He smiled at her confusion. 'You're going to the staff at HMS *Dryad*. I fixed it with Winnie. It's not beyond his power – something as mundane as the posting of an officer.'

'But why would the PM concern himself in my affairs? And where the hell is *Dryad*?'

'Near Southwick, Hampshire. You'll understand when you get there. And as for Winnie he wants you to survive the war and stand for election. You'll get a safe seat, have no fear.'

Behind her father's kind facade was a will of iron. Susan realised he was ruthless in his determination to succeed whilst at the same time looking after the interests of the family. Always, for him, the family came first – right or wrong.

'How's Richard doing?'

Madelaine drew in a deep breath. 'He says he's enjoying the training and looking forward to his first ship.'

'But?' Susan looked at her stepmother with interest. She could tell immediately something was up.

'I got your father to pull a few strings. Richard doesn't know it but he's going to be selected for a signals course. Isn't that right, dear?'

David nodded. 'It's the hardest course in the RN. Only the brightest get selected. Even with today's truncated training it'll be another three months before he joins a ship.'

'Does he know?'

'Not yet. He has to finish basic training first, before he's told where he's going, although any volunteers usually get what they want. Like gunnery or minesweeping, which are shorter specialisation courses.'

'It will be July at the earliest before he's sent to a ship,' said Madelaine, 'and anything can happen before then.'

'He'd be furious if he knew,' said Susan, 'As am I, dad – it feels wrong, you pulling strings. What if I don't want to go to *Dryad*?'

Her father shrugged. 'Your influence doesn't extend quite as far as mine, yet.' He smiled to take the sting out of the words, 'So you'll go where they send you.'

'But I want to fly.'

'And you will. Only not in combat missions. Susan, that's over for you. Accept it. If you want to go back to ferry work that can be arranged. But I suggest you take the staff job for a while. Think about John Phillipe, Susan. There's a limit to the amount a front-line pilot can take. It's standard practice now to rotate pilots from the front-line to training and staff jobs and back again. Your time was up anyway. In your heart you knew it.'

'What about the others in my crew, was their time up? What about Dog and Sandy, Scabby and Fish?' She could tell from her father's face that something was wrong. 'What is it? What's happened to them?'

'I'm sorry, Susan, there's no easy way to tell you. They were shot down over Dieppe two nights ago. A returning Messerschmitt attacked them.'

'Did . . . Did any of them survive?'

Her father shook his head. 'We don't think so. We haven't heard anything to the contrary.'

Tears welled up in Susan's eyes. Gone, just like that. 'Do you know what happened?'

'A little. An air raid had hit Portsmouth. It was over and most of the German planes had returned to France. There were a few stragglers as always. It seems the pilot of P for Peter was too high. The plane was at fifteen hundred feet. They didn't stand a chance.'

'Fifteen hundred feet? The idiot! He should have been down on the deck. What was he doing?'

Her father shook his head. 'Few pilots would or will fly as low as you. To be honest, they don't have your skill or experience. We pick the best but this one had only been flying for eight months. It's not enough. I'm sorry, Susan. I know how much you cared for them.'

If only she'd stayed with the squadron, they'd be alive today. *Or maybe*, a little voice whispered, *you'd be dead too*. She should have stayed with them, kept them safe. It was all her father's doing! He was to blame. Him and his ambition for her. Anger coursed through her and she stood up.

'Those boys are dead and it's your fault,' she said, fury making her voice tremble.

'Susan! Apologise to your father. Of course it wasn't his fault.'

David touched his wife's arm and squeezed gently. 'It's all right. Let her have her say.'

'If I'd have stayed with the squadron they'd be alive. I'd have hit the deck. Flown so low no fighter would have dared come after us.'

'You're right. And you may have been too low and gone into the sea. Or the Messerschmitt pilot might have attacked anyway and damn the consequences. Or the pilot who replaced you could have been a better flyer and flown lower. Whatever "maybes" we want to imagine, it doesn't change the facts. I'm very sorry about what happened to your crew, but not because they were yours. Because we can ill afford to lose men like them. They were damned good.'

'They were better than good, they were the best.' All the fight went out of her and Susan sat back down. Her flash of anger had been not so much at her father but at the whole rotten situation.

'We can't change things, Susan, only keep fighting. A lot more people are going to die before it's over. Some of us may live to see it through, some of us won't.'

He was right of course. 'I know. I'm sorry, Dad. It's just so bloody unfair.'

'I know, sweetheart.' David embraced her tightly, kissing her on the forehead. He cradled her in his arms, swaying gently from side to side as she wept. For the next hour they sat listening as she recounted stories of her crew, alternately laughing and crying. They were surprised by the sound of the doorbell.

'Are you meeting Robert?' Madelaine asked.

'Mmm. We'd meant to go to the theatre. I don't know if I feel up to it.'

'What about the cinema? Sit in the dark and relax.'

Susan shuddered. 'No, thank you, Madelaine. If I see another news-reel of myself I'll scream.'

David ushered Robert into the room.

'Sorry I'm late. I had a problem with the Delta circuit.'

'Solved?' David asked sharply.

'Yes. Crystal problems. It's okay now.'

'Blasted crystals. The sooner we find a better method of fixing a frequency the happier I'll be. Are you off?'

'Yes,' said Gill. 'I've checked and there's no unusual W/T traffic so it looks like it'll be a quiet night. No air raid.'

'Good. Well, goodnight, both of you.'

Susan and Robert left, her father watching their retreating backs.

'They make a handsome couple,' said Madelaine.

'They do. I like Robert. He's intelligent and diligent, a good combi-nation – one that makes things happen.'

Madelaine smiled at her husband. He was, she thought, looking tired. 'Let's pray they have a long and happy marriage.'

'Has Susan mentioned a date? For the wedding?'

'After the summer. That's all she's said.'

'Why so long?'

Madelaine shrugged. 'It's not that far away. Three or four months.'

'In time of war, that's an eternity.'

Susan could hardly concentrate on the review they went to see. Supper in a nearby restaurant was mediocre and they went home to Robert's flat in sombre mood. Mike was away and so they had the place to themselves. Susan was assailed by thoughts of P for Peter. It felt so disloyal to be out enjoying yourself while her friends had lost their lives that way.

She sighed. 'Damn, I hate this war.'

'It can't last much longer, that I'm sure of,' Robert tried to reas-sure her. 'You must know that the whole of Southern England is now sealed off? Nobody and nothing moves in or out without the right pass. This is the build up. Invasion is in June, sometime.'

'Should you be telling me this?'

'I didn't hear it from intelligence sources, I worked it out. And if I can, you can be damned sure the Germans can too. The only thing they won't know is exactly when. My God, what's that noise?'

'Sounds like an engine. It's stopped.' Less than a minute later there was a loud explosion.

'What the hell? I was sure there wouldn't be a raid.'

Gill opened the window and looked out, into the sky. 'I can't see anything. Listen! There's the sound of that engine again.'

Susan was by his side. 'I've never heard one like that before. It's stopped.'

A second explosion occurred about a mile away. It ripped the night apart and sent flames shooting into the air.

'Bloody hell,' said Gill, 'what's going on?'

'I don't know but I don't like it. Have you heard anything about the Germans building a new weapon?'

'Christ, yes. There are always stories but most of them are make believe. Only this time I think it may be true. One of our agents working a circuit near a place called Peenemünde reported a pilot-less rocket, stuffed with explosives, raining down indiscriminately, causing carnage. It looks like he was right.'

The following morning their worst fears were confirmed. The V1, jet-propelled bomb had become a reality. For the second time since 1939 schoolchildren were evacuated into the country for safety. Within days the V1s were coming regularly, killing civilians haphazardly, untargeted, bringing terror with them. When their motors cut out the people of London looked up at the sky and prayed. For many the fear proved too great; a million people were once more on the move, looking for safety.

Susan reported for duty three days later. HMS *Dryad* was a sprawling complex. It centred round a grand old house, which had been turned into the officers' quarters. Allocated a cabin in the women's wing, after dropping her bags she went to report for duty.

She was shown into the office of a Royal Naval Captain, Peter Loram, whose chest full of medal ribbons made it clear he'd been in the thick of the fighting. Loram was silver-haired, tall and slim, with an unlined face making it hard to guess his age. His eyes were a piercing blue, but somehow Susan had the feeling they weren't looking at her but at far horizons. She was to learn later that he'd seen action from the South China Seas, across the Indian Ocean, the Mediterranean and around

Britain. Provided he didn't blot his copybook he was tipped for the top, one day possibly making First Sea Lord.

After a few preliminaries he asked, 'Have you any idea what we're doing here?'

'No, sir.'

'Good. Then I'll tell you. In these rooms we are planning the invasion of Europe. Work has been going on for over two years but from now on every detail of Operation Overlord will be finalised here. Even the name is top secret. Everybody here has been vetted to the highest degree.'

'When will we invade, sir?' She was excited. To be at the heart of the invasion of Europe was more than she could have ever wished for.

'We don't know, not exactly. Late May or early June. Any later and we'll have to call the whole thing off. You can't hold a million men, ships and equipment in readiness forever.'

'I take it the deciding factor will be the weather?'

Loram looked at her in surprise. 'That's very astute of you. Good show.'

Susan smiled in return. 'It's the only factor over which we have no control. What exactly will my job be, sir?'

'We wanted someone with operational experience of flying bombers as well as a pilot who'd flown regularly over France. It came as a surprise to find the best candidate was a woman. But you fit the bill. We also need you to liaise between the RN and RAF. This will be a united services operation. The army has the task of retaking the land, the navy's job is to get them there. The air force has to fly cover and soften up the Germans. It's a huge undertaking. The biggest in the history of warfare.'

'You'll be sharing an office with a First Officer Wren. Her name is Letitia Kitchin and her area of expertise is convoy control. Right now we're bringing in vast amounts of equipment to an area stretching from Falmouth to Dover. We need air support of the convoys and logistic distribution once they get into harbour. Stuff is coming in small coastal vessels into ports that are more used to fishing boats. But it's the only way. You've a lot to learn. I want you up to speed by the end of the week. All right?'

'Yes, sir.'

'Good. That'll be all.' The door opened and a Petty Officer Wren

445

appeared. 'Show First Officer Griffiths to room two zero one, please.'

Letitia Kitchin was short and stocky. She wore her brown, grey-streaked hair tied back in a tight bun and smoked full strength, unfiltered blue-liners. Susan's new colleague had a mouth like a rat-trap and seldom smiled.

Her first words to her new colleague were, 'So you're the famous pilot. Your desk is that one. Do you smoke?'

At Susan's shake of the head she said, 'Good. In that case we'll get on well. Provided you take your issue of fags and give them to me.'

'I don't think so, somehow. Smoking's a filthy habit. If you do smoke in here I'll open a window. You don't mind do you?'

From the look on the First Officer Wren's face it appeared that she did. She wasn't used to anyone talking back to her and it came as a surprise. An unpleasant one.

46

SUSAN SPENT THE next three days reading files and attending briefings. She was utterly astonished at the size and scope of the operation. The files covering the first 24 hours of the Invasion were huge
and their attention to detail mind numbing. Some of the Allies' best
military brains had been working on the plan since May 1943, headed
by COSSAC, Chief of Staff to the Supreme Allied Commander, Lt
Gen Frederick Morgan. The plan had resulted in the production of
hundreds of thousands of documents, which had to be disseminated
through a multi-lingual command structure, a multitude of nationalities and every facet of modern warfare. It explained why tank regiments were lined up on the Winchester by-pass and why landing craft
filled every nook and cranny along the south coast. The logistics
required to feed, clothe and house so many men were staggering. As
she read, the statistics thundered in her brain. She often found herself
shaking her head at what she was reading. As she worked she made
copious notes, querying decisions, often finding the answer further
along.

During this time she sat with the window of the office wide open
due to her colleague's incessant chain-smoking. She had smoked in
her teens and early twenties and like all those who had given it up
was now virulently anti-smoking. The smell in particular appalled
her. She had tried to reason with Kitchin but to no avail. It seemed
the First Officer couldn't function properly without a lit cigarette in
her hand. Susan tried to ignore the problem and concentrate on what
she was reading.

At the end of one memorandum she came across a conclusive date
– the fifth of June! The day of the invasion was less than a month
away!

By the end of her first week she was up to speed on what was

447

happening and had a better understanding of what was expected of her. She worked a fourteen-hour day, as did the rest of the men and women there. It came as a surprise to know she was one of the most junior officers in the place. The rest of the staff were Air Force Wing Commanders, Naval Commanders and Army Lieutenant Colonels and above. There was a veritable plethora of one, two and three-star Generals. Commodores and Air Commodores, Vice-Admirals and Air Marshals abounded, and she was beginning to wonder what she was doing there.

Loram put her mind at ease. 'You'll be needed soon enough. We'll be stepping up all SOE operations from next week. It's imperative we have the Germans looking elsewhere and not at Normandy when the time comes. Your task is to optimise the use of One-Six-One Squadron with SOE operations. We want to fulfil the Prime Minister's original order, to set Europe alight.'

Susan nodded, but didn't correct him. Churchill's order was to set Europe ablaze. Same effect, she thought and then focused her attention back on Loram as she realised her mind had wandered.

'. . . by phone and signal. That means you won't have to leave *Dryad.*'

'Do I get a list of operations that are already planned?'

'Here it is. It came in this morning. It's just been decrypted.'

'What about the number of operational aircraft?'

Loram smiled at her. 'I hadn't thought of that. Also see how One-Six-One is fixed for pilots. If they can handle more planes we can do something about it.'

'I'm sure they can. Our limiting factor was the jobs given and the planes in service at any one time.'

'Good. Then get to work.'

'Thank you, sir, I will.'

'How are you getting on with Letitia?'

'Her smoking is, quite literally, getting up my nose.'

Loram nodded. 'Your predecessor was a sixty-a-day man and didn't mind. I can move you if you like. There's a Royal Marine Colonel who smokes like a chimney. He can go in with Letitia and you can share with a Naval Commander. I think it'll be for the best.'

Susan returned to her office. 'Letitia, you'll be delighted to know I'm moving out tomorrow. A bootie is coming instead.'

'Why? Where are you going?' Kitchin used the stub of a cigarette to light another.

'To his office. Apparently he smokes as much as you do so you'll be good company.'

Sitting at her desk she lifted the phone and asked for a number in London. Moments later she was put through to Mike O'Donnell.'

'Mike? It's Susan. I've been told to co-ordinate operations between SOE and One-Six-One in order to up the ante, so to speak.'

'I'd heard. We got the orders a short while ago. Robert is contacting all training establishments to see how many bods he can push through. We have a meeting of all circuit heads in an hour to discuss what's to be done. We should have preliminary ideas for tomorrow.'

'Good. I'll speak to the squadron, find out how many more planes they can use and see what I can find.'

'I take it this is for the big one.'

'I can't say, Mike.'

'Of course not. But we're throwing everything we've got at it, so something's in the wind.'

'It doesn't take a genius to work that one out. I'll speak to you later. Bye, Mike.'

Brian Ogilvie had been promoted to Air Vice-Marshall and sent to Scotland. His successor, Group Captain Stanley Hudson, was unknown to Susan. She elicited the information that he could use another six planes if she could find them. Apparently he'd been trying to get them out of Bomber Command but they wouldn't release them. 'You know we're low down the feeding line when it comes to planes and spares,' he said.

'That's about to change. Leave it to me.'

Twenty-four hours later, in her new office, where the air was fresh, Susan slammed the receiver down in anger. Bomber Command cited the orders of Air Marshal Portal, Chief of Air Staff, on the availability of aircraft to SOE. Any aircraft used by SOE was only of *potential* value, while dropping bombs was of *immediate* and *actual* value. The words were spoken with relish and had been quoted to her half a dozen times already.

She reported the situation to Peter Loram. 'Any ideas?' she asked.

'Draft a signal and I'll send it under General Morgan's authority. We have priority over everything that moves from now into the foreseeable future.'

'I think our best bet would be to get Griffins from St Athan. The Griffiths factory.'

'Griffiths?' Loram raised an eyebrow at her.

'My uncle,' she admitted.

'Good aircraft. I had no idea they were built by your family. Phone him up and tell him there's a signal on its way.'

It took an age but finally she got Sion on the phone. 'It's Susan, Uncle Sion. This is a courtesy call to tell you a signal is on its way authorising you to release the next six Griffin bombers to One-Six-One Squadron.'

'What about Bomber Command? They insist all planes go to them.'

'The signal overrides them. If you get any flack wave it under their turned-up noses.'

Her uncle chuckled. 'Don't worry. I'll send the planes to One-Six-One. Where are they based?'

'Tempsford. Near Bedford.'

'Ah, I know. The SOE flyers. Your old mob.'

'That's it. Got to go. Give my love to Kirsty.'

The SOE operations stepped up considerably. Agents, money and equipment were flown into France and all Maquis attacks intensified. The fear that communist cells would become focal points for post-war communism and undue Russian influence was ignored. One battle at a time was the cry.

The biggest demands from the resistance groups were for ammunition and explosives. Tons upon tons were dropped into France and the Benelux countries. Reprisals by the Germans against captured Maquis increased. Hundreds of brave men and women died at their hands, often following torture of the most brutal kind.

After two weeks of non-stop work Susan applied for weekend leave, which was granted, and she set off for Brighton and "*Fairweather*". Travelling along the south coast was slow. Everywhere she went she was asked to show some form of ID.

What she saw on her journey astonished her. Everywhere she looked men were bivouacked in fields of tents. Langstone Harbour, between Southsea and South Hayling, was jammed with the grey hulls of naval vessels, from destroyers to hundreds of landing craft. It wouldn't be for long, she reminded herself. In fifteen days they would be on their way – June 5th was a Monday. She couldn't help looking at the cloud-laden skies. Back at HMS *Dryad* they were obsessed with the long-range weather forecast. So far it was no better than uncertain.

Of course the date of the invasion wasn't sacrosanct. It merely marked the beginning of the window of opportunity for the attack. However, that window would only last a few short days. After that the men would have to disembark and Overlord would be postponed, possibly until September, which would be a potential disaster. Everything depended on the weather.

The carriage was packed and she had to fight her way off the train at Brighton. In a pub across the road from the station she treated herself to a gin and Angostura bitters then telephoned the house. To her joy Robert answered the phone.

'You made it, darling! I'm so glad. I've missed you horribly.'

He chuckled. 'My SOE pass gets me everywhere. I'll come and collect you.'

Ten minutes later he joined her for a drink.

'Here's to the weekend,' she raised her glass.

'Only twenty-four hours,' he grimaced.

'It's more than a lot of people get.'

'I'm not complaining, don't get me wrong. I feel a cheat somehow. Being here with you, while a million men are camped out, waiting to go to Europe. Many to their deaths.'

Susan looked around her, like a conspirator in a bad spy film and lowered her voice. 'Don't forget the work you're doing with the Department of Deception. It could save tens, even hundreds, of thousands of lives.'

'Trust you to know about that.'

'It's a vital part of our plan for the invasion. If we don't get enough men and materials into Europe before a counter-attack by the Germans it could be over in a few days and we'd be chucked out of Europe for possibly years to come. I gather it's working so far.'

Gill nodded. His smile was ruthless. 'It's amazing how the threat of a firing squad sharpens the mind. Our double agents have been feeding misinformation on the invasion for the last six months. All we can tell is that the German reserves are in place at the Pas de Calais, where we want them to stay.'

'The PM was as *Dryad* looking at the invasion plans and said "the truth is so precious it has to be protected by an armour of lies".'

Gill nodded in agreement. 'By the way, there's some good news. One of your old crew was picked up.'

Susan smiled excitedly. 'Who?'

'The navigator. Salmond?'

'Fish! Oh, Robert,' she clutched his arm, 'you've made my day!'

Their time together was a delightful, passionate interlude. All too soon they had to part. Susan managed a cheerful smile, although she could feel the tears threatening. She was being ridiculous, she told herself. After all, he was returning to London, not a posting overseas, while she was headed back to *Dryad*, hardly what you would call being in the front-line.

The train pulled out and she waved frantically to him until her carriage rounded a bend and he was lost to view. She spent most of the journey re-living the previous twenty-four hours, thinking about the future. Where would they live? What did she really want to do with her life? Another child would be a wonderful start. Could she settle for being a housewife after that? Even as the question formed she had her answer. No.

Back at *Dryad* she plunged into her work. The activity became frenetic with tension building as the date for the invasion drew nearer. Tempers became frayed and officers who should have known better snapped orders. This was the culmination of two years planning. Operational orders were pored over, errors looked for, contingency plans discussed. In the end it all came down to two factors: the weather and luck.

On the evening of Sunday the 28th of May Susan arrived in the mess for dinner. The bar was packed, but there was an oppressive air in the room.

She ordered a gin and tonic before she spied Letitia Kitchin in a corner and crossed the room. 'Why's everyone so glum?'

'You haven't heard? Nearly a hundred of our boys escaped from Stalag Luft III in Silesia.'

'A hundred escaped? That's wonderful.'

Letitia shook her head, lighting another cigarette. 'The Germans shot forty-seven of them. Killed them while "resisting arrest" or attempting to escape a second time.'

Susan looked at her in shock.

'How . . .' she cleared her throat. 'How many wounded?'

'None,' came the harsh reply. 'Fourteen are still at large.'

'But . . . But that's not possible. If you shoot at someone trying to escape some will inevitably be wounded.'

Letitia nodded. 'They were murdered. Bastard Germans! I wish I were a man. I would love to be able to kill some of the swine.'

Susan sighed. 'It's not much fun,' she said in a quiet voice.

Letitia's look was hostile. 'I've heard all about your exploits, seen the newspapers and the newsreels. How much of your story was made up for propaganda purposes? Having a pretty face must have helped.'

'You can think what you like, Letitia. I don't care. Now, if you'll excuse me, I want to speak to Captain Loram.' She joined her boss at the bar. 'I heard about the POWs.'

'We're still trying to get the details. The Swiss are working on it. Messages are being broadcast by the BBC threatening the Germans with dire consequences if they don't behave when it comes to our Prisoners of War.'

'I've heard some of them. War criminals will be tried and if found guilty, hanged.'

'It's all we can do at the moment. We can't exactly shoot forty-seven innocent Germans in a tit-for-tat operation, can we?'

'Hardly. Too barbaric for words. Besides, who would we get to do the shooting?'

'There are plenty of people who would do that. Fathers whose sons have been killed on active service, or mothers whose children have been killed by bombs. There would be plenty of volunteers. When it comes to the death of your child, no matter what his or her age, women are a damned sight more deadly than men. Interesting thought, isn't it? Our barbarism is being held in check by our laws and our government. But how would we all behave if the shackles were released?'

A week later embarkation onto ships began for the British 3rd Division. The ships were about to set sail when the report was received that bad weather was predicted for the 5th June. The sailing date was postponed twenty-four hours.

On the same day Rome fell to the Allies when the American General Mark Clark lead the rush into the Eternal City. Meanwhile the invasion fleet remained securely alongside in port, steam up, ready to go.

47

A PALL OF gloom hung over the men and women at HMS *Dryad*. They knew men couldn't be held indefinitely on small ships. If the weather didn't clear soon the invasion would have to be called off.

Then came the order. Force S, the invasion fleet destined to land on Sword Beach was to set sail. The ports of Southampton and Portsmouth emptied on a cold and blustery day, more like March weather than June. More prayers were uttered at that moment than at any other time. If the weather didn't clear the ships would have to be recalled and the invasion postponed. Landing hundreds of thousands of men and associated equipment on open beaches was hazardous at the best of times. In bad weather it would be impossible.

Then the miracle happened. The weather began to clear, the wind abated and the sea grew calmer. The countdown had begun. Later the history books would describe it so-:

5 June, 22.56hrs The British 6th Airborne Division takes off from airfields in the south of England to spearhead the invasion.

6 June D-Day 00.16hrs The 6th Airborne Division's first glider touches down in Normandy, near the Caen Canal. The liberation of Europe has begun.

03.00hrs Massive RAF bombing of the Atlantic Wall defences begin prior to the landings.

05.30hrs Troops disembark from the transport ships into the landing craft to take them ashore onto beaches code-named Utah, Omaha, Gold, Juno and Sword. A hundred miles of coastline from Quinéville in the west to Cabourg in the east is under attack.

07.25hrs 8th Brigade troops, part of the British 3rd Division, land on Queen Beach, a part of Sword Beach. Armour and tanks are landed at the same time.

08.30hrs 8th Brigade clears the beaches and moves inland towards Hermanville.

10.00hrs 185th Brigade, 3rd Divisions intermediate brigade, come ashore and drive towards Caen.

15.00hrs 3rd Brigade's advance falters.

19.00hrs 21st Panzer Division's attack take it to the sea between Lion and Luc sur Mer. The Germans fail to exploit the situation and no reinforcements arrive. Wave after wave of gliders land with the 6th Airlanding Brigade, causing panic at the German HQ who withdraw the 21st Panzer Division.

24.00hrs 3rd Division's attack stalls. They consolidate their position for the night.

All that day troops and heavy armour poured onto the beaches. Fighting had been fierce and it was touch and go as the Germans threw everything they had at the Allies. Heavy naval bombardments pounded the Germans, softening up positions, forcing them to keep their heads down. The explosions and pounding of shells all along the area were an assault on the senses of the men taking part. Continuous noise, revving engines, yelled orders, blowing whistles and unceasingly, the sound of gunfire. Men waded out of the sea to die as their feet reached the beach. But still they came, overpowering the German positions by sheer weight of numbers.

The 3rd Division had been evacuated at Dunkirk. Now it spearheaded the return to Europe. Revenge was a powerful motivating factor.

With the first day over there was no longer any doubt. It would be a long hard slog all the way to Berlin.

Susan and the other officers at *Dryad* read every signal and followed every event as best they could. During this twenty-four hour period the RAF and US Air Force bombers had been pounding the German positions along Western France. From far out to sea battleships had maintained a huge barrage, emptying their magazines onto the Germans, whilst closer to shore destroyers followed suit.

The weather continued to hamper progress, a strong north-westerly wind and heavy seas causing great difficulty for the landing craft. The outcome was finely balanced. The Allies had one major advantage – the German belief that the attack on Normandy was merely a feint and that the real attack would be around Calais, where the

Germans' heaviest tank armour was sited. If they were thrown against the Allies then the tide could so easily turn in the German's favour.

Hitler had been fooled by the SOE. For weeks, cardboard cut-outs and rubber blow-ups of guns, tanks and planes had been erected around Kent. A huge effort at misinformation had been master-minded by the Department of Deception to great success. The German armour was kept in readiness for an attack that never came. By the time the German High Command realised the deception it was too late. The Allies' tenuous toe-hold had strengthened to a degree that meant the deployment of the armour was no longer an issue.

It was a nerve-wracking time for the men and women in Eisenhower's HQ as events unfolded. Into the middle of it all came the King, the Prime Minister, and the South African PM, General Smuts.

Lt. Gen. Morgan gave the briefing. 'You can see, gentlemen, precisely the position as of one hour ago.' The huge mock-up of the Normandy coast and the Channel showed the disposition of the troops and ships. A wall chart was updated with the deployment and movement of the different air forces doing battle in the area. 'We have managed to destroy miles of railways, all the key bridges and most significantly, the radar stations along the whole area. Supply columns coming in from the east have also been destroyed, thanks to our air supremacy. We still have a long way to go, but we're getting there.'

'There is no turning back,' said Churchill. 'We can only go forward. No matter what the Hun throw at us we *cannot* fail. What are the casualty figures?'

'Sketchy. It's too early to tell although we have lost somewhere between ten and twenty thousand men. It'll be some time before we have accurate figures. Deputy Commander Griffiths, you have information on Maquis activity?'

'Yes, sir.' Susan referred to the file she held in her hands. 'There have been thousands of attacks across France, from single deaths to large-scale sabotage. Many of the strikes have been around Normandy, to prevent the Germans reinforcing their positions. The French have paid a high price. We're getting reports that SS troops obliterated the village of Oradour-sur-Glane.'

'Where's that?' the King asked.

'Near Limoges, your Majesty. As far as we can tell an SS officer was killed and the villagers massacred in reprisal. The men were taken

to a barn in groups of twenty and shot while the women and children
. . .' Susan faltered, licked her lips and continued. 'The woman and
children were all locked into the church. A large box was placed near
the altar, which exploded, setting fire to the church. Women were shot
as they tried to climb out of the windows. Children too.'

'How do we know their fate?'

'One village woman fainted and was left for dead. She escaped
later, your Majesty. The rest of the village was soaked in petrol and
paraffin and utterly destroyed. As far as we can tell only seven of the
seven hundred inhabitants survived.'

'And the children?'

'All dead, your majesty.'

The king's gentle manner failed to conceal the anger and sadness
he felt. 'Winnie, this is an atrocity. The soldiers responsible must be
punished.'

'They will be, sir. All war crimes will be investigated and those
responsible brought to book. We broadcast the fact every night in an
attempt to stop the Germans committing such acts of barbarity.'
Churchill sighed heavily and lit one of his ubiquitous cigars.
'Unfortunately there are still some who see themselves as the master
race. These atrocities must be stopped at all costs and Europe must
be liberated.'

The three VIPs adjourned to a private room for refreshments, taking
Susan with them. She didn't want to go but when your King and
Prime Minister insist, all you can do is nod and smile.

It was the only respite she had. For the next three weeks the atmosphere was one of organised chaos. Cherbourg fell to the Allies with
the capture of twenty thousand prisoners, and General de Gaulle
arrived in Bayeux to a rapturous welcome. Casualty figures were
published. In the first fifteen days of fighting the British losses made
grim reading: 1,842 killed, 9,599 wounded and 3,131 missing.
America: 3,082 killed, 13,121 wounded and 7,959 missing. Canada:
363 killed, 1,359 wounded, and 1,093 missing.

German casualties were far higher, although no exact figures were
available. *It was*, Susan brooded, *a terrible waste of life.*

One bright star shone on the horizon. The Germans were becoming
short of materials, evidenced by their desperate use of obsolete French
tanks, which were useless against the latest Allied guns.

After a month, Susan, along with other personnel, was granted a weekend pass. She longed to see John Phillipe and had contacted Connie by phone to make arrangements to meet. Arriving on Saturday morning she walked out of Paddington Station expecting to see them in the summer sunshine. They must be delayed, she reasoned, as she stood waiting. Suddenly the air-raid warning sirens began. Susan looked up at the sky, expecting to see enemy aircraft. Instead, with horror, she heard and then saw a "doodlebug" fly past, the noise of its engine already a well recognised and terror inducing sound.

Areas of Kent and Sussex had become known as "bomb-alley". Anti-aircraft guns were ineffectual and the RAF was unable to shoot them down. The only defence Britain had was to bomb their launch sites across the Channel, a priority now that the Allies had established a firm foothold in France.

Susan heard another rocket and then fear rooted her to the spot as the noise suddenly stopped. The engine had cut out – the rocket was dropping to earth. She had fifteen seconds until the explosion. But where should she go? She could as easily run into danger as away from it. As she scanned the area for a route to safety a scream stopped in her mouth. Connie was rushing towards her, dragging a terrified John Phillipe behind her.

That image was the last thing Susan saw as the explosion behind her blew out a wall. Mercifully she knew nothing more as she was buried under tons of rubble.

She became aware of two things – the smell and the pain. That all-pervading smell so unique to hospitals assailed her nostrils. Her right foot ached terribly, reminding her of the wound she'd suffered previously. She tried to sit up but found she couldn't and when she tried to speak all she managed was a low croak. But it was enough. A nurse suddenly appeared before her.

'You're awake. How are you feeling?'

'Water.'

'Let me help you.' The nurse poured water into a glass and helped Susan drink. 'Not too much, just enough to wet your mouth and throat. Good. Better?'

'Yes, thank you.' Susan sank back onto her pillows. 'Where am I?'

'Guy's hospital, on the south bank. Are you in pain?'

'All over.' She lifted a hand to her head and felt the bandage. 'Especially my head and right foot.'

The nurse nodded. 'Well, you need rest. I'm going to give you an injection now and you'll go back to sleep. When you wake, if you need anything, press this button. It rings at the nurses' station.'

'Thank you. My son . . .' the last word was heard only in Susan's mind as the narcotic took hold and she slipped into unconsciousness.

She slept for twenty-four hours. When she finally came to the pain and smell were still there. She groaned aloud and tried to sit up. Propped on her elbows she looked down the bed. From the waist down the bedclothes were lifted off her body and she wondered how much damage had been done. She wriggled her toes and felt them moving although her right leg and foot hurt like hell.

She had a raging thirst and realised she couldn't manage the jug of water. She rang the bell and a moment or two later a different nurse appeared. She helped Susan by placing a glass to her lips.

'Thanks.' Susan frowned. 'How long have I been lying here?'

'Four days.'

'Four days! As long as that?'

'Can you remember what happened?'

'Yes. A doodlebug landed nearby. But I don't know what happened after that.' A sudden horrific thought took hold of her. 'Oh! Where are Connie and my son? John Phillipe? Are they hurt?'

'I don't know, miss. I've just arrived on the ward.'

'Please, I must find out about John Phillipe.'

The nurse said. 'I know two children were brought in when you came in. He's probably there.'

'Please check.' Susan took the two painkillers the nurse handed her and sank back onto her pillows. Tentatively she moved her hands and arms, and tried to move her legs. That was more problematic. She gave up, exhausted and she fell back into an uneasy doze. When she woke it was to find Gill sitting by her side.

'Hullo, Robert,' she said weakly.

'Susan! You're awake,' Gill smiled at her, leant forward and took her hand. 'How are you feeling?'

'Like I've been run over by a number nine bus. But it's not me I'm worried about. How are John Phillipe and Connie.'

Gill licked his dry lips and took her hand. 'Do you remember the V-One flying over?'

'Yes. I heard the engine and then that awful silence when it cut out. I remember seeing Connie and John Phillipe. But then it all goes blank.'

'A wall was blown down behind you. You were almost killed.' Emotion took hold and he cleared his throat and blew his nose.

'Hey, we Griffithses are tougher to kill than that.'

He looked away for a moment, dreading what he had to tell her. 'You were trapped under a load of stones and bricks. A solid concrete lintel was over you, protecting your head and upper body from the worst of it. A passer-by dug you out. The ambulance arrived looking for casualties just as he got you clear. Your father pulled every string he knew to get the best attention for you, the best surgeons and doctors. You very nearly lost your leg.'

'God, I knew it was bad, but to have lost . . . lost . . .' she choked on the words. The thought of being crippled filled her with horror. Smiling at him tearfully she said, 'And Connie and John Phillipe? I understand that they're here too. Or at least John Phillipe is. Is he all right? I must see him!' Seeing the stricken look on his face fear clutched at her. 'What is it? Tell me, Robert! What don't I know? Robert, you're beginning to frighten me.'

'They died, Susan. Both of them. Their bodies were found in the rubble, Connie's arms around John Phillipe.'

'You're lying!' Her voice rose as hysteria threatened to swamp her. 'The nurse said two children had been brought in. One of them *must* be John Phillipe. Why are you lying? How can you be so cruel?' Ashen-faced Susan struggled to pull herself upright.

And then she looked at him and knew it was true. Tears welled up in her eyes and washed down the sides of her face. 'Go away, Robert.'

Gently he put his hand on her arm. 'Darling, I . . .'

'Just go.' She spoke quietly, but with great force. 'Please leave me.'

48

THEY WERE BURIED together at *Fairweather*, in the sandy soil of the small graveyard near the Channel. Seagulls and terns reeled overhead as their coffins were slowly lowered, prayers were said, their graves blessed and filled.

Susan refused to attend the funeral of her son and best friend. She was suffering a storm of grief and guilt so profound that her father feared for her sanity. She blamed herself for asking Connie to come to London with John Phillipe.

Days passed in utter desolation. Susan refused to speak about what had happened. Instead she sat looking out of the window of John Phillipe's room, towards the graveyard and the sea. Words of comfort were met with glazed-eyed indifference or a tirade of fury.

She replayed the details of the day again and again in her mind, playing the "if only" game – if only she hadn't asked Connie to bring him up to London on that day, if only they had agreed to meet elsewhere, if only the train hadn't been late . . .

If only she had stayed home to care for her son, as any loving mother should have done. It seemed to Susan that only with his death did she fully understand the profound love she had for her child. She blamed herself, not only for their deaths, but for the months of neglect and abandonment caused by her monumental ego.

Nights brought no relief. Sleep eluded her entirely. She floundered in a sea of self-loathing and grief.

Her father, already staggering under the loss of his grandson, and the terrible anxiety he felt for Susan, had a tremendous urge to protect her. But there was no way they could hide the fear and worry he and Madelaine felt when they opened the telegram issued by the War Office.

461

When he sought her out, Susan dimly registered how haggard he looked. 'Something happened?'

'It's Richard. He's Missing In Action.'

Gradually they pieced together the story. Richard had been on the flagship, part of a naval task force attacking northern Italy. Apparently he had been sent across to one of the escorts with signals and instructions for the captain. A routine event.

The task force was attacked by German planes and the ship Richard was visiting had been badly damaged. One of the bombs hit the bridge and several of the crew were killed. Others were missing. The blast had blown men over the side. Richard was one of them.

Knowing that their uncertainty was shared by thousands of other families made the waiting no easier. David tried hard to keep his anxieties to himself – full of hope one moment and despair the next. Madelaine wept in private, seesawing emotions leaving her raw. She was vaguely aware of transferring her anger onto David, blaming him for allowing Richard to stay in the navy, though in her heart she knew her son's idealism would never have allowed him to leave. She suffered terribly, fear for her son colouring every waking moment. Her every thought, every breath, was for news of him – news that he was safe. That he was alive.

Susan, for the first time since losing John Phillipe and Connie, felt needed. Later, much later, she knew that seeing her father's and Madelaine's agony started her own healing process.

Madelaine stayed in town, at the flat, waiting for news, carrying on with her work, while David and Susan remained at *Fairweather*, sitting for hours in the conservatory, overlooking the fields of vegetables which had previously been parkland. It was a peaceful place and they sat in silence, each lost in their own thoughts.

Finally Susan said, 'I think I'll visit the graves today.'

David looked at her with a tiny flicker of hope in his eyes. 'Are you sure?'

'Yes. I can't sit and grieve forever. Madelaine needs me. We need each other.'

Gibbs appeared and gave a respectful cough. 'Sir, Madame is on the telephone.'

'Thank you, Gibbs. I'll be right with you.' He turned back to Susan. 'Would you like me to come to the graveyard with you?'

'No, Dad, thank you. It's something I have to do by myself.'

'Right. I'd better see what Madelaine wants.' He braced himself as he followed Gibbs into the hall. He had come to dread every phone call.

'Darling! Darling, it's come.' Madelaine sounded ecstatic and he knew it was good news.

'What has come?' he asked stupidly.

'Richard's capture card. He's alive! He's been taken prisoner, but he's unhurt. The card says he's on his way to Northern Germany.' Madelaine broke down and wept. David's eyes filled with tears and he longed with all his soul to be with her.

'Thank God,' he breathed.

Madelaine pulled herself together, anxious to give David all her news. 'The card came via Switzerland. He was put in a POW camp near the Swiss border. I suspect that's how we got a card so quickly! Isn't it wonderful news?'

'Yes, my dear, wonderful. I'll tell Susan. She'll be overjoyed.'

'About what?' Susan was standing next to him, her coat on, ready to go outside.

'It's Richard. He's a POW. Madelaine? Listen, darling, I'll see you to-night.' Replacing the receiver he smiled at his daughter. 'Until recently it always took forever to learn whether someone is a POW – but now the lads are sending these capture cards home to their next of kin as soon as they get to their destination. As soon as the cards arrive they are passed to the War Office for processing. It used to take as much as three months to hear news of a loved one. With the capture card it can be as little as one. God,' he shook his head, 'what a relief.'

'All Richard has to do now,' said Susan, 'is survive.'

Richard and David's Story

49

I WAS EXHAUSTED. I could barely think straight. I just concentrated on putting one painful foot in front of the other in a kind of daze. Our progress was slow; I had plenty of time to reflect on how I found myself in my present predicament. Griffiths' stubborn pride, that's what it was.

Despite violent opposition from the family, I had been determined to do my bit. The way the war was going I knew it would be over before I could get my chance to fight the Hun. It was galling to watch as other, younger men joined up while I was expected to go to university. Mum wanted me to go in as an officer, of course, but officer training would have kept me away from the fighting. So I did a bunk and went to HMS *Ganges*.

It was almost like being back at Eton, only not nearly so academic and the food wasn't as good. Most of the others in my division came from working class backgrounds, and I had the Mickey taken out of me something rotten because of my accent. But I took it on the chin for the most part.

Things only got out of hand once. A Newcastle lad in another division called Warren – he deliberately picked on me; my plummy vowels annoyed him apparently. Fancied his chances rather. What he didn't know was that I'd boxed for Eton. In fact I'd been expected to get my blue up at Oxford.

I bent my head against the cold wind and trudged onwards, the memory a warm glow of satisfaction. It wasn't a proper fight. No Queensbury rules or anything. Just bare knuckles.

The scrap lasted approximately two minutes. He was bigger and heavier than me but a lot slower too. After about twenty seconds, when I'd got his measure, I toyed with him, very much like a cat with a mouse. A minute and a half later he still hadn't landed a punch, so I decided to end it. Two jabs to the gut, followed by an uppercut which sent him down. Nobody bothered me after that.

Dad had encouraged me to take up boxing, though Mum wasn't keen. He reckoned it was always useful to be able to defend yourself.

I'm almost sure he pulled strings behind the scenes after my initial training was over. Don't get me wrong, I enjoyed the signals course I was sent on. At the end of it I could send and read Morse at ten words a minute by light and sound, I understood the signals flags and had a working knowledge of wireless sets.

Then I got my first ship, a flagship with Admiral Carbonne, no less! It was so exciting! I'd only been there a few weeks when the squadron was deployed to the Northern Adriatic to support the attack on Italy. I'd spent most of my working day on or near the bridge, listening to what was going on, hearing how decisions were made. Then I was sent across to one of the escorts with a package of orders. Suddenly the air was filled with German bombers and all hell broke loose.

I remembered falling into the sea, but then I lost consciousness, I suppose. I awoke to find myself adrift, supported by my lifejacket, not a ship in sight. Luckily the September sea was warm, otherwise I would never have survived the next few hours. I drifted all night and must have dozed because when I awoke I could hear the sound of the sea. Even to my befuddled brain it could only mean land was nearby.

There was a slight swell and I caught glimpses of coastline as I bobbed up and down. It took an eternity, but I used the last of my strength, desperately kicking towards it, until I found myself standing waist-deep in the water. Thankful to be alive I staggered ashore and straight into the arms of a German patrol.

I have to say they were decent chaps, not at all what I'd been expecting. They were about my own age, or perhaps even younger, and pretty fed up, so far from home. Being able to speak reasonable German helped. They knew the war was going badly, in spite of what their officers told them. Italy was practically lost to Germany and now that the invasion of Normandy had taken place they saw that the end wasn't far away. Their greatest fear were the hordes of Russians coming from the east.

My first *Dulag* or *Durchgangslager* – transit or reception camp – wasn't too bad, though I wasn't there long. They let me write my capture card and issued me with a plate, fork, spoon and tin mug before assigning me a bunk in one of the huts.

Up until then, I hadn't really believed that I was a prisoner. Well, the barbed wire was proof enough. "Reorientation of priorities" I think they call it – all I knew was that my safe, happy life, with warmth, love, family back up – all those things I'd taken for granted – were suddenly gone. Within a few days my previous securities were shaken to the core. The monotony of camp life was soul-destroying, the food inadequate and the thought of being at someone else's mercy mind numbing.

Escape was impossible, although I thought of nothing else from the second I arrived. The perimeter fence was made of barbed wire, with watchtowers placed every hundred yards. Five yards from the fence there was a white line drawn in the dust. If you crossed the line you'd be shot.

The military hierarchy applied in the camp just as it did at sea. Being so far away from home, in such uncertain circumstances, I was glad of the order it imposed. As a mere Able Bodied Seaman the hierarchy placed me well at the bottom of the heap, so I kept my head down, my nose clean and went about my work.

Being a transit camp all the services were represented. Officers were in one section and other ranks in another. The officers and senior NCOs didn't have to work, but I was thankful I was made to labour, even if it was only picking tomatoes or olives.

We'd been there about three weeks when we were woken in the middle of the night. The door of my hut was thrown open and our German guards roused us from our bunks. I was terrified out of my wits. Was this it? Were they going to take us outside and shoot us? We'd all heard of such things.

'Gather all your belongings,' screamed the guard. 'You are leaving camp tonight. You go to Germany.'

There were forty of us in the hut, in bunks three high. Everybody stood stock still, not understanding.

Unable to bear the tension any longer, I asked, 'Why are we going to Germany?'

'We have orders to move all Prisoners of War. The British and Americans are advancing. We can no longer guarantee your safety. You are to be moved to the Fatherland.'

469

'Why not just leave us here?'

I got no further. The guard advanced towards me, his rifle raised. 'No more questions. Tell your friends to hurry.' Much to my relief he lowered his gun and backed towards the door. 'Tell them they have ten minutes.'

The hut had a number of corporals and leading seamen. One L/S, by the name of Taff Ellis was in charge. 'Look you, I didn't know you spoke *kraut*, Griffiths.'

'There's a lot you don't know about me, Taff. Tell the others to get dressed. They're moving us to Germany.'

Consternation broke out amongst the men, a feeling I shared. Here in the transit camp we were safe, though uncomfortable. We knew our place, our days were mapped out. As long as we did as we were told there was a strong probability we would survive the war. If we were moved to Germany, who knew what might happen?

'Here, Griffiths, what else did that swine say?' somebody asked.

'That our troops are coming and that was why we were being moved. For our own safety. We've got ten minutes to get ready.'

Frantically we packed our meagre possessions. I'd acquired a rain-coat since I'd been there. Quickly I shoved a tin of bully beef, which I'd swapped for a handful of smuggled tomatoes, into my pocket before following the others outside.

The whole camp was in uproar. Thousands of men were being herded onto the parade ground. Those who didn't move quickly enough were encouraged with kicks and blows.

On the *Appelplatz,* the camp adjutant addressed us in English. 'You men will walk to the station at Treviso, sixty kilometres away, where you will be put on a train for Germany. If you do not walk you will be shot. If you try to escape you will be shot. If you cause any trouble . . .'

'You will be shot!' hundreds of POWs yelled. The litany was one we'd heard many times.

'Good. We understand each other.'

Orders were given and different sections began the trek out through the main gate. We were near the end and it was a full hour before we were given the order to march. Throughout that time we were all prey to our worst fears. What made it even more galling was that we could hear the faint sound of heavy gunfire in the distance; the Allies were closing in. *So near, yet so far.*

Finally we moved out. Dread of the unknown is debilitating; I found myself on the verge of a blue funk for the first couple of hours. Our speed was slow, despite the guards using their rifle butts to chivvy us along. After four hours we stopped. I was glad of the chance to rest but the respite was short lived. All too soon we were back on our feet again.

My shoes were naval issue, fine onboard ship but totally inadequate for long marches. Pretty soon my feet began to hurt as I felt every stone I trod on. After a while a sort of numbness took over.

As far as the horizon I could see POWs walking ahead of me, most with bowed heads, some helping others along, some talking quietly, one or two singing. Although we were leaving what was technically a transit camp many of the other men had been there for several months, contending with dysentery, malnutrition and lice, as well as the treatment meted out by the guards. The war in Italy, I assumed, had prevented the Germans moving us to a more permanent site.

Now we were on the move, two thousand men and more. At midday we were given a weak potato soup. Although tasteless it at least took the edge off my hunger pains.

Hunger seemed my natural state. I couldn't remember what it was like *not* to crave something to eat, in spite of the tomatoes and olives I'd stolen from the local farms. The thought of a juicy steak or a leg of chicken made my mouth water. Things I'd always taken for granted. And that wasn't all I'd taken for granted – truth be told. I felt little connection to the young idiot who had signed up; the idealist who had thought only of the glamour of war and the prospects for heroism. What I wouldn't give to be in Oxford right now – reading politics and history as I'd intended.

My thoughts of home were interrupted by the guttural yells from the guards and we were wearily forced back to our feet. In a way I was glad – it hurt to think of the family, how worried they must be.

The afternoon wore on. As dusk fell, we reached the outskirts of an abandoned village. Fires were already burning and food was being cooked. We'd be staying there for the night. Most of the houses were crammed with men who had reached the place a full two hours ahead of us. Those who had arrived earlier had already eaten and were asleep in the dilapidated houses and barns, safe from the biting wind and the threatening snow.

I found a fire surrounded by *matelots* and I joined them, offering my tin of bully beef for the shared meal. They had scavenged the area and found a field of potatoes, most of which were rotten. The best had been added to the pot, along with maize supplied by the Germans and various tins we'd been carrying, courtesy of the Red Cross.

I hadn't met any of them before; they had been billeted at the far side of the camp. While the stew was cooking we exchanged stories. The most senior man was a petty officer who'd been held for a full year, taken when his ship had sunk during the North African campaign.

'This is my third move,' he said bitterly. 'Bloody Krauts, they've been shunting us up Italy as our lot advanced. At one point I thought I'd get away but we got orders to stay put until we were liberated. Bloody hell, even the Eyeties had left.'

'What, no guards?' I asked.

'None. Done a bunk they had. Our CO was debating what to do when the Germans arrived and honest to God, they just shut the gates on us again. I could have wept buckets, I could. We made our first move soon after. Aye, I've lost a lot of good mates in the last year.' He coughed and hawked up phlegm. 'What branch you in, son?'

'Signals.'

'Me too. Fifteen years, man and boy. What about you?'

'Seven months.'

He laughed. 'Not even a dog watch. Name's Westwood. Stan to me friends.'

'Richard Griffiths.' We shook hands.

'In that case I'll call you Dickie. Richard is for officers.'

Stan was in his early thirties. He was cadaver-thin and looked ill, but his eyes shone brightly enough. He smiled and handed me a bowl. I was so exhausted that for now I was happy to eat hot food, half cooked or not, drink reasonably clean water and fall asleep in a draughty barn, lying on rotting straw.

I snapped awake to a sharp pain – a rat was biting into the fleshy part of my hand, between my forefinger and thumb. Shaking it off in disgust, I watched it vanish under the straw and shuddered.

Squeezing the wound, I forced a few drops of blood out to clean it and hopefully prevent myself catching something. Did rats spread disease nowadays? Bloody things had been responsible for the Black Death. That was all we needed – bubonic plague, or some such.

We were crammed into the barn, sleeping so tightly together that

472

when you rolled over you could end up on the man next to you. My tussle with the rat had a ripple effect and the other prisoners began to come round and sit up. The darkness was fading, grey light filtering through from outside. Another day loomed ahead. I prayed by the end of it we'd be at the railway station.

I'd slept with my shoes on. I took them off to examine my feet. Blisters from the march had burst, caking my feet in blood. They hurt like hell. I massaged them, trying to get the circulation going again, knowing that by tonight they would be a lot worse. Examining the soles of my shoes, I saw the leather was wearing away. No wonder I could feel every stone and crack on the road.

The Germans fed us bread and cheese washed down by a cup of ersatz coffee. The bread was hard and the cheese mouldy, but at least the coffee was hot. The call to move out came and we lined up to go. Before we could move the sound of a horn held us in check and a convoy of German vehicles came into sight, led by a staff car, the driver leaning on his horn. As the convoy of trucks passed we could see they were crammed full of German soldiers, many of them wounded.

'I wonder where they're from?' Stan Westwood asked as he came up beside me. We soon had our answer.

The convoy came to a halt and I called to a soldier sitting next to the tailgate of the nearest truck. 'What's happened? Where have you come from?'

He was probably so startled to hear me speak German that he replied automatically, 'Trieste. The Yugoslavs and the Americans have broken through. We are leaving to defend the Fatherland.'

As the convoy jerked into movement again, I called out, 'They're on the run, lads.' As I repeated what I'd been told, a ragged cheer broke out and as we lined up to start walking again, someone began to sing, "It's A Long Way To Tipperary". "Keep the Home Fires Burning", and a host of other favourites soon followed.

For the first half an hour our spirits were buoyed by the news but one by one we fell silent as the effort to keep moving took its toll.

Westwood fell in alongside me. 'You fluent in German?'

I nodded. I had been dreading the question.

'Why aren't you one of the negotiators?'

'You know the score, Stan. Never volunteer for anything. I want to survive this,' I replied with honesty. 'So I've kept my head down.'

'Why talk to that soldier, then?'

Why *had* I spoken out? I licked dry lips. As far as the eye could see POWs were walking with heads bent, dispirited and weary. I'd gotten to know a lot of the men during the last few months. Despite inhumane, brutal treatment there was always a flickering of resistance, of fighting spirit within them. I knew it was there, it just needed encouragement. It was time to put my head above the parapet. I shrugged. 'We need and are entitled to better conditions. More food, better medical treatment, better everything. We're surviving on Red Cross parcels and what we can steal off the land. It isn't good enough.' Talking was taking my mind off my feet. I looked squarely at Westwood, 'In part I held back because I'm young and they don't come any more junior.'

'That's true. So any negotiating would have to be done by an older, more senior person, whilst you interpret. The last German speaker we had in the camp died a month ago. Since then we haven't been able to get anywhere with the Krauts. We need someone to represent us again.' Westwood tapped the side of his forehead. 'Survival in this place means surviving up here. Have you read the letters some of the lads have received from home? The *Dear Johns*?'

I shook my head.

'Even the married men have had them. It's like our women are ashamed of us POWs. As if we should have died fighting, rather than surrender. Lots of us have had letters giving us the heave-ho.'

'You too, Stan?'

'Me too.' There was no mistaking the bitterness in his voice. 'Good riddance to her, I say. Even after ten years of marriage. She says she's going away with a soldier from Scotland, a man who's "still fighting" is how she put it. Well, good luck to him. She did me a big favour, though she doesn't know it. That letter made me so angry I'm more determined than ever to survive. So like I say, it's all up here. Our last German speaker, he gave up, lad. Don't let it happen to you.'

'Surely there are other German speakers in the camp?'

'Although we're a *Dulag*, we're mostly other ranks. The few officers we've had who spoke German didn't stay long enough to make a difference. I'll talk to Jock McAllister. He's a good man – he'll be able to use you.'

McAllister was our Man of Confidence, elected camp spokesman and leader by the rest of the prisoners. A Chief Petty Officer, he had been in the last transit camp for almost eight months, although he'd been a prisoner for two years. I'd heard McAllister was renowned for his patience and quiet determination when dealing with the guards. His only drawback was he couldn't speak German.

We stopped talking. We needed our strength to walk.

The midday meal passed in a blur and then we were up and off again. My feet had stopped hurting, they'd gone numb. A cold wind came down from the Alps, threatening snow. But it held off and we made it to Treviso. When we finally came to a halt my vision was blurred with fatigue.

A long train of cattle trucks was waiting for us. We were herded on, packed together so tightly that we couldn't lie down. Eighty of us were forced into each truck, barely able to breathe, our heads propped up by the next man's shoulders. After what seemed an eternity the train jerked, throwing some men off their feet, and then we were moving. There was a slop bucket in the corner but few could reach it. As the hours passed the men urinated and defecated where they stood. I closed my eyes, numb, terrified of what lay ahead.

50

Churchill had reluctantly agreed to a meeting at Number Ten. I lost no time confronting him over the issue of our Allied POWs. Since Richard's capture I had devoted all my spare time to finding out how best to help those men held captive behind enemy lines.

'We simply *must* do more to protect them, dammit.'

Winnie had listened to my tirade of facts and figures from behind his desk, with beetling brows and obvious ill humour. 'There is little else we *can* do, Griffiths. We are broadcasting hourly to the German people, particularly the regular troops and the camp commandants. The warning is clear – the onus is upon them to protect our POWs from ill treatment. They will be tried for war crimes otherwise.'

'And do you really believe that will be sufficient?' At least he had the good grace to look discomfited. 'Winnie, you were a prisoner of war in Africa. You actually know what it's like. Nobody else in government or in the armed forces has any inkling. But surely *you* understand – we must give our men hope as well as practical help. I've heard the broadcasts. We know that the average citizen and soldier won't harm our men, but what of the Gestapo and the SS, the merciless scum who *enjoy* inflicting pain and death?'

'I repeat, we have made it clear that any attempt to shift the blame to the SS or Gestapo will not be acceptable, that the commandants *must* do their duty and protect our men. I'm sorry, David, but there is little else we can do right now. Since they started their damn doodlebug campaign, over four thousand civilians have been killed and ten thousand injured. V1s are raining down on us at a rate of one hundred and fifty a day. We may be winning the war in Europe but we're losing it back here. My priority is to locate and stop those rockets. It's imperative.'

'It's also imperative that we save the lives of over two hundred and fifty thousand Allied troops. Italy was a fiasco.' As deputy head of SOE I had argued bitterly against instructing our POWs to remain where they were until our troops relieved them. 'As soon as the Italians left the compounds the Germans turned up and simply took over. Now tens of thousands of Allied prisoners are being forced into Germany. They'll be used to blackmail us, as sure as night follows day.'

'At the time the orders were issued with the best of intentions.'

'With respect,' I said, with barely suppressed fury, 'we should have dropped arms and paratroopers to our men and have them fight the Germans. We could have added fifty, even sixty thousand fighting men to our lists. Trained men, ready to fight.'

'No, you're wrong there, Griffiths. I haven't been completely lax in this matter. I've spoken to psychiatrists and prison wardens.' Opening a drawer Churchill lifted out a buff coloured file and waved it at me. 'It's all in here. Other than the men who've been taken prisoner in say, the last six months, the rest will have become institutionalised. They will need to be helped back into normal society. For some of them simple, everyday decisions, which we take for granted, will be beyond them. To expect them to be able to fit back into fighting units is impossible. The likelihood is they'd be liabilities, rather than assets.'

'A small minority perhaps . . .'

He held up his hand. 'We have to trust the experts on this one. There are too many Allied troops in German hands. To repatriate them would take huge effort and resources. Turning them into useful fighting men and returning them to their units would take weeks if not months. We don't have the resources to accomplish the undertaking. It's far better to leave them where they are.'

'Why not drop a small contingent of men and arms to take over the camps? The POWs could hold out as our forces advance and overrun their positions.'

Churchill shook his head. 'We've discussed the possibility. There's a real danger that the Germans could kill those prisoners held in camps we can't get to as a pre-emptive strike, or in retaliation. Believe me, David, I have spent time and effort on the problem, but for now it's shelved. Our POWs are to stay where they are until we reach them.'

'What happened to the plan to get wireless transmitters into all the camps?'

Churchill shrugged. 'It was vetoed.' Fiddling with his cigar he looked abashed. 'I know how difficult this must be for you and your family, David, but my hands are tied. I've read your recommendations, and for what it's worth the High Command concurs. The War Office concurs. Parliament concurs. But for the moment we've done all that we can. We know now it's going to be a long hard slog into Germany. After Stauffenberg's failed assassination attempt nobody will be able to get to Hitler. A bunker mentality has taken hold. The Germans will fight like cornered rats – viciously and without mercy.'

'And when the Germans threaten to kill our POWs if we don't agree a peace settlement? What then?'

'There will be no settlement. Not unless Hitler is removed first and that won't happen. Even if we agreed, the Russians won't. Stalin made that abundantly clear. They'll overrun Germany and believe me they won't be going back to Russia. This is now a war of attrition. We will prevail. It's inevitable. Now we must consider the terms of peace. When the war is over I foresee two monoliths facing each other, the West on one side, the Communists on the other. So the more of Germany we have under our control the better. We won't make the same mistake with reparations again. Stalin is going to demand his pound of flesh. Whatever land he takes he'll bleed white. Germany will be a nation divided unless we can get there first. For that reason alone, we cannot spare resources from the main invasion effort to rescue prisoners of war.'

'Until they are used as bargaining chips.'

'There will be no bargaining, David. Not under any circumstances. The POWs have to take their chances along with everyone else. Here, read this.'

The memorandum the PM handed me was marked top-secret. As I read, I began to realise the true extent of the problem. As of August there were 160,000 British and Commonwealth prisoners in Germany, of whom 100,000 would eventually be in the Russian liberated zone. A further 22,000 Americans would also be in Russian hands. Soviet POWs, on the other hand, now languishing in the western part of Germany numbered 365,000.

Anthony Eden, the Foreign Secretary, travelled to Moscow to discuss the problem with Marshal Stalin. They had agreed the mutual return of prisoners of war. But I knew that meant nothing.

'We can't trust Stalin,' I said, shaking my head. 'Indeed, the good

Marshal claims the POWs are traitors to Mother Russia for having surrendered; back in Russia they will be summarily shot. The Americans are saying, quite rightly, that it's immoral to force Russian POWs to return to their certain death. You won't get any argument from me. But,' I sighed, 'that would mean non co-operation by the Russians with regards to our own POWs.'

'Correct. The moral high ground is a difficult place to occupy when you have to make life-or-death decisions. We both know Stalin. If we don't return the Russian POWs, he won't release ours.'

'What about a military option?'

Churchill nodded. 'It's not out of the question. But don't forget, the liberation of Europe is one thing. There's still a bigger war to be won in the east.'

'I hadn't forgotten.'

'So we'll send the Russians back and turn a Nelsonian eye to what happens to them. We've no choice. We must secure the release of our own men.'

Throughout the last four years the Russians had proven themselves to be the most duplicitous, difficult government to deal with. There was no doubting the bravery of the ordinary people. But the communist leaders cared nothing for their populace, their well-being or future. They had broken practically every treaty made and taken advantage at every opportunity. There was no official recognition of the hardships and dangers our convoys had suffered to keep the Russian war effort afloat. They believed they had a right to our aid, no matter what it cost us in men and materials. But then, for Stalin and his henchmen, lives were cheap. The Russian revolution had wiped out over twenty million souls. What did a few million more matter?

Churchill was sympathetic but adamant. I should expect no further help from him. Defeated, I returned to my office at SOE.

O'Donnell was waiting for me. He had news. 'Reports are coming in thick and fast about POW movements. All in one direction, towards the heart of Germany.'

'Any word about Richard?'

'He's being moved to Treviso. A cattle train is waiting to take them through the Brenner Pass.'

'Do we know where the train is headed?'

'We can guess. Marlag Nord.'

'Bremen?'

Nodding, Mike voiced my own thoughts. 'It's a hell of a long way.'

'Could we mount an operation to stop the train before it gets there?'

'In Germany? I don't see what good it would do. Where could the POWs go? At least if they get to Bremen they might be safe. They wouldn't stand a chance in the middle of the German countryside. A lot of our fliers have been killed by German civilians. Just because most of Richard's lot are sailors it doesn't mean they'll be any safer.'

I nodded. It was true. *Terrorfliegers* they called them. Our pilots were blamed for the destruction of Cologne and dozens of other cities. Already rumours of POWs being killed by irate German civilians were trickling through. The movement of prisoners was fraught at the best of times. Now it was downright dangerous.

Dangers threatened from every side, it seemed. POW trains had already been attacked by our own aircraft, the pilots unaware that Allied personnel were onboard. Partisans had blown up rail tracks and roadways, unwittingly killing our own men as well as their German targets. To add to the confusion vast numbers of refugees were on the move, fleeing from the Russians. Others were headed north and west, escaping from the Allies. Among them were shadowy figures, French, Belgian, and Dutch *collaborators*. If caught, those traitors were being summarily tried and punished. I looked at the wall map and pictured in my mind the seething masses criss-crossing Europe. How on earth was I going to keep track of one individual amongst that lot?

'We can only pray he arrives safely in Northern Germany,' I said.

'I didn't think you were much good at praying,' O'Donnell smiled.

'I'm not, Mike. Which is why I intend moving bods along the route, to keep an eye on things and report back to us on the POWs' progress. Can you fix it?'

'Probably. Anything else?'

'I've been thinking. Most of the time it's down to the Red Cross that our lads are surviving at all.' I paused, evaluating my plan. Mike, knowing me as well as he did, kept quiet. 'It's time we gave them a helping hand. In that mass of misery my son is unidentifiable. So we have to give blanket help to all of them. I want aid given at every opportunity to the men from Richard's camp. With luck it will trickle down to him. The one thing we've learnt about POWs is that they look after each other. Will Richard's train stop anywhere for any length of time?'

'At the Brenner Pass. The Italian side. They need permission to go through. Currently the hold-ups are running into a full day.'

I walked over to the wall map and examined it carefully. 'Brennero. I've been there. If we can get a Red Cross contingent to meet the train they might be able to distribute food and other items to the prisoners.'

'No can do,' said Mike. 'The Red Cross insist on neutrality.'

I pondered his statement for a few moments before nodding. 'What about using our own people disguised as Red Cross?'

Mike sucked in his breath and sat down heavily in the chair opposite my desk. 'That's a high-risk strategy, David. If anyone found out we'd be pilloried. And rightly so.'

'Have you any other ideas?' I asked irritably.

'Getting help inside Germany would be extremely difficult, though we do know some people who are anti-Hitler and anti-Nazi. All they want is for this bloody war to end, as do we all. But we still have good assets on the Italian side, agents who can give away as many food parcels as we can get to them.'

'In that case, use money to bribe local people to distribute the food. If we produce a thousand parcels can we get them to Northern Italy in time?'

'Where are we going to get a thousand parcels from?'

'We'll use the wireless factory in Wales to pack the items and Sion can deliver them. This is a humanitarian flight, so he could paint a plane with the Red Cross colours. The fact the flight isn't sanctioned by the Red Cross is immaterial.'

'You're insane,' Mike said with a wide grin, 'but I like it. What about putting Red Cross insignia on the parcels?'

'Leave that to me. Can you talk to Betty at the factory while I speak to Sion? I think there are restrictions on what we can pack. We need to hurry. We don't have much time.'

'Get Robert working on the problem too. He's got bods in the area, hasn't he? Right, we'd better get to work.'

A short while later Gill appeared with Susan. There were dark shadows under her eyes, an indication of how badly she was sleeping. Although there was still an indefinable air of sadness around her, it was almost as though our worry for Richard had brought her back from the edge of madness. She and Madelaine had spent long evenings talking together. Finally she seemed to have accepted that Connie and John Phillipe's deaths were not her fault. I admired her so much and wasn't surprised by her greeting.

'Tell me what I can do to help.'

'You could start by making us a fresh cup of coffee,' O'Donnell suggested.

Susan gave a mock salute and headed for the tiny kitchen. I glared at O'Donnell who shrugged.

'She can't be pampered forever, David. She needs to keep busy.'

'She's coping,' Robert reassured me. 'And she genuinely wants to help.'

I turned my attention to the problem in hand. The drop was a bureaucratic nightmare. For the last two years there had been almost open warfare between the Red Cross and the War Office's Directorate of Prisoners of War. The latter was totally inept, while the former was merely ineffective. Food parcels sent by relatives frequently didn't arrive at their destination. The Post Office denied it was their responsibility and the DPW blamed the Red Cross. I knew better.

The War Office was effectively ignoring the problem of the POWs, paying lip service but doing nothing. I looked at the map of Europe, picturing my son and the hell he and thousands like him were going through. I vowed I would do all in my considerable power to protect him.

Food parcels were a start, including a private parcel for Richard. It probably wouldn't reach him, but it was worth trying.

Susan returned, carrying a tray and we gratefully accepted cups of coffee, before discussing our plans.

'This operation will cost a fortune,' said Gill.

The three of us looked at him in surprise. He reddened and looked uncomfortable, but carried on voicing his thoughts.

'Loss of production at the factory, purchasing all the items. And where will you buy them? We don't have enough food vouchers.'

I was glad he said *we*, identifying himself with the venture. 'Money is no object,' I began and realised I was sounding pompous. I cleared my throat. 'Robert, this is family,' I emphasised. 'Money is there to be used when it's needed. To you it may seem strange putting in so much effort just for Richard. Selfish even. Well, I'm the first to admit both are true. But we'll also be helping thousands of others in the camp. But you're right about the vouchers. That's where you come in. You're an ex-policeman, use your contacts. The black market is awash with what we need.'

He looked at me in astonishment and then smiled. 'I'll be delighted.'

'And you have assets in Northern Italy, right? We need someone to organise the drop from that end,' O'Donnell said.

He nodded. 'I know just the person. A countess, believe it or not.'

'Can we use her?' I asked.

'I don't see why not. We had radio contact as of a week ago.'

'Good. Explain what we need. Offer her a substantial amount of money for expenses. Then I want you to get busy collecting food and clothing. The prisoners are going from autumn in Italy to a northern winter. Warm clothes are a priority.' We discussed the content of the parcels. 'Chocolate, raisins, oranges if you can get them. Or apples, if you can't. Where will you start?'

Gill smiled. 'I happen to know a black market dealer on the south coast. I'll start with him.'

'Will he co-operate?'

Gill nodded. 'Don't worry, I'll make him an offer he can't refuse.'

I raised a quizzical eyebrow. His reply told me Susan was marrying the right man.

'His life.'

51

THE TRAIN JOURNEY was a glimpse of hell. We moved slowly, accelerating in short, jerky bursts that threw us against each other. Stopping often in the same way, then held up for hours at a time. The stench in the car was overwhelming. As I looked around me, at the shut down faces of my comrades, it was hard to remember that these were men of pride and dignity. We'd been on the train for two days and were still in Italy.

On the third day we'd been travelling for about two hours when we heard the first explosion. The truck I was in rattled as debris hit the side. The train came to a screeching halt. Doors were thrown open and we piled out.

A Griffin fighter/bomber was climbing into a clear sky before turning to come back. *We were being strafed by our own plane.* The pilot opened fire, aiming at the back of the train. We jumped down into a ditch, desperately seeking whatever shelter we could find. He must have realised we were Allied prisoners – at the last second he stopped firing and turned away, waggling his wings. We stayed where we were, terrified he might return, but after a few minutes it was clear he'd gone for good. Back to his mess, I thought bitterly, for a bath, a drink and some decent grub.

Whistles blew. The guards came and herded us back onto the train. Climbing in I took a chance to see what lay ahead. In the near distance were the Alps, their tops wreathed with heavy cloud. The rail track meandered along a canyon floor before passing into a ravine a few miles ahead.

I was the last man onto the wagon and kept my head outside until the doors slid closed and we were locked up in that filthy hellhole once again.

Hours later we stopped in the complex of track at the southern end of the Brenner Pass. The doors were opened and we were ordered out. I jumped down and helped out a few of the others, weak from lack of food and the effects of dysentery.

'You *Kriegies* line up over there,' a guard ordered. *Kriegies* was short for *Krieggefangener*, meaning prisoner of war. One of the men moved too slowly and he shoved him with the butt of his rifle.

'Leave him alone,' I shouted furiously in German. 'You can see he's not well.'

'Make him move quickly or it'll be the worse for him.'

I put my arm around the man's shoulders and hustled him forward.

'Thanks, son, ' he mumbled. 'Here, if you speak German you should be helping Jock. He's a good negotiator but not speaking Kraut makes his life difficult.'

'The German officers speak English,' I argued.

'Only when it suits them.'

This was the second time I'd been asked to help the camp's Man of Confidence. My conscience was troubling me. There is a time to be still and a time to act. *Tomorrow*, I thought, *tomorrow* I'll introduce myself to the Man.

But matters were taken out of my hands. An altercation was taking place about fifty yards away and I realised that McAllister was in the middle of it.

Against my better instincts I went forward. McAllister was speaking to a group of German officers.

'This is disgusting. Half a loaf of stale black bread and mouldy cheese? You have an obligation under the Geneva Convention to feed and clothe us properly.' In response he received a mouthful of abuse in German, which, without the rhetoric, condensed down to the fact that there was no more on offer.

Addressing the most senior officer, I said in my best *Hochdeutsch*, 'The Convention is quite clear. We prisoners are entitled to the same food as a German soldier.'

The German officer, extremely tall and thin, one armless tunic sleeve tucked into his left hand pocket, looked at me in astonishment. 'The Geneva Convention does not apply here.'

'What did he say, lad?' McAllister asked.

I told him.

'The Geneva Convention applies under all circumstances,' said the

485

Chief Petty Officer, 'and if he doesn't conform to it he will answer for that when this war is over. Tell him.'

There followed a protracted discussion. Throughout, McAllister kept his voice even and his temper in check. I was having great difficulty doing likewise. The German major became angrier as he lost argument after argument.

McAllister was on a roll. 'Under the provisions of the International Convention relating to the treatment of POWs, published at Geneva, Switzerland, on the twenty seventh of July, nineteen twenty nine, of which Great Britain and the German Reich are signatory powers, you are in breach of the Convention for the following reasons; One, transferring prisoners in an unmarked train to the endangerment of their lives. Two, moving men in such conditions as to cause widespread hardship and distress. Three, failing to provide adequate facilities for sanitation. Four, failure to provide urgently needed medicine for those who are ill. Five, inadequate food and water comparable to rations a German soldier can expect in the field. Six . . .'

He didn't reach six. The Germans simply walked away from us.

'Bastards!' said McAllister in impotent fury. Then he turned to me, holding out his hand, 'What's your name, son?'

'Able Seaman Richard Griffiths, Chief.'

'You speak German pretty good. You had better travel with me. We have to keep reminding them of their obligations. Otherwise they'll run roughshod over us.'

'They do anyway,' I said, looking at the state of the men queuing up for their meagre food rations.

'Believe me it would be a lot worse if we didn't keep at them.' McAllister sighed and said, 'I fear that's what will happen when we reach Germany.' He looked about forty, though I knew he was ten years younger. Thin to the point of emaciation, his hooked nose and deep-set eyes were more pronounced than they should have been.

'Who was that major?'

'His name's Heinrich. He took over the camp the day we left. Major Fischer was called back to active duty. Fischer was bad enough but this swine appears a lot worse. Have you noticed the guards? They're either old or maimed or barely out of nappies; the old ones are bitter and the youngsters are afraid. That's a mix that makes for a very dangerous, unstable situation. I've picked up a bit of German since I've been a prisoner and I've talked with those who can speak

486

English. The older guards are mainly veterans from the Eastern Front. The stories they tell about the Russians make my blood run cold, even though the Germans are our enemy. It's why they're running back to the Fatherland. To save it from the Bolsheviks.'

I lined up with McAllister. A lump of black bread was thrust into my hands, along with a piece of cheese. My mug was filled with cold water, which I drank thirstily, emptying it without thinking. It made chewing and swallowing the bread and cheese all the more difficult.

The German officer returned. 'You will remain here for one day,' he announced.

I slipped back into my role as interpreter.

'Out in the open? What about tents? Blankets?'

The German shrugged. 'You will have to do your best with the wagons. You can sleep in and on them. If anyone tries to escape they will be shot.'

'What about setting up latrines?'

'We don't have the equipment,' he shrugged.

'This is intolerable . . .'

'*Genug!*'

Despite the major's attitude, I kept my voice even, following McAllister's example, and continued to interpret. 'There is nothing I can do for you or your men. There will be an evening meal. You may light fires.'

He was interrupted by the sound of approaching trucks, clearly marked by a white roundel and a red cross. We stopped in astonishment to watch them climbing the steep incline to where we stood.

A middle-aged woman climbed down from the first truck and walked across to us. She looked tired, her grey hair held back in a severe bun. Her round figure strained the buttons of the shabby coat she wore.

Without preamble she addressed the major in German. 'I am from the Red Cross. We have food parcels for your prisoners and wish permission to distribute them.'

The major nodded curtly. 'You have it.'

'Thank you.' She turned to us. This time she smiled and said in English, 'Altogether we have a thousand parcels. Can we have a hand to distribute them?'

'My God, you're an answer to a prayer. Listen up.' McAllister raised his voice and addressed the other POWs. 'We have a thousand food parcels. We're staying here for the night. Light fires. Line up for the parcels. We share whatever we get. Section leaders take charge.'

A ragged cheer sounded and the men turned to with a will. Some went skirmishing for wood for fires under the watchful eyes of the guards, while others headed for the trucks.

'I don't know how to thank you enough,' McAllister said to the woman.

She smiled wanly. 'That's quite all right, though you could do me a favour. Do you have a Richard Griffiths here?'

McAllister turned to me, looking as surprised as I felt. 'This man is Richard Griffiths.'

'It's a common enough name. Do you mind me asking who your father is?'

'David. Sir David Griffiths.'

'You're the one, all right. I have a parcel especially for you. Will you follow me, please?'

I walked beside her back to the lorry. She opened the door on the passenger side and reached in. Turning to me she handed me a large package. 'I have had strict instructions to give this to you personally. Can you tell me your mother's name?'

'Madelaine. Why?'

'Your father said he will know you received the parcel if I tell him your mother's name. Very simple. Very effective.'

'Thank you.' I was really puzzled now. 'What on earth is going on?'

She shook her head. 'All I can tell you is that at dawn this morning we had a large delivery.' She lowered her voice though there was nobody in earshot. 'Amongst the equipment we received were the parcels for this train.'

The penny dropped and I said, 'Resistance? So this drop was arranged by SOE?'

'Quiet. Yes, this has all been arranged by your father.'

I smiled. A warm feeling burst in my stomach and spread through my chest, threatening to overwhelm me. I swallowed hard. 'Dad's doing what he can to help.'

She nodded. 'Is there anything in particular you need?'

'Can I sneak into your truck and hide?'

She smiled sadly. 'If you were caught, the Germans would use it as an excuse to stop *all* Red Cross activity. Would you want to be responsible for such a thing happening?'

Crestfallen I shook my head. 'In that case, I need boots. My feet are killing me. And a warm coat.'

'Guiseppe,' she called over her shoulder. A young man came around the cab.

'Yes, mama?'

'This is my son. He's about your size.' There followed a rapid exchange in Italian, which ended with Guiseppe taking off his overcoat and handing it to me.

'I can buy another,' he said in good English. 'Try my boots on.'

He undid the laces of one of his boots and pulled it off. I yanked off my shoe and tried the fleece-lined boot, wriggling my toes.

'It's a little big but another pair of socks should fix that.'

With Guiseppe's coat and boots I felt like a new man. 'I don't know how to thank you enough.'

'Your father has paid handsomely,' said the woman. 'Are they finished unpacking?' She addressed her son.

'Yes, mama.'

'Good. Then we can go.'

I watched as the convoy turned and went back the way it had come, before turning my attention to the parcel I'd received. I had been itching to open it. I felt like a kid at Christmas.

The first thing I found was an envelope stuffed with German marks. A note had been wrapped around them.

Son,

The money is to be used when you get to Germany, to buy food from the guards if you can. If we are able to send more parcels we will. In the meantime we are following your progress closely.

The family are all well, so don't worry about us, just take care of yourself. Your mother sends her love and best wishes. Bite carefully when you eat the fruitcake. You know how brittle your teeth are! Once you get to Bremen I'll arrange more parcels and mail. Tell no one about the money.

Love, Dad.

Making sure I was well away from any nosy guards, I checked the rest of the parcel. Raisins, a pound and a half of chocolate, two bars of soap, *The Saint Goes West*, by Leslie Charteris, tins of Spam, corned beef and pressed tongue, pears in syrup, tangerines in syrup and 1lb of butter. A veritable cornucopia! The fruitcake was at the bottom, wrapped in greaseproof paper. I frowned at it, wondering what the hell the old man meant about brittle teeth. It was only then that the penny dropped. I lifted the cake out to find another small package underneath. I tore open the paper. My hand wrapped around a Swiss Army knife with just about every attachment you could think of. Good old dad! I opened the three-inch blade and tentatively prodded the cake. On my second try I felt it hit something hard. Checking that no one was looking I broke the cake open. To my utter astonishment I found two wireless crystals wrapped in greaseproof paper.

Very carefully I began taking the cake apart. When I'd finished I realised that there were enough parts to make a wireless. I knew something about how to put one together but I was also aware that there were men far better qualified than me who would do a better job.

McAllister, usually so controlled, was barely able to contain his excitement. 'With that and the gramophone parts in some of the other parcels we ought to be able to transmit and receive.'

'And look.' I showed him the knife.

'Good man. Keep it hidden or the Krauts will confiscate it. It'll come in useful.'

'That's what I thought. Chief . . . ,' I had to trust somebody and that man was obviously McAllister. 'I've also got a wad of German currency.'

He looked at me with real interest. 'Just who the hell are you? How did this all come about?' He waved his arm around him, indicating the activity around us. Fires had been started and already food was being cooked.

I wondered how much I should tell him. How could I explain that my father would move heaven and earth to help me? That he was obsessed with looking after the family? That no matter what it cost, he would do his damnedest to keep me alive? It was unfathomable to anyone who didn't know him and so I didn't bother trying. 'My father is Sir David Griffiths. He's a banker and was a politician. He's also number two in the Special Operations Executive.'

McAllister was looking at me shrewdly. 'If this is all thanks to your father, Griffiths, then you're worth your weight in gold to us. Once we arrive at our destination we'll be able to ask for more help.'

'Bremen,' I said.

'Is that's where we're going? How do you know?'

'My father told me in a letter. And don't ask me how *he* knows.'

McAllister nodded. 'It makes sense. I'd heard there was a camp for naval POWs somewhere around the North Sea. Christ, we've a long journey ahead of us.'

We spent the night on the ground, sheltering under the wagons. The sickest slept inside. We had eaten our fill, more food than we'd had in two months. Those with dysentery swallowed charcoal before their meal in the hope that it would help them retain the food and give them some much needed energy. Each parcel had contained two apples. By unanimous decision, these were to be stored for cidermaking once we arrived at our destination. After all, Christmas was coming.

We were woken by a tin can being beaten and yells from the guards. Stiffly I climbed out from under the wagon and went to find someplace to relieve myself. Fires were stoked and water put on to boil. We would have real tea, sweetened with sugar and condensed milk to wash down bacon sandwiches.

After our meal we sat in small huddles around the fires, wondering what was going to happen next. As always, the talk turned to escape. But we didn't have papers, clothing, anything to allow us to blend in with the general population. The guards were edgy, lashing out at every opportunity. Which was why the escape attempt, when it happened, was so ludicrous.

There was a fight. A dozen or more men were involved. The guards rushed in, clubbing the POWs, trying to break them up. I didn't see the men who slipped away until they were spotted high on an embankment, a hundred yards away. The guards didn't even order them to stop. They just opened fire, mowing down all three. Two died instantly. The medics tried to save the third. They failed.

'Idiots,' said McAllister. 'We all have a duty to try and escape but only if there's a chance of succeeding. Not in this half-baked, foolhardy way.'

By mid-morning I was becoming restless. The sky was darkening. It was obvious a storm was coming down from the north. The wind had freshened and there was the feel of snow in the air. Trains had been going through the Pass all day, many coming south with troops and armaments to reinforce the German positions. Even to my untutored eye, many of the soldiers were either very young or past middle age. Germany was scraping the barrel in defence of the Fatherland.

Finally, as sleet and rain began to fall, we were herded back onto the train. With a full stomach I was more optimistic but that feeling didn't last. The train jerked back and forth, throwing us against one another, until finally it started towards the Pass. The sleet and rain were now falling with a vengeance and hitting the roof, the sound like machine-gun fire. The temperature had dropped and I was grateful for the coat and boots I'd acquired. Suddenly the gloom turned to darkness as we entered the tunnel and I closed my eyes, praying this nightmare would end soon. The smell in the wagon was getting worse. I heard another poor sod void his bowels, adding to the stench. My father had always argued that the German people were more sinned against than sinning and I believed him. But at that moment I felt such an overwhelming hatred I could have killed every last one of them.

The train passed back into the open and a dim light penetrated through the cracks in the wooden-sided wagon. The staccato drumming of the rain and sleet hit once more and I shivered.

The train wound its way through the Alps, passing along open track, interspersed with tunnels of varying lengths. I fell into a stupor, propped up between the wooden wall and the bodies around me. Tears of self-pity welled up in my eyes. Surrounded by dozens of my comrades, I felt very alone.

52

THE SIMPLE CODE had worked. Richard had received his parcel. The report given us by the Italians gave me cause for concern, but I consoled myself with the thought that he was still alive and there were things I could do to help. I was aware I was abusing my position, but my son's life was all that mattered to me. I would do everything in my power to keep him safe.

The logistics of the parcel drop still left me numb. As we congratulated each other on our achievement Robert Gill recounted his side of the story, which impressed me greatly. He'd gone to Portsmouth and found a man involved in petty dealing on the black-market. A bribe or two gave Gill the name of the man who controlled the trade from Portsmouth to Southampton.

'There's always a Mr Big,' said Gill, a whisky in his hand as he, Mike and I sat in the United Services Club. 'The criminal fraternity is as regimented as the army. Funnily enough, I'd heard some of the stories about this man when I was with the force but I'd never believed them.'

'Why not?' I asked, signalling a steward to bring fresh drinks.

'He's a solicitor.'

I'd been sitting back in my chair but sat up with a jerk. 'You're joking!'

'No. He's spent his life defending crooks in court and I suppose some of it's rubbed off. There'd been rumours but nothing ever came of it. He's too well connected to be arrested and tried.'

'What did you do?' Mike asked.

'I had a meeting with him in his office. Laid it on the line.' Gill paused to sip his whisky, evidently enjoying telling the story.

'Come on, Robert, what happened?' Mike asked.

'I told him I wanted to buy enough supplies for a thousand parcels.

I gave him the list we'd drawn up and he shrugged, handing it back to me. He said that I should take it to a shop with the correct food coupons.' Gill paused and smiled. 'I really enjoyed the next bit.'

'What did you do?' I asked.

'I took out my service revolver, shoved the barrel under his throat, cocked it and told the scum his home address. I explained that I could either buy what I wanted from him or from his widow. Which was it to be? You know, as a way of enforcing the law, sheer terror is highly effective.'

Mike and I laughed.

'All it took was one phone call. He arranged it there and then, pretending he was acting for one of his clients. The whole transaction was conducted as a business deal, handshakes included. He tried to stitch me up with the price but I dissuaded him of that and paid a fair amount in the end. Here's your change, sir.'

He handed me an envelope, which I slipped into my pocket. 'What happened then?'

'We went to his warehouse near the docks in Southampton and drove away in a truck stuffed to the gunnels. You know the rest. Wales was waiting for me. The staff at the factory had the packages ready in under an hour and then Mike and I took them to Sion.'

My brother had painted one of the Griffins with the insignia of the Red Cross. He'd flown the plane personally. First to Portugal, and then on to the drop zone. In the meantime we'd made contact with Gill's circuit and agreed a price for their aid. It hadn't been exorbitant; money, guns and explosives. And as deputy head of SOE I could lay my hands on as much of the latter as I wanted knowing it would be used for effective sabotage. And money wasn't a problem when you owned a bank.

'What's next?' Mike asked.

I shook my head. 'The train has crossed Austria and is now in Germany.'

'It's taking its time,' said Gill.

'That's because it has such low priority,' I said. 'There is so much rolling stock on the move right now, the railways are clogging up all the time. And a lot of track is being pulverised, causing delays and a lot of re-routing. We expected the train to go north via Munich but there's no chance of that. The next city of any size is likely to be Regensburg, about fifty miles from the Czech border. Any assets there?'

Both Mike and Robert shook their heads.

'We're working on Germany,' said Mike. 'We've established contact with Stauffenberg's people but they're keeping a very low profile. And nobody in their right minds would blame them for that.'

After the failed coup Hitler had gone on a killing spree. Many good men and women had died terrible deaths. The Fuhrer's assassins had a preferred method of killing – tying a thin wire around the neck of the victim, who was then suspended from a meat hook. Many had committed suicide rather than be taken alive.

'Have you read the report on Himmler's approach to the Americans?' I asked.

Both men nodded. 'It's incredible,' said Mike. 'He actually believes he can negotiate a peace deal that will leave him in charge after the war. After all he's done!'

'If we take him alive he'll be hanged for war crimes. Now he's taken charge of all POWs they're more vulnerable than ever.'

'Our long range weather wallahs say it's going to be a cold, hard winter,' said Gill morosely. 'If the rumours are true and our lads are moved west out of Poland then I don't give them much chance of surviving. They'll be force-marched with lousy food, no chance of shelter, and under an increasingly brutal regime.'

'We have to pray that Richard's train gets them to Bremen before the winter sets in too deeply,' I said. 'Once he's there I can get more aid to him. Ah, my favourite people.'

Susan and Madelaine entered the clubroom. Gill rushed to his feet and went to greet them, kissing Susan's cheek.

Madelaine's greeting was always the same. 'Any news about Richard?'

'They're still en route. Once he reaches Bremen we'll attempt to get supplies sent in the same way. Apart from that there's nothing we can do.' I could see that Madelaine was about to bring up the same hair-brained idea again. 'Darling, we *can't* rescue him. We've been through it a thousand times.'

'Mike, please . . .' she began. But he shook his head.

'I agree with David, Maddie. It's impossible. You can't waltz into Germany and spring a POW. There are far too many imponderables and difficulties. What we're doing is for the best.'

Susan and Gill made their excuses, saying they were going up the west end to take in a show.

495

I watched them leave with a critical eye. It was practically impossible to tell how Susan was really doing, but she seemed composed.

Madelaine caught my eye and we exchanged smiles. 'She'll be fine,' she said. 'She's a Griffiths, remember, made of stern stuff.'

The following morning brought bad news. RAF bombing raids, coupled with sabotage, had forced Richard's train eastwards. I double-checked the wireless signals we had received overnight. The train had entered Czechoslovakia and was already only a few miles south of Prague.

I'd had my staff mark every POW camp on the wall map and I stood looking at it, wondering where they were destined. There were thirty-five little flags, stretching from East Prussia and the Lithuanian border, west to Bremen, south to Munich and east to Teschen in Czechoslovakia. In those camps were some 257,000 American and British prisoners, 90,000 of whom were in the zone that would soon be liberated by the Soviets, potential pawns for Stalin. And amongst all those men was one young boy I was desperate to protect.

I forced off the feeling of uselessness and despair that threatened to overwhelm me. There was nothing more I could do for Richard until he got off the train or it stopped somewhere accessible. Other matters needed my attention. I began working on the pile of buff folders stacked on my desk, each one an operation proposed for occupied Europe. Reading them through I quickly endorsed several operations. The last folder I opened was entirely different.

Circuit *Tunnelman* in Normandy had been betrayed. Two traitors had stolen significant funds and denounced at least three of our agents, possibly a fourth. I carefully read each piece of damning evidence. Innuendo and hearsay amounted to a convincing case, but were they *guilty*? If I made the wrong decision I'd have the deaths of innocent men on my conscience. The circuit was Mike's and he'd already annotated the file with his judgement. Guilty. I needed to speak to him.

'Mike? Can you come and see me for a few minutes?' I hung up the receiver and he appeared almost immediately.

'*Tunnelman*?' he greeted me.

I nodded. 'There isn't any real proof that they betrayed our bods.'

'I know, David. But even if they didn't, they're still a liability. They've been spending money like water, getting drunk in inappropriate places. You read about the incident in the restaurant? In the middle of Nantes, for God's sake? It's a wonder the police didn't pick them up. The only way to survive is to keep a low profile.'

It was true. If you fought in the resistance you kept your day job. Went about business as normal. Avoided any behaviour that might call attention to yourself. It was standing operational procedure.

'It seems that these two either don't care if they're blown or else know no harm will come to them,' I said thoughtfully.

'Suppose they're innocent and it's sheer luck they haven't been lifted?'

'That's not possible. Too much money and equipment have gone missing. Nobody's asked to account for every franc and we know some pilfering is inevitable. But the scale of losses with *Tunnelman* is totally unacceptable.'

Mike shoved his hands in his pockets and stared morosely at his feet. 'It's not my decision, David, thank God. It's yours. Just think about the agents we've lost. How the hell did that happen, if they weren't betrayed? And who else could have betrayed them?'

Mike was right and I reluctantly agreed. 'Pass the word. I want to know when sentence is carried out.'

A day later the two men confessed to stealing money, ration books and equipment sent to the resistance. The stolen gear had been sold on the black-market. Money and ration books were discovered in their homes. No more proof was required.

There was no way they could have gotten away with it for any length of time. To have embarked on a crime spree against the *Maquis* and by extension SOE, was stupidity itself. They claimed they were criminals, not traitors and should be handed over to the *gendarmerie*. But there was no question of arrest and trial. Justice was quick. They were executed and buried in unmarked graves deep in a Normandy forest, just another sordid episode in a sordid war.

December was fast approaching – we would soon be facing a sixth Christmas at war. As a sign that hostilities were drawing to a close the Home Guard was "stood down", though many members retained their weapons.

The Saar Basin was taken by General George Patton's tank regiments and the French broke past Strasbourg. All along the western lines the Germans were in retreat.

Reports were coming in that the Germans planned a major offensive, though we were unable to discover where and when.

The lights went back on in Piccadilly, the Strand and Fleet Street after five years of blackout. Londoners rejoiced in the streets while only a few dozen miles away armies were still pulverising each other into oblivion.

We received an invitation to Churchill's birthday, which we felt obliged to attend. On the evening of the party I stood in front of the mirror and adjusted my bow tie. I caught Madelaine's eye in the mirror and summoned a smile from somewhere.

'I don't want to go either,' she murmured.

'I know, darling, but we've accepted.'

'It seems so wrong, somehow. Going out to enjoy ourselves while Richard is facing God alone knows what at the hands of the Germans.'

'Richard would want us to go and enjoy ourselves. This is a special occasion, seeing as the old boy's seventy this year.'

Tears sprang to Madelaine's eyes and she sank onto the bed. 'I know.'

'Chin up, darling. He has only months to hang on. The war is coming to an end. If he keeps a low profile he'll be liberated sooner rather than later.'

'When, David? When?' The anguish in her voice tore at my heart.

Shaking my head I said, 'By spring, I should think. Now that the Russians have crossed the Danube it'll be a race, East versus West. And Germany will be the prize.'

53

THE TRAIN STOPPED and the doors were thrown open. Whistles blew and harsh orders were given for us to climb down. Some of the men next to the doors simply fell out. I realised we were in the middle of a wood. Was this it? Were we to be machine-gunned and left to rot? The others caught my mood. We looked fearfully at our captors. German Shepherd dogs on leashes were snarling and spitting, pawing at the ground.

It was mid-morning and the sky was overcast. A cold wind was blowing from the north and I shivered, in spite of my warm coat.

Jock McAllister nudged me and I went with him towards a German officer.

'Tell him we want to know why we've stopped,' began McAllister.

'I speak English,' said the officer coldly. He was in his late twenties, I guessed, very tall, wearing the uniform of an SS captain.

My heart sank. The SS were known for their viciousness and ill treatment of prisoners of war. Suddenly I realised that the guards who'd been with us for the last few days had gone. In their place were youngsters, wearing the uniform of the Hitler Youth. For all their innocent appearance those fanatics were as bad if not worse than the SS. Now the men had disembarked, the Hitler Youth strutted around with guns on their backs and unsheathed bayonets in their hands. Their hate-filled eyes followed us coldly.

The last drink I'd been given had been the evening before and I had a raging thirst. Now fear added to the dryness in my mouth and I tried to wet my cracked lips.

'I repeat,' McAllister spoke politely. 'What is happening here, captain?'

By way of an answer the officer slapped McAllister across the cheek with his open hand. 'You will not address me unbidden,' he screamed. 'You piece of filth. Stand to attention when you speak to an officer of the Third Reich or I will have you shot.'

McAllister didn't blink. He drew himself to attention and saluted. With his arm held to the side of his forehead he held the pose and said, 'I respectfully request an answer to my question, sir.'

The captain appeared to be about to strike again but held himself in check. 'You will form up in columns three deep and seventy long, then follow this road to the next POW camp. Anyone who fails to keep up will be shot. Anyone who tries to escape will be shot. Anyone who disobeys an order will be shot. Do you understand?'

'Yes, sir. I will inform the men,' said McAllister calmly. The man continually astounded me. His equanimity was an inspiration to us all. Walking back to the men, I noticed cameras and three film crews – I pointed them out to McAllister.

'What the hell are they here for?' McAllister asked as the orders were given to line up in columns.

With so many men it took a while. I was with McAllister in the first section. Looking down the road I saw two lines of Hitler Youth forming either side, cursing and shouting. They held rifles and unsheathed bayonets. Interspersed along the two lines stood guards, cradling machine-guns. The significance of the cameras was suddenly clear to McAllister. He turned to face the long columns and said in a loud voice, 'Listen up, men. We're being set up. Whatever the provocation *do not* run. If you do they will shoot us. The film crews are here to provide proof that we were killed while trying to escape. Pass the word along. Do not run.'

'Silence! Silence!' The SS captain screamed but to no avail. The message was passed down the lines. I hoisted my small scran bag on my shoulder and wondered yet again if I was going to survive the day.

The order was given, 'Column will move to the right in threes, right turn!'

We moved with a semblance of order and military bearing. What it cost some of the others I would never know but it took me all my will-power to obey the command. I was now in the middle line, second from the front. Jock McAllister was ahead and on my right. The tall SS officer suddenly appeared at the head of the column and faced us.

'Keep up or you will be shot,' he shouted, then gave the order to march.

That caused more consternation until McAllister called over his shoulder, 'Steady, lads. Remember we have the Geneva Convention on our side.'

'Silence!'

An open-topped staff car drove slowly past us, the SS captain standing on the running board. Dressed in immaculate white breeches and knee-length, highly polished boots, he was brandishing a pistol. The dogs were barking more frantically than ever and the two lines of Hitler Youth brandished their guns and bayonets with greater menace. What the hell was going to happen?

The column set off. The guards on either side of us urged us on, telling us to keep up with the car or else we would be shot. The German Shepherds were now only inches from us, snarling and slavering, making us walk faster. Marching in step lasted for seconds only. We were too tired, thirsty and hungry to keep it up.

As we reached the lines of Hitler Youth the swine began to swing at us with their rifle butts and bayonets. McAllister was hit in the arm and a slice was taken out of his cheek. One youth darted at the column, reached past the man next to me and stabbed me in the arm. The material of my coat was thick and he barely nicked me, though he cut open the cloth.

The Mercedes staff car drove back along the column and the captain was screaming at the top of his voice, 'Make them run! Make them run!' He fired two shots over our heads and turned his demented, hate-filled face to McAllister. *'Verdammter Gott im Himmel, laufen Sie.'*

McAllister lengthened his stride but that was all. More blows rained down on him. He stumbled but kept his feet. I looked back. The column was in total disarray. The Hitler Youth were screaming like banshees, indiscriminately striking at our men, slashing with their bayonets. Panic was settling in. At any moment the other POWs could break into a run, which would be fatal. I realised how close we were to the edge as the guards suddenly raised their machine-guns directly at us. I remember thinking, *Please God, no. Please, God.*

'Jock! Jock!' I called fearfully. 'Settle the men. Say something. *Do* something.'

His strained face looked back at me and he nodded. Raising his hand he called out, 'Get into the rhythm, lads. March at my speed!'

Like a balm the call was passed down the line and the men settled, the panic withering away, to the fury of the Germans. The Hitler

Youth continued to trot by our sides, swiping at us.

One called out, 'This is for Hamburg and Cologne,' and slashed twice at the man by my side, cutting his face and his arm.

'London, Liverpool, Coventry, you kraut bastards,' the man screamed back at him.

The Mercedes car drove back up the column, the captain still screaming at us dementedly. The dogs were going berserk with the smell of blood, straining at their leashes, snapping at our heels.

Suddenly there was a scream and one man fell into the roadway. Looking over my shoulder I saw him get to his feet and run towards the thick pine trees lining the route. God alone knows what possessed the poor bastard. Shots rang out and he fell, throwing his arms in the air. Two German Shepherds were launched at him and leapt onto his inert body. The way they gripped and worried an arm and a leg each I prayed he was already dead.

Another flash point threatened to erupt in the ranks. Panicked flight or bloody-minded attack, which was it to be? The mood of the men had turned from fear to blind hatred and suddenly the air was alive with the threat of menace. I think the Germans suddenly realised it too. If we turned on them, many of us would die, but we would take many of them with us. We outnumbered them fifteen – maybe twenty – to one. We would prevail, although the cost would be horrendous.

It was the SS captain standing on the running board of his Mercedes who came to his senses first.

'*Macht langsam,*' he yelled.

'Chief, he says slow down,' I translated.

McAllister slowed to a fast walk. 'Take it easy, lads,' he yelled over his shoulder. 'Not far to go now.' Of course, he didn't know how far we still had to travel but it had the desired effect.

The road branched and we went along a wide and heavily used track. The Hitler Youth began to fall behind, their savage attacks on us stopped. Suddenly and completely unexpectedly we came to a huge clearing. In its midst was a POW camp.

The sign over the gateway said *Stalag XXB, Marienburg*. I recognised the name from Uncle Sion's maps – we were in East Prussia, only a few miles southeast of Danzig. We milled around the open ground in front of the gates as more of the POWs arrived behind us. Now that we weren't being hounded and attacked most of the men collapsed to the ground, exhausted, many nursing wounds. A semi-circle of guards formed around the edge of the trees, machine-guns at the ready, dogs held on close leashes. Even the dogs seemed to have had their blood lust assuaged, if only for a few minutes.

McAllister came over to me. Blood oozed from the cut on his cheek and his clothes had been torn in several places. He looked like a scarecrow.

'The filthy bastards,' he said with feeling. 'Stick with me, lad. I may need your linguistic talents.'

I don't know how long we stayed there but it seemed like hours. I was thirstier than ever and desperate for something to eat. I lay down with my head on my bag, the straps tied to my wrist. It wasn't unusual for gear and food to go missing, stolen by fellow prisoners. The day was drawing to a close and there was a hint of rain in the air. I shivered and prayed that the day would end soon.

The usual yells and screams forced us to our feet and we were finally marched into the camp. After ten minutes, during which time nobody approached us, we simply sat on the cold, hard earth and waited. Patience was one of the virtues you learned as a POW.

There were the usual rows of wooden huts. The barbed wire fence was high and deep, with the standard no-go line painted on the ground. The sentries in the watchtowers stood looking down at us. An odd silence descended.

Our arrival had caused a commotion further down the camp and a small delegation of POWs approached us. They stopped a short distance away. 'Who's the Man?' one of them asked.

'I am,' McAllister approached the other man, his hand outstretched. 'Jock McAllister. Chief Petty Officer, RN.'

'Sergeant Major Bullmaster, Sixth Armoured Division. Tony.'

'You the man?' McAllister asked.

'I am. Got the job by default. The last one died of pneumonia only two weeks ago. Once I've shown you the ropes, it's yours if you want it.'

McAllister's shoulders slumped and I saw the look of despair on his face. Beneath the phlegmatic exterior he was living on the edge of his nerves, worn down by the terrible responsibility he shouldered.

Bullmaster saw it too and said, in a kindly, quiet voice, 'I know – you need patience and tact when dealing with the bastards. I'm running short of both.'

'Are there any German speakers amongst your lot?' McAllister asked.

'Some, I guess, but if there are they aren't saying. You know what it's like. Keeping a low profile and I can't say I blame them.'

McAllister looked at me and said, 'Seems you still have a job.'

I nodded and replied, 'In that case hadn't we better do something about shelter, and getting the men fed and watered?'

'This is Dickie Griffiths,' said McAllister. 'He's a Royal Navy seaman and my right-hand man. What about food and something to drink?'

'In the mess tent. We were told to expect more POWs but Jesus wept, not as many as this. The Krauts told us that tents were on the way but they haven't arrived yet. There are three empty huts. Each one holds forty but I reckon we can double that number for a day or two. Where have you come from?'

'Italy.'

'Italy? All the way up here? What're the Germans playing at?' Bullmaster asked. He introduced the other men with him. We exchanged nods. I was too weary to offer my hand to shake. I was sure the rest of the men were as desperately thirsty as I was.

'We need water,' I said.

'Lads,' Bullmaster turned to the other three, 'get billy cans. Tell our lot to come and help. I see from your face and clothes,' he turned back to us, 'that you were made to run the gauntlet.'

We nodded.

'How many did you lose?'

'One. Though we've a few hurt quite badly.'

'I'll get the medics to come and take a look, though there isn't much they can do. Only one dead? You were very lucky. Last month twenty-four men were killed.'

'What the hell is going on? This treatment is totally illegal,' said McAllister.

'We know. So do the Germans. You meet the SS captain, Schmidt?'

'Tall, skinny fellow, with a mouth like a rat trap?'

'That's the one. He arrived about six weeks ago. Ever since then things have gone downhill. Running the gauntlet is one of his little games, to soften us up, so to speak.'

'Any other little tricks we should know about?'

'Plenty, as you'll soon find out. He boasts that nobody knows we're here, not even the Red Cross. So he can do what he likes with us.'

'Is that true?'

'I've been here four months and we haven't seen hair nor hide of a Red Cross parcel, so it may be true.'

'What about the men who were here before you?'

'The place was empty.'

'It doesn't look that new,' said McAllister frowning.

'It's not. It was occupied before, but like I said, it was deserted when we arrived.'

POWs from the camp arrived carrying cans of water and started distributing them amongst us. In all my life nothing had ever tasted so good.

Some of our men, feeling refreshed, began calling out, asking questions.

'Where do we kip?'

'What about some grub?'

'We need a medic over here.'

McAllister slipped back easily into the role of command. 'Take it easy, lads. We've only got three huts. I'll take a look and see what we can do. Bring those who are most badly hurt forward. They'll get a bunk in one of the huts. The rest of you stay where you are. I'll see the Adjutant about tents. What about spare clothing?'

Bullmaster shrugged. 'Just the usual.'

I knew what that meant, *dead man's shoes.*

'Dickie, you'd better come with me. Who's the commandant?'

'Oberst Schlessinger. He's ineffective, not a bad man, just useless. Since Captain Schmidt got here life has gone to hell in a basket. The first thing he did was halve our rations. They were barely enough to keep us alive as it was.'

'With winter coming on God alone knows how we'll survive.'

'Have you made representation to the commandant?'

'Twice. He just shrugged and said there was nothing he could do about it.'

McAllister nodded glumly. The word amongst the POWs was that the SS were taking over the camps. It was a sinister move that would have horrendous repercussions. Ironically, the POWs needed the *Wehrmacht* to stand up to the SS.

'I'll have to remind the commandant of his obligations under the Geneva Convention,' said McAllister.

505

'We've tried. But I wish you good luck with that.'

'How many are in the camp?'

'Close on ten thousand with your lot.'

'Christ, but that's a big number. Anybody escape?'

'Where's to go? It's a long way to civilisation. We're close to the Baltic. There's a river about half a mile away, which we're pretty sure is the Vistula. There's a lot of traffic on it that's no use to us.'

'What about work duties?'

'There are logging camps all over the area. Five days work, two days of rest. Here we are.'

We had arrived at a guardhouse separating the German quarters from ours. The gate was closed and Bullmaster approached the hut diffidently. Four guards were inside, watching us approach. They said nothing, merely stared at us.

Finally a sergeant opened the door. *'Was wollen Sie?'*

'Feldwebel, we wish to see the Adjutant.'

There came a torrent of German and Bullmaster stood there helpless. 'What did he say?' he asked me.

'That we are only allowed to see the Adjutant between nine and ten o'clock in the morning.'

'Tell him this is an emergency. We have fifteen hundred men to house and feed and we need help.'

I interpreted back and forth but we were getting nowhere. Jock McAllister stepped in.

'Feldwebel, if you do not allow us to speak to the Adjutant, when the war is over we will report you as being in contravention of the Geneva Convention. You have obligations to look after us and you are failing in your duty,'

The sergeant was an older man with grey hair. He looked slightly shamefaced. Acknowledging McAllister he said grimly, *'Befehl ist Befehl.'*

McAllister interrupted, 'Orders are orders – that's no excuse. I insist we see the Adjutant.'

The guard nodded unhappily and opened the gate. He instructed two soldiers to accompany us through and we were escorted to a hut not far off. In the outer office, amidst desks, filing cabinets and all the paraphernalia needed to run such a large organisation, sat two shirt-sleeved officers.

'They wish to see the Adjutant,' said the soldier.

One of the men nodded briefly, donned his tunic and walked across the room to another office. After a few moments he re-emerged and beckoned to us to follow him in.

The Adjutant was in his fifties. The first thing I noticed about him were his weak, watery eyes, enhanced by pebble glasses. His hair was silver, his uniform slovenly and he needed a shave. He must have thought so too, for he greeted us with a wry smile. 'Excuse me gentlemen, I wasn't expecting a visit from the British, otherwise I would have observed the proprieties. However, I have been at my desk since five o'clock this morning. What can I do for you?'

McAllister saluted. 'Chief Petty Officer McAllister, sir. I am responsible for the men who have just arrived.' There was silence. Jock stood to attention and held the salute. The Adjutant looked uncomfortable. 'Tell him I am waiting to have my salute acknowledged and for him to tell me his name,' Jock directed me.

The pause lasted a few more seconds until finally the Adjutant gave a sloppy salute and said, 'Major Ernst Buchold.'

'Thank you. Sir, we have fifteen hundred more men in the camp. We need food, tents, mattresses, blankets, medical supplies, clothing . . . quite frankly, everything.'

'I see. Unfortunately, I am unable to supply you with most of your requests. Tents will be distributed during the next two or three days. Food will be supplied for your meal this evening. Medicines we do not have. Clothes we do not have.'

McAllister stood at attention and spoke respectfully. 'Sir, it will be cold and wet tonight. It could even snow. We must get help to the men. It's imperative. It is your duty, sir.'

In a tired voice the Adjutant answered, 'I do not need reminding of my duty. However, in certain matters my hands are tied.'

'Sir, the Geneva Convention is quite explicit,' McAllister challenged. 'My men need shelter and warmth. Anything less is a violation. We have the right . . .'

He got no further as the door crashed open and SS Captain Schmidt stood on the threshold. He carried a swagger stick, which he was swinging against his boot.

'What do you want here?' His voice was harsh and demanding and I stuttered over the translation.

McAllister, however, was unperturbed. 'We came to discuss with the Adjutant the well-being of my men, sir. It is the duty . . .'

'Silence!' Schmidt's eyes bulged and his face mottled red. 'Do not presume to tell me my duty,' he screamed. 'My duty is to my Führer and the Fatherland. You scum are lucky to be alive. If I had my way we would put you in the ovens along with the stinking Jews. You will be given tents when we are able to provide them. Now get out.'

'Sir, I must protest,' said McAllister but got no further.

With lightning speed the captain swung his swagger stick and struck McAllister across the cheek, leaving a large red weal.

The CPO staggered but kept his feet and stood to attention. 'Your action contravenes the Geneva . . .'

He got no further. Another blow sent him sprawling onto the floor.

'Do not quote the Convention at me,' said Schmidt, breathing heavily. 'Here only what I say matters.'

I bent down to help the CPO to his feet.

'Leave him,' said Schmidt. 'He can stand up himself.'

I ignored the captain.

'Leave me, lad, I'll manage.'

I glanced at Schmidt, turned my back to him and took hold of Jock by the shoulder. A stinging blow across my back made me flinch but I'd been expecting it. Gritting my teeth, I pulled Jock to his feet. Another blow across the top of my arm sent me staggering across the room.

'You cowardly swine,' I yelled at him. 'After the war I'll see you hanged as a war criminal.'

Schmidt's face went chalk white. He screamed an order into the next room. The two orderlies came in and dragged me out of the hut. Outside I was pushed towards a small wooden construction, about four feet square and four feet high. They threw me inside. The walls were solid, the floor was packed earth.

I hung my head between my knees and fought back the tears.

I spent two days in there. By the time the door was opened and I was dragged out I could barely stand. My legs had long since locked from cramp. I'd had no food, receiving only a pint of water a day to drink.

I willed my legs to move but they just wouldn't function. I was dragged across the compound by the arms. The massed POWs stood silently, watching as I was shoved into the main compound where I collapsed onto the earth. As I lay there, my primary emotion was not relief, but hate. One day, I swore to myself, I'd kill the bastard who put me in that hole.

McAllister and Bullmaster helped me up. By now the circulation was returning to my legs and they were on fire. Stubborn pride made me stand and I forced my legs to do what I wanted. I vowed that should I ever end up in the same predicament again I'd do more to keep the blood circulating properly.

'Are you all right, lad?'

'Yes, Chief. Thanks.' I shivered violently.

During my sojourn in the cell sleet had fallen. Now the dark black clouds gathering above us began to drop their heavy load. Snow fell thick and fast. It was going to be a long, cold winter.

54

We'd lost track of the bloody train somewhere in Poland. I'd harassed every contact we had, but to no avail. Then, by a sheer miracle, we got a message through. A short-wave transmission from a camp in East Prussia, picked up by one of our circuits in France, was forwarded to us.

The message read – *Tell Madelaine package arrived safely in XXB, East Prussia. Dad to send Christmas presents.*

I clutched the flimsy tightly in my hand. It told me all I needed to know. He was alive, he was in Marienburg and he wanted Red Cross parcels. That I could arrange.

'Mike, have you seen this?' I handed the flimsy to O'Donnell.

A beaming smile wreathed his face as he took the message. 'Thanks be to God. At least we can do something for him now.'

'Let's get a chain of communication opened. This came from *Apricot*. They're in Northern France, I think.'

'I'll check.' A moment later Mike said, 'Correct. Nancy to be precise.'

'Okay. I'll get their file, while you get hold of Robert. Tell him we want another load of parcels made up.'

From the file I saw that one of SOE's best and bravest agents was a courier with the *Donkeyman* circuit. Her name was Marguerite Knight, known as Peggy. I flicked through the file. Three of her colleagues had been shot as traitors, working as double agents, while another had survived after a bungled assassination attempt by two comrades. She had been despatched by us into France after less than a month's training due to the fact that we were desperately short of fluent French speakers. Peggy had been in the field for seven months and had done excellent work, recruiting as well as committing acts of sabotage. I saw she was only twenty-four years old, clever and

510

daring. Her file photograph showed an attractive young lady with a wide smile. Peggy Knight would be my conduit to Richard.

Her radio operator was *George 61*, a man by the name of Leon Cabaldi. Italian by birth, he had lived in France for many years, training as an operator early in the war. He had been active now for nearly five years. Something of a record, I realised grimly.

I knew that the better organised and bigger POW camps had wireless detection equipment and so messages would have to be kept brief. The likelihood of there being such equipment in Marienburg was slim but I wasn't going to take any chances.

Signals were sent back and forth. Each was short and concise. It took days to get all the information I wanted. Finally I had a picture of the camp's operation and it wasn't a pretty one. The treatment of our POWs was disgraceful – totally at odds with the message parliament was sending out to the country. To listen to our Members of Parliament you would think that our men were being held in holiday camps, not under the direst of conditions. One MP even made a joke about "our boys" fraternising with German *Fräuleins* in the local bars and cafes.

The POWs at Marienburg were in urgent need of food, medicine and clothing. They also needed practicalities – blankets, crockery etc. In fact, anything we could lay our hands on. The biggest problem I could see was the distance to the camp. I knew of no plane with a range great enough to reach Prussia and back. I needed to talk to Sion. It took three telephone calls before I managed to get hold of him.

'Sion, I need another parcel drop, this time to the south of Danzig.'

'On the Baltic? That's a distance of about eighteen hundred miles from London. Bloody hell! We've nothing that can fly a round trip of nearly four thousand miles. Not only is there the possibility of evasive action, but we have to take into account the weather, battling headwinds and so on. How big will the payload be?'

'That's the other huge problem. The camp currently houses over ten thousand men. A standard seven pound package for each amounts to seventy thousand pounds all together.'

'Jesus wept. That's an impossible amount.' The line went quiet for a second. 'Let me get back to you. I've a glimmer of an idea.'

Sion phoned me back less than ten minutes later. 'We're on. Payload fifteen thousand pounds, and her range is two thousand three hundred and fifty miles. Only trouble is, you'll have to requisition one from the Air Ministry.'

'What is she?'

'A Catalina Flying Boat.'

'My God, yes! There are what? Five hundred with Coastal Command?'

'Nearer seven hundred.'

'How the hell,' I spoke aloud, 'am I going to get my hands on one?'

'That, Bro', I can't help you with. But I'm sure you'll think of something.'

Replacing the receiver I sat in thought for a few minutes. I made a phone call to the War Office and got the name I wanted. Within minutes I had the connection.

'Air Vice-Marshal Coggins? My name is Sir David Griffiths, SOE.'

'I've heard of you, Sir David. What can I do for you?'

'I need a Catalina for a special operation. It's totally hush-hush – Winnie's instructed me to carry out a certain task. I can go through the usual channels and requisition an aircraft but I thought it would make more sense to talk to you. Winnie,' I gilded the lily without a hint of shame, 'suggested I contact you directly.'

'Winnie said you should talk to me?'

'Your name did come up in conversation, yes. He said you were a man to get things done. It's all terribly rushed and secret, so I'm cutting through the red tape. Can you help?'

'Well . . . I don't know. It's pretty unusual.'

'Ah! Sorry!' I decided to back off. 'Never mind. I'll go through the correct channels and let the PM know. Thanks for your time, anyway.'

'Please, Sir David . . . Of course I can put a Catalina at your disposal. When do you want it?'

Keeping the smile out of my voice I said, 'Day after tomorrow. It needs to be delivered to St. Athan in Wales. Our own crew will take the plane for the operation itself. That's Standard Operating Procedure for us.'

'Right. Leave it with me. I'll get a plane there for first thing Thursday morning.'

'I don't know how to thank you enough.'

'Please, all part of the job. You will tell the PM won't you?'

'Certainly. You can count on it.'

Breaking the contact I telephoned my brother and told him the news. We discussed what else needed to be done and I hung up the receiver feeling satisfied. Staring across the room at the wall map, I found Stalag XXB and tried to picture my son there. I had overstepped the bounds of acceptable behaviour as SOE's second-in-command, but I didn't give a fig. By the time anyone found out what I was up to the bloody war would be over.

I caught Robert's eye and beckoned him over.

'Sir?'

'I've got a little task for you. I need ten thousand Red Cross parcels again. Think you can do it?'

Gill grinned. 'It took a little coercion last time, but the man got his money so he was happy in the end. This time it will be a lot easier.'

'Good. I'll get on to Mike to warn Betty. Time he had a few days off at home. I might even join him this time.'

Mike and I took the midday train on Tuesday from Paddington. We'd heard from Gill and he was on his way with a small convoy of lorries from Portsmouth to Wales. The purchase of the goods had been simplicity itself. Papers supplied by SOE under my signature would ensure that, should the police stop them, they wouldn't be detained for long. Handling black-market goods was an offence punishable by five years in prison and I didn't think Susan would appreciate her fiancé becoming a jailbird. Gill had spent nearly two thousand pounds of my money acquiring the goods, but it was worth every penny.

This operation was far more complex than one simple plane trip to East Prussia followed by an airdrop. I wanted ten thousand parcels delivered to Marienburg, a huge logistical undertaking. I had discussed maximum payloads with Sion and he had agreed that by making certain adjustments to the plane we'd be able to deliver the whole lot in four trips at 17,500lbs a time.

The entire operation had been condensed to one sheet of paper which Mike and I dissected as we travelled westwards. Crews were the bottleneck – the x-factor that could blow the mission out of the water. The round trip meant approximately twenty hours flying time. Eighty hours in total. Time to load the plane, refuel and turn around, about another three hours. One flight a day. I needed two full crews.

Men I could trust. Particularly to keep quiet. Mind you, I did have a sheaf of Official Secrets Act forms with me, another trick up my sleeve.

After the first trip we wouldn't have so far to fly, as the next three would be made from the east coast. I still needed to decide which airfield, though I was thinking of Great Yarmouth.

The train deposited us in Cardiff. Betty was there, a one-woman welcoming committee. A peck on my cheek and a warm hug and a kiss for Mike, then we were heading for the car.

'Robert arrived about half an hour ago. We're already working on the parcels. With three hundred willing hands we'll be finished in a few hours.'

'Excellent. Robert made good time. Is he at the factory?'

'Yes. He's helping with the parcelling. Are you going to prepare a special parcel for Richard?'

Regretfully I shook my head. 'No. I don't want to draw too much attention to him. It would look strange if he was the only person to receive a package with his name on it. Better he stays anonymous. A low profile will help to keep him alive.'

We found Robert in the middle of the factory at one of the work-benches, wrapping brown paper around tins and other stuff.

'You got here more quickly than I expected,' I greeted him.

'It was plain sailing after Bristol. The police stopped us there. I showed them my authorisation from you and my ID card. It satisfied them and they didn't look too closely in the lorries or ask too many questions. Traffic was non-existent and the lorries ran smoothly. Couldn't have been better.'

'Good. Once we've seventeen and a half thousand parcels ready we'll take them to St Athan. When the rest are finished I want them taken to Great Yarmouth.'

'Why there?'

'It'll cut flying time down by an hour in each direction. It's not a lot but it all helps. Can you see to that?'

'Certainly. Though I think it's a mistake.'

'Why?' I frowned. I wasn't used to having my decisions questioned.

'We got away with the police stopping us once. A second or third time we may not be so lucky. The additional flying time isn't rele-vant. What we don't want is anyone taking too close a look at what we're doing.'

I took his point and reluctantly I nodded. 'There's also a question of fuel, flight times and payloads.'

'Refuel at Great Yarmouth by all means. Only don't take the parcels across country. When I was in Portsmouth I met up with an old friend of mine, a sergeant in the police down there. Apparently Red Cross parcels are being stolen in their thousands and the contents sold on the black-market. Our operation in reverse, in fact. The post office and the Red Cross are arguing about who is to blame. There's going to be a question asked in the house in the next twenty-four hours. The police forces are going to be more vigilant than ever. You can see where it could lead.'

I did indeed. 'You're right. Okay, we'll get this lot to St Athan and keep it all there.' I looked around the huge room. Women of all ages were busy putting together the parcels, their nimble fingers making light work of it. 'What have you got?'

Gill reeled off an impressive list of food and other items.

'What about medical supplies?'

'A chest full. Including penicillin. I also got charcoal tablets and de-lousing powder.'

'How on earth did you manage to get penicillin?'

'There's a big black-market in the stuff – it sells for a fortune. Don't worry,' he added, catching my look of alarm, 'I didn't pay over the odds for it.'

'That's not what I'm worried about. It's not counterfeit?' There was, I knew, a huge trade in counterfeit penicillin. It killed more people than it cured. I was assured ours was the real thing. 'How much longer will you be?'

'I don't know. You'd better ask Betty.'

I checked with her. 'Two hours at the most. We might even get in an hour of wireless production before we go home. You know,' she frowned, 'this costs us a lot of lost sales. Just don't blame me when the monthly figures are down.'

'I won't. You and Mike enjoy your night together, but don't forget we'll need you tomorrow.'

The factory hooter was sounding when we finally threw the last parcel onto the back of the last truck. We left in a convoy of five lorries. Taking the back roads to Llantrisant we went through Talbot Green. I looked up at the round tower on the hilltop known as the Billy Wynt.

'You know, Robert, I crash landed just on the other side of that tower up there.'

In his surprise he took his eyes off the road and looked at me. 'You're kidding?'

'It was back in the twenties. Mike had had some trouble with the IRA and we ended up flying to Ireland and back. We ran out of petrol and landed just over there. There's a row of houses you can just see near the top. One of the men there came and helped us. Name of . . .' I frowned, my memory not as good as it used to be. 'Bill!' I snapped my fingers. 'That's it. Bill Whalley. His wife was pregnant at the time. I wonder if he had a boy or a girl? It was such a long time ago. Take the next left for Pontyclun. At this rate we should be there in time for dinner.'

It was a joyous welcome. Sion and Kirsty had gone all out and killed the proverbial fatted calf.

'Where did you get all these vegetables from?' I asked in wonderment.

Kirsty smiled. 'I grew them. I have a large and expanding allotment out the back. I'll show you in the morning.'

Sion smiled. 'She's even purloined sheets of glass from the works to make a glasshouse. Hence the garlic and other herbs.'

'Purloined my foot. You know perfectly well they were scratched and damaged pieces, which I've merely put to good use.'

'Some, maybe,' Sion conceded with a smile, 'but not all.'

After dinner we retired to Sion's office and discussed the next few days.

'I agree with Robert,' Sion nodded at Gill. 'It's better we leave from here now that the parcels are all safely stored in a hangar. I've made some arrangements of my own.'

Impatiently I said, 'Out with it, man.'

'I've arranged for a fuel lighter to meet us off the Wash, south east of Skegness. They're used to fuelling flying boats whilst at sea, so we can leave from there with as much fuel as we can squeeze onboard.'

'Excellent. Well done,' I said.

'What about crews?' Gill asked.

Sion pulled a glum face. 'I only know one flier who's been checked out on Catalinas.'

The penny dropped as he spoke. 'Susan,' I said.

'Correct. Because of her ATA days. There's almost no pilot alive with as much experience as she has on such varied aircraft.'

It was true. She'd flown everything from single-engined Lysanders to multi-engined bombers. But I had grave reservations about involving her.

'After what she's been through I don't think we can ask her,' said Gill.

'I agree with Robert,' I said.

'It may be the best thing for her. Doing this won't diminish John-Phillipe and Connie's memory in any way. Susan needs to be needed, now more than ever. We have to get her to stop brooding, feeling sorry for herself. Self-pity is as corrosive on the soul as acid.'

'She feels guilty,' said Gill, 'for being a rotten mother, as she says. Not spending more time with the boy. Leaving him to Connie, pursuing her own selfish ambitions and desires. She's making progress but it's painful watching her torture herself.'

I knew and understood what she was going through. Hell, I mentally beat myself up everyday over not saving Richard. The heart told me one thing, the head another.

'Regardless,' said Sion, 'I took it upon myself to contact her at *Fairweather*. She'll be arriving to-night.'

'I don't want her flying to East Prussia,' I said with feeling. 'It'll be too dangerous.'

'Try and stop me,' said Susan, making a dramatic entry, which made me wonder how long she'd been listening.

'Susan, darling,' Gill leapt to his feet and rushed across to her.

She gave him a kiss on the lips and a hug. 'How are you?'

'All the better for seeing you. More to the point, how are you?'

I could see that she was looking tired. Crow's feet had appeared at the corners of her eyes and a few grey hairs showed in her shiny, dark hair.

'Drink?' Sion asked.

'A gin and it will be fine, thanks.' With a glass in her hand she settled in the chair by the fire. 'I needed this. Now, let's talk business, the flight to East Prussia. I'm the only one here who's flown a Catalina. I've got a hundred and eighty hours in them, ferrying to Coastal Command mainly. So that makes me the expert. Ergo I take the first flight to, what's it called?'

'Marienburg,' Sion replied. 'It's ten hours flying time in total.'

'All right, in that case I suggest we have two pilots. I take off and fly the Cat for, say, three hours and show the second pilot the ropes. He takes over for the middle stretch and I land. Same in reverse. In the meantime, uncle Sion, why don't you get on to Coastal Command and explain that you'll be doing some of the maintenance on Catalinas and coerce them into letting you get some time on one. Hell, they aren't difficult to fly. You just need to learn a few basic rules.'

'That's a good idea. There's a squadron based in Pembrokeshire.'

'Any problems, dad?'

Reluctantly I shook my head. She'd solved one of the biggest hurdles we'd been facing.

Susan took a mouthful of drink, grimaced and added, 'Is Mike coming along?'

'He'll be here tomorrow,' I replied.

'In that case if he comes with me we need a second pilot for uncle Sion. What about Juan or Raphael?'

Sion's friend and chief engineer had two sons, skilled pilots as well as excellent engineers.

Sion answered. 'Juan is in Scotland with the RAF and Raphael is at an aircraft factory in Bristol. I'll send for them straight away. I suppose Peter could come.'

'No disrespect, uncle Sion, but isn't he a bit old?'

Sion shrugged and said, 'So am I and your father too.'

'You aren't coming, dad,' Susan said with alarm in her voice.

'Yes, I am. Somebody needs to shove the containers out of the plane.'

We settled once more to discuss the flight and manning. Each Catalina had two gun turrets, one in the bow and one in the rear with a ventral hatch. If we included somebody to manhandle the containers and parachutes we needed five men per plane. We were still two short.

'What if we only take four?' said Susan. 'The second pilot does the cargo handling. It's simple. I fly with Raphael . . .'

'I'm coming with you,' said Gill.

Susan nodded. 'That's what I thought.'

'Good, that's settled. Shall we continue?'

Sion and I exchanged wry glances and we carried on making our plans. The older she became, the more natural Susan found it to take command. Even of her father, I thought with amusement and pride.

The plane arrived the following morning. Soon she was hidden inside a hangar, having her RAF roundels painted out and the Red Cross emblem painted in their stead.

The next day I watched as the Catalina took off for the east coast of England. Sion had already been busy on the phone making sure the fuel lighter was there to greet them when they landed. All we could do now was pray.

55

THE HUNGER NEVER left you. It was there constantly, nagging at your consciousness. The best way I knew to beat it was to keep busy. We'd smuggled the radio crystals into camp hidden in a tin of tooth-powder. A camp loudspeaker "went missing" one night and canni-balised before its carcass was returned to the pole it had been removed from. Between a signals engineer and myself we managed to make a crude wireless that transmitted and received. I had the task of sending the messages, using a bent spoon as a key.

The transmitter/receiver's existence was known to only a handful of people. We hadn't told anyone of the aircraft that was due to fly over us some time in the next twelve hours, bringing Red Cross parcels. It took willpower not to stand and stare at the sky, willing the plane to arrive. Finally, on Sunday afternoon, we heard it, the steady drone of a twin-engined plane coming directly towards us.

'There it is!' I yelled pointing towards the west.

Prisoners all over the compound stopped what they were doing and looked upwards. I could see the German guards preparing to shoot at the aircraft and I ran towards one of the watchtowers.

'Nein, nein, nicht schiessen. Don't shoot. Red Cross! Rotes Kreuz!'

Two guards looked down at me and up at the sky again. The plane was angled in the wrong direction to see the Red Cross symbols but suddenly it banked and there was the red cross on the white background.

The aircraft came straight in and almost immediately started drop-ping containers by parachutes. The plane kept circling and the mush-rooms kept blossoming. The camp was in a fever of excitement as we started to collect the bounty falling out of the sky.

'Manna from heaven,' said the camp's chaplain standing next to me, looking up and crossing himself.

'It certainly is,' I replied.

'Our Father hasn't forsaken us after all,' he said piously.

I grinned at his sanctimonious face and smiled. 'My father certainly hasn't.'

The first container landed with a thud and POWs swarmed around it. Jock McAllister took charge, yelling orders at the top of his voice.

Suddenly whistles were blowing and armed guards rushed into the compound. Our men were pushed away and ordered to leave the containers alone.

'These are ours, dammit,' said one corporal and pushed back at a guard. The German hit him across the side of his head with the butt of his rifle. He dropped like a felled tree.

McAllister stepped into the middle of the fracas, beckoning to me to join him. Nervously I took my place next to him.

'Tell them these are Red Cross parcels, for prisoners use only.'

I began the laborious task of interpreting once again.

'We have been ordered to impound them,' said a sergeant, looking uncomfortable. We argued with the guards to no avail.

As container after container landed, the Germans were unable to take charge of more than a few at a time. When they could, the men quickly broke open the wooden crates and handed out the parcels. It was pandemonium. Within minutes the crates were empty and the parcels spirited away. Into this fiasco strode SS Captain Schmidt, his face absolutely livid.

'What is the meaning of this? I ordered these containers to be collected and taken out of here.'

'They're ours,' said McAllister with dignity, no trace of fear in his eyes.

'They are yours only if I say so,' said Schmidt with venom. 'And do not, under any circumstances, quote the Geneva Convention at me.'

'The Convention governs us all,' said McAllister. 'You included.'

'I told you before,' screamed Schmidt, 'that the Convention and the Red Cross have no influence here.' Spittle flew from his lips and I realised for the first time that the captain was not quite sane.

'You just saw a Red Cross plane fly over,' said McAllister, 'so I beg to differ.'

Schmidt did what he always did when he was verbally bested. Without warning his swagger stick struck Jock across the chin.

McAllister staggered. Perhaps it was the violence against a good man. Perhaps it was the thought of losing our bounty that accounted for what happened next.

As one man the POWs let out a ferocious growl of anger. Suddenly the German guards were facing ten thousand hunger-maddened prisoners prepared to launch themselves at them. It was the sergeant who realised their danger, not Schmidt.

'Come, sir. We should leave them.'

The Germans were nervously fingering their rifles. In the watch-towers the guards brought their heavy machine-guns to bear on us, but a collective madness seemed to have gripped us all. I didn't know what was going to happen next. But one thing I was determined to do – get Schmidt. Whatever it took.

The sergeant shook the captain's arm and pulled him away towards the gate. Reluctantly he gave way and backed off while the men followed him step for step. It was McAllister, as always, who brought the situation under control.

'Leave it!' he ordered. 'Take the parcels to the cookhouse. That's an order.'

Like a tyre deflating, our anger drained away and we watched the Germans leaving the compound. It had been a tense few moments. There was no doubt the captain and the dozen guards would have been killed, but at what cost? It didn't bear thinking about.

Jock fingered the weal on his chin and smiled. 'A fair price for what we've just received.' He stepped over to me and dropped his voice. 'There are going to be another three deliveries, yes?' Suddenly he looked immensely pleased with himself. 'Ask if they can come here at eighteen hundred. When the Krauts are being fed.'

'Same time as us.' I grinned. 'Bloody good idea, Chief. The next wireless sked is in an hour.' We had two schedules a day when we could send and receive. The first was 06.00 and the second was 18.00. The morning slot was when the Krauts were getting up to start a new day, and the evening transmission during their supper.

'The aerial needs fixing. You'd better go. I need to supervise the ration issue.'

Nodding, I hurried towards my hut. Half the open space in the compound was now taken over by large tents. Three days after our arrival Jock had been sent for and told to bring along twenty POWs. He was given entry to a hut filled with rows and rows of tents. They had been there all along. The bastards had deprived us of them for no reason other than sheer bloody-mindedness.

Keen to get to work, I slipped into my hut and called to three lads who were lying on their bunks, 'Watch the doors and windows, please chaps. I need to send a message.'

The huts were forty-feet long and twenty wide. Tiers of bunks down each side left a central aisle where we had placed tables and chairs. The roof was pitched, with a wooden ceiling. We had cut a section of the ceiling away, creating a trap door which was carefully camouflaged, barely visible even to a thorough search. Placing a table underneath, I climbed up and hauled myself into the roof space then closed the hatch behind me. I heard the lads move the table away and get a pack of cards out and deal a hand. The cards were immediately abandoned while they moved to the windows and doors to keep a lookout. Should any of the guards appear they'd simply slip into the chairs and continue with their card game.

We'd purloined a roll of copper wire a few days previously, when we'd been on work duty outside the camp stringing telephone wire after an air raid. One of the lads had managed to steal about three yards of the stuff, which was ideal for an aerial. I strung it across the roof space and back to the corner where we had the wireless and battery. Silently I placed a wire and bulb across the terminals and checked the voltage. I was relieved to see it was adequate, though it needed to be topped up soon. I had been working slowly and quietly and had taken my time but I still had fifteen minutes to wait, so I tuned into the BBC, finding an announcement that Allied convoys had sailed into the Belgian port of Antwerp for the first time, thus shortening the supply lines to the battlefront. The Russians had crossed the Danube and were penetrating the German defences in the south of the country. I closed my eyes. Didn't the Germans know it was all over? It was only a matter of time. Why didn't they surrender and save lives, prevent more needless destruction? And let us go home. My daily mantra, *Please God, let me survive another day and go home.*

Still a few minutes early I re-tuned the wireless and began transmitting. Almost immediately I got an acknowledgement. The new aerial worked a treat. Slowly I tapped out the message – **Drop at 18.00. Drop at 18.00. Guards at meal. Guards at meal. Over.**

Short and sweet, I received a *wilco* and signed off. Dismantling the terminals from the battery I prepared to climb down. I listened but could hear nothing so I tapped three times lightly on the trap-door. Scraping sounds meant the table was being moved, so I opened the door and clambered down. Seconds later the hut was back to normal. All we could do then was pray the message had gotten through. I was looking forward to a damned good meal for once. I felt my mouth filling with saliva.

That night I stuffed myself, as did every other man in the camp. The meal was a hotch-potch of babies' heads – tinned steak and kidney pudding – tinned potatoes and carrots, followed by apricots in syrup, with custard made from powdered milk, and as much tea as I could drink. It was amazing how the spirits of every man in the camp lifted as a result of such basic fare.

We had a medical orderly in our hut by the name of Corporal White, known to all as Chalky. He was cock-a-hoop over the medicines we'd received. We had also received a pile of blankets and a box of fifty pairs of boots.

There was one sour note. None of us really expected Captain Schmidt to leave matters as they were. Which was why, I suspected, Jock McAllister wasn't looking as happy as might have been expected.

'What's up, Chief?' asked one of the others. 'You look like you found two bob and lost five pounds.'

'Bloody Schmidt is what's up,' he replied, confirming my thoughts.

'Think there'll be trouble?' I asked.

'Sure to be, unless I can nip it in the bud. Especially with another load coming.'

'If it comes,' I said.

'Aye, lad, that's true. If it comes. What do you think? Will the plane come back?'

He was the only one who knew it was my father organising the drop. It must have sounded ludicrous to question an ignorant able seaman but, to him and I it made perfect sense.

'If it's possible. The Red Cross don't make promises they can't keep, or so I've heard.'

'Well, with tomorrow's drop Schmidt will go off his rocker.'

'What can we do about it?' Corporal White asked.

'I'll request a meeting with Otto. Try and pre-empt any problems.'

'Schlessinger does what Schmidt tells him.'

'We know that but he has certain obligations which I'll remind him of. I can but try.'

'I suppose . . .' I said hesitatingly but trailed off as all eyes turned to me.

'Well, speak up lad,' said McAllister.

I took a deep breath, blew out my cheeks and took the plunge. 'We could offer Otto some of the spoils. Hell, we know the Germans don't exactly eat off the fat of the hog.'

'They eat a damn sight better than us,' said McAllister. But he turned to Bullmaster and said, 'What do you think, Tony?'

'The youngster's got a point. By law the parcels belong to us. If we offer to share them we might get to keep them. Strike a bargain before Schmidt can take the lot. Mind you, we'll still need to have our wits about us tomorrow, assuming the plane comes. We need to get the parcels distributed p.d.q., just in case. If Schmidt does try and confiscate them we ought to be able to lose a hell of a lot before he can get at them.'

'We'll do that anyway,' said McAllister. 'All right, Dickie, you'll come with me to see Otto in the morning.'

Glumly I nodded. So much for keeping a low profile. I knew of at least three other POWs who spoke good German. They just refused to volunteer, keeping their heads well down and out of the limelight. A quiet life was the best way to survive as a POW. It looked like I wouldn't be enjoying one.

The countryside was covered with a blanket of snow. In the camp we shovelled the stuff to one side and kept the place fairly free of it. But with the snow came biting cold and one of our biggest headaches was keeping warm. Jock McAllister had negotiated a deal with the commandant that we could go into the forest and cut wood for burning. Each day a detail would march out with axes and saws and fell trees and split logs. There was something satisfying about the work and there were plenty of volunteers. I liked to go as it kept you fit. Though it also meant you worked up an appetite. Even the Germans weren't so stupid as to not feed us properly on the days we went logging.

'I'm on logging detail in the morning,' I said.

'Not any more you aren't,' said McAllister. 'Carruthers, you go instead.'

Steve Carruthers nodded. 'Glad to. Sorry, Dickie.'

In the morning we had bacon and powdered eggs, seasoned with salt. A real luxury! I had coffee and thought it the finest I'd ever tasted. I vowed to myself that should I survive and get back home I'd never complain about a meal again.

I cut my bacon using my Swiss army knife. It was my pride and joy and I kept it close at all times. Pilfering amongst the prisoners wasn't unheard of though it wasn't very common. Anyone found thieving was dealt with as severely as possible but as the Germans refused to become involved there was a limit to what punishment could be meted out. Usually it was something innocuous like cleaning detail or working in the vegetable patch. Camp life, I had come to realise, was like no other. We existed by a set of rules that reflected civilisation but we lived in a barbarous world. We had no recourse to justice when the Germans treated us badly. I'm sure that like me, many of us dreamed not only of freedom, but also of making Schmidt pay.

McAllister came for me at 09.50. He had arranged to meet the commandant at 10.00. Somehow he had learnt that Schmidt would be away for the morning and intended to take advantage of his absence.

I had spruced up my uniform as best I could and followed Jock across the compound. We were escorted to the commandant's hut where we were kept waiting in the outer office for half an hour. Finally we were marched in.

'Sir.' McAllister and I saluted, standing stiffly to attention in front of his desk.

'What do you want, McAllister?' Schlessinger spoke classic *Hochdeutsch* and I interpreted easily.

'It's with regards to the Red Cross parcels, sir.'

There was a twitch at the corners of the Oberst's mouth and I could have sworn he was holding back a smile.

'I gather there was a . . . shall we say . . . little local difficulty about the matter yesterday. The good Captain Schmidt was forced to retreat?'

'That is the case, sir. However, the captain was at fault.'

'That is one interpretation of events. The captain begs to differ. He was all for storming the compound, arresting you and a few other ring-leaders and confiscating the parcels you'd received.'

'Why didn't he, sir?'

'Let us just say wiser counsel prevailed. But do not cross Captain Schmidt too often, Chief Petty Officer, or you will definitely come off worse. The SS have overall control now and command of POWs.

My hands are being tied more and more. A new edict arrives every week, it seems. Believe me when I tell you that things will become a lot worse before they get better.'

'Sir, with all due respect, you are the Commandant.'

Schlessinger sadly shook his head. 'In name only. Germany is changing. The SS under Himmler are taking control of the *Wehrmacht* and the railways.'

There was genuine sadness in the colonel's face and for a second I felt sorry for him. 'So, gentlemen, why have you come to see me?'

McAllister looked him in the eye. 'We propose we share the parcels. You can have twenty percent. No arguments. My blessing.'

The *Oberst* sat for a few seconds strumming his fingers on the desk. 'Why should you give up the parcels you have?'

'We don't trust Schmidt. I wouldn't put it past him to come into the compound later today and stir up trouble. Men will be hurt. Possibly killed.'

'That is very astute of you, Chief Petty Officer.' Schlessinger leant back in his chair, the wood creaking under the strain. 'One third.'

'Sir?'

'One third of the parcels. And I will keep Captain Schmidt away.'

'I agree, sir. I will arrange for them to be collected and delivered to the guardhouse.'

'Good. Is there anything further?'

'No, sir. Thank you, sir.'

We saluted, about turned and marched towards the door.

'One other thing, CPO McAllister, this agreement covers future drops as well.'

'Future drops, sir?' I translated.

'Yes. You understand me, I think, mein Herr, "*Man of Confidence*".'

'Blimey, you'd think he was psychic. Oof . . .' A dig in the ribs shut me up. Back in our hut I rubbed my side and said, 'What was that for, Chief?'

'The corporal in the outer office speaks English.'

'How do you know?'

'I've watched him listening to us. Understanding what we say.'

'Sorry. I'll know better next time.'

'I know you will, lad. Right. If the message got through we expect a delivery at eighteen hundred. In the meantime I want hut leaders brought here. We must keep our end of the bargain before that bastard

Schmidt returns. The men aren't going to like it but there's nothing we can do about it.'

The plane appeared exactly on time. As it circled the camp German troops rushed from their messes to see what was happening. The plane was low and the parachutes flared open for seconds only, breaking the fall of the containers. We leapt on them like maniacs, tore open the crates and dispersed the parcels as rapidly as possible. Gunshots were fired, though they were sporadic, and whether they were aimed at us or at the plane, I couldn't tell. Although it was dark, the sky was clear and a half-moon lit the scene. The white background and dark-looking red cross showed clearly on the wings.

Ten thousand pairs of hands made light work and the containers were quickly emptied. The wood was taken into the huts. It had multiple uses – like making bunks and tables.

The senior man in each hut arranged for a third of the parcels to be given to the Germans. McAllister still didn't fully trust the commandant not to welch on our deal. Especially if Schmidt turned ugly.

A commotion at the gate attracted my attention. Captain Schmidt was there with a detachment of guards, all armed.

'Come on, lad,' said McAllister, 'we're needed.'

'Bring all the parcels here to me immediately or my men will shoot.' I did my best to keep up as Schmidt ranted.

'The commandant and I have an agreement,' said Jock, his voice controlled.

'There will be no agreement!' Schmidt was beside himself with rage. 'You will bring the parcels here now or your men will watch you die.' Schmidt raised the Luger pistol he was carrying and pointed it straight between the CPO's eyes.

Somehow McAllister managed not to flinch. He was, without doubt, one of the bravest men I had ever met.

'You get a third of what we have received. That is the agreement.'

He got no further as Schmidt pulled the trigger. The bullet just missed McAllister's head. The CPO flinched but held his ground. How the hell he didn't wet himself I'll never know.

The sound of the shot brought *Oberst* Schlessinger running. His tunic was undone and he was hatless. His gait was unsteady but there was a determination in his stride.

'Captain Schmidt.' Schmidt ignored him. 'Schmidt!' The colonel roared, 'What is the meaning of this?'

'*Oberst* Schlessinger, I suggest you return to your bottle and leave me to deal with this matter.'

I can only presume it was the bottle that gave Schlessinger the courage to do what he did next. 'I am a colonel, you are a captain. *You* will do as you are told. I have an agreement with the prisoners. We get a third of the parcels for our men. Legally the parcels belong to the POWs. They have been generous with their offer.'

'We do not broker deals with scum!' Schmidt was working himself up into another towering rage. 'Let me remind you that I an SS officer. As such I outrank you.'

The other guards were all regular *Wehrmacht* troops and Schmidt's words cut no ice with them.

Schlessinger's chest full of ribbons testified to the courageous soldier he had once been. Despite his dalliance with the bottle, that soldier now bellowed, 'And I out gun you, Captain Schmidt. I have an arrangement with these prisoners and it will be honoured. Please return to your quarters.'

Schmidt turned furiously to Schlessinger but there had been a subtle shift in the way the other guards pointed their guns. It appeared to me, and to Schmidt as well, that he was now in the firing line. He looked about in impotent fury.

'You have not heard the last of this, *Oberst*.'

'I am sure you are correct, Captain.'

Schmidt stormed away, his face thunderous.

'CPO McAllister, I trust everything is in order?'

'Yes, sir. Thank you, sir.' McAllister saluted, as did I.

We returned to our hut where Jock collapsed into a chair, his face chalky white, his hands shaking. God alone knew what it had taken for him to face down Schmidt like that.

'Get the Chief a drink,' I said to Chalky. 'The good stuff.'

The glass rattled in the Chief's hand as he poured a combination of surgical spirit and tinned fruit juice down his throat. Gasping, he placed the glass on the table in front of him.

'Another?' Chalky asked.

'No. That's enough. I've never been much of a drinker but by Christ, I needed that. I would never have thought Otto had it in him. It was a close call.'

'What happens tomorrow?' I asked.

'Dickie, lad, we'll worry about tomorrow when it comes.'

The drop was a carbon copy of the previous day – except that Captain Schmidt did not interrupt us. The guards had become friendlier as a result of sharing the parcels. Their diet was as poor as ours on the whole.

There was no drop the next day.

56

I DECIDED TO fly with Susan on the third trip. This time we crammed in additional items like boots, blankets, books, gramophone records, shirts, toilet paper, pairs of trousers and a container-load of duffel coats. Betty had managed to procure these from somewhere as if by magic. When I asked where she had tapped the side of her nose and told me that Robert had made a few suggestions. I didn't pursue it.

As we'd known, we were too far north for the Germans to take much notice. As on the previous two trips, there was no sign of enemy aircraft activity and very little ack-ack was fired at the Catalina. Which was why it was shocking when north of Flensburg, on the return leg, the Catalina was picked up by a mobile searchlight and battery unit. It was just after midnight and our concentration was at its lowest. I was jerked awake when Susan flung the plane into a steep dive to port. Ack-ack guns opened fire and chunks were knocked out of the port fuselage and wing.

Robert, in the bow turret, opened up with his two 0.3 inch machine-guns and managed to hit one of the lights. The ack-ack ceased and the plane was suddenly flying in blessed darkness again.

'Everybody okay?' Susan asked. 'Can you see the damage, Mike?'

'Bloody difficult in this light. It looks like a few chunks missing from the wing but it's hard to tell. Engine looks okay. Gauges all okay. No smoke and no fire. Christ, that was close.'

'Feels sluggish,' said Susan. 'Like the hydraulics have been hit. Possibly even leaking.'

'Mike, can you see any hydraulic leak out of the port wing?' Mike asked.

'Can't see a thing. Want me to shine a torch on the wing?' A few moments later he said, 'Something's leaking. I guess it's hydraulic fuel.'

531

'That's what I thought,' said Susan. 'I can level off here. We're at fifteen hundred feet and under the cloud base. Damn, damn and blasted damn.'

'Tut, tut, Susan,' said Mike with an attempt at levity, 'that's not very ladylike.'

'I don't feel very ladylike right now. The controls are getting heavier. All I can do is fly straight and level and put the minimum of strain on the hydraulic system. If the pumps aren't pushing too hard the system might last a bit longer.'

'Isn't there a wire system as back up?' I asked.

'Fraid not,' was the sobering reply.

Susan isolated the port hydraulics, freezing the flaps flush with the wing. Things settled down and the plane droned on. It was a tense time as the miles ticked away and the coast of England drew nearer.

'What are you going to do?' Mike asked. 'Land as usual? Or head for an airfield?'

'By rights we ought to land at an airfield. But look at us. We're the most disparate crew you can imagine. We've the red cross painted on the wings and fuselage which won't hold up to close scrutiny and we're shot to pieces. Can you think of a suitable cover story?'

'Off hand, no. But nobody is going to castigate us for flying supplies to POWs.'

'What if they ask where we got the supplies?'

'They won't. We've nothing to connect us with any black-market dealings. I'm sure we can land at one of the east-coast fields without any problems. Hell's teeth, three of us are SOE and you're a well-known pilot.'

'I guess you're right. I'd be happier landing at an airfield. Okay. Where do we go?'

Mike had an inspiration. 'The American airbase at Letchfield. There'll be no one to ask any awkward questions. Sion can get his men in to fix the plane and we can finish the mission. Worth a try?'

'Good idea! Once we close the coast I'll try and raise Letchfield on the radio.'

'No! That won't work. We need to be near there to ask for an emergency landing. Otherwise they'll wonder why we didn't land somewhere more convenient.'

'You're right. In that case we keep going. I need a new heading.'

'I'm just working one out for you. Come left twenty degrees.'

Finally we could see the coast. 'I reckon that's Great Yarmouth. About an hour to go,' said Mike. 'How are the controls?'

'Okay. Steady flight isn't a problem.'

'Want me to spell you?'

'Would you mind? I need a trip.' She headed for the tiny toilet situated in the middle of the plane. Mike took the controls while she left the cockpit.

'That's better,' she greeted Mike when she returned. 'Not long now and we can call the base.'

We established contact and explained we were a Red Cross flight inward bound and needing an emergency landing. Permission was granted and we lined up on the runway, which had been lit for our approach. Susan took the controls and connected the port hydraulics again.

The Catalina was fifty feet up and three hundred feet out when all hydraulic power failed and the plane ploughed into the runway. The undercarriage collapsed and the fuselage scraped along the concrete, sparks flying, the plane completely out of control, speed bleeding off quickly.

Susan shut down the engines and isolated the fuel. A fire truck raced alongside us, ready to pour foam onto the plane if needed. The Cat slewed round in a slow circle, swept off the runway and onto the grass and came to a shuddering halt in the middle of a frost-covered field.

Inside the plane we sat and counted our blessings. One thing was clear to me. There would be no more flights. I had helped one child and endangered the life of another. Sion sent his own people to repair the crashed plane, repaint the roundels and make arrangements to return it to the RAF. There was no point in wasting the food parcels we had stored at St Athan, and so we gave them to the legitimate Red Cross for distribution to other POWs. I arranged a radio message informing Richard there would be no more flights for the foreseeable future.

I knew the leading light of the Red Cross in Britain, my old friend, Major-General Sir Richard Howard-Vyse. I made an appointment to see him a few days later, a mere two weeks before Christmas. We met at his home in Belgravia.

Since the débâcle with Prince Edward, Howard-Vyse and I had often been in contact on one matter or another and as a result something of a friendship had developed. I knew I could trust him; he was one member of the establishment who didn't suffer fools or bureaucrats gladly. One and the same thing, he always maintained.

After the usual pleasantries and the offer of a glass of sherry I got down to business.

'My son, also named Richard by the way, is a POW in Marienburg in East Prussia.'

'Nasty place. At least it's in the wilds and not likely to be caught in any crossfire. Too many POWs have died as a result of friendly fire at targets near to camps.'

'Conditions there are particularly tough. Especially where food is concerned.'

'How do you know this, David?'

I told him the story of how we got supplies to Richard's camp in Italy and about the airlift to Marienburg. Naturally, I omitted to tell him about our use of the Red Cross insignia. I didn't think he would appreciate the liberty we had taken. 'I now need another way to get supplies to Marienburg.'

Howard-Vyse stroked his chin thoughtfully. 'It's something we hope to achieve as well, to camps all over Germany. We put a proposal to the Chiefs of Staff a little while ago. Expected them to call for action. All they did was call for more discussion. I have a memorandum here.' Opening a file he took out a sheet of paper and handed it to me.

Glancing down it my blood ran cold. 'This only mentions administrative and organisational problems then asks for further information or consideration of the facts. It is, to coin a phrase, utter bunkum. Good grief,' I ejaculated. 'The Foreign Office is to gather further information and the War Office to prepare a report. Useless nonsense.' I barely had my temper under control. 'What's this about a convoy of lorries?'

'Transportation across Germany is breaking down. As is law and order. We proposed sending convoys of lorries to the camps, driven by Swiss members of the International Red Cross. We had asked for armed troops to protect the convoy. The Germans have refused. Claiming with good reason that they don't have the men to spare. So we suggested using trains. Easier to protect but a target for Allied planes. We suggested clearly marking the tops of the trains with the red cross, but our high command pointed out that the Germans were not beneath using such a ruse to move troops and weapons. Another sherry?'

'No, thanks. What's this about ear-marking the supplies?'

'The War Office is concerned that supplies sent by us should go to British and American prisoners only. A very senior source at Whitehall has stated that we aren't in the business of taking relief to the Russians or French.'

'They're our allies, for God's sake.'

'David, I'm telling you all this so that you fully understand the picture.'

'Sorry. I do appreciate it. What's to be done?'

'I'm meeting Eisenhower this evening to discuss the problem. Would you care to accompany me?'

'Where to?'

'SHAEF headquarters, in Hampshire.'

I nodded. 'I know where it is. If you think I can be of any use I'll gladly accompany you. What are you hoping to achieve?'

Howard-Vyse frowned and fingered his glass for a few moments before replying. 'The General is a real soldier's soldier. He understands the men. I like to think that I, too, have a similar knowledge. You must understand it's not just a case of doing everything possible for the POWs, we must be *seen* to be doing it. Our troops need to know that they aren't abandoned when taken prisoner. Does that make sense?'

'Naturally. I have a few ideas we might be able to use. Richard, I hope you don't mind me saying but I also have a great many resources I can bring to the table. Particularly financial.' I paused.

'Go on. You interest me greatly.'

I smiled. 'I'll do all in my power to try and help my son. If you need money or information I can give you the former and help with the latter.'

'With all your banking connections, why don't you just offer a substantial bribe and get Richard taken to Switzerland or some other neutral country?'

'I've thought about that. But if the Germans think he has influence they are just as likely to send him to Colditz with the rest of the VIP prisoners.'

'I take your point.'

'His best bet to survive is to keep a low profile and await the outcome of hostilities. We know we'll win. It's merely a matter of time.'

That evening I accompanied him to SHAEF HQ. Our meeting with Eisenhower was totally satisfactory and we made our way back to London in a better frame of mind than when we left.

'Thank God for men like Eisenhower,' I said.

'Agreed. He's cut through the red tape and taken the problem away from the politicians and bureaucrats. With the hundred lorries he's ordered, as well as two relief trains, we can get something done. How the hell he got the Germans to supply a guard for each truck is beyond me. The IRC will have to make certain that all trucks and trains are clearly marked with our symbol.'

'The convoys and trains are all leaving from Switzerland and heading north,' I said. 'Which means none of the supplies will get as far as Marienburg.'

'I'm sorry about that,' began Howard-Vyse.

'Don't be. It's inevitable. But it does give us a precedent to work with.'

'What are you suggesting?'

'I'll finance a convoy from the north. Sweden to be exact. It's too far to go to Marienburg from Switzerland. Will you use your influence with the IRC to supply Swiss drivers and German guards?'

He thought about it for a few seconds before nodding. 'I don't see why not. Petrol for the trucks will be the main problem.'

'I've thought of that. In Sweden they use a lot of wood-burning trucks as petrol is scarce and they have wood a-plenty.'

'Good. That's one problem solved.'

'Richard, have you heard the rumours about more of our POWs being shipped into Germany? According to my information the process will speed up considerably in the new year. Particularly as the Russians get closer. Marienburg is an obvious target. That'll mean ten thousand POWs on the move west.'

'What's your point?'

'I don't agree with the government that transfers of POWs will be done quickly and smoothly, by train or convoy. I believe the POWs will be made to walk.'

'I agree.'

'So if we get can a convoy of trucks filled with rations to Marienburg for Christmas we could leave the vehicles there.'

'What about the drivers?'

'Arrange for them to have safe passage and sufficient funds to purchase train tickets.'

'It could be done. But have you any idea of the cost?'

'Let me worry about the cost. Can you implement the idea in time for Christmas?'

'Probably, if I piggyback on Eisenhower's orders.'

'I'll arrange funds to be transferred to the IRC's bank in Geneva first thing in the morning. I want them clearly ring-fenced for the operation in Sweden. Can you do that?'

'I should think so.'

'I need your assurance.'

'In that case, yes I can.'

'What about purchasing supplies in Sweden?'

'We have agents who can do that. The Swiss. They may be neutral in this war but they are amazingly good at organisation and attention to detail. They've saved many lives and continue to give support to those in need, no matter which side they're on.'

'Very admirable,' I said dryly. 'When you know how much the operation will cost I'll underwrite the bill plus ten percent. The additional money is for IRC general funds.'

'That's extraordinarily generous of you.'

'I only have one son,' I said. 'And though there are many families in the world in the same position as mine, very few are able to do anything about it. I happen to be in the fortunate position of being able to influence events and *perhaps* save my son's life. What I do for Richard I do for ten thousand other families in the same position.'

Things moved smoothly. The Swiss were past masters at organising events. Thirty wood-burning lorries were bought and paid for. Three hundred tons of food, medicine and other goods were purchased and drivers allocated. The question of the guards came as a shock. I learned how Eisenhower had managed to get German troops to accompany the trucks: he had paid for them. A substantial bribe to a Swiss bank account in the name of Himmler. I did the same and within hours the guards were allocated.

All that was left now was to pray the lorries got through. In the meantime Christmas was upon us again and we congregated at St Athan to celebrate. It was a subdued affair given the circumstances, but we did our best. The food and drink were plentiful. Toasts to a rapid end to the war in Europe and Richard's health made for poignant moments. I was certain of one thing. 1945 would be the last year of the war.

56

I WAS HUNGRY again. I was always hungry. Hungry and cold. Twice I was allocated the wood cutting detail but the cold outweighed the benefit of the extra food we were given. The food we'd had dropped only weeks earlier was virtually all gone. There were still some cans left, but they were being hoarded by individuals. I was tempted to trade my penknife for a tin of peaches but had managed to resist so far. Of course, if we hadn't given the Germans the parcels we would have been far better off but there was no doubt in my mind that we had done the right thing.

Some of the men were putting on a pantomime, Snow White and the Seven Dwarves, known to us by its more telling title of Snow White and the Seven Huns. Given our numbers there were obviously some highly talented people in the camp and work had been going on for a month. I had no talent at all in that direction, so took little to do with it. Besides, I was kept busy helping Jock McAllister as his interpreter and general dogsbody.

It was amazing how one adapted to our position. From housing, feeding and clothing to policing and medical needs, there was always something that needed doing. As the camp's Man of Confidence, many issues inevitably ended up on Jock's table, even though his prime task was to negotiate with the Germans. Since the showdown between the commandant and Schmidt we had rarely seen the captain.

At every opportunity I listened to the broadcasts by the BBC and passed the news to the lads by way of a bulletin for each hut and tent. As there were a hundred huts it took a lot of arranging but I had writers to make fair copies of the news I scribbled down. We'd asked dad for reams of paper and he'd sent ten packs. Nothing went to waste. When we'd finished writing on them we cut up the sheets of paper into eight pieces and used them in the heads. Toilet paper was still a luxury, along with soap, shampoo and toothpaste.

Three days before Christmas the commandant sent for McAllister and I tagged along as usual.

'Chief Petty Officer McAllister,' Schlessinger greeted us, 'I have good news which I want you to announce. A convoy of some thirty lorries has been given permission to come here. They are from the Red Cross, and are loaded with food and other goods.'

Jock and I beamed at each other and at the commandant.

'That is very good news, sir,' said McAllister. 'Naturally we would wish to share some of our good fortune with you and your men.'

'That is very generous of you, Chief, and on behalf of my men, I thank you.'

'When will the convoy arrive, sir?'

'Tomorrow morning sometime. We don't have an exact time.'

We were dismissed and left the hut.

'Why in hell did you give away our stuff like that?' I asked in amazement.

'Because, son, we're going to need the commandant and soon. I'm not a complete moron – I speak good German.'

My jaw dropped.

'Not as good as you, I own, but good enough. I have you along as a witness to what's said, but your being there also creates a delay while you translate, giving me time to think. That way I'm not hurried into decisions I may regret later. It also means I can listen to our German friends speaking to each other, safe in the knowledge that I don't understand. Schmidt will be back in two days and this time he will have a contingent of SS with him. Probably as many as ten, maybe twenty men. When that happens the balance of power, which has been precarious to say the least, will tip in his favour.'

Jock's information put the fear of God into me.

'Don't tell the rest of the lads, not yet. They'll learn soon enough,' I said and he nodded.

The following morning the minutes seemed like hours. The whole camp was tense with nervous anticipation. Squabbles and fights erupted for no reason and the NCOs were kept busy settling matters. It was bitterly cold but we stamped about, keeping warm as best we could. It hadn't snowed for a few days but the hills and landscape around us were covered with deep snow. Around mid-morning it came; the noise of trucks labouring over the track – the sweetest sound we had ever heard. We could see a thin line of smoke in the near distance as the first truck came wheezing into sight.

A ragged cheer went up. The Germans opened the gates and we stood back as the trucks came slowly through.

Raising his voice Jock called out, 'Steady lads. Let the lorries park up before we unload them.'

A short, podgy man jumped down from the first truck and came towards us. 'Are you in charge?' he asked in German.

'Yes,' I replied for Jock. 'This is Chief Petty Officer McAllister.'

'Good. We have come from Sweden with these provisions. My men and I are from Switzerland. I have been instructed to leave twenty-eight lorries and take only two to transport ourselves back to the railway. If the commandant will supply two drivers they can bring the lorries back.'

'Why are you leaving them? Don't you need them for other jobs?'

'Usually, yes. However, this is a somewhat unusual situation. I can tell you that the Germans are retreating all along the lines from the east, west and south. POWs are being transhipped into Germany. We suspect you will be going soon. These lorries have been purchased specially for your use. Those were my instructions. We will travel back to Sweden by train.'

Two lorries were quickly unloaded and driven out of the compound. We spoke to the commandant who agreed to send two drivers to bring them back. In a short time the provisions were stored, the Germans given their share and the lorries were parked up outside the camp.

Christmas Eve was a joyful one. The pantomime was hilarious, the food as good as anything we'd had since arriving in the camp, and the cider that we'd made from the apples we'd stored was as potent and full of flavour as one could hope for.

Christmas Day lunch was equally good. We toasted an end to the war and our families back in Blighty. I went to bed warm and reasonably content and slept peacefully until 06.00.

I awoke as the door of our hut was unceremoniously flung open and a harsh German voice ordered the men to get out and be quick about it. In near panic I dressed and put on my boots and coat. I could hear pandemonium as the rest of the camp was rudely awoken from a deep sleep. Fearful, we stumbled into the freezing cold air. The sight that greeted us struck real terror into me. A line of German soldiers, bearing the insignia of the SS, stood outside, machine-guns pointed at us. In front of them stood Captain Schmidt, his peaked cap pulled down low over his nose.

He ordered the *'Appel'*, warning us to comply or be shot.

During roll call it was common for us to try and thwart the Germans where we could; we would bugger about, making it difficult for them to take a proper tally. A man might answer, slip along the lines and answer again. Others would sneak off and hide in the huts, making it next to impossible for the Germans to keep track of who was there. The idea was that, should anyone try and escape, their departure would go unnoticed for as long as possible. Or so we hoped. Being so isolated, nobody had tried to get out of Marienburg, although escape plans were being fomented all the time.

The usual malarkey continued for about ten minutes, before Schmidt made good his threat. One of the men, Sergeant Wilkinson, a Liverpudlian wit, was moving along the lines, a trick he was famous for. Schmidt walked up to him, placed his pistol to Wilkinson's head and fired. The sergeant's brains and skull splattered over the men standing around him. A huge yell of anger and fear erupted from our throats. As we surged forward the machine-guns opened fire into the air and then pointed down at us. The threat wasn't enough, I could feel it. We paused, our anger building as we prepared to launch ourselves at the Germans.

Again Jock McAllister saved the situation. Without his calm intervention many men would have died that day.

McAllister raised his voice. 'Keep your line. Stand to attention. Roll-call will proceed as normal.'

The line held and the moment passed. The roll-call was concluded in record time. Then Schmidt addressed us.

'You are leaving the camp this morning. Thirty minutes from now we will march out of here and head west.'

'We need time to light the fires in the trucks,' said McAllister.

He was rewarded with a harsh laugh.

Schmidt waved an arm above his head and we were rocked by a series of explosions as the Swedish lorries burst into flames and were destroyed before our eyes.

'As I said, you will march!' Schmidt screamed.

'Parade will dismiss,' said Jock loudly. 'Dismiss!'

We turned right and then almost ran for our huts. I could have wept as I stood looking at my collection of tins and packets of processed food. How much could I realistically carry? As I made my preparations I opened tins of meat and crammed the food into my mouth. I knew I would need all the energy I could muster over the coming days. Climbing into the roof I lifted down the crystals, just in case we had the opportunity to make another wireless. I hid them in my tooth-powder tin again, wrapping the possessions I was taking with me inside a blanket and tying the ends in a knot. I wrapped a second blanket around my body before putting my coat back on. When I'd done everything I could think of I put a third blanket over my head and under my arms, where I tied it in place using a piece of rope.

Already the Germans were harassing us to fall in outside and reluctantly I left the hut. The men cursed and ranted as they got into three lines. McAllister beckoned me over.

'We need to speak to the commandant. Come on.'

I followed him as he led the way to the guardhouse. We were stopped as usual and asked to see the *Oberst*. Uneasy looks passed between the guards but the call was made. We were kept waiting for a few minutes and then, much to my disappointment, Schmidt appeared.

'I understand you wish to see the commandant.' He spoke pleasantly enough, which should have been a warning to us.

'That is the case, yes,' said McAllister.

'Regarding . . . ?'

'That is between me and the commandant.'

'I see.' Schmidt tapped the side of his leg with his swagger stick. For a second I thought he was going to take a swing at Jock but he didn't. 'In that case you gentlemen had better follow me.'

We did as we were ordered. In the outer room the commandant's orderly sat white-faced, looking as though he was about to throw up.

'In there,' Schmidt indicated the door to Schlessinger's office.

I followed Jock, who stopped suddenly in the doorway. The commandant was hanging from a beam, a rope around his neck. His swollen tongue protruded from his mouth and his face was a mottled red and blue.

'So die all traitors to the Third Reich,' said Schmidt.

We turned our horror struck eyes away from the grotesque sight and looked at Schmidt. 'You did this?' I whispered.

'*Ja.* He was a traitor. Now what did you swine want with him?'

McAllister licked his lips. Was there any point in even asking? 'Eighteen of our men are too ill to move. I request they stay here, bury Wilkinson and wait for Allied forces to arrive.'

'No.'

'But they'll slow us down,' said Jock in desperation.

'Then they will be shot.'

'You bloody bastard . . .'

Schmidt swung the swagger stick at Jock's head with such force that if it had connected it would have split his cheek to the bone and probably knocked him out. But McAllister ducked and the stick missed. Before Schmidt could recover Jock was on him like a tiger. He hit Schmidt twice, once in the face and again in the stomach before two shots rang out and Jock arched backwards, blood pouring from the wounds in his back. A guard, watching the scene from the door, had fired in panic.

'You bastard!' I screamed at the guard, kneeling next to Jock, lifting his head.

His breath was ragged. 'Good lad . . .'

Then his head fell back and he was dead.

A blow to the side of my head sent me sprawling and Schmidt yelled at me to get up. Awkwardly I rose to my feet, my blanket of provisions still bound over my shoulder. Ordered outside I stumbled through the door, in complete shock. What the hell were we going to do without Jock? Without his encouragement and guidance?

Bullmaster met me at the guardhouse.

'Where's the man?'

'Jock,' I managed to say, pulling myself together, ' Jock lost it. He snapped and attacked Schmidt. A guard killed him.'

'What about the commandant?'

'Hanged by Schmidt for crimes against the Third Reich.'

As realisation sank in Bullmaster said, 'You mean we're on our own? With that bloody swine Schmidt?'

'Yes!' My voice was a whisper. Of all the horrors I'd lived through this was the worst. It was as well I didn't know what was ahead of us.

We lined up and marched out into the teeth of a snowstorm. It came down in driving sheets. The cold quickly seeped through our clothing, costing us our strength and energy. The guards trudged alongside us, as cold and miserable as we were. The contingent of

SS troops travelled in the two lorries they hadn't destroyed, whilst Schmidt was driven in a Mercedes staff car.

After eight hours of sheer hell we reached a small village. Its inhabitants had fled westward some weeks earlier and we took possession of the cold, damp houses, barns and sheds. As I lay down on a bare wooden floor I made a promise to myself. Jock deserved justice and I would see he had it. I swore it, on everything I held sacred.

In the morning we were kicked awake and told we had half an hour to get ready to leave. Fires were lit and cups of tea magically appeared. I opened a tin of bacon, which I shared with Corporal White and Leading Seaman Carruthers who somehow had ended up sleeping alongside me. The tea put a little heart into us before we went out into the biting wind. Thankfully no more snow was falling.

Jock's death cast a deep pall over us all. I felt rudderless. It was astonishing how dependent we had all become on him, how his character and strength had sustained us.

Schmidt's Mercedes drove past and I looked at him with hatred. I must have spoken out loud because Carruthers asked me what I'd said.

'I'm going to see that bastard hanged for what he did.' Throwing my makeshift bag over my shoulder I added, 'We'd better get going.'

The second day was worse than the one before. Two of the prisoners who were ill collapsed and it was only thanks to Bullmaster that they weren't shot where they fell. A cart was commandeered and the two men were placed on it under a couple of blankets. Half a dozen of us took turns pushing the cart, which further sapped our waning strength. *Christ*, I thought, *we've only just left the camp and already we're falling apart.* Finally we stopped in the middle of a clearing in a pine forest. There was no shelter for the night and we lit fires to keep warm. Food was barley soup and black bread supplied by the Germans, supplemented by some of the cans of meat we still possessed. All that remained of my store of food was a can of prunes in syrup.

In the morning I awoke almost frozen stiff. I forced myself to move, shivering, my guts aching. There were no latrines and like 10,000 other souls I went a little way into the woods.

Where on earth were we going? How long were we going to be on the road, out in the open like this? I went to find Bullmaster to ask him.

He was sitting on a bank of snow, a cup of tea in his hands, hollow-eyed. I put my questions to him.

'I've no idea, Dickie.'

'Shouldn't we try and find out?'

'How?'

'By asking Schmidt.'

'You ask him if you want. I'm not risking it. Schmidt is as likely to shoot you as give you an answer.'

I looked at him in disgust. 'It's our duty . . .' I began.

'Don't talk to me about duty,' he spoke harshly. 'Look where it landed Jock. Well, Sergeant-Major Anthony Bullmaster ain't no hero. I'll keep my head down and hope for the best. You got that? And youngster, I suggest you do the same thing.'

'But we need a Man of Confidence. Someone to lead us.'

'Why not you?'

'Me? Don't talk rot. I'm too young. Too junior. Nobody will listen to me. And nobody would vote for me either. It's ludicrous.'

I left him and went to find my own cup of tea. I'd barely taken a sip when we were called on to get moving. Another day began. I was in the middle of the massive column, which disappeared ahead out of sight and dwindled behind in the distance.

We came to a town about mid-morning and trudged through it. The name of the place had been removed. Its people stood silently and watched as we walked past. Their round, pasty faces had a Slavic look and from the signs above the shops I knew we were in Poland. Nobody offered us anything to eat or drink, but as the shops we passed looked empty I guessed they had nothing to offer.

We crossed three rivers that day and finally arrived at another town, where we stopped. Some arrangements had been made; field kitchens were waiting for us. They gave us a thin soup to drink and black bread to eat. It was barely enough to keep a man alive and certainly not enough to counter the effort we had to make, walking westwards.

That night we were billeted in a school and the town hall, which stood next to each other. From the sign over the town hall I knew we'd reached Tczew. I had no intention of talking to Schmidt but I did seek out one of the other *Wehrmacht* guards. He was an elderly man who had shown small acts of kindness whenever he could back at the camp.

Offering him a cigarette I asked, 'Do you know where we are going?'

'Germany. That's all I know.'

'How far is it to the border?'

'Three hundred kilometres at least.'

'How the hell are we going to get there?'

'We are going to walk. All the way.'

'But that's ludicrous. We are covering about fifteen kilometres a day. That would take twenty days. Three weeks! In this weather? It's impossible.'

'Schmidt is mad. We've been told that if we don't make it we will be shot, along with you *Kriegies*. So somehow we will make it to Germany.'

I slept on the floor, wrapped in my blankets and coat, hungry, and tired to the point of exhaustion. When I woke up to a dark dawn I saw it was snowing again. To move in that weather was senseless. Men would die needlessly. Somebody needed to speak to Schmidt. I went to find Bullmaster again, to plead with him. I found him in a large hall that had been turned over to a kitchen where a breakfast of some description was being prepared.

I asked him again to speak to Schmidt. By way of an answer he banged his cup on a wooden table. Silence fell and the men looked our way. There were about three hundred in the room, a cross section of the services.

'Listen up. You know Jock is dead. We need a new Man of Confidence and I propose Dickie here. He speaks the lingo and has been dealing with the Germans since he got to camp. How say you? Raise your hand if you agree.'

'No! I don't want it,' I yelled as they raised their hands. They weren't listening. They didn't care who did the job as long as it wasn't them and for that I couldn't blame them. But this was ludicrous. I was nineteen years old. Suddenly I realised I would be twenty in two weeks. Jock had told me that the average age of the POWs was just over twenty-one. So maybe I wasn't too young. But I was too scared.

I didn't want to face Schmidt. I'd never negotiated with the Germans. McAllister had done that. I'd merely translated. I looked out of the window and saw that the snow was falling really heavily. *Somebody* had to speak to Schmidt. If we went out in that many of us would die.

'I'll go and see him,' I said, and walked out of the hall, which was

547

now silent. All eyes were on me as I left. I felt a fool. Schmidt wouldn't listen to me.

I knew where he was staying as his car was parked outside a hotel. Crossing the street I entered the foyer. What struck me immediately was the warmth and the smell of cooking food. Schmidt was in the dining room, a napkin tucked into his tunic, fresh coffee in a cup at his elbow.

He watched me enter, march up to him and salute. Rigidly I stood to attention, sweat breaking out on my face, which I told myself was due to the heat in the room and not my nervousness. He looked at me coldly for a number of seconds and I wondered if he was thinking of talking to me or shooting me.

'What do you want? You are interrupting my breakfast.'

'I am the new Man Of Confidence,' I began but got no further. He threw back his head and laughed uproariously. There were a number of other SS troopers in the room and he repeated what I had just said. Their laughter steadied my nerves. It was like a weight being lifted from me; I knew now I had to do this and I would do it to the best of my ability. Or die trying.

'Captain Schmidt, with respect, it is snowing heavily. I must request that we be allowed to remain here until the snow stops and we are able to continue.'

'That is not possible.'

'I don't know what your orders are but presumably we are no use to you dead. If we are to be bargaining chips with the Allies then you need us alive.'

His eyes flickered and he looked past me. I seemed to have struck a chord. I pressed on. 'Whether we starve or freeze we are dead either way. If we stay here for a few days, get some food and warmth, wait for the snow to stop, we might all make it. Which would be to your credit.'

His eyes focused on me and I felt dread. If he reached for his gun I would . . . Do what? I was a sailor, not a soldier. There was a knife on the table. Perhaps I could grab it and stick it in his black heart before I too was shot. I licked my lips but my mouth was dry.

'We will stay until the snow stops. Just this once. Then it's a straight road to Berlin and Luckenwalde.'

'What's at Luckenwalde?' I had the temerity to ask.

'Your new camp. Now get out of my sight.'

I saluted, about turned and marched out. My heart was singing. I'd done it! I'd faced the bastard down.

We stayed for three days, eating thin gruel and drinking weak tea that got progressively weaker the more often we used the leaves. We burned tables and desks for warmth. The last day I had an unwanted visitor. It bit me in my stomach and I reached through the layers of my blankets and clothing to crush it between my finger and thumb. The likelihood that I had only one louse was hardly realistic, so I stripped off until I stood in my underpants, shivering. Carefully I worked my way around very inch of my clothing, finding the foul little creatures that could cause such discomfort. Discomfort which, with the advent of typhus, meant death as well. As I removed them I crushed them. There were others doing the same thing. An infestation of lice was almost inevitable but the longer we kept it at bay the better.

It stopped snowing and all too soon we were on our way again. Sometime, somewhere, the New Year had begun and we didn't even notice. Or if anyone did, they didn't comment on the fact. New Year and parties belonged in another life.

We now passed other refugees, men, women and children, fleeing Poland before the Russians arrived. The fear and panic in their faces were clear to see. We had heard that the Russian army was engaged in an orgy of raping, pillaging and killing.

When my unwanted visitors returned there was little I could do about it. Like the other POWs I scratched until I bled. Most nights we had somewhere to sleep, sometimes we didn't. On the nights we had no shelter the sick and injured had to fend for themselves. Sometimes they didn't make it. Or they gave up. On two occasions I saw guards trying to prod some poor bugger awake and when he refused to get up they shot him where he lay. The SS troops who carried out such vile acts would pay for it one day. I memorised their faces and made a vow. It was the promise of revenge that kept me alive.

Thirst became an issue. We would grab mouthfuls of snow as we marched along and stuff it in our mouths. Although we tried to be careful it was all too easy to pick up snow that was discoloured by the excreta of the men in front. The result was rampant dysentery. You knew you had it when sudden cramp sliced through your guts and you couldn't get your trousers down fast enough. The first time

I soiled myself, I threw my underpants away. The second time I soiled my trousers. From then on I didn't care.

In an attempt to lighten my load of anything that didn't contribute to keeping me alive I threw away the radio crystals. It made no difference.

Each day was an eternity. After a while my legs didn't really hurt. Numbness settled on them.

Every chance I got I bought provisions from the people we passed in the towns and villages. At first I shared, but soon I only bought enough for Steve Carruthers and myself. I was paying well over the odds and dad's money wouldn't last forever. Still, it gave us strength when there was none. I realised that I'd turned twenty two days before. I doubted I'd ever see twenty-one.

57

WHERE THE HELL had they gone? If they'd gone westwards, where
were they now? Who had burnt the lorries? Why hadn't they been
used to help move the POWs?

I was desperate. Richard's birthday had come and gone. The
weather across Europe was atrocious and our armies were becoming
bogged down in heavy snow and driving rain. But they kept moving
forward relentlessly. The Ardennes breakout by the Germans a week
before Christmas, coined the Battle of the Bulge, had finally been
contained. They were being steadily but surely wiped out. Our heavy
bombers had been busy pulverising the German troops and supply
lines, causing German fuel and ammunition to run low. The steady
attrition meant that when the drive for Berlin finally came there would
be few troops standing in the way.

I was incensed when Sir James Grigg, the Secretary of State for
War, told the House of Commons that, while the POWs were being
moved west under harsh conditions, representatives of the Protecting
Power in Germany were doing all they could to secure improvements
from the Germans. What the Swiss could do was beyond me. I sought
a meeting with Churchill.

'Grigg is a fool. It's not true. We've been getting reports in from
our SOE bods all over Europe. Sick POWs are *not* being transported
by truck and train. They are *all* exhausted and seriously sick with
dysentery and typhus. We know transfers have been going on for
weeks and will last many more weeks yet. Hell, Winnie, February is
only two days away and some of our prisoners have just reached
Eastern Germany from Poland.'

Winnie looked every day of his seventy years. 'I understand the
Red Cross have delivered record amounts of food parcels, medical
supplies and other necessities.'

'It's not enough, Winnie. Grigg also said that any request by the International Red Cross for vehicles, fuel and maintenance stores were being quickly and effectively dealt with. That's a damn lie.'

'David, do not presume so much on our friendship. I cannot and will not allow you to call a minister of the crown a liar.'

'All right then,' I said angrily, 'what should I call it? A verbal inexactitude? Or some other ludicrous parliamentary bit of verbiage which means the same thing? It's a lie. Our prisoners of war have been abandoned to their fate and are having to fend for themselves. Our men are in serious trouble and will die by the thousands if we don't do something damn quick.'

Churchill looked up at me from under beetling eyebrows. He hated being put on the spot but I had no choice. Right then I had no idea whether Richard was still alive. All I could do was hope and pray. Prayers often needed a helping hand or a hefty kick to work.

'We have Operation *Eclipse* well in hand. Do sit down, David, you're blocking out the light.'

Like a recalcitrant schoolboy I sat down. Operation *Eclipse* was well intended, but it envisaged an orderly end to the war, with Germans surrendering, handing in their weapons and being permitted home to their families. An elaborate and complex plan to repatriate our POWs, it included details from delousing, to supplying daily newspapers and sending ENSA entertainers to the camps to keep the men happy while travel arrangements were made. But the reality was very different. I had a copy of the document in my briefcase.

'Winnie, I don't know if you've read this . . .'

'I haven't had the time.'

'Let me read you one sentence. *Information does not reflect the considerable movement of POWs that is taking place.* That sentence alone makes a mockery of the rest of the document. *Eclipse* assumes the Germans will feed our men when hostilities cease, when they can't even feed them properly now. The idea that medical aid will be forthcoming is ludicrous when, according to my information, four out of five men are already laid low with dysentery and typhus.'

I lifted another sheet of paper. 'This is a copy of a memorandum from one of the planners at SHAEF.' I handed it over. 'Here's another.' I tossed more copies of government memoranda on his desk. Each one represented the doubts of senior government officials and army officers as to the viability of *Eclipse*. 'Grigg *must* have seen these. Which is why I said the man is lying.'

'He's is being expedient with the truth.' Churchill busied himself lighting one of his foul cigars. It was, I knew, a delaying tactic to give him time to think.

'Our military attaché in Sweden came across a particularly frightening piece in a German language newspaper in Stockholm. I have the transcript here, which discloses that Himmler has a plan to be put into force on the day the Germans deem themselves defeated. *Niederlagstag* – N-day. Preparations have already been made for the liquidation of *all prisoners* in Nazi hands. That includes political prisoners, the inmates of concentration camps and, worst of all, all prisoners of war and foreign workers in Germany. The larger prison camps are to be liquidated by bombing and machine-gunning, or, where there are sufficient SS guards, by shooting. Reliable SS personnel are being infiltrated amongst the regular camp guards. Camp commandants are being provided with Nazi Party advisers who will have total authority for N-Day.'

'My God,' Churchill looked shocked as well he might. 'You have proof?'

'It ties in with information my office has received from the Red Cross.' I paused and looked out through the window at a wet, miserable day and thought of Richard. Firmly I concentrated on the matter in hand. 'And I have a report here from our embassy in Switzerland. Rumours are rife that the Germans intend to liquidate all POWs rather than try and remove them or let them fall into Allied hands. We need an official warning to the German people that they will be held responsible for the lives of the POWs.'

Churchill sat in silence for a few moments. Then he nodded his head. 'I agree. We will implement the policy immediately. Mass coverage using the BBC and Radio Luxembourg, as well as leaflets we can drop into the camps. I want you to work with SHAEF to create a plan of action to protect our POWs when the time comes. Let me have your ideas ASAP. Is there anything else?'

'Yes, though you aren't going to like what I have to say.'

'Since when has that ever stopped you voicing your opinion?'

'Never, I hope. We should call a halt to the carpet-bombing of German cities. The deaths of civilians achieve nothing. Quite the reverse. I think it makes the German more dogged, more determined to fight to the bitter end. If people have lost loved ones they wonder – what's the point of living? It's also ethically wrong, dammit. We don't wage war on women and children. Enough have died already. Let's try and save as many as we can.'

Winston looked grim. 'It has played on my conscience too. I will speak to Eisenhower. We need a special war room at SHAEF to monitor information about prisoners and co-ordinate a plan of action. I see a roll for SOE in that. With hundreds of thousands of our men in German hands we must do all in our power to protect them.'

'I agree.'

Churchill held up his hand. 'Any strategy has to be commensurate with winning the war.'

'The lives of our POWs are worth more than a few days off the end of the conflict,' I said coldly.

'The quicker we beat the Germans the sooner our men will be safe. Don't underestimate the role of the Russians in all this. They aren't to be trusted.'

'Meaning?'

'Meaning we need to take control of as much of Europe as we can before the Russians get there. Believe me, it's vital. I don't trust Stalin. If our POWs fall into Russian hands what'll happen? Our men will be used as bargaining chips for land.'

I struggled to stop the 'I told you so' forming behind my lips and settled instead for, 'Thank you, Prime Minister, for your time.'

'A pleasure. Get that report to me ASAP.'

When Dresden was virtually obliterated on St Valentine's Day I was incandescent with rage. The city's peacetime population was 600,000 but because of the fleeing refugees it had swollen to a million. Around midnight on the 13th February eight hundred four-engined Lancasters dropped tons of high explosives and incendiaries. Then, at noon on the 14th, American B-17s continued the destruction. Casualties were estimated at between 60,000 and 130,000 dead, but might be as high as 400,000. It was a total and utter obscenity.

The claim that the city was an important industrial and communications centre for the German armies on the Eastern Front didn't wash with me. Air Chief Marshal Sir Arthur Harris, Chief of RAF Bomber Command was quite simply wrong to continue with his policy of terror bombing the Germans into submission. I spoke to my contacts at the War Office and many of them agreed with me. We would do better to attack the German aviation fuel and petrol production plants.

Such actions put our POWs in serious jeopardy. I tried to get hold of Winnie, but was told he was in the Crimea, at Yalta, meeting Roosevelt and Stalin to discuss the post-war carve-up of Europe. The meeting had been going on for a week in total secret.

We soon learned that Poland would be ruled by the Soviets. A situation which filled my colleagues and I with a great deal of uneasiness.

Having finished my report for the PM, I had a meeting with senior staff at SHAEF headquarters and we were agreed. Operation Vicarage was born.

In essence I proposed that Army Group Command be prepared to send relief columns to POW camps near their axis of advance. This was conditional on such action not hindering the Command's main objective at the time. Furthermore the First Allied Airborne Army were to prepare to despatch airborne detachments of at least battalion strength if Ground Forces could not advance quickly enough.

POWs would be sent west by road but the RAF and USAAF would also be on standby, ready to help with the evacuation.

However, this grand plan lacked one vitally important aspect – up-to-date intelligence of the situation at any camp, at any given time. In order to deal with the problem I proposed dropping small reconnaissance teams behind enemy lines, close to the camps where they would go to ground. Their task would be to send information back and, at the same time, open two-way radio communications with the prisoners.

My proposal was agreed and volunteers were asked for; one hundred and twenty teams of three men each, to include over a hundred British and American officers. Brigadier J. S. Nichols was appointed leader and the group was named SAARF – the Special Allied Airborne Reconnaissance Force. Training was organised and conducted by SOE with help from America's Office of Strategic Services. The objective was to have sixty teams ready to enter Europe by the beginning of May.

As February drew to a close we were battering Berlin ceaselessly. The American Ninth and First Armies had crossed the Ruhr and broken into the plain of Cologne. The Russians had crossed the Oder and were well on their way to Dresden, threatening the German capital from the south. I looked at the reports flooding in to SOE and I wondered what the race into Berlin was for. By the time we'd finished bombing the place there would be nothing left.

In the middle of the month an old adversary of mine raised his ugly head. On the 16th of March the Duke of Windsor resigned as Governor of the Bahamas and in an obscenely short space of time left the islands for America, without warning effectively abandoning his post. Reading this latest act of cowardice, part of me sincerely regretted dropping that decanter of port.

I still had no definite knowledge of Richard's whereabouts. There were millions of people on the move across Europe. Roads were jammed with refugees, fleeing German soldiers and POWs. Most were heading west as news of the atrocities being committed by Russian soldiers reached us. German men, whether in uniform or not, were being hanged or shot as the Soviets advanced across eastern and southern Germany.

Throughout this period our workload was staggering. My staff and I often slept on camp-beds in our offices. Madelaine and I rarely saw one another.

Once the war in Europe ended we still had the war in the Far East to contend with. Would Richard be sent there, once his leave and recuperation time were over? Not if I had anything to do with it, I vowed.

On the 27th of March Argentina declared war on Germany. Cynically we added her name to the list. In the last two months thirteen countries had declared war, starting with Ecuador on 2nd February. Then, in quick succession, declarations came from Paraguay, Peru, Chile, Venezuela, Turkey, Uruguay, Egypt, Syria, Lebanon, Saudi Arabia and Finland. The aid we received from our new allies was minimal, but like rats returning to the ship, it proved Britain was no longer sinking.

I was tackling a mountain of paperwork when Robert Gill barged into my office without knocking. 'We've got him – Richard – he's in Luckenwalde.'

I had never before understood the expression 'to weep for joy'.

'Phone Sion. Use your contacts on the black-market. I want the biggest parcel drop we can organise.'

He grinned at me. 'Sion's on line one.'

58

WE HAD TAKEN almost three months to cross Poland. Now spring was in the air and I, like many others, felt a stirring of hope that I might survive after all. On the nightmare march across Poland and Eastern Germany, I had lost about two stones in weight. When we finally arrived at the gates of Luckenwalde we thought it was a sanctuary.

They left us outside for hours in the freezing cold. Finally I managed to get hold of the Adjutant and begged him to let us in. After a long delay he agreed and we struggled through the gates. Twenty-four hours later I was wishing with all my heart to leave the place.

Luckenwalde, or Stalag IIIA, was hell on earth. Fifteen thousand strong in the camp and more prisoners were arriving every day. In my hut alone there were two hundred bodies, crushed together. I had gladly sunk back into anonymity, no longer the Man of Confidence.

There were vicious SS guards in the camp who made free with their blows and kicks for the slightest infringement of the rules. Schmidt and his cohorts were absorbed into the camp machinery, but I made it my business to know where he was and what he was doing at every opportunity. My hatred of the man and my determination to get justice for Jock were all-consuming.

The sanitation arrangements were the worst anyone had ever encountered. Pervading the camp like an evil cloud was the stench of the latrines. The lavatories were primitive, wooden hut with pits and boards stretched across them. No privacy and the pits were never emptied. You gripped a pole to crouch over the pit. I had nightmares about my hands slipping and falling into one of them. I couldn't think of a worse way to die. There was no paper – *The Saint Goes West* was long gone – and limited washing facilities, so the horror of the place was overwhelming.

Still the prisoners kept arriving. Bunks were four-high. The barracks were crammed to bursting point and the tents overflowing. Water and food were at a premium, our clothes and bodies were infested with lice, and dysentery was a continual problem, in spite of the charcoal we forced ourselves to eat.

News arrived continuously as more POWs joined the camp. We knew that the Russians were closest but everyone prayed that the Americans or British would get to us first.

The parcel drop came out of the blue. A Griffin simply appeared one day and began parachuting in supplies. Four or five aircraft in total dropped thousands of parcels and it felt like Christmas. We had sardines, jam, butter, tins of meat, raisins, chocolate, peanut butter – everything was shared.

Shortly after the drop a stranger entered my hut and spoke to my mate Steve Carruthers. Steve pointed at me and the man approached. He was a corporal, a few years older than me and as skinny as the rest of us.

'You named Griffiths?'

'Could be, why?'

'Nothing to worry about. I was told to fetch Richard Griffiths.'

Alarmed I asked, 'Fetch him where?'

'To see the Man.'

'Why?' I climbed off my bunk and stood up. Alarm bells were ringing in my head and I wanted to know what I was letting myself in for.

'There's nothing to worry about. Just come with me.'

He walked out and I followed. Steve Carruthers and I exchanged puzzled looks and he got to his feet.

'I think I'll join you.'

'Thanks, Steve.' In spite of the deprivations we'd survived on the march Carruthers was still a tough-looking man. He was a few inches taller than me and I knew he could handle himself in a fight. There was a calmness about him that had inspired me many times on our journey – he was rock solid, salt of the earth, a good man.

We crossed the camp to a hut much the same as our own. Inside was a table, with half a dozen prisoners seated around it. As I looked at their faces one of them spoke. 'Are you Richard Griffiths?'

'Yes. Who are you?'

'Name's Whitaker. Sergeant-Major, Third Infantry.' He pointed to the red inverted triangle with three black triangles attached to each side, sewn on his sleeve. 'In this part of the camp I'm the Man.'

The camp was so large it was separated into smaller sections with barbed wire. I knew that one part was run by a Norwegian General and another by an RAF Wing Commander, though I'd not seen or met either.

'I gather you were the Man for Marienburg.'

'Only on the march. Since that bastard Schmidt shot Jock McAllister.'

'That's what I heard. Sit down.' He pointed to a chair on the other side of the table and I slid into it, as wary as hell. 'Who's your friend?'

'Just that. My oppo. We did the walk together.'

Whitaker knew what that meant. Many of us teamed up as we struggled on the march, looking out for each other, helping one another. It was an odd comradeship brought about by a combination of necessity and real friendship. I doubted I would have made it without Steve's help. But then I liked to think the same went for him.

'We have a radio here,' Whitaker said, which came as no surprise. 'We knew about the parcel drop and what to expect. After the drop we were asked whether we'd received the parcels and asked to identify a Richard Evan Griffiths. That you?'

I nodded, unable to stop a smile splitting my face.

'If we send a code word tonight we'll get a second drop in five days. Actually, not so much a code word as the answer to a question.'

I nodded and tried to look co-operative.

'What's the name of your father's house?'

'*Fairweather*,' I replied instantly.

'Just who the hell are you? I don't like mysteries,' said Whitaker. The sergeant major was a tough-looking individual with piercing eyes.

'My father arranged the drop. He'll arrange the next one. He might even send a third if he knows I'm alive. Tell him we need medical supplies, books, anything. If he can get the stuff he'll deliver.'

Whitaker nodded. 'Right, Griffiths, I want you to move huts. To come into this one. It's not safe out there. The men are becoming desperate and we can't do with losing you and your connection. We've had one suspicious death in the camp already. The man who died was suffocated. All he had was a tin of pilchards. They were gone when his body was found.'

I put my hand in my pocket and fingered my Swiss army knife. It was an odd source of comfort when I felt in a tough spot. Ludicrous, I knew, but it had become my talisman. 'Sir, there's no point in me moving. No one knows who I am. I'll just stay where I am, thank you.'

'All right. Only be careful. We'll send the signal and hope we get another drop. We've more men arriving today from the east and we've nowhere to put them.'

Steve and I left them to it. I was so relieved I was no longer the Man; the responsibility was hellish. We'd gone half way back to our own hut when we heard a commotion in another. Approaching cautiously we saw an argument that was getting out of hand.

'That's my bread, you bastard.'

The youth he had cornered was holding a piece of black bread. The lad couldn't have been much more than seventeen and was obviously terrified out of his wits. His accuser was older, tougher and wielding a wicked-looking home-made knife.

The other POWs were lying on their bunks or sitting around the stove, which was lit, waiting for something in a pot to cook.

Steve and I exchanged looks. I shrugged and Steve nodded.

'Leave him alone,' I said entering the hut. The chap with the knife wasn't much bigger than me, but he looked a damn sight tougher than I felt.

'Keep out of this. It's none of your business.'

'I'm making it my business. Leave him alone.'

As the man turned his attention on me, the youngster slipped past and out the door.

'Hey! Come back, you little swine.' As he took a step to follow, I hit him a glancing blow on the side of the head and Steve grabbed his hand and forced him to drop the knife.

The man looked at us for a few seconds and then crumpled. 'He did steal my bread, I tell you. It was mine. I'd hid it under my mattress.' Tears welled up and the man began to sob. It was a shocking sight.

One of the others came over and led him away to a bunk. When he came back he said, 'You'll have to excuse Johnny. He was captured in 'Forty, after Dunkirk. He's had five years of camp life. He's escaped three times and been brought back. And he was telling the truth. That boy is a light-fingered little bastard who's been thieving all over the camp. He'll get a knife in his gullet one day.'

'Bloody hell, I'm sorry. I didn't know.' I had a small piece of bread in my pocket and I held it out. 'Give this to Johnny, will you? Tell him we're sorry.'

Receiving a nod we left the hut.

'I feel an utter prat,' I said. 'That'll teach us to rush in.'

The following day our rations were cut. Each loaf of bread was to be shared by seven men and last a day. We were to get three-quarters of a mug of soup, the same of potatoes, enough margarine to cover one slice of bread and cheese or meat paste sufficient to be spread thinly on a quarter slice. Twice a day we were to get a mug of mint tea or acorn coffee. The food parcels had helped but as they had been shared one between four men they had assuaged our hunger for a few hours only.

The skies were filled with aircraft and we could hear bombs exploding in the far distance, so we knew the roads would be impassable. It would be weeks before a proper convoy of aid arrived. I lay on my bunk that night, staring at the wooden frame above, thinking of home and freedom. We only had to survive a few more weeks.

With April the weather turned and spring was finally with us. It took away the bone-biting cold but brought with it spring rain, turning the compound into a mud bath.

Rumours were rife in the camp. The threat of being moved always in the air. Then, on the 11th of April, we were told to be ready to leave. So far the rumours had always been connected to the Russian advance. This time we heard we were going to Berlin, to be held as hostages. We walked out in a bedraggled line, leaving behind the few hundred men who were too ill to travel. Steve walked beside me.

We climbed into railway trucks, mercifully not as crowded as before. In sharp contrast to previous moves, the guards behaved themselves. They spent the journey assuring us that Hitler was a *Schweinhund* and that they were anti-Nazi.

For a day and a night the train shunted from one siding to another. At night time we slept in the trucks, in the daytime we sat in the sunshine when we could. POW was painted on the top of the trucks in bright yellow but as an American Thunderbolt aircraft attacked further up the line I wasn't confident of our safety. A few trains passed us, travelling north, obviously carrying guns and troops to defend Berlin. The Germans looked like what they were – a defeated army.

We were finally ordered onto the train which we believed was headed for Berlin but after only a few hours we were told to disembark and return to the camp. I didn't know whether to be relieved or not. Steve and I trudged back to our hut to find that our bunks and everything else had disappeared. The Poles had stripped our section of the camp bare and taken anything useful into their own.

In spite of the confusion I felt a stirring of optimism. Surely the end couldn't be far away?

That night I was awoken by loud explosions and bright flashes in the sky. Looking out I saw the sky filled with aircraft. Germany was being obliterated.

Word came through to the camp that we were to stay put, no matter what happened. The rumours that we were being moved to Berlin were scotched. For days nothing happened, then, in the middle of the night, we were woken by the guards and told to get dressed. Their orders had arrived.

We left the hut thinking we were about to be moved. Instead we were given the news that the Germans were going to defend the camp to the last man against the Russians; we were to expect heavy casualties. The Germans appeared to have no further interest in us. Uncertain what to do, we stood in the compound for a while, then wandered back to our huts. I spent a sleepless night but the following morning had brought no change.

Two German fighters flew low over the camp and for one heart-stopping moment I thought we were going to be strafed. But they flew off, leaving us relieved but confused. Almost instinctively I looked around for my nemesis. Schmidt was standing talking to a POW I recognised from Whitaker's mob. The man *knew my identity*. Alarm bells sounded in my head. I knew I was in trouble now.

The following morning a hush seemed to have fallen over the camp. I stood in the compound and looked around. Many of the POWs were in their huts. With uncertainty came fear. There seemed to be fewer guards than usual. I was suddenly aware of a man approaching me, wearing civilian clothes, and for a few seconds I didn't recognise him – Captain Schmidt. He was pointing a gun at my chest.

'You will come with me, Griffiths,' he ordered. 'You are my "ticket out of here", as you so quaintly put it.' He jerked his gun to the side and I raised my hands.

Steve, realising I was in trouble, ran across shouting, 'What the hell's going on?'

'Schmidt says I'm to go with him.'

'Leave him be, Schmidt.'

'Shut up! The Third Reich is finished. It is every man for himself. Already guards are taking off their uniforms and leaving. Going west before the Russians get here. I am an SS soldier and I've served my country well. But I know what will happen if I am caught. As a good soldier, I plan ahead – in exchange for a tin of meat a prisoner told me your friend Griffiths' father is an important man in Britain.' He looked at me. 'A phone call to a contact in Berlin confirmed that your father was a politician and is also a wealthy banker. Now, unless you want to break your father's heart, I suggest you come with me.'

I couldn't believe it. Betrayed for a tin of meat! Not a handful of silver? The stupid thought clouded my mind as I tried to think.

'I'll come with you.'

'Most sensible. Now move!'

I walked towards him and he stepped aside.

'Put your hands down. Make it look natural,' he ordered.

Moving forward, I put my hands into my pockets and felt for my knife. My coat hung loose on me and I put my hands round the front and managed somehow to open its saw blade.

I heard a noise behind me and turned just in time to see Steve leap at Schmidt, who unhesitatingly shot him in the side of the head. Steve went down and lay sprawled on his stomach, his hands and legs outstretched, unmoving. In a blind rage I leapt at Schmidt. Weakened as I was from lack of food and a bout of dysentery, I should have been no match for the wiry SS officer. But surprise was with me and I slashed at the inside of his gun hand with my knife and cut deeply into his wrist. He screamed and dropped the gun, blood pouring from the wound while I swiped at his face, striking him in the left eye. Falling back, blood pouring down the side of his face, Schmidt turned on me with a snarl.

Even now I knew I couldn't put up much of a fight against him and so I dived for the pistol that was lying on the ground between us.

My hand curled around the butt and my forefinger slipped through the trigger-guard. I'd fired plenty of shotguns in my time and had used a .303 on the range when I joined up. But a pistol was an officer's weapon and I had never fired one. My finger had barely touched the trigger when it went off. Mercifully the gun was pointing at Schmidt and he screamed and fell backwards, clutching his leg. I looked at him in astonishment – I hadn't expected the gun to fire so easily. Besides, I wanted him alive, then arrested and tried for murder. *Double* murder – Jock and Steve.

As I looked over to where my friend lay I saw him move. Overwhelmed with relief, I went to him, kneeling beside him on the packed earth.

'Steve! Steve, speak to me.'

Steve groaned and made as if to sit up.

'What happened?' he groaned.

'Schmidt shot you.' I looked over at Schmidt in time to see him get to his feet and lurch away. I wondered why the guards hadn't been to investigate the shooting. As soon as Schmidt got hold of one I'd be dead.

I scrambled to my feet and ran after him. Nobody tried to stop me, no guards yelled out. He was about thirty yards away. I shouted at him to stop. He ignored me and I fired at him. I missed but had the gratification of seeing him duck his head. Suddenly he swerved to the left and ran into one of the huts. The fool – he'd gone into a latrine. There was no exit.

I hurried after him and staggered through the door, the stench over-powering as always. Schmidt had crossed some of the planks and stood over one of the filthy pits. I didn't hesitate. I fired, my hand shaking.

I hit him in the back. He fell onto the board and rolled into the pit full of excreta. He was holding on to the board when I reached him, up to his waist in a pit I knew to be at least eight-feet deep.

'Help me, please.' His face was white with effort and pain. I looked into his cold eyes.

'Like you helped us? Like you helped Jock?'

'*Befehl ist Befehl.*'

I held on to the post and looked at him with utter contempt. With every last ounce of strength in my body I kicked him in the face. He let go the plank and sank beneath the surface. Incredibly he came up spluttering out of that incredible filth, his eyes ripped open, horribly bright in his filth-covered face before he sank out of sight again. I waited but he didn't reappear.

I managed to get outside before I threw up. *At least*, I thought, *I don't need to hide the body.*

564

Steve had been shot along the head. The wound had bled profusely but done no real damage. Corporal White even managed to find a clean bandage to wrap around it.

The riddle of the missing guards was soon solved. They had left, simply walked away, leaving us to fend for ourselves.

'What should we do, Dickie?' Steve asked.

'I don't know. Stay put like we've been told and wait for the Russians, I suppose.'

They turned up the next morning. Our senior officers welcomed them with smiles and handshakes. I stayed in the background, instinctively wary. There was talk that we were to be relocated to a different, better camp but the Senior British Officer refused to move.

As a result the Russians manned the watchtowers and guards patrolled the camp once again. We were prisoners of our own allies.

59

WE ONLY MANAGED to organise and execute two drops of Red Cross parcels. Even they had been achieved more by luck than good judgement. The crowded skies over Europe were a dangerous place for single planes or a small squadron. Sion supplied Griffins but after the second drop we agreed it was too hazardous to make a third. Besides, we were closing in from all sides and it could only be a matter of time before Luckenwalde was liberated.

The information we were receiving about the state of the camps was very disquieting. But even the conditions under which our POWs had been held paled into insignificance beside the emerging horror of the concentration camps. The names would go down in the annals of infamy – Dachau, Belsen, Buchenwald, Auschwitz . . . The systematic extermination of millions of innocents defied the imagination.

Roosevelt died in the middle of the month and Harry S. Truman, Vice-President, was sworn in as the 32nd President of the USA.

SOE's task to "set Europe ablaze" was now complete. Already we were focusing our efforts into the war in the Far East. It was a fight I didn't have any stomach for, but I was determined to do my duty.

I knew the Russians had arrived at Richard's camp and that the Americans were about thirty miles away, pushing towards the western side of Berlin. The Russian stranglehold on Germany's capital drew tighter. Their aircraft strafed the streets of the city with impunity, killing men, women and children indiscriminately.

Berlin was in a state of panic. Soldiers were throwing away their rifles and abandoning their uniforms. Fanatical SS units were hunting them down and summarily executing them. Millions of people were on the move, many fleeing west, away from the retribution of the Russians. Prisoners of war from both sides had to be dealt with. Since

D-Day the allies had taken over 2,250,000 prisoners, a million in the last three weeks alone.

Then, amazingly, word came through that Hitler had shot himself and poisoned Eva Braun, his wife of one day. Mussolini, his aides and his mistress Clara Petacci had been shot in Milan and their bodies strung upside-down from the facade of a petrol station in the Piazza Loretto only two days previously.

The war in Europe was effectively over. Russia's perfidy came to the fore as Stalin tried to use our POWs as bargaining chips for control of central Europe. Everything Churchill had predicted was coming to pass.

I had no intention of allowing Richard to become one of Stalin's pawns. I needed to get to Germany as soon as possible and the only person who could get me there was my brother. First I armed myself with diplomatic papers. Winston had balked at the notion initially but I reminded him of one or two services I'd rendered him in the past and he'd acquiesced. I also received a letter of special appointment, written in English and Russian. It named me as a special envoy for the Prime Minister, and asked that every courtesy be extended to me. For travelling I chose to wear the uniform of a brigadier, a promotion I'd been given shortly after joining SOE.

I was in my office, making last minute arrangements when Mike and Robert suddenly appeared at my door.

'We heard you were planning a jaunt into Germany without us,' said Mike.

I nodded. 'I have to go alone. He's my son. And I'll not risk any more lives.'

'We don't think that's your decision, with all due respect.' Mike's smile took the sting out of his words.

'Mike, I can't ask you two to come to Germany. You know what it's like over there. People are being killed for a loaf of bread. It's too dangerous.'

'Which is why you need us. To cover your back.'

'I'll manage.'

'David, don't be ridiculous. How do you expect to pull this stunt off?'

I explained my role as Special Envoy to Churchill.

'If that was the case you certainly wouldn't be travelling alone. You'd have a retinue. Aides, assistants, God knows what.'

There was truth in that; I'd decided to say there was nobody available to accompany me.

'What reason are you giving for your visit?'

'Officially I'm there to find POWs whom we deem to be VIPs. After the mess at Colditz it's natural for us to be looking.' Allied Prisoners of War had been removed from Colditz just days before it was liberated on the 16th of April. Generals, senior officers and certain men with important relatives had been spirited away from the legendary Oflag IVC. The *Prominente,* as they were known, had included John Winant, the son of the American Ambassador to London, shot down early in the war, Winston's nephew, Giles Romilly, Lord Lascelles and the Master of Elphinstone – both nephews of King George VI. Field Marshal Haig's son and the cousin of Field Marshal Alexander had been among them too. They had ended up near Berlin and held until the bitter end. There were still others who merited special attention. So my task wasn't unreasonable.

'Good. Then we'll be your aides,' said Mike.

'Mike, I can't ask you to come. What about Betty? What about Susan?' I looked from one to the other. Both their faces bore the stubborn look I'd come to know very well.

'To be sure, I would rather face a German division of SS than tell Betty I let you go alone,' said Mike.

'Agreed,' said Robert. 'Susan would probably marry me just to spend *her* life making mine a misery for having let you go alone.' His smile belied the words.

I made one more feeble effort to dissuade them. 'I won't be alone. Sion will be with me.'

'One geriatric looking after another,' said Mike. 'Well, we'll be there to look after you both. Someone,' he added reasonably, 'needs to carry your bags.'

Both men were in uniform. Mike was now a full-blown commander and Robert a major. I grinned at them, to hide my brimming emotions. 'I appreciate it,' I managed.

Sion picked us up at Biggin Hill in a Griffin. The plane displayed the roundels of the RAF, and was fitted out to drop paratroopers. We sat on the canvas seats lining the port side, just behind the pilot's seat, with the door to the cockpit open.

Sion was piloting and Mike navigating. Clearance had been obtained from the different air traffic control stations as far as north-eastern France. There was little chance of being bounced by a German fighter, but always the chance of being attacked by an over-zealous Allied fighter pilot. The Americans were getting a reputation for attacking first and identifying their target later.

'There's the airfield,' said Sion. 'About two miles away.'

We landed without mishap on a strip of grass south of Potsdam. A track, a windsock and some wooden huts were all there was to proclaim it as a working airfield. Taxiing over to the huts, Sion pulled the fuel stops to the engines. As they wound down a blessed silence descended. Two men came out of the nearest hut and approached the plane. Robert opened the fuselage door and I stiffly climbed down, working the kinks out of my joints.

The two officers saluted. 'Captain Meredith, sir, and Lieutenant Smith.'

I returned the salute. 'Brigadier Sir David Griffiths. These men are Commander O'Donnell and Major Gill.' Sion joined us at that moment wearing flying gear without insignia.

'We have a staff car available, sir. A Mercedes, courtesy of the Germans. We've painted a Union Jack on both the front doors and a Union Jack standard flies on the bonnet. I also have an invitation for you to dine with us at Potsdam this evening.'

'That's very kind but we'll have to decline. I need to get to Luckenwalde as quickly as possible.'

'Yes, sir.' The keys to the car were handed to me and the two men saluted once more before departing.

We had decided that it made most sense for Sion to stay with the plane and look after it. While he went about seeing to refuelling we stowed our gear in the open-topped staff car and climbed inside. Robert drove, while Mike and I sat in the back. The three of us had Sten Mk II sub machine-guns, as well as Webley pistols at our sides. Mike also had a satchel of grenades. We were going into territory rife with fanatical SS troops, Hitler Youth and desperate civilians. We weren't taking any chances.

Close-up the destruction was mind-numbing. Acrid smoke bit into my throat as we drove through the wreckage. Buildings were nothing but jagged and blackened stumps pointing at a mocking blue sky. Refugees, stumbling along in a pathetic sea of terrified humanity made me despair. Hollow-eyed and frightened, they were like lemmings in a headlong rush. But from what, and going where? I didn't, in all honesty, understand. There was nothing ahead of them to flee to. I quickly realised they were Germans fleeing the Russians but there was nothing for them in the west. Europe had been devastated as far as the Channel. And they certainly wouldn't be welcome in France, the Benelux countries or Scandinavia. As I watched them my overriding emotion was pity.

We were stopped by an American patrol, which quickly waved us through. Only a short distance from Luckenwalde we hit our first major snag. A Russian roadblock.

A Russian officer swaggered up to the vehicle and looked inside insolently. 'Papers!' He said in English, holding out his hand.

He was a squat brute, with long arms and an unshaven face. I recognised his shoulder pips to be those of a captain.

In a mild voice I asked, 'Do you speak English?'

'Papers! Papers!' He repeated himself, his voice rising.

I was about to climb out of the car but Mike restrained me. First he pointed at my shoulder red tabs and epaulettes, then at his three stripes. Indicating the Union Jack on the side of the car he roared, 'Stand to attention and salute or I'll have you on a charge. Where is your senior officer?'

The captain looked at him sullenly but made no move either to salute or acknowledge the question, which he probably didn't understand. There were two soldiers by the makeshift barricade, watching us with interest. We obviously didn't present a threat as their rifles remained slung over their shoulders.

For a few seconds there was a silent impasse, while we glared at the Russian and he glared back. Finally, with another scowl, he indicated to the two men to lift the barrier and we drove through.

With a thankful sigh I sank down into my seat, then looked back at the three Russians. They had already forgotten about us as another vehicle approached them. 'So much for Allies and mutual respect,' I said.

'We can't count on it,' said Mike. 'I've never trusted the Russians, not since we sold those planes to them back in the twenties. We'd better keep our wits about us.'

The road was clogged with refugees and as we were going against the tide we had no choice but to drive slowly. The twenty-five miles to Luckenwalde took nearly four hours. We'd met more Russian soldiers but they'd ignored us. Then, on the outskirts of Luckenwalde, we came across a column of Russian T34 tanks. We pulled over and waited as they came closer. At the head of the column was a staff car, with two officers and a driver. The car stopped alongside ours.

'Who are you?' one of the officers asked in heavily accented but understandable English.

'Brigadier Griffiths. Special envoy for Prime Minister Churchill.'

'Ah, Churchill, very good man. Great man.'

'That is so. And you are?'

'Major Orlov,' he saluted, 'and this is my commanding officer, Colonel Satoff.'

I returned the salute with a smile.

The colonel said something in Russian and the major turned to us.

'My colonel would like to know what you do here.'

'We are going to the POW camp in Luckenwalde, looking for certain men.'

'If you go down road you will see Soviet HQ. Please to report there.'

I nodded and smiled, uncertain whether I intended reporting anywhere. On the other hand, with the Russians nominally in control, it might be best to keep on the right side of them. So I nodded, waved and tapped Robert on his shoulder. 'Drive on.'

We moved away after a further exchange of salutes. The road was much clearer all of a sudden, as though the refugees had somehow disappeared into thin air.

A cluster of army trucks and other vehicles, each emblazoned with the red star of Russia, were parked in a large square near the town hall. The Russian hammer and sickle flew outside an isolated, enormous marquee and we stopped beside it. A guard stood to attention beside a tent flap, tied open to reveal trestle tables and chairs. There were several officers inside.

We all three approached the guard who saluted. I returned the salute and we walked inside. There was a table on the right, with a major seated behind it. He took a look at my tabs and shoulders, stood and saluted. I returned the gesture then asked, 'Do you speak English?'

'A little, sir.'

I explained who I was and my reason for being there. He took my letter, read it and smiled.

'Please to follow.'

Our arrival had caused a small stir of interest and the others in the marquee were watching as we approached a table at the back of the tent. The man seated there was obviously a senior officer.

There was an exchange of Russian and the senior officer's scowl turned into a broad smile.

He spoke rapidly in Russian, which a very attractive young lady interpreted. I learned later that most of the Russian/English interpreters were attractive young female officers. Cynically I wondered if they were employed solely for their language skills.

'The General says welcome to Germany. It is a great pleasure to meet you and he hopes you will join him for dinner.'

So frustratingly close to the camp I had no intention of stopping until I had found Richard. Knowing I would be dealing with Russian officers at some point I had come prepared. Smiling warmly, I answered, 'Please tell the General that I would be delighted. However, I wish to contribute to the meal, if I may.'

'Certainly,' she translated.

Mike and Robert saluted and promptly returned to the car to fetch a basket we'd brought with us. The General watched as they returned, weighed down by its contents. They heaved it onto the table and I opened it with a flourish. The General leapt to his feet with an even bigger smile and addressed the assembled officers.

Reaching inside he removed four bottles of malt whisky then followed them with packets of cold meats, a leg of ham, *paté*, fresh white bread and a host of other items. His thanks were as profuse as one might expect from someone who'd been eating field rations for months. I knew that the gesture would go a long way with the Russians.

Having hopefully made a friend, I explained why I was there.

'Your son is in the camp? Then we must find him immediately. Come.'

The General lifted his jacket from behind his chair and slapped his hat onto his head. With the interpreter in tow and several other Russian officers we set off for the camp, a short ride away. Within minutes our convoy of cars drew up at the camp gates which, as I later learned, had been smashed open by Russian tanks.

Prisoners of War were standing in groups all over the compound. I was horrified to see the state they were in. Many looked like walking skeletons.

'A terrible sight, is it not?' The general said in English.

I looked at him in some surprise.

'I speak English, though not perfectly. Interpreters have their uses, on occasion. Come, let us find your son.'

For the next thirty minutes we wandered through the camp. *Please let him be here.* The mantra kept repeating in my head. We eventually reached a field hospital only to be told that over a hundred injured men had been removed from the camp hours earlier.

A group of bedraggled POWs stood outside one of the furthest huts watching us as we approached. One of them detached himself from the rest and took a hesitant step towards us. Emaciated, filthy, barely human, I recognised my son immediately.

'Richard,' I yelled rushing towards him, tears blurring my vision. *Thank you, God, thank you.*

Richard was crying too, holding me tightly, his thin frame wracked with sobs. My strong boy, he was all skin and bone. What had the bastards done to him?

'It's okay. It's okay, Richard. Mike's here and your uncle Sion. We're taking you home.'

It wasn't quite that simple but it wasn't too difficult either. The general was happy enough when I told him we would prefer to leave immediately. Especially when I handed over another six bottles of whisky. In exchange, we departed Germany with a plane filled with sick POWs, as well as Richard, his friends L/S Carruthers and Chalky White, who helped to look after the sick. On the plane we had handed out sandwiches, bags of apples and bars of chocolates, all of which they had devoured to the last crumb. What I remember most about that flight is the stench of their bodies. Although we were cooped up together for the best part of three hours I couldn't get used to it. How had they borne the humiliation, the degradation, the pain of their war behind barbed wire?

Sion radioed ahead to Biggin Hill to tell them about our cargo and ambulances were organised to meet us. We also radioed St Athan and told Kirsty the good news. We left it to her to network the information around the family.

A contingent of Military Police were there when we landed. They wouldn't allow anyone to leave the airfield until names and numbers had been taken. I wasn't to know it then but this was a foretaste of the disgraceful maltreatment of all returning Prisoners of War. I pulled rank and took Richard away. He insisted on Carruthers coming with us and I saw no reason why he shouldn't.

It was now nearly midnight. I could see from their haggard faces that Richard and Carruthers were close to exhaustion. My elation had worn off and I was feeling punch drunk. I was, I knew, getting far too old for such goings-on, but the truth was I wouldn't have it any other way.

On the outskirts of Biggin Hill was a large, country hotel. We'd used it often in the past and we went there now. The manager was less than pleased to be knocked up at that hour, but when he realised who we were, and I'd slipped him a fiver, he welcomed us with open arms.

The first order of the day as far as Carruthers and Richard were concerned was to have a bath. My son confided in me afterwards that he'd changed the water four times and still didn't feel clean. Their clothes were incinerated and fresh clothes given to them by the hotel staff after the exchange of a few more pounds.

Richard had tried unsuccessfully to get his mother on the phone. I now had my second wind and we were just sitting down to a cold supper when there was a commotion at the door. Kirsty had contacted Madelaine at the flat and she had driven straight to Biggin Hill. Once there she had quickly learned we were at the hotel. Madelaine ran towards us calling Richard's name. As mother and son embraced I felt a lump in my throat and my vision grew blurred.

I looked at Richard with a feeling of pride. Despite all he had been through, he appeared stronger, more self-assured. He was a man now – a good man, I hoped.

We talked the night away. Finally, reluctant to be parted, we went to our beds. As the dawn broke I held Madelaine tightly, as she cried unashamedly, the tears streaming down her face.

'It's okay, my darling. He's back safe and sound.'

'I know. I'm just being silly. It's a mixture of happiness, relief, anger, knowing what he went through. It's all of those things and it's none of them.'

'If it's any consolation, I've wept a few tears in the past few hours too.'

With Madelaine's head on my shoulder we silently watched the sun appear on the horizon. For the first time in five years I had a sense of inner peace.

*　　*　　*

On Monday, the 7th of May, Germany surrendered in a small red schoolhouse in Rheims. The Germany signatory to the unconditional surrender was General Alfred Jodl, Army Chief of Staff. General Bedell Smith, Eisenhower's Chief of Staff, signed for the Western Allies and General Ivan Suslapatov was witness for the Russians. During the previous fortnight German armies had been surrendering all over Europe, from Italy in the south to as far north as Norway. Five days earlier the garrison in Berlin had surrendered. Hundreds of German generals and senior officers were taken prisoner and shipped to Bridgend in South Wales, to work on farms.

Life in Britain was gradually returning to normal. Richard was given POW leave, along with young Steve. Both of them had been through a terrible trauma, but I knew their youth would help them recover. And listening to them talk I knew that they were both survivors.

Two weeks later the coalition government resigned and elections under the old party system were called. The King asked Winston to form a caretaker government until the election could be held on the 5th of July.

In June, Germany was carved in half and Russia took over the eastern part. This meant moving battalions, divisions, even armies around Europe as positions of occupation coalesced.

At the end of June delegates from fifty countries signed the World Security Charter to establish an international peacekeeping body, to be called the United Nations. Its purpose? To provide peace with teeth. The first to sign were the Chinese, followed by the Americans as the host nation. The claim made by many – that if such a body had existed a few years earlier millions of Europeans would still be alive – I personally doubted. But then, I was always cynical where governments were concerned.

At the end of July, Labour won the election with an over-whelming majority. Churchill, so revered and loved as a wartime leader, was out in the cold, comprehensively rejected by the British people. Clement Attlee became Prime Minister and would be leading the delegation back to Potsdam to negotiate with Russia regarding the future of Europe. I didn't hold out much hope, knowing Attlee as I did.

Now all our attention was focused on the Far East and the war against Japan. Emperor Hirohito told his armed forces that there would be no retreat, no surrender. No "foreign devils" would be allowed to set foot on the sacred soil of Japan. At SOE we estimated we could expect to take a million casualties before Japan would be forced to surrender. It was an incredible number but we all agreed, probably close to the truth.

The Manhattan Project saved those million lives and probably years of warfare. The first atomic bomb, wiping out the city of Hiroshima, should have ended it. However, it took a second bomb dropped on Nagasaki on the 9th of August to get the desired results. On the 14th of August Japan surrendered unconditionally.

A week later I resigned from SOE. I was sad to say goodbye to the many friends I had made there, each individual an indispensable link in the chain we had forged.

The following fortnight was completely taken up with the preparations for Susan's wedding. When the big day came, I was proud to walk my beautiful daughter up the aisle. Her new husband, Robert, was a fine man.

Once we'd seen the happy couple off, Madelaine and I sat over a nightcap in our bedroom at *Fairweather* and discussed the future. What would it mean for our children? Europe, indeed the world, needed rebuilding. New lines had been drawn in the sand and tensions were already high in some trouble spots around the world. With sadness we spoke of brave Alex and our darling John Phillipe, needless deaths, but only two amongst millions. What a tragic waste – the second time in thirty years. I prayed to God there wouldn't be another world war. But whatever the future held, I knew that the Griffiths family would be in the thick of it.

Epilogue

'SIR,' SAID TIM Hunter, 'I've spoken to a publisher in America.'

Sir David Griffiths looked up from his desk.

'They weren't convinced about publishing your biography until I told them about the "D" notice. That got their attention and fast.'

'And?'

'They've agreed. There's only a small advance but it was all I could screw out of them.'

Waving away the question of money, Sir David said, 'I fully intend giving all royalties to charity by way of a trust. How soon can we get the project off the ground?'

'Volume one is ready. I'm sending it special delivery tomorrow. I guess we'll have the printer's proofs in about three months and the finished book not much later.'

'Good. This calls for a celebration.'

'I was under the impression, sir, that you weren't allowed to drink. Your wife . . .'

'. . . is a wonderful person whom I love dearly, but she's too bossy by half. Besides, I'm feeling much better and I'm off the antibiotics. Anyway, I wasn't suggesting a proper drink.'

'Oh.' Hunter was at a loss for words. He'd actually been looking forward to a snifter, as the old boy tended to let slip a few little gems when he'd had a drink or two.

'I thought we'd try a rather special port I have in the cellar. It's about a hundred years old and drunk only on special occasions.'

'Is this such an occasion?'

'You're sure they're going to publish?'

'Oh, yes, one hundred percent. I know the editor very well. There's no doubt. First print run one hundred thousand copies in hardback. As he says, if there's a 'D' notice the book must contain information

577

the Brits don't want known. And they love washing British laundry in public. Sorry, sir. Of course, there is the added advantage that your father was elected President of the US of A.'

Sir David's face darkened, the memories flooding back. When was it? 1921 or 22? He had been the mastermind behind his father's election campaign. He summoned a smile. It was so long ago. 'Then we deserve the port.' Ringing the bell, Sir David sat back with a look of anticipation. The butler appeared, took his instructions and departed.

'I wanted to ask, sir, about the king.'

'His majesty? What about him?'

'He said you would not find him ungrateful if you helped with the problem of his brother. But nothing seems to have happened.'

Sir David sat back in his chair and nodded. 'Actually, it did. After the war I was sent for by his majesty and he offered me an earldom. I declined. Respectfully, of course.'

'Why?' Hunter frowned in puzzlement.

'I think titles are baggage. An anachronism in the modern world.' Sir David shrugged. 'I still believe in the monarchy. It's the rest I don't think is necessary.' He held up his hand. 'Illogical, I know, but there it is.'

'Reading the archives I was also intrigued about your nephew, Paul. He's hardly mentioned.'

'The work he was doing was top secret and is still heavily classified. No doubt it'll all come out after the fifty year rule expires. You know it was thanks to him that computers took such a leap forward. If he hadn't gone into academia after the war I'm convinced he could have made a huge fortune in industry. But there it is. Money, *per se*, has never motivated him.' Sir David smiled. 'The patents he's registered could have made him wealthy if he hadn't given most of the money to the university.' He abruptly changed the subject. 'How are you getting along with Sian?'

'Very well, thank you, sir.' Hunter was no longer quite so alarmed when the old man asked after his granddaughter in such a forthright manner.

'She's a wonderful girl, though a bit headstrong. Fine looking, too.'

'Yes, sir. If you say so.' Hunter looked considerably less happy now.

Sir David threw back his head and laughed out loud. 'Jesus, man, this is the sixties. I may not agree with free love and all that nonsense but I'm no prude.'

The butler reappeared, carrying a silver salver on which sat a decanted bottle of port. The bottle was alongside. He placed the tray on the desk and departed.

Tim Hunter picked up the bottle and looked at it. 'Eighteen sixty-five. The last year of the American civil war.'

'Most people don't realise it, but there were more American soldiers killed during that conflict than in either of the world wars. Interesting, eh?'

Hunter nodded. 'All this century America's been bailing Europe out. When will it end?'

'When Europe finally takes responsibility for itself, and stops bickering. But that won't be in what's left of my lifetime. Or even the next forty years. Not with the French involved. They're the only people I know who kiss you on both cheeks, give you a hug and steal your wallet at the same time. They've reneged on every international agreement we've ever signed. Young man, please don't get me started on European politics. Hand me two glasses from behind the bar.'

Sir David poured the wine. They raised their glasses in salute and sipped. 'Like nectar,' said Sir David with satisfaction.

Hunter agreed, 'Delicious. What do you intend doing about the 'D' notice, sir?'

'Intend doing? Nothing.' Sir David squirmed a little in his chair and looked a tad uncomfortable.

Interesting, thought Hunter, *I seem to have struck a nerve*. Suddenly he sat up, almost spilling his drink.

'My God, you crafty old so-and-so.'

'I beg your pardon?' Sir David looked rather startled at being addressed in that way.

'Sorry. It just slipped out, but you are – incredibly crafty.' Throwing back his head it was Hunter's turn to laugh out loud.

'Why on earth are you making such a row?'

'You arranged that "D" notice, didn't you? You knew it would make the Yanks pay attention. So when do you propose having it lifted?'

About to protest his innocence, Sir David pursed his lips and then smiled. 'Very astute of you. That's why I like you so much; you're a good match for my granddaughter. The notice will be lifted in six months, after we publish in America.'

The door opened. 'Gramps, have you seen Tim? Oh, there you are.

579

Come on, darling, we're going to be late for Fee's party in Brighton. You finished with him, Gramps?'

'Yes. Have a pleasant evening, you two.'

The last thing Sir David heard as the door closed was Susan asking, 'What's the matter, Tim? What's so funny?'

'Your grandfather is amazing. You'll never guess . . .'

Sir David didn't catch the remainder. Leaning back, he took a satisfying mouthful of port. *As I've said many times, if I need to, I'll cheat.*

Author's Note

IT'S TRUE WHEN it's said that fact is often stranger than fiction. This novel is drawn from actual history and my imagination. Many of the secondary characters you meet in the book were real people.

During the war many different kinds of men and women wore uniform. Some with pride and great heroism, others were self-serving crooks and scoundrels. In this story you will come across them all. Many of the incidents I've written actually took place, names and circumstances changed to suit the narrative.

Most of the remarkable men and women who risked their lives deserve our lasting thanks and admiration. Others were not so noble.

All the incidents connected to the Duke of Windsor were true – from his attempt to avoid Britain's strict quarantine laws for his beloved dogs to the decision to assassinate him. He was, without doubt, a vain, shallow and self-centred man. In my opinion he was also a coward.

Although this book is based on real events it is primarily a story about a family. It is their story, but it is dedicated to everyone who gave so much, so that we can enjoy the freedom we often take for granted today.

Paul Henke

A Million Tears

'The summer's best holiday read . . .'

Scottish and Universal Newspapers

'An unquenchable thirst for daring and creativity . . .'

The Sunday Times

'As a literary publicist we receive over 50 books a week to evaluate – we knew instantly that *A Million Tears* was a classic.'

Tony Cowell, *PressGroup UK*

'Henke has written a gripping story . . .'

Corgi Books

'I smelt the coal dust in Wales and felt the dust in my eyes as I fought alongside Evan.'

Dr Peter Claydon

'Henke tells interesting and exciting stories. He doesn't use bad language and writes good English. A joy to read.'

The Sun

The Tears of War and Peace

Silent Tears

Paul Henke has always enthralled readers with books full of passion and adventure. In Silent Tears his readers will be captivated as three generations of the Griffiths family struggle to meet the challenges of their time.

From the depths of the depression and the rise of fascism to the abdication of Edward VIII and the Spanish Civil War, Henke's meticulous research brings the period and vibrant characters to life.

David, powerful and dynamic, at the centre of political intrigue, his love for the family is put to the ultimate test . . . Meg, stalwart and determined, guides the family with humour and devotion . . . And Susan, beautiful and tempestuous, fighting for justice. No sacrifice is too great for those she loves.

Packed with excitement, Silent Tears is a masterpiece. A novel that vibrates with sheer narrative power and relentlessly builds the emotional pressure until it explodes in a firestorm of passion and high-octane adventure. A spellbinding epic.